T J Vertigo's

Caution:

Under
Construction

ISBN   0-9744121-9-8

First Printing 2004
Cover art and design by Anne M. Clarkson

Published by:
Dare 2 Dream Publishing
A Division of Limitless Corporation
Lexington, South Carolina 29073

Find us on the World Wide Web
http://www.limitlessd2d.net

Printed in the United States of America and UK by

Lightning Source

Introduction to Caution: Under Construction
By Vertigo

Meet Sheridan Landers - an attractive, muscular, little blonde, flirtatious and somewhat cocky construction worker who "thinks" she has the world by the balls. By day, she works for her father's construction company, and gives as good as she gets, just like one of the guys. At night however, she becomes the ultimate object of desire for every woman in the club as she dances for her pleasure and every woman there, soon to be her conquest no doubt. She is exquisite to watch on the dance floor and she knows it. Bare biceps, pert ass and a killer smile. Never at a loss for companionship, Sheridan's ego, among other things, is constantly stroked. Sheridan is ruled by her libido. She knows she will not be alone this night or any other she chooses.

But, she has another side that most never see. A solid family that includes her beloved developmentally-disabled brother Steven, a quixotic young man, with clear bouts of genius at unexpected times, but no verbal edit mode. Together they form a marvelous pair and keep us in stitches. Their love for each other is palpable and it is clear he adores the ground she walks on, and she him. Last but definitely not least are Sheridan's life are her two "boys" Zeus and Pharaoh...not exactly the best mannered four-legged gentlemen, but they give her joy and show us her softer side and something more...Sheridan isn't quite what she would have the club goers think… there is much more here.

Enter Keefer Gibson - a leggy, graceful, somewhat self-effacing beauty of thirty-something with cerulean eyes. She is an inspector for OSHA – Occupational Safety & Health Administration.

The inspector is somewhat sexual repressed and trapped in a loveless, abusive relationship with a domineering, moderately unhinged woman by the name of Dani. Keefer's greatest love and solace is her loving, disfigured dog, Fifi, a real little trooper and like her mom a consummate lady. The inspector's days go on and on and she accepts what life has given her, little does she know what is to come.

On one fateful day, Sheridan and Keefer's paths collide at a worksite. Sheridan is instantly and thoroughly smitten. Keefer is every woman's desire and Sheridan decides she *will* have this one. Keefer feels

V

something too, something unfamiliar. Something about Sheridan pulls her, but she has Dani to consider and she runs as fast as she can away from Sheridan. Her feelings for Sheridan are strong but there are issues to consider…Sheridan makes her feel, really feel. She is scared, and in that instant does something no other woman has ever done before…she has turned down the great lothario Sheridan Landers.

This story takes us on a journey of love, in all its aspects, from blinding passion and undiscovered sensual pleasures, to trust in another. In the case of Keefer, we find basic human empathy. Sheridan finds unexpected patience and kindness.

Watch as these two women grow into love cautiously and passionately, forever under the watchful gaze of the maniacal and somewhat dangerously jealous eyes of Dani, who will stop at nothing to put a spanner in the works. Will she succeed? Well, read the story. Time will tell, because here you have love under construction.

Vertigo is a past winner of **The Amazon Ice Award** as well as **Tigg's Too Hot Award**. She has been reviewed by **Lunacy** and has been a favorite among internet readers for years. This is her first published book.

Dedicated to Stacey Jan Wilson, my life partner, my wife; and Teryl Cardella, who was there when I needed it most. Without both, I never would have gotten it right.

Thank you to Geebs, Stacia and everyone at Vertigo's World for their endless faith in me.

TJ

Chapter 1

"God damn it! There's never any fucking parking!" Sheridan Landers glanced at the clock on the dash, pulled an illegal U-turn and drove her little black Corvette onto the sidewalk, making her own parking space. It was almost midnight and time for her to make a grand entrance into her usual haunt. She checked her hair one more time in the rear view mirror before grinning slyly at herself, "You look fierce, Sher...as usual."

After crawling out of the low car, the blonde smoothed her hands down the ass of her tight-fitting Levi's and shook each leg out, readying herself for another night of fun. Her boots thunked loudly in the deserted streets as she approached the nondescript gray doors to the club. She self-consciously looked behind her as she took hold of the handle and, when she noticed nobody around, pulled open the door.

The dizzying throb of the bass-laden dance music caused her to blink rapidly and the thick wall of smoke that followed reminded her to light a cigarette. She jumped the three steps down into the club and stopped in front of the doorman, handing him a ten.

"Come on, Sher, you know I don't take your money."

"Just this once, Billy? Please?" She stuck out her lip and made puppy-dog eyes.

The bouncer ruffled up her hair, earning him a glare and a smack in the iron-like abs.

"Well then, I'll have to tip real good tonight." The blonde sauntered deeper into the club, stuffing the ten into her pocket. She stopped in front of the coatroom and leaned over the half-door. "Where's my sugar, Sugar?"

The coatroom attendant, Verna, a well-passed middle-aged woman, came out from the back and smiled a motherly smile. "You just like seeing an old lady blush, don't you?"

"Well?" Sheridan puckered up and Verna placed her cheek on the young woman's lips. "Thanks, Ma."

"You be careful, okay?" Verna called after Sheridan, who was already on her way.

The club was huge, by Brooklyn standards, and it was the only gay disco in the borough that guaranteed a good crowd most nights. There was a large dance floor and a smaller raised stage area where they held drag and strip shows. Up a few carpeted steps were two levels of lounge area, peppered with small platforms and tiny tables which most people used for making out and doing drugs. There was a small patio off the second level, where they sold barbecued hot dogs and hamburgers for a buck in the summer.

Once she stepped into the large room, Sheridan was in her element. Green eyes squinted and adjusted to the darkness. Tonight was Ladies Night, and she was bound to find a lady or two to her liking. Her hips started to move to the music as she scanned the crowds. Pounding beats and blinding strobe lights made her forget everything else; the only thing left on her mind at the moment was dancing. She pushed up the sleeves on her leather jacket and jumped up on the stage.

Sheridan was well aware of the many eyes trained on her as she moved to the music. There were plenty of women there and it was a sure bet she had either dated or at least sucked face with the majority of them. The attention drove her on and she danced for her admirers, but didn't look at anyone; she had a look of determination on her face when she danced, full concentration reserved for the release that only dancing gave her.

A small group of Sheridan's friends gathered at the foot of the stage to wait for her to acknowledge them. They knew the blonde went there with an agenda. The first and foremost intention was getting rid of the day's stresses, and once she was satisfied, the hunt for women began. Sheridan's friends were a motley crew. Dawn, the car mechanic, stood 5'8", was built like a Mack truck and sounded like the horn when she spoke—loud and obnoxious. Marie, who was missing her two front teeth as a result of being jumped in a gay-bashing incident, was short and squat. Her job in a pizzeria kept her that way. Sharon, the cop, cocky as all get go, but no where near as lucky with the women as she made herself out to be. She was a tall and lanky woman, but strong as an ox. In fact, they were all masculine women, since Sheridan couldn't keep a feminine woman at arm's length—it was just too much temptation for her.

Suddenly a loud shriek pierced through the music and Sheridan was lifted off the ground in a bear hug. Greg, her oldest friend and poster child for queer stereotypes, twirled her around in circles. He stood 6'2" and dressed in the finest couture, right down to his shoes. They looked like the most severely mismatched couple, but when they danced together, it was the most amazing thing anyone had ever seen. They liked to brag that they were the only white people in the world who mastered the lambada. Sheridan loved dancing with Greg; it was like they had an unspoken connection and they fit together perfectly—except when he started voguing. She drew the line at voguing. Old dances die hard in Brooklyn, and that was one of them. The Bus Stop was another, and it wasn't uncommon to see all the patrons in the club line-dancing en masse to an old, crusty disco song. That was usually when the blonde jumped off the stage for a bottled water.

Keefer Gibson swung her long legs off of the side of the bed and rubbed her hands over her face. She focused bleary eyes at the bedside clock and grimaced. *Two a.m. Fabulous.* Sighing, she stood up and let the blanket drop from her body onto the bed. She looked over her shoulder at the figure that was sprawled out and snoring and rolled her eyes. Slipping out of the bedroom, the tall woman closed the door silently behind her and padded into the den. As soon as she flipped on the light, she heard the clicking of toenails on the kitchen linoleum. Soon enough, a fairly unattractive mixed-breed dog appeared at her side with a very chewed piece of rawhide in her mouth. "Looks like me and you again tonight, Fifi."

Fifi wagged her bald tail rapidly and jumped up on the futon beside her mommy, turned around a few times, and then plopped herself down in a heap. "What'll it be, hmm? News, infomercials, old movies, Nick at Nite..." Keefer flipped through the channels on the television, the dog in her lap being more interested in chewing on her rawhide than the screen. "Oh, look at this, Bob Vila." She curled her feet up on the futon and watched the television with interest.

Keefer hadn't always been up at all hours; this was a new development, only starting when Danni had moved in with her. Not accustomed to sharing her bed or her life with another, she started to have trouble sleeping in the bed. More and more, Keefer would escape to the den in the wee hours, sometimes falling asleep on the futon with her dog.

This didn't go over big with Danni, who began to accuse Keefer of loving the dog more than her. The arguments should have upset the tall woman, but they didn't, and she found herself agreeing with Danni just to

3

shut her up. This was also a new development. Keefer Gibson never backed down from a fight in her life. Lately, she just didn't care anymore.

Danni was Keefer's first girlfriend and her first relationship. The tall woman was instantly drawn to the lanky redhead, and Danni was totally in lust with the brunette. When they met at a company picnic, they had both had a few too many and the night had flown by in a haze to Keefer. Waking up the next afternoon with Danni had been shocking. Losing her virginity was supposed to be a wonderful experience, and she couldn't remember a thing. Things went very fast from that day forward and Keefer just went with the flow. She wasn't happy with the way the relationship was, but having nothing to base it on gave her nothing to fight with. She believed Danni and her constant chant of, "You have to work hard to make a happy ending."

Keefer wasn't entirely convinced that she loved Danni anymore. She wasn't sure if she ever had, but being in her mid thirties, she was afraid to be on her own. Oh, she liked being alone and she craved solitude, but she also liked having someone tell her she cared about her, loved her. She knew if she left Danni, there would be no one else in her life besides Fifi. She didn't think relationships were worth the fight and she wasn't the one-night-stand type. Sure, she liked sex...it was okay. Danni seemed attentive enough, making sure she was satisfied each time they made love, which was hardly at all anymore...but the idea of having sex with any one else, someone she didn't know, made her cringe. Keefer was a very private person. She didn't like to share too much of herself with anyone. Getting naked in front of Danni was hard enough—exposing herself to a stranger was never going to happen.

Danni hated that about Keefer and reminded her often that it drove her crazy that Keefer was so quiet... especially in bed. She would beg Keefer to make some sort of sound to let her know she was doing something right. |It took forever for Keefer to reach orgasm, and Danni had adjusted their love making, always tending to Keefer first. If Keefer made love to Danni first, she'd be too tired to see that Keefer was taken care of. Keefer knew that it drove Danni a little crazy that she was so inhibited. They never made love with the lights on and never anywhere but the bed -- nothing out of the ordinary and no unusual positions. She couldn't let Danni look into her gorgeous blue eyes and watch her come; she always covered her face as if embarrassed by her orgasm. It had taken a whole year, the entire time they were together, before Danni was able to coax Keefer to straddle her face and that had only lasted a few minutes before the tall woman scooted down and said she was too tired. Keefer suspected that Danni was losing interest in their relationship, but the thought of Danni cheating on her had never crossed her mind.

Sheridan leaned both elbows on the bar as she waited for her turn. The area was pretty crowded, at least three people deep, but the crowd parted for her. After many winning smiles, kisses on the lips, and firm handshakes, she propped her foot up on the railing and leaned forward to kiss the bartender. Dawn elbowed her in the ribs and nodded in the direction of the doorway. Green eyes followed and spotted what had captured Dawn's attention. A good-looking Spanish woman stood in the doorway scanning the room. Sheridan smirked to herself; having a new toy to play with always made her night.

"You gonna go for it, Sher?" Dawn's deep voice resounded in her ear.

"Maybe." the blonde shrugged, but her cocky grin told a different story.

"Shit, Sher! Why don't you leave anything for the rest of us?" Marie complained half-heartedly. She would never have the nerve to go up to any good-looking woman and they all knew it.

"Yeah, like you have half a chance, stud," Sharon teased. She rolled her eyes and fixed the collar on her jacket.

Sheridan chuckled quietly and swiped her water off of the bar, leaving a five in its place. She slipped through the crowd of women and made her way toward the door and the cute Spanish woman.

"You fuckers are so busy arguing, you let Sheridan get there first." Dawn laughed out loud, pointing with her beer at their friend.

The blonde drank down a few gulps of cold water, enjoying the shiver as she felt the cool path it made traveling down inside her overheated body. She felt her nipples harden against her white T-shirt and she smirked to herself at the sensation. Sheridan propped herself against the large doorway and waited for the Spanish woman to catch her stare. Once the brown eyes turned in her direction, she blatantly ran her gaze the length of the woman's body, letting her know she liked what she saw. As the Spanish woman began to blush, Sheridan crossed her arms over her chest and cocked her head, a charming little smile on her face.

"So, tell me, are you here alone or are you waiting for someone?"

"Alone...and you?"

"Oh, I was just waiting for you to get here."

The woman blushed again and smiled.

Ha! The blonde turned her head slightly and winked at her friends. This evening was going to end on a high note.

Danni turned over and felt the empty bed. She frowned angrily and sat up. *Again! What the fuck is her problem?*

Keefer looked up at the doorway when she heard the heavy footsteps making their way toward the den. She knew what to expect and she sighed in anticipation.

"I knew I'd find you and that dog in here. Keef, it's four o'clock in the morning! You have to be up for work in a few hours!"

"Thanks Dan, I had no idea," she replied sarcastically.

"What's up with you, anyway? Why don't you sleep anymore? Is it me?"

The tall woman shrugged, never taking her eyes from the TV.

"Fine, be like that." Danni turned to leave the room, but spun around again. "Let me just tell you one thing, this has got to stop. We hardly see each other during the day and now you run away from me at night. You're my girlfriend and you belong in bed next to me. Are you even listening to me?"

"Yes, I'm listening to you." Keefer gave Danni a withering look.

"Would it help if I let the dog sleep in the bed with us? If that's what would make you happy, then okay, I give in."

"That's not the problem." *She sleeps with me anyway, and you have no fucking clue.*

"Well, figure it out, Keef. I'm tired of sleeping by myself."

Danni stormed out of the room and slammed the door behind her. Blue eyes fixed on the closed door as Keefer waited to hear the bedroom door slam too. Once that was done, the tall woman laid her head back on the futon and rubbed her face with her hands. "What the hell am I supposed to do?" Fifi stood up, stretched, and licked Keefer's chin. She smiled and shook her head. "I'm hungry, Fifi, how's about you?"

"Last call for alcohol!"

"Mmmph." Sheridan tore her mouth away from Maritza's and dug into her pocket. "Want a last drink?"

"Sure." The Spanish woman attempted to smooth out her shirt and got up from the blonde's lap. "Water?" she asked as she took the money.

Sheridan nodded and leaned back against the wall. Turning to the left, she looked in the mirrored paneling and shook her head. *What is it with red lipstick these days?* She tried to wipe it off of her mouth but it was not going anywhere. *And what do they make it out of, anyway?*

"Whew, Sher, she's a hot one! I thought for a second you guys were gonna fuck right here!" Marie smacked her friend on the back.

"Hey, I have *some* class," the blonde laughed. "I'm cutting out as soon as I say good night to Maritza. See you guys tomorrow?"

"Yeah, sure thing," Dawn winked. "Have fun, Sher. You're gonna have a hard time explaining that face to the guys in the morning."

"Don't remind me," she groaned. "What the fuck is in lipstick anyway?"

"Who the hell knows? You could probably take it off with paint remover," Marie joked.

"Yeah...like I want that on my lips. Thanks, guys." Sheridan waved as they took off and smiled as Maritza stood in front of her.

"Wanna come home with me, Sheridan?" she asked coyly.

"Why the fuck not?"

Keefer jumped out of her skin and her newspaper went flying all over the place. The homeless man who woke her up in a very unpleasant manner continued to blow his trumpet, oblivious to the very ugly glare he was receiving. While trying to get her heartbeat back to normal, she glanced around the crowded subway car and found a few sympathetic faces pointed her way. Gathering her paper, Keefer stood abruptly, startling the people around her who recovered quickly and dove for the empty seat. The tall woman squeezed her way toward the door and followed the throng of people up the stairs and out onto the street. She wore a scowl as she stopped at the coffee cart for her morning cup. She was tired, cranky, and had too much on her mind.

She took long strides to her office building, stopping only momentarily as she did every morning to hand her newspaper to the homeless man that begged for change on the corner.

"Hey, tall lady, why the long face?" he asked with a toothless smile.

Keefer frowned as she turned to look at the dirty man. *You think you got problems? Snap out of it.* "Just thinking bad thoughts." She offered him a big smile in return.

"Oh, now there's a beautiful face," he grinned. "Thank you, ma'am." He held up the paper and bowed his head.

"Welcome." She returned her attention to the street and entered the skyscraper.

"Daily News, 50 cents!" he shouted.

Once up in her office, she closed the door. She could expect at least a few hours of quiet now that she was bumped up to a private office. When she first started her job, she was forced to go out on site to inspect, always being watched by her superiors. Now, she didn't have to go anywhere, it was just her and her research and paperwork...no people. Keefer winced as the phone rang. *So much for quiet.*

Sheridan pulled her car into the spot in front of Landers and Sons Construction Co. She turned off the ignition and leaned her head on the

7

steering wheel. A yawn threatened to swallow her face, and the tears that sprang to her eyes from the action made her squeeze her eyes shut. She heard the footsteps crunching on the gravel walkway and sighed. It was bound to be her brother Steven...always cheerful, always smiling. *Bite me,* she thought with a closed eye roll as he knocked on the window.

"C'mon, Sher, the old man is waiting for you."

Sheridan opened the door and her brother watched in amusement as she literally rolled out of the low car and sat on the ground. "Coffee. Much coffee. Now," she grumbled.

"Well, what the hell do you expect? If you didn't run around 'til all hours, you wouldn't be in this condition." Steven mimicked his father.

The blonde glanced up through her dark sunglasses and eyed the tall, muscular man. Yep, he was smiling and cheerful. She took the extended hand and allowed him to lift her off the ground and onto her feet. Wiping off her ass, she sighed, which turned into a yawn, and she had to lean on the car with the force of it.

"Was she worth it?" he teased.

"Yeah." Sheridan started toward the door of the office.

"You know, you're going to have to explain that stain all around your mouth better than the last time."

The blonde chuckled. "I thought the pistachio nut thing worked just fine."

Steve opened the door and gestured for his sister to enter first. She half snorted at the action and smacked him on the shoulder as she entered the office.

"Hiya, Sher!"

"Hey, Pop." The blonde made a beeline for the large coffee urn and seriously contemplated sticking her face under the spigot. She grabbed the biggest mug and dumped in sugar, milk, and then coffee.

"You are so weird, Sher," her brother snorted and rolled his eyes.

"It's the lazy way; no stirring required. I figured you'd know all the lazy ways out, Stevie-boy."

"I hate it when you call me that, shrimp toast."

"Eat me, you whiner."

"Okay, that's about enough from you two." Mr. Landers shook his finger, signaling the end of the argument. "Sher, I have some good news for you."

"What is it?" she asked, sipping the hot liquid carefully from the mug.

"I hired a new secretary, so you don't have to help me out here anymore."

Sheridan put down her coffee, hopped onto and over the desk, and wrapped her father in a bear hug. "You fucking rock, Pop!"

The large man chuckled. "I don't see what you can possibly like about working with those guys." He shook his head in amusement as his daughter hopped back over the desk. "They're just pigs."

"We get along," she grinned. "Can I start working today? I have my hard hat in the car."

"Sure, go on." He sat down in his chair. "Oh, and hon, I don't think that color lipstick suits you," he teased.

"Uh...yeah. Thanks," Sheridan stuttered, hating when her father caught her off guard. "I'll remember that next time."

"Yeah, be more choosy about whose tongue you suck on," Steve yelled as she opened the door.

"Love ya, Pop. Bite me, Stevie-boy."

The tall woman threw her pen across the room. "Damn!" That was not the phone call she wanted. It seemed the man scheduled for on-site inspections that week had called in that morning with a broken ankle. *The idiot probably fell out of his own shoe.* Keefer would have to fill in for him all week, something she absolutely hated to do, especially in a monkey suit and heels. *So much for peace and quiet,* she scowled to herself. She picked up the paper with the job lists on it and frowned even more furiously. *Queens? I should have stayed in bed. I'd have had the whole house to myself.* She was even crankier than she was before she walked in. Not owning a car or having the desire to do so, Keefer was going to have to take cabs and or the subway to these sites. Even though it was spring, the trains were stuffy and the cabs were intolerable with the thick partitions and the safety windows.

Shit! She tossed the paper in the direction that she'd tossed the pen and narrowed her eyes at it when it floated slowly down to the desk. She leaned back in her chair and sipped her coffee, stewing in her bad luck. Reaching for the evil paper that she had been glaring at, she looked it over again and sighed. "At least tomorrow I'll be dressed more appropriately for this construction site." Just as she was about to get up, the phone rang.

"Keefer Gibson."

"Hiya, Keef, it's me."

"Yeah, Danni, what?"

"You ran out of here so quickly this morning, I never got the chance to tell you that I won't be home 'til at least after midnight tonight."

"Yeah, well, whatever."

"Don't you want to know where I'll be?" Danni asked with irritation in her voice.

"Actually, no. I'll see you tomorrow." Before Danni had the chance to reply, Keefer hung up the phone and walked out of her office.

TJ Vertigo

Chapter 2

Sheridan found her energy reserves by the time she arrived at the construction site, helped by two cups of coffee and two donuts. The guys were very happy to see her there and welcomed her back enthusiastically. Although there were plenty of people working, she was going to be with three of her best buddies: Tony, Phil, and Bobby. All three men were typical New Yorkers in their twenties, married and living vicariously through the boss's daughter. They loved to tease Sheridan, or Patch as they called her, about her nightly exploits, each harboring a smidgeon of jealousy about her prowess.

"Glad to see you!" Bobby yelled. "I need someone to help me whip these guys into shape!" he laughed, turning down the radio.

"What happened, Patch? The old man catch you doing the new secretary?" Tony joked, knocking on her hard hat.

"Quit it, you idiot, I had a long night and, no, I never even saw the secretary." Sheridan smacked Tony in the stomach and took a good look around the half-gutted building. "What the fuck are you guys doing here all day?"

"Ooh, Miss Cranky, didn't you get any last night?" Phil asked, making an obscene gesture with his hands.

"You're a pig, Philly." She shook her head, but her chuckle let everyone know she loved it.

"You love me because I'm a pig. So? Did ya get lucky?"

"Of course she got lucky, you chooch, look at her mouth," Tony laughed.

Sheridan pursed her lips and shook her head. "It won't come off," she explained quietly.

"It never does, stud muffin. Hey, you been working out more than usual? Your arms look bigger," Bobby wondered.

"No, just the usual." The small blonde shoved up her sleeve and flexed her bicep. In a flash, all three men were at her side, doing the same thing, comparing biceps.

"Ooh, Tony, she's got at least an inch on you," Phil teased.

"Fuck off, she does not!" Tony pouted.

"She's got me beat, too." Bobby pulled down his sleeve and walked away dejectedly.

"Yeah, well, my ass ain't got nothing on you guys. I'm surrounded by tight buns," Sheridan said, in order to raise the confidence level in the room. All three guys turned their backs on her and flexed their buns. It was all she could do to not laugh. "Oh, baby...stop it, I'm getting hard."

They all laughed when Tony began flexing his ass cheeks individually to the music.

"That's attractive," Sheridan teased. "Ooh, stop, I can't take much more." She fanned herself dramatically.

"I bet you said that last night," Bobby winked.

Sheridan pulled her T-shirt to the side, exposing a fresh set of hickeys and bite marks. "You could say that, boys," she gloated.

"Fucking shit! I swear, girl, you get more women than all of us put together," Bobby exclaimed.

"Uh, yeah. That would be three women between you. I can get three women on a Tuesday," she bragged.

"I hate you, Patch," Phil chuckled.

"I hate you, too." She blew a kiss at him.

"Hey, how's Stevie?" Tony asked.

"Hey, he hates that name. Don't call him that to his face," Sheridan said in warning.

"Whoa, just asking."

"Yeah, well, he's okay. He's working with Pop now. He hated the group home."

"I don't want to be nosy, but weren't they teaching him how to work there? Wouldn't it be better for him to stay there?" Phil asked, genuinely interested.

"Pop coddles him too much. Steve whined and Pop took him home. He's in good hands. Pop did a great job raising us when Mom died." The blonde narrowed her eyes at Tony. "He loves us all equally. Besides, Pop doesn't treat him any different, so neither should you."

"Since when did I do anything?" Tony looked surprised.

"At the last job. You wouldn't let him do anything. He was hurt," Sheridan said angrily.

"Jesus Christ, Patch, he's six foot two and got the mind of a thirteen-year-old. He wanted to use the power tools!" Tony shot back.

"So? Plenty of thirteen-year-olds use power tools. He pouted about it for days. He thinks you hate him. It was eerie seeing anything other than a smile on his face."

"Shit. I'm sorry. I'll apologize to him next time I see him," Tony said sadly.

"Here," Sheridan whipped out her cell phone. "Speed dial number one." She smiled triumphantly as Tony spoke to her brother. No one was allowed to fuck with him. Only her.

Keefer trudged up the walkway to her house and grimaced. Fifi's nose prints were all over the front window, and she knew Danni would get on her about that. Sighing, she put her key in the door and was instantly greeted by a very excited mutt. Suddenly, Keefer's bad day dissipated and she smiled as she knelt down to hug her dog. "Hiya, sweetheart. Did you miss me?"

"She snotted all over the window."

"It's not snot." Keefer started to defend the dog to Danni but thought better of it. "Give me a minute to change and I'll clean it off."

"You kiss the dog hello, but not me?" Danni asked from the kitchen.

Keefer ignored her lover, closed the bedroom door behind her, and changed into sweatpants and a T-shirt. She let her hair out of its ponytail and ran her fingers through it a few times. Scratching at the door made her grin and she opened it just enough for her dog to enter, closing it again behind her. "Feefs, up." She instructed the dog onto the bed and smiled sinfully as Fifi began rubbing her back all over Danni's pillow.

"You eating dinner or what?" Danni called from the kitchen.

Keefer opened the door, let Fifi out, and then replied, "I'm going to walk the dog first. You eat."

"Suit yourself." Danni shrugged and made her way to the couch with her plate. "Don't forget the snot."

Blue eyes shot the woman a look before Keefer disappeared with the dog.

Danni was almost done with dinner when the phone rang. She let the machine pick it up.

"Danni? You there?"

It was Susan. Danni jumped up to get the phone; Keefer couldn't hear this. She grabbed the receiver and erased the message.

13

The tall brunette came home to find her lover hanging up the phone. "Who was that?" she asked absently as she went to the kitchen to fetch her dinner.

"It was nothing. Hey, I'm going to go out with the guys tonight." Danni met Keefer by the stove after putting her plate in the sink. "You mind?"

"Why should I? Go on, have fun." The brunette left the kitchen and sat on the couch, reaching for the remote.

Danni was pissed. *Doesn't Keefer care?* "I'll be out late," she stated with annoyance.

"So?" Keefer shrugged. "What else is new?" She flipped through the channels and settled on Animal Planet. Fifi jumped onto the couch and sat attentively by her side, waiting for the piece of food she knew she would get.

"Don't you give a shit, Keef?" Danni stood in front of the television with her hands on her hips.

Ice blue eyes pinned Danni to the spot. "No, not really. You know I don't like clubs or bars and I know that's where you go, so...enjoy yourself. Just get out of the way." Keefer made shooing gestures and tried to look around her lover at the TV.

"Okay, fine. We gotta talk, Keef." Danni threw open the coat closet and tossed her coat on angrily.

Keefer watched with a bored expression. "We always gotta talk, Dan. Problem is, you're never home to do that."

"How can you be so nonchalant when our relationship is on the rocks?" Danni asked, red faced.

"It's easy. Our *relationship* is always on the rocks, or so you say." Blue eyes returned to the TV screen.

"Don't you even care about that? Our relationship—"

Keefer threw down her fork and glared. "What relationship?" She wasn't yelling, but the controlled tone of her voice told Danni she was angry. "When do you care? You think we'll talk tonight? You'll go out, get drunk, come home, and pass out. I'll be in the den watching TV and you'll be in the bed snoring away. It's the same thing every night. If *you* were so concerned, *you'd* stay home and talk."

Danni stood, shocked.

Keefer regretted her outburst. She really didn't want Danni home right then and she certainly didn't feel like talking. "Look, you go out and have fun. I really would rather be alone right now."

"You only want to be alone," Danni said sarcastically as she slammed the door behind her.

"Who wouldn't? Huh, Feefs?" Keefer fed her dog a piece of chicken. "Maybe I do need to go out once in a while, huh? You think?" She scratched Fifi behind the ear and leaned back on the couch. "Maybe I need to see where Danni goes, one of these days," she thought out loud. "And it's not snot," she added.

Fifi cocked her head and raised her ears. Keefer stared at the TV and ate mechanically. After she was finished, she went to the kitchen and started the dishes. The dog followed. Danni cooked and Keefer cleaned. She cooked and she cleaned. It didn't make sense, and the tall woman shook her head. "Something's gotta change, Feefs. I don't think this is a relationship." *It's more like maid service.*

Sheridan pushed open the door to her apartment and braced herself. As soon as the door opened, two hundred pounds of dog came at her and she wound up on her butt, as usual.

"Okay! Okay, kids!" the blonde laughed as she was greeted by her babies, a large, male brindle-colored pit bull named Pharaoh and an even larger Rottweiler named Zeus. They licked her enthusiastically, pouncing all over her as she squirmed on the floor.

"I get the picture, guys! I missed you, too!" she said as she grabbed Pharaoh's face and kissed him on the snout. She wrapped her arms around Zeus's neck and did the same to him, then used his massive body to pull herself up from the floor. "Now, you let me take a shower to wash all this dust off and we'll go out for a walk."

Sheridan had said the magic word, and both dogs began doing the happy dance all around the apartment. Zeus leapt for his leash, which was hanging on the back of the door, while Pharaoh continued to jump and prance in circles by the bathroom door.

The blonde stripped off her clothes as she walked toward the bathroom, laughing out loud at her dogs.

When she had gone to the shelter, she had no intentions of having a big dog, let alone two monsters. Having grown up with dogs and cats, she wanted a companion in her new place and was simply going to the shelter to look at options. She swore Zeus was smiling at her and still stuck to that story. As she was about to leave with her new puppy, she heard a painfully sad howling. Following her ears, she wound up on doggie death row, and there was Pharaoh, singing for all he was worth as if he knew he was going to die. He couldn't have been more than seven months old. Sheridan's heart hurt.

Pharaoh was trouble, at first. He'd been abused terribly and was fearful of humans. He was most likely beaten for not being a fighter, and

15

he wore the scars of his defeat. A long, pink, hairless scar swept across his big square head and his left ear was permanently damaged, the result of either a fight or a bad ear cropping. It didn't matter to Sheridan; to her, it added to his charm. These were her babies and she loved them like children. They were a family.

The blonde walked out into the living room in her underwear to survey the damage inflicted while she showered. Not too bad, she noted. Zeus had finally gotten his leash and was whipping it around the living room as he threw his massive head from side to side, killing the thick leather strap repeatedly. Pharaoh was standing on the couch looking guilty for something that Sheridan was no doubt going to find when she least expected it. "You guys being good?" she asked rhetorically. They were never good.

Zeus dropped his leash and panted at her, and Pharaoh cocked his big head.

"Okay, give me a second...wait," she held up her hand.

Both dogs sat where they were and waited.

"Thank god for hand commands," she muttered as she ran into her bedroom to dress.

Keefer didn't even bother going to bed. She changed into her pajamas and went directly into the den. The thought of sharing the bed with Danni that night didn't sit well with her. She settled under the comforter and propped a pillow behind her head. She waited for Fifi to get settled and then reached over to the table for her glass of milk. As she dunked her Oreo, she thought about her lover's behavior.

Keefer watched the television off and on, changing the channels every so often as she tossed thoughts around in her head. She and Fifi shared the Oreos, and she let the dog lick up as much of the milk from the glass as her short snout would allow. Once again surfing through the channels, she found a cable talk show, and something a guest said caught her attention. He was talking about cheating spouses and suddenly Keefer wondered if Danni might be having an affair. Her lover showed all the signs of it, according to this guy. She sat up straight and paid close attention to the talk show.

Dawn elbowed her friend, "Hey, Sher, it's Susan."

Sheridan's head swung around quickly. "Well, I'll be. Who's the redhead she's with?"

"No wonder she's been MIA. Looks like she's hooked a new one." Marie raised an eyebrow as Susan and the redhead sucked each other's tongues.

"Yeah, well...good for her," Sheridan said bitterly.

"Hey, at least she's not stalking you anymore." Dawn patted her friend on the back.

"Give her time; she'll get on my nerves eventually." The blonde made a sour face and walked away from her friends.

Sure enough, Susan and her new friend migrated to a spot directly in front of Sheridan as she danced. Susan glanced every so often at Sheridan to try and gauge her reactions. The blonde was getting aggravated; she came to the club to avoid stress, and here she was with agita. She squatted down on the stage and tapped Susan on the shoulder. "I see you, now go away."

Susan tore her lips away from the redhead. "Oh, hi, Sheridan. I didn't see you there." She blinked rapidly.

"Bullshit, you're practically making out on my fucking lap all night. Now get out of my face."

"Hey, don't talk to her like that," the redhead spoke up.

"Now, now, ladies," Susan giggled. "Sheridan, have you met Danni?"

"Charmed." The blonde rolled her eyes.

"Mutual." Danni narrowed her eyes.

Sheridan walked off the stage and over to her friends. "That bitch gets me so mad. I don't know why I let her get to me!"

"Sher, she's nothing. Just blow it off."

"Her new pet has an attitude, too. I'd like to kick her in the ass," Sheridan fumed.

"Shit, don't let her get to you. Come on, loosen up. Let's find us some chicks, release some tension, okay?" Marie offered, smiling at her agitated friend.

"Yeah, I need to fuck this tension away." Sheridan patted the bulge in her pants. "I came prepared."

Dawn and Marie looked at their friend's crotch and laughed. "You fucking rule, Sher!" Marie choked out between laughter. "I didn't even notice it until you showed me."

"I'd certainly hope you wouldn't be looking at my dick. I'd have to kick your ass," Sheridan chuckled.

"Ooh, blonde at the bar," Marie announced.

"Go get her, tiger," Dawn laughed, turning Sheridan around and shoving her in the direction of the bar.

It was after two a.m. and Keefer had been tossing and turning all night on the futon, her thoughts about Danni not allowing her to fall asleep at all. She stood up and stretched, grabbing the half-empty glass of milk from the table. She stood in the dark kitchen and rinsed out the glass as she heard Danni come home. Her lover was trying to be as quiet as she could, but Keefer could tell she was drunk just by her clumsy stumbling.

"I'm up, Danni," she said loudly as she flipped on the living room light.

"Jeez!" Danni squinted and covered her eyes.

"How'd you get home?" Keefer asked, watching as her lover's eyes adjusted to the light.

"I got a lift. I didn't drive tonight." Danni looked Keefer up and down. "Where'd you get that nightie? I like it." She grinned wolfishly.

"I've had it a while. You've seen it before." The tall woman rolled her eyes. *Great. Horny and drunk.*

"Yeah? You'd think I'd remember something like that," she leered. "Why don't you come to bed tonight, babe?"

"You're drunk, Dan," Keefer sighed.

"So? You're my girlfriend. Now come to bed and prove that."

Keefer tracked Danni's movements until she was half naked and in the bedroom before turning out the living room lights.

A short while later, Danni was snoring and blue eyes were staring at the ceiling. Keefer had talked Danni into lying back while she made love to her. It was over rather quickly and Keefer was grateful for that. Danni reeked from perfume, and it was not a scent Keefer had ever smelled before, and it made her want to gag. She sat up and leaned over her snoring lover, studying her face. Danni's lips were swollen. Keefer leaned down and sniffed her face...her neck...it was as if Danni had bathed in another woman's perfume. Blue eyes narrowed.

Keefer threw off the covers and inspected her girlfriend's body. *Nothing.* She turned her over and did the same to her back. *Hmm,* she thought as she squinted at a mark on her back. Turning on the bedside lamp, the brunette stared at the mark again. *It looks like a scratch...but still, that could have been anything.* She looked again at Danni's front and saw a faded bruise on her collarbone. *Could have been a hickey at one time?* She froze. *What are you doing?* Keefer turned off the light, ashamed at herself. Inspecting Danni's body like she was embarrassed her. She felt guilty for doing it, but the talk show guy had really made her think. Now that she opened her eyes, she had a good idea that her suspicions were confirmed.

The blonde struggled out from under her sleeping dogs and slapped the alarm clock. "Shit!" she yelled as Pharaoh's head fell heavily onto her bladder. "Up!"

The pit bull yawned widely and stretched all his legs, giving Sheridan the chance to wiggle out from underneath him. "Thanks a load," she muttered as she ran to the bathroom.

While the hot water cascaded down her tired body, she thought about the woman from the night before. Grinning, she remembered how they'd wound up in a bathroom stall, never making it out of the club. Sheridan loved women like that—slutty women who didn't give a shit who knew what was going on. The woman wasn't quiet, either, and when they finally did leave the stall, it was to rounds of applause from the other women waiting in line for the bathroom. The woman she had bent over the toilet took a few bows and blew kisses at the clapping people, and Sheridan winked at a few. *What was her name again?* She thought hard as she soaped up her body. For the life of her, she couldn't remember.

A big black head appeared around the shower curtain and the blonde flicked water at the dog. "Can't I even shower in peace?" She shook her head and chuckled silently as a brindle head appeared next to the black one. "You guys are too much. I'm coming, I'm coming." Sheridan rinsed off quickly and turned off the water. "Make yourselves useful and fetch a towel, will ya?" She pointed at the dogs, who just sat there and stared at her. "All right, then tell me where you hid my shoe...Pharaoh." Se stepped out of the shower and shook her head over the dogs. They didn't appreciate that and trotted off out of the room in a huff.

Keefer propped her sneaker-covered feet on her desk and looked over the list of places she had to be that day. She narrowed it down to three places and decided to get the construction site done first. She despised construction sites. The men always gave her a hard time, spouting cheap comments, coming on to her, making obscene gestures, acting like they were God's gift. She hated dealing with all that testosterone and wanted it out of the way as soon as possible. After that, it was smooth sailing with a few food service places.

Pulling her hair back into a ponytail, the tall brunette stood up and stopped in front of the door. Her reflection in the cheap mirror she'd put up made her do a double take. She was not used to seeing herself dressed this way in this particular mirror. She gave herself the once over and turned sideways to check out her ass. *Danni's right, my ass looks good in these jeans.* Keefer grimaced. *Let's not think about Danni today,* she told herself. *Well come on, Keef, let's get this over with.*

The tall woman took a deep breath as she stood in front of the construction site. *This is the place,* she told herself. *Time to face the*

19

animals. Keefer braced herself for the comments that were sure to be tossed at her as soon as she pulled open the door.

"Hey, look at what we have here!"

Sheridan's head turned in the direction of the wolf whistle. She knew that meant a good-looking woman was in the vicinity and far be it from her to pass up a look-see.

"Yo, Patch, you may want to come and take a look at this!" one of the guys called from downstairs.

Sheridan snickered; she was too busy at the moment and she had a screwdriver in her teeth. She shook her head and resigned herself to the fact that she'd miss out on this opportunity.

"Oh, that has to hurt," Bobby teased her. "A sweet lady and you can't see her."

The blonde had to admit she was very intrigued by the amount of clamor downstairs regarding this particular female. She spit out the tool and stood up. "She sounds like a looker, though. Maybe I should—"

"I'm sending her up, she needs to speak with Patch!" a voice called, followed by a ruckus of teasing comments directed at Sheridan.

"Must be my lucky day, boys." The blonde winked and rolled up her sleeves, exposing overworked arm muscles.

"Oh, sure, call out the big guns," Phil joked as Sheridan wiped the dust off of her butt.

Keefer stood there with her hands on her hips, already steaming over her greetings downstairs. It took her way too long to acquire a hard hat and find out who was in charge. *Patch...what kind of a name is Patch?* she wondered as she looked at the men in front of her. "Which one of you is in charge?" She raised an amused eyebrow as the seemingly mesmerized men all pointed to the short guy in the corner. *Men...she* thought disgustedly. *Although check out the ass on the short one...that's some body, too, come to think of it.*

"Jesus Christ!" Bobby whispered, just loud enough for Sheridan to hear.

Sheridan's heart picked up speed at the sultry-sounding voice. She almost didn't want to turn around, but Bobby's exclamation caused her to act. She looked over her shoulder directly into the inspector's denim-covered breasts. "Holy shit..."

"Uh, Patch, you said that out loud."

Sheridan blushed and looked up into the bluest eyes she'd ever seen. A wolfish grin appeared unbidden as she studied the gorgeous face in front of her.

Keefer lost her breath. *She's a woman?*

"I'm in charge, Miss..."

"Gibson." Keefer stood dumbfounded at the cocky expression on Sheridan's face.

"Miss Gibson. Sheridan Landers, what can I do you for?" She smiled and wiped her hands on her pants.

The tall brunette took a deep breath and shook her head. *Get a grip, Keef!* "I'm with OSHA, I'll need someone to show me around."

I'll show you around, baby..."I'd be glad to." Sheridan grinned boldly, assessing the tall woman's body.

The tall woman stood there for a second, watching as the muscular blonde turned to walk away. She caught herself staring at Sheridan's ass and blushed furiously. Hurrying to catch up with the smaller woman, Keefer rolled her eyes to the many catcalls and comments that followed her out of the area.

Sheridan turned around and graced the tall woman with a forgiving grin. "You'll have to excuse them, Miss Gibson, they have no class." She turned to the small crowd. "Shut the fuck up, assholes."

"I see you're just oozing with it, Miss Landers." The tone of her own voice made Keefer blush again. *Am I flirting with this woman?* She noticed green eyes twinkling back at her. *Curiouser and curiouser.*

TJ Vertigo

Chapter 3

Sheridan stormed up the stairs and shouldered her way through Bobby and Tony, not stopping until she was in a space all by herself. She was fuming. She lit a cigarette and threw the pack against the wall. *What the fuck was that all about?* She paced back and forth, swinging her hands in the air. *What, does she think she's so goddamned special?* The muscular blonde stopped by an opening in the wall and watched as Keefer scrambled into a cab. She adopted a stiff-shouldered pose and aped the tall woman. "No, I don't want to inspect the closet, and I'd appreciate it, Ms. Landers, if you'd stop staring at my tits."

The guys exchanged confused looks as they watched Sheridan bound past them. They could hear her muttering and stomping around, and all three men raised their eyebrows at the same time.

"No way..." Tony said.

"I think Patch has just been turned down," Bobby pursed his lips.

"By the most beautiful woman I have ever seen!" Phil added.

"Jeez, that's gotta suck. I wonder what happened." Bobby looked to Phil, who just shrugged and nodded his head at Sheridan, who had just entered the room.

"What are you all staring at?" she asked angrily.

"Come on, hon, it's not the end of the world," Tony said sympathetically. Sheridan scowled and flicked her cigarette at him. "Hey, what are you, stupid or something? You coulda took out my eye," he said as he stepped on the butt.

"Mind your own business for a change," the blonde bit out as she folded her arms across her chest and looked miserable.

"What happened? You were only gone a few minutes," Phil dared to ask.

"Nothing. She inspected. And if you wanna know, she was flirting with me! I saw it plain as day! Who is she to get all offended, anyway? I know she's queer, I knew it immediately, she was checking out my ass, for Christ sakes!" Sheridan kicked a bag of cement in anger and regretted it instantly.

Bobby grimaced. "Hey, so she turned you down, what's the big deal, really? You've been turned down before. Why are you so pissed off?"

Sheridan frowned. "I don't know," she admitted. *Why am I so upset? So the most gorgeous woman I ever laid eyes on took offense to my advances.* Now she pouted. *Fuck...is she hot though.* "I'm over it. Let's get to work." She limped back to the guys and turned up the radio real loud.

Keefer leaned her head back on the seat and sighed. *Well, that was certainly...interesting,* she thought. *God, she was worse than the men! And what did I think I was doing, looking at her ass?* The tall woman felt a blush creep up her chest. *It was a very nice ass. But God, she caught me staring...and that cocky little smirk she had on her face pissed me off.* She closed her eyes and swallowed hard. *And the way she kept staring at my breasts...I* know *she saw my nipples get hard, I just know she did.* The blush traveled to her cheeks as she recalled the twinkling green eyes meeting hers. *She* knew *I was flirting with her. What the hell was I thinking? But that hard little body—Stop it! Stop it now, Keef!* Keefer put her face in her hands and groaned. *I paused. I goddamned paused. And she grinned. I actually* thought *about the closet and she knows I did.* She cringed. *What on God's green earth did I think I was doing, anyway? I do not flirt.*

Blue eyes popped open as she sat up straight. *Oh, I certainly did. Shamelessly. I stared at her ass like she stared at my chest. And why did I get so mad? I gave her all the reason in the world to come on to me.* Keefer shook her head and groaned out loud again. *Dammit. I want her.* She stared out the window and her heart pounded furiously. She wished she'd never gone to the construction site that day. Meeting Sheridan Landers changed everything.

Sheridan's mood had improved as the day went on. No one mentioned the tall inspector; in fact, they avoided the subject like the plague. The guys had never seen her so miffed over a snub before and they didn't know how to act. Instead, they joked and goofed around for the rest of the day and were all relieved to see her laughing along with them. They were sure she was going to go out that night and all weekend, for that matter, inevitably getting lucky. She would be back to her old self on Monday.

Pharaoh danced his happy dance and Zeus looked on with interest as Sheridan tied her boots. She was going out tonight with an agenda. *I wonder what kind of underwear she was wearing?* Green eyes widened as the thought sprung into her mind without warning. "What the fuck was that?"

Zeus seemed to shrug and Sheridan ran her hand through her hair. "I know I wasn't thinking about her underwear." But now that the seed was planted, she couldn't think of anything else. *A thong. Had to be a thong. I don't think I've seen jeans look quite so good before.* Her eyebrow rose as she recalled the long legs and how they met a perfectly round rear. Her belly tingled with a familiar feeling. *Oh no...*She stood up suddenly and flung her arm in the air. "What are you doing?"

Grabbing her car keys and leather jacket, she ran out of the house like a woman on a mission.

Keefer turned up the heat in the den and closed the door. She then grabbed two towels, took off her shirt and bra, and knelt by the bathtub. "Here, Feefs! Bath time!" she said cheerfully, laughing as she heard the dog running full speed through the house.

When Keefer had found Fifi, she had been a mess. The prognosis was not good for the poor dog. She'd been tied up in an abandoned garage that somehow caught on fire. It just so happened that the tall woman was walking by as it burst into flames. She didn't see how it happened and she didn't care either—all she heard were the panicked barks of a burning dog. She broke through a window and climbed through the wreckage to free the dog, then knocked on people's doors until someone was kind enough to rush her to the hospital. There was no doubt in her mind that she would be taking the dog home, if she lived. She had been burned over 50 percent of her body and the vet didn't give her a chance in hell.

Keefer visited the dog every day and was shocked to learn that she was recovering well. The dog went through so many painful procedures that the brunette thought it might have been more humane to have put her down before trying any heroic deeds. But one look into those soulful brown eyes convinced her she'd made the right decision. She was living all alone and became attached to the little dog very quickly. One day when she arrived at the hospital, the dog began to thump her raw tail in happiness, and Keefer cried. The dog was terribly scarred and the tall woman needed a pretty name for her, so she came up with Fifi. The dog tried to lick her face when she asked her if she liked her new name, and so it stuck.

"Okay now, sweetie, let's go." She patted the edge of the tub and smiled as the dog scrambled to get in.

Fifi required medicinal baths every week to keep her skin healthy. Keefer didn't mind, and it became part of her weekly schedule. Friday nights were reserved for bath time and Fifi loved her bath. So much so that the brunette had to strip from the waist up as the excited dog repeatedly jumped up on her to lick her face, splashing her in the process.

In the beginning, Danni used to bitch and complain about how much time Keefer spent on the dog, but one day she happened by the bathroom. Seeing her tall lover topless and unashamed while she bathed her dog gave Danni reason to set aside time on Friday nights to stand outside the door and secretly watch her lover. It was the only time Danni could openly admire Keefer's breasts, and Keefer never made the connection as to why Danni was so amorous on Friday nights.

After Fifi was rinsed off, the tall woman wrapped her in towels and carried her into the den where she placed her on the floor. Fifi was used to this ritual and once she was unwrapped, she shook for all she was worth. Only having half of her fur, the spray wasn't too bad and Keefer never minded, anyway. The dog lay down obediently and waited for her mommy to tell her it was okay to leave the room.

Keefer closed the door behind her and left the dog to air dry in the warm room. She whistled as she cleaned up the bathroom, then stripped the rest of her clothes off to take her own shower. She briefly wondered where Danni was, then shook the thought away. *I don't care where she is,* she told herself, but it didn't work. She found herself thinking about her lover and with whom she might be cheating on her. She tried to figure out what the woman looked like, what her name was, what she did for a living. Images of Danni rolling around in bed with faceless strangers barraged her mind; she couldn't shake them away. Working herself up to just short of a panic attack, Keefer took long deep breaths to calm down. *Why do I care? If she is, she is. It doesn't matter with whom.*

She dried off and wrapped a towel around her long hair. She walked naked into the bedroom and slipped on a nightshirt. Looking at the clock, she realized she had spent longer in the shower than it seemed and went to the den to retrieve the dog. As she opened the door, she had a flashback from that morning. Sheridan Landers's cocky smirk flashed before her eyes. She felt her heart pound in her chest. *Where did that come from?* She let Fifi out of the den and returned the temperature to normal. *I know I wasn't thinking about her just now.*

While she wondered about that, another image came to mind. The little blonde's ass as she followed it down the stairs. *Mmm, mmm. You could bounce a quarter off that butt...*Blue eyes went wide. "Oh no...what is wrong with me? I don't say things like that." *But you know you want to see what else bounces off that ass, now don't you, Keef?* A hot blush covered her cheeks and a curling feeling developed in her belly. *And those abs, I could see them plain as day through that tight T-shirt...*The feeling traveled down between her legs and she stopped in her tracks to assess it. She tested it. She pictured Sheridan's breasts and gasped. "Oh God," she whispered, never having felt that sensation before. "Oh, Feefs," she groaned, "I think I just found out what horny really means."

Sheridan watched the women trickle into the club from her vantage point on the stage. She had finished working off her day's stress but couldn't put a dent in her libido. For her, seeing all the good-looking ladies filing into the club was like a kid with ten dollars in a candy store. She had stopped dancing a while ago and just stood there letting the sweat dribble down her back as she watched the procession of potential conquests.

Sharon hopped up on the stage and stood behind her. She turned Sheridan's head in the direction of a petite strawberry blonde and spoke into her ear. "Got called to her house today. She tried to throw her girlfriend out and the girlfriend made a scene. Blondie, there, finally succeeded. She's one tough little shit, but she's got something to prove tonight."

Sheridan digested this information. Sharon had a point, this chick had something to prove to her ex, and wouldn't it be lovely if Sheridan were the one to prove it? On the other hand, this was a serious rebound situation. *Can't have any emotions involved.* "Nah, I'll pass. Go get her, Shar." The blonde gave her tall friend a pat on the leg and went back to making her choice.

Just as Sheridan was about to jump off the stage on a mission, Susan walked in with her redhead in tow. *Shit. Can't they go somewhere else?* she thought as she squirmed her way to the bar. Finally standing close enough to the woman she was eyeing, Sheridan presented her with a toothy smile. "Hi there, can I get you a drink?" she asked, her voice dripping with sensuality.

The woman took in the muscular form, her tight shirt and black jeans. "Um, sure, why not?" She smiled back and moved as close as she could to invade the adorable blonde's space. "Beth," she offered her hand.

"Sheridan," she grinned triumphantly as she accepted the hand.

From a distance, Susan narrowed her eyes, then grabbed Danni in a hungry kiss.

Danni tore away from the assault and took a deep breath. "Lemme guess. It's that short butch chick from last night." Susan looked guilty but nodded. "Hey, I don't care, I just want to know, why does she work you up like that?"

"She turned me down." Susan shrugged. "You don't mind that I'm using you like this?" she asked seriously.

"Hell, no! I'm doing the same thing," Danni laughed. "My Keef ain't giving me any," she admitted.

"Well, that's her loss, sweetie. She don't know what she's missing," Susan purred.

"Oh, believe me, she does. She's just a cold fish in the sack. You, my dear, are a wild woman." Danni wiggled her eyebrows and leaned in for a kiss.

Sheridan over heard the last part of the conversation as she made her way up to the second level with her new chick. Danni pissed her off. Susan she could understand; she was fucked up and why Danni ever got involved with her was beyond Sheridan's imagination. However, Danni had a lover and she was cheating on her—not too subtly, either. *Poor Keef.* "Red there needs her ass kicked," she muttered as she purposely banged into the couple. *I bet her girlfriend hasn't got a clue.*

"So, Sheridan, are you into fucking women?"

"Oh, Beth, you hit the nail on the head." The blonde grinned and pulled Beth down onto her lap. Green eyes watched Danni and Susan for a while until Beth's tongue reached her ear, and then her eyes rolled shut.

Keefer scanned the channels as she did every night, but she didn't see what was on the screen. Her mind was abuzz with thoughts of Danni and Sheridan. She'd be so angry with her lover she'd want to scream, and then a sexy thought about the cute little blonde would pop up and erase everything. Her stomach was so confused, it was in knots. Keefer was switching from acid to arousal so often her insides couldn't keep up.

Fifi nudged Keefer's hand until she began to stroke the dog's head. "Sorry, Feef. I'm so distracted tonight." She stretched her fingers to scratch behind the dog's ears. "There, is that better? Does that feel good?" The dog pressed her head into the hand and wagged her tail.

"I think I'm going crazy," the tall woman announced to the room. She lifted one leg onto the couch and rested her chin on her knee. "Why do I keep thinking about her? She's obnoxious and rude, she has no class, and she has way too high of an opinion of herself."

Fifi rolled over onto her back and sighed. Keefer scratched the dog's belly and smiled. "You are spoiled rotten," she told her happy dog. Danni's voice popped into her head. *You spoil that mutt, Keef. I wish you'd touch me as often as that dog...*

Keefer shook the voice away. She was so angry with Danni that if she were to walk in the door, she'd throw something at her. "Why doesn't she just leave me for this other woman?" she asked Fifi. "Apparently she's happier with her, she spends all her time with her now." She sighed loudly in defeat. "I want to know what she looks like. I need to see her so I know it's true." Keefer stewed a bit. "Then, after I see her...them...I'll throw that shithead out in the street." Tears sprang to her eyes and she sniffled, "You will not make me cry, Danni. I refuse."

Fifi turned back over and saw her mommy in distress. She immediately leapt up and licked the tears away. She kept it up until she heard the wonderful sound of mommy laughing, and then was satisfied to lay her head in her lap and go to sleep.

"Holy hell, Sheridan. That was...whoo." Beth lay exhausted in her bed.

"Yeah," Sheridan agreed as she rolled off of Beth and stood up.

"Where ya going?" Beth sat up in alarm.

"Home. I can't leave my dogs alone. Where's my other sock?"

"Oh, yeah, well I understand," Beth said sadly.

Sheridan pulled on the missing sock and searched for her shoes. "Hey, you wanted me to fuck you, no strings...right?" she asked with annoyance.

"Well, yeah, but do you have to run away right this second?"

"Uh...yeah."

"But I didn't touch you, aren't you...needing a little something?" Beth asked with a smirk.

"Nope, came already, sorry." Sheridan pulled her shirt over her head and tucked her bra in her coat pocket. "Maybe next time."

Beth laughed. "Who are you kidding, Sheridan, your reputation proceeds you. I know all about you. I'll never get the opportunity again."

"You never know." She shrugged. "Hey, look," she sat on the bed and softened her voice, "I'm usually not like this, but I have a lot on my mind tonight. I think I need to be with my dogs." Beth gave her double-raised eyebrows. "Oh, man, that's not how I wanted that to sound..."

Beth smiled, "I gotcha. You need to be with your babies. It's okay. Go home, Sheridan."

"Thank you. I'm sorry about this, really." She kissed Beth quickly on the lips and jumped out of bed.

"And just so you know, you live up to that reputation of yours, stud." The blonde chuckled as she closed the door behind her.

Keefer woke up in a sweat, her heart pounding loudly in her ears. "Wow. That was...something," she whispered hoarsely. The dream had been so real, she could still feel the fingers on her body. "Wow," she repeated, shivering from the erotic visions in her head. "I never did that before."

Whatever force had been making her think of the blonde construction worker all day had just invaded her subconscious. Keefer had her first erotic dream and Sheridan was the star. A deep red blush covered her face as she tried to erase the images flashing before her eyes. "God, I really am going crazy." She was highly aware of the feeling between her legs, and it scared her. She was so wet, she feared she might have peed herself. Lifting the covers, she spread her legs and looked, just in case. *Nothing on the couch.* She hesitantly reached under her nightshirt and made contact with a slick inner thigh. She gasped out loud. "Jeez, I'm dripping wet!" She tentatively touched her sex and jumped a mile high from the sensation. "From arousal!" This made her blink rapidly. Danni complained repeatedly about Keefer's lack of natural lubrication. She hated the artificial, sticky stuff and was offended that Keefer couldn't produce any of her own for her.

The tall brunette sat back on the couch, stunned. "I don't believe this. Danni could be touching me for hours and I can't even get wet. I have one dream about that little cocky construction worker and I'm Niagara Falls." Just the thought of Sheridan made her tingle between her legs. A strange scent wafted toward her nose. "What is that?" She sniffed under the blanket. "Good Lord...that's me!" The thought crossed her mind to touch herself again, but then she blushed furiously and shook her head. She'd never done that before and she wasn't about to now over some silly dream. But then again, she'd never felt like this in her life, and it was beginning to make her head spin. Another image of the dream flashed by and she inhaled sharply as a throbbing began between her legs. She started to slide her hand toward the ache, slowly, until she felt her pubic hair under her fingers. She took a deep breath and slid lower, shuddering fiercely as she felt the pools of wetness between her legs. A groan escaped her lips and she snatched her hand away in shock at the sound. She sat up quickly and flipped on the television.

"Sheridan Landers, what have you done to me?"

The blonde construction worker was beat that afternoon. In order to keep her mind off of the tall inspector, she went to the job site and busied herself with just about every activity that came up. She was confused at her behavior the night before. While she was doing her thing with Beth, she saw the inspector's face every time she closed her eyes. It bothered her in a way that wasn't familiar. Sheridan was a little angry with herself for not being able to control the visuals that kept popping into her head. While she didn't lie to Beth about coming last night, she failed to mention it was to the image of the tall brunette writhing beneath her. *What is with this woman anyway? She was a total bitch!* The muscular blonde didn't understand why she couldn't keep the other woman off of her mind. *Hell, I don't even know her first name!*

Sheridan couldn't have been more ready for a hot shower and a soft pair of sweats. She had big plans involving a TV dinner, the television, and the couch. The Saturday evenings that she stayed home were few and far between and she was going to enjoy it. Sheridan took the dogs out immediately, before her shower, so she could relax the rest of the night. Once the dogs recognized the change in routine, they were happy as could be. They pulled her to the park quickly, did their business fast and pulled her home. If she thought she was tired before, she was exhausted after the tug of war that was their walk.

Keefer left her office in relatively good spirits. She didn't normally work on Saturdays, but she wanted to get rid of the last few inspections and go back to her nice quiet office on Monday. Not to mention, she didn't really want to spend the whole day with Danni. Work was certainly a good distraction; her thoughts were less about Danni and more about Sheridan and the effect the cute, yet arrogant blonde had on her. At first, she was afraid of the new feelings she'd developed while thinking of her, but just being able to experience them at all gave her a pleasant rush. All these years she had been thinking that sex was a chore—an overrated chore. Now when the images came to her, the tingling she felt in her groin made her smile. She wondered if a thought could make her feel so good, so alive, what would actual sex feel like with Sheridan Landers?

The subway ride seemed shorter than usual with her constant daydreaming. Keefer worried briefly that it might be unhealthy to be thinking about a stranger in the ways she was, but once the twitchy feeling appeared between her legs, a blush covered her face and she couldn't imagine a feeling that was so good as being bad.

She let her hair loose as she walked to her house. She felt somewhat confident and walked with a little spring in her step. Reaching her front door, she smiled as Fifi danced for her. "Hiya, sweetheart! Who's mommy's baby? Who's my big girl?" The mutt wagged her whole backside in response, twirling circles around Keefer's legs as she locked the door behind her. The inspector stooped down and let Fifi climb up on her knees, showering her face with hello licks. "That's a good girl."

Making her way through the house, Keefer was surprised to find it empty. Danni was nowhere to be found, and the tall woman startled herself by smiling and heaving a sigh of relief. "Well, that oughtta tell me something," she chuckled to Fifi. Since it was safe to assume Danni wouldn't be home until the wee hours, Keefer decided it was going to be a pampering night. She started a bubble bath and while the water was running, grabbed a bottle of wine and a bunch of magazines. "It's going to be a good night, Feefs." She smiled happily and took off her clothes.

Sheridan lay on the couch in her pajamas, eating ice cream out of the pint container. Zeus's big head rested solidly on her thigh, his eyebrows alternating between "please" and "I love you." Pharaoh sat on the floor at her side, his good ear standing at attention, licking his chops intermittently. The blonde tried to ignore them; they'd already gotten more of her TV dinner than she did. "I don't see either of you," she said out loud. Pharaoh leaned forward until his nose was an inch from her face and huffed. "I still don't see you." Zeus nudged Sheridan's thigh with his wet nose and started a pathetic whimpering noise. She was quickly losing her cool. Pharaoh's soulful eyes watched attentively as the spoon lifted to her mouth; he stared at the hunk of ice cream, begging it to fall off.

"Oh, fine!" she yelled and directed the spoon to the pit bull's open mouth.

Zeus was very unhappy with this turn of events and he leapt up onto the prone woman, standing his 100-pound-plus weight on all her sensitive parts.

"Jesus! Fuck!" She held out the pint of ice cream and Zeus tore at it until the contents fell out into her lap. It was a feeding frenzy on Sheridan's naked thighs as the two dogs licked up the ice cream in earnest. The blonde squirmed and shrieked, swatting at her babies until they were finally convinced they'd gotten every last drop.

"Well, thank you very much...both of you," she growled as she stripped off her wet boxers. The dogs converged on her and attempted to snatch the boxers out of her hand, Pharaoh to hide them and Zeus to kill them. Sheridan lifted them way over her head and ran to the bathroom to wash her legs.

When Sheridan came out of the bathroom, the phone rang. It was Sharon telling her about the scores of eligible women just waiting for her to arrive. Sheridan wasn't feeling much like going anywhere, but now that the cop mentioned the women, she started to reconsider. *All those hot* *women just waiting for me to choose...*In a matter of seconds, the blonde's mind was made up and she told her friend to expect her in a half-hour.

Keefer lounged in the bathtub with her magazines and her wine until the water became too cool to bear. Totally refreshed and having the house to herself, she slipped on a short silk robe and decided to give herself a much-needed manicure. Bringing all the necessary items into the living room, she turned the ringer off the phone and she and Fifi settled on the couch for a girl's night. Keefer flipped on the TV and hummed to herself as she filed her nails.

A short while later, the answering machine came on and Keefer cursed herself for forgetting to turn the volume down. A dark eyebrow lifted as a strange woman's voice floated through the room.

"Hey, Danni, it's me, pick up. You there? Well, okay. I thought you were coming to meet me tonight?"

Keefer's gut twisted.

"Oh, well. You must be in the shower. Anyway, I'll be at the club, see you later."

Blue eyes narrowed to slits as she stared down the machine. *So, you're the floozy Danni's been sleeping with...*Keefer stood up and began pacing. *Maybe I should show up at the club and see what Miss Voice looks like.* She became more agitated the more she thought about it. *If I only knew what club.* Keefer stopped pacing and turned her head to face the coat closet, an evil smile taking over her face. Storming over, she threw open the door and began rifling through her girlfriend's pockets until she found what she was searching for. *Bingo!* A matchbook advertising the club with a phone number scrawled on it. *Susan, huh?*

Sheridan pulled her black car onto the sidewalk and marveled at how packed the club was. There wasn't a parking spot for blocks. This was sure to be a night she would have regretted missing. Once inside, she made her way over to Verna for her nightly sugar.

"Hey, Sher, I didn't think you would make it."

"Would I let you down, sweetheart?" The blonde winked.

"Well, what are you waiting for? The world is your oyster tonight, girl!"

"I count on it, Verna." Sheridan wiggled her eyebrows and strode away.

Green eyes scanned the packed dance floor. She instantly spotted Susan and squeezed her way in the opposite direction. *Wonder where Danni is tonight?* She chuckled to herself. *Probably already tired of Susan and her bullshit.*

33

"Sher! Over here!" Dawn yelled out, waving over her head with both hands.

"Whassup?" Sheridan asked, slapping her friend on the shoulder.

"Would you believe Marie hooked up?" Dawn asked, wide-eyed.

"No fucking way! Where? I gotta see this!" The blonde stood on her tiptoes and looked in the direction Dawn pointed to see Marie dancing her heart out with a cute woman in a low-cut dress. "Well, well...Marie's gonna get some," she teased.

"I know. Good for her. Have you seen Sharon?"

"Are you kidding? This place is so packed I barely saw anything." Sheridan lost her balance as someone rammed their shoulder into her side.

"What the fuck?" she asked angrily, turning to face the smirk of the dreaded redhead, Danni.

"Oops, sorry, guess I didn't see you," she snickered.

Sheridan bristled. "You got a problem with me, Red? 'Cuz I already want to kick you in the fucking ass. Just give me half a reason."

Dawn intervened and pulled her friend back a few paces. "Yo, Sher, chill out," she said in her ear.

"I don't like this bitch, Dawn. She's a lowlife," she said loud enough for Danni to hear.

"What was that?" Danni asked, posturing in Sheridan's personal space.

"You heard me. You're trash. You got a woman who probably has no fucking clue you're dicking around on her and you have the nerve to disrespect her with a cheap tramp like Susan."

"Hey, Sher, it's not your business. What's up with you?" Dawn signaled for Sharon as soon as she spotted her.

"You're right, Dawn." Green eyes never left Danni. "She's nothing. Just get out of my face, Red, before I shove my foot up your ass."

"You have some nerve to judge me," Danni yelled. "The fucking whore of the club is telling me who I'm disrespecting. Who I fuck is my own business, so butt out." She poked Sheridan in the chest, and it took both Sharon and Dawn to hold her back.

"Let it go, Sher. Let her walk."

The blonde was too riled up. "Maybe I should find this Keef and show her what a real woman is all about," she spat after Danni's retreating form.

The redhead turned around and laughed. "Good luck, her legs are sewn together at the knee." Danni wiggled her eyebrows. "But she's a hell of a looker. Good to keep around." Then she disappeared into the crowd.

"That son of a bitch," Sheridan muttered. "Poor fucking Keef. I hope she has three women on the side and gives Danni fucking herpes."

34

Chapter 4

Sheridan shouldered her way toward the dance floor, Dawn and Sharon right behind her. It took a while for them to calm down their friend and even when she convinced them that she was okay to go off on her own, they still tailed her, as all good friends should. She knew that they totally understood her behavior, that they themselves felt bad for this woman named Keef. They knew that Danni had really got to her with her crack about being a whore. In fact, they seemed to be a little surprised at how quickly they talked Sheridan down from her anger.

The blonde stood before the stage, seeking out a good space next to a woman with potential. Every so often, she'd get angry and have to take a deep breath to calm herself. *I can't let that fuck get to me!* she'd remind herself. *Who the hell does she think she is? I'd just love to meet this Keef and walk her in circles around that redheaded bitch.*

Sheridan fucked women on a nightly basis, so it would seem ridiculous for her to be so upset over this stranger, Keef, being disrespected, but Sheridan Landers never disrespected women. The women she fucked wanted to be fucked, and she never did anything to them that they didn't want to be done. She never forced anyone and she never crossed any lines. She respected women as a gender and it pissed her off to see one get hurt or played for a fool. There had been plenty of times she herself was almost thrown out of the club—her home away from home— for protecting a crying female from a disrespectful woman.

With her two very conspicuous tails, Sheridan climbed up on the stage and took a deep breath. Soon the anger dissipated and the throbbing bass took over. Her hips began to move, followed by her body as she danced rather aggressively to the beat. This is what she needed, her mind becoming a blank as she moved, sporadically singing out loud to the music.

Keefer paced the living room, picking at the matchbook nervously. *What do I do when I get there?* she wondered. *What if she sees me? What if it's a hole in the wall kind of place where every one looks at you when the door opens?* She sat down on the couch and bounced her leg. "Feefs, should I go? Should I go see what this woman looks like? Should I even bother?" She sighed. *You know you want to see what Danni finds so attractive. Why put it off?*

"What do I wear?" she said as she ran to the bedroom. She quickly threw on jeans and a tight blue T-shirt and looked herself over in the mirror. "I look like a tramp! Everything's so tight!" She turned around and looked at her ass. "Well, what exactly *should* I look like when I'm going out to catch my girlfriend cheating on me?" Keefer was becoming frustrated. "You look fine. It's not like you're going out to pick up someone. You don't even know *how* to pick someone up," she told her reflection.

As she ran a hand through her hair, a thought came to her. *Bullshit. You knew just what to do with that obnoxious, yet adorable, construction worker.* Blue eyes went wide. "Now why'd you have to go and bring *her* up?" she yelled at the voice in her head. "I haven't thought about her in hours. Now look at what you did!" she pointed to her hardening nipples in the mirror. *What if she's there? I know she wants me.* A huge grin spread across her face and Keefer shook her head violently. "Oh no, Keef, two wrongs don't make a right. Just because Danni's cheating doesn't mean you should." Her eyes narrowed. *Yeah, but she wants me...and I want her.* Just admitting that to herself caused the now familiar pulsations between her legs. Her heart beat loudly. "What if she *is* there? What do I do?" *Oh, come off it. What are the chances that the woman you've been fantasizing about is in the same club that your girlfriend is cheating on you in?* One last look in the mirror and Keefer left the room to pace in the living room again, debating even further with herself.

Wanda sat on the toilet tank, legs spread, one hand holding her bunched-up skirt against her stomach, the other clutching a fist full of Sheridan's hair. "Oh, fuck, yes..." she whispered as three fingers speared in and out of her, hard and fast.

Sheridan stood, straddling the toilet bowl, her mouth glued to a nipple. The anger she'd felt before was slowly leaking out as she fucked Wanda, who was no worse for the wear, despite the aggression. She egged Sheridan on with words of encouragement, groans of approval, and yanks on her hair. The rhythmic thumping of the toilet tank against the wall made the blonde's nostrils flare.

"Yeah, baby, harder...come on..."

36

Sheridan grunted and chewed Wanda's nipple, adding a fourth finger, pumping faster and harder than she thought possible. She needed this, she was so hot, Wanda was making her so hot. She needed relief of her own and would have to wait until she finished with Wanda to get any. She felt as if her clit were on fire and there was nothing to ease the burning.

"Fuck yeah, baby..." A hoarse whisper blew right into the blonde's ear. "I'm gonna come..."

Sheridan groaned. This was what it was all about, making women come. She never felt more of a rush then when she felt a woman quaking around her fingers, knowing she was the reason for their pleasure. She planted her feet and growled as sharp fingernails dug into her neck. She smiled triumphantly as Wanda came, shaking quietly in the public bathroom, biting her lip to hold back the sounds. Not that it mattered; Sheridan could hear another couple going at it in the next stall.

Not a second after Wanda caught her breath, Sheridan was tearing open her belt in hopes of reciprocation. She didn't know why she was so turned on, but she was, and she needed to come. She stopped at the button on her leathers and stared into hungry brown eyes. "You up for this? I promise it won't be long."

"Sure, baby," Wanda cooed. "Drop them leathers and let me take care of you."

Just as Wanda's warm hand touched Sheridan's hot sex, a voice came from the next stall, "Oh yeah...Danni..."

Sheridan grimaced and tried to block the voices out of her mind. She grabbed Wanda's wrist and pushed her fingers harder. She was right there.

"God, Suz...that's so fuckin' hot."

Green eyes squeezed shut and Sheridan thought for a split second to cover her ears. She jerked her pelvis frantically; she was so close she could touch it.

"I bet Keefer doesn't touch you like this."

Keefer? Her name is Keefer? Well that would explain Keef, now wouldn't it? Stop, Sher! There's a woman fucking you!

"Oh, Sheridan, you're so wet, so ready..."

I wonder what Keefer looks like. I mean...that's an unusual name. She's probably unusual, too. Then again, mothers don't know what their kids are going to grow up looking like when they name them. Keefer could be gorgeous! Hell, she could be better than that bitchy inspector! Once the thought came, it wouldn't go away. *Oh yeah, now that's a woman I wouldn't mind bending over this toilet...*

"Hello? Earth to Sheridan." Wanda snapped her fingers in the blonde's face.

Sheridan had the good grace to blush. "Uh, sorry." She pulled up her pants and looked at the floor. "I, uh, got distracted," she apologized lamely.

"Well, anyone would with the noises from the next stall." Wanda banged on the wall. "Keep it down in there, we're trying to fuck!"

Sheridan laughed. "You okay? I didn't hurt you, did I?"

"Oh, no, I liked it. Thank you." The brown-eyed woman bent over and kissed Sheridan sweetly. "I'm just sorry things didn't work out in your favor."

"No problem. I'm good." *Yeah, right. As soon as you walk out of this stall, I'll have my hands down my pants so fast...*"I'll see you later? I gotta pee."

As soon as Wanda left the stall, the blonde opened her pants and leaned on the wall. She could see the tall brunette smirking at her, her nipples poking through the T-shirt she'd worn that day, hear her smoky voice flowing over her, giving her goose bumps. She was so close again in seconds.

"Ooh, Danni!"

Fucking shit! Sheridan pulled up her pants and kicked the wall to the adjoining stall repeatedly before stomping out of the bathroom entirely.

Dawn was waiting in the bathroom line and didn't seem the least surprised to see Sheridan. "What the fuck happened?"

"Danni happened." Realizing she'd have to elaborate and not wanting to even try, she shook her head. "Nothing. I'm fine. Blue balls." She adopted a pained expression and limped out to the giggles of the women in line.

Keefer waited outside the club for almost an hour, hiding behind a van, watching as people came and went, none of them Danni. None of them Sheridan. She was floored by the size of the club. She knew there was no way Danni could see her in a place that big and, by the amount of cars parked nose to fender for blocks around, she imagined it was packed. Every so often when the doors would open, a cloud of smoke would billow out and she'd hear the loud music and sounds of people laughing and talking. She grimaced at the sounds, knowing she'd be miserable if she went inside and had to hear that banging bass beat up close and inhale the lungfuls of secondhand smoke.

There was a line of private car services around the corner from the entrance, all waiting patiently for their turn at the head of the line. She contemplated jumping in one and running home a few times, but stopped herself. She knew she wanted to do this. The problem was, she wasn't sure if it was Danni or Sheridan she was hoping to find inside the loud, smoky club.

"Okay, Keef, it's now or never."

The tall brunette straightened up and walked toward the door. While she stood there, willing her hand to touch the handle, the door flew open and two women spilled into the street, separating on either side of her as they passed.

"Whoa...maybe I should re-think this going home thing." One woman ogled Keefer openly and wiggled her eyebrows.

"Come on, Casanova. Sorry, hon, she's a bit drunk." The other woman smiled and dragged her tipsy friend away.

Keefer stepped into the darkness and stood there, waiting for her eyes to adjust. She wore a sour expression, instantly hating the loud music and the smoke that was sure to stick to her hair and clothing. She took the steps down into the club hesitantly, stopped at the doorman and smiled weakly.

"Ten dollars cover."

The tall woman wiggled her fingers into her pants pocket and produced a ten-dollar bill. She grinned at her luck. A large man grabbed her hand and she almost bolted, but calmed as she watched the man stamp the inside of her wrist with a loud purple smudge that was sure to mean something. "Thank you," she managed, before slinking away toward the large doorway that led in to the dance floor.

A very irritable blonde construction worker stared daggers into the back of Susan's head. Sheridan leaned on the bar and fumed. *Leave it to them to screw up a perfectly good wank,* she grumbled to herself. She felt uncomfortable and wet in her panties and wondered if she should just leave when Danni turned and met her eyes. The smirk that Sheridan saw was enough to make her visibly cringe. She gave her the finger and turned her back to the couple.

Sharon squeezed in next to the blonde and gave her a curious eye. "What's up? Dawn tells me you got screwed?"

"Nah, she wanted to and everything...never mind." Sheridan frowned; she was really getting into that fantasy about the tall inspector. *This ain't over,* she promised herself.

"Okay, now why the grin, Sybil?"

"Oh, nothing, just thinking," the blonde evaded answering.

"It must be good, 'cuz a second ago I thought you were going to kill somebody."

"And I would have, too, but jail just ain't my gig," she snickered. "I have no intention of being anybody's bitch."

"Oh yeah, you'd go over real big!" the cop agreed with a rapid nod.

39

Dawn waved frantically on her way over to the two women. She apparently had something very important to say and made a scene all the way through the club.

"What the fuck is she flapping around about?" Sharon asked with a chuckle.

"Beats the hell outta me." Sheridan shrugged and for a split second thought she caught a glimpse of the very woman she'd been fantasizing about. *Whoa, creepy.* She shook it off and turned to see what Dawn's commotion was about.

"Guys, you gotta see this!" She dragged the two women toward the doorway, and when they were close enough she pointed. "There, by the cigarette machine."

Sheridan paled; her heart beat in her throat.

"Holy shit...baby...come to Papa!" Sharon made a rude gesture with her hips.

"Oh, no. I saw her first...that one is mine!" Dawn shook her head and folded her arms in defiance.

"Uh, Sher, pipe up any time now..." Sharon elbowed her friend, who appeared to be stricken. "Sher, you okay?"

"Uh, yeah...and nobody's going after her," she said, never taking her eyes from the woman in question.

"No way, Jose. You get every single fucking good looking woman that walks into this place. This one's mine," Dawn protested.

"I said fuck off. I...know her." *Good one, Sher.* She mentally slapped herself.

"What the hell else is new!" Sharon threw her hands up in the air in exasperation.

"Hey, I don't mind sloppy seconds," Dawn chuckled.

Sheridan snarled and backhanded Dawn in the stomach, "I said, lay off!"

Both friends raised eyebrows at this. Sheridan had never minded sharing before. This was very unusual. Protective even. Sharon shrugged and mouthed "back off" to Dawn, who nodded and mouthed the word "wow."

Keefer's blue eyes carefully scanned the sea of women for her girlfriend. She had never seen so many women in one place at the same time and it overwhelmed her. She stood half hidden behind the cigarette machine, in hopes that Danni might be within range. She was aware of a whole lot of club left for her to scan, but was reluctant to move from her safe spot. She was afraid to find Danni, but needed to also. *With this many women in one place, maybe Sheridan is here.* A blush began to creep up her neck at her spontaneous thought. *Oh, please, there's got to be more than one gay club in all of New York. Now, find Danni and get out.* The tall woman crept slowly toward the gaping doorway, unaware she was scaring the shit out of a small, blonde construction worker.

Dawn jumped as Sheridan ducked behind her. "What the fuck are you doing?" she asked in confusion.

"I don't want her to see me," she said quickly and panicked.

"All right, Sher, what did you do to her? Better yet, is she looking for you?"

"No, nothing; I never touched her. I have no idea who she's looking for." Sheridan watched closely as the expressions changed on the inspector's face. She could have sworn she saw a blush and liked the way it looked. Taking a good long look from behind her friend, she narrowed her eyes at the tight shirt the tall woman was wearing. As she snuck out from behind the cigarette machine, Sheridan was treated to the long, denim-covered legs and the ass she so fondly remembered.

Sharon stared openly at Sheridan. She couldn't believe what she was seeing. "Who is this woman to you?" she asked, dying of curiosity.

"No one. I mean, she's an inspector with OSHA, she came to the job site the other day." The blonde snuck behind Sharon now.

Keefer scanned to the left slowly, her stomach in knots, afraid at what she'd see. Then it happened; there, leaning on the speaker cabinet was Danni, thoroughly engrossed in sucking some woman's face off. *So. That's Susan.*

Green eyes took in the sudden change of expression and she felt a twisting in her gut. She knew that look and what it meant. *Where is the bitch; I'll fuck her up!* She followed the tall woman's pained gaze and gasped out loud. *It can't be!* She double-checked, even going so far as to step in the inspector's line of vision and see for herself. *Danni?* She looked once more at the tall brunette who looked as if she'd been stabbed in the guts. *That's Keef?!?*

"Sher, what's up? Where you going?"

Before Sheridan knew it, her legs had propelled her in Danni's direction. Without her knowledge, her hand shot out and grabbed Danni by the hair. "You fucking piece of shit!" she spat. Her left hand, again without her knowledge, came up at the speed of light and her fist connected with Danni's face. Susan screamed, Sheridan screamed louder. "You goddamned worthless scumbag!" Before she had the chance to strike again, Sharon's hand was wrapped around her bicep, holding her from doing any further damage.

Keefer watched in total shock at the scene unfolding before her eyes. Not only was the blonde construction worker in the club, she was beating

up Danni! *Why? What happened? How do they know each other? God,
please don't tell me Danni's kissing her girlfriend!* The tall woman
couldn't move; she was rooted to the spot and could only watch in shock
as another woman intervened and held the construction worker back.

"Have you totally lost your fucking mind?" Sharon screamed in
Sheridan's face.

"You broke my nose! You little shit! You broke my fucking nose!"
Danni spat blood onto the floor and shook herself off as Sheridan loosened
her grip.

"What the hell was that all about?" Dawn yelled.

"Fuck off! Both of you," Sheridan was shaking with anger. She
grabbed Danni by the front of her shirt and dragged her away, leaving
Sharon to comfort the screaming Susan as Dawn ran after Sheridan.

Keefer watched with wide eyes and a pounding heart as Sheridan
dragged Danni in her direction. She felt as if she might throw up. Danni
was bleeding badly. The small blonde had fire in her eyes and although it
frightened the hell out of her, she felt a small twinge of excitement.

"Does *this* belong to you?" Sheridan bit out through clenched teeth.

Keefer nodded mutely. Looking into those wild green eyes had her
mesmerized.

"Do you want it anymore?" The blonde's nostrils flared.

Keefer shook her head in the negative.

"Danni, apologize to this woman. Now!" Sheridan tightened her hold
on Danni's shirt and the redhead gasped for air.

Keefer felt light-headed. She wasn't sure it was from the blood or
from Sheridan.

"Now, you fucking worthless shit."

"Sher—easy!" Dawn worried.

"I'm sorry, Keefer." Danni sobbed pathetically. "I love you...please,
we have to talk...please..."

"That's enough." The construction worker shook Danni to shut her up
and watched closely as Keefer seemed to shrug. "Do you want her back?"
she asked hesitantly.

"No."

Sheridan felt a shiver slide up her spine with that one word.

"Please, Keef...I'm sorry...I love you..."

"Shut up! You don't love me. I want you out, Danni. I never want to
see you again." Keefer raised her voice and Danni's eyes went wide.

Green eyes twinkled at the bleeding woman and Danni became
furious. "You're fucking her, aren't you? That's what this is all about!
You're fucking the club tramp!"

42

Before she knew what happened, Keefer slapped Danni across her bleeding face—hard.

"Good for you," Sheridan commended. "Shall I get rid of her?"

"Yes, please, she's making me nauseous," Keefer smirked.

Susan finally broke free of Sharon's grasp and ran into Danni's arms.

"Are you going to walk or am I throwing you out on your ass?" Sheridan asked with a cocky grin.

Keefer shivered this time.

"Get off of me and I'll go," Danni sniffled, shook loose from Sheridan's grasp, and disappeared into the crowd with Susan in tow.

Keefer and Sheridan looked at each other in silence for long moments, neither knowing what to say.

Sharon yanked Dawn by the elbow, and the truck driver reluctantly allowed herself to be pulled away from the unusual scene.

"Um, are you okay?" Sheridan asked quietly.

"I think so. I mean, I knew it was happening..." Keefer trailed off.

"You just had to see for yourself. I understand."

Keefer nodded, her gaze traveling to the muscular, leather-clad legs of her savior. "Thank you."

"Please, I hated that bitch from the moment I laid eyes on her...uh, what I mean is..."

"You know her? How long?" Keefer asked with tears in her eyes.

"Since...well...since Susan." Sheridan felt awful. This beautiful woman was hurting and she wanted to make it better. "Look, I'm really sorry. I don't know what to say to make you feel better."

The tall woman shrugged. "You know, today didn't start out half bad. It's tonight that really sucked." *Why is she looking at me like that? God, those leather pants! Hey! You're supposed to be heartbroken!*

Sheridan raised an eyebrow as she watched the blue gaze travel up her thighs for the second time. "Well, are you okay to drive home alone, Keefer?" It was the first time she'd said the name out loud and it made her tingle in her stomach.

"I don't drive. I took a car service." Keefer melted at the way Sheridan said her name.

"Let me give you a lift. You're pretty tall, but I think I can fold you into my car." The blonde smiled devilishly.

Keefer felt her knees weaken. *I don't know...in a car alone with this one...and that smile...*"Okay." *What?*

The construction worker grinned from ear to ear, "Come on, let's get out of here." She took Keefer by the hand and marveled at the softness of her fingers compared to the roughened calluses of her own.

Keefer just tried to concentrate on breathing; the mere touch of Sheridan Landers made her excruciatingly wet. She had no idea how she was going to make it home without the small blonde smelling her.

Chapter 5

Keefer allowed herself to be led into the entrance area and waited with her heart in her throat as Sheridan kissed and tipped the coat-check women. *Odd, she's wearing her jacket.* Keefer's baby blues almost rolled back as the woman the construction worker called Ma commented on what a beautiful drink of water she was and how the blonde should keep her around for a while. *She's the club slut? Isn't that what Danni said? Oh, Jesus...what am I doing?*

"You all set, Keefer?" Sheridan released the tall woman's hand to dig in her pocket for her car keys.

Ohh, how she says my name...

"Hey." Sheridan touched the tall woman's cheek and turned her to face her. "Are you okay?" she asked with concern.

Look at her eyes. They're blue and green at the same time. "Oh...yeah. I'm good. Sorry, I must have zoned out for a moment." The brunette blushed bright red.

"Aw, that's all right. I understand. Do you still want me to give you a lift? I'll send you home in a car service if that's—"

"No, it's okay, take me home." *Oh God, did I just say that?* "I, um, I mean..."

Sheridan chuckled and held the door to the club open. "I know what you meant. I may be the club slut, but you can trust me." Green eyes twinkled with amusement at Keefer's completely flustered expression.

"It's not that," the brunette stammered.

"Lighten up, Miss Gibson," Sheridan winked. "I'm just foolin' with ya."

45

Keefer smiled. "I can be so clueless at times." She closed her eyes briefly as a hand rested against her lower back, guiding her toward the car. "Oh wow. Is that your car? Are you sure I can get in there?"

"I don't know, but think of all the fun we can have trying." The blonde snickered and Keefer followed suit when the door was opened for her.

"Maybe I'd be better off stretched across the dashboard," the tall woman joked.

Oh, don't tempt me, Keef. "Nah, you'll do just fine, lemme push the seat back."

Blue eyes narrowed as Sheridan bent over and leaned into the car. *Oh, dear Lord, would you look at that ass in leather pants?* Keefer's mouth went dry as she let her gaze wander down to the blonde's thighs. *Oh, they're even more wonderful from behind.* Not believing the things that she was thinking, she blushed profusely.

Sheridan backed out and stood up, catching the red flush. *Hmm? Did I do that?* she smirked to herself. *You know you did, Sher...go slow with this one.* "Your chariot awaits, m'lady." Sheridan bowed and swept her hand out dramatically.

"You are but too kind," Keefer replied in a fake accent. *What do you know? You're heartbroken not twenty minutes and you're playing games with the classless construction worker.*

Once in the car, Sheridan got Keefer's address and then the two women fell silent. Sheridan had a million things to say, all of them inappropriate for her to bring up, most of them involving Danni. Keefer had a million things to say as well, but she would never say them. She was already mortified that her private life played out so publicly and not to mention with, of all people, Sheridan Landers. Blue eyes darted to the left, catching a glimpse of Sheridan in her peripheral vision. She really wanted to turn her head and stare at the construction worker. A hard hat and dust did no justice to her at all.

The blonde was dying to know what Keefer was thinking. She could feel the nervous energy in the car and wanted to cut through it so badly that she was breaking a sweat.

"Sheridan?"

The tall woman's barely audible voice gave the blonde goose bumps. Even in a nervous whisper, it was still sexy. "Yeah?"

"How did you know Danni was cheating on me?" Keefer forced herself to face the driver.

"I, uh...was kinda watching you," Sheridan admitted. "I saw you come in."

"Oh."

The car fell silent again. Sheridan began to get very uncomfortable. "Look, I wasn't watching you to spy on you or nothing. I just noticed you there and then I saw you get upset. I put two and two together."

"You knew Danni was cheating on me all along, didn't you?" Keefer hung her head.

"No!" *Jeez, Sher, scare her half to death.* "I mean, I knew she was cheating on someone. Someone named Keef. I didn't know your name," Sheridan babbled.

"You hit her when you found out it was me. How come?"

The blonde shrugged. "I always wanted to kick her ass. She gave me a reason."

Blue eyes picked up the blonde's nervousness and Keefer smiled. "You did it 'cuz you were protecting me."

"Maybe." Sheridan wanted to end this conversation. The way Keefer was grinning made her feel tingly.

"Thank you, Sheridan," the brunette said before she leaned over and kissed the blonde on the cheek.

"No problem." Sheridan felt pretty good about herself at that moment. "You're home, you want me to walk you to the door? Danni was pretty drunk tonight."

Is she cute or what? "If you'd like. I can take care of myself just fine, but it's nice to know I have my own personal bodyguard."

"Cut it out," the construction worker snickered.

Before they got to the door, Danni, still bloody, flung it open and glared angrily at the two of them. "I *knew* you were fucking her!"

"Danni! The neighbors!" Keefer hissed.

"Fuck the neighbors. Hell, fuck everybody while you're at it!" Danni bellowed.

Sheridan fumed, but she did notice a few bags by the door and it made her feel a bit better.

Keefer pushed Danni into the house and threw her on the couch. She had never been so embarrassed before. "*You* don't have to live here anymore, I *do*! Shut up and get out!"

Sheridan moved in behind Keefer just in case she needed a hand.

"What's *she* now, your fucking lapdog?" Danni slurred and laughed.

Sheridan growled.

Speaking of dogs..."Where's Fifi?" Keefer panicked, not noticing her anywhere.

"In the bathroom; she pissed me off."

"How dare you?" Keefer ran to the bathroom and let the dog out. "It's okay, baby, Mommy's home," she cooed to the whining Fifi.

"Hey, shit for brains," Sheridan spoke low. "You get off on fucking with women and dogs? Does that make you a tough guy? Huh?" she sneered, daring Danni to come after her. She could hear Keefer in the kitchen running water, probably for the dog to drink, and it angered her more.

"Fuck off and mind your business." The redhead swiped at her nose with her sleeve. "You already broke my nose, asshole. It's only a stupid dog."

Oh, looky, another reason. Sheridan stepped forward with a menacing growl.

Keefer came back in the room to find Sheridan smirking and Danni doubled over on her knees. "What happened?" she asked loudly.

"Danni here has no respect." Sheridan narrowed her eyes at the redhead.

"Get out now, Danni. I'll send the rest of your stuff to your mother's house. You explain it to her."

They both watched as the redhead stumbled to her bags and slinked out the door. Keefer melted into the couch in tears.

Sheridan didn't know what to do and stood there motionless. *Shit! What do I do? Do I hug her? Does she even want me to touch her? Should I say something? I'm sorry?* Just then a strange-looking dog appeared at Keefer's side, her bald tail wagging furiously as she tried to lick away her mommy's tears. Sheridan was reminded of how many times her babies comforted her and she smiled fondly at the dog.

The tall woman hugged her dog and cried. "Oh, man, this has been a huge nightmare. I'm so sorry you had to be involved, Sheridan." Keefer continued to weep. She couldn't pick up her head and was too mortified to look the blonde in the eyes.

"Hey, no problem. I don't mind." *Very comforting, Sher. Get your ass over there and make her stop crying.*

Keefer started when she felt the blonde sit down next to her. "You don't have to stay here, I'll be okay," she sniffled pathetically. "I'm so embarrassed by all of this."

Sheridan noticed Fifi giving her the eye, and so she gave her a hand to smell and Fifi licked her fingers. "Hey, I want to be here. You shouldn't be alone now, anyway. Danni could come back." The construction worker rummaged around in all her pockets. *I know I must have a napkin in here somewhere...Dunkin' Donuts, I'm sure...*

Keefer smiled through her tears as the crumpled-up napkin with pink and orange writing on it was thrust into her line of vision. It had dried coffee stains on it and that made her smile even bigger. She took the napkin and found a clean spot to wipe her nose. "Thank you...for everything." She held up the dirty napkin and grinned slightly.

Sheridan nodded and smiled back. Even miserable, Keefer was gorgeous. She felt horrible for getting aroused by the crying woman, but she couldn't do anything to stop it. She stood up abruptly and shoved her hands in her jacket pockets. "Uh, why don't you get cleaned up and comfortable and I'll get something for us to drink." At Keefer's nod she continued, "Just point me in the direction of the kitchen."

Keefer stood up, too, and forced herself to look at the blonde. "It's over there. Why are you still wearing your jacket?" *Not that I mind, all that leather is incredibly appealing.* The errant thought made her blush. She watched as the construction worker peeled off her coat and tossed it on the couch, baring the tightest black T-shirt she'd ever seen. Her heart picked up speed and she stared openly at the blonde's torso. *You have some nerve!* she mentally berated her body for reacting to the blonde.

Sheridan couldn't contain her smirk. Keefer was most definitely checking her out and, by the way she kept staring, was pleased with what she saw. She watched with amusement as the tall woman swallowed and nervously ran her hand through her hair. "I'll get those drinks," she said as she brushed past her.

Keefer smacked her hand to her forehead. *What is wrong with you? You should be devastated; instead, you drool all over the living room?* She shook her head and went to the bathroom to wash her burning face. Stopping in front of the mirror, she was horrified. *Look at you!* She splashed cold water on her face and neck, trying to get rid of the heat from crying and the evidence of her blush. *You're a mess, Keef. You're all swollen and ugly.* Even as she thought those things, she could still feel the twinge of arousal from seeing the blonde standing there in front of her. "You've gone your whole life not knowing what it felt like to be truly aroused and you picked a fabulous time to finally react," she told her reflection. The knowledge that Sheridan was sitting in her house with her, alone, made her gasp. *Oh no, what do I do?*

Sheridan waited patiently in the living room. She chose some iced tea and poured two tall glasses and set them on the coffee table. She studied Fifi and wondered what in the world had happened to her. It warmed her heart to know that Keefer loved this dog for all her flaws. The tall woman was a good person and she respected her more for it. She looked up when she heard the brunette clear her throat. Her mouth went dry when she saw that Keefer had changed into shorts and a baggy T- shirt. All those legs for her perusal—and she perused, all right.

49

"I hope Fifi didn't give you a hard time. She's a little protective of me." The tall woman sat down on the couch next to Sheridan and raised an eyebrow as the blonde flinched.

"No, she gave me the once-over, but seems to approve."

"She knows decent people when she smells them," Keefer joked.

"Well, then it must be my shower gel, 'cuz I'm far from decent." Sheridan wiggled an eyebrow. *Stop that! She's not one of the chicks at the club.* "I'm sorry..."

"That's okay, I have proof otherwise."

"Yeah, well, don't go spreading it around."

Keefer winked. "Don't worry, I'll keep your reputation intact."

Green eyes watched as a long arm stretched out to pick up the glass of tea. She felt her nostrils flare as she imagined those fingers wrapping around her arms, the tips digging into her skin as the tall woman lay beneath her. *Shit!* Sheridan closed her eyes and banished the thought. It would do no good for that earlier fantasy to make itself known right now.

"You know, I don't feel as bad as I thought I would about Danni. I think I feel relieved," Keefer admitted.

Grateful for the interruption from her mental musings, Sheridan leaned back on the couch and stretched her legs out. "Were you expecting it? I mean, you were pretty upset when you saw them, but I've seen much worse."

"I've known. I probably made her do it." The brunette couldn't tear her eyes from the blonde's body.

"Why would you say something like that? That's not fair." Sheridan frowned. *How could anybody throw this away?* Her eyes scanned the expanse of leg next to her. *Then again, Danni was telling the world how dead Keefer was in the sack...*She pulled her gaze from the smooth thigh and brought it to meet baby blue eyes. Seeing the inspector react to her stare made her avert her eyes. Her need was apparently evident and she didn't want to scare her.

"I wasn't a good enough girlfriend." Keefer forgot to breathe for a moment when she read the hunger in Sheridan's eyes. *I've seen that look before. Danni used to look at me like that right before we—* A powerful jolt of arousal traveled down her body.

Sheridan watched in fascination as Keefer's nipples tightened. She licked her lips and crossed her legs as she felt herself get damp between them. "I don't believe that for a second. Cheaters don't need reasons, they just cheat." *Fuck...I want her.*

Keefer looked away. She couldn't bring herself to confess to the blonde the real reason why Danni cheated. She wasn't any good in bed and Danni told her so often. She couldn't even imagine talking about sex with

Sheridan. She didn't think she could even say the word. "Trust me. I gave her reasons." She saw the blonde narrow her eyes and she changed the subject. "Are you planning on staying here the whole night?"

"Do you want me to?" Sheridan asked hesitantly.

"Well, I don't mind if you do." Keefer petted the dog to distract her thoughts about the construction worker spending the night at her house.

"If I won't be in the way..."

"You can crash in the den. The futon is very comfortable, I often sleep in there myself." *Why did you just say that? No one had to know that...*

Really? Hmm...I bet it smells like her then. I'll get no sleep tonight. "Sounds good to me. Just lead the way."

Keefer led her guest into the den and left her there while she went to fetch a sheet and pillow. *I can't give her Danni's pillow, can I? That just seems so wrong. I'll give her mine.* The inspector chose a clean sheet from the closet and stopped to gather her pillow. She was suddenly struck with the thought of the blonde's naked flesh touching her sheet and had to catch her breath. *I don't understand this. I am so entirely turned on by this woman...why is she doing this to me? Why now?*

Lost in her thoughts she was taken completely off guard as she walked into the den. Sheridan was standing there looking around the room, oblivious to Keefer, with her bra in her hand. Blue eyes were riveted to the construction workers breasts and Keefer felt her own nipples harden as she stared at Sheridan's. *She's not wearing her bra; her breasts are right there under her shirt.* The tall woman raised both eyebrows at herself. The thoughts that were taking over her brain the last few days had never even crossed her mind before. She had never been attracted to anyone, let alone thoroughly aroused. This new way of thinking was shocking her; she had little else on her mind lately except sex—sex with Sheridan. She swallowed hard. *And here she is, in my den, in the middle of the night...taking off her pants!* She threw the sheet and pillow in the room and turned her back quickly.

Sheridan jumped as the pile came flying at her. She caught the pillow and inhaled it without thought. *Man, this is her, all right.* She felt her crotch twitch. *I can't go to sleep this horny. I'll just have to take care of this when she goes to bed,* she decided.

"Uh, do you want some sweats or something? I'm sure Danni's will fit you." The quiver in Keefer's voice was very noticeable and she squeezed her eyes shut in embarrassment.

"That's okay, I'll just sleep in my underwear." *Like I'll get any sleep at all.* Noticing the tall woman hadn't turned around yet, the construction worker shook out the sheet and covered herself with it. *Damn, she's so shy!* "Hey, you can turn around, I'm covered."

Keefer turned slowly, and relief washed over her to see the blonde holding up the sheet. "The couch flattens to a bed if you want. The remote is over there." She pointed to the table. "We get all the channels."

Sheridan nodded and picked up the remote. She flipped on the television and out of habit checked through her favorite channels. Scanning quickly past the porno channel, she chuckled to herself. *Yep, all the channels I'll need.* "Thanks, Keefer. If you need me, just holler. I'm a light sleeper."

"I'll be all right. I guess I just need another presence in the house. Good night."

"Night."

Keefer left the den and went over what she had just said. She'd never needed another presence in the house before. The way the words fell from her mouth without hesitation made her wonder. She had a feeling that it wasn't just anybody she needed there tonight, but Sheridan. *I can't understand this. Everything is changing; I don't know what I feel anymore. I want her here. I never wanted anybody.* The tall woman slid into bed; as soon as she lay down, her entire body thanked her. *I must be more tired than I thought.* She stretched out her limbs and sighed loudly. *Sheridan Landers is sleeping in her panties...in the den.* That was the last coherent thought that skipped through Keefer's mind before she fell deeply asleep.

Sheridan waited until a long enough amount of time had passed before tiptoeing through the house to check on Keefer. Finding the bedroom, she looked in and saw the woman dead to the world, curled up in a small ball on the left side of the bed. Fighting the urge to approach the sleeping inspector, she hurried away and headed for the bathroom. Once she returned to the den, she turned down the volume on the TV and scanned through the channels. Wide awake and painfully aware of the throbbing between her legs, Sheridan turned to the porno channel in hopes of finding something else to inspire her instead of the woman in the bedroom down the hall. She wasn't quite sure she could control her moans if she continued with her Keefer fantasy. Unfortunately for Sheridan, the scene playing out on the television did nothing to help her. It was two women already heavily involved with each other, and all she could see were her and Keefer...panting and groping...sweating and groaning. She turned off the television in frustration and sat in the dark, quiet room for a few minutes before lying down on the futon, face first. She inhaled the pillow deeply and became wet instantly. *Oh, fuck.* She slipped her hands between her legs and sighed blissfully. *I can't help it; she's just too fucking hot.*

The tall woman turned over and groaned. She felt terrible; her head hurt and her eyes felt scratchy. *That's why you never cry,* she scolded herself. Looking at the clock on the night table, she scrunched up her face in distaste. *Eight in the morning on a Sunday. Yuck.* Throwing back the covers and swinging her long legs off the side of the bed, Keefer yawned widely.

Ohh, man. What a night. Her heart suddenly beat frantically. *Oh, my god! Sheridan is in the den!* She stood up and hurried to check on her guest. Peeking her head around the doorway, Keefer saw Sheridan sprawled on her stomach with her mouth hanging open, obviously still asleep. The sheet had twisted itself around the blonde's upper body, leaving her uncovered from the waist down. Blue eyes took in the small black panties, hardly covering the construction worker's muscular backside. The muscles in the back of her thighs were relaxed, but they were still pronounced and the tall woman's mouth watered. Still not quite comfortable with the way she was feeling about the blonde, Keefer backed out of the room with the vision of Sheridan's partially naked butt firmly imprinted in her mind.

After going through the morning bathroom rituals, the brunette put on a pot of coffee and unsuccessfully fought the urge to spy on her guest as she slept. As she stood outside the door to the den, Keefer's gaze drifted up and down the blonde's body several times, causing the fluttery feeling she'd been experiencing every time the construction worker entered her mind lately. Not knowing how she got there, Keefer found herself squatting down in front of Sheridan's peaceful face, tracing her full, parted lips with her eyes. The tall woman licked her dry lips as she received an unexpected image of those lips leaning in toward hers. Her heart picked up speed and she blinked a few times, trying to dispel the image. Tearing her gaze from Sheridan's lips, she let it wander down her body again, stopping to explore her firm rear with her eyes.

Keefer's body was reacting on a whole new level of awareness. She had never before felt anything like it. She struggled to keep her hands on the floor as she gaped openly at the half-naked blonde. She had the overwhelming urge to reach out and touch Sheridan's body, an urge so strong she feared she might not be able to control it, but still, she couldn't bring herself to stand up and leave the room. She could feel her shorts dampening as she became increasingly aroused, and she marveled at the feeling she got in the pit of her stomach when she once again let her eyes wander to the construction worker's lips.

Sheridan drifted toward wakefulness with the eerie feeling of being watched. Not fully aware of her surroundings, she peeked open an eye and was very surprised to find Keefer watching her. The blue eyes seemed to be tracing her body, and a fierce pang of arousal traveled through her groin. Sheridan struggled not to move, concentrating on her breathing, and closed her eye. *I wonder how long she's been here. What the hell time is it, anyway? Damn, why am I so fucking horny?*

She lost the battle of her will and peeked open the eye closest to the pillow. She felt the blood pounding through her veins when that eye focused and she saw the way Keefer was staring hungrily and with wonderment at her lips. She begged her body to lie still and her tongue not to wet her lips. She kept her eye mostly closed as she took the opportunity to steal a sweeping glance of the tall woman. Keefer was crouching, and Sheridan's line of vision narrowed between her legs. She could see the tall woman's shorts stretched tightly over her vagina, the seam parting her lips. Her own crotch throbbed when she spotted the small wet spot there, and she desperately fought the urge to inhale deeply in an attempt to smell the woman's arousal. She kept her eye cracked open a sliver; she was sure Keefer couldn't tell she was awake. The inspector was sure to be mortified if she knew, and Sheridan didn't want that to happen.

Keefer's tongue wet her lips again; the thoughts that were raging through her mind both shocked and aroused her to new heights. She couldn't stop imagining those perfect lips caressing parts of her body that lips had never touched before. She shifted her weight and bit back a gasp as her shorts dug between her legs. She reached down, slipped a finger through the side of the crotch and pulled the material away from her body. Her eyes closed involuntarily as the back of her finger grazed her sex. *Wow,* she thought as she pulled out the finger and held it to her face. It was wet, very wet. *This is incredible! I feel like I'm on fire!* The urge to put out the fire was slowly consuming her, a thought that hadn't occurred to her before Sheridan entered her life. She craved to ease the ache that the blonde's body had caused and she even thought, for a split second, about doing it right there as her hand once again fell to her crotch. Suddenly realizing what she was doing, Keefer snatched her hand away and stood up. Her heart was pounding like a drum in her ears and she thought she might even faint. She took a deep breath, fled from the room, and locked herself in the bathroom.

She sat on the side of the tub and tried to get her breathing back to normal. She felt confused and a little ashamed at what just happened. All sorts of new urges she'd never felt before overwhelmed her at once. She sat there with her arms resting on her legs and her head in her hands, trying to gain some control back from her own body. Her sex wasn't just giving her signals, it was ringing bells and blowing whistles. It had been a fantastic feeling when she touched herself and as she replayed that moment in her head, the same image of Sheridan filled her mind. A groan escaped her lips and she opened her eyes to chase the image and the feelings away.

As she looked down at her wet shorts, the tall woman automatically touched the darkened spot and she gasped at the feeling. She left her hand there and closed her eyes, the construction worker's half-naked body flashing behind the lids. She moved her hand and bit her lip; the sensations spread all throughout her body and she was afraid that she might make an embarrassing noise. Her hand kept moving tentatively, her breathing changing drastically. Quite against her will, she found herself imagining the blonde's hand between her legs. She felt her shorts get wetter and her sex get hotter. The feelings were incredible now, traveling through her entire body, making her feel things she'd never—she couldn't stop if she wanted to. She moved her hand more confidently, struggling not to make any noise; the pressure was building from the inside out and her legs started to tremble. The sensations overwhelmed her, and a quiet hiss escaped through her teeth as her body jerked uncontrollably. Blue eyes popped open and watched in disbelief as her thighs clamped closed around her hand.

Sheridan sat upright and ran a shaky hand through her hair. She was beyond aroused and thanked every power there was for making Keefer stop and run. She was certain she would have tackled the tall woman and taken her on the spot, though after witnessing Keefer's amazement at her own wetness, she was beginning to understand more and more about her. Keefer was not going to be on her list of conquests. While Sheridan already knew that and respected that from the get-go, she now realized just how much work it would be for the tall woman to open up, let alone have sex. She suddenly hated Danni with a vengeance. Now that she knew a little bit more than when she went to sleep, all of Keefer's comments made sense. *Of course she thought she wasn't a good enough girlfriend, of course she thought she drove Danni to Susan. Of course Danni would say she was a cold fish in bed. That uncaring little fucker...*Sheridan wished Danni were there. She could guess what the real problem was, and if Danni were any kind of human, she would have helped Keefer, not hurt her. *Keefer has major sex issues. I bet that bitch never once gave her any support.*

It had been too quiet for too long. Sheridan knocked on the bathroom door. "Hey, you okay in there?"

Keefer jumped up to attention and turned on the water. "Yeah," she croaked out. "I'll be right out." Her heart was pounding and she couldn't breathe. *I have never felt anything remotely like that before with Danni,* she thought in awe, staring at her hand. *I can't believe I did that! What has gotten into me?* She washed her hands thoroughly before doing the same to her flushed face. *I have to get out of these shorts.*

Sheridan watched Keefer closely as she exited the bathroom. She shivered at the telltale afterglow. *Oh, boy! What I wouldn't have given to be part of that!* All of a sudden, she realized why the tall woman was so flustered, and she groaned to herself, *I don't have the patience for this...*Keefer reappeared dressed in jeans and a long-sleeved white shirt, her hair pulled back in a ponytail. She smiled quickly at Sheridan and then looked away guiltily. *Well, maybe I have some patience left somewhere.*

Chapter 6

The blonde construction worker tidied up the den as Keefer poured the coffee. She wanted to go home to her dogs as soon as possible, but at the same time she didn't want to leave the tall inspector. Usually, her dogs were her best excuse to go running from a woman's house, but not this one. Whether it was the sudden protectiveness she felt for Keefer or the lust she was experiencing, Sheridan wanted to be near the sexy brunette as much as possible.

Keefer stood with her back against the edge of the counter top, holding her mug of coffee. She was still stuck, replaying the events of the morning in disbelief and embarrassment. Oh sure, it felt good, very good to touch herself like that, but it was *why* she did it that gave her fits. She had never wanted to be touched so badly before, and the only times she ever did crave attention were long after Danni had been touching her already. Sheridan hadn't even been awake and Keefer was so aroused, she couldn't control the need to touch herself. Danni often begged her to do it, not only for her own selfish pleasures, but hoping that it would help Keefer's climax come quicker so she could go to sleep. The tall woman never gave it a second thought and always refused. She'd never done that in her life, not even as an inquisitive child. Keefer wasn't by any means a sexual person, not in the way that she'd read about or heard people talk about. She'd never thought of herself as abnormal until Danni started telling her she was. She had even begun to wonder if maybe Danni was right, that she was a sexual freak of nature.

Until now.

She had never experienced the depth of arousal that she felt that morning while watching Sheridan sleep. She craved and felt things that took her completely by surprise, but that she was unable to process at the time. She was too hot to think about it; she couldn't stop to analyze if she wanted to. *God, is it hot in here?* She fanned herself and pulled a box of donuts off of the counter. The whole train of thought was making her blush deeply and she had to stop before Sheridan appeared.

Sheridan joined Keefer at the kitchen table and picked up the steaming mug with a smile. "How did you know how I take my coffee?" she asked, snatching a donut from the open box. "And donuts, too. Ms. Gibson, have you been spying on me?"

Keefer paled, dropped her coffee all over the table and jumped up from her seat.

"Jesus! What happened?" Sheridan asked as she ran to the roll of paper towels. *Shit all I said was—fuck! Way to go, Sheridan!*

"It, uh...it must have slipped. I better go change," Keefer said with a shaky voice as she ran from the kitchen.

"Shit, smart mouth, how are you gonna fix this?" the blonde asked herself as she wiped up the coffee.

"Oh, my god! She saw me...she goddamned saw me...what am I going to do?" Keefer felt like crying again. Her entire body felt hot. Her mind played back the earlier events quickly and she took a deep breath. "Get a grip, Keef. She was fast asleep." She peeled off her wet pants and grimaced. "Christ! There's coffee all over me. I need a shower," she yelled out to Sheridan.

The construction worker turned off the water in the kitchen, thinking she had heard Keefer call to her. She dried her hands on the towel and took it with her as she walked toward where she thought the tall woman might be. The bedroom door was open a crack and Sheridan was looking right through it. Like a fantasy come true, there was Keefer standing by the bed, pulling her shirt over her head. She wore nothing but panties and Sheridan suddenly felt light-headed at the sight. The brunette had the most perfect breasts she had ever seen in her life, and she'd seen enough to know. Her mouth watered as she imagined what one might taste like. Her eyes traveled downward; Keefer's abdomen was beautiful, flat and smooth.

Sheridan had to swallow. She was actively drooling and she still hadn't gotten to those legs. Green eyes widened as Keefer hooked her fingers in the elastic of her panties and Sheridan backed up, away from view, desperate to see what came next but not willing to be caught. She watched, her heart beating loudly as the tall woman bent at the waist and pulled her panties down to her shins before standing up and kicking them off of her feet. Keefer bent to speak to the dog on her bed and Sheridan almost gasped out loud. Green eyes clamped shut and the blonde woman took a deep breath, opening them again very slowly. The tall woman was facing her dresser, rummaging through the drawer, her bare ass staring Sheridan right in the face. *Hot shit...would you look at her...there's not one single flaw on that whole entire body.*

Her eyes wide open and her mouth gaping, the blonde watched as Keefer turned around and walked toward the doorway. Sheridan scanned every single inch that was bared to her—the firm, large breasts with perfect nipples standing proudly in the center, her delightful stomach, and her dark black, neatly trimmed thatch of pubic hair at the apex of two gloriously long, sculpted legs. Keefer reached for something on the back of the door and Sheridan hightailed it back into the kitchen. Her head was swimming with naked Keefers, her heart pounding in her ears. She tried to associate that woman with the bitchy inspector that she'd first encountered at the job. They were two completely different people. Fifi appeared by her legs and she reached down absently to pet her head.

Keefer stood in the kitchen with her head cocked in question. Sheridan looked all out of sorts and from the way she was clutching the dishtowel, the tall woman thought she had hurt herself. "Sheridan? Is everything all right?"

Jarring back to reality, Sheridan focused on Keefer in her big fluffy robe. She swallowed hard before she spoke, "Yeah, everything's fine."

"Oh, okay. Are you sure? You look upset."

"No, really, I'm okay." At Keefer's raised eyebrow, she smiled. "Honest."

"Well, then I'm going to take a shower, I'm all sticky from coffee."

"Listen, I gotta go take care of my dogs. As much as I'd love to stay here with you all day, and I would, I have to feed and walk them or they will tear my place apart," she said with regret. This was the one time where she wished the dogs could use a can opener.

"You really want to spend the day with me?" Keefer blurted before thinking.

"Well...yeah. Why wouldn't I?" Sheridan grinned at the blush that Keefer wore. *I'm getting mighty attached to that color.*

"No reason. I'm just surprised, you hardly know me and after all that's happened..."

"Oh, I know you better than you think, Keefer." The blonde startled herself by saying that out loud.

Keefer's eyes widened considerably. "What do you mean by that?" she asked nervously.

"I mean, that I know you have a heart of gold. Fifi is testament to that. I know you had a shit for a girlfriend; I know you deserve much better. I also know that you can still find that special person who's willing to treat you with the respect that you deserve." *Phew!*

Keefer expelled a loud breath. She was taken for a loop. No one ever said those things to her, not even Danni—and she claimed to love her. She looked at Sheridan differently now. "You know all that, do you?"

"Yes, I do...and I believe it."

Keefer had the sudden urge to kiss the shorter woman, but held herself back. Not being a touchy-feely person, it worried her how she suddenly needed to have physical contact with Sheridan. It worried her still more as to how she'd react should she actually make that contact. "Um, thank you. I'm going to shower now. Just lock the door behind you." She got as close to the blonde as she could without touching her. "Thank you so much for staying here last night. If I can do you any favors, just tell me."

Sheridan, not having Keefer's reserve, reached out to the tall woman and took her hands. "Don't you worry, I'll think of something." She kissed one hand and winked before heading into the living room.

Keefer watched breathlessly as Sheridan picked up her jacket and left the house. The blonde's leather-covered rear was the last thing she saw as the door closed. "Whew, Feefs. I think I'm in big trouble here. I didn't want her to go."

Keefer finished her shower and wandered around her house in a daze. Standing in the living room, she noticed a mangled napkin on the coffee table with writing on it. Upon further inspection, she found that Sheridan had written her phone number on it and a small note that said if she ever needed her for anything to call. Keefer smiled at the donut shop napkin. She'd have figured Sheridan to carry around little cheesy business cards that said, "For a good time call..." Smoothing out the wrinkled napkin, she folded it in half and held it as she walked into the den.

Fifi was already sprawled out on the couch, her head resting on the folded sheet that Sheridan had left there. "The baby likes Sheridan, doesn't she?" Keefer sat next to her dog and scratched her behind the ear. "The mommy likes her too," she said as she picked up her pillow and hugged it. "Oh no..." Under the pillow was a black sports bra. Keefer picked it up and stretched it out, inspecting it. She could never wear one of these—her breasts were too big. She held it up to her body and snickered at the difference in size. Suddenly her stomach clenched as Sheridan's cologne wafted up to her nose. She hummed in the back of her throat as she brought the bra up to her face. *My mouth is where her tits were,* she thought fleetingly.

Fifi gave her mommy a curious look as she flopped back on the futon with the bra on her face. The tall woman lay there for a long while smelling the bra, feeling all sorts of good sensations tingle through her body as she thought about Sheridan's breasts. Her tongue poked out on its own volition and she tasted the fabric briefly before she jolted upright and pulled the bra off her face. Thinking about what she'd just done, and the things she'd done earlier, she came to a conclusion. "Okay, Keef, you're now officially obsessed."

I am never going to shake those images... Sheridan mused while she watched her dogs run wild in the park. *Those tits... that ass... mmm... she's fucking perfect.* She absently tapped her fingers on her thigh. *What now, Sher? She wants you and you know it. You wanna fuck her so badly... but you can't, and you know that, too.* She reached down and turned on the radio. *The woman has issues, lotsa issues. But did you see her? She touched herself thinking about you this morning,* she thought. A grin curled the side of her lips. *You did the same fucking thing, you perv.*

A thought popped into her head that made her heart palpitate. *Imagine doing it together...* She remained lost in the thought for a long time, the wetness growing between her legs. *Oh, yeah...imagine those long fingers doing their thing right there in front of you...* A small growl fell from her lips and the blonde shook her head and whistled for her dogs. *Just cut that out—now! That's an image you really don't need.* Zeus came to a skidding halt at her feet and she reattached his leash. Pharaoh was still hogging a Frisbee from a collie and she had to walk over to him to wrestle it free. She apologized to the collie's owner at the condition of the toy and promised to replace it next time. She hooked Pharaoh up to his leash and walked toward the gate, mulling over her dilemma. *It's Sunday night and you need to get laid. How the fuck are you gonna do that? The goddamned club is closed for renovations until Tuesday.* It was going to be a long two days. Sheridan was horny as hell.

Keefer returned home after walking Fifi and as she put the key in the door fear, washed over her. *Uh-oh...what if Danni's in there?* She turned the key slowly, swallowing hard, bracing herself for her ex-girlfriend-to-be on the other side. Hesitantly opening the door, she waited. "Is she there, Feefs?" The dog offered no answer, but the way she was shoving her nose through the small opening in the door made Keefer felt a little more confident. "Okay, go on then," she told Fifi and pushed the door open all the way. Taking a look around the living room, she was relieved to find it intact, though she was scared to check the rest of the house. *This is ridiculous. You took all those self-defense classes and you're acting like a frightened little girl.* Keefer knew she could never hit Danni with intent to harm, though, and that's why she was so afraid to find her there. The redhead never acted like she had last night—so hurtful and full of spite.

61

The tall woman walked quietly through the house, Fifi on her heels, sensing her mommy's trepidation. "It's okay, Feefs, the house is empty." She patted the worried dog and let out a sigh of relief. She never thought she'd ever be afraid of Danni and she wasn't sure it was actually fear that she was feeling; nonetheless, she wasn't at all comfortable with the knowledge that the redhead still had the keys to the house.

Sheridan sat on the couch in her underwear with her feet up on the coffee table. Zeus had his head on her left thigh and Pharaoh was curled up next to her with his body under her right arm. She idly scratched his back as she flipped through the boring Sunday television programs and waited for the microwave to ping, telling her dinner was ready. She drank Pepsi out of the one-liter bottle and belched loudly, snickering as all four doggie ears twitched at the sound. *Oh, man...this is my entertainment? I am so pathetic.* She laughed at herself as she jumped up and did a happy dance when her oven pinged. "Woo hoo...Hungry Man chicken."

She fed herself and her dogs and then turned the apartment upside-down, looking for something to do. So far, she had done pretty well keeping the tall brunette off of her mind and intended to keep doing so until the club opened up again on Tuesday. If she continued to think of Keefer in the ways that she had been that morning, her right forearm was sure to look like Popeye's—and that would never do. Besides, "Why do it yourself when you can have someone else do it for you?" was her motto. Not that she'd knock it—she had been doing it as long as she could remember –it just felt so much better when someone else did it.

Her thoughts drifted back to the expression on Keefer's face when she'd touched herself. If Sheridan didn't know better, she'd think it was the first time the woman had ever done such a thing; she'd looked totally surprised by both the feeling and the wetness she'd encountered. *Poor Keefer...missed out on so much fun...*She shook her head in sadness. *I'd love to teach you everything there is to know,* she thought with a smirk.

"Oh baby!" She chuckled out loud. "Wouldn't that be something, showing her all the finer points of pleasure?" Sheridan narrowed her eyes. *I told you not to go there; you have two whole days to go until you get laid.* The reprimand did no good as her mind wandered all over the place. Unfortunately, all images and thoughts included the tall inspector, every one of them erotic. "Fine! Stay horny; see if I care!" she yelled at her crotch.

It was almost lunchtime on Monday afternoon. Keefer closed the folder she had been staring at and placed it neatly on top of the stack on her desk. She leaned back in her chair and stretched out her long legs, kicking her shoes off of her feet. *I hate stockings...*She frowned at her feet and wiggled her captive toes. The phone rang and she stiffened. Danni had been calling her all morning, alternately begging for forgiveness and being hurtful. Keefer didn't want to answer her phone, but had to—it could be important. "Keefer Gibson," she said into the receiver, closing her eyes and bracing herself.

"Babe, don't hang up on me, please!"

The inspector threw herself back in her chair and blew out a frustrated breath. "What," she said with annoyance.

"Listen to me, please. I'm sorry. Why can't you believe me?"

"Danni, you're not sorry. Now leave me alone." Keefer sighed; she was getting tired of this.

"But, Keef!" Danni whined.

"What could you possibly give as an excuse that would make me forgive you? You slept with another woman—you didn't even bother being discreet! Half of Brooklyn knows that you played me for a fool, Danni!" Keefer was getting angry and it was showing through her voice. "You embarrassed me, you disrespected me, and you weren't the least bit concerned about who knew it."

"You're just pissed that the little construction worker knew. Keefer, she's nothing but a slut! She's a fucking asshole! I love you!"

"Sheridan isn't the asshole, you are. Now stop calling me."

"Sheridan is a fucking loser! She's only out to fuck you. Do you think she cares about you?" Danni barked a laugh. "You're wrong, she wants to nail you and add you to her collection of conquests. Keef! She broke my nose!"

Keefer smiled. "Yeah she did break your nose. You deserved it." She slammed the receiver down and dropped her head into her hands. *Oh, shit. What if Danni is right? What if I'm reading Sheridan all wrong...what if she only wants to sleep with me?*

She slipped the folded napkin out from under her desk blotter. She thought about calling Sheridan and just plain asking what her intent was, but then she changed her mind. *What if Danni is making all this up to hurt me?* She stood up and put on her suit jacket, shoving the napkin into her pocket. *I should just ask her what she wants from me. She'll be honest.* She stopped on her way to the door and looked in the mirror. *What if she does only want me for sex...then what? Do I sleep with her anyway? Oh, no. I could never...could I? I've never wanted to so badly before in my life. Would it be so bad if I did?*

The tall woman blinked a few times and forced the thought out of her mind. She'd gone all morning without thinking of the muscular blonde, and she intended to keep up the good work for the remainder of the day.

Sheridan did nothing for her concentration—thoughts of her confused her body and her mind. Once the woman popped into her head, she found it hard to think about anything else. Her eyes, her body, her hands...

"Her hands? Why her hands?" Keefer asked out loud. She remembered the way those callused hands felt as they held hers, the roughened skin scratchy against her palms. A shiver coursed through her body as she imagined the feeling of those fingers elsewhere. She felt her nipples tighten and she glanced down at them in confusion. "Why do you keep doing that?" she asked them. Thankfully, they didn't respond and she blushed as she studied them. She had never been aware of her nipples reacting in such a way to any thoughts or situations before, except a chill. She looked away from the mirror as she thought about Sheridan's hands on her breasts and gasped audibly as she felt her nipples tingle in response. *Hmm...* She reached up with one hand in curiosity. The instant her fingers brushed against her nipple a surge of feeling washed over her and settled between her legs. Eyes wide, she stared at her reflection, the warmth in her sex a steady reminder of her body's inability to control itself when it came to the little blonde construction worker. *Again...would it be so bad if she only wants to sleep with me?*

Sheridan flopped down on a pile of cement bags and opened her lunch. Phil sat on the floor in front of her and opened his lunch, too. They ate in silence until Bobby sat down next to Sheridan and hip-checked her.

"Watch it, asshole," she threatened, nearly sliding off the cement bag.

"Cranky much?" he asked with a raised eyebrow. "You've been biting our heads off all morning. What gives?"

"I'm not cranky, I'm horny. Unless you plan on doing something about it, get off my lap," she growled.

"Ooh..." Bobby mock shook. "Okay, tough guy, I'm moving." He moved to the floor and exchanged looks with Phil, who shrugged and bit into his monster sandwich.

"What's going on, Patch? It's not like you to go without," Bobby dared to ask.

"Ah, it's not that...I had some trouble Saturday night. I had to tend to a lady in trouble. Kinda fucked up my plans," she said with a frown.

"Always the gentleman. That's cool, though, it's not so bad to help out a lady," Phil said with a grin. "The benefits are well worth it."

"Yeah, but it's not that kind of thing, buddy. She's not someone I want to dick around with; she's got a few issues," Sheridan explained.

"Issues? Forget it, Patch, you don't need issues." Phil held up his hand and shook his head. "Plenty other fish in the sea."

"That's what I keep telling myself," she muttered, biting into her lunch.

"Huh?" Bobby furrowed his brows.

"Nuthin'...forget it," she said around a mouthful of food.

They ate their lunches in silence. Sheridan stayed lost in thoughts of Keefer and her glorious nakedness, Keefer touching herself, Keefer blushing, Keefer in the shower...She suddenly stood up and cleared her throat. "I need some air, guys."

Phil and Bobby watched in curiosity as she ran down the stairs.

"What do you think has gotten into her?" Phil wondered.

"I think it's this damsel in distress. She seems pretty bothered by it; she's been distracted all morning," Bobby said, polishing off his lunch.

"If this thing happened on Saturday, she's been stewing in it since then. I wonder what this woman is like to get Patch all fucked up?"

"I dunno, Philly, but she must be something else. I've never seen her act like this before."

Sheridan stomped around outside for a while, trying to think about something other than Keefer. She climbed up onto the back of a high pickup truck and swung her feet back and forth. *Why is she still on my mind? What has she done to me?* she wondered. *Sure, she's a hell of a fine-looking woman, but I can't fuck her. That should be the end of the whole thing, but it's not. I still can't stop thinking about her.* The blonde jumped down from the back of the truck and moved some gravel around with her foot. *I should have taken her phone number, see if she's all right. What if that bitch-face came back to bother her?* Sheridan felt panic. *Oh, no...what if she did? What if she needed me?* She paced back and forth. *Okay, I gave her my number. If she needs me, she'll call me. Stop worrying, Sher.* She took a deep breath and adjusted her hard hat, rubbing the tension out of her neck. Her cell phone chirped and her heart beat faster. Looking at the phone, she saw it was her dad and she felt somewhat let down at the familiar number; she'd hoped it was Keefer. *Why is she doing this to me?*

"Whassup, Pop?"

"Steven wants to work with you tomorrow, is it okay?"

"Sure...I'll pick him up in the morning on my way over."

"Thanks, sweetheart."

Sheridan clipped the phone back into its holder and started back toward the guys. *At least I don't have to think about her tomorrow. I'll be too distracted,* she thought with relief.

Keefer strolled back into the building after a long walk on her lunch hour. She looked around briefly to make sure Danni wasn't in the lobby and headed toward the elevator. She hated feeling like she did, looking around every corner for her ex, but they both worked for the same company and she was bound to run into her somewhere.

Standing in the safety of her office, the brunette noticed that she had a few messages blinking on her voicemail. She sat down and thought about transferring out of the building, maybe to another location, so she wouldn't have to worry about Danni while at work. It was bad enough that Sheridan distracted her, but that was a good distraction; Danni's was bad. Thinking about Sheridan made her feel very good things. Danni made her feel sick and nervous. She couldn't possibly continue to work in a productive manner with all the distractions.

Playing back her messages, she flinched at Danni's voice, instantly deleting the voicemail without listening to it. All the messages were from Danni and she deleted them all. Closing her eyes, she wondered if she should be afraid that Danni would come back to the house. She sounded desperate enough, and Keefer became worried. She fingered the napkin in her pocket, entertaining the idea of calling Sheridan and asking her to come over. *For what? What would I be asking her to come over for? Protection?* She grimaced and shook her head. *Be a big girl, Keef. You can deal with Danni all by yourself. You don't need to put Sheridan in the middle of this.* She sighed out loud. *You want Sheridan somewhere, though, don't you? How? Why?*

Keefer's boss stuck his head in her office and she immediately dropped all thoughts of Sheridan and Danni, knowing it would be a brief respite.

The blonde pushed open her apartment door and laughed out loud as her dogs greeted her with the same enthusiasm as they did every day. "You'd think I was gone for weeks!" she mumbled around the paw that covered her face. "Phew, Zeus, your feet stink!" She made a sour face that didn't last long as she was licked to death by warring tongues. "Pthbht." She chuckled and blew big gusts of air in the dogs' faces. "Okay...that's it! Enough!" she yelled, twisting her body around beneath the giant dogs. Finally getting herself in an upright position, she gave the animals a long look. "You guys are so dusty and dirty. You both smell."

Pharaoh actually looked offended and he cocked his good ear along with his eyebrows.

"Well, you do. Both of you need a bath. What do you say we hit the groomer's tomorrow morning?"

Zeus turned over on his back and sighed pathetically, Pharaoh smelled Zeus's bared belly and then sneezed.

"See? I told you so," Sheridan stuck out her tongue at the dogs and proceeded to get undressed as she walked to the bedroom. "Tomorrow it is, then," she said to herself.

Pharaoh followed her into the bedroom and jumped up on the bed.

"Hey, get your smelly feet off of my bed! And where is my black bra, you thief?" she questioned the dog as she sifted through her underwear drawer. "You're the underwear stealer, go get it," she ordered Pharaoh, who lay down and yawned. "Fine, I won't wear a bra then," she told the dog and then disappeared into the shower.

Keefer pulled off her stockings and twisted them up in a ball before throwing them on the floor, "God, I hate those things." She frowned at the balled-up nylon. "Why do I have to wear them anyway? Tomorrow I won't wear stockings. Heck, I won't even wear a dress, I'll wear pants to work," she decided as she pulled on baggy sweats. Looking at herself in her mirror, she scowled. *These are Danni's sweats.* Keefer went through her dresser and her closet and pursed her lips in thought. *Hmm...I never thought about that before.* Realizing she had no sweats of her own, she made another decision and grabbed her wallet. *Time to go shopping.*

"Feefs!" she called and the dog came running. "Go get that leash, we're going for a long walk."

Chapter 7

Keefer hummed as she waited in line at the coffee cart on a bright Tuesday morning. She was in a very good mood, despite being woken up by a phone call from a pleading Danni. As soon as she refused her, Danni became vicious and said some things that made Keefer's stomach hurt, but she refused to let it get to her. Following her previous night's plans, Keefer dressed in chinos, a white button-down shirt and comfortable shoes. *No pantyhose!* She sighed happily to herself when the soft cotton pants moved against her legs as she descended the stairs to the subway. It had been so long since she felt comfortable sitting on the train that she had intentionally let her long legs sprawl open, taking up more room than necessary, despite the glares from standing passengers. Accepting her cup of coffee and bagel, the tall woman made her way to her building with a spring in her step.

"Whoo-ee, tall lady, you sure do look different like that!" The homeless man clapped both dirty hands together in approval.

"Thanks, bud, here's your paper. Have a great day," she smiled.

"I sure will after seeing that smile!" he replied in all honesty.

Keefer got some curious looks from her co-workers as she headed to her office. She wasn't sure if the women were looking at her with jealousy or contempt. She made sure to smile at all of them. She had been feeling quite confident since buying new clothes the previous night and she couldn't care less if these people hated her or not. It didn't matter to her; lately she didn't much care about anyone's opinion. Her whole attitude had suddenly changed after she broke up with Danni and met Sheridan. She hadn't given it much thought, but if she did, she would have seen how much more attractive she had become with her newfound cockiness —one of the reasons Danni was being so persistent.

Sheridan picked up her brother and dropped off the dogs at the groomer's, then the pair went directly to the do-it-yourself car wash. It was still early and if her dogs were going to suffer a day at the groomer, then the least she could do was clean the car.

Steven was content to do the exterior, so she fed the machine quarters and cranked up the radio as she vacuumed her side of the car first. Singing out loud with the radio, she failed to notice the car pull up beside her until she saw the feet standing next to her. Backing out of the driver's seat, she stood up to face the one person she thought she'd never see again. *Danni.*

"What the fuck do you want?" Sheridan immediately adopted a defensive stance. Steven stood straight up and watched protectively from behind the car.

"Nice to see you, too," the redhead smirked. "Ya nail my girlfriend yet?"

"She's not your girlfriend any more, Danni. Deal with it." Sheridan crossed her arms over her chest and flexed her biceps for effect.

Danni took a good look at the construction worker's body. She'd never seen her in the daylight or in a T-shirt. Sheridan was in great shape. She re-thought her initial intentions of menacing the blonde and stepped back a foot or two.

"Is that all, Danni, because me and my brother have to get to work," Sheridan said, feigning boredom.

"Yeah, well, I'm just warning you—Keefer ain't worth the effort. She doesn't know how to fuck and I doubt she's had any practice since we broke up."

Sheridan felt the anger welling up inside her at Danni's chuckle. *How dare she laugh at Keefer's expense?* "Oh, I wouldn't be so sure of that, Danni-girl." She wiggled her eyebrows suggestively.

Danni couldn't believe it. *Did she really sleep with her or is she fucking with me?* "What exactly are you implying?"

"I'm just saying that maybe she *does* know how to fuck. It could have been her partner that sucked ass in the sack," Sheridan said with a big shit-eating grin on her face.

"You lying sack of shit," Danni fumed.

"Hey, maybe you just didn't know what to do to please her. Perhaps she's a wild woman in bed and you just never knew it. Mmm, mmm, mmm. She's a fine-looking woman, Danni. So sorry she kicked your ass out."

Danni wanted to throw a punch so badly her fingers twitched, but she was sure she'd never even land the blow before she was bleeding from one of her orifices again.

"Well, bye-bye now. If you'll excuse me, I gotta finish making my car clean. You never know what pretty woman I may drive around in it."

Sheridan stepped toward Danni and she backed up even further. The redhead certainly didn't expect that kind of encounter. Was Keefer really fucking Sheridan? The construction worker pretty much spelled it out, but could she trust her? She might have been fucking with her head. Danni watched through narrowed eyes as the blonde went back to vacuuming her car, singing with the music. *That cocky little shit,* she thought angrily. *She can't be fucking Keefer and Keefer can't be a wild woman. She just can't!* She stomped to her car and slammed the door behind her. *She just can't be fucking her, can she? Only one way to find out. Keefer...*

The tall inspector came back from her lunch hour with a few new purchases, the most important being the caller ID units she was about to install on her office phone and at home as soon as she arrived there. Danni wasn't going to ruin her days anymore. The second thing she bought was a giant pack of dress socks. If she was going to be wearing comfortable shoes, she needed comfortable socks to go along with them. It would seem no one said anything about the way she was dressed; she'd even made sure to have an impromptu chat with her supervisor and he didn't seem fazed. She was a little pissed, at first, that she could have been dressing this comfortably all along, until she remembered that it was Danni who told her she should dress like that for work. *Why did I ever listen to her? Why was I so damned wishy-washy?* Keefer felt a new sense of power even as she purchased her socks. She was in charge of her life and how she should live it. She felt stronger than she had in a long time. When she started thinking about what happened to her life and how she'd lost control of it, she felt bitter and all her resentment pointed toward Danni. She wasn't happy with that feeling and pushed it away, opting for a much brighter mood by thinking about a trip to the Gap for all new work clothes.

Settling down and hooking up the caller ID, Keefer sat behind her desk in her comfortable clothes and went back to work. Not soon after she picked up a pen, the phone rang. Blue eyes darted to the little screen and she grinned when she noticed the phone number. With an evil little chuckle, she picked up the receiver an inch off the cradle and let it drop back down. Feeling very good about what she had just done, she leaned back in her chair and smiled.

After the initial greetings were over, Sheridan led her brother back outside to the trucks. He was very excited to be helping his sister; he looked up to her and lived for her acceptance. She never let him down and always told him she was proud of him.

71

"You and me are gonna unload the trucks, Steven, okay? These bags of cement are pretty heavy but us Landers kids can handle it," she grinned, smacking Steven on his shoulder.

"No problem, Sher. Where are we going to put them?"

"We just gotta empty the trucks, it don't matter," the blonde shrugged.

"Wouldn't it be better if we can put them where they should be so no one has to lift them again?" he asked with concern. "They're heavy."

"You got a point there, Stevie." Sheridan stepped back and thought a minute. "Okay, but they have to go inside, you think you can carry them all that way?"

"Yes, I ate my Wheaties this morning," Steven replied confidently and with his ever-present smile.

Sheridan smiled back, "Well then, let's get moving there, brother." She hoisted a bag up over her shoulder and walked off.

"'Kay! I'm coming, Sher!" he yelled excitedly and mimicked her actions.

Keefer glanced up at the clock and her eyes widened in shock. She had been daydreaming for the better part of an hour. Shaking her head in disbelief, she stood up and stretched, groaning out loud as her shoulder popped. "You were doing so good, Keef, what happened?" she asked herself, visions of the muscular blonde still clouding her brain. Somehow, Sheridan had managed to slip into her head and Keefer couldn't shake her. Right now, even as she tried to dispel the images, she couldn't. The construction worker's hard little body invaded her thoughts.

Moments passed with Keefer growing increasingly aware of her body's reactions to her less than pure thoughts. She scrubbed her hands over her face in an effort to wash away the visions. This led to her hands sliding down her neck and to her chest, as she imagined them to be Sheridan's hands touching her. A small sigh of pleasure slipped through her lips as her hands reached her breasts. She lingered there and let her palms feel her nipples tightening, her heart beating faster. *Will her hands feel this good?* she thought as she moved them ever so slightly across her pebbled flesh. *Will I ever know?*

Keefer's phone rang and she jumped, pulling her hands from her body, staring at them in amazement. "What the hell am I doing?" She looked to the caller ID and saw Danni's number appear. "Persistent, aren't we, Danni?" *God, if she didn't call, what would I have done?* The idea that she was touching herself again stunned her; the fact that she was doing it at work mortified her. Images of why she was doing it flashed in her head again. Sheridan Landers was becoming more than a distraction and it scared her. She needed something to keep her busy. Looking around the room, Keefer spotted something. She stood up, grabbed the latest issue of OSHA's safety handbook and started reading out loud.

Sheridan dropped the bag of cement and Bobby whistled, "Breaking quite a sweat there, Patch!"

She looked down at her soggy black T-shirt. "Yeah." She wiped a dirty arm across her forehead. "Not a bad thing at all."

"I always say there's only three good reasons to sweat: sex, workouts, and hard labor."

"Hear, hear," she agreed with a high five.

"Hey, Sher, can we take a break? I'm really thirsty," Steven whined.

"Yeah, go get some soda or something," she rummaged in her jeans pocket and took out money. "Here, get me a big, cold soda too." She handed Steven the crumpled-up bill.

"'Kay, Sher."

"He's a hell of a worker, Patch," Phil said as he watched Steven go.

"Well, he's strong, that's always good." The blonde sat down on a bag of cement and watched the sweat drip off her face onto the floor.

"You know, I'd never know he was...you know..."

"What, Bobby, you can say the word. Re-tard-ed. It's okay." Sheridan got annoyed.

"It's not that, it's just...they should come up with a better word, is all. Retarded seems so harsh for him."

"Well, actually, he's developmentally disabled, which means his development is retarded," she said offhandedly.

"Yeah, well, both things sound so serious. He's slow, that's all," Phil added.

Sheridan laughed. "I dunno, guys...for a slow guy, he's doing your jobs pretty quick. He's saving your sorry asses an awful lot of work."

Bobby snorted, "You got that right, *chica.*"

Just then, Steven appeared with a big brown paper bag. Sheridan winked at him. "Hey, we're cutting out early today, soon, in fact. I left the kids at the groomer's and I don't want to leave them there all day." She stood up and lifted the bottom of her shirt up to wipe her face with.

"Jeez!"

"Patch!"

Sheridan looked at them in puzzlement.

"Wear a bra, for Christ sake!" Steven clarified with a red face. "My own sister's tits..."

"I couldn't find it this morning." The blonde blushed furiously. "Ain't nothing you didn't already see before, guys."

"Well I never saw them," Steven said with a snicker.

"Half the women in New York have seen them already, Steven," Bobby teased.

"Fuck you," Sheridan laughed.

"Nah, you'd kill me."

"Damned right!" she chuckled.

Resigned to the fact that she'd never get any more work done, Keefer called it an early day. She stopped by her supervisor's office and told him she'd be leaving early. He didn't mind; in fact, he told her that she'd been doing a great job lately and should think about taking a vacation. Keefer thought about it as she sat on the subway. She hadn't taken a vacation in three years. *Where would I go? What would I do?*

The inspector remained deep in thought about potential vacation spots and traveling when she noticed the train had stopped moving. Looking out the window, she saw they were still on the Manhattan Bridge. She stood up and stared out the window in search of something. *Hmm...isn't Sheridan's work site just off...that street?* Scanning the area, she located the construction site, searching frantically for any signs of the muscular blonde. Keefer was far enough away to squint but not so far that she couldn't make out the blonde's form as she hoisted a heavy bag from the tailgate of a truck. *God, there she is!* Keefer's heart beat rapidly and she licked her dry lips as she watched Sheridan work. When the muscular blonde disappeared from view, she turned her back on the window and closed her eyes. She welcomed the now-familiar feelings of arousal and she concentrated on them, pinpointing every individual tingle in her body.

She turned back around, her eyes falling on the small blonde figure that had reappeared on the ground below. She and a larger man were leaving through the wooden gate and heading to the black sports car. *She's leaving?* Blue eyes squinted as she tried to recognize the man with Sheridan. *Who is that?* Not recognizing him from her day on the site, she shrugged and continued to follow them with her eyes. *What are the odds that she took a half-day, too?* The tall inspector jolted as the train began moving again. Losing sight of the small black car, she went back to her seat.

The hungry feeling that enveloped her body made her swallow hard. *Look at what she does to you, Keefer,* she thought with a silent groan.

You want her so badly, be daring. Why don't you just call her? You know she'd be willing to sleep with you and you know you are more than willing to let her. What do you have to lose? She thought about it again as her body calmed down, and she blushed. *You know better than that, you know these feelings will never go away, even after you sleep with her. Then what? Sleep with her again? What if she doesn't want you again? What if you're no good? What if it takes so long for you to climax, she gets tired and leaves, like Danni?* Keefer's body cooled down quickly and she closed her eyes and leaned her head back. *Better leave her alone, Keef. She can have anybody she wants. She doesn't need you.*

Steven flung the Frisbee as far as he could and laughed as Pharaoh leapt high in the air to catch it. The pit bull then threw his head back and forth, as he killed the plastic toy over and over again. Zeus was running fast circles around Sheridan as she tried to get the ball from him. Finally giving up, she made tracks toward her brother and stood next to him as he threw the slimy Frisbee once again. She chuckled as he wiped his hands on his pants.

"You all right, Stevie-boy?"

"Shut up, Sheridan," he pouted.

"Aww, I'm just foolin' with ya. Are you having fun?"

"Yeah, a lot. Thanks for letting me come with you. I like hanging out with you much more than Pop."

"Why is that?" she asked with concern.

"Ha! Zeus just stoled the Frisbee!" he laughed. "Pop is Pop. I like coming to work with you better, I like Bobby and Phil and Tony. Where is Tony, anyway?"

"He twisted his shoulder, he should be back soon. Why do you like hanging with us? We're just a bunch of dirty-mouthed pigs." *That's what Pop says, anyway.*

Steven grinned. "That's why," he admitted sheepishly.

"Heh heh. I see." Sheridan raised an eyebrow. He might look like a grown man, but her brother was an adolescent. "Sorry about my tits, then. The last thing I wanted was to traumatize you."

"It ain't the first tits I ever saw, you know," he said defensively.

"Oh?" The blonde whistled for her dogs. "Just where did you see them?" she asked curiously.

"In a magazine. Yours are the first real ones I seen. It figures they would be my sister's." Steven rolled his eyes.

Sheridan had to laugh. "Sorry 'bout that. Hey, I better be the first to know if you get lucky, buddy boy, or there will be hell to pay." She hooked on Zeus's leash and threw Pharaoh's at her brother. "Good luck."

"Oh, I'll tell you. I'll tell you everything. Pharaoh! Sit!" he yelled at the spinning dog.

"You'll have to be more firm with him."

"Sit!" Steven yelled loudly and grinned big when the dog obeyed. "There ya go. Let's get back to the house."

"I can walk him?" Steven asked excitedly.

"Sure. Why the hell not? Just hold on tight, okay?" Steven's enthusiasm made her smile.

"Cool! Let's go, Pharaoh. Let's go home."

Keefer closed the door behind her and was about to pull off her clothes out of habit when she realized that she was already comfortable. She laughed as Fifi came flying across the living room, throwing herself into her.

Keefer squatted down to the dog's level and hugged her wiggling body. "I know, sweetheart, I'm home early today. Gimme kisses."

Fifi obeyed and gave her mommy tons of kisses, whining and barking excitedly as she did.

"Oh, boy, someone's glad to see me!" The tall woman stood up with her dog in her arms and made her way into the kitchen. She felt like a cup of coffee.

No, I feel like cold coffee...coffee ice cream, maybe. She stood in front of the freezer and frowned. "No ice cream. Feefs, let's go get ice cream, okay?"

As they were heading out the door, the phone rang. Keefer cursed herself for not hooking up the caller ID first thing when she came home and waited to hear the message. It was Danni and she was irate.

"Where the fuck are you? I've been trying to call you all goddamned afternoon and now they tell me you left for the day. Keefer, call me, I want to talk to you. It's important...please."

Keefer closed the door behind her as Danni spoke into the answering machine. "Gotta change that number, Feefs." As she locked the door, another thought came to her and she felt the hairs stand up on her arms. "Shit, Fifi, I gotta change the locks, too! Maybe we'll go to the locksmith after the ice cream place. What do you think?" She bent down and ruffled the dog's ears. Both eyebrows lifted as she heard a voice in her head answer for the dog. *Why wait for a locksmith when you have a perfectly good construction worker to call?*

Keefer stood up straight and looked her dog in the eye. "You may have something there, Feefs." A slow smile spread across her face. "Hmm, yeah, just may have a good reason to call." She started walking with the dog. "Of course, we'll have to do something about that bra I've been sleeping with."

Sheridan and Steven sat on the floor in the living room after taking turns in the shower. The dogs lay in various stages of relaxation next to them. Steven was idly scratching Zeus's belly, and Sheridan was flipping through the TV guide.

"Find anything yet?" Steven asked as his sister stopped throwing the pages.

"Not really, just a movie I like is on later tonight." *Yeah, a lesbian porno, you perv.*

"When's the pizza guy getting here, I'm fainting!" he whined.

"Hold your shorts, he's coming. And I doubt you're fainting," she snorted.

"These shorts are too tight, Sher, they're pinching my privates." Steven grimaced.

"They're all I had for you. The laundry will be done in a few minutes, just hold your breath," she chuckled.

"Hey, Sher? Who was that woman this morning? She looked pretty mad. I thought she was going to hit you," Steven asked with worry.

"Aw, she wasn't going to hit me. She's an asshole, don't worry about her."

"Did you sleep with her girlfriend?"

"Her *ex*-girlfriend and no, I didn't sleep with her."

"You want to though, don't you," he stated instead of asked.

"Why do you say that?"

"You pretended to her that you did and, just now, you looked sad when you said that you didn't."

Well I'll be. "You're too smart for your own good, kiddo."

"Well, do you? Do you want to fuck her?"

"No, I do not want to fuck her!" Sheridan growled.

"Okay, just asking. It sure seems like you do." He dropped the subject, seeing his sister scowl.

The doorbell rang and the dogs went crazy. Steven jumped up and yelled, "Yay! It's about time!"

Sheridan sat there on the floor in thought. *But you do want to sleep with her, don't you. You just don't want to fuck her. Shit, Sher, just when you thought you had no morals...*

"Come on, Sher! Pay the man!"

"I'm coming, I'm coming."

The tall brunette lounged indulgently in the bubble bath, stirring her coffee float with a long spoon. She had turned off the phone and put the bolt on the door and was now enjoying the rest of her evening. She'd had to lock Fifi in the den for fear that she'd jump into the tub; she'd done it before.

Sighing and sinking lower into the tub, she closed her eyes and relaxed. The music from the living room stereo floated into the bathroom and she began humming to the melody. The scent of lavender from the bubbles calmed her senses. *This is just what I needed,* she thought as she sipped from her tall glass.

Long moments passed and Keefer emptied her glass. The water had gone lukewarm and she reluctantly pulled the plug from the drain. As the last of the water gurgled down, she stood up and turned on the shower to wash the suds from her body. As she ran the sponge down her body, she felt a small chill from the open bathroom door. Her nipples hardened and she was reluctant to touch them, remembering what had happened in her office earlier. She leaned her chest forward under the shower spray to rinse it off and her back arched from the sensations. Her hands immediately came up to cover her breasts, protecting them from the hard spray.

Wow!

She backed up from under the water and moved her hands. She studied her pebble-like nipples in curiosity. *I've been showering all my life and that has never happened before,* she mused. Her right hand came up and hovered over her breast; she didn't want to touch it for fear she'd not be able to stop, but her hand had other plans. She rubbed her palm over her nipple and felt the jolt all the way to her crotch. Looking down at her sex, she did it again, with the same warmth spreading between her legs. She squeezed her breast and groaned out loud as her pelvis jerked on its own. *I'm not even touching it and it feels so good.* She explored her breast with her fingers, learning that she liked it when she pinched her nipple lightly, even more when she twisted it a little. She felt herself growing wet between her legs, and her other hand reached down to explore that area as well. As her fingers touched her wetness, she moaned out loud again, surprising herself.

"Well, well, well. What do we have here?"

Keefer grabbed the shower curtain and attempted to wrap it around her body as she caught her breath. "What the hell are you doing here?" she shouted in shock.

Danni chuckled. "You know, I've been trying to get you to do just that for a year. Tell me, what made you decide to do it now? Or have you been having your way with yourself all this time without sharing?"

"Get out of here! You do not live here anymore!" Keefer hollered, her heart beating wildly.

"I came to see if you were okay. You haven't answered any of my calls; I was worried about you," Danni said, still not budging from the bathroom.

"Bullshit! You weren't worried about me, you were worried about you and how it would look if you showed up to the next party without me there."

"That's not true!"

"Danni, if you don't get out of here right this minute, I'll call the cops."

"I spoke to your little construction worker this morning. She seems rather fond of you," Danni held out a towel.

Oh yeah? She does? Wait a minute..."You spoke to Sheridan? Where? When? What did you say to her?" Keefer accepted the towel and quickly wrapped it around herself.

"Bumped into her, if you will. So, has she found out what a dead fuck you are yet?"

Keefer felt sick.

"I know you she wants to fuck you, Keef. Too bad she'll have to find out the hard way that you're not worth the energy."

The tall woman sat down on the toilet with tears in her eyes.

"Were you thinking of her just now, Keef? Is the feeling mutual? Does she make you want to touch yourself?"

Tears fell from blue eyes and landed on Keefer's thighs.

"Poor baby. No one will want to fuck you after she tells them all what a dry hump you are."

She's right; I'm so fucking pathetic.

"Only I know how to make you feel good." Danni knelt in front of her. "Come on, baby, let me make you feel good. Just like when we were together. I can make you stop crying. You know I can."

Keefer felt like throwing up, not like making love—especially with Danni. She looked into Danni's eyes and saw a spark of triumph mixed with jealousy. It infuriated her.

"Come on, honey, let's go to the bedroom." Danni ran a hand up Keefer's thigh.

Keefer's body stiffened in anger. *Why, you little shit!* She slapped Danni across the face so suddenly and so powerfully that the redhead wound up sprawled out on the bathroom floor.

Keefer stood up and clutched the falling towel to her body. "Don't you *ever* touch me again! You sneaky, *cocky* son of a bitch! Get out now, Danni, before I really hurt you!"

Danni lay on the floor holding her cheek in shock. Fifi began barking wildly from the den at the sound of her mommy's anger.

79

"Now! Get out *now!*" Keefer couldn't wait for Danni to stand up and she reached for her arm, mindless of the towel falling on the floor, and jerked Danni upright. She pushed the stunned woman out of the bathroom door and watched as she stumbled into the living room.

"Okay, okay. I'm going!" Danni stuttered as she backed into the couch.

Not realizing Danni's shock, Keefer couldn't understand why she hadn't left yet and grabbed her by the neck. "Don't you ever come back here again, Danni. I swear I'll break every bone in your body," she said coolly.

Danni wrenched away from the vise-like grip and ran for the door.

Sheridan flopped down on the couch with a bag of pretzels to watch her movie. She questioned the intelligence of watching porn when she was already horny as she was. Coming to a grinning conclusion that whoever she was to pick up that night would be a lucky camper for it, she sat down and got comfortable.

While she waited for the movie to start, she ran into the kitchen for a soda. Seeing Steven's hard hat on the counter made her laugh. He was so happy to be back in his own clothes he'd forgotten about his hat. She felt bad about driving him home so soon, but she was going out and there was no way she was going to leave him there alone for the night. There were too many things for him to find and she really didn't want to explain why she had many variations of the male anatomy hiding in her room. It was bad enough he knew she slept with women; he didn't have to know details.

Settling back on the couch, she contemplated what to wear to the club later. *I could wear my brown leathers...no, the zipper sticks. Maybe the black jeans...no, too tight. I need easy access tonight. My loose fit 501's. That's it, and a white tank top. I'll wear my black work boots; I don't have to untie them to kick them off. Damn, I need to get laid tonight!*

The movie started and she smiled when her favorite female porn stars appeared on the screen. *Most people follow movie stars, I'm so pathetic that I follow porn stars,* she snickered to herself.

Not halfway into the movie, Sheridan had her hand in her pants, evenly stoking the fire that had started days ago with the tall inspector. She wasn't trying to get off, but damn if she wasn't turned on. She watched her favorite women doing all sorts of things that she would hopefully be doing in an hour or so. She closed her eyes for a second to enjoy the feelings she was invoking and before she knew it, her mind had the perfect picture of Keefer, her mouth open and making the sounds that were emanating from her television. She soaked her fingers. Sheridan pulled her hand out of her pants and opened her eyes wide. "Fuck! I almost came," she nearly shouted. "Why the hell does she have to pop up all the time? You can't have her, so get over it already!"

The blonde frowned as she turned off the TV. Stalking into her bedroom, she started stripping off her clothes; her sweatpants were soaked and she would have to wipe herself before she could put on clean underwear. "Fuckin' shit," she muttered, walking toward the bathroom. Wadding up some toilet paper, she rubbed it between her legs and groaned pathetically. "God...I can't." She sat down on the toilet and reached between her legs.

"Fucking Keefer..." she groaned as she worked herself to a quick orgasm. It did nothing for her state of arousal and she was a little bit startled by it. Usually, a quickie was able to take away some of the ache, but this did nothing for her. Washing her hands and face, she wondered about that.

Chapter 8

Keefer picked herself up off of the floor where she had been for over an hour. She was naked, cold and emotionally exhausted. She'd sat there crying for a long time after Danni left. Keefer wasn't even sure she knew the reason why she was crying, but she couldn't stop once she'd started and just let it go.

She had let Fifi out of the den as soon as Danni left and the mutt hadn't left her side since. She whined at her mommy, for her mommy, frustrated that she wouldn't stop crying even when she licked her face.

Keefer took a couple of deep breaths before she took out a folding chair from the closet and wedged it under the doorknob to the front door. Then she went into her bedroom, yanked her robe off the hook, and marched back into the bathroom. She muttered to herself as she turned on the water and tested the temperature.

"Who does she think she is...goddamned son of a bitch...trying to take a shower...like she owns the place...break her fucking legs..."

Fifi watched curiously as her mommy dropped the robe and walked into the shower, flinging the curtain violently as she did.

Keefer angrily worked the shampoo into her long black hair. She had gotten past the shock of Danni's sudden appearance, the humiliation of getting caught with her hand between her legs, and now she was angry. She was angry with herself for crying, for hitting Danni, and for allowing Danni that moment to make her feel like she was weak and helpless.

"I am *not* weak. I don't need *her* to make me feel good. That stupid shit. Wait 'til I get out of here...call Sheridan...change those locks..." She soaped up her body roughly as she continued to mumble. She had never been so angry in her life and the fact that she had let Danni get her in this state of mind pissed her off even more.

Sheridan bounded down the steps into the club, blew a kiss at Verna, and jumped directly on the stage. She stood there scanning the half-empty building, cursing each time the swirling red light hit her in the eyes. She was sure there was a woman out there with her name written all over her, she just had to find her.

Sharon and Marie stood by the bar and watched her searching through the crowd. They both knew that particular look on Sheridan's face and were already taking bets on which woman would be the lucky one.

Greg was about to shriek his hello when Sheridan jumped off the stage and walked through the crowd with a purpose. He snickered to himself and shrugged his shoulders. *No biggie,* he thought with a smirk. There were plenty of good-looking men to dance with tonight. Sheridan wasn't planning on staying very long.

Green eyes locked on the shyly grinning woman. Sheridan had fucked her before and, if she remembered correctly, she was very good. *Melanie?* She was about 5'9" in her heels and had a body to die for. The construction worker felt a pulling in her groin when the woman smiled seductively, crooking her finger and beckoning the blonde to come over. *Or was it Donna?* Sheridan nearly leapt to cover the distance between them, coming to a halt in front of the sexy woman. She lifted her arm up and braced her hand against the wall near the woman's head, whose curly brown hair tickled her wrist as her leather jacket rode up on her arm. *Maybe it was Rachel...*

"Hi, Sheridan." She smiled as she spoke.

"Hey there, sexy," the blonde winked and grinned.

The curly haired woman ran her fingernails across Sheridan's abdomen and delighted in the way the smaller woman twitched at the touch. "Ooh, I'd say you're on a mission," she teased, her nails raking up and down the blonde's torso. "Anyone in particular?" She cocked her head and licked her lips, loving the hitch in Sheridan's breathing.

"Touch my tits again and, so help me, I'll fuck you right here."

The woman snaked her hand up the back of Sheridan's jacket and pulled her neck down, teasingly licked the blonde's lips, and rubbed herself against the trembling muscular body in front of her. "Do it, baby," she breathed against Sheridan's lips.

The blonde growled and scooped her up, practically throwing her over her shoulder, and marched up the stairs toward the bathroom.

Keefer groaned loudly, licking her dry lips as the hungry mouth closed around her sensitive nipple. She opened her legs wider to allow the muscular blonde to slide between them, a lewd invitation that Sheridan accepted. Their slick bodies slid against each other; the friction felt delicious and Keefer opened her knees wider. Sheridan licked a hot path from nipple to neck, biting and sucking hungrily, marking the skin, and Keefer trembled. Blue eyes popped open at the sudden loss of sensation to find swollen lips hovering above her mouth. She reached up and wrapped a long arm around Sheridan's neck, pulling her down into a long-awaited kiss. Keefer groaned desperately, trying to suck as much of the frantic tongue into her mouth as she could.

Sheridan braced both hands on the stall dividers and dropped her head back in pleasure, her exposed breasts pointed skyward as her back arched. The hot lips sucked at her throat, biting and nipping their way on a downward path. Hands slid into her pants, clutching her naked ass as the nails dug into her skin. She lifted a booted foot onto the toilet seat, thrusting her hips forward, urging the hands to touch her where she needed it. She licked her lips, still tasting the lipstick smeared all over them from frantic kisses.

"Touch me...now..." she begged.

"Patience, Sheridan," came the hot reply in her ear.

"Fuck patience..."

The construction worker reached down, pulled a hand from her ass and thrust it down the front of her pants, and moaned at the blissful contact. An image blinked behind her eyelids, a flash of the tall inspector's face. *No...not now...*She opened her eyes and focused on the curly haired woman's face.

"Oh, my god...you are so fucking wet!"

"Just touch me...shit, yeah," Sheridan gasped as the fingers dug into her ass and into her sex.

"You're so fucking horny, Sheridan," the woman stated breathlessly, rubbing her cheek against a straining nipple.

"Don't stop..."

Keefer sat up on the couch, taking in huge gulps of air. Her heart was pounding in her chest, her neck cold and damp. Her sex was soaking wet and throbbing painfully.

"Good God!" she exclaimed as her whole body shook with arousal.

The dream felt so real. She rose on shaky legs and ran to the bathroom to check her neck; she moved her hair all around but found no marks. Somewhere in her addled brain she knew she'd find nothing there, but she had to look; she could still feel the hot wet mouth on her skin.

Sitting down on the toilet, Keefer ran her hands through her hair. It was wet at the nape of her neck and at her temples. She let her fingers slip through the damp hair, marveling at it. *It's not hot in here...why am I so sweaty?*

She shivered and crossed her legs tightly when goose bumps spread down them, and her hips jerked uncontrollably. Her body was hypersensitive and she had no idea what was going on. Her nipples were harder than she'd ever remembered them being. She stretched her T-shirt over her breasts to look at them, and the fabric pulling against them made her shiver violently yet again. Wetness gathered between her legs and she uncrossed them to try and get the cool air on her hot flesh. Lifting the hem of her shirt, she fanned it over her crotch, completely in awe at her own body.

"Holy shit...what a dream!" She shook her head to try and shake the feelings that were coursing through her body. "Wow. Can she possibly do that to me?"

Keefer sat there on the toilet, not believing what her sleeping mind had dreamed up, in total shock at her subconscious reactions. Finally, her body began easing down from the bowstring tension that had taken it over and she breathed a sigh of relief.

Getting up and looking at the clock, she saw it was only eleven thirty. Her first thought was of what Sheridan was doing at this moment...and with whom.

"Do you need me inside?" the woman asked as a strong grip on her wrist pushed her hand down lower.

"Yeah," Sheridan gasped.

The brown-haired woman slipped her fingers inside the drenched opening, the muscles there grabbing her tightly. "Hard or slow?"

"I don't care." The blonde moaned in frustration.

The Ride of the Valkyries started playing from the general area of Sheridan's ass.

"What the hell is that?"

"Never mind it...it's my phone..." Sheridan grabbed a handful of brown hair and pulled the woman toward her breast.

"Sher, it's not stopping. It's pretty late, maybe it's an emergency."

The blonde growled dangerously, yanked her phone out of her back pocket and began to yell. "I don't know this fucking number..." She suddenly stopped and yanked her shirt down over her tits. *Keefer?*

The brown-haired woman pulled her hand out from between Sheridan's legs and waited.

"Hello?"

"Hi, Sheridan? It's Keefer."

Sheridan pushed the other woman out of the way and left the stall. She covered the mouthpiece and mouthed for her to wait for her. Loud music blared over the phone.

"Sheridan?"

"Yeah, just wait a second, I gotta go outside to the patio to hear you better." She was trying to tuck her shirt back in her pants with a shaking hand, her bra was all twisted up around her tits, and she was breathing very heavily. "Yeah, I can hear you now," she said with a slight tremor in her voice.

"Are you all right? You're not busy, are you?"

"No." *Not anymore.* "Are you all right?" she asked hesitantly, worried by the tone of Keefer's voice.

"Um, well, Danni was here before and well...I just wanted to know..."

"Are you okay? Did she hurt you? Do you need me to come over?"

There was a long pause.

"Keefer! Are you okay?"

"Yeah. I mean, if it's okay with you. I don't want to pull you away from...something..."

"I'll be right there. Don't open the door until you see me."

"Um, can I ask you something?"

Sheridan swallowed hard. *Oh God.* "Anything."

"Would you be able to change my lock?"

The blonde blew out a breath. "Sure. I'll be right there."

The brown-haired woman found Sheridan on the patio banging her head against the brick wall. "Stop that! Is everything okay?"

"Look, I gotta go. A friend is pretty upset and she needs me there," Sheridan said, her forehead resting against the wall.

The woman ran her nails down the construction worker's neck. "Must be some friend, Sheridan. I was gonna fuck you 'til you couldn't stand."

Sheridan groaned pathetically, her sex clenching at the words. "Yeah...I know. I'm sorry."

"Maybe next time then."

"Yeah." *If I live that long...*

Keefer hung up the phone and panicked. "Oh, no. I can't look at her in the eyes! Not after what I just dreamed! The things I've been feeling, the things I've been doing!" The brunette ran around her house in an attempt to clean it up. She quickly rinsed out the tall glass and washed her dinner dishes. "Oh, my god—I'm not wearing underwear!" she shrieked and ran into her room.

Fifi followed her frantic mommy in confusion from room to room.

Keefer ran into the den and straightened up the futon, hesitating briefly, wondering if Sheridan would stay the night again and if she'd be able to control herself this time. "Oh, my god! Her bra is on my bed!"

She ran around the house like a lunatic until she was sure everything was perfect. She had no idea why she was acting this way, but didn't have time to think about it. The club was only minutes from her house; she had to hurry.

Sheridan glared at the man in the next car as he watched her shove her hands up her shirt and fix her bra. Leaning her head out the window she yelled, "Yeah, buddy! I'm a stupid moron! Keep staring at me!" She banged on the steering wheel hard and glanced in the car on the other side. She opened the passenger window and leaned over to that side. "That's right, lady, I coulda gotten laid...but nooo." The light changed and Sheridan peeled out, startling the two drivers, who gave her obnoxious looks. "Oh yeah, she had her fucking hand in my pussy...and I'm going to keep Keefer *company*! The hottest woman on the face of the earth needs a hug...*and I'm going!*" she yelled out into the night.

"Jesus fucking Christ! What is wrong with me?" She questioned her sanity as her clit steadily reminded her of her need. She tilted her head down and pointed at her crotch. "You shut up! I know I'm an idiot, I don't need you to remind me." The man from earlier raised both eyebrows at this action. Sheridan growled at him. "You have no idea, buddy. Just keep driving."

Keefer watched as the small black sports car pulled into her driveway. She saw the blonde get out of the car and punch at the air several times, then jump up and down like a child having a tantrum. She cocked an eyebrow and stared curiously at the construction worker as she took three steps toward the house, then three steps back to the car and continued to do this ritual for long moments. *What the hell is she doing?* Blue eyes opened wide as she watched the woman in her driveway point at her crotch and speak to it. *Oh, God, I know exactly what she's doing.* Keefer felt terrible all of a sudden. It all clicked just then: Sheridan's shaky voice on the phone, her heavy breathing, her little temper tantrum. She was most definitely in the middle of something back at the club, and Keefer felt miserable for interrupting it. *Well, it's true then, she really is a slut,* she thought briefly, watching the short blonde compose herself before walking up to her door. After the bell rang, Keefer opened the door and the sight that was before her made her heart pound. *Oh boy, that's what she looks like when she's...needy...*

"Hey." Sheridan waved slightly.

"Oh, I'm sorry, come in." Keefer blushed at being caught staring and stepped aside to let Sheridan in.

"Are you okay?" the blonde asked.

Keefer noticed the stiff movements and shook her head. "Are you sure I didn't interrupt something, Sheridan? You seem rather tense."

She had her fingers inside me and I was going to come! "No, it's all right. I'll get over it." *What's another day?* She groaned inwardly. "Um, believe it or not, I have cylinders in my car, I can change the locks right now."

"You do? Why would you have them in the car? Are they for work?" Keefer asked as she motioned for Sheridan to follow her into the living room.

"Well, they *were* for work, but we didn't need them. I was going to bring them back, but keep forgetting. No one will notice one set missing." The blonde smiled deviously.

Keefer's stomach fluttered at the look. She couldn't hide her expression of want.

Sheridan blinked rapidly. *Oh God...oh God...please don't tell me she wants to have sex...not now, not with me...* "You okay?"

"Uh, yeah. Just thinking." Keefer took a deep breath. "I'd like very much if you could change those locks now."

"Did Danni hurt you? What happened before?"

"No, she didn't hurt me. She surprised me."

"How did you get her to leave?"

"I hit her."

"You hit her?" Sheridan laughed out loud. "Boy, she must have really pissed you off. What did she do?"

"She just caught me off guard, is all." Keefer looked away and cleared her throat. She couldn't tell Sheridan what really happened. She'd rather die first.

Sheridan sensed there was much more to the story, but let it rest. "I'll go get the locks. I'll be right back."

Keefer sat on a chair in the kitchen watching discreetly as Sheridan tinkered with her door. Blue eyes traveled up and down the kneeling frame, hesitating on a flexing bicep as the blonde twisted the screwdriver, on a straining thigh as she held the door in place. She was fidgeting in her seat; Sheridan sure looked good when she was working. Keefer started thinking about what other things she needed done around the house and if she could get the blonde to do them.

"Hey, Keefer?"

The brunette wiped the silly grin off of her face and walked quickly to Sheridan's side, squatting down to her level.

Keefer's closeness made the blonde's eyes narrow. She could smell how clean she was, and she closed her eyes momentarily to compose herself. "I need you to hold both these doorknobs for me while I tighten this."

"Sure." Keefer stood up and did as she was asked.

Sheridan almost swooned. If she turned her head to the side, her face would be in Keefer's crotch. She didn't know if it was wishful thinking or not, but she swore she could smell Keefer's arousal. She took a deep breath and turned her head slightly; a vision of Keefer's naked body immediately came to mind and Sheridan's imagination went wild. Her mouth watered and she swallowed, physically shaking the images from her head.

Keefer watched Sheridan curiously, wondering what was going on with her until the blonde inhaled and swallowed. *Oh! Is she smelling me? Can she really smell me? Oh God, I think she can...*Keefer's breathing came in nervous spurts. She closed her eyes. *Is she imagining me naked? The look on her face...she likes what ever it is she sees very, very much.*

Sheridan gathered her wits just enough to finish the job. She stood up abruptly, ducking out from the circle of Keefer's long arms before she straightened out. "I uh..." she wiped a hand over her face, "I'm gonna need a drink." *And pour it down my pants, please—I seem to be smoldering.*

Keefer took note of Sheridan's nervous demeanor and couldn't help a grin from spreading across her face. *I did that to her! She's all flustered because I was standing so close to her! Do I have that kind of power over that kind of woman?* Her heart was beating quickly as she wiped her sweaty palms on her T-shirt. "What would you like?"

"Anything. Cold, it has to be very cold," Sheridan managed through clenched teeth.

Oh, wow! She's really a mess! Over me! "Sure. Feel free to turn on the television."

Sheridan watched as Keefer left the room and she grabbed at her crotch and groaned. *I can't believe this is my life.* Her underwear felt uncomfortably wet and she was sure her clit was actually turning blue. *Why me?*

Keefer appeared quickly with a cold bottle of water and handed it to Sheridan. She giggled as the construction worker shoved the bottle up her shirt. "Hot, Sheridan?"

"You have no idea," she groused, taking the bottle out and opening it. *Would she think I'm completely insane if I poured it down my pants?*

"Um, I'm sorry. You didn't have to come over. I obviously interrupted something and I feel terrible." Keefer hung her head.

"No, it's all right. She'll keep. It's me I'm worried about." Sheridan raised her eyebrows after she said that out loud. "I mean, I'll live." She gulped down the water.

"I don't know about that," Keefer teased, finding the blonde's embarrassment to her liking. "You look like a wreck."

What's this? She's talking sex? "Well, it's been a while, and the phone call came at a very odd moment." The blonde waited to se how far Keefer would take this line of conversation.

"Odd? Or do you mean just plain awful?"

Sheridan held up her hand and made a "teeny" gesture with her fingers. "I was this close."

Keefer blushed profusely. "Oh." She sat down on the couch and continued to blush.

Sheridan grinned and sat next to her, knocking into her with her shoulder. "Hey, it's okay...no harm done. I can always take care of it myself."

Keefer felt her ears burn. *Oh, please don't give me that food for thought...*

Sheridan stifled a snort. *Her head is going to explode!* "Keefer, I didn't mean to embarrass you. I'm sorry."

"No, no. I'm just, well I don't usually talk like that with anyone."

"I know, I'm sorry." She stuck out her bottom lip and ducked her head under Keefer's. "Forgive me?"

The tall woman laughed at the sight. "You're good at that. I forgive you."

"Cool!" Sheridan stood up and stretched her arms over her head. "Look, it's one in the morning. I should go."

"You don't have to go," Keefer blurted out quickly.

"I don't really want to intrude. With your new locks and all, you might want to run around the house naked or something," she snickered.

"I don't run around the house naked!" Keefer laughed.

"Sure you do. Admit it," Sheridan teased, catching the pillow that was thrown at her.

"I do not! You run around your house naked, I bet." Keefer giggled.

"Yeah, it's a wonderful thing. In fact, maybe I will stay over here and run around *your* house naked."

Keefer turned red. *I wouldn't survive. I'd drop dead in seconds.*

"Okay, I'm just fooling ya, but by all means, feel free if you want."

"You're a pig, Sheridan." Keefer blushed.

"Hey, always willing to see a beautiful woman naked." Sheridan winked.

The brunette blushed even more. "Oh, stop that."

"Okay, okay, but I never lie to you."

"Oh, yes you did. You came over here to replace my locks instead of...you know," she smiled sheepishly.

"I can get that anytime. It's not often I can sit in the company of such a beautiful woman."

"Oh, you're really good. I almost believe you." Keefer swatted at Sheridan's shoulder. *God, that's hard!*

"I speak the truth. Come on, beautiful, let's get you all tucked in." *I have matters to attend to.*

The brunette still blushed, but felt all warm and fuzzy at the same time. *She's so full of it, but damn is she cute.*

The two women sat on Keefer's bed. Neither one was tired at first, and they got to talking about nonsense things just to keep each other close. Neither one knew the other had the same agenda, and so both sat willingly and chatted. After some inane conversation, Keefer fell silent. Sheridan wondered if it had anything to do with what had happened earlier and figured there was no better time to ask. She sat cross-legged facing Keefer, who had trouble looking her in the eyes.

"So, do you want to talk about what happened with Danni earlier?"

"Nothing happened, really."

"Something happened bad enough for you to want your locks changed real quick."

"She came in while I was in the shower...scared me a bit," Keefer said nervously, picking at her nails.

"That would be pretty scary." *Fucking asswipe. I could kill her.* "Are you sure she didn't hurt you?"

"No, she never hit me or anything like that. I can't believe I hit her. Man, was I mad."

"What happened?" Sheridan asked, genuinely concerned. She couldn't imagine Keefer getting mad enough to hit anyone.

"I can't tell you," the brunette whispered sadly.

"Was she talking about me? Is that why you can't tell me?" The blonde reached out and turned Keefer's chin so she was facing her.

Blue eyes still looked away. "A little, but mostly she was talking about me," she admitted quietly.

Sheridan saw the tears forming in Keefer's eyes and it hurt her stomach. She was on autopilot as she pulled the tall woman close and wrapped her arms around her. "It's all right. I'm sure she was only trying to get you upset. I bet none of what she was saying was true."

Keefer hesitantly wrapped one arm around Sheridan, ducking her face in the crook of her neck.

"Am I right? I bet she was talking nonsense." *Except the part about me.*

"No, she was telling the truth," Keefer breathed into the blonde's neck.

Sheridan rubbed gentle circles on Keefer's back; her free hand slid up into thick black hair and cradled her head. "What..." Sheridan had to stop and breathe a second as long fingers wrapped around her bicep. "What did she say? I'll tell you if it's true."

Keefer breathed Sheridan's scent in deeply, wondering if the construction worker could feel it when her nipples stiffened. "Please don't make me tell you." *You'll find out soon enough if we don't break this up.*

Sheridan pulled back and looked into teary blue eyes. *I bet I know what she told her, that stinkin' little fuck. Let me go out on a limb here...*"I'll bet you any amount of money that whatever she said about you is a big fat lie. In fact, I bet that one day, I'll give you proof."

Keefer gulped loudly at that. *Jesus. I think I just got wet!* "Um, I don't think you'll get the opportunity, Sheridan." *I don't want you to find out.*

Bingo! I knew it! Only one way to fix that...

Keefer's eyes opened wide when she saw what was about to happen. Suddenly, all the blood in her body rushed to her head as Sheridan's soft lips covered her own. It was over so quickly that Keefer almost didn't believe it happened.

Sheridan felt her heart beating madly against her chest. She didn't figure on her own body reacting to that small innocent kiss as it did. She had to bite her tongue to keep it in her own mouth. *God! That was a stupid thing to do!* Every bit of arousal came screaming back between her legs when she looked at Keefer's dreamy expression.

Keefer took a moment to catch her breath before licking her lips. They felt suddenly empty and she wanted desperately to pull Sheridan in for more. Realizing she was clutching the blonde's bicep tightly, she snatched her hand away and looked guilty.

"You are an extremely desirable woman, Keefer, and anyone who is stupid enough to treat you any less than you deserve to be treated isn't worth crying over."

"Thank you," the inspector whispered.

"Aw, there's plenty more where that came from," Sheridan joked.

"I meant for the kind words." Keefer smiled, then added quietly, "But the kiss wasn't so bad either."

Sheridan grinned knowingly. "You ain't kidding, woman. It jump-started me all over again," she laughed.

Keefer blushed. "One kiss?"

"Yeah, well, I'm easy," she kidded.

"So I hear," Keefer retorted in kind.

"Good news travels fast. Are you sure you don't mind having me in your bed? All sorts of rumors may fly."

"Actually, I don't give a rat's ass about rumors. I'd like it very much if you stayed in here tonight." *There, I said it.*

"Yeah? In the same bed? Are you sure?" *It's gonna be a long night!*

"I'm positive. I really don't want you to go," Keefer said shyly. "I mean, if it's okay with you."

"Sure, you only live once." The blonde laughed, flopping herself back into the pillows.

"Oh, would it be so terrible to sleep in a bed with a woman and not have sex?" *I said sex?*

"Depends on the woman," Sheridan said, wiggling her eyebrow.

"I'm sure you'll live. You said it yourself."

"I'm not too sure now," she muttered into her pillow.

Chapter 9

Fuck, her skin is so soft.

Sheridan was having a wonderfully sensual dream. Keefer was lying next to her, naked, allowing the blonde to touch her...explore her body. Sheridan's fingers drifted up over a perfectly curved hip and she flattened her palm against the skin of Keefer's lower back.

Ohh, baby...I may never wake up...

Callused fingers traced the brunette's spine all the way to her shoulder blades and then back down again, chuckling silently as the tall body shivered.

It feels so real...

A nervous prickly sensation began in Sheridan's stomach and wiggled its way up into her brain.

Wait a minute...

Green eyes opened carefully and focused on silky black hair as it spilled over Keefer's shoulders.

Fuck!

The construction worker panicked, realizing that her hand was indeed up the back of Keefer's sleep shirt, splayed across her lower back. While Keefer was facing away from her, Sheridan had no doubts that she was awake. She could feel the woman's heart beating insanely hard, matching her own hysterical rhythm.

Ohmygod, ohmygod, ohmygod.

Keefer was breathing erratically, the sexy curve of her backside tucked snugly into the front of Sheridan's body. A smaller muscular leg was wrapped possessively around two very long ones.

Did I do this? Oh, fucking hell! What do I do now?

Keefer was beside herself with panic. She had been lying there, trying to count sheep as a last ditch effort to fall asleep, when Sheridan had migrated behind her and snuggled into her body. That was enough contact to set her body on fire. Just when she thought she was calmed down enough, a leg wrapped around hers, pulling her backside as close to Sheridan as possible. At that moment, Keefer began to panic, and it just got worse from there. Her whole body was tingling with arousal and her sex began to clench. The knowledge that her right butt cheek was touching Sheridan's crotch made breathing an effort. When a hand snaked its way up under her shirt, Keefer was panting. She wanted so badly to run away, but that strong leg held her tightly. Goose pimples sprouted all over her body, even in places she never knew goose pimples could appear. Her mouth was open with the effort to breathe and yet, she was as petrified as she was aroused.

*Should I wake her? What if she wakes up and finds herself doing this? What do I say? Oh, my god, her fingers feel so good...*Keefer shivered uncontrollably as Sheridan's fingers touched her body. *Jesus, she's only touching my back and I could scream from excitement! I can't even fathom what would happen if she touched my front.* Sheridan's hips rocked gently against her backside and Keefer stifled a groan. *It's touching me, it's so hot, I can feel the heat. Oh, God...*Suddenly all movement from behind her stopped and she froze. *She woke up!* Keefer held herself still, not wanting to let Sheridan know she was awake, allowing her to touch her like she was.

"Keefer?" Sheridan whispered, still afraid to remove her hand.

The brunette stayed immobile, still trying to breathe.

"I know you're awake. I'm so sorry," she whispered sincerely.

"It's okay."

"No, it's not. I'm so sorry," Sheridan repeated.

"You don't have to apologize. It's really all right."

"You're not mad at me? I didn't know what I was doing. I was sleeping...and before at the club..."

She sounds so pathetic. Do I tell her what I'm feeling? Can I tell her what I'm feeling? She listened to the stuttering blonde continue to make excuses and swallowed hard. *Oh heck...*"Sheridan?" she interrupted.

"Yeah?"

"I liked it," she admitted in a low whisper. "You don't have to stop."

"Excuse me?" Sheridan sat up and stared at the black hair.

Keefer exhaled loudly when her legs were freed and the hand disappeared from her skin. She focused on the bedside clock and took a deep breath before speaking. "I liked it, it felt very good," she said quietly. "It still does," she added almost imperceptibly.

Don't push her. Go slow, Sher. You can do it. "Do you want me to keep touching you?"

Keefer nodded, closing her eyes in anticipation.

On the inside, Sheridan screamed and jumped up and down. On the outside, however, she closed her eyes and smiled, all her teeth glowing in the dark. "Well, that's great, 'cuz I really liked it, too."

Keefer flinched nervously as she felt the warm body press up against her back and Sheridan's hand rest gently on her hip. Another hand began sifting through her hair softly, as if Sheridan was examining it in the dark.

"Is that okay?" the construction worker asked.

"Yes." Keefer felt her heart beat speed up when Sheridan's breath blew across the back of her exposed neck. *What are you doing?* Keefer questioned herself.

"Turn around, I want to see your face," Sheridan whispered hopefully.

"I can't...I'm sorry."

Sheridan slowly slid her hand over the curve of Keefer's hip and onto her thigh. "That's okay," she said with understanding. *Slow, babe, take it easy.* She slid her hand back up and worked her fingers under Keefer's shirt. "May I?"

Keefer nodded, afraid to speak. She had all her attention focused on that hand. The other one danced around her shoulders and neck, but this one was more important, she had to keep track of it. She gasped as the rough skin of Sheridan's hand met her sensitive flesh. It felt so good; she was afraid she'd make a noise and bit her lip. She felt the slightest of kisses on the back of her neck and her nipples tightened painfully.

"God, you feel like silk," Sheridan mumbled into Keefer's hair, before inhaling the scent and memorizing it. She ran her hand up along the brunette's side, dipping her pinky down toward her belly. Keefer let out a loud breath through her nose and Sheridan grinned. "Can I?" she asked as she ran her pinky back and forth along the soft skin.

"Yes," Keefer responded hoarsely. Her throat was dry and she swallowed nervously. *You've lost your ever-loving mind! Stop this!*

Sheridan boldly slipped her hand down onto Keefer's stomach and let it rest there. She was thrilled with what was happening between them, but she knew Keefer was going to need some time, some coaxing for it to go any further. "Are you okay?"

Am I okay? I have no earthly idea. "Nervous," she admitted. "I know it's silly..." Keefer took a deep breath; she couldn't seem to control her breathing.

"No, it's not silly. Does it feel good?" Sheridan asked while still palming her stomach. She could feel the trembling inside and knew the brunette was more frantic than she let on.

"It feels very good. I'm just afraid that you might want me to, well...you may need...I don't know that I can..."

"Shh. Don't worry about me." Sheridan kissed the back of her neck again and let her tongue poke out and taste the skin.

Oh, God...that was her tongue! Keefer swallowed hard again. "But I do. I know how you felt when you came here tonight." She didn't go on because Sheridan's fingers began moving on her stomach.

She has no idea. Sheridan mentally rolled her eyes. She was hornier than she had ever been in her whole entire life. She'd have to do something but she couldn't scare Keefer—not now, when she was touching her beautiful body. "It doesn't have to go that far, babe. How's this?"

Keefer shook again, unable to control her body's reaction to the roughened fingers on her skin. "I trust you, Sheridan." *You better, Keef, this has gone much farther than you imagined.*

"Good, 'cuz I'd never hurt you. I promise," Sheridan swore. She shook her head in disbelief. There wasn't a woman in this world who trusted her, and she'd never given a pledge like that to anyone. Yet her hand stayed respectfully within the boundaries of ribs to waistband, controlled by a force Sheridan had never known.

Keefer closed her eyes and concentrated on the feelings she had never experienced before. Her body had never been so receptive, as if all of her skin was an erogenous zone, shooting wonderful sensations between her legs.

Smoke billowed from Sheridan's crotch. Well, it didn't really, but she swore it was blazing. Her thighs clenched together to provide some quick relief, but it didn't help—the fire was too hot. Being in a constant state of arousal for three days was torturing the muscular blonde, but just then there was nothing she could do about it. Touching Keefer was not exactly making it any easier, but she couldn't stop. Feeling her perfect ass pressed into her lap was more than just arousing, it was intense. She fought every instinct to wrap a leg around Keefer and ride her ass for all it was worth.

Keefer arched her body uncontrollably when Sheridan slipped the hand from her hair up the back of her shirt. She was assaulted with sensation on the back and the front. Her breath was coming loudly from her flared nostrils, her nipples were practically throbbing, and wetness was pouring from her sex. *Jesus Christ, nothing has ever felt this good! I really want her to touch my breast, but I can't tell her that. Her hand keeps coming so close, but she doesn't touch it; she's being so nice, so controlled.* A smile lit Keefer's face. *Maybe she cares about me; it's not her style to go slowly...*

Sheridan was practically panting like a dog. If she opened her mouth, she was positive her tongue would come rolling out across the bed. *You better stop touching her, Sher. You might not be able to control yourself much longer.* She crossed her ankles and begged her legs to stay still. Her fingers wanted so badly to touch Keefer's breasts. They were so close, and she'd never let them down before. She wanted to feel their smooth softness in her palms, weigh them, squeeze them, hold them. Her sex spasmed painfully and she saw stars. *Okay, stop right there. Do not pass go. Step away from the breasts!*

Keefer was surprised when Sheridan's hands left her body completely. She waited for the blonde to speak, but all she heard was heavy, erratic breathing from behind her. *She sounds worse than I do...she got that way by touching my body?* Keefer waited some more, and this time she heard a stifled groan. *She's bad, all right. She couldn't have gotten so turned on from touching me; she was already horny from the club. That's it.* The bed shifted and she knew Sheridan had turned over onto her back.

"I gotta get some sleep. I got work in the morning," Sheridan's voice was thick with arousal.

God, she sounds so sexy like that. "Yeah, me too." *Ha! Sleep.*

"Good night, Keefer."

"Night, Sheridan."

The muscular blonde pleaded with her crotch to stop hollering at her. It didn't work. She threw an arm over her eyes and sighed heavily. *Now what?*

Keefer's body was singing arias and the racket was deafening. She concentrated as hard as she could, and finally slowed down her breathing and her heart rate and began to relax. She managed to ignore her nipples long enough so that she was able to turn over onto her stomach and get comfortable. Her mind was racing with thoughts of what had just happened. Sheridan Landers was in her bed, touching her naked skin and breathing on her neck. She'd even tasted it. The contact was brief, but it was enough, and she couldn't help imagining that feeling everywhere else on her body.

She heard a quick inhale and furrowed her brow in confusion. *What the hell?* Her eyes opened wide in astonishment when she heard the strange breathing pattern next to her. *Oh, sweet Jesus. She's not!* Sheridan's leg shifted and it leaned lightly against Keefer's, yet she could feel it quivering. *She is! In my bed! With me right here!* Despite her shock, Keefer found herself getting turned on all over again. *I wish I could do that,* she thought jealously. The idea of Sheridan touching herself right next to her made her mouth water. Keefer wanted to do the same—she even moved her arm, resting her hand on the bed by her hip—but she couldn't go any further. *Go on, it's not like she'll ever notice. She's doing it, too.* She couldn't do it. As wet as she was and as turned on as she was by what was going on beside her, she couldn't bring herself to do it. Suddenly, Sheridan stopped breathing and grunted quietly. *Was that it?* Keefer heard the blonde's breathing slow down and even out. *That was it. Damn, she's quick. Either that or she was really, really horny.* She felt Sheridan turn over onto her side and heard her sigh. *Could I have really done that to her?*

"Kee-fer," Sheridan whispered, crouching down beside the brunette's side of the bed.

The inspector stirred, a small smile creeping across her lips. "Mmm," she hummed.

"Come on, sleepy head. Wake up." The construction worker brushed black hair off of the sleeping face. *She's so beautiful.* "Keefer...I gotta go."

Keefer rose to consciousness with a lengthy stretch, turning over on her back.

"You awake?" Sheridan whispered.

Blue eyes opened slowly and widened when they focused on Sheridan's lopsided grin. She sat up quickly and looked away.

Shit...she's probably mortified at what happened last night.

"Um, you're leaving? What time is it?" Keefer asked the blanket, unable to make contact with green eyes.

"It's seven. I don't know what time you need to be at work, but I have to go now. I made coffee, if you want it." She pointed to a steaming mug on the nightstand.

Keefer's sleep-addled brain finally made sense out of everything and she blushed hotly. She lowered her head and glanced sideways at Sheridan. "Thank you for the coffee and for waking me up. I must have forgotten to set the alarm last night."

Man, she is really uncomfortable. Do something! "Look, about last night...I um, I got carried away, I don't know what happened when I was sleeping, but I sure enjoyed it when I was awake."

"Me too," Keefer mumbled, turning her head to the side to catch a glimpse of the blonde. Sheridan's smile made her stomach flutter.

"Yeah, so, I gotta get going." Sheridan stood up. "If you don't mind, maybe we could...I don't know..."

"That would be nice." *Jeez, Keef, at least let her finish the sentence!* She blushed redder.

Well, that answers my question. "You have my number. Give me a call, okay?"

Keefer nodded, afraid she'd say something embarrassing if she opened her mouth.

Can this be any more awkward? "See ya, Keef."

Blue eyes ran the length of Sheridan's body as she walked out of the room. A sudden urge to run after Sheridan and kiss her goodbye startled Keefer. *But did you see that ass?* After hearing the front door click closed, she threw herself onto her back and groaned out loud. *She called me Keef.* A smile spread across her lips and she giggled. "Oh, man, you are in trouble." Turning over onto her stomach, she fished out the black sports bra from under her pillow and smelled it, memories of the night before flooding her brain and making her heart pound. "So much trouble."

Sheridan couldn't show up to work in the clothes she had slept in and she refused to walk around all day stinking of her own arousal. Stopping home, she took a long, hot shower and ran the dogs around the block twice, with great apologies for staying out all night, before she hopped into her car and drove to work.

The radio was blaring, the bass pounding in the pit of her empty stomach. She made a quick run to Dunkin' Donuts and screeched into a parking spot.

Tony laughed and tsked when Sheridan flew up the stairs, half a donut hanging out of her face. "Well, well, well...look at what the cat dragged in," he snickered.

"And look at that, almost ten to boot. Late night, Patch?" Phil pointed to his watch and wiggled an eyebrow.

"Uck oo, illy." Sheridan spit the uneaten portion donut out of her mouth and narrowed her eyes at all three of her smirking co-workers.

"So, still cranky, eh? I'd have thought maybe you got laid or something," Bobby gestured to the misbuttoned flannel Sheridan had thrown on that morning.

The blonde shrugged and began to blush. "Yeah, well, you thought wrong." She rolled her eyes at him and fixed the buttons on her shirt. "I was in a rush, is all."

"I don't know that I believe you, Patch. I mean, all the signs are there. You even look like you got some."

"Looks can be deceiving, boys," she snickered. So what if she did get some, doing it herself didn't count.

"I know. Body check!" Phil yelled and all three men pounced on the smaller blonde, pulling her clothes all over the place, looking for telltale signs.

101

Sheridan laughed loudly and allowed them to check her body, if for no other reason so that she could gloat when she proved them wrong. "You guys suck ass!" she yelled into Tony's thigh between attempts to bite it. She never said she'd let them do this willingly.

"Anything?" Bobby grunted while trying to control the flailing arms.

"Nope," Tony replied.

"Ditto," Phil agreed.

They let her go and watched her rearrange her clothes with curious looks on their faces.

"I told you so." She stuck out her tongue and gave them the finger.

"I don't know. This is all too weird. It's been three days and you haven't gotten any?" Bobby frowned, trying to figure it out. "By now you should have exploded."

"Yeah, all that tension, and especially after that woman...Hey," Phil grinned wickedly. "It's this woman, ain't it!"

"Fuck you, leave her out of this," Sheridan snapped.

"Oh yeah, that's it. It's that woman, the one with issues."

Green eyes narrowed dangerously and Sheridan flexed her arms as she folded them across her chest.

"Whoa, okay...just a thought." Phil backed up and returned to work.

"Keep it to yourself, Philly-boy, I ain't sharing." She stomped off to smoke a cigarette.

Conversation stopped as the guys contemplated this new development. From Sheridan's reactions, it was apparent that it was definitely something to do with that woman...but what?

"Do you think she feels something for this woman?" Bobby wondered out loud.

"I don't know, but whatever it is, this woman is off limits." Tony made the button gesture on his lips.

"No kidding, I thought she was gonna hit me!" Phil worried.

"Pussy," Bobby teased.

"Yeah, well, you take a slug from those arms and then call me a pussy."

The blonde calmed down enough to think rationally and it occurred to her that she had just gone a little off the deep end protecting Keefer's honor among these morons. *What the hell was that all about? Why is she all of a sudden so special? What is she doing to me?*

Sheridan noticed the guys looked too innocent when she came back. "What the hell were you guys talking about?" she asked angrily.

"Your sex life, stud."

"Rather, your lack of a sex life," Tony laughed.

They're teasing you, Sher, lighten up! "Whoa, hey, I never said I didn't have a sex life, I always got me a steady." She held up her right hand and wiggled the fingers.

"Jeez, Patch! That's a visual I didn't need!" Phil shook his head and grimaced.

Sheridan snickered at his discomfort. *Let him chew on that one for a while.*

The day passed quickly for Keefer and before she knew it, it was time to go home. She made neat little piles of work on her desk and stood by the window to stretch.

All that day, when she thought of Sheridan, she had physical feelings to recount. Drawing on those feelings made her crave more of the same and soon she was running her own hands up and down her body, imagining them to be Sheridan's. Hours flew by as she stopped every so often to entertain herself with thoughts and sensations of the blonde's hands all over her body. Especially her nipples.

Sheridan's fingers had come so tantalizingly close to her breasts the previous night, driving her to the brink of sanity. Every so often, a finger would brush the underside of one and Keefer strained to keep her groans to herself. She wondered about that, too. She had never made noise during sex, yet the night before she wanted to scream out loud. She wondered— with a blush, of course—what would happen should Sheridan actually touch her breasts? Would she be able to control herself? The previous night was not even close to sexual, but Keefer was beyond aroused from the innocent meanderings of the construction worker's hands. The sounds that had welled up and threatened to spill out of her mouth from the roughened fingers gently exploring her skin frightened her. Would Sheridan think she was crazy if she let them out? Could she let them out? The mere thought of letting loose a groan in front of the blonde made her blush in embarrassment.

She closed her office door behind her and walked through the carpeted halls toward the elevator.

"Gibson!"

Keefer jolted from her thoughts at the sound of her boss's voice. "Yes?"

"You never submitted a report from that construction site...what was it...Lanson..."

"Landers and Sons. I didn't?"

"No, you didn't. Any reason? Too many violations?"

"Uh, I don't know, sir." Keefer strained hard and couldn't remember anything about the construction site, except the muscular blonde who showed her around. *Did I even bring my clipboard? I can't remember a thing!*

"You don't know? What the hell, Gibson?"

"I, uh...I'm sorry?" she gave him a pleading look. *Please don't send me back there...not now. I can't look at her yet...*Keefer watched miserably as he stepped into the elevator.

"I want a full report. Tomorrow. On my desk. Have a good night," he said curtly before the doors closed in front of his face.

"Dammit!" she growled and stalked back into her office to retrieve what she needed for the next day. *Great. She's going to think I'm an incompetent fool! Better yet, she's going to think I needed an excuse to see her. I can't even face her! Not with what I've been doing.*

Keefer frowned furiously as she banged the elevator button. "Damn."

Sheridan wrapped her leg around the woman's neck and grabbed fistfuls of hair, pushing her face deeper into her sex. She banged her knee into the steering wheel but ignored the pain, briefly wondering if this woman's neck was gonna snap from the position she was in.

"Mmph...mmm," the woman hummed into Sheridan's crotch. The blonde was so receptive tonight, even more so than last night. She thanked her luck. Not many women got to taste the muscular blonde.

"That's it, baby...don't stop..." Sheridan grunted between loud breaths.

The brown-haired woman shook her head in agreement, shoving her fingers deeper, sucking harder. Why would she even think of stopping? Okay, so maybe her neck was in danger of breaking, but shit, she was eating Sheridan Landers!

"Fuck!" Sheridan gasped, tightening her hold in the brown curly hair. "I'm gonna come..." she rasped.

The woman grunted approval and doubled her efforts. Sheridan was so hot that night, it was incredible.

The blonde's legs tensed and she began to tremble. She focused on the head between her legs and the much-needed release flooded through her body and she groaned languidly. As the orgasm began to subside, she released the brown hair and closed her eyes. Keefer's face appeared in her mind and hungry blue eyes bore into her. "God!" she yelled, grabbing the steering wheel for leverage as her orgasm renewed itself, her pelvis bucking uncontrollably. When she settled down a little, she pulled the woman's face from between her legs. Her legs were still twitching and her clit was spasming even without the contact. "Oh shit, Keefer..." she muttered under her breath, amazed at the effect the inspector had on her.

"Keefer?" the woman asked as she sat up, arranging herself in the passenger's seat.

Fuck me... Sheridan groaned and banged her head against the steering wheel.

"Who the fuck is Keefer? I know you fuck a lot of women, Sheridan, but is it too hard to remember who you're with at the time?" she asked angrily, yanking her skirt down roughly as she opened the car door.

"Look, wait up! Hey!" Sheridan called after her, struggling to get her pants back on while trying to chase after the hurt woman.

"Hey?" she called back. "Hey? I bet you don't even *know* my name, do you?"

Sheridan looked guiltily at her feet.

"You son of a bitch!" the woman yelled, beginning to attract attention from the people entering and leaving the club.

"Hey, I'm sorry. It slipped out!" Sheridan yelled back in frustration, glaring at the passersby.

"Fuck you, Sheridan!"

Green eyes flashed with anger and embarrassment. She flung herself back in the car and slammed the door so hard, the widow rattled. "Fucking shit!" she yelled resting her head on the back of her seat. Reaching down and adjusting her underwear, she shrugged. "Well, at least she licked good pussy," she snickered as she turned the key in the ignition. "That'll keep me for a few days."

Chapter 10

Keefer trudged around her house in misery all night, wondering what she was going to say to Sheridan when she saw her in the morning. She had no idea how to face her after what happened the night before. Not only had she allow the blonde to touch her body, but Sheridan had actually touched herself, too. The inspector knew she'd never be able to look her in the eyes after that. Keefer was sure Sheridan knew she was awake; she knew the construction worker was aware of what she did to her by touching her, too. Keefer had been breathing so loud and her body had been shaking so hard, it was all but impossible to ignore. Millions of thoughts ran through Keefer's mind.

What and whom was Sheridan dreaming about when she wrapped her leg around my body? Why didn't she stop when she woke up? Did she purposely continue to touch me for her own selfish needs? If so, why did she go as slow as she did? Why did I allow it in the first place? What came over me to admit to Sheridan that it felt good? Will it ever happen again? Will I allow it again? Did Sheridan know what she did to me when she touched herself? Did she do that often? Did she do that on the futon?

"Come on, Feefs." She nudged the sleeping dog at the foot of her bed, then turned off the lamp and went into the den. *No sense trying to sleep now.* Fifi jumped up on the futon and settled down into a ball. Keefer wrapped the blanket around herself and lay down, turning on the television with the remote.

"Huh?" Keefer sat straight up. Blue eyes threatened to pop out and roll away. *What the hell is this? I wasn't watching this...* It occurred to her that the last person to watch television in that room was Sheridan. *She was watching porno?* Keefer covered her eyes with a hand and felt the heat of her face against her palm. *I didn't even know I had this channel.* Keefer

107

glanced through her fingers at the number display on the cable box and closed her eyes again. *Forty-six. How did she find this channel? I certainly didn't program it into my favorites.*

Keefer moved her hand away and flipped through her favorite channels, suddenly pausing with a thought. *I don't think I even programmed these at all! Didn't Danni program these?* She punched in forty-six again just to make sure she had it right. *You'd think Danni would have wanted me to watch porno, the way she was always going on about doing new things,* she thought bitterly, peeking at the screen again before changing the channel to something she could watch without her ears blowing off from embarrassment.

She spent much of the rest of the night flipping around the channels, never really concentrating on one particular program. It was well into the wee hours when she made another attempt at channel forty-six. Her eyes widened and she covered her face again. "Feefs, did you see that?" she asked in astonishment. Peeking through her fingers, she felt her mouth drop open. Two women were on a bed; one was lying on her back while the other sat on her face. All camera angles were close-ups and all were very graphic. Keefer blushed beet red, but continued to watch the scene. She lowered the volume, afraid that someone might hear the noise and think it was her. She watched wide-eyed as the woman on her back reached between her own legs and touched herself while she licked the other woman. *Everyone does this but me?* Suddenly there was a close-up of the woman sitting on the other's face; her vagina filled the screen and Keefer was mortified, but still kept watching. She was completely astounded that these women could do this in front of crews of people...for others to watch.

She turned to her sleeping dog. "Can you even imagine?"

After various position changes and a few loud orgasms, Keefer found herself breathing very heavily. "I can't believe I just watched that whole thing! I can't believe they do that on television." She paused a moment to stretch. She hadn't moved from her original position and her legs were cramping. She blushed profusely as the damp crotch of her underwear pressed up against her body. "I can't believe I got turned on by that," she chuckled with embarrassment. "I wasn't even thinking about Sheridan."

There, the seed was planted and her mind took it and ran. The entire movie started to replay itself, with two new stars. Keefer squirmed with the visions and squeezed her eyes shut tightly. She was sitting on Sheridan's face. Extreme close-ups of the blonde's tongue against her sex flashed larger than life in her mind and she could almost feel it happening. The scene switched to Sheridan touching herself and Keefer gasped, beads of sweat forming on the sides of her face and between her breasts. "Oh, my god...this is so not good."

She stood up and paced the floor, trying to erase the images that bombarded her senses. It wasn't working, and a small pathetic whimper sprang from her mouth. She immediately looked to Fifi to see why she had made the sound when she realized it came from her. Keefer stopped pacing and put a hand to her chest. Her heart was beating madly, her breath coming in heavy pants. "This is really not good." Sitting down on the futon she attempted to gather herself. "Why does she do this to me?" she whined, dropping her head into her hands. "I don't believe how turned on I am. I'm sweating, for God's sakes! How am I ever going to look at her tomorrow? I just know I'm going to see her naked, I just know it!" Keefer couldn't shake the images replaying in her head; her sex begged for attention, she couldn't make it stop.

"I'll never get to sleep now," she mumbled to herself. "Unless..." She licked her lips nervously and thought about it. "I mean, if everybody's doing it..." Blue eyes darted around the room and fell on the dog. *I can't do that with her in the room,* she thought. Keefer got up and tiptoed into her bedroom, shutting the door behind her. She felt her heart pound at what she was going to do. She was very nervous as she slipped her hand under the covers and into her underwear. Her fingers were so cold, she jumped. Once she encountered the wetness awaiting her, she groaned. It felt so good. She opened her eyes and looked around. No one was there to hear her and she groaned again. Soon the room was echoing with sounds of pleasure.

It was unseasonably hot in New York City that morning, so Sheridan dressed for the occasion. She knew it would be unbearable in the partially erected building and pulled on a pair of cut-offs and a tank top, tossing a long-sleeved denim shirt over her shoulder as she left, just in case.

Driving to work, she wondered if any of the guys were going to wear shorts. She loved to tease them about their hairy legs, often sneaking up behind them and pulling the short hairs just to watch them jump. With a snicker from the thought, she pulled into the donut shop parking lot and hopped out of her car. She left the radio blasting and the windows down. She loved warm weather and wished it would stay like this all year round.

Waiting in line for her morning coffee, she noticed a new girl working behind the counter—a cute, leggy blonde who seemed to be giving her the once-over. Sheridan worked it and before she knew it, she had a free cup of coffee. *Damn, you're good,* she smiled to herself as she winked at the blonde and left. As she was about to pull away, the blonde appeared at her window, handing her a piece of paper.

"What's this for?" The construction worker smiled.

"It's my phone number." She adjusted herself so her tits were practically leaning on Sheridan's shoulder.

Green eyes took the bait and stared wolfishly at the sight. "Well, thank you," she glanced at the card, spotting the name, "Sara. When can I call?"

"Any time. I'm a sucker for a girl in work boots."

Sheridan laughed out loud and drove away, waving over her shoulder as she did. *I wonder if she gets a lunch break,* she mused as she merged back into traffic.

Bobby was wearing shorts and Sheridan couldn't resist the temptation.

"Ow! Hey! You shit! That fucking hurt!" he yelled, grabbing his inner thigh. "I think that one was attached to my balls," he grumbled.

"Serves you right, showing off all that leg in my face," Sheridan teased. "I just can't resist a good leg."

"Patch, if you ever encounter legs like that on one of your nightlies, run—run away!" Phil joked.

Everyone laughed but Bobby, who narrowed his eyes at the bunch.

"Oh, lighten up, sweet cheeks!" Sheridan smacked him on his butt and winked.

"Yeah, and if I did that to you, I'd lose an eye."

The blonde bent over and shook her ass. "Give it a try, I dare you."

It was tempting, but Bobby declined. "No thank you, I'm not that stupid." He held up his hands and backed away.

"Thought so," she laughed.

"What lucky lady do we thank for this pleasurable mood, Patch?" Tony asked with a wiggling eyebrow.

"I forgot her name," she said sheepishly.

"Ooh, not good. I hope she didn't know that." Phil shook his hand and whistled.

"Unfortunately, she did. Let's just say it didn't end on a high note. But all's not lost, fellas, I got this chick's number at the donut shop this morning!" She held up the paper and leered at it.

"You are such a fucking hole, do you know that?" Tony shook his head in wonderment.

"I wanna be you when I grow up," Phil chuckled.

"*If* you grow up, Philly-boy," Sheridan snickered. "You left yourself wide the fuck open there, dude."

"Yeah, well...hey, when did you bang up that knee?" he asked with concern. "It's pretty ugly."

She closed her eyes and shook her head slowly. "Steering wheel got me last night."

"Oh, man, that must have put a damper on the mood. That had to hurt!" Bobby winced in sympathy.

"To tell the truth, I didn't even feel it at the time. I had more *important* things on my mind," she smirked deviously.

"And between your legs," Tony laughed.

"You betcha." Sheridan winked at the guys. "Damn, she was good."

"Shit, Patch, I wanna follow you around one night so I can see how you do it. Women just fall at your fucking feet, you rock."

"It's not such a good thing, boys. Some women, you just don't want to fall," she said with a hint of sadness.

"That mystery woman with issues?" Bobby asked, only realizing he'd said the wrong thing when Tony whacked him on the back of the head.

For the first time ever, Sheridan spoke openly with the guys. "Yeah, her. She's not meant to be fucked and frankly, I don't think I know any other way."

The guys didn't know what to say and just looked around uncomfortably.

"I don't want to hurt her, she seems so fragile. I never met anyone like her before," she continued, more to herself than to the men in the room with her.

"Well then, just stay away from her," Bobby offered.

"I can't. I don't want to, but when I'm around her, I want to be somewhere else! It's so goddamned frustrating!" She kicked the wall and sat down on a stepladder.

Phil had never seen his friend look so confused. It bothered him, but he knew what Sheridan was going through. The same thing had happened when he met his wife. Sheridan was falling for that woman...hard.

"I act like a whole other person, too," she added.

Oh yeah, she's got it, all right! Phil thought. *I wonder, who is this woman?* He knew she must be something special; he'd never seen Patch so freaked out.

"If you don't mind me butting in here, what do you mean by 'whole other person'?" Tony asked with a curious look on his face.

"I don't know, almost romantic, overly respectful...so not like myself. Totally patient," she said while still looking at the floor.

The three guys exchanged knowing looks. They all knew what Sheridan was going through, but no one was going to enlighten her. They were way smarter than that. You didn't tell a woman like Sheridan that she was falling in love.

Keefer waged a mental war that morning regarding when she should go to Sheridan's job site, and if she should go at all. She stood in her living room for a long time, holding her phone, ready to call in sick. *If I call in sick, they'll send someone else to do it,* she thought. Then she thought about Sheridan seeing someone else come to inspect and perhaps she'd think Keefer had given them reason to send someone for a second inspection. That made her panic. The next thing she thought was that Sheridan would think Keefer was avoiding her. That made her even more panicked. She finally decided that she'd go to Sheridan's job site herself, but she'd do it in the late afternoon. Maybe she'd feel less nervous by then.

The morning dragged for Keefer. She couldn't concentrate on anything for any length of time without worrying about having to explain her second appearance at the construction site. She mentally beat herself up about actually forgetting to even make a report the first time. If she had done what she was supposed to in the first place, she wouldn't be having this nervous breakdown.

She stared at the clock as it turned to noon and stood up from her chair. She made a snap decision to go and get it over with. She ran her hands through her hair nervously as she left her office.

"Gibson? You got that report for me?"

"I'm going now. I'll be a few hours." She tried not to sound annoyed but failed.

"I'm surprised at you, it's not like you to be so half-assed. You got a thing for construction workers, Gibson? Something catch your eye and distract you?" Her boss was joking, but she still choked on her own saliva. As she wheezed and coughed, her boss gave her a curious look. "You gonna live?" he asked with concern when he saw her face was bright red.

Trying to hide her embarrassed blush, she ran into the open elevator. "I'm fine," she choked out, covering her face with her hands. *You better be nothing less than the consummate professional, Keef...this report better look good.*

She sat restlessly on the subway, getting up to look out the window several times and then taking a new seat. People were starting to stare at her as she gestured to herself and covered her face repeatedly.

You don't have to look in her eyes. Pretend. That's it. Look at a spot just beyond her face. Her ear, look at her ear. Yeah, Keefer smiled triumphantly, *keep looking at her ear and you'll be fine. Oh, come on! You know you can't just look at her ear! You've imagined her body naked!* Keefer stood again, shaking the thought away and starting on a new one. *Okay, just tell her you lost the old report and have to make a new one. Act nonchalant about it and get out as fast as you can. Professional, Keef, this is work. You get paid to do this, so do it right.* She held her head high, confident with her pep talk.

By the time Keefer was facing the wooden gates to the construction site, she was licking her lips obsessively, her hands were clammy, and her heart was pounding. She caught herself fixing her hair for the thousandth time and clasped her hands together in front of her body. *Primping, Keefer? Come on! You'll be wearing a hard hat, for God's sake.* She pushed open the gate and took a deep breath. Her hands were shaking. *Everything is fine. This is work and you are a professional. Just don't think about what you did last night.* Blue eyes opened wide in disbelief at her own mind's betrayal. *Are you insane? What did you go and think that for! Oh, no.* Keefer swallowed repeatedly until the boulder in her throat went down.

"Hey lady, you lost or sumpthin'?"

He's talking to you, idiot. "Uh, no, actually." She flashed her credentials and the guy sighed heavily.

"Patch! Get down here! Someone here ta see you!" he shouted, scaring an already frazzled Keefer half to death.

"No! That's okay, I'll go. I know where she is," she replied quickly.

"Never mind! She's coming up!" he yelled again. "You'll be needing a hat. Go into the trailer, there should be a clean enough one in there." He pointed her in the direction.

"Thanks." She smiled nervously and headed off.

"Ooh! Patch has a lady coming to see her!" Bobby teased.

"Maybe its whassername from last night comin' to smack ya around some more," Tony said with a raised eyebrow.

"Knock it off. She never hit me." Sheridan was very curious as to who the lady was. It could be anybody. She grinned wickedly and chuckled.

"Now they're comin' to you for a nooner. I tell ya, Patch..." Phil clapped Sheridan on the back.

"What can I say, buddy, when you got it, you got it," she said, wiggling both eyebrows.

"I can't wait to see the lucky woman. You musta really did her good for her to be coming here," Phil joked.

"Maybe she didn't do her good at all and she's coming for a refund," Tony laughed.

"Fuck off, assholes, I'm always good." Sheridan dusted herself off as best she could before the mystery woman appeared. For all she knew, it could be her aunt Sadie, her pop's sister, with some of her famous cookies, but she did so love to play with the guys.

Keefer stood immobile on the top step, completely stricken, unable to close her mouth. *God! She's gorgeous!* Sheridan stood mere feet away, hardly dressed, dusting herself off, sweat glistening on tons of exposed skin. *I can't move my legs.* Keefer was totally taken by surprise.

Sheridan felt the smack on her back and was about to frown when she noticed Keefer standing on the top step. *Oh, no...what is she doing here?* Sheridan started to panic; her heart started beating loudly in her ears. Keefer looked adorable to the blonde and she let her eyes drink in the sight. She was wearing tight-fitting, tan chinos and a white oxford shirt with the sleeves all rolled up to her elbows. Green eyes scanned upwards still to the odd expression on the inspector's face. *Why is she looking at me like that?* Sheridan self-consciously looked down at herself. Finding nothing hanging out, she looked back up at into the inspector's eyes. *Oh, I see,* she cursed to herself. *This is very bad.*

Move, you idiot! Keefer screamed at herself, forcing her feet to carry her into the room. She broke her gaze from the wonderful body and glanced around at the men in the room. They were all looking at her like she was the Messiah and it made her very uncomfortable. She began to blush and cleared her throat nervously.

"Um...Kee...Ms. Gibson...to what do we owe the honor of a return visit?" Sheridan managed to croak out.

"I, uh, I..." *Her ear, Keef, her ear!* "I seemed to have misplaced the first report I made. I'm sorry for the hassle, but I need to run another check," she said as apologetically as she could, given the circumstances.

What the hell is she looking at? Sheridan touched her ear self-consciously. "No, it's no problem at all." She approached the tall woman, who took a step back. *How weird.* It happened again. "Um, Ms. Gibson, you're gonna take a header down the stairs." *Damn, she's totally spooked by me! What the hell happened? Is this 'cuz of the other night?*

Keefer blushed at her actions and took a hesitant step toward Sheridan. She could not take her eyes off of her exposed body, as hard as she tried. Her mind was taking pictures, capturing every inch of skin, every muscle and sinew, for future reference. She couldn't speak; the blood was rushing around in her head so loudly she was afraid she'd shout.

Once they got close enough to each other and far enough away from the guys, Sheridan whispered, "Hey, Keef, you all right?" The closeness of the tall woman gave her a twinge in her stomach.

The inspector nodded and looked at her shoes.

"You sure? Hey..." The construction worker went to touch Keefer's hand and she jumped, pulling her whole arm away. "What did I do? Why are you acting like this?" she asked, hurt clearly evident in her voice. *Why is she so afraid of me?*

"It's not you. It's me."

Keefer had said it so quietly, Sheridan had to hit rewind in her head and replay it. "You? What's going on? Did you really lose the report?"

"Yes. I'm just here for business, please don't touch me right now, okay?" Keefer begged, her blue eyes wide.

Whoo-ee, she's really fucked up over that night! "Well, then, Ms. Gibson," Sheridan said loud enough for the guys to hear, "shall we inspect?"

Keefer followed Sheridan away from the scrutiny of her co-workers, breathing a small sigh of relief once out of the spotlight. She squeaked when she was grabbed by the arm and turned around. She used every bit of strength she had not to turn and attack out of instinct.

"What the hell is going on here? Why are you so afraid of me? What did I do to you? You said you liked it!" Sheridan asked in rapid-fire succession.

Keefer was focused on flashing green eyes and she swallowed very nervously. "Nothing, I did like it. Too much...please, I can't help it..."

Sheridan let go of the tall woman's arm and cursed herself. "Fuck. Keefer, I'm sorry I acted that way. Really. I don't know why I did that." The blonde closed her eyes and leaned her head on the wall. "You scared me, is all. I don't know why you make me feel so crazy sometimes."

"Tell me about it," Keefer agreed with a nod.

"Really, forgive me, I don't know what came over me." Sheridan was genuinely sorry and she felt like shit.

"It's all right, just know that I have all sorts of colorful little belts in my closet and if you ever grab me like that again, I'll break your arm."

Sheridan looked up into serious blue eyes and raised both eyebrows. "You're not kidding me, are you?" she asked in wonder.

"No, I'm not," she smiled. "Okay, let's start over again. I lost the report and I have to inspect. Do you want to show me around or should I get one of the guys to do it?"

"Hell no! You stay away from those guys, they're nothing but trouble."

"And how about you, Sheridan, are *you* nothing but trouble?" Keefer asked, only half teasing.

"Yes, and it would do you a world of good to stay away from me," she answered truthfully.

Keefer stopped and let Sheridan walk ahead of her. She scanned the blonde's body from head to toe before shaking her head in defeat. *I just can't do that.* She ran to catch up with the smaller woman and jumped in front of her. "I'm sorry, Sheridan, but I just can't do that. I want to be around you," she blurted out, shocked at her own words.

Sheridan closed her eyes and swallowed hard. The words hit her like a physical slap. She couldn't keep Keefer around without hurting her or, worse, sleeping with her. The tall woman would fall in love with her, she was sure of it. Keefer wasn't the type of woman Sheridan wanted to get involved with. Most of all, Keefer scared her witless.

"Can we be friends?" Keefer asked hopefully.

Hmm...friends? The construction worker rolled it around in her head. "Sure, we can be friends." She smiled brightly and felt her stomach twist when the smile was returned just as brightly. *Damn, she sure is beautiful, though.*

"Thanks, I like having you around," Keefer said as she walked ahead.

"Me too. So, you liked it too much, eh?"

"I knew I shouldn't have told you, of all people, something like that." The tall woman laughed in embarrassment.

"Who else has been touching you, then?" Sheridan asked with a smirk.

"Just you," Keefer whispered. "We can still touch, can't we? I mean, if it's okay with you," she asked shyly.

"Try and stop me." The construction worker grinned confidently.

Yes! Keefer raised an eyebrow at her internal comment.

"And I think it's your turn," Sheridan teased, expecting the blush that crept up Keefer's neck.

Chapter 11

Sheridan led the inspector around the job site and Keefer scribbled diligently as she went along. The construction worker would find herself lost in thought as she watched the tall woman pause and write on her clipboard. She'd trace the long fingers with her gaze, imagining them roaming up and down her body, remembering how they'd felt digging into her arm that night. She'd catch herself on occasion watching Keefer's ass and hips move as she walked in front of her, tripping over things as she did. Keefer would look over her shoulder with a raised eyebrow and Sheridan could hardly hold back her embarrassment.

Keefer found it hard to believe that Sheridan was so clumsy, at times stumbling over her own two feet, and wondered if maybe she was giving the construction worker a reason to be so distracted. She remembered the look on Sheridan's face the first time she saw her in her sleep shorts and a silly grin crept up on her. *Maybe I am doing this to her. Maybe she* does *find me distracting.* She forced herself to concentrate on her job before she screwed it up a second time.

The guys stood around, looking at each other with knowing expressions. They knew that was the mystery woman who had Patch so flustered. They had never seen her lose it like she did when the inspector showed up unannounced. The guys had seen their co-worker in all sorts of uncomfortable situations, including being pushed into a wheelbarrow full of wet cement by an unhappy woman. All three of them had to agree—this was very different.

"That's her, you know." Bobby nodded as he spoke.

"It's gotta be," Phil agreed.

117

"I gotta hand it to her, I don't know how long I'd be able to hold out on that one. Damn! She's one hell of a looker!" Tony whistled his pleasure.

They all agreed—Ms. Gibson was "the one."

"Poor Patch. She's got it bad," Phil said sympathetically. "How long ya think it's gonna take her to figure it out?"

"I dunno. Ya know, she said this woman has issues...big-time problems. She may never stick around long enough to find out," Tony stated, looking expectantly at Bobby.

"I ain't gonna tell her...no way!" Bobby backed up and shook his head.

"Well, neither are we." Phil shook his head too.

All three men frowned. It was going to be a bumpy ride.

Sheridan wrestled playfully with her dogs, feeling guilty for not spending her usual amount of quality time with them lately. They stayed in the dog run at the park for hours and then she roughhoused some more with them at home. Finally tiring them out, she filled up their food bowls and plopped down on the couch to catch her breath. Some time later, while watching television, her cell phone rang.

Damn! I forgot to call that girl, what was her name? On her way to find her phone, she dug in her pockets for the number. *Aha! Sara. Gotta call Sara,* she thought with a smirk. Finding the cell, she glanced at the incoming number as she hit the talk button. *Shit...it's Keefer.* She wasn't expecting her to call. "Hello?" she answered warily.

"Hi, Sheridan, it's Keefer."

"I know. What's up? Bad news to tell me? The site was a problem?" she asked while sitting back down on the couch.

"Uh, no. It's actually pretty by the book," Keefer replied.

"Well that's good. So what's up?" Sheridan was curious.

"Well...I was just wondering if you're doing anything for dinner tonight."

She wants me to come over there? Already? "I'm not...why? You cooking?"

"Actually, I was thinking about it and I hate to cook for myself really...so maybe you'd like to come over or something?" Keefer sounded very hesitant.

"I'd be more than happy to eat what you cook. I was going to settle down with a frozen pizza." Zeus trotted over, hauled himself onto the couch and flopped his big body across Sheridan's lap. "Oof!"

"What was that?" Keefer asked with a chuckle.

"My dog just sat his fat ass across my stomach." Just then, Pharaoh jumped up from his nap and began barking at the air. "That would be my other dog barking at his own shadow," the blonde laughed. "Hey, knock it off!" she yelled away from the phone.

"He sounds pretty big. What kind of dogs do you have?" Keefer asked.

"A pit and a Rotty."

"*You* have a pit and a Rotty?"

"Yeah," Sheridan laughed at the shocked tone of her friend's voice. "They're good boys."

"If you say so." Keefer played like she didn't believe her.

"I'll introduce you one day." Sheridan's stomach growled. "Hey, what time should I be over there?"

"How about in an hour or so? Is that too soon? Do you have things to do?"

"Take it easy, babe, an hour is fine. Just gotta jump in the shower, okay?" Sheridan heard the tall woman's nerves jangling from where she was sitting.

"Okay. Thanks."

"Don't thank me until you've had dessert," Sheridan teased.

"Dessert?"

"Well, I was gonna bring Aunt Sadie's famous cookies," the blonde smirked to herself, "but if you had something else in mind..."

"No! I mean, that sounds great."

I know just what you're thinking, 'cuz it crossed my mind too, Keefer. Bad girl. "Okay then, see ya soon."

Immediately after hanging up, Sheridan called Sara and made a date for later that night at the club. She hummed as she showered. It had been a long time since she had any home-cooked food and she was looking forward to it. Dressing in jeans and a T-shirt, she ditched her jacket, due to the warm evening. Slipping into her boots, she called her good nights to the still-napping dogs. "I promise I'll be home tonight, kids!" she vowed before she left.

Keefer fretted for a while about what to make for dinner and she finally decided on steak. Sheridan looked like a meat and potatoes kind of woman and Keefer looked forward to pleasing her. She made homemade mashed potatoes and salad to go with it. She was just about finished when she saw the headlights shine into her front windows. *Perfect timing!* she thought as she headed toward the front door. Fifi remained where she had been from the moment Keefer started cooking—sitting directly in front of the broiler, licking her lips.

Sheridan had her hand poised to ring the bell when the door opened up to the wonderful vision of Keefer. *I swear she gets prettier and prettier.* "Hey, psychic or something?" she asked with a wink, letting herself into the house.

"Yeah, you've found out my secret." Keefer smiled and shut the door.

"I seriously doubt that, Keefer. If you could read my mind, you'd have run away screaming the first day you met me," Sheridan said with an eyebrow wiggle.

I bet she's so right. "You don't scare me, Sheridan Landers," she said with much more confidence than she felt.

"I should. Remember that," the construction worker half teased.

Keefer took in Sheridan's half grin, her confident stance, her clothing and the delicious body they were hugging and knew she was right. She should be very afraid of this woman. She had some sort of power over her. Keefer was drawn to her like a moth to a flame, but she had a reputation and she didn't hide it. The tall woman glanced up into knowing green eyes and true to form, she blushed.

She was definitely checking me out. Tread easy, Sher, this is very iffy. "Mmm, it smells damned good in here." She closed her eyes and inhaled dramatically.

"Hope you like steak." Keefer was grateful for the change in conversation. "I have wine, beer...vodka, or would you like soda?" she asked with her head buried in the fridge.

Sheridan stared at the perfect ass aimed directly at her and exhaled a heavy sigh. *What did you get yourself into? You'll never be able to say no to her. Not with that body, those eyes...that ass. She wants you, Sher, in a bad way. Thank God she's as shy as they come or you'd be all over her like flies on shit.* Keefer stood up and Sheridan remembered that she'd been asked a question. *So, what exactly is stopping you from jumping her bones? She certainly does want you, and you definitely want her. So what's the deal?* "Soda's fine. I'd usually go for the beer, but I'm driving tonight."

"Sorry, I forgot. Do you mind if I have some wine?" *I can't do this without some help.*

"No, suit yourself," Sheridan waved her hand. *Please don't get drunk, I beg of you...please...*

Keefer grabbed a can of soda, a bottle of wine, and a glass and nudged the dog with her bare foot. "Feefs, you're going to have to move."

"Hmm, maybe you do have some powers, the dog is damn near hypnotized." Sheridan narrowed her eyes playfully.

"Trust me, it's not me, she'll sit there all night if she has to. She loves steak."

"My kinda woman."

"So, there is such a thing?" Keefer asked before she could censor herself.

"Maybe. I like all kinds." *Lately, tall brunettes with crystal-clear blue eyes seem to be at the top of my list.*

Keefer got warm at the way Sheridan was looking at her and looked away. She motioned for the blonde to sit down and began bringing plates to the table.

Sheridan popped right back out of her seat and protested, "Let me do that, you cooked."

"No, it's all right, I want to do it," Keefer argued, holding the plates over her head out of Sheridan's reach.

Sheridan sat down and pouted.

Jesus, she's adorable when she does that. "Just you sit there and let me wait on you."

"You're going to spoil me." The construction worker shook her head and wagged her finger.

Perhaps that is the plan... "Please, when's the last time you sat down and someone served you?"

Sheridan smiled wickedly and chuckled.

"Food! I meant food, you pig." Keefer swatted her in the back of the head and then covered her mouth in shock at the familiar gesture. "Oh, I'm so sorry, I don't know why I did that."

Sheridan rubbed her head and frowned, "You better be careful there, Keefer, only certain women are allowed to smack me in the back of the head. Certain women with certain privileges."

As much as she didn't want to hear it, she found herself asking, "Oh? And what makes them so special?"

Sheridan leered.

Keefer gulped.

She is turning out to be so much fun, Sheridan thought as she changed her expression to a cocky smirk. "You may just find out yet," she teased.

Keefer drained her glass of wine.

Keefer found it very hard to eat with Sheridan sitting across from her. She tried to stay focused on her plate, but her eyes kept drifting of their own accord to the blonde. She would catch herself stopping in mid-chew to admire the way Sheridan would lick her lips or the way her muscles moved as she lifted her soda, both sights causing pleasant feelings in her groin.

"This was fanfuckingtastic, Keefer," Sheridan said with enthusiasm. "You did good." She leaned back and smiled at the brunette.

Keefer fell into the green eyes, her wine glass resting on her lips. Catching herself staring once again, she put down the glass and smiled back, feeling very pleased with herself. "Thank you."

"Fifi agrees." Sheridan winked at Keefer, then reached down to pet the dog at her side.

"I better keep my eye on you, she's going to be waddling soon if you keep feeding her like that."

Sheridan raised an eyebrow. "If I didn't know better, I'd say that was an invitation."

Keefer looked like a deer in the headlights. *What the heck? Why not...*"I suppose it was," she said distractedly, Sheridan's grin making her forget what she was saying.

"I'd like that, Keefer, I enjoyed the food and the company. It's not often I get to eat a meal with such great scenery." Sheridan smiled and stood up with her dish. "Do you have a dishwasher or should I put this in the sink?"

Her smile does such strange things to my insides, or is it the wine? No, wine never made me feel like that before, it must be her.

"Keef?" Sheridan knew that look and she mentally patted herself on the back.

Oh God, I love it when she calls me Keef.

"Hey, Earth to Keefer..."

The tall woman jumped up out of her seat. "Oh! I am so sorry. Just rinse it off, I'll load up the dishwasher," Keefer apologized, thoroughly embarrassed.

"No you don't! The least I can do is clean up." Sheridan put the plate down and walked over to Keefer, turned her around, and led her into the living room. "Sit," she ordered, pointing at the couch.

Keefer grinned and obliged. "Okay, but don't make a habit out of this," she warned, loving the warmth of Sheridan's hand on her back.

"I think I'm already addicted," Sheridan mumbled on her way back into the kitchen, looking at her hand.

Keefer leaned back and smiled to herself. The wine made her pleasantly relaxed and she felt so comfortable with the blonde in her kitchen. She stretched her long legs out in front of her and sighed happily. *This is nice,* she thought. *Sheridan's not so bad, once you get used to her. I'd like to keep her around; she makes me feel good just by being here.*

"Hey, you done with this or do ya still want it?"

The object of her thoughts was standing there holding the half-empty wine bottle; she had already placed the glass on the coffee table. *Jeez, Keef, she had to see you smiling like a nut job.* The tall woman blushed and accepted the bottle with a shy grin.

"Be careful, Keef, I don't want you getting drunk and taking advantage of me," Sheridan teased.

It took her a moment to figure out the comment since she was already rather tipsy. When it made sense, she sat straight up and moved her mouth a few times without saying anything.

Sheridan snickered. "Gotcha," she teased and sat down next to the flustered woman. "It's okay, I know you'll control yourself," she added playfully.

"You are so bad, Sheridan." Keefer paused to glance at the blonde, regretting it the instant she felt her face get hot. Shaking her head, she looked at her hands. "I think you like to tease me."

"Oh, you don't know the half if it," Sheridan grinned, noting Keefer was much more relaxed than usual.

Keefer let the comment slide, her mouth going dry at the implications. She lifted her glass and toasted the air. "Here's to new friends." She drank, grateful for the cool wetness sliding down her throat.

"Tonight is kinda special," Sheridan added with a chuckle.

Keefer laughed, "You really are bad."

"I'm so bad, I'm good." Sheridan wiggled her eyebrows.

"I just bet you are." Keefer's mouth opened wide and she hid her face. *Where the hell did that come from?*

"Hey, did anyone ever tell you you're beautiful when you're mortified?"

"No, I've never been so embarrassed before," Keefer admitted, her face still in her hands.

"Ooh, I'm special then. Cool."

You certainly are, Keefer thought as Sheridan pulled her hands away from her face.

"Hey, no harm done. If you must know, I like it that you are so shy around me. It makes me smile a lot."

Keefer turned her head and looked into deep green eyes, the feeling in her stomach making her eyelids flutter. Sheridan was so attractive to her; everything about her turned her on, even when she teased her mercilessly. *Look away, Keef...*

Sheridan felt her own flutters, a little lower than her stomach. Keefer's eyes were so blue, she felt as if she could drown in them. She knew the brunette was pretty vulnerable after drinking half a bottle of wine and she felt a little protective as well as turned on. She knew she shouldn't stare into her eyes any longer, but she couldn't stop herself. She had already caught herself licking her lips and she noticed the vein in Keefer's neck throb furiously after she did.

Oh, my god, she's going to kiss me! Keefer's blood rushed frantically through her body, giving her a head rush. She closed her eyes briefly to gain her equilibrium and when she opened them again, Sheridan was looking away, her green eyes closed. *Breathe, Keef, breathe,* she reminded herself as she too looked the other way.

Sheridan took a long slow deep breath. *Okay, Sher, that was almost very stupid. You know you can't fuck her, so drop it. Besides, Sara is waiting for you.* Sheridan jumped as she felt Keefer's hand touch her arm. *What is she doing?* Her eyes popped open and she watched as Keefer seemed to be studying her arm. The inspector's fingers traced her muscles and Sheridan couldn't contain a shiver. *She's going to kill me.* She felt her nipples harden as goose bumps appeared. *Oh, shit...I gotta get out of here.*

Keefer couldn't stop herself and she watched her hand reach out and touch Sheridan's forearm. The muscle had been flexing while the blonde sat with her thoughts and it called to the tall woman. Her fingers drifted up and down the smooth skin, delighting in the feel of the soft, blonde hairs. She glanced up and saw Sheridan's half-lidded gaze following her fingers and warmth flooded her sex. *Wow, that look is so hot.* Keefer stopped when she saw the small shiver and the goose bumps her touch was causing. *I did that? To Sheridan?* A small triumphant smile flickered across her face and she tried to wipe it away.

As soon as the fingers disappeared, Sheridan stood up and smoothed her sweaty hands on her jeans. *She looks mighty pleased with herself, doesn't she?* she thought, noticing the ill-hidden expression on Keefer's face. *You know? I should just—Hold up, hot stuff, she's learning here, and you're the willing subject or you wouldn't be submitting yourself to it by being here.* Sheridan calmed her breathing and noticed Keefer had stood up, too. *Just why are you allowing this, anyway?*

"I'm sorry, Sheridan, I couldn't seem to stop myself."

"No, that's quite all right. It felt very good. Besides, it was your turn anyway, remember?" She smiled reassuringly.

"That's all I get?" Keefer's eyes widened enormously. *That's it!* She put down her wine glass and blushed bright red.

Sheridan couldn't stop herself and a snicker escaped. Keefer was completely horrified at herself. "Whoa, easy there. It's okay." She rubbed her hand on the tall woman's back. "There's plenty more of me for you to touch."

The tall woman felt her stomach flop at the touch. If possible, Keefer's eyes widened even more.

"Hey, relax, Keef, we got all the time in the world, right?" *We do? What am I saying?*

Keefer managed to calm slightly and she nodded. "I really don't know why I'm acting like this. It must be the wine." She pointed at the offending bottle.

"Well then, I'll remember to bring some wine the next time I come. I like you like this." Sheridan smiled and tucked a stray black hair behind Keefer's ear. The tall woman shivered and Sheridan's eyes narrowed with arousal. *Gotta get out of here,* she reminded herself.

The tall woman nearly groaned out loud at the gentle gesture. "Didn't you mention something about cookies?" Keefer hugged herself to hide her hard nipples.

"Shit! They're in the car. So much for dessert, huh?" Sheridan smacked herself in the head. "I'll go get them."

"Nah, save them for next time," she said. *I think I've had too much dessert for one night, anyway,* Keefer thought with another shiver.

"Um, I gotta get going, I have um, something tonight and..."

"Sheridan, I know all about it." *That's what you get for falling for the neighborhood slut. Did I say falling?* Keefer pushed the thought away. "Go have fun. I had a great time tonight," she said with a hint of sadness.

"Me too. I look forward to spending time with you again," Sheridan said, trying to make Keefer feel better.

Keefer smiled. "I bet you say that to all the girls," she joked.

"Actually, no, I don't. Good night, Keef." Sheridan blew a kiss to the tall woman.

"I like when you call me Keef. Good night, Sheridan, be careful."

Keefer watched as the door closed behind the blonde and she sat down in the couch heavily, reaching for the rest of the wine.

Sheridan arrived at the club and spotted Sara first. She was wearing a barely-there mini skirt and a tiny half-shirt. Green eyes drank in the long, sexy legs and flat belly and she made a beeline for the attractive blonde. *Oh yeah, just what the doctor ordered.*

"Well, hi there, Sheridan. I was wondering if you were going to show up at all." Sara smiled seductively, inviting Sheridan to move closer.

"I'd never stand a pretty lady up. You look great." The construction worker openly appraised the tall blonde.

"So do you." Sara tickled her fingers from Sheridan's shoulders to her hands.

Small talk out of the way, Sheridan reached up and pulled Sara down into a kiss. As soon as their tongues met, she pulled away with a curious look on her face. "What are you drinking?"

"Wine, why?"

"Nothing." Sheridan resumed the kiss. *It just fucking figures.*

125

Sheridan leaned into Sara's back as the cashier's face pressed up against the wall. She was sucking on the back of the tall blonde's neck, running her hands all over her long legs.

"I never figured you for a leg woman, Sheridan," Sara breathed out into the cool tiles.

"I'm not," Sheridan replied into a burning ear. *Just can't control these impulses lately.* She trailed her hands up the inside of Sara's thighs and growled at the wetness she found at their apex. "It doesn't look like you mind the attention, now, does it." *I wonder if Keefer gets this wet.*

"Mmm, not at all, baby." The taller woman stuck her ass out, pressing it into Sheridan's body, begging her to continue. "Do it."

Forget Keefer, dammit! Just drop it! Green eyes narrowed at the back of Sara's head. "You horny bitch, you wanted me to fuck you like this from the second you laid eyes on me, didn't you?" Sheridan whispered hotly into Sara's ear, shoving her fingers inside her waiting entrance.

"Yes...harder!" Sara gritted her teeth to stop from screaming.

"I bet you wish I had a cock so I could shove it into you right now." Sheridan grabbed a handful of Sara's hair and pulled her head back, thrusting her hand into her sex, her crotch into the round ass.

"Fuck me, Sheridan!"

"You're damned right I'll fuck you." The muscular blonde yanked Sara's hair harder and rode her ass, pumping her fingers hard and fast. "I'm going to make you scream, Sara," she growled, reaching for Sara's hand and thrusting it between her legs. "Touch your clit," she instructed.

"Ohh...I'd much rather...touch yours," Sara groaned between breaths.

Sheridan grinned wickedly, wiping her sweaty face against Sara's shoulder. She guided the slender hand behind the woman to her own crotch. "Find it, and you can have it all you want."

Sara fumbled around behind her, hand at an awkward angle; finally tearing open the buttons on Sheridan's pants, she shoved her hand into her underwear.

"Oh, fuck...you got it," the construction worker grunted, thrusting her hips in time with her hand.

Keefer lay on the couch in a pleasant haze from the wine. She ran her hands gently up and down her arms, watching as the hairs stood up, imagining they were Sheridan's hands, softly exploring her body once again. She brought them across her chest, using the slightest pressure over her breasts, shivering at the sensations. Her imagination allowed Sheridan to touch her everywhere, skimming her callused fingers over her cheekbones and into her hair. Her nipples were straining for attention and she teased them gently, slowly and patiently, paying close attention to the twitching between her legs as she did. The alcohol made her relax, able to accept her fantasy lover's touches, and she closed her eyes as the teasing fingers slipped across her belly. Slowly lifting her shirt, she touched flesh to flesh, hand on breast, and arched her back dramatically.

"Oh, Sheridan."

Marie saw Sheridan exit the bathroom first and smirked knowingly. She had heard that her friend was there somewhere and when her search turned up empty, she knew just where Sheridan was. She motioned to Dawn, who waved Sheridan over to the bar.

"Whassup, girl?" the blonde asked a little louder than she should. She was still worked up from the wild scene in the bathroom.

"I should ask you that. Who's the tall drink of water?" Dawn asked, taking a good long look at the marks peppering the leggy blonde's neck.

"Sara, this is Dawn," she turned to Marie who had just made it over to the bunch, "and this is Marie. Where's Sharon?" Sheridan asked, scanning the crowd for her tall friend's head.

"Aw, they switched her to night shift yesterday. She must have pissed somebody off." Marie frowned. "Sharon's a cop," she offered the newcomer.

"Hi, guys, nice to meet you." Sara smiled as politely as she could with Sheridan's hand squeezing her ass. "If you'll excuse me," she said to the bunch and pecked Sheridan on the cheek, "I gotta get going. It was fun, sweetie, call me." She winked and was gone.

"That's my kinda date, Sher!" Dawn laughed.

"Well, she's just what I was looking for tonight," Sheridan said with a smirk.

"Hey, what ever happened with that tall woman with the black hair? The one Danni fucked over?" Marie asked with a thoughtful expression on her face.

"Nothing happened and I'm going to keep it that way," Sheridan answered sharply.

"You mean you never fucked her? Come on, Sher!" Dawn laughed out loud at the ridiculous statement.

"What's the big fucking deal? No, I didn't fuck her and I'm not going to, so butt the hell out!"

The two women watched as their friend stormed off to the dance floor in a huff.

"What was that?" Dawn asked in surprise.

"I haven't the slightest idea. Why would she be so determined not to fuck a gorgeous women like that?" Marie puzzled.

"And one who's right on the edge, too. Rebounds are the best kind." Dawn shook her head.

"You don't think that the tall chick turned Sheridan down, do you?" she asked, eyes wide.

"No way. No one turns her down." Marie watched her friend dance out her frustrations. "You know, something just ain't right with her lately. Did you see that chick's neck? She never marks women like that."

"Yeah, I saw that, and look at her now, she's pissed as all hell since we brought up that other woman. I wonder what happened." Dawn furrowed her brow.

"Who the fuck knows. Apparently, that woman and her don't get along and Sher's not talking. Hey, let me buy you another drink," Marie pulled out some money.

"Sure." Dawn thought for a minute and then shook her head with a laugh.

"What happened?" Marie asked her chuckling friend.

"Nothing. I just thought for a split second that maybe Sheridan *can't* fuck that tall woman, you know, because she cares about her or something."

Marie laughed too. "You're right, that is funny."

Sheridan was exhausted by the time she fell into bed. The dogs piled in with her and soon they were comfortable, but their mommy was not. "Must you always dig your foot into my head?" she asked Zeus, pushing the paw away with her shoulder. "I mean, sheesh, I wouldn't complain if you were a woman and all, but really, this is pathetic." She chuckled at her own misfortune and moved away from the offending limb.

Sleep wasn't coming. Sheridan's mind was filled with multiple images of the night. Sara's ass banging into her crotch...Keefer's surprised look when she said things before thinking...Sara's neck after she sucked it relentlessly...Keefer's bare toes curling into the carpeting...Keefer's hand in her pants, making her come...*Wait a minute, that was Sara.* Sara's face as she sucked on her nipple...Keefer's lips forming her name as she came...*Okay, that's just about enough.* She turned over and beat her pillow. *Keefer is slipping into the worst places...and how would I know what she looks like when she comes, anyway?* The image appeared again and Sheridan growled at it, swatting at it in the dark room. "God damn it." She frowned and crossed her arms over her chest. After pouting for a while, she started to chuckle. "Why waste a good imagination?"

She finally fell asleep with a grin on her face from the wonderful scenes in her wild imagination.

Chapter 12

Keefer came to consciousness and the first thing she realized was that she had a headache. "Ow," she complained quietly. The second thing she realized was that she had a hand on her breast and the other in her underwear. "Oh, Jesus!" Sitting up quickly, she hissed as the pain flooded into her stiff neck. *I fell asleep on the couch? Like that?* Focusing a little better, she noticed her shirt was pushed up to her neck. Yanking it down quickly, she leaned forward and covered her face with her hands. "What a night," she breathed into her palms, only to inhale the scent of her own arousal all over her fingers. She pulled them away and stared at them, the whole night coming back to her in a great flood of images. "Oh, no..." She blushed dark red. "I can't believe I did that!"

Eventually, the more she remembered about the night, the more her embarrassment faded. "She really liked it when I touched her," she recalled out loud, still able to feel the strong muscles under the soft skin. "I wonder if she's that hard and soft everywhere." Her musings made her squirm as embarrassment returned. *I pretended she was touching me all over, didn't I?* She glanced down at her disheveled clothing. *Well, from the looks of things, I guess it went very well.* She vaguely remembered beginning her little fantasy last night, but remembered distinctly how it ended. "Oh, no!" She hung her head again in shame. "I yelled. I yelled out her name...Good Lord!"

Keefer sat, mortified with herself, until she heard her alarm go off in the bedroom. Music filled the house and she stood up and went to the kitchen to make coffee, yawning loudly and waking her dog. *Let's not dwell on the uncomfortable, shall we?*

Fifi came running into the kitchen as Keefer was setting down fresh water. "Hiya, girl! How come you never wake up to the alarm?" Fifi didn't answer and Keefer giggled. The dog was as immune to the noise as Danni was. *Ew, don't go there,* she reprimanded herself. "Did you enjoy all that steak Sheridan fed you last night?" The dog wagged her tail quickly. "Yeah, well, don't get used to it, I'm going to watch her like a hawk next time." Keefer's brows knitted together in thought. "I wonder when the next time will be."

"Nail marks on your neck, Patch?" Bobby snickered. "Must have been one to remember."

Sheridan's hand went to her neck. "Where? I didn't see anything."

"On the back." Phil grinned. "Four of them, straight across."

The blonde grinned slyly. "Well then, I guess I'll have to get another mirror for the bathroom."

"Why? I know you don't want to cover them with makeup or nothing," Tony called from the other room.

"No, so I could stare at them and gloat, asshole," she yelled back. "How the hell did you see them?"

"Kinda hard to miss, Patch, they're practically glowing."

Now that she thought about it, it had stung a little in the shower and when she'd sweated while she was doing her push-ups that morning. "Yeah well, thanks, guys, now I'll be aware of them all day," she grumbled.

"Our pleasure." Phil spoke for the crew.

"Anyone we know?" Tony asked in curiosity.

"Chick from the donut shop. Nothing special, really," she answered distractedly as she began to work.

The guys exchanged glances and shrugged. Not bragging about her sexual escapades was terribly unusual.

"Nothing special? With those marks? I'd have thought it was an all-nighter," Bobby mentioned casually.

"Nope, it was a quickie. I had dinner at Kee—a friend's house and then ran to the club to meet Sara. She cut out on me as soon as it was over," Sheridan replied, bored.

The slip didn't get past the guys. Sheridan had called the inspector the same thing when she visited the second time. This certainly was different, Sheridan eating dinner at a woman's house—one whom she wasn't sleeping with. They already knew that their friend was falling for the tall woman, now it was a matter of the blonde realizing it for herself.

A little after Keefer returned home, her phone rang. She looked at the caller ID and her heart sped up. She quickly picked up the phone. "Hi, Sheridan," she said a little breathlessly.

"Now I know you're psychic," the blonde laughed.

"I hate to burst your bubble, but caller ID. Sorry."

"I hope you don't mind me calling; I had your number in my phone from when you called me."

Mind? Are you crazy? "That's perfectly okay with me," she said, almost excitedly.

"Hey, I didn't interrupt anything, did I? You sound out of breath."

"No, no, I just walked in the door," Keefer covered, holding the phone away from her ear to take a deep calming breath.

"Oh, do you want me to call back later?"

"No, that's all right, I'm sitting now." Keefer blushed at her reactions.

"I was just wondering...how does Fifi get along with other dogs?"

Odd question..."She's okay, why?" Keefer asked in confusion.

"Well, I take my dogs to the dog run, the one a couple blocks from your house. I was thinking maybe we could meet up there tomorrow, since it's Saturday."

Keefer covered the mouthpiece on the phone, leaned back on the couch and kicked her feet in excitement. Once she settled, she uncovered the phone. "That sounds great. What time do you want to meet?" She sounded like the picture of composure, but her smile threatened to split her face in two.

"I was thinking about ten-ish, is that okay?"

"That's fine. I'll see you then."

"Later, Keef."

Oh, I just love how she says that. Keefer smiled for the rest of the night.

Sheridan hung up the phone and took the pizza out of the microwave and brought it to the couch. Pharaoh jumped up on the coffee table and sniffed at the food. "Oh no you don't, you beggar! Mine!" She pushed him off the table and propped her feet up in his place. "I gave you dinner," she reminded him. Zeus looked up at the drooling pit bull from his position on the floor as if to say, "I told you so."

After dinner, the blonde turned to her dogs and shook her finger. "Now you listen to me, guys, you are to be on your best behavior tomorrow morning. Fifi is a small thing and from the looks of her, she doesn't need you apes traumatizing her any more than she has already been."

Zeus snorted and licked his face. Pharaoh wagged his tail rapidly.

"That's right, I don't want you jumping on Keefer either, you got it?"
Pharaoh yawned; Zeus got up, stretched, and walked away.

"I thought you'd see it my way." Sheridan rolled her eyes. "Maybe this was a bad idea," she thought out loud as she watched the pit bull roll onto his back.

Keefer hardly slept at all, waking up every hour to look at the clock, afraid she'd oversleep. She finally got out of bed at sunrise and she wasn't the least bit tired either. She was excited about the day, hanging out with Sheridan in the park. It was almost like a date and the thought made her toes curl.

"Hey, Feefs! We're going to the park today! You want to meet Sheridan's boys?"

The dog wagged her tail fast when she heard Sheridan's name. She liked the blonde woman, she gave her steak and she made her mommy smile.

"I'll take that as a yes. Come on, let's get some breakfast."

Keefer sat at the kitchen table, absently chewing on a toasted bagel, thinking about Sheridan's phone call. *I wonder why she called me so soon after seeing me? I think she likes me more than she lets on. I think she likes me that way.* Keefer smiled at the thought. She broke a small piece of her bagel off and watched as Fifi licked off the cream cheese.

I like her that way, too. Maybe I should make it more apparent to her...you know, show her I'm interested in her that way. Keefer blushed and stared into her coffee cup. *I can't do that. I'll blush my fool head off. She thinks it's funny that I am so shy. I think she likes to tease me so I'll blush.* Keefer narrowed her eyes in deep thought. *Hmm. She's so damned cocky...and she can be, she probably has them lining up in front of her when she goes out.*

That thought made Keefer frown. She emptied her plate into the garbage and took her coffee into the living room. *That's funny. She's apparently the neighborhood slut; she's not afraid to admit it, either. I think she's even proud of it. Hmph. I bet she and the guys at work brag to each other about their little exploits.* Keefer's eyes widened in shock. *Maybe she said something about me! That's probably why they were looking at me like that. No, no...Sheridan hasn't given me any reasons to doubt her. She's been honest with me from day one.*

Fifi came trotting over with her leash in her mouth. "Okay, honey. Mommy has to take a shower, and then we'll go to the park." Fifi's head cocked at the word. "You like the park, do you?" Keefer laughed at the dog's excited response. "Just keep your fur on, honey, we'll go in a little bit."

Keefer walked to the bathroom, still lost in thought. *Okay, she's a runaround; she can have any woman she wants. I know this about her, and yet, she hasn't made any fast moves on me. Maybe she doesn't like me like that?* She turned on the water and took her clothes off. *Wait a second...you saw how she reacted to you; she definitely is interested in you. So why isn't she acting on it? Did you do something to turn her off?*

Keefer sighed in pleasure as the hot water cascaded down her body. She stood motionless under the heavy spray, letting it wash all the nervous tension away that all her thinking created. *Think about it, Keef, would you really be ready for Sheridan if she did make a move on you? You don't even know what she's capable of. She could be everything you don't want. This may be a good thing for you, you know.* Keefer began to wash her body, her stomach having unknotted considerably after her last thought. *You see? You're not ready for her yet. She must have her reasons for not approaching you, Keef. Maybe that's what you have to find out—what her reasons are.*

She lathered up her long hair and bent her head down, letting the hot spray beat against the back of her neck, still stiff from sleeping on the couch the previous night. She blushed when she thought of why she fell asleep there in the first place. *That's why she hasn't come on to you, you idiot! You blush at the drop of a hat, she probably thinks you have no idea what that thing is between your legs, better yet, how to use it. God, she must think I'm so naive!*

Keefer washed the shampoo away and groaned pathetically. *Face it, you are naive. Sheridan will never want you if you keep that up. You need to find out what she likes, what she hates, what makes her smile...find out how she likes to be touched and what makes her feel good. Oh yeah, you got some serious work to do. You need to get out more, Keef.* To her deep surprise, Keefer didn't blush at these thoughts; instead, she felt a sense of determination.

She stepped out of her bathtub that morning with a whole new agenda.

When Keefer arrived at the park, she noticed Sheridan off in the distance. Immediately, her pulse started racing and she was grateful she had brought along a bottle of water because her mouth went dry as well. The construction worker was wearing a carbon copy of her outfit from the job—frayed cut-off shorts that exposed her very strong legs and a tight tank top, showing off her powerful arms. She had a baseball cap on backwards, and a tuft of blonde hair poked out from the front. Keefer put her hand on her chest to feel her heartbeat, then looked down at her own attire. *Okay, shorts and a T-shirt, that'll do.* While appraising her clothing, she noticed her hand moving with every beat of her heart and she panicked. Removing the hand, she could visibly see her breast pumping. *Oh, no...you gotta calm down, you know that's the first place she looks!* She opened the water and took a healthy swallow, followed by some deep breaths. Letting the last breath out slowly, she felt a lot calmer and her chest stopped bouncing. "Okay, baby, time to meet the boys."

As Keefer got closer, she was able to take a better look. Sheridan was standing there, hands on her hips, with her shoulders pushed back, smiling as she watched the dogs run amok. She looked incredibly adorable and the brunette willed herself not to drool. Keefer tried to locate the blonde's dogs but didn't have much to go on, except their breed. Suddenly, Sheridan squatted down and waited with her arms open. A huge Rottweiler barreled into her and toppled her over, a well-chewed Frisbee in his mouth. *That's one...*Out of the corner of her eye, Keefer spotted another dog, a brown pit bull running full speed ahead at the blonde. *There's two...*Keefer watched in amusement as Sheridan wrestled around on the grass, laughing and screaming with her dogs. They were at least as big as she was, and the inspector had to wonder what possessed the small woman to want such huge dogs. They seemed harmless enough and Fifi was tugging relentlessly on her leash as soon as she spotted Sheridan, so Keefer walked quickly to the fracas.

"Hey, Sheridan, are you under there?"

Zeus came flying out of the fray with Sheridan's hat in his mouth and took off. The blonde stood up, not even bothering to dust herself off, and took off after the dog.

"Hiya, Keef, be right back," she yelled over her shoulder, chasing the dog around the run.

Keefer laughed out loud, shielding her eyes from the sun to get a better look at the strong sexy legs in motion. *Mmm,* she hummed to herself, watching as the blonde ran around in circles after the dog.

Fifi was already sniffing the pit bull's butt and Keefer figured it was okay to introduce them. "Hiya, what's your name, big fella?" She knelt down and scratched his neck. "Damn, but you're all muscle! Wow." She let her hand run along the sides of the dog's body and shook her head. "Just like your mommy, huh? Here, let me see your tag." She twirled his collar around and read the name. "Pharaoh, huh?" The happy dog wagged his tail and attempted to lick her. "Oh, no you don't, not to offend you or anything, big guy, but you really need to wipe your face." Keefer dug around in her pockets and came up with some paper towels reserved for Fifi's poops. "Here, you owe me," she said as she held his face with one hand and wiped his drool off with the towels. Pharaoh shook his big head after Keefer let him go and jumped up onto her, his tail wagging wildly.

"Oh, you like me, do you?" She pulled Fifi out from behind her legs and made her sit in front of her. "Pharaoh, meet Fifi."

"Pharaoh! Down!" Sheridan yelled breathlessly as she trotted over. She was clutching her hat in her hand and was red faced from running.

"It's all right, he's a good boy. Fifi is terrified, though." Keefer laughed as her dog ran right back behind her, her nose poking out from between her shins.

"Pharaoh, sit."

The dog sat and Keefer squatted down to his level, bringing her frightened dog around to meet him. After a few moments of socializing, Fifi wagged her tail and sat next to the big pit bull.

Sheridan took the opportunity to catch her breath, as well as give Keefer the once over. She looked great with her hair pulled back, and that T-shirt left nothing to the imagination. She wanted Keefer to stand up so she could peruse those long-ass legs in shorts. When Keefer finally did stand up, Sheridan's mouth watered. "How ya doin' this morning?" she asked, taking a good look at the long bare legs. *Maybe I do have a thing for legs...those are hot shit!*

Keefer studied the blonde; she was sweating and dirty and had just about caught her breath. "Pretty good. I brought some water, you look like you can use it."

"Thanks, I do." After a long swig on the bottle, green eyes glanced up into blue. "You look great in shorts, Keef."

The tall woman blushed. "You've seen me in shorts before," she reminded the smiling blonde.

"Yeah, but I don't think I told you how good you look in them. Just an observation." Sheridan shrugged.

Uh-huh. Likes my legs...remember that. "Where's your other dog?" Keefer asked, looking out at the many dogs playing.

Sheridan stood and let loose a shrill whistle, startling Keefer. Pharaoh jumped to his feet and waited excitedly.

"Whoa!" The inspector took a step back as Zeus came flying at breakneck speed.

Sheridan braced herself for the impact as the Rotty tackled her to the ground, holding her forearm in his mouth, slobbering all over it. Pharaoh jumped onto Sheridan also, slobbering all over her hair. Keefer snickered as Fifi tried to jump in as well. She let her off the leash and watched, laughing loudly as her small dog ran straight for the blonde's face and began licking her mercilessly.

"Fifi! You traitor! You were supposed to be...ptth...my friend!" Sheridan yelled from somewhere under the pile of playfully snarling dogs. "Keef! Help!" she laughed.

135

Keefer squatted down next to the wrestling match and rooted around in the pile for Sheridan's hand.

"Hey!"

"Sorry." *Oh! I think that was her breast!* Keefer blushed and resumed her search, coming up with a thick bicep as a reward. *Mmm...that's nice.* She felt along the slippery arm, slick with sweat and doggie drool, until she found the hand. Grasping it, she tugged a few times before Sheridan tumbled out of the pile with the strangest look on her face.

What the hell was that all about! I think she was feeling me up! Sheridan looked quizzically at her tall snickering friend.

Keefer had to cover her mouth so she wouldn't guffaw. The blond was sitting, legs spread on the grass, filthy and covered in drool. Her hair was wet and sticking up all over the place and she was wiping her arms and hands on the small area of denim her cut-offs provided.

"Yuck it up, Keefer." Sheridan attempted a glare but failed.

"I'm so sorry..." Keefer bit back a snort of laughter. "If you could only see yourself." Keefer pointed at first to Sheridan's hair, but then noticed the dirt clinging to her neck and moved to point there, then gave up entirely when the blonde fell back on the grass and groaned.

"Zeus, gimme." Sheridan held out her hand and moved her fingers. The dog soon plopped her hat into her hand. She held it up over her face and grimaced. "Ick."

Pharaoh grabbed the Frisbee and dropped it at Keefer's feet. She bent down, picked it up, and then threw it. She watched him chase it, still snickering at her groaning, mumbling friend. "You all right there, Sher?"

"Peachy." She wiped her hand over her head and put the mangled hat on.

"Just checking." Keefer winked.

Sheridan studied her tall friend from her spot on the grass. *What's different about her today?* she wondered as Pharaoh retrieved the Frisbee and dropped it obediently at the brunette's feet.

"Fifi's turn, Pharaoh, okay?"

Sheridan watched in shock as her dog sat down and stared at Keefer, his body twitching to go after the Frisbee, but letting Fifi run after it instead.

"Good girl, baby!" Keefer praised her dog. "And you're a very good boy." She knelt down and kissed the pit bull on the snout, earning her a gape from Sheridan and a snort from Zeus as he pushed his big head into her leg. "Okay, you too, big boy, you're a good doggie too." Keefer followed that by grabbing the dog's cheeks and planting a kiss to the Rotty's huge head.

She is a whole other person! Maybe it's the dogs?

Keefer glanced over at the blonde and raised both eyebrows. "You look like you swallowed a bug," she told her as she sat her long body down next to Sheridan and hugged her knees.

Green eyes fell immediately to the back of Keefer's right thigh where it disappeared into her shorts. *Jeez, that looks so soft.* She sighed.

"Did you?"

"Huh?" the blonde asked in confusion, tearing her eyes away from their admiration.

"Swallow a bug?" Keefer repeated.

"What the hell are you talking about?" Sheridan chuckled, looking at Keefer like she'd grown another eye.

Hmmm, totally distracted, I see. Keefer stretched out her long legs in experimentation and leaned back on her hands, watching Sheridan's reaction out of the corner of her eye. "Nothing, you just had the most curious expression on your face. What were you thinking?"

"Nothing!" she answered quickly, trying desperately to not stare at the goddess laid out next to her, but failing miserably.

Keefer averted her eyes and turned her head to avoid showing Sheridan her blush. *Directly at my breasts. I knew it.* She mentally nodded, glad that she wasn't facing the blonde.

Sheridan suddenly stood. "I'm about ready to go, how about you?" Keefer nodded, so she whistled for her dogs. If she didn't know any better, she would have been certain the tall woman was teasing her. This confused her terribly. *Maybe it was innocent after all. It's hot and the sun is nice, maybe she's just taking it in or something?* She glanced over her shoulder at the reclining brunette and received an innocent smile that she returned. *Keefer doesn't know how to flirt...I don't think. Does she?* she wondered, wiping off her dirty butt.

Keefer had a perfect view—Sheridan's backside was directly in front of her. She began to blush as she followed the sinews of the construction worker's legs until they disappeared under frayed denim. *God, she needs a shower,* she mused as she saw Sheridan swipe at her butt a few times. Letting her eyes travel upwards, she traced along the sculpted triceps and across strong shoulders until she came to her neck. *Ohh, looks like one of the dogs got her.* She frowned for her until Sheridan grabbed the back of her neck and her fingers covered the scratches perfectly. *How coincidental do you think that could be?* Keefer narrowed her eyes. *Must have been one of her lady friends.. if you can call them ladies...* Blue eyes were fixated to the back of Sheridan's neck. *I wonder how they got there? What was she doing for the woman for her to leave those kind of marks? How were they entwined?*

Sheridan turned around and cocked her head in curiosity at the look on Keefer's face. *What the hell is she thinking about? Oh, she's blushing. That could be just about anything.* She smiled deviously. "You coming, Keefer?"

This caused the poor woman to blush darkly. "Uh...yeah." *If she only knew how true that was just then.*

Chapter 13

Sheridan decided to walk Keefer to her house, since it was so close, and then she'd walk back to the park to retrieve her car and drive the dogs' home. Keefer fell behind as Sheridan and her dogs led the way up the street.

The blonde's neck was itching and she was unable to let go of the dogs to scratch it. Besides, she knew it would burn if she actually did scratch it, so she kept twisting it around in an attempt to stop the itch. She jumped suddenly as cool fingers gently scratched the back of her neck, then gulped in panic realizing that Keefer had to know what the marks were and how she got them. Sheridan shivered at the sensation of Keefer's fingers touching the back of her neck. *Since when is she so touchy-feely? She must have touched me ten times so far...*

"Better?" the tall brunette asked.

"Much, thanks." *I always wanted to walk down your block with my nipples a mile in front of me.* "Um, about those marks..."

Keefer was suddenly in front of her. "I know what they are, Sheridan. I'm naive, not stupid. I just hope they were worth it." She smiled a little bitterly.

"Yeah, well..." *That was certainly interesting.* "She was good." *Why did I feel the need to explain them to her anyway? It's not like she's my girlfriend. I shudder at the thought...that's just what I need,* she thought sarcastically.

Keefer nodded and resumed walking toward her house. *Why should I be so twisted over this? I know what she does and I know it's who she is. Just cut it out, you don't own the woman, for God's sake.*

139

Sheridan continued to think. *So, maybe not as a girlfriend, but I need to have her around. Just look at that ass in tight shorts—I'd swear there's a little more shake to that walk than yesterday. What's going on with you, Keefer?*

Keefer stopped at her front walk and waited for Sheridan to catch up. *I wonder what she's thinking about. I wish I could get into her head.*

"Thanks for meeting me today, it was really fun." Sheridan smiled at the tall woman and then reached down to pet Fifi's head.

Keefer smiled back and touched Sheridan on the shoulder, noticing that the green eyes darted to her hand as she did. "I enjoyed myself immensely," she said a little teasingly.

Sheridan furrowed her brows at her tall friend. *I think she's hitting on me!* "Maybe I'll catch you later?" she asked.

Keefer laughed quietly as she walked up her front walk with the dog. "Who are you kidding, Sher, it's Saturday night." She turned around and winked knowingly.

"What's that supposed to mean?" Sheridan asked in confusion.

"You can't pass up a Saturday night at the club. There are probably twenty women waiting on your arrival tonight." Keefer put the key in her door and opened it.

Sheridan couldn't make sense out of it and frowned. "So? What are you getting at?"

"Go get laid, Sheridan, I'll see you some other time." The trap set, Keefer disappeared into her house, leaving the blonde bewildered and slightly angry.

Sheridan began walking back toward the park, her face in a permanent scowl. "What the hell was that all about, guys? It's like she fucking turned on me or something. So I like to get laid, since when has this been a problem? What do I care what she thinks anyway?" A man stepped out of her way, a nervous look on his face. "What are you looking at?" she asked him, anger seeping through her pores. "Jeez, some people...they think they own you 'cuz they're your friend. What does she think? I need to get laid or I'll die? I don't need anything." Sheridan fumed all the way home.

Keefer sat restlessly on the couch, wondering what Sheridan was thinking. She knew what she'd said could possibly piss the blonde off and turn her away, but she also knew Sheridan was stubborn and would probably want to prove her wrong, should she get over her initial anger. It was risky, but she had to try. Keefer hadn't watched all that late-night television without learning something. Talk shows ran rampant in the middle of the night and she loved them, often comparing her life to some of the guests. She hoped that this would work, forcing Sheridan to look at Keefer in a different light and question her own actions.

If Sheridan should choose to stay pissed and walk away, then Keefer wouldn't lose anything, but if she chose to stay and prove her wrong, then Keefer gained something. Both scenarios scared the pants off of the brunette. She had grown really attracted to Sheridan and would probably be very hurt should she go away, but she'd survive. If Sheridan decided to stay and possibly pursue Keefer, then she would be petrified. She had no real experience dealing with anyone even remotely like Sheridan. Relationships? Danni was hardly a role model and Sheridan probably didn't know the meaning of the word. Keefer wasn't prepared to be Sheridan's sex object, but she really wanted more from the blonde than she had right then.

Keefer paced her house, looking at the clock. *She's probably just getting to the club now. I wonder what she does there. Does she know how to dance? How does she pick up the women? Do they come to her or does she use that totally disarming grin of hers to call to them? What does she want with them...from them...once she has them? I saw on that* Sally *repeat that some women only like to give pleasure...is she like that? Does she let them touch her, too?*

Keefer stopped moving long enough to capture an image of Sheridan in the throes of passion, some mysterious woman touching her between her legs. She felt a twinge of jealousy and held her belly with both hands. *Oh, that's just great. Now you're* jealous? *How are you going to learn anything about her if you can't even stomach the thought?*

The tall woman's plan initially involved her going to the club to spy discreetly on the blonde, watching her interact with the women and her friends and possibly finding out secrets. Now, she wasn't too sure she could. The rush of confidence she'd felt all day was running out on her, leaving her a little defeated and a lot insecure. *I just know I screwed everything up.*

Sheridan was in rare form when she entered the club. She went straight out to the patio and flung herself into a chair.

Dawn followed her out and sat across from her, a concerned look on her face. "What's wrong, Sher?" she asked, leaning forward toward her obviously angry friend.

Sheridan flew out of the chair, forcing Dawn to teeter in her own chair momentarily as she tipped backwards. "Fucking shit! Who does she think she is?"

"Who?" Dawn stood up to follow her friend as she paced in agitation.

"Keefer, that's who!"

"Keefer?" Dawn wracked her brain. "Oh! Danni's ex!" she said excitedly and then she frowned. This was the chick that Sheridan was having some sort of trouble with, the one that pissed her off the previous night. "What did she do?"

Sheridan blew out a loud breath. "Nothing...forget it." She held up her hand and waved the whole conversation away.

"You sure? You're pretty steamed over something. Maybe I can help?" Dawn ventured forth.

"She thinks she's my girlfriend or something! Well, she's not!" Sheridan blurted once again, tossing herself angrily into a chair and lighting a new cigarette off of the old one.

"Hey, I don't know what's going on here, so start at the beginning, okay? Why would you get the impression that she thinks she's your girlfriend?"

The waiter came over and handed Sheridan a bottle of water, and she gave him money and sulked. "It's not that. We were fine as friends. Don't get me wrong, I'd do her in a heartbeat if she weren't so fucked up, but I like her, ya know? So we're friends." She glanced up at Dawn, who nodded for her to continue. "She's got problems and she's way too shy about stuff—not my type and all that. Well, anyway, we hang out and stuff, she cooks me dinner, and today we went with our dogs to the park."

"Cool, she has dogs?"

"One, Fifi, she's a mess and a half. She looks like she got burned or something. I think Keefer rescued her."

"That's real nice, Sher, she's got a love for animals, just like you. Good heart." Dawn smiled, noticing that Sheridan was calming down. "So, what happened?"

"Well, all the while since we met, every time I got the least bit flirty with her, she freaked out and blushed her ass off. I played with it a little, but not as much as I could have; I didn't want to make her too uncomfortable."

Dawn raised her eyebrow. *Really now? What's this I see? Sheridan cares for this woman? Wait 'til I tell the girls!* "That's awfully sweet of you, Sher," Dawn teased.

"Yeah, well...so all of a sudden today, it's like she can't keep her hands off of me and she's shaking her ass and stuff. I swear she was on my shit the whole time."

"What's wrong with that?" Dawn asked, totally confused.

"She knows I ain't gonna go for it! I don't need that shit right now! I'm happy with my life just the way it is. I don't need someone else's crap fucking up my life." She paused and drank from her bottle. "She gets all pissy with me about going out tonight and getting laid. She knows what I do, I don't hide it from her. She doesn't need someone like me as much as I don't need someone like her."

Dawn's eyebrows got higher and higher as her friend rambled on.

"The thing that gets me is, I like her, she's fun to be with and she cooks great, too. She's gorgeous and smells good...aw, fuck me. I'm so hot for her and she knows it, but she hasn't played me until today."

"Maybe she wants you, Sher. Maybe she just realized it."

"Oh, no, she wanted me from the get-go. I can tell. I tell you it's so damned hard to keep my hands to myself when she touches me..."

She touches her? Sheridan controls herself? Quick, call the tabloids...

"I can't fuck her, 'cuz then I'd have to move on. She doesn't deserve that and I really don't want to go away." Sheridan paced again, flicking her cigarette across the patio.

Dawn was dumbfounded. *Did she just hear what she said? Sheridan doesn't want to fuck this woman because she wants to keep her around. She cares about her more than she knows. How stupid can you get?* "Sher, sit down, you're making me dizzy. I still don't see where she thinks she's your girlfriend."

"Maybe I read into it wrong, maybe she was just being cute. I don't know. Maybe I overreacted. Do you think I need sex?"

"What kind of question is that? We all need sex," Dawn laughed.

"Never mind." Sheridan lit another cigarette and left Dawn sitting on the patio, shaking her head.

The blonde was a hellcat at work Monday, and the guys stayed away from her for their own safety. Sheridan was cranky, nasty, and mean, and they banded together to try and figure out what to do about it. It was so bad by mid-week that they actually thought about contacting the tall OSHA inspector and begging her to talk to Sheridan. Then they thought about their own health should that backfire and hunkered down for the long haul.

Sheridan had spent most of Sunday at home doing laundry and working out. The only time she left was to walk the dogs. She didn't even take them to the dog run; she didn't feel like having fun. She tried to analyze her feelings, but came up empty. She felt as if she had lost her best friend, but she couldn't understand how that could be when she'd only known Keefer for a short time. She already missed her terribly and cursed her weakness repeatedly. She saw Sara on Monday, but the sex didn't cheer her up. In fact, she felt a little guilty afterwards, like she was doing something wrong, and she cursed Keefer for planting that seed in her head. She wound up prowling the club on Tuesday, reveling and gloating after she fucked two women at the same time. She neenered at Keefer in her head afterwards, strutting around like she owned the place. Wednesday went much the same way. By the time she got home from work on Thursday, she realized what she was doing and felt awful about proving Keefer right. The tall woman knew her all too well and it made her angry. She vowed to stay away from the club that night and prove her wrong. She didn't need sex.

When Keefer didn't hear from Sheridan for almost a week, she resigned herself to the fact that the blonde didn't really want her and that she had lost her friendship, too. She sulked all day at work and puttered around her house, beating herself up for acting the way she had. *It's all my stupid fault. That'll teach me to think I'm worth her while. I should have known. What the hell would she want from me anyway? I'm a prude and she lives for sex. What a team we'd make.*

Keefer trudged home on Thursday evening and kicked her shoes off as she flopped dejectedly on the couch. She looked over to her answering machine and found no new messages blinking. "What did I expect? Did I really think she'd drop everything and run to me? I must be stupider than I thought." She sighed out loud and laid her head on her dog's belly. "I'm sorry, Feefs, I know how much you liked Sheridan," she mumbled, frowning as the dog's tail wagged at the mention of the blonde's name.

Keefer decided to change into baggy sweats before she walked the dog. She felt miserable. As she was hooking the leash on the dog, a thought occurred to her and she brightened up. "Hey, girl, it's a nice enough night, what do you say we go down to the dog run?" Fifi wagged her tail and jumped up on Keefer's leg. The tall woman smiled deviously. "Just let me change my clothes first, girl." *I can't let her go like this.*

Still not sure she could stay sane without going out, Sheridan drove the dogs over to her father's house to spend time with him and Steven.

"Hiya, Sher! To what do we owe this honor?" her dad teased, enveloping her in a big hug.

"Hi, Pop, just thought I'd see what eats you got in the fridge," she replied with a guilty grin.

"I was just going to call Steven to the table, I made a pot roast."

Sheridan's mouth watered. "Sounds good to me!" she said, running to the kitchen sink to wash her hands.

"Sher!" Steven yelled, sliding across the kitchen linoleum in his socks. As soon as he came to a complete stop, the blonde jumped up and wrapped herself around him, messing up his hair and giving him a wedgie all at the same time. "Sher, you suck so bad!" he shrieked like a kid.

"Sheridan, why do you insist on fucking with your brother?" Her dad slapped her in the back of the head lightly, but with enough gusto for her to wince.

"Sorry." She gave her best sad face and smiled when her father rolled his eyes. "Come on, Stevie-boy, dinner's ready." She laughed as her brother dug deep to retrieve his underwear.

"Cool!" Steven said excitedly. He loved when his sister came over.

"Oh, the dogs are in the back yard, we'll toss around a ball after dinner, okay?" She knew this would make her brother very happy and smiled warmly when he nodded almost violently, his mouth full of food.

The conversation revolved around work and related subjects. Steven sat patiently as his father and sister talked, dying to go out and play with the dogs. At the first lull in the conversation, he jumped up out of his seat. "Are we done? Can I go play with the dogs? Can we go to the park? Please, Pop?"

The eldest Landers laughed at his son's enthusiasm. "Go get some shoes on and we'll leave that decision to Sheridan. She's gotta put up with you."

Sheridan pursed her lips to the side, pretending to think really hard, knowing it would drive her brother nuts. Finally, she nodded. "Okay, grab a few balls. We got some toys in the car."

"Yes! I love you, Sher!" Steven yelled as he ran to his room.

"I love you, too, asshole."

"I love you back, moron," he yelled through the house.

"I love you more, Jolly Green Giant!" Sheridan snickered.

"Me more, Pee-wee Herman!" he said as he ran to the back door.

"Me even mo—Ow! Pop!" She rubbed the back of her head and frowned.

"Enough already."

Keefer scanned the dog run for Sheridan, knowing the chances were slim of the blonde actually being there, but she had to try. She had to see her, maybe talk to her and, if she was lucky, touch her. There was no sign of the construction worker so she sat on a bench and let Fifi off of her leash to play. Keeping an eye on her dog, she wondered what she would say to Sheridan, should she show up...how she would start a conversation after she'd acted so badly the last time. Thinking about it made her feel disgusted with herself. *What was I trying to prove? I'm not that tough, I shouldn't have played with fire.* Just when she felt at her worst, she heard it, the piercing whistle that she'd only heard once before. She stood up quickly and then sat back down, trying to look inconspicuous as she looked for the source of the sound. She squinted as she tried to see far off at the other end of the park. It looked like Sheridan, but who was the big guy with her? She couldn't talk to her about last weekend with someone else around. *Oh, no! Feefs!* She watched with a pained expression as her dog took off at lightening speed toward Sheridan. Keefer got up and started to run after her.

"Hey, Sher, there's a dog gonna attack you!" Steven said in a panic, turning his sister around.

Sheridan furrowed her brows at the dog headed her way. "Hey...Fifi?"

"Who's Fifi?" Steven snickered.

The small dog ran into Sheridan and practically climbed up her body. The blonde reached down and lifted her up, letting her lick her face frantically.

"This," she patted the dog on the back, "is Fifi."

"Damn, she's ugly," Steven observed, petting her on the head anyway.

"She's different, is all, Stevie," Sheridan said before returning the dog to the ground. She scanned the area with a deep frown on her face. "Where's your mommy?" she asked the panting dog.

"Right behind you."

Sheridan spun around and blinked repeatedly. *Goddamn, she's hotter than last week!*

"Wow...you are gorgeous!" Steven blurted out.

Keefer blushed, never taking her eyes off of Sheridan, who seemed to be taking inventory of every body part Keefer had.

"I'm Steven, Sheridan's brother." He held his hand out politely.

Keefer tore her eyes away from the blonde to shake his hand. "I'm Keefer, Sheridan's...friend?"

"Uh, yeah, my friend," Sheridan agreed, swallowing the drool that developed while drinking in the tall woman's legs.

Keefer almost laughed with relief. She smiled so brightly that Sheridan had to return the gesture.

Steven watched the two women stare at each other and realized this must be one of his sister's "lady friends." He remembered that she'd told him to play with the dogs should she run into a good-looking woman. "I'm going to play with the dogs now, okay, Sheridan?" He winked conspiratorially at his sister.

"You do that, Steven." She winked back, making him feel like he did something good, when in reality he'd just embarrassed her.

The two women stood there silently until it became uncomfortable.

"You look good, Keef," Sheridan broke the silence.

"You too. Look, about Saturday..."

"Forget it. It's done." Sheridan waved it off.

"I'm still sorry. I was way out of line. It's none of my business what you do or who you do it with." The tall woman tried not to blush at that thought.

Sheridan grinned. "You're beautiful when you blush," she teased.

"Yeah, well, I do it so often." Keefer looked down.

"I think it's cute, really." The blonde grinned at Keefer's embarrassment.

"Well, I must be downright adorable right now." Keefer laughed, then made eye contact again. "I think you make me blush on purpose."

"Guilty as charged," Sheridan snickered.

"Anyway, I felt awful all week about what I said to you. I really thought you'd never want to talk to me again," Keefer said while looking everywhere but at the blonde.

"I was pissed at you at first, but you're right about me—I lived up to your expectations very well," Sheridan said with regret.

"I don't have any expectations of you, Sher."

"Then you're the first." The construction worker glanced sideways at her tall friend. "I have a reputation...you may get caught up in it."

"I really don't care about your reputation; I think I know a different Sheridan, anyway. I like the one I know."

"Thanks, Keefer. I like you, too." Sheridan reached out impulsively for Keefer's hand.

The tall woman started and stared down at their linked hands. *Well, that was unexpected!* She smiled at the feeling of the warm, rough hand in her own. "What did you do all week—and leave out the blush factor, please," Keefer joked, feeling much more comfortable with Sheridan than she expected.

They began to walk toward Steven and their dogs. "Nothing unusual. I went out, I did my laundry...nothing special. What about you?"

Okay, Keefer, honesty is the best policy. "I missed you," she whispered.

Sheridan nodded. "Me too."

"You did?" Keefer asked in disbelief.

"Yeah, I did. Why does that surprise you?"

"For starters, I have far less to offer you than any of your other women."

"Hold it right there." Sheridan held up her hand and stopped walking. "Have I ever asked for anything from you?" she asked with annoyance.

"No, but—"

"But nothing. I did a lot of thinking these last couple of days and I came to the conclusion that I like having you as my friend."

Keefer was happy and sad at the same time. *Just a friend, huh? I guess I could live with that.*

"Why the weird face? Don't you want to be my friend?" the blonde asked nervously. She had to have Keefer in her life one way or another.

"Yes, of course!" Keefer smiled.

Sheridan began walking again and Keefer followed. "Have I told you how good you look in shorts?" the blonde asked without turning to look at the tall woman.

"I do believe you have." Keefer smiled triumphantly to herself.

"Just checking."

The brunette looked down at her legs. *Buy more skirts.*

Steven came over to them slowly. "Is it okay to come over?" he asked his sister nervously.

Both woman laughed and they let go of each other's hands.

"Yeah, it's safe, Steven." Sheridan looked at Keefer who was, as she figured, slightly pink. "There you go again," she teased.

"Well, you know what he's thinking." Keefer pointed to Steven.

"Keefer's my friend, Stevie-boy, you don't have to worry about interrupting anything," she explained.

"Oh, are you sure, Sher? She's so pretty. I'd marry her," he said innocently.

Keefer's eyes went wide and Sheridan laughed nervously. "You'll have to excuse him, he speaks his mind." She glared at Steven.

"I can't help it...I'm a retard!" he whined, hating that he got his sister mad.

Sheridan rolled her eyes, but wrapped an arm around him anyway, rubbing his back. "Hey, don't you say that. I'm not mad at you, I promise. You just embarrassed me and my friend," she soothed.

Keefer watched in fascination. *Oh...well, that makes sense.* Blue eyes softened. *Look at her; she doesn't care who's watching now, so many facets...*

"Are we leaving now?" he asked.

"Are we?" Sheridan asked Keefer.

Keefer leaned over to the small woman's ear. "Don't you have to get ready for tonight?" she asked. "It's ladies night."

Sheridan shivered involuntarily at the breath in her ear. *I wasn't, but after that...*"Yeah, you're right, we should go."

Keefer watched her friend close the car door behind her. She mentally gave herself two thumbs up, one for the shorts and another for the shiver. Things were working out just fine.

Chapter 14

"Sheridan and Keefer, sitting in a tree..."

"I said cut it out, Steven!" The blonde took a hand off the steering wheel and smacked him in the stomach.

"K-i-s-s-i-n-g."

"I'm gonna fuck you up."

"You and what army?" Steven teased, sticking his tongue out.

"Why do you keep singing that song anyway? I told you we're not like that." Sheridan rolled her eyes.

"I'm not blind, you like her a lot, I can tell. You were holding her hand," Steven said smugly.

I was, wasn't I. I think I even initiated that, didn't I? Sheridan stopped the car in front of her dad's house. *She didn't seem to mind that at all, though.* One eyebrow rose with the thought of Keefer's hand in hers.

"See? You have nothing to say. Ha! I'm right!" he gloated.

"I never said I don't like her, I just said we weren't fucking," Sheridan countered defensively.

"You want to fuck her, you can tell Stevie-boy, Sher."

"See, there's the problem, Steven, I don't want to fuck her," she said sadly.

"You don't? Shit, Sheridan, she's gorgeous! Are you crazy? Why not?"

"Ah, I'm thinking I may just be a little crazy. I think I like her too much to just fuck her."

"Well, what the hell else would you do?" Steven asked in confusion.

"There's having sex, and then there's making love..." Sheridan started to explain before she scared herself.

"Which one is fucking?"

149

"Stevie, is that all that's on your mind?" The blonde laughed.

"Well, yeah! Have you really looked at Keefer?"

Great, my brother has a woody for my woman. Sheridan shook her head and then her eyes widened. *My woman?*

"She's so pretty...and she's got great legs."

"We definitely are of the same blood, baby brother, those are some fine-looking legs."

"Are you going to have sex...or make love with her?" he asked expectantly.

Yeah, answer him, Sher, she thought sarcastically. "I don't know. Go on, get outta my car, I gotta get home and shower," she said with a phony smile.

When she got home, Keefer ran through the house and grabbed the black sports bra, thrilled that its owner had held her hand. She held it to her face and smelled it, giggling like a teenager, remembering the warmth and the feeling of Sheridan's fingers against hers.

After eating quickly, she retired to the den to watch television. Flipping through the channels only proved what she already knew—there was nothing worth watching on her 75 cable channels. Looking around the room shyly, she punched in channel 46 and looked up at the screen through her eyelashes. *What is this, the lesbian porno channel?* she wondered as again, the image of two women appeared. *I shouldn't complain now, should I?* she scolded herself and leaned back on the futon more comfortably.

While the women were touching, kissing and caressing, she was able to handle that very well. In fact, she felt pretty good about it when she didn't even blush. One of the women reached off camera and when her hand appeared again, it was holding a large dildo. Keefer did blush at that and her eyes widened in fascination. *Danni didn't have one of those,* she thought fleetingly. The woman holding the dildo leaned over and started licking and biting the other woman's nipples and Keefer felt hers perk up in empathy. She watched intently, her brain soaking up the information like a sponge. The woman strapped the dildo to her body with a leather harness and Keefer sat straight up. *I wonder if Sheridan has one of those.* The errant thought made her blush deeply. *Why would you want to know that?* she wondered and then chuckled at her own internal question. *You know damned well why you want to know that.* She looked back to the screen and shook her head rapidly, attempting to dispel the image of Sheridan lying on top of her wearing the dildo.

Hours later, Keefer was completely frazzled. Every new position the women took up brought a different image of her and the blonde into her head. She watched it all, sometimes gasping, other times blushing, but stuck through the whole thing. She found herself feeling sympathetic for the woman on the bottom as the second woman paid close attention to her breasts. Keefer even rubbed her own nipples every so often, enjoying the feeling it sent between her legs. *The things I've been missing,* she thought.

Aroused and enlightened, she took a quick, cool shower and went to bed. Her mind worked feverishly with the images that it had just absorbed, not giving her the opportunity to sleep. She wondered what Sheridan was doing at that moment, picturing her in the midst of many different sexual acts and narrowing her eyes jealously at the faceless women. She wanted Sheridan to touch her in these ways, but knew if the blonde tried, her own first instinct would be to run away. Keefer knew she needed to be stronger, but she wasn't sure she could actually accept the blonde's advances should it happen. *I'll probably push her away; I'm such a nerd,* she thought sadly. *Come on, Keef! You want her so badly...you have to do something! Tell her how much you want her.* She wrestled with that idea and tried to come up with ways to tell the construction worker what she wanted from her. *Oh, God...you can't say that!* she thought of one particularly blunt scenario. *Go back to your first plan of action, Keef, find out what she likes.* With that last thought, a plan put itself in motion and Keefer went to sleep with a great big grin on her face.

Greg, Sheridan's full-time dancing partner, was thrilled to see his friend dancing with a smile and jumped on stage behind her. They danced provocatively, humping and gyrating while the rest of the dancers looked on with amusement and jealousy. By the time Sheridan peeled off her leather jacket, she had quite a crowd of female admirers offering her a drink or a napkin to wipe her face. She winked at a few women and threw her jacket at one in particular, giving that one goose bumps while the others frowned and glared at her. "Ooh, she's a cutie!" Greg yelled into Sheridan's ear.

"Yeah, she is," the blonde yelled back, barely heard over the music.

"You're in a great mood tonight, thank God. I thought you were going to self-destruct all week!" he shouted.

Sheridan shrugged, a little embarrassed by her behavior.

"Well, I'm glad you're back to your old self. The girls and I were getting worried."

"Yeah, well, I'm back—better than ever," she joked, making a muscle.

The woman holding Sheridan's jacket nearly swooned at the display and was grateful Sheridan had picked her for the night.

Sharon and Marie watched their friend with a curious eye. Sharon, having been working all week, had missed out on the angry Sheridan but had heard all the rumors. She wasn't entirely convinced that Sheridan acted as badly as they said. She had known her a long time and she never was that much of a bear.

Dawn made her way back from the bar with their drinks and joined the others in watching the blonde. "So, what do you think?" she asked the others.

"Maybe she just decided to drop the whole Keefer thing?" Marie thought.

"Or maybe she got lucky with her," Sharon offered.

"You think? I don't know. With the way she was going on, if she did nail Keefer, she would be in a worse mood than before," Dawn said.

"What do you mean?" Sharon asked, gulping her beer.

"I think she's falling in love with Keefer, if she hasn't already fell, and if she fucks her, she'll have to either face how she feels or drop her like a hot potato. I don't think she has the balls to do either. It would be awful for her either way."

They all contemplated what Dawn said while they watched Sheridan squat down on the stage in front of the woman holding her jacket.

"Hey, she kinda looks like Keefer," Marie noticed.

"Yeah, tall, dark, and sexy," Dawn agreed.

"If her eyes are blue, ladies, then we know what Sheridan's thinking." Sharon laughed out loud.

"Twisted." Marie laughed too.

Sheridan had to turn the tall brunette to face her numerous times during their fling on the patio. Although she had a thing for the tall woman's ass, she had to see her face as well. She kept imagining this was Keefer; from behind, they could be identical and it was blowing her mind.

The muscular blonde backed the other woman against the wall and pulled down the front of her shirt, attaching her mouth to a nipple. The taller woman bent her head down and her long hair tickled the back of Sheridan's neck, causing her to shiver.

In Sheridan's aroused brain, it became Keefer's hair and Keefer's breast; she began sucking in earnest. She wrapped her arms around the curvy body and pulled her close, sliding both hands down to her ass. She could see Keefer's blue eyes half closed with the pleasure she was invoking. She manhandled the flesh in her hands, drawing groans from the woman. She found herself pressing herself into the tall woman's leg, imagining Keefer's head thrown back in delight as she did.

"Oh yeah, that feels so good, Sheridan."

The high-pitched voice was not the low sexy one that she was imagining. *Shit! What am I doing?* Sheridan pulled away in a panic, her heart beating loudly in her chest.

"What happened?" the woman asked, noticing that Sheridan looked pale.

"Um, nothing. I think I'm getting a migraine or something. I gotta go." The blonde bolted from the patio and darted through the crowd to the lobby.

"Hey, sweetie, what's wrong?" Verna asked with concern at Sheridan's apparent dismay.

The blonde leaned on the half-door of the coat check and breathed deeply. "I think I'm going crazy."

Verna laughed. "Honey, you have been crazy as long as I know you. What enlightened you?"

"I can't get this woman off of my mind." Sheridan dropped her head into her hands.

"What woman?"

"It doesn't matter, she's haunting me. She invades my dreams, my fantasies, my everyday thought processes, and, just now, she slipped into my reality, fucking with my head."

"Well, sugar, I don't think she's aware of it, so don't take it out on her."

"No, she doesn't know anything about it!" Sheridan almost shouted in panic.

"Okay, okay, honey! I don't know her, it's all right!" *Jesus H. Christ! I think she's in love!*

"What am I supposed to do about this? It's cramping my style, if you know what I mean." Sheridan frowned deeply.

"How old are you?"

"Thirty-one, why?"

"How many times have you been turned down, Sheridan?"

"Never," she boasted.

"So, why haven't you told this woman how you feel about her?"

"What do you mean, how I feel? I don't know how I feel."

"Oh, I think you do. Think about it. Tell her. What is she going to do, laugh at you?"

Sheridan paled dramatically at the thought of Keefer laughing at her advances. "Oh, God."

Both Verna's eyebrows flew up. *I don't think I've ever seen her so scared! Time for something she can relate to.* "Sheridan! Now you stop being a pussy and do it!"

The blonde blinked a few times at Verna's outburst. "Yes, ma'am." She grinned and leaned over to kiss the older woman on the cheek.

"And remember what I said; think about it."

Keefer stared distractedly out the window, her back toward the desk, swiveling slowly from side to side in her office chair. *Boss says I should take a vacation, so maybe I will. A few days off won't kill me. Maybe I'll redo the house...paint or something.* Blue eyes gazed down at the people rushing quickly from one place to another and Keefer scrunched up her nose in distaste. *Do I look like that too? Zipping and running like a chicken without a head. Yeah, maybe a long weekend...maybe five days or so. I always wanted to redo the bathroom, maybe put up some shower doors.* The more she thought about it, the more determined she became to make it a reality. She turned to face her desk and began to make a list of things she needed to make her dream bathroom. Halfway down the list, a thought occurred to her and she smiled deviously. *And I know just the woman to call to help me with this little project.*

Keefer stopped by her boss's office and made sure he was okay with her taking that many days off. He was more than happy to give her paid time; she'd never taken any before and he was afraid, after that little mishap at the construction site, that she really needed one. Not one to believe all the rumors that he heard, he couldn't help wondering if the one about her and Danni from accounting was true. Keefer had been acting so funny lately; it would make sense that she was having a personal crisis.

The tall woman was in an extremely good mood as she rode the crowded subway home. She even found herself standing up and giving her seat to another woman, just because she couldn't sit still. She was excited about her weekend plans, and not just about hitting the Home Depot—she had a very big idea for the next night involving the club and a dark corner. Keefer was already wishing for Saturday to come. She would have done her spying on Sheridan that night, but it was Friday, Fifi's bath night. Despite her resolve, Saturday couldn't come soon enough for Keefer.

She stopped at the deli and got some cold cuts and beer for dinner. She didn't feel much like cooking, but she did feel like kicking back and having a few beers. She rarely indulged in this kind of behavior and felt a twinge of excitement at being able to do whatever she wanted. It had taken a while, but she was finally realizing that she was her own person and she could do whatever she wanted, without worrying about what others thought. She wasn't totally there yet, and that's why she was so excited about sitting home on Friday night, drinking beer with her dog. It was out of the ordinary for Keefer and, lately, out of the ordinary seemed to be the norm for the usually reserved woman. Her plans for Saturday night alone should have sent her screaming into a corner, but she was bound and determined to see her plans through. Keefer Gibson was turning over all kinds of new leaves and it was thrilling for her.

Sheridan whistled her way through the gate Friday morning, much to the delight of her co-workers. She tossed a box of donuts on the floor and smiled smugly.

"Ooh, thanks!" Phil rubbed his hands on the back of his pants and snatched a donut out of the box.

"One of the perks of fucking the counter girl. Dig in." Sheridan chuckled.

"There's this cute girl working at the Lexus dealership—" Tony started but never finished, as he had to catch the donuts being thrown at him.

"Screw you, Tony," Sheridan laughed.

Tony blew kisses. "Come on, stud," he joked.

"I'd kill you," the blonde replied with a grin.

"Well, well, well." Bobby looked his friend up and down. "What do we owe this mood to, Patch? The donut chick?"

"Nah, nothing like that. By the way, guys, thank you for dealing with me, I was a real fucker, I know it."

"No problem, Sybil," Phil said as he ducked behind a doorway.

"So you didn't get laid last night? Jeez, I woulda thought you fucked goddamned Jennifer Lopez to get you outta that mood," Bobby said around a mouthful of jelly donut.

"Ooh, wait a sec while I imagine that, boys," Sheridan joked, then made an overly dramatic show of looking dreamy.

"Me too." Phil stood next to her and mimicked her. "Oh man, looks fucking good from where I'm standing," he laughed.

Sheridan back handed him and snickered. "It looked just as good from my point of view."

"Jesus, welcome back, Patch. We sure missed you around here." Tony smacked her on the shoulder.

Sheridan got embarrassed and smacked him back, signaling the end of discussion.

On the way home from work, the blonde had a sudden urge to call Keefer; she even began to speed dial her number on her cell phone before realizing she had nothing to say. Putting the phone on the seat, she thought again about what Verna had said to her the night before. She still didn't get it. Sheridan had thought half the night about it, and still she couldn't figure out what she felt for the tall, sexy brunette besides the obvious: lust. *Lotsa lust,* she grinned. *Well, I kinda like her...a lot more than I like the guys at work, so that means I like her more than I like my friends,* she thought. *I like her even more than the girls I fuck. That's 'cuz I couldn't care less about the girls I fuck...uh-oh...that means I* do *care about Keefer, which means...*

Sheridan swallowed against the nervous feeling in her stomach. *So the fuck what! I care about Keefer, so what?* Sheridan peeled away from the red light and turned the corner to her block. *That's why you can't fuck her, Sher, you care about her...and that includes her feelings. You don't want to hurt her by treating her like the others...that's why. That's the reason...nothing else,* Sheridan convinced herself of that as she walked up the stairs to her apartment. *It's not like you* love *her or anything...right?* She snickered nervously at the thought. *You just don't want* her *falling in love with* you. *That's why you can't fuck her.* Totally convinced that this was the answer, the construction worker breathed out a sigh of relief. *Yeah, I hate when they fall in love; boy, that sucks.*

She turned her key in the lock and braced herself. "Hiya, kids!"

Sheridan dressed slowly for the club, changing her outfit a few times before settling on plain old Levi's and a white T-shirt. She felt almost lazy about going out; it didn't seem as exciting as it usually did and it was bugging her. She looked herself over in the mirror and didn't like what she saw. It wasn't the clothes, her hair, or her boots. *What the fuck?* She put on her leather jacket and had to admit she looked damned good, but still she wasn't satisfied with herself. She felt a small sense of longing in the pit of her stomach and chalked it up to her abrupt exit from the club the previous night. *Yeah, that's why I feel so weird. I'm totally out of whack. I need to get laid tonight and I'll be just like new.*

Sheridan plunked herself down on the sofa, jacket and all still on, and sighed heavily. The dogs lifted their heads at the sound; Pharaoh raised an eyebrow, causing a tiny grin to appear on the blonde's face. "We're not going anywhere, guys. I'm just thinking." This satisfied the pit bull and he dropped his head back onto his paws. Zeus took a little more convincing and he walked over to his mommy and laid his head on her thigh. Sheridan scratched his head, then bent down and kissed his nose. "I'm good, baby," she told him and he seemed to buy it. *How come they always know when something's not quite right?*

She wandered into the kitchen; she was hungry, but didn't feel like eating anything in the house. Looking at the clock, she saw it was too early to go to the club, but too late to bother her pop, so she decided to grab a slice or two of pizza at the shop on the corner. *Yeah, pizza...no garlic.* She ran her fingers through her short blonde hair before heading out the door.

After a shared dinner of ham and turkey, Keefer and her dog began their Friday night bath ritual. Fifi waited patiently as her mommy attached the special hose to the tub faucet and readied the medicated shampoo. Once the water temperature was suitable, Keefer patted the inside of the tub and her dog climbed in obediently. The tall woman stripped off her shirt and bra and knelt down beside the tub, spraying the water all over her baby. As usual, Fifi shook off the excess water as soon as it touched her body, making Keefer laugh at the predictable action. "That's why I take my shirt off, Feefs. Here you go, this is probably cold," she said as she squeezed the shampoo onto Fifi's back.

Sheridan stood in the middle of the stage and scanned the club restlessly. She couldn't seem to find what she was looking for and it was beginning to annoy her. There were plenty of great-looking women dotting the club, but she didn't find any of them to her liking. She began dancing again, the frustration easing a bit as she moved to the music, sidling up behind Greg to work off her unusually nervous energy.

"Hey, gorgeous, you're going to make ugly wrinkles with a frown like that," Greg said into her ear.

"I just don't feel right tonight, Greg. Maybe I'm getting sick," she said, her frown deepening.

Greg nodded silently and studied his friend. She had been acting out of character lately. He wondered briefly if maybe the rumors were true, maybe she was falling for a certain tall, black-haired woman. *Sheridan in love? It couldn't happen. Then again, she has been acting so strangely.* Marie said that Dawn said that Sheridan cared for this woman, even respected her, which was wonderful, but a whole new concept for his friend. Dawn also said that Sheridan said that this woman wanted her badly too. This woman supposedly wanted Sheridan from the get-go. *So what's the big problem?* His eyebrows furrowed in thought.

"Hey, you're gonna make ugly wrinkles," Sheridan teased him.

"I'm worried about you. You haven't been acting right. You wanna talk about it?"

Sheridan thought for a second and nodded, grabbing his hand and pulling him from the stage. They settled on the patio and sat at a table.

"What's up, Sher?"

"I feel like I'm waiting for something to happen. I feel kinda anxious," she started.

"Maybe you forgot to do something?" Greg had an idea, but wanted to work up to it slowly.

"I don't think so. I even felt weird about coming out tonight. That's never happened to me before."

"Can't you find a woman tonight?" he asked innocently.

"There's plenty here, believe me, I'd do at least ten of them in a heartbeat, but I get this feeling like I shouldn't be here...with them."

No, you'd rather be playing house with a tall, blue-eyed woman, wouldn't you? "Hmm." Greg narrowed his eyes. "Maybe you'd rather be somewhere else? Perhaps with someone else?" Sheridan raised her eyebrows at him. "You know, like maybe you should be visiting a sick aunt or something," he blurted out. Blonde eyebrows rose higher. "Or maybe you should be visiting a sick friend, maybe?"

"None of my friends are sick, Greg." She narrowed her eyes at him, not knowing what he was up to.

"Oh, well, my mistake then." He sat there grinning at her like a fool.

"What the hell is wrong with you?" she asked in irritation.

"Nothing. If none of your friends are sick, then there's no reason to visit them, is there? It's much too late in the evening to just drop by unannounced anyway, unless they were expecting you. Or maybe they wanted to see you, but didn't want to impose on you, it being Friday night and all. You know, big night at the club for you."

Go on Sher, go get laid. Keefer's voice popped into her head. She winced.

"Just a thought. Ooh! Is that Randy? He's so hot!"

Greg was gone in a second, leaving Sheridan alone with her thoughts.

Keefer was just about to grab a towel and wrap Fifi in it when her doorbell rang. "Who in the hell?" The possibility that it was Danni outside her door frightened her. She grabbed her T-shirt off the floor of the bathroom and threw it on, took Fifi and her towel and deposited them both in the heated den. The doorbell rang again and she hesitated at the front window, peeking through the curtain. When she saw the little black sports car in her driveway, her heart leapt into her throat and she flung open the door.

Sheridan stood riveted on Keefer's soaked T-shirt, more specifically at her nipples that were entirely visible through the wet material. Her mouth went dry and she was totally embarrassed when a hand lifted her chin up.

Keefer was too excited to think about her attire; once she'd seen Sheridan's car, she lost her mind. Now she was blushing as red as she'd ever been while the construction worker stared open-mouthed at her breasts. Somewhere among the mortification was a feeling of excitement, knowing that Sheridan was so interested in her breasts. When she looked down, Keefer's eyes went wide as she noticed that her T-shirt was not leaving anything to the imagination. Feeling the need to divert Sheridan's eyes, she lifted her face up to meet her eyes.

Green eyes lingered at the spot even after her chin was lifted but she finally made eye contact and a slow smile spread across her face. Keefer looked adorable. Her hair was all disheveled, her shirt was inside out, and she was soaking wet, not to mention the sexy flush that covered her face and neck. *Say something, you idiot.* "Hi."

"Hi. Do you want to come in?" Keefer asked, sweeping her arm into the room for Sheridan to follow.

"Yeah, if it's okay. It's not too late or anything, is it?" The blonde practically ran into the living room.

Keefer watched with a curious eye. *Wonder what's going on with her?* "Hey, are you all right? Is something wrong?"

"No, I'm okay, I was just in the neighborhood..."

"It's Friday night, Sher, why aren't you at the club?" Keefer asked skeptically.

"Nothing appealed to me," she admitted.

Keefer stood there digesting that bit of information. *Nothing appealed to her at the club so she came here? Does this mean I am what she finds appealing tonight? Oh, Lord!* Keefer panicked. *Okay, no panicking. Take a deep breath, that's better. Offer her a beer or something...and for God sakes, cover your breasts, Keefer, before her eyes fall out.* She folded her arms over her chest, forcing Sheridan to make eye contact again. "Do you want a beer?"

"Yeah, sure." *Can't you control yourself?*

She seems mighty uncomfortable. Something's wrong. "Are you going to take off your jacket or what?" Keefer asked from the kitchen.

"Uh, yeah." *Jeez, Sher, you didn't come here to sit and stare at her, talk already!* "Um, what were you doing, if you don't mind me asking?"

Keefer appeared with two beers and stood there with one hand across her chest. "I was washing Fifi; she needs a medicated bath once a week for her skin. I actually have to go into the den to dry her. It's pretty warm in there, but you're more than welcome."

"Sure, why not? So, what happened to her, how'd she get burned?" Sheridan felt a ton better than she did when she walked in the house and followed Keefer into the den, wearing a great big happy smile.

Chapter 15

Sheridan rolled over in her bed and draped her arm around Zeus's neck. "Morning, big boy," she mumbled as she stretched out her legs, scratching Pharaoh with her toes as she did. "You know, guys, I could never bring a girl here with the way you lay all over the bed." Zeus yawned widely and licked his nose, then dropped his head back down heavily on the pillow. Sheridan laughed at him. "Lazy fuck," she snickered, grabbing his snout and shaking it playfully. The Rotty snorted through her fingers and turned over into his back, displaying his belly for a scratch. Sheridan did as she was expected while Pharaoh stood up and stretched, making a high-pitched sound as he yawned. "Jealous?" she asked the pit bull, who shook off the sleep and slid from the bed.

Sheridan was pleasantly happy that Saturday morning. The previous night was so cool. She and Keefer had hung out late into the night, drinking beer and chatting like two old friends. She'd learned a lot about the tall woman and also blabbed a lot about herself, something she wasn't usually comfortable with. She didn't stop to think about that at the time, she now reflected; she'd just felt so comfortable sitting around in the presence of the inspector.

Learning what little she had about Keefer's life gave her more insight into why she acted like she did. Her mom had Keefer late in life and Keefer never knew her father; he was a one-night-stand that her mother never talked about. Sheridan felt a pang of sadness as Keefer casually mentioned this information. She'd grown up in a large family, and being around her extended family was a big part of her childhood. She shared losing her mother with Keefer, but she confessed that she couldn't imagine life without her pop. It made Sheridan wonder, though, the way Keefer described her mother as a "loose" woman. Knowing that her mom was a run-around probably added to Keefer's need to stay away from sex and boys. Sheridan had wondered how Keefer wound up in bed with a woman, especially one like Danni. When Keefer explained how she and Danni met and became involved, Sheridan was appalled. Keefer had no experience and no say in the relationship; it seemed like Danni abused that to the nth degree. Sheridan now hated the redhead even more than she had before.

Rolling over again onto her back, Sheridan stretched once again, a smile lighting up her face. *Damn, but she has nice tits!* Her eyes had returned to them numerous times throughout the night and sometimes she felt as if Keefer were purposely displaying them to her, but then she thought better of it. *Not sweet, innocent Keefer.* Sheridan remembered those breasts with a happy sigh. *Hmm, come to think of it, the conversation, brief as it was, that we had about sex was not as sweet and innocent as it should have been.* Green eyes narrowed as she recalled the conversation. It all started when Keefer turned on the TV and the porno channel appeared. She immediately changed the channel, but Sheridan caught the deep blush before she turned her head. At first, she thought that maybe Keefer hadn't watched television in the den since she'd spent the night, but now that she thought about it, perhaps Keefer was watching the porno channel by herself. *She did ask that odd question about dildos, didn't she?* Keefer never actually said the word, but Sheridan got the idea, and her answer was yes, she had a few of them in her collection.

The blonde rolled out of bed, thoughts of Keefer, sex, and dildos filling her brain. She was already aroused from staring at Keefer's breasts all night, and now the visual that her mind concocted with Keefer and a dildo was making her ache. She wondered about how the blue-eyed woman was watching her hands and how she'd breathed out a sigh of relief after Sheridan took up her offer to help her redo the bathroom. *You know, I think she wanted to see me as much as I wanted to see her last night,* she thought. *It wouldn't kill me to give up a night or two at the club to spend time with her.* Sheridan stopped moving and blinked a few times. *Did I really think that? What does that mean? It means that I don't need sex.* She smiled triumphantly, then widened her eyes in shock. *Does it mean I need Keefer? Oh, Christ! I think I do! What is happening to me?*

The tall inspector wandered the aisles of Home Depot, thoroughly engrossed in memories of Sheridan's visit the night before. While totally unexpected, it was a very welcome surprise. They'd talked all night long about their lives and childhoods. Keefer never told anyone about her childhood, but she felt so at ease around Sheridan—even if she had been staring at her breasts half the night. She wondered about her own behavior toward that, how she didn't bother to change her shirt and even stopped covering her chest after a while. She was totally embarrassed at first, but found she enjoyed Sheridan's attentions. A few times, she imagined the construction worker's hands on her breasts and caught herself staring at the roughened fingers. She even felt her nipples tightening as she stared, and she knew Sheridan saw it too. It gave her a little thrill to know that the blonde was fixated on her nipples when it happened. *I wonder what she was thinking. Was she wishing she could touch them too? I wonder what she would feel like, would she be gentle or would she be rough? How would her fingers feel? Not mine, not Danni's...Sheridan's fingers touching them...*Keefer cleared her throat and excused herself as a woman passed by with a cart full of children. *God, Keef! Get a grip!* Her nipples were hard all over again.

As she studied the towels, she remembered how Sheridan's face lit up while she talked about her family. *I bet that was so nice to have.* She thought about how hard it must have been for Mr. Landers to lose his wife, but she was sure it was so much easier to have all that family around. *She sure does love her brother...he's so handsome, too. Good looks run in the family.* She grinned at her thought. *Muscles, too. I about died when she flexed for me. I can't believe I asked her to do that!* Keefer blushed her way down the aisle. *But, damn, she has all the right muscles in all the right places.* Keefer caught herself licking her lips and scolded herself. *Stop that! You're in Home Depot! Think tools...*Keefer blushed harder. *Oh God...I asked her about that too, didn't I? What came over me last night? However, she did say she has a few. I wonder what they look like.* Lost in thought, she didn't realize she was blocking the aisle until the same woman with the kids tapped her on the shoulder. *Okay, that's enough now. Get what you need and get out!* The tall woman commenced to shop, trying very hard not to think about spending the next day alone in the bathroom with Sheridan.

Sheridan didn't feel like breakfast, so she went right to the weight bench after walking the dogs. One might think walking the dogs was a workout in itself, but Sheridan liked to feel the burn and worked herself to absolute failure when she did hit the bench. She wasn't crazy about working out, though she did it occasionally, when the mood struck her. She used to be fanatical about it, she and Steven waking up at five in the morning to work out together before school. She was blessed with a wonderful metabolism and she only needed to work out a few times a week to stay in shape. This was one of those days when the mood hit her hard, and she worked up a hell of a sweat before her stomach started growling.

While she was in the shower, Sheridan thought about what Keefer had planned for her bathroom. If she wanted to, she could have all the work done in one day, but she wanted to stretch it out and spend more time with the tall inspector. Keefer had taken the whole week off. Sheridan knew she couldn't possibly stretch it that long, but she could make it last until Monday if she wanted. *Sure, I could tell her it takes much longer for the grout to dry than it does, or the caulking. I can do that,* she thought with a devious smile. *I can't imagine being cramped up in that bathtub with her while we put up those doors. I know I'm gonna lose my cool and do something stupid.* She frowned at the thought. *You know, I don't think she would exactly mind if I did something stupid...like kiss her, maybe. I think she'd like that. I bet she'd even kiss me back.*

The blonde grinned. *Yeah, how slyly can I manage that without jumping up and down on my tippy-toes? She's too tall for an ambush, gotta plan...what am I doing? Planning a kiss? Get real, Sher, when you want something, the general rule is, you get it. You don't have to plan.*

Keefer had already looked over her purchases numerous times and was impatiently waiting for time to fly. It was too early for her to show up at the club, since she wanted to make sure she got there long after Sheridan had arrived. She needed to find her and then find a good spot to hide and watch her in action. Keefer was determined to see what the construction worker was like in her element, how she picked up women, what she did with them. She knew she'd probably never have the nerve to watch Sheridan with another woman, but seeing her body language was important to Keefer. She really wanted to see how Sheridan kissed another woman, how she turned her head, if she put her lips outside, sucking on the other woman's lips, or sideways, giving them both the same amount of lip contact. *Phew! Just that vision was enough to get me started!* she thought, fanning her heated face. She looked to the clock and frowned. It was still early and she was way too restless to just sit here and wait. She turned on the television and attempted to watch.

The blonde stood with her friends by the bar, not so casually cruising women as they stood and waited for drinks.

"Why are you slumming tonight, Sher? It's not like you to hang by the bar," Dawn said while watching a sexy blonde squeeze by.

"That's why." Sheridan laughed, purposely leaning into the good-looking woman as she passed.

"No one said you were stupid." Marie snickered.

"Hey, don't look now, but guess who just walked in with Susan."

164

Sheridan grimaced. "Fucking Danni. She knows how to ruin a perfectly good night."

"Fuck her, Sher. It's a big club, ignore her." Sharon shrugged.

"Yeah, what the hell, but if she so much as looks at me wrong...Ooh, coming your way, Dawn!"

Dawn leaned into the top-heavy girl as she pushed her way through the crowd. "Thanks, Sheridan, I owe you." She winked.

Keefer winced hard. *Danni!* That was the last person she wanted to see or be seen by. Now she needed to keep three people in her sights, and it was going to be hard. Once she caught sight of Sheridan, she was frozen to the spot. She'd only noticed Danni because of Sheridan's expression, following her gaze and cursing silently. That was all she needed. It had taken Keefer a long time to work up the nerve to enter the club and now that she was there, she wasn't backing out. She hid discreetly behind the amplifier stack, marveling at how her hair seemed to move with the bass beat. Not one for loud music to begin with, she knew it was going to be a long night.

"Hey, Sher! There's one for you!" Sharon pointed at the doorway.

Sheridan gave the woman a good look but scrunched her face up. "Nah, I'm good."

Dawn and Marie exchanged surprised looks. "What do you mean you're good? You got laid today?"

"Why does everyone think I need to get laid like I need air? Jeez!" Sheridan stomped through the crowd and climbed on stage.

"What the hell?" Sharon asked the others.

"I'm telling you, she's fucking weird lately," Marie replied with a shrug.

"Whoa...isn't that..." Dawn trailed off.

"What? Who?" Marie wondered.

I could have sworn that was Danni's ex. "Nothing, I thought I saw someone."

"Worth investigating?" Sharon asked.

"No, not like that. I'll be right back." Dawn excused herself and disappeared. She followed her instincts and spotted what she was looking for. *Bingo! It **is** her...and she's watching Sheridan. Ooh...this is getting better and better.*

Keefer watched with an open mouth as Sheridan gyrated and humped with a tall, flamboyant man. Blue eyes stayed fixed on the blonde's perfect ass as she moved it in ways that made Keefer's sex hurt. *God, if that's how* *she dances, imagine how she...*Keefer swallowed hard and took a deep breath. *I can't watch this...maybe I should go.*

"Hey, gorgeous, you wanna dance?"

Keefer turned around quickly and stared.

"You wanna dance with me?" the biker chick from hell asked again.

"Um...no, thank you," Keefer choked out as she tried desperately not to draw attention to herself. Her eyes sought out Danni and darted to the still-dancing Sheridan before she backed up again.

"You want a drink, then?"

"No, thank you," she said, rolling her eyes.

Dawn watched with concern as the bigger woman moved closer to Keefer. She was ready to jump in at any moment, but with the size of the monster woman, she knew she needed help.

"Why, your girlfriend gonna get mad or something?"

"I'm not thirsty and I don't want to dance. Now, if you'll excuse me." Keefer tried to walk around the large woman, but she sidestepped into her path.

Sheridan watched Danni out of the corner of her eye as she danced, keeping tabs on her. While she glanced up to check on her, she noticed Dawn watching something intently, her body tense, and she followed her line of vision to the back of a big woman apparently menacing someone else. Dawn caught her eye and pointed her chin in the direction of the potential altercation, so Sheridan jumped off the stage to see what was going on. Danni, who hadn't once taken her eyes off of Sheridan, saw the whole thing and couldn't resist drama, so she followed too.

"Trouble, ladies?" Sheridan asked the back of the big woman.

Large Marge turned around and laughed at the construction worker. "No problem, shorty, butt out."

"Looks like a problem." Dawn stepped closer to the troublemaker.

Crazy woman stepped away and, to Sheridan's utter amazement, there was Keefer! Her eyes almost fell out of her head and she closed the distance between them quickly, standing beside her protectively.

"I said, butt the fuck out! The lady here was just going to dance with me, weren't you, sweetie?" The big woman smiled at Keefer.

"Oh, this is too fucking good," Danni said to Susan, who agreed whole-heartedly. "That chick is gonna wipe the floor with Sheridan."

"I don't see a ring on her finger and I don't see a girlfriend anywhere." The stranger stepped too close to Keefer for Sheridan's comfort.

"Back off, fucker, she's with me," the construction worker threatened.

Danni practically guffawed. "Yeah, right," she snickered obnoxiously, making Susan giggle.

Sheridan's eyes narrowed and her fists clenched. She wrapped an arm possessively around Keefer's waist and pulled her close. "I said back off, and you better move on, too, Danni."

Danni pushed her way in front of Sheridan and Keefer. "Prove it," she smirked.

"What do you mean, prove it, asshole?" Sheridan sneered at Danni's attitude.

"Yeah," the annoying stalker woman agreed. "If *she* was with *me*, I'd have a fucking neon sign around her neck."

Danni's smirk pissed Sheridan off in the worst way. She glanced up at nervous blue eyes, trying to convey a plan, but Keefer was looking at the floor.

"So, prove it," Danni dared. "Keefer doesn't have the balls to lie to me, and she wouldn't be caught dead showing affection in public, so," Danni turned to Sheridan, "kiss her." She smiled smugly.

Keefer swallowed nervously and looked at Sheridan for help. Green eyes pleaded desperately with her as she felt Sheridan's hand reach up her back toward her neck.

Sheridan felt the resistance and turned to Danni. "Fuck off," was the best she could do with Keefer feeling so uncomfortable. All of her muscles flexed at once with the effort not to punch Danni right in the mouth.

"I told you, Keefer doesn't want any part of this whore, any more than she wants to lie to me," the redhead boasted to the rest of the crowd.

Sheridan didn't expect it, but suddenly Keefer was holding her face and kissing her senseless. Her black hair fell around their faces like a curtain, tickling Sheridan's neck, making her shiver. In a moment of clarity, she reached up, pulled the teasing hair back, and held it with her palm against the back of Keefer's head. The tall woman made a sound in her throat that left Sheridan suddenly breathless and she inhaled loudly through her nose.

This sound drove Keefer on; she felt wonderfully powerful and she deepened the kiss, pulling Sheridan's face closer, pushing her tongue through soft lips, completely oblivious to where she was and who was there.

Sheridan's knees weakened when she felt the tongue force its way into her mouth. She sucked it in quickly, tightening her grip in the black hair, wrapping her other arm around Keefer's neck, pulling her down harder. Their tongues dueled and Sheridan moaned. There was a buzzing in her head that she'd never heard before and it would have scared her if Keefer's tongue wasn't swirling around in her mouth.

Just like it started, it ended, leaving Sheridan stunned. She caught a glimpse of two very dazed blue eyes as they parted, giving her a jolt to all the important parts, and she was forced to hold back a gasp. She let her hands trail slowly down Keefer's back and she gripped her hip with one hand. Keefer's expression was one of both complete confusion and total arousal, turning Sheridan on to no end. The construction worker's grin was a mile wide as she turned and faced the group.

"Holy shit, Danni, I'd say that was big-time proof." Dawn laughed loudly.

Danni was speechless; she couldn't believe she had just seen that with her own eyes. Keefer sucking face with anyone in public was just impossible. Keefer sucking face with the club slut was way too much for her to handle. Her mouth was hanging open, and Susan closed it with a look of distaste.

"Well, Danni, buh-bye now. Gotta go." Sheridan flashed her best cocky smile before turning around a still-stunned Keefer and leading her out.

The club was littered with dazed women.

Once outside, Keefer leaned against Sheridan's car and closed her eyes. "Well..." she cleared her throat, "that was...wow." She felt so alive, so good, and very turned on. She opened her eyes to see Sheridan with her arms folded across her chest, a confused look on her face. "What?"

"Why did you do that?" Sheridan asked, her head cocked in curiosity. "I mean, it was fucking great, but I would have never expected that in a million years."

"That's why I did it, I guess. Danni really started to make me feel stupid and I just reacted. I'm sorry, I don't know what happened." Blue eyes looked at the ground and she had a regretful tone in her voice.

"Don't you dare apologize for that. Jeez, Keefer! That was the single most delicious kiss I've ever had," Sheridan said as she moved to stand directly in front of the tall woman.

Keefer looked up from the ground into wide green eyes. "You mean that?" she asked in disbelief.

"I never lied to you before, did I?" Sheridan smiled sincerely.

"Damn...it was good, wasn't it? Phew." Keefer smiled in return, comfortable with Sheridan being so close. "I never did that before."

"What? Kissed? You sure are good at it, left me pretty dazzled," Sheridan said, joining their hands.

"No, silly," Keefer grinned. "Initiated something like that. I know I did it for a bad reason, but I'm glad I did it. It felt good to do that...with you." She looked directly into green eyes.

"Feeling's mutual, babe. Oh, and you can go and initiate that any time you want...no complaints from me."

"Friends don't usually go around doing that." The tall woman blushed, her lips still tingling from the kiss.

"I know." The construction worker lifted their hands. "They usually don't hold hands, either. Do you want me to let go?" she asked, leaning closer to the taller woman.

"No," Keefer whispered, her eyes sending very clear messages of acceptance.

Sheridan lifted one set of their hands and used her index finger to trace Keefer's lips. She could still feel them on hers and she wanted to feel them again.

Keefer closed her eyes; feeling Sheridan's touch made her heart flutter. When she opened them, she focused on half-open lips and licked her own.

"Are you gonna do it again?" Sheridan asked, her voice husky.

"Yes," Keefer answered before touching their lips together once again.

Their hands broke apart quickly as they both reached for the other's body, holding heads and pulling each other close. They kissed hungrily, tongues spearing wildly, each of their desires finally fulfilled. Sheridan leaned into Keefer, pressing her tightly between her body and the car. Keefer let her weight fall backwards and soon the only thing holding her up was the muscular leg between her own two shaky ones. She whimpered slightly and tried to pull away in embarrassment, but Sheridan held her tighter, shaking her head, telling her it was all right with a small series of satisfied hums. Keefer felt her stomach clench as the construction worker nibbled on her lips. She bent her knees and slid down lower, her body reacting on its own, pushing against Sheridan's thigh.

The blonde pulled away from the kiss, feeling like she couldn't breathe. She opened her eyes, groaning loudly at the sight of Keefer's blue eyes, bright with arousal; her ragged breathing was turning Sheridan on even more. The inspector's lips were wet, swollen and so inviting. She pulled Keefer's face down again, but was stopped with a hand pressed into her chest.

"Stop," Keefer said breathlessly.

"Why?" Sheridan asked, trying to maintain control of her senses.

Keefer stood up straight, losing contact with Sheridan's thigh. "It's too much."

If it were anyone else, Keefer would have cried at the small tirade, but it was Sheridan and she looked so damned cute when she was having a tantrum. "Do you really think I would let things go any further out in the middle of the street?"

Sheridan stopped her fit and stared at Keefer, both eyebrows in the air. "What are you saying?"

"I'm saying that I liked what we were doing, but this is neither the time nor the place to be doing it." Keefer colored slightly at the admission.

"We could do more than that?" Sheridan asked as if she were a child asking for more cake. Sheridan did a happy dance in the middle of the street. "Woo hoo!" she yelled, giving the air a high-five sign. *Think, Sher! Stop jumping like an idiot and think about this!* "You bet." Sheridan zipped over to Keefer and smiled adorably. "When can we do more?" she asked expectantly. *Warning...danger...you're begging.*

"Soon, Sher, soon. You'll have to be patient with me; I'm sorry." Keefer started to hang her head.

"Oh, no!" The blonde dropped into a squat under Keefer's face. "You look at me, missy," she scolded playfully. "When it feels right, it will be right. I'm not going to force you into anything." *And that, ladies and gentlemen, was the alien that just took over my brain.*

"That's just it, I don't know that I'll ever feel right. You may have to nudge me along a little bit. I don't want to cause you to explode," she said truthfully.

The construction worker popped back to her feet. "I have plenty of ways to take care of frustration, Keef, don't you worry," she said with a sly grin.

"Please don't go there," Keefer mumbled, the images already flooding her brain.

Interesting, Sheridan noted.

Chapter 16

Sheridan stopped the car in front of Keefer's house and waited, her palms sweating. She felt like a teenager on her first date—all expectant and full of anticipation.

Keefer wasn't faring any better. She was nervous and her back was sweating. They hadn't talked much on the way home, and the comfort that they had shared just a little while ago had turned to uncertainty for the tall woman. She was unsure how Sheridan would accept her need to take it slower; she was afraid that she might have blown everything.

"So...what time do you want me to come over tomorrow?" Sheridan asked, staring out the windshield. *Should I kiss her good night? Is that too much?*

"Um, I get up pretty early, so I think it would be better for you to give me an appropriate time," Keefer answered, glancing sideways at the driver. *I'd die for a kiss right now.*

"Okay, how's ten sound?" Sheridan asked, turning to face Keefer.

"Good." Blue eyes darted everywhere but at Sheridan.

"Keef?" Sheridan ran a finger down Keefer's arm.

"Yeah?" She shivered noticeably at the touch.

"Would it be too much if I kissed you right now?"

"God, no."

Sheridan chuckled as she slid over as far as she could and wrapped an arm around the tall woman's neck, pulling her face close. "Good, 'cuz you have the sweetest lips."

Keefer would have gasped from the comment but her mouth was covered by Sheridan's. *Oh, wow! What a wonderful thing to say!* She felt her heart warm and her mouth open to invite Sheridan's tongue inside.

171

Keefer practically floated into her house, still high off of Sheridan's kisses. They'd had to actually count to three and separate in order for Keefer to get out of the car.

"Feefs!"

The dog came bolting into the living room.

"Sheridan is the most incredible kisser! Okay, I only have one person to compare her to, but oh, my god! Wow!" Keefer picked up her dog and twirled her around. "I kissed her first; can you even imagine that? It had to have been in front of at least two hundred people! Danni too! I bet she swallowed her tongue when she saw that!"

Keefer blushed. "She said I have the sweetest lips. Can you believe it? She must have kissed every woman in that club and she said I gave her the most delicious kiss! Do you think she meant it? You think she was just saying that?" The brunette recalled the wide-eyed look of surprise on Sheridan's face. "I think she meant it...Me, I did that...I kissed that expression onto her face!"

Keefer was so excited; she had finally gone for it and it worked out perfectly. Of course, she hadn't planned on kissing Sheridan that night—she didn't even want the blonde to see her at the club—but Danni had pissed her off and she couldn't help herself. Keefer felt great; she felt all tingly with the knowledge that she'd not only initiated this whole night of kissing, but Sheridan had enjoyed it as much as she did.

"I could kiss her forever, Feefs! She has such delicious lips. Oh, no, I have to spend the whole day with her tomorrow! I hope she doesn't wear shorts...or a tank top. Who knows what I'll do?" She laughed at the thought of herself making the moves on Sheridan. "Yeah, like that'll ever happen. Uh-oh, what will I wear? I saw the way she was looking at my breasts. If she touches one, I know I'll faint. That would never do." She frowned, honestly believing she'd pass out if Sheridan touched her breasts. "I'll have to wear something so that she can't see them. She promised to go slow; I don't need to shove them in her face." She thought about the literal meaning of that statement and shivered. She could picture Sheridan's face nestled between her breasts and almost feel the sensations that it would cause. "Oh, boy...I'd really pass out!"

Keefer started rooting through her drawers, looking for a big enough shirt, and she came up with one of Danni's—a big orange Gap shirt. "I can't wear this to redo my bathroom, she'll think I'm nuts." She held up the shirt to her body and looked in the mirror with a sour face. "I don't want to wear something of hers anyway. What is it still doing here?" she wondered as she threw it into the garbage. Staring at herself in the mirror, she stuck out her chest. "She really likes them, doesn't she?" She turned sideways and looked at her chest. When Danni stared at her body, Keefer had always felt bad. However, when Sheridan stared at her body, she felt very good. "I wonder why that is? They both had the same piggish look in their eyes..."

She wondered about that as she crawled into bed. "Maybe it's because I want Sheridan to look at me that way? I want her to touch me and I couldn't stand Danni touching me. God, I want Sheridan to touch me, but I know I'll just faint." Various images came to her as she closed her eyes, sights she saw on channel 46 and other things that were purely her imagination. "You better stop that, Keef...you'll never be able to look her in the eye tomorrow if you wind up touching yourself tonight!"

"The sweetest lips...can you *be* any more sappy? God!" Sheridan banged her head on the coffee table after she kicked off her boots. The dogs sat and stared at her like she was crazy. "Read any poetry lately, Sher?" she groaned. "Now she'll think I'm a romantic or something. Jeez, where did that come from anyway? The sweetest lips..." The blonde shook her head and got undressed. The dogs followed and jumped into her bed. "But she does have the best lips though...totally kissable...thoroughly suckable," she thought out loud with a faraway look. "Mmm, I could get very used to kissing her, very used to it."

Sheridan snuggled into the mattress with a big smile on her face. "I can't believe she kissed me in front of the whole club. Way to go, Keefer! Danni just about croaked!" She laughed out loud. "Damn, she kisses good." She got comfortable amidst the dogs and sighed. "Last night all I could think about were her tits, and tonight, her lips. I'm fucking obsessed! I have to be trapped in the bathroom with her all day tomorrow...shit, how am I going to do that without touching either her lips or her tits? Maybe we can take kissing breaks..."

She snorted at how childish that sounded. "God, I sound like a horny teenager...I am horny. I haven't been this horny in a long time—since the time I spent the night at her house." Zeus huffed as if to say shut up. "You shut up, I'm sensing a pattern here...Keefer has control of my crotch somehow," she told the dog. "I see her, it wakes up and becomes louder with every passing minute I'm around her." She concentrated on that for a while before an unexpected but pleasant visual danced through her head. "Oh, yeah, she has such nice tits," she mumbled as she tried to keep that image for her dream. "I bet they taste as good as her lips."

Keefer woke up early, as usual, and took the dog out for a long walk. She was so excited about the prospect of spending the whole day with Sheridan, she was smiling nonstop. She stopped at the bagel store to get something for them to eat and took a shower when she got home, relishing the hot water as it ran down her body. "Shit!" She realized she probably

173

wouldn't be able to shower after working all day and stomped her foot. *Maybe we should do the shower door first? Does she need to use any glue stuff on it? How long will it take to dry?* She pursed her lips as the questions ran through her head. *Guess I better ask her about that first.*

Sheridan cursed herself to hell. All she'd dreamt about was Keefer's tits and how good they'd taste, should she have the opportunity. She wasn't grouchy about it; she was damned horny from the moment she opened her eyes. She took the dogs out and ran with them, trying to work off the frustration, but that didn't work. Now she was sitting in her car and she could smell her own arousal as she drove. "Fuck!" Keefer was sure to smell her eventually in such close quarters. Green eyes scanned the back seat to make sure she had brought everything, and she grinned when she spotted the duffel bag. "Cool, spare clothes. I'm gonna need a shower after this." She smiled evilly as she imagined herself in the shower behind the new doors with Keefer. "Oh yeah, Sher, that's taking it slow. What the hell came over you anyway? Talking like the ever-so-patient girlfriend. Crap. She's *not* your girlfriend," she insisted. "So what the hell is she then?" she thought as her eyebrows furrowed deeply. "If she isn't your girlfriend, what exactly is she? She's not anything...yet," she said to herself. "Wait until you sleep with her and then think about it."

Sheridan spotted her brother sitting on the deck as she pulled her car into her father's driveway so she blew the horn and pretended she was going to crash into the deck. What she didn't expect was her father to open the door at that exact moment. She cursed silently and put on a remorseful expression as she got out of the car.

"Sheridan's in trouble," Steven teased.

The blonde walked up to her father and took off her baseball cap, baring the back of her head.

"Why do you do such stupid things?" he asked as he biffed her on the back of the neck.

"Love ya, too, Pop. Hey, where's that caulking gun?"

"In the garage, what are you gonna do?" Mr. Landers asked.

"I'm helping a friend fix up her john. I'll be right back," she replied as she ran for the garage.

Steven ran up behind her with a hopeful look on his face. "Can I help, too? Please?" he begged with a puppy-dog face and clasped hands.

"Not this time, Stevie-boy." Sheridan began gathering tools and things while her dad and brother looked on.

"Where are all your tools, Sher?"

"Mine are all grungy and nasty. I'll bring these back, I promise." She put on her puppy-dog face this time.

"Who are you trying to impress?" the older man asked with a knowing grin.

"Nobody! I'd just rather use yours," she rushed to explain.

"Nobody, huh?" Mr. Landers teased.

"I'm just going to help my friend Keefer out with her john, that's all," Sheridan said with as much boredom as she could.

Steven pretended to fluff his hair and made kissy-lips. "Ohh...Keefer, can I hold your hand?" He giggled like a girl.

"Bite me, Steven!" Sheridan blurted in embarrassment.

"Hey, stop fucking with him, Sher." Her father couldn't contain his smirk. He had never seen her so flustered. "So, is she pretty?"

"Pretty? She's gorgeous! I want to marry her and she's so tall, too. Great legs!" Steven said in a hurry.

"Oh? You met her?" Mr. Landers raised an eyebrow at his son.

"In the park. Sheridan was holding her hand and I thought they were gonna kiss, so I went to play with the dogs."

"That's enough, Steven." Sheridan glared at him.

"Your brother sounds just as smitten by this Keefer as you, Sheridan." The older man smiled.

"I am *not* smitten. She's damned hot and her legs do go on for days, though."

"Uh-huh. Well, take your time with the tools, then," he smirked. He knew better—his daughter was definitely gone.

"Thanks, Pop. I gotta go, I'm gonna be late!" She practically ran to the car.

After she peeled away, Mr. Landers patted his son on the shoulder. "So, she's really something, heh, Steven?"

"She's prettier than anyone I ever saw, Pop. She was wearing shorts and her legs gave me goose bumps." He shivered at the memory.

"I can imagine. Your momma had long, beautiful legs, too." He shook his head in sympathy for his daughter. If she was anything like him, she was a goner.

Keefer and Fifi waited on her front steps for Sheridan and when the car turned the corner, Keefer wasn't surprised to find herself blushing already.

"Hi." She waved as the blonde got out of her car. *Oh, no...shorts and a tool belt?*

"Hey. Is that coffee for me?" Sheridan asked, indicating the second mug on the steps. Fifi jumped up on her legs and she scratched her ears.

"Yep, there's bagels inside, too, if you're hungry."

"I am, thanks." Sheridan leaned into Keefer and gave her a quick kiss on the lips before picking up the mug. "Good morning," she said with a lopsided grin, then sat down next to her.

"Morning." Keefer smiled shyly. *I love that grin.*

All Sheridan wanted to do was tackle the woman beside her and kiss her senseless. Just being next to her made her feel good. She didn't understand the concept but wasn't going to question it. Keefer wanted to go slow and Sheridan was sure that jumping her on the front stoop was pushing things, so she tried to make conversation instead. "So, are you ready for all the work today?" she asked before sipping from her coffee.

"Very. Is that okay? It's not too cold, is it?" Keefer asked worriedly, indicating the coffee.

"It's fine, relax. I'm used to drinking hours-old coffee with a layer of dust on top."

"I can't help it. You make me nervous," Keefer admitted with a small blush.

"Me? I do? Am I sitting too close?" Sheridan asked nervously.

"I see I'm not the only one. Do I make you nervous, too?"

"No...a little, I guess. I don't know how to behave around you. I don't want to make you uncomfortable; I feel like I'm not being myself and it's a little nerve wracking," Sheridan said while she fidgeted.

"Really?" Keefer raised both eyebrows. "Sheridan, you don't have to change how you act to be around me. I'm sorry I made you feel that way."

"You didn't make me feel that way, I am the one who feels like I have to be different. Keef, I'm usually so rude and piggy. I don't want to be like that around you," Sheridan said with a serious expression.

Keefer looked into those deep green eyes and felt her belly flip-flop. *She respects me! How cool is that?* "Please just be yourself. I don't have any expectations of you, I like you the way I met you." She smiled sincerely.

"Yeah?" Sheridan grinned.

"Yeah. Starting now, you just be your own piggy, rude self. Just act how you normally would. I'm a big girl." *Just kiss me already.*

"You sure about that, Keefer?" Green eyes twinkled.

"Positive." Blue eyes twinkled back.

Sheridan put down her coffee mug, took the brunette's away, and did so. She slid her hand up the back of Keefer's neck and pulled her down for a kiss. Keefer exhaled in a rush as their lips touched, then wrapped her arms around Sheridan tightly. They kissed hungrily, both tongues pressing into each other's mouths, circling and wrestling with one another until Keefer let go of a barely audible groan and pulled away.

Sheridan gave her a curious look. "Why are you embarrassed by making noise, Keef?"

Blue eyes looked everywhere but at Sheridan. "I just am."

"Okay then, I won't push the issue, but just know I think it's really hot to hear a woman moan."

Keefer blushed brightly. Sheridan chuckled at the predictable outcome.

Sheridan was standing in the bathtub next to the tall inspector as they both admired the new shower doors. They'd worked perfectly in sync with each other, falling into a comfortable pace rather quickly. There were plenty of times where body parts brushed against sensitive regions, but they both diplomatically ignored the sensations. It got pretty dicey there a few times as the two women had to work extremely close to one another. There was a point where neither of them could let go of the freestanding doorframes and Sheridan needed to get to the other side of Keefer. She sidled under Keefer's arms, and the taller woman's breasts pressed tightly into Sheridan's back and rubbed into her as she shimmied by. There was much silent prayer and lip biting at that moment, but they both survived. Now they stood, sweaty, horny, and proud of their achievement.

"God, do I ever have to clean this tub!" Keefer exclaimed after looking at the various footprints and small debris.

"Yeah, well, you'll have to wait to be sure this stuff dries," Sheridan said apologetically.

Keefer slid the door open carefully and stepped out of the tub. Being trapped in the enclosed space with nothing to take her mind off of the blonde was excruciating. She could feel Sheridan's body heat, hear her breathing so close, smell her sweat...it was turning her on like crazy. She had to escape before her nipples did their thing and alerted the construction worker to her dilemma.

"I'm sorry. You probably want to take a shower now, don't you?" Sheridan followed her out of the bathtub.

"It would be nice. I'm sure I'm pretty ripe," Keefer said as she lifted her wet hair off of the nape of her neck.

Mmm...looks salty. Sheridan eyed the expanse of skin momentarily until she noticed the inspector's breasts pushing against the confines of her shirt when she lifted her arms. *Hello, girls!* she thought as she traced both globes with her eyes. *You don't know me yet, but give me time,* she promised them silently.

Keefer brought her hands down and crossed them under her breasts, noticing green eyes widen slightly as she did so. "Why don't we get to the rest of the work, then, since we have all the time in the world?"

"Okay, but I could use a drink," Sheridan mentioned as she washed her hands in the sink. "Wanna come with me?"

Keefer blushed.

Sheridan smirked, then added, "To the kitchen?"

"I want to wash my face, can you grab me something cold?" Keefer grinned sheepishly at Sheridan's knowing expression. After the construction worker left the room, Keefer rolled her eyes and shook her head. *You are such a jerk*, she chastised herself for blushing at Sheridan's innocent comment. *The one time she's not flirting...*

"I brought you a beer, is that okay?"

Keefer jumped and nodded. "Yeah, I didn't hear you come in. I usually don't drink beer but...why the hell not?" She smiled and opened the can. "Cheers."

"Yeah, why the hell not..." Sheridan repeated with a devious grin.

Her tits are taunting me! The blonde rubbed a dirty hand over her face. *That's the hundredth time they've poked me!* She tried to turn the screwdriver confidently but her hand was sweating. Five beers later and Sheridan still couldn't cool off. She could see the tall woman's reflection in the mirror and she was as turned on as Sheridan was. *Dammit all to hell. Slow, I said...how can I possibly go slow? Just look at her face!*

Keefer stood behind Sheridan, holding the new medicine chest in place while the blonde fastened it to the wall. Every time Sheridan pulled her elbow back to twist the screwdriver, her shoulder bumped into the taller woman's breast. Keefer was sweating profusely; her nipples were rigid as could be, especially the one that was being constantly jostled. Every so often, Sheridan's butt would bump back into her crotch, causing an electric current to flow down her legs. To say Keefer was turned on was an understatement. She was on fire. Watching the construction worker's muscles playing under her sweat-slickened skin was driving her insane...and the way she was standing, sort of straddled, made her leg muscles pronounced and in those shorts, Keefer couldn't miss a thing.

Sheridan was grateful that this was the last touch in the bathroom. She turned the screwdriver the last time—mercifully so; it was the last time she'd touch that godforsaken breast. "That'll do it!" she exclaimed proudly.

Keefer stepped back and tried to compose herself. She wanted to curl herself up in a ball and crawl into the freezer right that second.

"Well?" Sheridan gestured around the bathroom.

"It looks great. Everything looks great, Sher! Thank you so much!" The construction worker standing there with her arms outstretched looked too much like an invitation to the overheated brunette. She reacted entirely on impulse and walked into the open arms, pinning Sheridan against the wall.

Sheridan's heart beat loudly as her arms encircled the tall woman. They were both hot and sweaty—it reminded her too much of sex, and she found herself taking deep breaths to control her impulses.

Oddly enough, it was Keefer whose body adjusted until they were face to face. The smaller, muscular body felt incredible pressed up against her own. She made the mistake of looking Sheridan in the eyes and drowned at the look of lust in them.

"You're very welcome," the blonde said in a husky voice, her hands traveling slowly down the expanse of the tall woman's back.

Keefer licked her dry lips while her eyes fixated on Sheridan's wet full ones.

Their lips came together hard and fast, both mouths opening simultaneously as tongues probed and searched hungrily. Keefer pressed hard into Sheridan's body and the blonde groaned deeply and pulled away.

"Keefer, if you truly want me to go slow, you're going to have to move away from me very quickly," the construction worker said breathily, her fingers hooking into Keefer's waistband.

"Okay." The brunette nodded, her eyes never leaving Sheridan's lips, her body never moving from its place.

"I mean it," Sheridan warned.

"It feels so good in your arms...kissing you," Keefer said quietly, glancing up into half-lidded eyes.

"I want you so badly right now, Keef. Unless you're ready for me, please back up." This time, she begged.

Keefer backed up slowly, reluctantly. A part of her wanted Sheridan to take her right there on the bathroom floor. Another, saner, part of her realized she wouldn't have allowed it to happen. *Not in broad daylight, not this sweaty and dirty, and not this soon.* "I'm sorry...I don't know why..."

"No harm, Keef. Just don't touch me for a little bit," Sheridan said while closing her eyes and leaning her head back on the wall.

Keefer's gaze traveled the length of the blonde's body, ending at her smooth neck, watching as she swallowed heavily. That insane part of her wanted to throw herself at the construction worker in all her sweaty glory like some slut; the other part fought for control. *Look at the effect you have on her! She can hardly stand up!* Keefer felt rather cocky for a few moments. *Get a grip. You can't handle it yet; you're not ready for this and you know it.*

"Okay, I'm good."

"I'm really sorry, Sher," Keefer said sadly.

"Look, if you're not ready, you're not ready." The blonde shrugged.

"I don't know," Keefer said in frustration. "A part of me is. Really is. Another part of me is scared. I don't know that I can let myself...what I mean is, when I really am ready, I don't know that I'll allow..."

"I know. Don't you worry. I won't force you into anything, I promise. If I sense you really don't want something, I'll stop. Scout's honor."

Keefer smiled in relief. Sheridan really did understand her. "You were never a girl scout," she teased.

"Hey, don't I look the type?" Sheridan pretended to be offended.

"No, and don't even try to tell me that you ate a brownie," Keefer smirked.

"Never." The construction worker smiled at the old joke.

They stared at each other in silence for a long while, comfortable with each other again.

"Thank you, Sher. I didn't mean to put us in that position."

"No problem. Hey, I think you can shower now."

"Bless you!" Keefer couldn't resist duckling in for a quick kiss before darting to her bedroom for some clean clothes.

Sheridan relaxed on the couch while Keefer prepared a late dinner. She felt much better after showering away all the dirt and sweat, and was far less horny, too. She was very comfortable sitting there, watching television, and it made her think. She'd never felt this relaxed in another woman's home before...not to mention a woman like Keefer who made her blood race just by looking at her. In fact, she couldn't remember ever spending this much time in any woman's home without sex being involved in one way or another. Sheridan didn't ponder it too long; she was far too at ease to get deep.

"Almost ready," Keefer called from the kitchen. "Do you want to eat in there?"

"I'll eat wherever it's convenient."

"Okay, I'll bring it in."

Sheridan was up on her feet in a heartbeat and heading for the kitchen. "Don't think you have to wait on me, Keefer. I'm not Danni."

Keefer gave Sheridan a puzzled but annoyed look. "I never said that you were."

"Well, I can carry a dish, you know. I don't want you to feel like you have to cater to me."

"I don't. I suppose it's habit," Keefer admitted, still slightly miffed at the insinuation.

"Hey, I'm sorry about that crack, it was wrong of me," Sheridan said with sincerity.

"It's okay. I guess I just got used to tending to her. Anyway, I would never compare you to her."

They walked into the living room with dinner and more beer. They settled down at the coffee table and ate in silence for some time.

"I don't think you are anything alike," the brunette said while raising a fork full of food.

"Come on. Your first impression of me wasn't so great." Sheridan grimaced with the memory.

"I thought you were classless—at first, that is. I thought you were arrogant and rude," Keefer confessed with a small smile.

"And then what happened?"

"You broke Danni's nose in my honor." Sheridan puffed up. "Then I thought you were a brute." Keefer grinned as Sheridan deflated. "Then I looked into your eyes and they were full of fire." She looked down and studied her plate. "It turned me on."

Sheridan puffed up again. "I was plenty pissed off."

"I could tell, but I also saw the way you looked at me." Keefer blushed.

"How was that?" Sheridan teased.

"Hungry," Keefer said and quickly drank some beer.

"Was I ever. That was a horrible night. There I was, horny as I ever been—" Sheridan stopped short. This was not a story to share with Keefer: Danni and Susan in the next stall ruining her masturbatory fantasies about her.

Keefer was going to ask Sheridan to go on, but to her great surprise, the blonde began to blush brightly. "Well now...that's a switch!" she giggled.

"Yeah, well," Sheridan stuttered with embarrassment.

"Do go on," Keefer urged teasingly.

"Uh, no. Not that story. Trust me." Sheridan cleared her throat nervously.

"I know some of it. I know that you told me you were this close," she held up her thumb and pointer in a teeny gesture, "and you never got...there." Keefer grinned. "What happened?"

"We were interrupted. I was distracted." Sheridan blushed hotly. "Hey, since when do you want to talk about sex, anyway?"

"Since about three beers ago." Keefer smiled lopsidedly.

"Well, no more beers for you, then. Lush."

"Puh-lease. Those are exactly the type of women you look for. Drunk and easy."

Sheridan's eyes widened. "Why listen to you talk, Miss Potty Mouth."

"God, I'm sorry!" Keefer blushed dark red. "I am so embarrassed."

Sheridan chuckled. "Now, that's more like the Keefer I know."

"Well, since I'm on a roll, and I'm just about as red as I'll get, what distracted you that night?"

"Nosy, aren't you?"

"You're avoiding the question, Sher, why?" Keefer teased. She was so close to daring Sheridan to tell her. She had no idea why she was so curious in the first place—maybe it was the alcohol—but for some reason, she felt she needed to know.

"Because. Finish eating so I can tuck your lush ass into bed," the blonde said while pointing to Keefer's plate.

"You won't tell me and you can't lie to me, huh? It must be juicy. Was she doing something wrong?"

"You're way off track," Sheridan said with a smirk.

Keefer pretended to think real hard.

"Don't hurt yourself," the blonde laughed.

"Someone walked in on you?" Keefer guessed.

"This is killing you, isn't it?"

"You opened your eyes and the woman wasn't who you wanted it to be?"

Sheridan paled and cleared her throat, drinking a large gulp of beer to cover her nervousness.

"That's it, isn't it? You were fantasizing about someone else! I guessed it!" Keefer got up and did a silly little victory dance.

"Yeah, so you guessed it, sit down and sober up. I don't like you drunk anymore." Sheridan pouted.

Keefer got on her knees in front of the pouting woman and smiled triumphantly. "Who were you thinking about?" she questioned with a smirk.

Sheridan looked everywhere but at Keefer and licked her lips nervously.

Keefer's smirk faded as she read the blonde's facial expression loud and clear. Her mouth hung open and she pointed to herself in shock. "Me?" she squeaked.

"Yeah, you. Are you happy now?" Sheridan stood up abruptly and took her plate into the kitchen.

Keefer sat there on the floor, suddenly very sober. "Oh, my god," she muttered to herself before getting up and taking her own plate inside.

Sheridan moved a little to the side to make room for Keefer by the sink. She was embarrassed for some reason and it made her confused. "Just for that, you have to confess something to me." She pouted at the sink, not willing to look at Keefer.

"Okay."

"You agree? Just like that? You really must be drunk." Sheridan chuckled.

"Actually, I'm pretty damned sober right now. You really fantasized about me?" she asked in amazement. "You can have any woman you want and you wanted me?"

"Well, at the time, you popped into my mind. I couldn't help it," Sheridan confessed.

"It happened to me, too," Keefer said directly to the fork she was washing.

Sheridan laughed out loud. "No way! While you were with Danni? How cool is that?"

"I was...alone," she said quietly, this time to her knife.

Ooh... Sheridan grinned cockily. "Oh yeah?" she asked, trying to make Keefer look at her.

The tall woman nodded.

Okay, she's way too embarrassed here. "I did that a few times myself." Blue eyes darted to green. "You know, by myself, thinking about you."

"You did? You're not just saying that to make me feel better?" Keefer turned to face Sheridan.

"Nope. Want me to name days?"

Just the thought of Sheridan touching herself had Keefer turned on all over again. The very idea that she was thinking of her while doing it made her break out in a sweat. "No, you don't have to name days, I believe you."

"Wanna know what you were doing to me?" Sheridan teased, testing Keefer's breaking point.

"No!" The tall woman blushed furiously.

"Just asking," she chuckled.

Keefer threw the sponge at the blonde and left the room.

"Okay, just teasing you," Sheridan laughed from the kitchen.

"Just get in here and sit next to me, please," Keefer called from the living room.

"You got it."

TJ Vertigo

TJ Vertigo

TJ Vertigo

TJ Vertigo

184

Chapter 17

Sheridan sat in her car outside the club. She wasn't ready to go in yet; she was still going over her last few minutes with Keefer from earlier. The two of them had been making out like a couple of starving, hormonal teenagers for quite some time before Sheridan had made an attempt at escape.

The blonde untangled her fingers from the mass of black hair she was grasping and pulled back. "I better go, Keef," she breathed out against the brunette's lips.

"Yeah," Keefer agreed just as breathlessly, poking her tongue out and tickling the kiss-bruised lips of the woman pressed against her.

Sheridan groaned painfully, her hips jerking at the sensation of the wet, hot tongue tracing her lip. She jumped back and out of the circle of the long arms. "Jesus, woman! Are you trying to kill me? I swear I'm going to just explode into a million little pieces!"

Keefer averted her eyes to look at the carpeting. "I'm sorry. I just can't stop kissing you," she admitted quietly.

"I'm so turned on right now, Keefer..." Sheridan started to explain but Keefer's highly aroused eyes met her own and she shivered, losing her train of thought. "I, uh...better go," she stammered, backing toward the door. Keefer started to follow her and she held out a hand to stop her. "Step away from the horny lesbian!"

Keefer giggled, "Huh?"

"Stay right where you are, hands where I can see 'em and nobody gets hurt," Sheridan half joked.

Keefer obeyed, holding up her hands and standing where she was. "Better?" she smiled.

"Much," Sheridan grinned back. "I'll call you tomorrow," she said as she winked and was gone.

Sheridan squirmed from the memory of Keefer's lusty blue eyes watching her back from the front door. "God, she turns me on!" She closed her eyes and took a deep, cleansing breath before getting out of the car and, reflexively, smoothing her pants over her butt. *At least I know she's as turned on as I am. I wonder how long I'll have to wait to finally touch her where I really want.*

After jumping down the steps to get into the club, the blonde sauntered over to Verna and waited for her sugar fix.

"Hiya, Sher, you look good tonight. Hot date?" the coat-check woman teased.

"Yeah, something like that." Sheridan winked.

"Hey, what's the story with you and the tall looker? The rumor mill has been working overtime on this one."

Sheridan winced. "Great, just great. What's the general feel, Ma?"

"That leggy brunette dragged you outta here and had her way with you out on the avenue. You submitted like a puppy dog."

Sheridan grimaced. *Not so far from the truth, is it?* "Looks like I have to consider some serious damage control then, huh?"

"No truth to the rumors?"

Sheridan shrugged cryptically and pursed her lips in thought.

Interesting, thought Verna.

"Well, she's a hell of a kisser, that's for sure," the blonde said with a smirk before wandering off to the bar. A quick scan of the place alerted her that all four of her closest friends were huddled by the bar, waiting for her. *Fabulous.* Apparently, they'd heard all the talk and needed an explanation.

Little did Sheridan know, but they had all already had an inkling as to how special Keefer already was to Sheridan and were just waiting confirmation. After all, their eyes couldn't collectively betray them at once. They had seen Sheridan literally melt into Keefer's mouth and it was a good thing, too. They never would have believed it if they hadn't seen their normally in-control little friend totally lost in one single kiss—a kiss that was designed to arouse jealousy, not libidos.

Sheridan mustered up her patience and waved at the small crowd as she worked her way through the bodies to get to the bar.

"Well, well, look who it is. Gimme." Greg grabbed her chin and studied her face.

"What the hell are you doing?" Sheridan asked in annoyance, pulling away.

"Nope, no change. She didn't sleep with her yet," Greg observed with a cluck of his tongue.

Sheridan furrowed her brows and backhanded him in the stomach. "Fuck you."

"Ew!" he exclaimed with a small attack of the willies.

Dawn, Marie and Sharon snickered.

Sheridan scowled. "So are you all just gonna stand there and stare at me all night or what?"

We just want to know what happened," Marie started.

"Yeah, did you guys go back to her place?" Sharon asked with excitement.

"I know you already wanted her, Sher, that kiss was hot!" Dawn said, fanning herself.

"You guys are so fucking nosy. She kissed me to piss off Danni. That's that," Sheridan said with a shrug, turning her back on the group to order a drink.

They all exchanged confused looks.

"Hey, since when don't you kiss and tell?" Dawn asked with a hint of annoyance, giving voice to their desire to hear what was true and what was not.

Sheridan rolled her eyes and turned back around to the very curious looks of four nosy-nellies. "We kissed out by the car, then again at her place, then this morning, then again this afternoon, then more tonight. There, I told." She threw a hand up to wave the conversation away.

Eight stunned eyes stared in disbelief as she casually drank her water.

"Did you do her?" Sharon asked.

Sheridan frowned. "No, I didn't *do* her. End of conversation, *capisce*?" To make sure it was over, Sheridan wiggled through the crowd and jumped up onto the dance floor.

"Shit, that was strange," Dawn said with a shake of her head.

"I told you, she's got it bad for this Keefer chick. Mark my words, she's falling," Marie stated confidently.

"Oh, my! Our little Sheridan, falling in lurve!" Greg pretended to wipe a tear and sniffled.

"Don't joke, buddy, I think it's serious. Did you see her face when she talked about them kissing all those times?" Sharon asked the group.

"Yeah, and she's so protective over her, even before the kissing thing. Hmm." Dawn wondered if it was true.

"Well, we'll see about that," Greg said suspiciously. "Wait to see if she fucks some floozy in the bathroom before we make that assumption."

"What makes you say that, Greg?" Marie wondered.

"I've been there—in love, I mean. It changes everything. She won't be able to fuck some stranger senseless if Keefer is really what she wants. It will screw with her head."

"Don't be too sure. This is Sheridan we're talking about. She'll fuck some nameless woman *because* she can't take her mind off of Keefer," Marie answered.

"You have a point." Greg frowned. "Okay, we'll see what happens. I really hope she doesn't fuck this up. Did you see the way Keefer looked after that kiss? Totally gone. Then again, that's how they all look after Sheridan kisses them, don't they?"

"Yeah, but Keefer kissed Sheridan and Sheridan looked about to keel, too," Dawn reminded them.

"Too true. Okay, so now that we've established that the feeling is mutual between them, how do we make it work for them?" Greg wondered.

"We don't. We just sit back and let nature take its course," Marie replied seriously.

"That's what I was afraid of," Greg groaned.

Sheridan was dancing with abandon to her favorite song when a familiar scent wafted to her nose. Her heart beat wildly in anticipation as her eyes scanned the immediate surroundings until she found the culprit. Some blonde bimbo had the nerve to wear Keefer's perfume. Sheridan narrowed her eyes at the poor woman until the bimbo danced toward the end of the stage. *Who does she think she is, making me think Keefer was here?* It was an irrational anger, but she couldn't help it. Her excitement had built so quickly at the scent. The thought that Keefer might be there, looking for her, missing her, needing her...*Well, she has some nerve, is all.*

Sheridan wouldn't admit how much she actually missed Keefer—that would be crazy; she had just left her a few hours ago. She amused herself with thoughts of the brunette missing her, which turned into thoughts of kissing her, which turned into thoughts of Keefer needing her, which became panting her name as she touched herself...*Did they just turn off the AC in here, or what?* The blonde shed her jacket and dropped it onto the stage in front of her. A sexy redhead picked it up and shook it out, draping it over her arm with a sultry look to its owner. *Not bad...and you are damned horny right now.* Sheridan glanced briefly around the club and shrugged. *Why not?*

"So, what's your name?" Sheridan asked with a sexy grin.

"Barbara," the woman answered in a high-pitched voice.

Sheridan winced. *Oh no, that can't be her real voice, can it?*
"Sheridan."

"I know. I've been watching you for a long time."

I think Gramma's china just broke all the way in Detroit. "Oh?"

"Yeah, so why don't we cut the small talk and get down to business?"
Barbara asked with a lick to her top lip.

Okay, so that was hot. I can ask her not to speak..."Business? What
do you have in mind?"

"Oh, you take me out to your car and have your way with me."
Barbara traced a fingernail over Sheridan's bicep.

*That was even hotter...*She shivered.

"Until, I scream out your name."

Oh, no, I am not *paying for new windows.* "I tell you what, Barbara,
let's say you have to be quiet. Can you do that?"

"I guess, but my fantasy involves me screaming." She traced that nail
down Sheridan's throat and then across her breasts.

Lordy! That did it. Sheridan grabbed her hand and dragged her up the
stairs, past four frowns and into the bathroom.

Keefer lounged around her house with a big smile. She felt so good
and tingly that evening. Sheridan Landers had made her feel like a new
person, and she welcomed the sensations. She and Fifi sat on the floor by
the sofa, eating cookies and watching television. It was already very late,
but Keefer felt so awake and energized that she had no desire to sleep.
Sheridan's kisses awoke something inside of her that she never knew
existed. At first, she was frightened, but now...now she eagerly awaited the
tremble in her legs and the fluttering in her stomach.

I can't believe I drank all that beer! she thought with a lopsided
smile. *I hate beer, don't I? I should be exhausted after all that work today,
plus all that beer.* She flipped the channels and settled on a talk show. *I
can't believe I survived the whole day with Sheridan. God, her kisses are
incredible! Argh! I want her to touch me so badly, but I know I'll push her
away when it gets too intense.*

Keefer knew she'd sabotage any attempts at deepening their
relationship. She didn't know why she was scared, but she was. She wasn't
so scared about touching Sheridan, though. She wondered if the blonde
would shirk her advances, should she make any. *Could I actually make the
first move? What if she wants to reciprocate? What if I back out? That
doesn't seem fair, and I want her to touch me so badly!*

Keefer sighed heavily, letting her head loll back on the seat cushions
of the sofa. She was thinking too much again, but she couldn't help it.
There were so many instances that day where she had caught her hand

from reaching out and tracing Sheridan's muscles, from touching her hot skin, from swiping up a drop of sweat that was trickling down her neck. *Would she let me? I'm driving her crazy, I know I am, but she's being so good about it. I don't think touching her is a bad thing. I think she's perpetually horny. She'd welcome my advances...I'm sure of it.*

Keefer decided that the next time they were together and she had the urge to touch, she was going to go for it, despite the consequences. *At least I get to touch her that one time. Even if she makes me stop, I'd have still touched her.* With that thought, Keefer yawned. *Oh, looks like it's time for bed.* "Come on, Feefs, beddie-bye."

The redhead's hands were all over the muscular blonde. It bothered her that Sheridan was so unresponsive, but she hadn't heard much about the other women touching the construction worker and decided that this was how she responded. She pulled the blonde's shirt out from her jeans and scratched her nails up her back.

Sheridan groaned and shivered, her body reacting to the stimulus on its own. Her nipples hardened as the nails traveled back down. *Okay, this is better.* She broke the kiss and nuzzled Barbara's throat, biting down at the sensitive skin, eliciting a high-pitched whining sound from the woman. *Could that be any more annoying?*

Barbara thrust her chest out in hopes of some attention. *Boy, she works slowly, doesn't she? I thought she was supposed to be a good fuck!*

Sheridan wrapped her hands around the offerings and squeezed them. They were awfully large. *Bigger than Keefer's,* she thought briefly. She moved the lacy bra aside and studied the large pink nipples. *I bet Keefer's are prettier.* Rubbing her thumbs across them had no effect. She did it again. Nothing.

"I like it hard, Sheridan. Pinch them."

*Shit, all I have to do is look at Keefer's tits...*She bent forward and took one in her mouth. It felt soft and rubbery. She bit down on the nipple and received a small groan in response. *What I wouldn't give to hear Keefer...but this isn't Keefer, is it?* "Look, Barbara," Sheridan fixed the redhead's clothing, "I'm not into this."

"I thought you were a better fuck, Sheridan. You're pretty lame, if you ask me," Barbara said with disgust.

"Yeah, well, fuck you," Sheridan said defensively.

"I'd rather fuck myself!" Barbara said loudly as she slammed open the stall door.

"Yeah, well, you do that!" Sheridan yelled after her, exiting the stall to the shocked faces of the women waiting. "What? Her voice could peel paint!" she said as she stomped out of the room angrily.

Sheridan came storming down the steps from the upper level and threw herself against the bar.

"What the hell happened in there?" Sharon asked in confusion. "That chick came flying out of there so pissed off, I'd swear you got slapped."

"I didn't get slapped. The bitch has a problem, is all," Sheridan bit out angrily.

"This is so wrong, Sher. I never saw that kind of reaction before. What happened?" Dawn wondered.

"I wasn't in the mood, so I told her and she freaked out." Sheridan tried to sound nonchalant but failed. She was far too annoyed to be convincing.

"Well, you do have a reputation, Sher, it's not like she was expecting the impossible," Marie stated the matter of factly.

"Yeah, well, I wasn't in the mood! What's the big fucking deal? She was annoying—she fucked it all up," Sheridan gave as an excuse.

She fucked it up, my friend? Marie mused.

"What the hell is that for?" Sheridan asked of Marie's expression.

"Nothing. Are you sure it was all her fault? Perhaps your head wasn't where it was supposed to be."

"Fuck off!" Sheridan barked, pissed that her friends could read her so well. "Her voice made my teeth hurt." She turned her back on them and pouted to herself.

"Uh-huh." Greg nodded with an innocent look. *It wasn't Keefer's.* He winked at the rest of the women and they all smirked knowingly.

"I'm cutting out. I'm tired. See ya tomorrow," Sheridan said as she left abruptly.

Various high-fives went up amongst the four friends. "I told you!" Marie said proudly. "Totally gone."

"Can we live through this?" Greg asked with concern.

"We shall see," Dawn sighed.

Sheridan had been horsing around in the dog run with her babies for a long time before Zeus finally tore apart the Frisbee. She held up the mangled plastic disk and sighed. "It took you long enough. What's a'matter, Zeusey, tired today?" she chuckled.

Pharaoh attempted to snatch the Frisbee remains out of Sheridan's hand. "Oh, no. This one's finished. All gone, no more." Both dogs looked genuinely sad and the blonde rolled her eyes. "Okay, it's time to go home, anyway. Let's go, guys. I want to shower." *And call Keefer.*

She had been constantly distracted with thoughts of the tall brunette that morning. She was surprised to find herself smiling as she got lost in her thoughts; she expected to be pissed, especially after the previous night's fiasco. The more she thought about Keefer, the better she felt...until she started recalling their kisses. Then she just felt lonely. That confused her; she had never felt lonely a day in her life, except when her mother died. Even though she had been lonely then, it was a different kind of loneliness. Now she felt like something was missing when she thought about kissing and holding Keefer. It made her want to go to Keefer's house and kiss her the minute she opened the door. While not being an unpleasant idea, the neediness worried her. Sheridan had craved women before in her life. She craved the feel of a woman's body in her arms, the sensation of a woman's vagina closing around her fingers, the sound of a woman's voice moaning her pleasure, the feel of a woman's tongue in her mouth or, even better, a nipple. But with Keefer, she just simply craved her presence. Oh, sure, all those other things would probably blow that craving out of the water, but for now, she just wanted to smell her.

Am I going crazy? she wondered as she loaded the dogs in her car.

Keefer stretched and welcomed the new day. The sun had already been up for hours and Fifi was doing a pee-pee dance at the foot of the bed. She hadn't slept in in a long time. Having this mini vacation was a blessing. Not only did she get to sleep late, but she also got to spend all of the previous day with Sheridan. *Maybe I'll see what she's doing today.* The brunette smiled and shook her head. *You haven't even opened your eyes yet and what's the first thing you think of? Shame on you.* "All right, Feefs, let Mommy get dressed." She petted the pooch's head before padding off to the bathroom.

As soon as she came back with the dog, the phone rang. She looked at the caller ID and grinned brightly, her heart already beating faster before she heard the voice on the other end.

"Good morning, Sheridan."

"Good morning to you, too."

"Would you believe I just got up a little while ago?" Keefer eased comfortably into the couch and closed her eyes.

"No...alert the presses."

Sheridan chuckled and Keefer smiled warmly at the vision it invoked. "Did you have a good time last night?"

"Actually, no, but I don't want to talk about it." She waited a beat and then asked, "Hey, you wanna hang out today or something?"

"Sure," Keefer replied quickly.

Sheridan chuckled again. "Well, don't let me twist your arm or anything."

Keefer blushed.

"I bet you look adorable right now."

"Yes, I'm blushing, for your information. I hate being so predictable." She covered her face.

"Don't cover your face, it's so cute when it's all pink."

"How did you know that?"

"I just do. So, did you miss me last night?"

"Yes. Did you?"

"Oh, yeah."

Sheridan's purr shot right between Keefer's legs and she sat up a little straighter.

"So, what's the plan for today?"

"Why don't you come over here and well take it from there," Keefer said as she tried to ignore the throbbing at her center.

"Is a half-hour too soon?"

"No. That's perfect."

Sheridan fulfilled her earlier desires as soon as Keefer opened the front door. She backed the taller woman into the house and kicked the door closed behind her. At first, Keefer was caught off guard, but she quickly adjusted and kissed Sheridan back with gusto. She didn't realize how badly she needed that kiss until she was already lost in it. They kissed hungrily for a long while until Keefer's knees threatened to give out on her and Sheridan assisted her in sliding to the floor.

"Mmph." The blonde lost her breath as the taller woman pushed her down on her back and crawled on top of her, never stopping the devouring kissing.

Keefer's hands held the sides of Sheridan's face as she explored her mouth with her tongue. She pulled back enough to suck the blonde's lips into her mouth, nibbling on them until Sheridan was squirming beneath her. The writhing of the blonde alerted her to the fact that she was probably torturing her again, but she couldn't bring herself to stop her explorations. She felt Sheridan's hands pressing up into her shoulders trying to push her away, but she didn't care. Her mouth traveled to the side and she dropped wet kisses all over Sheridan's cheek until she reached her ear.

"Keef..." Sheridan gasped. The warm ragged breath in her ear made her sex physically hurt.

"Uh..." She breathed into Sheridan's ear before poking her tongue out and tasting it. She could feel Sheridan's heart pounding against her chest and it thrilled her.

"God, no...you have to stop!" the blonde begged. The weight on top of her was delicious and she feared she'd throw Keefer over and attack her at any second.

"Please..." Keefer whispered, sending violent shudders down Sheridan's spine. The tall woman pulled back at the tremors and looked into a pair of very aroused, yet panicked, green eyes. She scrambled to her feet, leaving Sheridan on her back, panting and gripping the carpet.

"Oh, God...Keefer..." Sheridan groaned.

"I'm sorry, I got carried away," she said remorsefully. Her own body was at a heightened level of arousal she had never felt before. "It felt so good."

"You're telling me?" Sheridan said as she crawled to her knees and took a deep breath.

"Why do you do this to me, Sheridan?" Keefer asked seriously.

"Probably the same reason you do it to me. I can't tell you how hot I am right now. Jesus Christ!" She scrubbed her hands over her face and leaned against the wall. "All we did was kiss!" *Can I live through anything more?*

"I can't seem to control myself when it comes to you. You're being so kind, too, I really do apologize for my behavior," Keefer said with genuine sadness in her voice.

"Hey, now, that's no reason to apologize." Sheridan walked over to the tall woman and took her hands. "I'll wait. I'll live."

"You didn't seem so patient a moment ago." Keefer blinked away her embarrassment.

"Well," Sheridan grinned, "a moment ago, I had the hottest-looking chick I ever met breathing in my ear."

"God, what came over me?" she asked, burying her face in their linked hands.

Sheridan smiled knowingly. *Poor Keef. This is all new to her. That fuck-off Danni could have prevented all of this, but no, she had to go and—wait a minute. If it weren't for Danni being such a dick, I wouldn't be here right now. Hey, thanks, dickhead! I owe you one.* "Hey, Keefer, believe me, I didn't mind the attack. I just wasn't prepared for it."

Keefer grinned and showed her face. "How can you be prepared for that," she giggled.

"Oh, a few hundred orgasms oughtta do it." Keefer's eyes widened and she blushed deeply. "I don't know what it is about you, but all you have to do is look at me and I'm a goner. Maybe it's those baby blues, they trap me in there."

"Stop that." Keefer blushed harder.

"Oh, no, I mean it. If you were to look directly at my crotch I'm sure I'd come. I bet you're trying not to look at it now, huh?" she teased.

"I'm going to kill you!"

"Ooh, hurt me, baby." Sheridan laughed and ran into the living room with Keefer hot on her heels. "Catch me at your own risk, baby!"

That's true. If we wind up on the floor again, who knows what will happen? Keefer hesitated and watched the blonde settle down on the floor in front of the couch. *That's exactly where I sit, how cool is that?*

"Chicken?" Sheridan flapped her arms and squawked.

Keefer narrowed her eyes. "Them's fighting words, shorty."

"Ooh, I'm scared!" Sheridan hugged herself and shook dramatically.

As soon as she was close enough, Keefer dove at her and pinned her arms over her head. "How many women have had you in this position, Sheridan?"

"Not many. None," Sheridan said nervously. Keefer's nipples were taunting her again. They were hard and perfectly outlined as they pressed against her worn, white T-shirt. Sheridan could see them clearly, the low neckline exposing more cleavage than was safe for her. *Is she even wearing a bra?*

God, having her under me like this is intoxicating. I'm so hot! Keefer thought as she unconsciously pressed her hips down into Sheridan's abdomen. "So I'm the first?"

Sheridan nodded, fixated on Keefer's breasts as they pushed to break free. She could feel the heat emanating from Keefer's sex, burning her stomach. She tried with all her might not to grab her hips and press her down firmly.

She's staring at my nipples. Blue eyes glanced down. *They're hard? How did that happen?*

"Okay, you win, you better get up now."

Sheridan's voice cracked and Keefer gave her a raised eyebrow. "I win," Keefer said breathlessly.

"Any time now."

"Can I touch you?" the brunette blurted out.

"Where?" Sheridan squeaked a bit.

Keefer released her captive's hands and rested her own on Sheridan's strong shoulders. "Here."

Sheridan nodded and willed herself not to react. Keefer explored the muscular shoulders with her fingers, sliding them under the sleeves of the blonde's shirt, relishing in the feel of the soft skin over the hard muscles. Sheridan felt her sex get wet and her nipples harden at the same time, making her squirm. Keefer ran her fingers down the length of Sheridan's arms, exploring every inch of skin.

Sheridan watched the other woman's face as she touched her. Her blue eyes followed her hands, first one and then the other, as they journeyed torturously up and down her arms. Sheridan's hands twitched to reach up and reciprocate, but she'd made a promise and she'd keep it. Keefer gasped as Sheridan flexed her arms in an effort to keep them where they were. Green eyes focused on half-opened lips, and Sheridan was a goner. "Kiss me, Keefer."

She didn't have to tell her twice. Her nails dug into Sheridan's biceps just like she always wanted to do as their lips met in a bruising kiss. Once again, Keefer was leaning over the blonde. Sheridan could feel her nipples poking at her, just beneath her own, and it was driving her insane. She squirmed and fidgeted, desperate to relieve some of the fire between her legs.

Keefer inhaled sharply as Sheridan's stomach flexed into her sex. She pulled away from the kiss, breathless and highly aroused. *I want her to touch me now. Anywhere. How can I tell her that?*

The blonde struggled and sat up. She looked around the living room a few times, trying to not look into Keefer's heavy-lidded blue eyes, knowing that would be her downfall. She prayed to all the powers that be that this would be the day that the brunette made the first move. *She wants it; just look at her.*

They separated. Sheridan needed time to cool down and Keefer needed a way to voice her needs. The way Keefer looked right then wasn't making it easy for Sheridan to cool off any time soon. The construction worker was staring at her hardened nipples as they invited her in for a taste. She was afraid that she'd never be able to resist.

"Sher?" Keefer asked shakily.

"Yeah?"

"Um..."

Sheridan let it go. She couldn't get her hopes up like that.

"Sheridan?"

"Yes?"

"Will you touch me?"

Chapter 18

They sat facing each other on the floor of the living room, the hum from the refrigerator the only sound in the house. Sheridan wondered how she was going to be able to go slowly after being given permission to touch Keefer. *Those tits, I need to touch those tits!* was her first thought. Her second thought was of Keefer's possible discomfort at being attacked in the way that Sheridan had craved. She had an idea that was sure to work well for both of them. She smiled crookedly at Keefer and bit back a chuckle at the look of want on her face. She backed all the way up, until she was leaning on the couch, and beckoned Keefer to follow by crooking her finger.

Smiling shyly at the sexy grin on the construction worker's face, Keefer walked on her knees to sit beside the blonde.

"No," Sheridan whispered and patted her lap, "here."

The tall brunette stopped moving and sat back on her heels, resting her arms on her thighs. She wanted so badly to follow the instructions...needed to feel Sheridan wrap her arms around her and lay her head on her breast, making her feel safe and secure. *I know I said I wanted it, but can I do that?*

Sheridan reached over, wrapped a strong hand around Keefer's forearm, and tugged loosely. "Please?" she pleaded quietly, her smile never wavering.

Keefer found herself rising up and moving to straddle Sheridan's muscular thighs, quite against her better judgment. She hovered over the outstretched legs, not wanting to make the final contact, fearing her own reactions to such closeness. She hadn't counted on that. She merely wanted to feel Sheridan's hands on her skin. *This may be too much.*

197

Sheridan released Keefer's arm and brought her hand to the nervous face above her, cradling the chin with her fingers. "Sit, baby," she whispered, her eyes bore into insecure blue ones.

Keefer felt the stare right down her body to her toes and shuddered slightly, finally lowering herself to sit astride Sheridan's lap. Once her backside made the contact, she sighed nervously and licked her lips. She didn't know where to look or to put her hands, so she rested them on the couch on either side of Sheridan's head.

"Look at me, Keef."

Blue eyes lifted to meet green. She saw trust and assurance in them.

"Do you trust me?" Sheridan asked as she palmed Keefer's lower back securely.

The inspector nodded, afraid that her voice would crack if she spoke out loud.

Sheridan never lost eye contact as she slowly brought her hand up the middle of Keefer's back. The taller woman gasped, the warmth from the hand burning a path right through her thin T-shirt and spreading out all around her body.

"Does this feel good?" Sheridan asked, nodding along with Keefer as she answered, placing her other hand on the sexy body on her lap.

Keefer wanted to close her eyes—they kept fluttering with every touch of Sheridan's hands—but she was deeply lost in her eyes and didn't want to find her way out.

Sheridan leaned her head forward until she was a mere inch away from the enticing cleavage. She watched for signs of fear and saw none. She inched closer and inhaled slightly, a low groan in her throat signaling her approval. Her hands soon included the front of Keefer's ribs in their journey.

Keefer felt herself responding and had no control over it; her hands slithered through soft blonde hair until she laced her fingers and cradled the back of Sheridan's head. It felt good...too good, and she breathed out a shaky breath. Her heart was pounding double-time and she swore it must have skipped a few beats when Sheridan's nose accidentally brushed her skin.

Green eyes were the first to succumb and flutter shut. The smell and feel of Keefer all around her caused great twinges of arousal to electrify her nerve endings. Sheridan felt the sweat beginning to slide down her back and between her breasts, giving her little shivers now and then. She readjusted her legs, causing Keefer to straddle her left thigh.

Keefer still stared at Sheridan's face, even after green eyes had closed. The construction worker seemed to be in pure ecstasy as she touched and smelled her way around her body. One of the strong hands brushed the underside of her breast and Keefer's back arched uncontrollably. *Oh, God, yes...*

Green eyes popped open and focused on sky-blue ones, pupils fully dilated from arousal. Wetness pooled between the blonde's legs at the sight of Keefer's bottom lip being trapped between her teeth. She brought her hand back, grazing her breast consciously this time, and watched the face above her intently as she did.

Keefer strained not to move as Sheridan's fingers tickled her sensitive skin a second time, but she failed to stop the tiny whimper the feeling caused. She blushed deeply and tried to avert her eyes.

Sheridan held her ground and, with her other hand, pushed Keefer's chin upward so they were looking at each other again. "Does it feel good when I touch you like that?" she asked very quietly.

"Very good," Keefer whispered, still red with embarrassment.

"Then I don't mind you complimenting me. Sounds of pleasure make me feel as good as you," the construction worker explained soothingly as she stroked the soft skin under Keefer's left breast.

Keefer nodded, this time sucking both lips into her mouth as she breathed in sharply through her nose. Making noise was embarrassing to her and she wasn't comfortable with it, but she'd be damned if she didn't want to scream out loud right then.

"It's okay...relax," Sheridan murmured, rubbing her cheek softly against Keefer's right breast. The nipple was already as hard as a rock and the shudder in Keefer's frame told her just how sensitive her nipples were. She drew the material of the v-necked T-shirt to the side and exposed more skin for her to touch, quickly inhaling the scent and then rubbing her cheek against the hot but smooth skin.

Keefer didn't think she could control herself anymore. She was beginning to sweat heavily, her hips were straining to move, her sex was on fire, and she still had her clothes on. This was not how she'd envisioned their first time together and it scared her. It was too much sensation all at once. "Sher...wait," she said in a shaky voice.

"Shh...Keef, just let me do this..."

Sheridan's breath blew across her breast and this time her hips jerked. "God," Keefer blurted out uncontrollably, gripping Sheridan's head tightly to her chest. Suddenly there was a burst of sensation as a hot tongue began to bathe her already burning skin. "Sher!"

"Mmm," the blonde hummed. Hearing Keefer rasp out her name made her sex gush. She wormed her tongue deeper inside Keefer's shirt, until she felt the pebbled flesh of her areola. The saliva actually dribbled off of her tongue as it tasted the puckered skin. Fingers tangled painfully tight in her hair and she groaned in pleasure.

Keefer bucked into Sheridan's body, the feelings exploding from her breast and going directly between her legs, ending up as a strong pulsation in her clit. She couldn't sit still if she had wanted to and squirmed against the muscular thigh beneath her.

Sheridan had tortured herself long enough. "I'm gonna lick your nipple, baby," she whispered into Keefer's shirt before doing just that.

"Oh, my god..." Keefer whispered, dropping her forehead onto Sheridan's head.

The blonde whimpered, her scalp throbbing from Keefer pulling on her hair, but the taste of her nipple made it all worthwhile. "Mmm...yeah..."

Keefer couldn't contain her pleasure any longer. She opened her mouth and her breath came out in heavy pants. Sheridan's hand held her snugly in the middle of her back while the other one cupped her breast, kneading it from underneath, as her tongue swirled a path of fire across her nipple. She was vaguely aware of her own loud gasp through the buzzing in her ears as her entire breast was suddenly exposed. She pulled her face up from on top of Sheridan's head and looked down in time to watch her nipple be enveloped completely by a hot mouth.

The sound that Keefer made forced Sheridan to thrust her hips up to satisfy the sudden throb. It was a delicious whining sound and reverberated right down to her clit. She opened her eyes and glanced up to see Keefer's eyes riveted to her own breast. Sheridan inhaled sharply at the sight and sucked the nipple a bit more roughly.

The pulling sensation was phenomenal and Keefer's hips began to move rhythmically; it was completely beyond her control and she didn't even notice she was doing it until the sparks began igniting from her sex outwards. She arched her back, pressing her chest into Sheridan's face as she felt her shirt rip open.

Sheridan tore the T-shirt down the middle, fully exposing the objects of her desire. Once Keefer started to thrust against her, she switched breasts and didn't waste any time attacking the new nipple with a renewed hunger. She heard the heavy, uncontrolled breathing and knew the tall woman was enjoying this as much as she had hoped. Once she'd found out how sensitive her nipples were, she knew she had to taste them.

Keefer bit back a moan as Sheridan's teeth teased her nipple. She was so wet, she knew Sheridan could feel it on her leg, and she wasn't the least bit embarrassed about it at the moment. All she could think of was the incredible pulling at her nipples...first one, then the other, and the feeling shot straight between her legs. Her sex was burning up. She was burning up. Sweat dripped down her neck and onto her breasts and she could feel Sheridan's tongue swiping at the droplets in between sucking and biting.

Sheridan dropped her hand from Keefer's back to her ass, holding it steady while she bucked up into her body. She felt Keefer pull her head even closer, so she let go of her breast, now confident that Keefer wasn't going to pull away any time soon. She brought that hand around and held the tall woman's other ass cheek, pressing her down into her thigh. The result was instantaneous and she felt Keefer begin to shudder almost continuously.

A strangled groan bubbled up from Keefer's chest and she pressed her forearms to the sides of Sheridan's head. Her sex spasmed deliciously and she began to tremble. *Oh, my god...I'm going to...*

"Mm-hmm, mm-hmm." Sheridan shook her head, humming in encouragement. Her nostrils flared as Keefer bent backwards slightly. A whimper escaped her open lips and the tall woman began to shake all over. *God, I wish I was seeing this!*

"Ohh...Sher..ohh..." Keefer whispered breathlessly as she jerked and twitched on the muscular leg.

Sheridan sucked and bit the nipple in her mouth for all she was worth, wanting to make this last as long as she could, savoring every breath from Keefer's mouth at that moment.

The inspector shuddered and shivered, breathing loud and erratically, her sex pressing hard and fast into Sheridan's leg. The more she stayed there, the more she twitched, and somewhere off in the back of her mind she heard herself say, *Woo hoo!*

Sheridan relaxed her movements as the fingers loosened their grip in her hair. She immediately released the nipple and searched out Keefer's face. The tall woman wrapped her arms tightly around her back. She hid her face in Sheridan's neck, breathing heavily into the sweaty crevice, causing skitters of electricity to travel up and down Sheridan's spine. She reached up and ran her fingers under Keefer's hair, starting at the neck, loving how wet it was there at the nape.

"Oh, my god..." Keefer breathed.

"Let me look at you." Sheridan tried shrugging her shoulder but Keefer wouldn't budge, instead shaking her head where she was. "Why not?"

"I'm so embarrassed," she mumbled, licking her lips, tasting the sweat off Sheridan's neck.

"Oh, Keef...that was fantastic. You're so beautiful."

"No. I'm never moving," she promised.

"Please?" She bucked her hips to dislodge her.

"Nuh-uh."

Sheridan chuckled quietly. She had been afraid this would happen. She found it so incredibly cute that Keefer couldn't look her in the face. *I bet that's the first intense come she's ever had...probably mortified now.* "You can't possibly breathe in there."

"So I'll die." Keefer loosened her grip on Sheridan's body and let her stomach relax. She had never felt like that before in her life and she was stuck between thanking Sheridan profusely and hiding under the rug.

"I bet you look so hot right now, Keefer, all flushed and sweaty. God, what I wouldn't give to see your eyes right now." The blonde ran her hands soothingly up and down Keefer's back.

"I'm not looking at you ever again."

"Don't punish me like that. It would kill me if I couldn't look at your face ever again." She tried to pry the brunette away from her neck. "Keef, you're driving me crazy breathing on my neck like that."

"Sorry." Keefer turned her head.

Sheridan snapped at the opportunity and pulled the sweaty face toward her own. Keefer tried to shy away, but Sheridan held her ground. The tall woman really was embarrassed. It was broad daylight, her tits were hanging out, and she had orgasmed louder and harder than she ever had before in her life.

"Oh, yeah, you are so beautiful right now," Sheridan said as she wiped errant locks of hair away from Keefer's face. "Kiss me, baby."

Keefer glanced at Sheridan's face and saw nothing but truth. She almost felt like crying as she lowered her head and kissed the blonde. *She means it! She thinks I'm beautiful!* she screamed inside her head as she devoured Sheridan's mouth.

Sheridan groaned into Keefer's mouth. The taller woman wrapped her arms around her and crushed their bodies together. Keefer's naked breasts were so tantalizingly close; Sheridan was going to go mad in a moment.

"Thank you," Keefer murmured against Sheridan's lips, "thank you so much."

"Hmm?" Sheridan was reluctant to break up their liplock but she wanted to know why she was being thanked.

Keefer sat back and looked into Sheridan's eyes. All traces of embarrassment were gone and a satisfied smile lit up her face. "You mean it."

"That you're beautiful? Of course I mean it. Have you looked in a mirror lately?" Sheridan asked in all seriousness.

"You have the most incredible eyes, Sheridan."

The blonde would have blushed, but her senses were overloaded as Keefer began kissing her again. Large hands left their place on her muscular back and began to roam up and down Sheridan's torso, coming dangerously close to her aching nipples.

Keefer felt light-headed as her hands discovered all of the new places to touch. She felt bolder than she ever had, egged on by the confidence that Sheridan gave her. She wasn't worried about satisfying her lover, she knew she'd done a damned fine job with Danni, if she said so herself. She was worried, however, about her own reactions to seeing Sheridan's naked flesh, touching it, and tasting it. She also remembered that she was half naked and the sun was streaming into the room, illuminating her breasts like a neon sign.

Sheridan jumped as fingernails slipped under her shirt and scratched her torso teasingly. She turned her head to the side and panted a bit before speaking in an aroused husky voice. "You sure you're up to this, Keefer?" She didn't receive an answer as the brunette's lips trailed down the side of her neck. Sheridan grabbed both wandering hands and held them still. "Keef?"

"Yes," Keefer breathed into her ear. "Never wanted anything more," she added before sucking in the salty flesh of the blonde's neck.

"Sweet Jesus!" Sheridan let go of Keefer's hands and held onto her shoulders.

The strangled exclamation drove Keefer on. She brought her teasing fingers up higher until they hovered over two perfectly round breasts. *Here goes...*

Both women gasped at the contact. Sheridan arched into the touch and Keefer touched her more demandingly.

Finally! Sheridan thanked the gods for listening to her prayers.

Keefer wasn't satisfied with the cloth barrier and she lifted Sheridan's shirt and bra up to expose her breasts. Once they were bared, blue eyes narrowed with even more arousal and Keefer replaced her hands where they were.

"You feel so good, Keef," Sheridan groaned, the hooded blue eyes looking down at her making her shiver.

"So do you," Keefer whispered, once again seeking out the sensitive crevice in Sheridan's neck.

Sheridan squirmed uncontrollably as long fingers teased her nipples. Her eyes rolled back and she let her head fall onto the seat cushion behind her as those fingers began to pull and squeeze with a purpose. She could feel the uncomfortable wetness in her panties and wanted so badly to take them off and let the air from the room cool the heat that caused the pooling. Keefer's tongue traced paths of fire all over her throat, stopping only to torture her with sharp nips and delicious sucks to her oversensitive skin. The blonde groaned pathetically as Keefer's fingers worked with the same rhythm as her mouth, pulling as she sucked, pinching as she nipped. *And I thought she was shy!*

Keefer had never been so lost in her life. She was drowning in Sheridan. The smells, textures and tastes were driving her on with a force she hadn't thought she possessed. She slid one hand down and palmed Sheridan's rock-hard stomach, smiling into her neck at the small tremors she encountered under the soft, hot skin. Struck with an urge to taste what she was feeling, the brunette began sliding down the smaller woman's body.

Sheridan opened her eyes and managed to focus on her tormentor long enough to get the idea of what was to come. Her heart pounded in her throat; she was so turned on, she couldn't concentrate. This had never happened to her. She had *never* been so out of control with a woman before. Keefer was in total command of her body, making it tremble and jerk as her wonderful mouth blazed a trail down her left arm. She watched as Keefer crouched lower and gasped at how cold the room's air felt on her leg when the inspector's body raised off of it. *God, she's so hot...*The blonde writhed and made fists, not sure if touching Keefer would ruin the moment.

Keefer wanted to shout. She wanted to tell the world how delicious Sheridan tasted...how sexy her straining bicep felt under her tongue. She sucked at the spot and shivered at the strangled sound Sheridan made. *She's loving this as much as I am,* she thought confidently. Keefer wasn't at all worried about pleasing Sheridan. If anything, this was one thing she *knew* she was good at doing. *And watching hours of porno didn't hurt...*she mused briefly. She was positive that she would satisfy the sexy construction worker and she intended to prove that right then.

Sheridan sat upright and groaned as her fingers were enveloped in hot silk. *Un-fucking-believable!* It felt so much like being inside a woman that Sheridan made it a point to watch Keefer's mouth as she bathed her fingers, just to be sure she wasn't. The tall woman's breasts hung dangerously close to her crotch as she crouched over her body. Sheridan couldn't control her desire any longer and her hips lifted, brushing the stiff denim of her pants across Keefer's right nipple.

Keefer gasped and arched her back, totally aware of her exposed breasts and the sharp jolt that ran through one of them. She composed herself and lay completely down; her eyes squeezed shut at the sensation of her nipples pressing against Sheridan's jeans. The knowledge that one of her breasts was nestled between the blonde's legs made her sex burn with need. *Oh, my god...I want it again!* she thought in shock. She'd never been turned on while making love to Danni; she did had just done what she had to do and that was that. Now, however, she would have given anything to have Sheridan touch her between her legs. She hadn't done that yet, and

Keefer's center craved it. She blushed profusely at her needs and lifted up on an elbow to adjust her position.

The construction worker watched as Keefer hovered over her body. She opened her legs wide and invited the taller woman between them. Keefer accepted and they both whimpered when their breasts touched. "God, Keef...you are incredible," Sheridan breathed out in the midst of a groan.

"Me?" Keefer said with a stunned expression.

Sheridan watched as Keefer drank in what was exposed of her body with a hungry gaze. She swallowed hard as blue lasers pinned her right nipple in their sights. *Oh, Jesus...*Sheridan braced herself but couldn't have prepared herself for the feeling of Keefer's mouth surrounding her nipple.

"Have you looked at yourself in the mirror lately?" Keefer smirked into Sheridan's breast.

Touché, thought the blonde, whose lower half started a slow grind into Keefer's body.

The brunette closed her eyes and tried to concentrate on the nipple she was ravishing, but Sheridan's crotch was pressing into her stomach, driving her crazy. She looked up to meet unfocused green eyes staring into her own. A twinge of arousal shot through her groin and she hummed uncontrollably at the pleasurable sensations.

Sheridan whimpered and brought both of her hands to Keefer's head. "Shit, baby...yeah," she grunted as the taller woman nipped at her nipple.

Seeing Sheridan watching her, with her mouth lolling open and her tongue twitching out repeatedly to wet her lips, made Keefer incredibly wet. She felt powerful over this goddess, the woman she'd been fantasizing about since the moment they'd met. She had the power to reduce this cocky woman to the trembling pile of mush that she was at the moment, and they both still had their clothes on. The thought thrilled the inspector. She switched breasts, but not before dragging her tongue through the salty, damp space between them. Sheridan's hips rose and fell at a steady pace—one Keefer found intoxicating. She was reveling in her abilities and sucked the new nipple like a starving baby.

"You're killing me, Keef!" Sheridan whined pathetically, pulling the dark head closer to her body.

Keefer looked up into wild green eyes. The same feeling of electricity that she'd first felt at the club when she had encountered Sheridan's fire traveled through her bloodstream, ending as a pounding between her legs.

"I need you so badly," Sheridan said with a dry throat. She released Keefer's head and peeled the taller woman's hand from around her forearm.

Keefer allowed her hand to be led between them. Sheridan's knuckles brushed over one of her nipples and she grunted out loud, glancing up nervously to find the construction worker's nostrils flared, her eyes sparkling. "Yeah, I love your sexy sounds," she whispered.

Keefer let her hand rest on the waistband of Sheridan's jeans. She wasn't afraid to go any further, but she had to calm her racing heart before she did. She feared a dead faint when she first touched the blonde's wetness. She had done so numerous times in her dreams and she now thought the real thing might kill her.

Keefer sat up on her heels between Sheridan's legs and blushed as she tried to cover her breasts.

"They're beautiful, just like you."

Keefer blushed harder and looked away.

"It's okay," Sheridan said as she leaned forward and gently pulled the material of the torn shirt over each breast before lying back against the couch.

Keefer found that gesture so endearing. The look on Sheridan's face was close to worship when she looked at her breasts. *She really likes them...a lot. She always has. She's so good to me...*Keefer warred briefly with herself before reaching up and moving the material to the sides, baring first one and then the other breast for Sheridan's pleasure. She dipped her head lower, still very embarrassed by being on display, but seeing the look on Sheridan's face was worth the exposure. "You really like them, don't you?" Keefer asked quietly.

Sheridan nodded and forced herself to look into Keefer's eyes.

The brunette smiled, still embarrassed, but not as much as she thought she'd be. "Yours are perfect," she said while reaching forward to touch them.

Sheridan groaned. This was far better than she thought it would be. Keefer was torturing her, but she loved every damned second of it.

"They fit perfectly in my hands, too. See?" Keefer demonstrated by covering each one of them with her whole hand. After lingering there for a moment, she slid her hands lower, with a firm touch and splayed both hands on Sheridan's abdomen. "You're so soft...and hard at the same time." *Nothing like Danni, but you wouldn't know that, would you...you never did anything like this with her.*

Sheridan had had about all she could take and she lifted both hands and palmed Keefer's breasts. The brunette breathed out in a rush and leaned forward into the touch. She couldn't ever remember a time when sex felt this good, this hot. She wanted to please Sheridan in the worst way, but she loathed it to be over. Danni just came and rolled over; she wanted this to last forever with Sheridan.

"What are you thinking, Keef?"

"I want to touch you forever."

Sheridan smiled brightly. "No one's stopping you."

Keefer leaned even further down until their lips touched. The kiss that followed was hungry and sensual at the same time. Each one tried to capture the other's tongue, fighting and then pulling back, forcing the other to come and get it.

Sheridan arched her back when fingers toyed with her fly. She captured Keefer's nipples between her fingers and pleasured them, causing those long fingers to suddenly dig into her skin.

Keefer tried desperately to concentrate on opening Sheridan's pants. Her nipples felt so good, and she felt it all the way between her legs. She was finally able to pop open the button and then lowered the zipper. Sheridan groaned into her mouth and it gave her goose bumps. If those insistent fingers didn't stop touching her breasts, she was afraid she'd lose it again.

Sheridan felt Keefer stiffen and slipped her hands around the back of the tall woman's body. The last thing she wanted was for the inspector to stop what she was doing. She was almost there. Keefer breathed a sigh of relief across Sheridan's face and began tugging at the open jeans. The blonde lifted her hips and Keefer had to break the kiss to sit back and watch as the denim was pulled away.

Sheridan took the opportunity to get rid of her shirt. Once she was completely unclothed, Keefer crawled back between her legs. Sheridan wasn't the least bit modest and couldn't wait to be naked. The effect her body had on Keefer wasn't planned, though, and she found it hard to control herself at the look of sheer starvation in those piercing blue eyes.

*Oh...my...god...*Keefer was speechless. Sheridan was naked, gloriously naked, waiting for her. "You are stunning," she said in awe.

Sheridan suddenly felt embarrassed and felt a small blush creeping up on her.

"My god."

"Take off your shirt, Keef. Please."

Keefer obeyed immediately. There was hardly anything left to take off anyway.

"Gorgeous," Sheridan breathed in admiration. "Come here, I want to feel you."

Keefer unfolded her legs and lay down on top of Sheridan. The feeling was indescribable and when the brunette couldn't stifle a moan, Sheridan replied in kind. Keefer's hungry lips attached themselves to the arched neck below her. Her hands were constantly in motion, touching every place she could reach. Thighs, arms, chest, belly, the sides of

Sheridan's ass...it all felt incredible. Sheridan bucked up into her as she brushed her nails over a particularly sensitive spot and Keefer gasped at the wetness she felt on her skin.

"Keef, you have to touch me."

The tone of desperation in Sheridan's voice told Keefer that playtime was over. She sat up completely and backed up, confusing Sheridan for a second, but when she pulled the blonde's ankles, forcing her to lie flat on her back, Sheridan whimpered in anticipation.

Keefer's mouth watered at the sight. She drank in the smooth, tense body before her, stopping briefly to admire the inviting tuft of blonde hair, begging for her touch. She had the sudden need to rub her face in the seemingly soft curly hairs but held back. The desire to touch the beautiful body overrode that need and she laid both her hands on Sheridan's calves, sliding them up slowly, but with determination.

"I'm gonna die," Sheridan breathed out through her teeth, tensing her legs as the teasing hands reached her upper thighs.

"You don't know how long I've wanted to do that."

"What else have you wanted to do?" the blonde groaned.

"I want to..." Keefer began blushing, but found the courage to continue, "I want to lick your abs."

"Go with it," Sheridan grunted and steeled herself for the certain onslaught of sensations to follow.

Keefer slid down until she was lying on her stomach, her lips hovering over Sheridan's navel, and looked into hooded green eyes. She lowered her head slowly until her lips touched the damp skin, then flattened her tongue as she took a long leisurely swipe.

"Ohh...too good," Sheridan moaned.

The twitching muscles under her tongue gave Keefer even more confidence and she slipped her tongue lower until the tip touched curly hair. Her mouth watered so dramatically she had to snap it shut for fear of drooling all over Sheridan's crotch. *What the hell was that?* she puzzled as she swallowed. Sex had always been mechanical, but this was fueled by an insistent desire, an intense craving to please Sheridan. Keefer was also driven by her need to learn every inch of the blonde's skin. Sheridan spread her legs and her strong scent hit Keefer like a brick. She glanced down at Sheridan's sex and groaned loudly, not even bothering to blush at her outburst. *Even that is gorgeous.*

"Please, Keefer...do something..." Sheridan pleaded miserably, her hands finding the brunette's shoulders and pressing her closer to her burning need.

Keefer nodded absently as she brought up her right hand to touch what she had been loving with her eyes. She rested the heel of her hand on

Sheridan's pubic bone and glanced up at the construction worker's face. Her expression looked almost pained, and the inspector slid her hand down until her fingers were buried in slick heat.

"Yes...God, yes..." Sheridan nearly shouted with relief, her hips thrusting hard, pressing herself desperately into Keefer's hand.

Keefer's heart pounded in her throat as she let her fingers explore every nook and fold of Sheridan's inflamed sex. The scent was making her mouth water again. She had never felt the need so strongly to make love; it was overwhelming. She licked her lips and inhaled long and deep. "So wet..." she muttered when her fingers made audible sounds as they slid through the soft hot place. *I need to taste it.*

"Fuck!" Sheridan was practically airborne as Keefer suddenly slid her stiff tongue up through her lips. The blonde's hips rose high and she gripped Keefer's head like a vise, silently begging her not to stop.

"Mmm..." Keefer hummed to herself, not realizing she did so out loud. Sheridan tasted so delicious—she couldn't get enough. She worked her tongue up and down, back and forth, first in a point, then flat. She slid it all the way down and dipped inside with the tip, then back up again, resting on the hard, throbbing bud that was begging for attention.

"Oh, baby...I'm not gonna last long..." Sheridan threatened through clenched teeth.

Keefer's mouth was wide open as she responded. She wound up making an unintelligible sound in the back of her throat as she pressed her tongue insistently against the desired location.

"Please...do it..." Sheridan choked out. Keefer read that plea like a cue card and promptly wrapped her lips around the blonde's straining clit.

"Oh, fuck!"

Sheridan's knees came up and clenched Keefer's head, her fingers digging painfully into the brunette's scalp.

Oh, yes...this is heaven...so good...so delicious...yes... Keefer was panting from her own excitement as she sucked at Sheridan's sex. The feeling of being enclosed by the strong limbs that surrounded her made her own clit throb. *Please come for me, Sher...*

Oh God...that's so...shit...

Keefer added her tongue to the mix and began flitting it across the tip of Sheridan's clit.

"Oh yeah...oh yeah..." Sheridan was there. The constant suction with the added feel of Keefer's tongue drove her hard and fast over the edge.

Yeah, Sher...that's it...

The blonde's stomach clenched and she sat halfway up, exhaling a loud groan. Her thighs trembled around Keefer's head and her fingers twitched in her hair. The brunette never stopped what she was doing.

Sheridan fell back down to the floor as her hips bucked with a life of their own. "God, Keef!" she whimpered.

Keefer slowed down and waited until Sheridan started pushing her away before stopping entirely. The strong, quivering thighs slid down over her shoulders, and her arms fell limply at her sides. Keefer could hear Sheridan's heavy, erratic panting and feel her uncontrollable twitching and a sly smile spread across her face.

Sheridan glanced down at the expression on Keefer's glistening face as it lay on her lower belly, and a slow smile spread across her face.

"Good?" Keefer asked as she ran her fingers lightly up and down Sheridan's still-trembling torso.

The blonde shivered. "Outrageous. Fantastic. Super spectacular."

"Really?"

"God, woman...get up here and let me hold you."

Chapter 19

Sheridan wrapped her strong arms around Keefer's back and rolled them over until she was on top. The look of surprise on Keefer's face caused a smile to spread slowly across her lips. "You're so beautiful," she said before leaning down and capturing the swollen lips.

Keefer felt glorious. Her mind kept replaying the moment when Sheridan's body curled around her head and her name sputtered from her lips. Right now, even as her mouth was being thoroughly devoured, her scalp still tingled where the construction worker's fingers had reflexively dug into it as she climaxed. Her nose still smarted from when it was crushed into Sheridan's pubic bone as the blonde's thighs locked around her head. She couldn't take it anymore. The excitement at what she had just done made it hard to breathe and she pulled away from the kiss with a gasp.

"What happened? What's wrong?" Sheridan asked worriedly.

Keefer exploded up from underneath her and stood in the middle of the room, mindless of her topless condition. "I feel so incredible!"

Sheridan laughed at Keefer's joy. "I gotta agree with ya there, Keef, you feel incredible." She hoisted herself up onto the couch.

"No, I mean it! I feel so...so...proud!"

Fifi came bounding into the room, wanting to join her mommy in her happiness.

Sheridan still chuckled at Keefer's exuberance. "I know what you mean." She smiled warmly, knowingly. "Come back here and let me make you feel even better," she proposed with a devious twinkle in her eyes.

Keefer scrambled to the couch and pushed Sheridan back into the cushions, kissing her senseless. "Thank you for that."

"I have no idea what you're thanking me for, but with a reaction like that...mmm...any time. Any time," Sheridan smirked. She gently pushed Keefer's head against her shoulder and held her securely.

"Mmm. This feels good," the brunette practically purred.

"Yeah," Sheridan agreed with a blissful smile. She usually wasn't one for cuddling, but she felt the urge to do so now.

Keefer inhaled deeply in preparation to release a heavy sigh of contentment, but Sheridan's scent filled her senses and the exhale came out as a long moan.

The blonde raised an eyebrow at the sound. "Mmm. What was that all about? Not that I minded much, but if you keep making sounds like that, there's no telling what I may do," she joked as she stroked Keefer's long black hair.

"Oh, God...I made that noise?" Keefer buried her face in the construction worker's chest, which only made matters worse. She groaned again as a nipple wound up at her lips.

"Keefer..." Sheridan warned.

"I can't help it." The inspector blushed profusely and stared at the nipple.

"Do you have any idea what those sounds do to me? Hmm?" Sheridan's nails skittered up the middle of the taller woman's back.

Keefer shivered hard. *Should that have turned me on as much as it did?* she wondered while her mouth watered more and more as she looked at Sheridan's nipple.

"Keef?" The blonde shrugged her shoulder, jostling the taller woman. "Whoa!"

Keefer couldn't control herself, the shrug put Sheridan's nipple within tongue's reach and she took advantage of the situation.

Sheridan leaned back and allowed Keefer ample room to adjust her long body. It was apparent that the brunette wasn't just tasting, she had one hand holding the breast she was enjoying and the other wrapped around the neglected one. Keefer uncurled her legs and moved so she was straddling Sheridan's thighs.

Green eyes watched with great interest as the brunette's cheek and jaw muscles moved and flexed. She let her fingers slide repeatedly through the long, soft black locks that fell all around Keefer's face. This was heaven.

Blue eyes lifted and Keefer stifled a whimper when she saw Sheridan watching her. Their eyes met and the look that passed between them was one Keefer had never experienced. She liked it...a lot. It made her heart pound fast and a strange twisty feeling overwhelm her gut. She didn't think too long about it as Sheridan's fingers wound their way back up to the top of her head again. Keefer couldn't remember a time when she'd felt this wonderful.

Sheridan groaned quietly but gratefully as Keefer worked her way across her chest. Of all the things she could think of, this was not how she'd seen this day turning out. Keefer had surprised her; she wasn't the prude she had thought she'd be. In fact, the way she was using her tongue at that very minute was causing feelings in the blonde that she hadn't ever felt before. Keefer was apparently very confident in her ability to give pleasure, something Sheridan wished she could thank Danni for. *Fuck it, I will thank that bitch next time I see her,* she thought with a smirk—but that smirk was short lived. Keefer was sliding lower.

I love this! She's letting me do anything I want! The brunette's breath was coming in excited spurts as she traced the indentation between Sheridan's prominent abs with her tongue. She kept her eyes open and marveled at the way those muscles twitched and rolled under her exploring mouth. The blonde shuddered, driving Keefer on, feeding her curiosity to explore further.

Sheridan wound her fingers in the hair behind Keefer's neck and held on. Nobody had ever taken the time to pleasure her so thoroughly; she had never given them a chance. Now, at that moment, she wondered why. Her whole body responded to Keefer's tongue as it slid confidently down her stomach. "Arr," she growled when the wet muscle teased the crease where her thigh met her body. Her pelvis jerked uncontrollably.

Keefer was far beyond excited by Sheridan's reactions. She was so aroused, she felt drunk. The taste of the construction worker's skin and the smell of her sex drove her on, making her extremely intent on giving Sheridan pleasure. The reactions in the muscular body gave her a very new, intense sense of accomplishment. Each time Sheridan groaned, Keefer's heart sped up; each time her body jerked and spasmed, Keefer's sex responded in kind. She felt totally empowered and reveled in it.

Sheridan squirmed and grunted under the onslaught. Keefer's lips nibbled all her sensitive spots. The torturous mouth stopped every so often to nip and suck in areas that caused her to whimper. Nobody had ever made her feel so thoroughly cared for; no one had shown the need to do so. Sheridan felt the uncontrollable urge to cry. She wanted to pull the brunette up and hold her, squeezing her until the feeling passed. It startled her that she wanted to hug Keefer right in the middle of the most wonderful sensations she had ever felt.

The inspector's mouth hovered over Sheridan's center, her hot breath blowing puffs of electricity on her aroused flesh. She contemplated whether to touch or taste and before she had decided, Sheridan was lifting her up off of her knees.

"I want to touch you, Keef. Let me touch you."

Keefer allowed herself to be rearranged on top of Sheridan's lap. She didn't understand. Sheridan's face was flushed with need, her eyes screamed in hunger and yet, she'd made her stop. "Did I do something wrong?" she asked nervously.

"Fuck no! I just need to feel you, too. Please, let me touch you."

Keefer looked deeply into pleading green eyes. It didn't take long for her to figure out exactly what Sheridan was asking of her. "Um, here?"

"We could go in the bedroom, if you want, I don't care. I want to feel you," the blonde said, even as her hands touched every part of Keefer that they could.

Keefer slid away from Sheridan and stood up between her legs. She looked like she might run away at first and Sheridan's heart jumped into her throat, but then, Keefer took blonde's hands and placed them on the waistband of her jeans.

Sheridan's nostrils flared at the vision of trust standing in front of her. She leaned forward and rested her cheek on Keefer's stomach as she lowered the zipper of her fly. "Thank you," she whispered before placing a sweet kiss on the skin by her lips.

Keefer drew in a ragged breath, she was petrified and she didn't know why. Her eyes closed tightly and she tried to remind herself that this is what she'd wanted all along, this is what she'd been dreaming, fantasizing and craving.

"It's all right...it's just me, Keef."

The soothing whisper relaxed the taller woman enough for her to open her eyes. As she glanced down at the tousled blonde hair at her belly, a tiny smile formed on her lips. When did she get on her knees? she wondered. Oh God, she's on her knees at my feet? No one had ever treated Keefer like Sheridan was; it made her feel special and wanted.

"You smell so good." Sheridan breathed the words across Keefer's belly, causing her to shiver.

Keefer wanted nothing more than to have Sheridan make love to her, but there was still that part of her that freaked out over everything. Her mind raced with what ifs as her body reacted all on its own to Sheridan's hot breath. She stiffened slightly as strong, knowing hands began sliding her jeans down slowly.

The blonde sensed Keefer's nervousness and did everything in her power, power she didn't know she possessed, to calm her.

Keefer smiled nervously when green eyes met hers. "I'm okay," she lied.

Sheridan led Keefer to the couch and gestured for her to lie down. Once she did, the blonde lay down next to her and held her with one arm as the other pushed Keefer's pants and panties down lower. "Is it all right?" she asked, forcing herself not to look down at Keefer's exposed sex.

Keefer could only nod. She felt as if she had become mute. The blood was rushing through her veins so fast she could hear it. The pounding in her ears was deafening. She wanted Sheridan to touch her so badly.

Green eyes slowly lowered in tandem with the blonde's body as she moved to slide off Keefer's clothes. *Jesus, she's beautiful!* was Sheridan's only thought.

Why is she staring at it? Oh God, I'm gonna faint...

"You're so fucking gorgeous, Keefer," Sheridan stated with feeling.

Keefer let go of the breath she was holding and her whole body seemed to relax a notch.

"Oh...I can't wait to touch every single beautiful inch of you," the blonde whispered in awe.

Keefer bit her lip when Sheridan's hands started to wander up her legs, starting at the ankles. The roughened skin of her hands felt arousingly scratchy as they slid up her soft thighs.

"You're so soft...everywhere I touch..." Sheridan observed out loud.

Keefer didn't know what to do with her hands; they were dying to touch the blonde. Tentatively, she draped them on Sheridan's shoulders.

"You can touch me, too, if you want. Actually, I'd like that."

Keefer blushed at being so transparent, and at being naked in the middle of the day. That embarrassment faded fast, though, as Sheridan's hands palmed both of her breasts at once. "Oh!" she gasped as the hard calluses rubbed roughly against her nipples.

"Mmm, you like that, huh?" Sheridan asked with a sexy grin.

Keefer blushed again but nodded.

Sheridan dipped her head down and traced Keefer's lips with her tongue until she squirmed.

"That tickles!" she giggled breathlessly.

The sound was music to the blonde's ears. She enveloped the sexy bottom lip with her mouth and sucked it until blue eyes rolled shut and a stifled whimper vibrated in Keefer's throat. The inspector's hands wandered lower as if they had a mind of their own and began caressing Sheridan's backside, causing the shorter woman to groan in pleasure. "That feels so good, baby," she mumbled in between sucking on the brunette's already swollen lips.

Keefer ate Sheridan's excitement up and touched her with more purpose. She reached as low as her hands could go and cupped the blonde's cheeks, squeezing them in time to the suction on her mouth.

215

Sheridan's hand traveled even further down until she was stroking Keefer's lower belly. Feeling the muscles tighten and flex under her fingers delighted her. She'd never paid that much attention to another woman's reactions and she promised herself to do so from then on. It was incredible. The feelings, the sounds, the textures...it was like Sheridan was learning all over again.

Keefer was aware of the strong fingers sliding even lower. She was so turned on and ready. The things Sheridan was doing with her mouth drove her crazy; she could feel the sensations in her sex and it was hard keeping her body from wrapping itself around the blonde and quenching her fire. Her body twisted and moved on its own, reactions that surprised her— she'd never done that before. *God!* Sheridan's fingers were killing her. By the time they reached her pubic hair, she was panting with need.

Sheridan ruffled through thick, dark curls teasingly with two fingers, not wanting to force Keefer's legs open, yet dying to proceed lower. She could tell Keefer was very nervous and she wanted to make this right. She continued to kiss the brunette hungrily and just a little bit roughly, in an attempt to distract her from thinking. It worked. Long fingers dug into her thighs and Keefer moaned quietly. She was breathing so hard that the blonde knew she was doing the right thing. She let her fingertips slide lower...and lower...until they were suddenly surrounded by soaking-wet, hot flesh.

The exquisite groan Sheridan let loose into Keefer's mouth made the brunette's scalp tingle with excitement. The feeling of those fingers touching her made her gasp loudly. She sucked the construction worker's tongue into her mouth as her legs reflexively opened wider, welcoming more of Sheridan's hand between them.

The feeling was delirious. Sure, there were plenty of times Sheridan's fingers had been swallowed up in wetness, but between knowing it was Keefer's sex and Keefer's copious arousal...Sheridan could do no more than release a shaky sigh of pleasure as her fingers sat motionless, surrounded in the divine feeling.

Both of Keefer's hands suddenly moved from Sheridan's thighs to her forearm, holding it still. If those fingers were to start moving, she knew she would lose all control and that would be horrible. She had waited so long for this moment, she wanted to make it last.

The construction worker got the message and she pulled away from the kiss breathlessly, resting her face between Keefer's neck and shoulder. "You let me know when, baby," she whispered.

Keefer merely nodded, overwhelmed with sensation after Sheridan's breath tickled her skin. She gave the muscular arm a good squeeze as a reminder before she brought her hands to the blonde's waist. She wasn't going to let the opportunity pass to touch Sheridan.

"God, Keef, you're so wet," the construction worker groaned into the brunette's ear, concentrating on the feeling surrounding her fingers.

"Your fault," Keefer whispered into Sheridan's hair, flattening her hands and sliding them up the blonde's torso.

"Um." Sheridan squirmed until those large hands settled on her breasts. Her back arched, forcing her begging nipples firmly into Keefer's palms.

Keefer circled her hands, something she had just found that she liked herself, hoping that Sheridan would, too. She was very pleased when the blonde moaned.

"Now?" Sheridan questioned while nibbling at Keefer's ear.

"I don't know," Keefer responded weakly as a hot tongue traced the vein on the side of her neck. She wrapped one arm around Sheridan's neck and slid the other down to the top of the blonde's pubic mound.

"Oh yeah..." Sheridan growled in anticipation. "Go ahead," she urged.

Keefer inched her fingers lower and smirked a little when Sheridan gasped. She slid her fingers around until they were soaking wet, her own sex twitching.

"Now?" Sheridan groaned pathetically. Her hand was about to rebel.

Keefer nodded, burying her face into Sheridan's shoulder, sucking a bit of skin into her mouth before wandering to her throat.

The blonde's insides screamed in relief when her fingers began to move. She loved the shuddering breath Keefer exhaled and the way her thighs trembled from her touch. Keefer was, in no doubt, marking her neck as she sucked hungrily, but that made no difference to Sheridan. She'd wanted this from the moment they'd laid eyes on each other. It had been haunting her every hour and, now, she was doing it.

Keefer's world was spinning; she tried to stay still, not wanting to look desperate but dying with need. Sheridan's fingers knew exactly what she liked. They touched her sex expertly, in all the right places at all the right times. It felt so delicious—she couldn't control herself. "Oh, God, yes..." she groaned as two fingers circled her world. Her hips jerked into the touch.

"Baby...that's it..." Sheridan coaxed the brunette to speak her pleasure. She never knew how it turned her on until she heard Keefer's husky, sexy rasp.

Keefer was dangling at the edge of bliss, but something was missing. She needed something else and she knew what. She unwrapped the arm from around Sheridan's neck and turned her head to face her. "I want to feel you...all of you," she bit out, nervously and quietly as the blonde's fingers never stopped moving. She yanked on Sheridan's shoulder until the construction worker comprehended.

Sheridan adjusted herself until she lay fully on top of the brunette; Keefer's legs fell open, accommodating her body. "Ohh..." she sighed happily when their sweaty hot skin met in all the right places. Keefer wrapped her arms immediately around her back, but Sheridan needed her elsewhere. She pulled on Keefer's arm until she moved it and brought it between their bodies. "You gotta touch me."

"I can't think," Keefer whimpered.

"That's okay." Sheridan placed Keefer's hand where she wanted it and moved her own body as she continued to circle her other hand between Keefer's legs.

The inspector groaned wordlessly and sought out Sheridan's mouth. The blonde caught a fleeting glimpse of the expression on Keefer's face before her mouth was covered in a sloppy, unforgiving kiss. Black eyebrows were furrowed in what would otherwise look like deep concentration, but Sheridan knew different. She'd watched many women come and she knew this was a prelude to bliss.

Keefer tried to stop the feelings from surging out of control but failed. The heavy weight of Sheridan's body blew new life into the fires already raging out of control in her body. One of her legs instinctively wrapped around Sheridan's lower back and her body twitched with impending release.

Sheridan would have given anything to see those beautiful blue eyes at that moment, but she settled on the feel of the long body wrapping around hers. Her own release was imminent; she was spiraling quickly toward climax from just the notion that this was Keefer she was pleasuring. The long fingers trapped between her legs didn't hurt matters much and she thrust her sex against them harder and faster as Keefer began to whimper into her mouth.

Keefer's free hand groped blindly for Sheridan, finally grabbing her strong, hard shoulder, her fingertips digging in painfully hard. Her body reacted on its own and she couldn't stop any of it. Her pelvis jerked and her body stiffened as the leg that was wrapped around Sheridan's back pulled the blonde impossibly close.

Sheridan groaned loudly into the crazy kiss, trapping Keefer's top lip between her teeth and trying desperately not to draw blood as her body succumbed to the pleasures.

Keefer's long body trembled briefly before being overcome by large, violent shudders. Her hips spasmed so hard, she lifted them both off of the couch.

Sheridan arched dramatically, riding the long fingers hard and fast. Her head fell back and she groaned loudly. "Ohh, Keefer...shit, yeah!" Keefer's unoccupied mouth fell open and a long erotic groan burst forth, causing Sheridan to shiver with renewed vigor. Without thinking, she suddenly thrust her fingers inside of Keefer.

"Sheridan!" Keefer's body spasmed hard and she sat halfway up and snatched her arm out from between their bodies to hold on with both hands. *Oh, my g—I can't...Ohh...God, this is good...*

Sheridan held Keefer tightly with one arm as the brunette shuddered and quaked through the powerful orgasm. She didn't know why she'd done it, but she was glad she did as she felt the strong muscles pulsating around her fingers. "Keef, you feel so fucking good...oh, yeah, baby...yeah..."

Keefer finally fell back down onto the couch, her chest heaving and her body twitching. Her breath was coming in audible huffs and Sheridan couldn't think of a more beautiful sight. Her face and chest were glistening with sweat, both flushed deep red, and both more gorgeous than the last time she saw them. Sheridan withdrew her fingers slowly, savoring every twitch of the long body beneath her.

Keefer was trying with every thing in her being not to get up and run away from Sheridan's open gaze. While taking deep, calming breaths, she heard an odd sound and peeked open her eyes to find Sheridan sucking her fingers clean. "Oh, my god..." she breathed and immediately covered her embarrassed face with her hands. That wasn't a smart thing to do, as the scent of Sheridan's sex assaulted her senses. She looked at her hands and then past them at the very pleased expression on the blonde's face. Blue eyes narrowed playfully before she opened her lips and slid her fingers between them. The taste was better than before and she devoured it.

"Oh, Jesus, Keef! That's too damned hot!"

"Uh-huh," she agreed. "You taste so good," she said around her fingers.

"Oh, baby, you too." Sheridan wiggled her eyebrows. "Maybe I could..."

"Are you trying to kill me? Have you any idea how hard I'm trying to not run away and hide under the bed right now?"

"I'm sorry, Keefer," Sheridan said pitifully and lay her body back down to cover the brunette's exposed one. "Would you want me to get a blanket or something?" she asked.

Keefer smiled warmly. "That's okay. I'm really trying to change."

"You don't have to do that all in one day," Sheridan reassured, kissing Keefer's ear.

"I want to...for you."

Sheridan got a funny feeling in the pit of her stomach. *What the hell was that?* Keefer was putting too much trust in her and she was afraid she wasn't worth it. "I don't deserve your trust, Keefer."

"You've done nothing but earn it." Keefer tickled her fingers up and down the wide strong back.

"Thank you." *I think.* Sheridan felt awkward. This was where she usually left. *Now what?*

"You know, I don't think I've ever felt so good."

And I've never felt so confused. Sheridan frowned. It felt so good to lie there and hold Keefer, something she'd never done in the past, and she didn't know what to do next.

"Sher?" Keefer asked nervously.

"Hmm?"

"Are you okay?"

"Perfect," she answered believably.

"Me too."

"Hey, I gotta pee," Sheridan said as she got up from the comfortable circle of Keefer's embrace. The minute she sat up, she felt cold and it puzzled her.

"Okay," Keefer said sadly. The second Sheridan was gone from the room, Keefer began to put her clothes back on. She felt suddenly naked without Sheridan there. *What's going on here? I've never felt like this in my life. Then again, all I had was Danni...yuck, why does she keep haunting me?* The brunette tried to get her feelings together before Sheridan came back from the bathroom. *Why do I feel like this? My stomach is all tied up in knots and she's only been gone a second.*

She didn't have time to analyze it as Sheridan's naked form wandered back into the room. She looked troubled. "Hey, what's wrong?" Keefer asked as the blonde began dressing.

"I don't know. I'm not sure what to do now."

"What do you usually do?"

"Make up some excuse and leave," Sheridan said while putting on her socks, not looking at Keefer.

"Well...do you want to leave?" Keefer asked as her stomach flipped sickeningly.

Sheridan stopped dressing and studied the brunette's fearful face. "No," she admitted with frustration.

Keefer blew out a relieved breath, "Then don't. Stay with me."

"Okay." Sheridan nodded, already feeling better, seeing Keefer smile.

"Are you hungry?" Keefer asked as she hesitantly sat next to the blonde.

"Yeah, you?" Sheridan instinctively reached out and wrapped an arm around Keefer, feeling infinitely better for it.

"Yeah, but I'd rather you just hold me for a while."

"You got it."

Two sighs of relief filled the room as four arms wrapped securely around two needy bodies.

"God, Sheridan, I've never felt like that in my life," Keefer said as she buried herself in the blonde's neck. "You made me feel incredible."

"You *are* incredible."

Keefer blushed. "You, too. This feels good, too."

"It does, doesn't it." Sheridan decided not to think about it. It felt too good to pick apart. There would be time to think later. All that mattered was that Keefer was in her arms.

"Thank you," Keefer sighed.

"For what?"

"For making me feel."

Sheridan held her tighter. She didn't know what to say. "You're welcome." Her stomach felt funny again and she willed the feeling away.

TJ Vertigo

Chapter 20

Keefer hummed as she made her way around the kitchen; she was in a great mood as she cooked. Sheridan had left with the promise of returning for dinner. The two had shared some cookies earlier, but that wasn't enough after all the energy they had both expended, so Keefer suggested dinner together. Sheridan was all for it, but needed to get home to tend to her babies. It was hard for them to tear away from each other's lips when the blonde finally left, yet another moment in time for the tall woman to replay in her head as she cooked.

Keefer had never known such a good feeling as when she thought about time spent with Sheridan—especially when they kissed. She could kiss her for days. The construction worker had a way with her lips that curled Keefer's toes. When she thought about it, though she tried not to, she and Danni had hardly ever kissed. Keefer hadn't felt the urge. She certainly felt the urge to kiss Sheridan; she hardly wanted to do anything else when in her presence. She knew, after their first kiss in the club, that she wanted to do just that forever. She blushed as she thought about how bold a move that was, but in the end, she couldn't have asked for a better outcome.

There were things that worried her, too. Things she'd rather not linger on, like, "Will Sheridan be going out tonight?" and "Will she be with someone else?" "Was this a one-time thing for the blonde?"

Will I ever get to be with her again...like that? Keefer thought for a moment. *What exactly was that, anyway? It wasn't just sex. I know what sex is like. What we did was more, it was incredible, it was...intense.* Keefer dumped the pasta into the strainer as she pondered that.

With Danni, sex wasn't nearly as fulfilling; it had been a chore, if anything. The redhead just did what she wanted and Keefer struggled through the whole thing for a forced, unpleasant orgasm. With Sheridan, though...*Oh, with Sheridan...*Her cheeks flushed deeply with the memory of a myriad of sensations. Everywhere she'd touched was an erogenous zone. Everything she did had a definite reaction, a good reaction from Keefer's body.

Keefer poured the spaghetti back into the pot and started to season the sauce. *The way she felt under my fingers...Danni was never as receptive and hardly as patient, either. Then again, I couldn't have cared less what her stomach muscles were doing...or what they tasted like.* Keefer cleared her throat, noticing that Fifi was staring at her, head cocked as if she were reading her mind. "What? You'll get your meatballs; just wait until Sheridan gets back. I'm sure she'll see to it."

Fifi's tail swept the floor at the sound of the blonde's name. She was the one who made Mommy so happy. Fifi was smart, she could tell the difference in her mommy. The good-smelling blonde woman made her smile and laugh and Mommy acted in a way she never had as long as Fifi could remember. *Wait a minute---did she say meatballs?*

Sheridan let the hot water beat on the back of her neck. It felt great. Everything felt great...except for a little part of her that felt confused. It gave her the impression that something big was going on, it was as if she were anticipating something monumental, but she couldn't quite put her finger on it. Every time she tried, it slipped away and she forgot about it until it popped up again. It presented itself in the form of a persistent tugging in her stomach. She originally thought she might be getting sick, but she couldn't be. She was starving and so looking forward to dinner. With Keefer. *There it is again.* Sheridan puzzled over it while she dried off, but just like it appeared it was gone and she shrugged it off.

The blonde smiled as she relived some of the day's moments. Never before had she felt the insistent desire to simply kiss another woman. Her encounters were usually brief and often anonymous, she'd never had the desire to kiss the women. Once in a while, yes, but not like she desired Keefer's kisses. She almost *needed* to kiss the inspector. She couldn't tear herself away from her that afternoon, it felt so good to hold her in her arms and just neck like a couple of teenagers.

Sheridan looked all over the place, but still couldn't find her black bra. She threw her towel at Pharaoh, knowing he had something to do with its disappearance and decided against the bra. *Fuck it, she's seen my tits already.* At that thought, the blonde smirked, *Did she ever...I think they're her favorite part of my body.* Sheridan chuckled out loud. *And hers are mine, well, next to her pussy, that's pretty damned wonderful, too. Man, I can't believe how wet she got for me! Shit, she tasted so good. I can't wait until she lets me taste her.*

Sheridan wasn't aware of it yet, but she'd just given Keefer more deliberation with that one thought than she'd ever given a woman in her life. "Guys! I'm leaving now!" Sheridan called from the door. Two large dogs came running through the apartment to see her off. "Now, you guys be good, I don't know if I'm coming home tonight. I love you both," the blonde said as she kissed both dogs on the nose before leaving.

Keefer stirred the sauce once more before turning the flame all the way down. "Sheridan should be here any second, Feefs." She smiled with that realization and went to go look at herself in the mirror. "You look good, Keef," she told her reflection, smiling even wider. The doorbell rang and she darted into the living room to answer it.

"Hey," the blonde smiled.

Sheridan was leaning against the doorframe in such a way that it made Keefer's heart speed up. "You look good," she said coolly, despite her sudden need for air.

"You look beautiful," Sheridan answered and sauntered in.

Keefer couldn't keep her eyes from tracking the blonde's rear as it passed her by. *Jeez, I've turned into a perv,* she thought with a blush.

"What are you thinking about, Keef?" Sheridan teased the tall woman after spotting her red face.

"Nothing," she lied and sat down next to the blonde on the couch.

"Oh, I thought you were staring at my ass."

"Sheridan!" Keefer blurted in embarrassment, slapping the hard shoulder next to her.

"'S okay, babe, I was checking out yours, too, and it's so nice." She purred the last two words.

Keefer's eyes widened.

"Before you explode with mortification, can I have a kiss?" the construction worker asked as she already had her hand behind Keefer's head.

"Absolutely," the brunette replied a second before her lips were covered. The slight whimper slid right from her throat and she did nothing to hide it, it just felt so good kissing Sheridan.

The blonde growled a little into the kiss, her tongue slipping past the brunette's open lips, searching out its mate.

Every kiss felt the same, if not better to Keefer, all of them devastatingly delicious. She allowed her mouth to be invaded while she gathered her wits and then retaliated by thrusting her tongue past Sheridan's and forcing the blonde's tongue to retreat. She loved the throaty sound Sheridan emitted when she overtook a kiss. She planned on doing it often.

Fifi had had enough. There were meatballs in the kitchen, for goodness sake, and no one was giving her any. She jumped up on the couch and began walking around on top of the two women.

"I think someone's trying to tell us something," Sheridan whispered against Keefer's lips.

"Yeah," Keefer replied breathlessly. "Maybe we should eat," she added, reluctant to break the kiss, but starving just the same.

"I'm pretty hungry anyway," Sheridan agreed.

Once they stood up, Fifi was thrilled and did a circular happy dance around their legs.

"She only loves me for my meatballs."

"I doubt that, Keef." *There's plenty about you...* Sheridan bit off the end of that thought with a panicked expression.

Keefer didn't see Sheridan's face, since she was in front of her as they walked from room to room. She merely chuckled at the dog's dancing and thanked Sheridan for her vote of confidence.

"Are you all right? You've been pretty quiet." Keefer had been watching the blonde as they ate and something seemed to be bothering her.

"I'm okay, I think. Maybe I'm coming down with something, I just feel weird lately."

"I know what you mean. Maybe we gave it to each other."

"Yeah, well, get used to it. I don't plan on stopping myself from doing this." Sheridan leaned over the table and kissed Keefer on the lips. A rather chaste kiss, but it left them both smiling like goofs.

"I could get very used to that," Keefer said with her eyes still closed.

Sheridan had the urge to gather the brunette up in her arms and kiss her senseless like they do in the movies, full dipping scene and all. *What the hell is that all about?* she wondered, yet found herself in front of the grinning inspector without hesitation.

"I take it dinner is over?" Keefer said with a sexy smile.

"Totally," Sheridan replied as she straddled the brunette's legs and started what would be called a steamy kiss, had it been in the movies.

Keefer wrapped her arms around the blonde and inhaled deeply. Sheridan always smelled so good, no matter what she wore. Showered or not, her scent was always overwhelming. It made Keefer's insides turn to jelly and her knees feel weak. She was grateful they were sitting; her scent, combined with one hell of a kiss, was making her whole body weak.

Sheridan laced her fingers through the long black hair and kissed Keefer deeper. She couldn't control her need to do so and though it caused her great confusion, the urge to kiss was greater than the urge to think about it. She finally pulled away from the kiss and looked into the slightly unfocused blue eyes. Her belly flipped again and for a second she thought she might be ill—it was that strong—but it went away.

"What's wrong?" Keefer asked with concern.

"I don't know," Sheridan said quietly, confused.

"Did I do something?"

"I don't think so." Sheridan couldn't tear her gaze from Keefer's eyes. It was as if she were seeing all the way inside the brunette and it was fascinating to her.

"Can I do something?"

Sheridan glanced down at Keefer's lips as she spoke. "Yeah, just kiss me."

Keefer made herself comfortable on the couch and watched with amusement as Sheridan fed Fifi meatballs. The blonde had Fifi sitting, giving her paw, and doing all sorts of new things for the treats. "I told you she could learn, you just have to have proper motivation," Sheridan said with a smile.

"You're pretty proud of yourself, aren't you?" Keefer grinned as her dog sat and waited patiently for her meatball.

"Absolutely." Sheridan winked and made Fifi roll onto her back.

Keefer chuckled as the blonde wiped her hands off and held them up empty.

"No more, sweetie, all gone," she said with a surprised look, like she was also at a loss.

"Do you even know how cute you are?"

Sheridan smiled shyly as she sat down next to the brunette. "Please." She waved the compliment away, which was weird, since she prided herself on being a lady-killer, but from Keefer it was embarrassing.

"You are," Keefer said as she covered the blonde's hand with her own. She glanced at the clock nervously, still anticipating that Sheridan would leave for the club that evening.

"Hey, I never asked you, did you and Danni buy this house?" Sheridan asked after taking in the large living room.

"No, this was my gramma's house," the inspector answered with a sad smile.

"She left it to you?" the blonde asked.

"Yeah, I was raised in this house. It's almost exactly same now as it was then."

"So it was about time you redid the bathroom." The blonde's fingers idly stroked the hand within them.

"Well, Gramma had the kitchen redone about a year before she died. She did it for me, really, since by then I did all the cooking anyway."

"Your parents lived with her?" Sheridan mentally counted all the rooms and realized that they would have been a little cramped.

"No, I don't have parents," Keefer said with a little contempt.

"Oh." Sheridan felt like an ass for bringing it up and winced at her lack of tact.

"Hey, it's all right. Gramma raised me pretty good." Keefer closed her other hand around their already joined ones and squeezed. At the pained look on Sheridan's face she continued, "Don't feel bad, really."

"I lost my mother when I was really young. My dad became the center of my existence. I can't imagine living without him. I feel bad, Keefer, I can't help it."

"My mother was useless as a parent. I got the better end of the deal living here with Gramma. Sure, there was a generation gap, and I'm certain I have plenty of unidentified problems stemming from my unconventional upbringing, but still, I was better off this way."

"Unconventional?" Sheridan questioned, now idly stroking Keefer's entire arm. She didn't know why, but she needed to have the contact.

"Well, I didn't know it then, but after I had been let loose on the world, I found out my childhood wasn't typical. Gramma was a stern old broad, she was pretty strict and set in her ways. I didn't go out to movies much, play video games, go bowling, or anything else you probably did with your family. It was just me and her and I pretty much took care of her from as far back as I can remember."

Sheridan was intrigued. "Did you date any?"

Keefer barked out a laugh. "Date? Gramma had me terrified of boys! She said that men were the devil and I believed her until I turned sixteen."

"What happened then?" The blonde turned so that they were facing each other.

"I met a boy in school who didn't seem like the devil at all. Mind you, I knew nothing about sex, God forbid Gramma mentioned that word." Keefer sat in thought for a moment. "Anyway, I remember I had to lie to her about going on a date and, let me tell you, when he kissed me good night I thought I would die."

Sheridan chuckled, "He was that good, huh?"

"I don't know. All I do know is that I was mortified. He tried to touch my breast and I almost cried. I didn't know anything but what I learned in school. I had no friends to talk to; I was always busy with Gramma. I thought what he did was horrible." Keefer laughed at her reaction.

"Why did she want you to believe that about men?"

"I think it's because of how I was conceived. My mother was a junkie; she prostituted herself for a fix. I think I was an accident. No one ever told me for sure, but I think it was pretty obvious," Keefer said with a frown. She hadn't thought about this in years.

"I'm so sorry, baby. I wouldn't have asked..."

"It's okay. I really don't know why I'm telling you all of this..."

"You don't have to, I'm being too nosy. It's all right, Keef."

"It's just that I never felt like talking about it with anyone before." The brunette wondered why she felt so comfortable with the blonde.

"But didn't Danni—"

"I don't want to talk about Danni."

Sheridan searched Keefer's eyes and found sadness. "Why does it make you sad?"

"Because Danni used me." There was anger in those blue eyes.

"I would never use you," Sheridan declared with conviction. It surprised both of them.

"I have to believe you," Keefer said quietly. She had to believe or she knew somehow she wouldn't survive.

Sheridan needed to change the subject. She was way too uncomfortable with where this conversation was going. "Are you going to fix up any other rooms? I'd love to help you."

Keefer leaned back into the sofa and relaxed, grateful for the obvious change as well. "I'd love to do the whole damned thing eventually. Think you're up for that?"

"I'm up for anything you throw at me," Sheridan said with a cocky smile.

"I just bet you are," Keefer chuckled, looking at the clock again.

Keefer smiled, allowing the rough fingertips to soothe away some of her anxiety. Some of it—it was getting late. All thought processes stopped as those delicious lips descended on her again.

Sheridan couldn't explain it if she wanted. She needed to kiss Keefer; it felt so good. She felt it all over her body when their lips met and it made her breathless to feel the inspector in her arms.

The construction worker buried a hand in dark hair as her other hand held Keefer's face. *Her skin is so soft...it feels so good.* Soon, her face wasn't enough and the blonde's hand was working its way up under Keefer's shirt.

The brunette shivered in delight as the callused fingers slid across her stomach. It had never felt this good to be touched before. It was like Sheridan was getting all the same pleasure she was as she touched her. The blonde made the most wonderful sounds as she caressed her abdomen, reminding Keefer of exactly why Sheridan liked to hear her, too.

Keefer broke the kiss. "You make me feel so good when you touch me."

Sheridan knew how hard that was for Keefer and she smiled warmly. "And you feel so good to touch," she replied before burying her head in Keefer's neck.

Keefer knew *that* groan had come from her own mouth, since it was wide open. Sheridan's mouth was sucking on her neck and it felt like heaven.

Suddenly Sheridan's phone rang and she sat up to answer it.

Keefer caught her breath and watched as the blonde tried to do the same as she nodded on the phone. After Sheridan hung up, Keefer's anxiety returned. Sheridan sensed the change, leaned over, and placed a soft kiss on her lips.

"Are you going to the club?" Keefer asked quickly.

Green eyes watched the lips as they spoke and she was momentarily distracted. She didn't hear the fear in the question. "Yeah."

"Oh," Keefer sat up straight and pulled Sheridan's hand from her mouth.

"What's wrong? Do you wanna come with me?" Sheridan asked in confusion.

Keefer's eyes widened. "You'd want me there?"

"Well, yeah. Why wouldn't I?" Sheridan asked with a furrowed brow. "Do you know how to dance?"

Keefer leapt into Sheridan's arms and rained relieved kisses all over her face.

"Whoa!" the blonde laughed, attempting to kiss Keefer as many times as she was being kissed.

The brunette would rather not have gone to the club—she hated such places—but just knowing that Sheridan would welcome her there as a date made her giddy.

"So, are you coming?" Sheridan had to hold Keefer away with a hand on her head to ask the question.

"No, I hate that place. You go, have a good time," the taller woman said with enthusiasm.

"Uh, okay." The blonde looked entirely confused by the whole scene. "You're sure you don't wanna go?"

"No, really! Go," Keefer said as she pushed the construction worker toward the door.

"What the hell has gotten into you?" Sheridan laughed.

"I'm just happy. Dance for me, okay?"

"Now?" Sheridan teased.

Keefer's stomach twirled. *Would she really do that?* "I was only kidding," she admitted. "I meant at the club."

The blonde smirked at Keefer's blush. "I know and I will."

Chapter 21

The little blonde was hot. She was sandwiched between two attractive women, all three dancing sensuously to the slow, thumping bass beat. Hips pumped and pelvises gyrated. It was scene worthy of Sheridan Landers. All eyes that weren't closed were focused on the sexual performance.

One girl shimmied her way down the front of the muscular blonde while the other held her from behind, hips grinding in perfect synch with each other, simulating the most private of acts in a most public place. The girl in the front stood up and when Sheridan clasped her hands behind the girl's back, the girl leaned backwards, the strong hands of her dancing partner the only thing holding her up. Her breasts pointed skyward, daring Sheridan to look, to take. The girl in the back clasped her hands around Sheridan's middle, leaning herself backwards as well. It was a sight to behold, and the patrons of the club were enjoying the show immensely.

"What do you make of this?" Sharon asked Marie, never taking her eyes off of the stage.

"I haven't the slightest idea," the pizza-maker said with a confused frown.

"I thought her and that Keefer woman were an item. You said she hasn't left her side."

Marie's eyes widened along with the rest of the onlookers as the girl in the front pulled Sheridan's face into her cleavage and shook her torso. "She hasn't! She was there when I called earlier, too! Holy shit, would you look at that?"

The girl in the back twirled the blonde around and jumped into Sheridan's arms, her legs wrapped around her back.

"Sher doesn't seem to mind at all," Sharon thought out loud.

"I wonder what happened tonight. Maybe they had a fight?"

"Who the hell knows?"

The song ended and Sheridan lowered the girl back to the stage. She was dying of thirst and needed to get to the bar. "Thanks, ladies," she said as she winked at the two girls before jumping off of the stage to loud hoots and applause from the crowd.

The two girls stood there in shock. They were certain at least one, if not both of them would be dragged off to the bathroom or the car. They were confused and they weren't the only ones. They shrugged in defeat at the redhead by the mirrors.

"Son of a bitch!" Danni cursed loudly and kicked the stage.

"Calm down, honey. Maybe she'll be back for more. You *know* Sheridan, she can't turn down a hot woman, and they are hot."

"She went to the fucking bar and now she's headed up the stairs! She turned them both down! I don't believe it!"

"Dan, please, you're getting all blotchy." *Well that's not gonna happen now, is it?* Dawn smiled deviously, wondering if Sheridan had any clue as to how perfectly she'd fucked up Danni's little plan.

"Hey, Sher, wait up!" Marie called after her as she stepped out onto the patio.

The blonde turned around as she stripped off her leather jacket. She pulled out a pack of cigarettes and lit one, leaning her drenched back against the cool brick wall. "I needed to cool off," she explained, dropping her jacket at her feet.

"No doubt. Damn, that was a hot little show you put on there."

"No fucking kidding. My pussy's on fire." Sheridan leaned her head back and blew a slew of smoke rings. "What?" she asked, her eyes narrowing at the look on her friend's face.

"Why did you walk away from them, then?"

"One chick's perfume gave me a headache and the other one was too short," she said matter of factly.

"Really," Marie said, more questions appearing in her raised eyebrows.

"What the hell are you getting at?" the blonde asked in frustration, holding her wet shirt away from her hot skin.

"Nothing," she said as plainly as she could.

Sheridan eyed her skeptically, but only for a second, She wasn't kidding—she was a horny mess. She clenched her vaginal muscles and groaned out loud.

"What was that all about?"

"I'm fucking dying here. Damn, they turned me on." The blonde banged the back of her head against the brick wall in frustration.

Marie pursed her lips at her friend's strange actions. "So, why don't you go back inside and get some relief?"

"No one looks good."

"Shit, Sher, there's at least two dozen women in there that I *know* you wouldn't mind fucking," Marie said as convincingly as possible. She had an idea exactly what Sheridan's problem was.

"Nah." The blonde shrugged and pushed off of the wall to find an ashtray.

Okay, Sheridan, talk to me. "So, what did you do by Keefer's all day?"

Sheridan lit up like a Christmas tree, then seemed uncharacteristically embarrassed.

Interesting, Marie thought with a barely hidden smirk. "You guys have been hanging out a lot lately."

"Yeah, we are. So?"

Marie noticed that her friend hadn't looked her in the eyes since she brought up the tall woman's name. "Just curious. Sharon tells me you fixed up her john."

"Yeah. What are you, writing a book?" the construction worker asked with annoyance.

"Well, she's a hot number and all. Just wanted to know—"

"That's none of your business, is it?" Sheridan started to walk away, but Marie stopped her by grabbing her arm.

"Since when can't you talk to me, Sher?"

"Look, Keefer's different. I don't want to talk about her when she's not around. It doesn't seem right."

Oh, boy! This is news! "Oh, I get it. Respect and all."

"Yeah, respect, that's it." *I guess...*

Marie released Sheridan's arm and the blonde put on her jacket. They stood in silence for a while. Sheridan stared at her boots, mulling over the last comment, and Marie mused over Sheridan's mulling.

By the time Dawn and Sharon came bursting out on the patio, Sharon knew all about what Danni had planned. At first, they weren't so sure about sharing it with Sheridan, but after watching Danni chew out the two dancers, they decided that Danni should get what was coming to her.

Danni stiffened her shoulders when she saw the angry blonde construction worker headed directly toward her. *Aw, fuck me.*

Sheridan saw red as she approached. *How dare they try to make me look bad to Keefer. Hasn't Keefer had enough?* Sheridan was outraged. She barely noticed Susan step in front of her frightened lover until she was standing directly before her. "Beat it," Sheridan warned the blonde.

Susan stood defiantly. "You do anything stupid and they'll throw your ass out of here," she said with a cocky smile.

"Does it look like I care?" Sheridan said answering with a more menacing smile. She didn't wait for Susan to move, she shoved her away herself.

"Hey, don't touch her." Danni stepped forward.

"Oh, you protect this piece of crap but slander Keefer to the world. Funny how that works," Sheridan spat as she poked Danni in the chest.

The redhead winced and Susan ran to get the bouncer. Sheridan's friends saw this and pulled the blonde off to the side to tell her.

"What the fuck is your problem?" Danni bellowed, now that Sheridan was securely surrounded by her friends.

The muscular blonde exploded out of the circle and grabbed Danni by the throat before she could even process what had happened. "What's my problem?" she yelled into the redhead's face. "I'll tell you what my problem is, you little shit for brains. How dare you..." She shoved Danni against the wall so hard her own teeth rattled. "What were you trying to prove with that little setup? Did you think I'd take them into the bathroom and fuck them just because you wanted me to?"

Danni gulped, looking frantically for the bouncers. Her hands dug into the construction worker's biceps, trying to pull her off.

Sheridan shook with rage as she thought about Danni telling Keefer she'd fucked two women in the bathroom. She didn't know why it upset her so much, but she was wild. "Or were you going to run to Keefer and shout 'I told you so'? Huh?" She tightened her grip on the redhead's throat. "Do you want to see her cry? Is that what you want? Would that make you feel good?" She shoved Danni again, making her whimper. "I tell you what makes me feel good, you insensitive shit." Sheridan chuckled evilly. "Keefer makes me feel good...really good," she purred dangerously. "I just wanted to thank you for fucking that one up, Danster."

The bouncers came and Marie and Sharon wrestled Sheridan off of the petrified, yet steaming woman. They smirked as the redhead fell to her knees, gasping for air. Dawn just smiled madly, scaring Danni even more.

Sheridan was not done yet. With a strong grip on each arm, she squirmed a bit as she promised Danni one more thing. "So help me, Danni, if Keefer sheds so much as one tear over you and I find out about it, I'll fucking kill you."

The conviction in those green eyes scared them all. They had no doubt she meant it.

"Let go of me, I'm fine."

Brian, one of the bouncers, put a beefy hand on her shoulder and bent down to her ear. "You have to go for the night, Sher. I'm sorry, but rules are rules. Come back later when they leave, if you want."

"No problem, Brian. I understand. I'd rather not be in the same room as her anyway," Sheridan said as she shrugged off his hand.

Danni looked a little too smug as Sheridan was led out the front door, so Sharon had to do something about it. She wrapped her long arm around Danni's shoulder and walked her away from the wall. "You know, if Sheridan finds it necessary to protect Keefer, we all find it necessary. I would watch my back if I were you," she said with a shit-eating smile. "No one here likes you anymore."

As if on cue, a whole crowd of onlookers with disgusted expressions stared at the redhead. They had no idea what had gone on, but it was well known that Sheridan had a beef with her, and now the popular blonde had been eighty-sixed because of her. No one was too pleased with Danni.

Dawn and the girls moseyed back to the bar, lost in thought.

"Sheridan acted totally out of control. It really mattered to her what Keefer thought about her," Sharon said, trying to figure it all out.

"Yeah, and she wouldn't tell me anything about the two of them, either, out of respect for Keefer," Marie added.

"Respect, that's a new concept for her. Did you see how nuts she was? Guys, I think she's really in love with this woman," Sharon said nervously, "and I don't know that she can understand it."

"I know what you mean. I never saw her so serious as she is about Keefer. I thought she was going to kill Danni on the spot, all because she was going to tell Keefer that she fucked someone else."

"She didn't, though, did she," Dawn stated.

"Nope. She didn't and now we know that she slept with Keefer. Damn, Sher really cares about her and what she thinks. She never cared about that before, she reveled in her nicknames. She has a shirt that says *slut*, for shit sakes," Sharon reminded them.

"Keefer really started something. Sheridan got thrown out of the club because of her. That never happened before. It's eerie."

"Love works in mysterious ways, my friends."

Keefer woke sometime after two and she had no idea why. She assessed herself and found she wasn't thirsty and she didn't have to pee. Fifi was lying peacefully by her side and nothing was odd. No phones were ringing and no alarms were going off, yet she felt like she had to get up. Stumbling half-awake out of her bedroom, she stopped in the living room and began to panic. Bright lights flowed into the room through the front windows and her heart sped up in fear. *Who's in my driveway?*

Danni? She tiptoed to the door, her mouth dry and her hands sweaty, and peeked out of the side of the window. "Sheridan?" she questioned out loud. Her heart was still pounding in her ears and it took her a while to actually comprehend that it was indeed Sheridan's car in her driveway. "What the hell...?"

Sheridan jumped out of her angry funk and peeled her hands off of the steering wheel when her cell phone rang. "Who the fuck is calling me at this hour?" Seeing the familiar number flashing on the phone, she couldn't help her upper lip from curving into a half smile. "Hi," she said sheepishly, remorseful for waking the brunette up.

"Are you all right?" Keefer's worried, sleep-scratchy voice asked with concern.

"I don't know."

"Um, do you want to come in?"

"If it's not...I'm sorry I woke you...I can just go..."

"Sheridan, get in here."

The blonde looked at her phone for long moments after Keefer hung up on her. When she noticed the tall woman standing by the side of her car, Fifi at her side, tail wagging happily, she finally shut off the car and opened the door.

The shy smile Sheridan offered melted Keefer's heart. She felt infinitely better to see the construction worker in one piece, but she could sense the tension rolling off of her in palpable waves. Seeing no movement from the blonde, she wrapped her hands tighter around herself and shivered in the breeze. "It's cool out here, Sher, come inside."

Sheridan followed obediently, still not understanding why she'd even turned up that block in the first place. She'd been busy trying to figure that out when her phone rang, and she felt plain stupid for disrupting the tall woman's night. She closed the door behind her and leaned on it, watching Keefer rub the cold out of her arms. She instinctively shrugged off her jacket and held it out to her, feeling much better, less intrusive when she put it on.

"What happened, Sher? Is everything okay?" Keefer asked, holding out her hand to draw the uncomfortable woman away from her door.

Sheridan took the hand and allowed herself to be led into the kitchen and to a seat. She watched as Keefer started preparing coffee. *She looks so adorable in her nightgown and my jacket.*

"Sher?"

"I don't know why I came here. I should have just gone home. I'm sorry I woke you up. I should go," she said as she stood.

The tall woman moved in front of her and put a hand on her shoulder, forcing her to sit. Only then did she notice the red marks on both of her biceps.

Green eyes gazed down at what blue eyes were studying. *What the fuck? I didn't even realize she was doing that. Jeez, I must have been really out of control!*

Keefer ran her fingers along the marks with a very unhappy frown. Besides being bruised, Sheridan's arms were as hard as rocks, the muscles coiled and attentive. Letting her hand drift up toward a shoulder, she frowned even deeper at the tension she found there as well. Looking her straight in the eye, she pursed her lips and then said, "Spill it. What happened?"

Sheridan let out a shaky sigh. Should she tell Keefer everything? Did she want to mention Danni? The girls? She'd never lied to the inspector before...should she start now? No, she couldn't. *Danni would be sure to tell her the whole sordid story from her pathetic point of view, better she hears it from me.*

Keefer became worried at the silence and the look on Sheridan's face as she sat there. "Talk to me, Sher. Are you in trouble?" She reached out and clasped hands with the blonde.

"Define trouble." She grinned somewhat.

"Sheridan, don't piss me off," Keefer said with a dangerous glint in her eye.

Ooh, that was hot! The blonde's eyes widened at the sudden errant thought.

"Do you want coffee first?"

"Yeah, I'll take some." Sheridan nodded, grateful for the extra time to gather her thoughts. When Keefer set down a steaming mug in front of her, she merely sat and stared into it.

"Sheridan, whatever happened can't be that bad, can it? Who hurt you?"

"Danni."

Keefer's eyes blazed. "Danni? Danni hurt you? What for? Why was she even touching you?" She stood up and made angry fists.

Sheridan's mouth hung open. Keefer was livid. She'd never seen this side of her before and she was totally caught off guard. *She's protecting me? What for?*

"Tell me why she was touching you!" Keefer said loudly, obviously terribly upset.

"I was, um, sorta...choking her," Sheridan whispered regretfully.

Keefer sat down with a thud, apparently not expecting that answer. "Okay, why were you choking her?" she asked unusually softly.

"It's kind of a long story." Sheridan squirmed.

"I got all night," Keefer said without any signs of sleepiness.

"Okay then." The blonde took a deep breath and proceeded to tell her exactly what happened.

"You mean to tell me you nearly choked Danni to death because of...me?" Keefer asked in disbelief.

"Hey, it's not so ridiculous. I seem to remember a few minutes ago when you looked like you were ready to behead her for touching me," Sheridan said defensively.

Keefer blushed. "Yeah, I guess I was..."

Both women got lost in thoughts of why they'd reacted so strongly.

Fifi couldn't stand the tension. She slinked out of the room and disappeared.

Keefer watched the expressions change on the blonde's face as she thought. *I would have killed Danni if anything happened to Sheridan. Of all the stupid, childish things to do...trying to set her up in some twisted— hey, Sheridan walked away from those girls, didn't she? Maybe she did it because of me. Could that possibly be, or did she really hate her perfume? She said they were hot as all get-go, and she did mention they turned her on. I wonder why she didn't...maybe it was me?*

Sheridan noticed the cute little grin on Keefer's face and cocked her head in question. The tall brunette stood up and moved behind her, both hands resting on her stiff shoulders. "What are you doing?"

Keefer began to knead the hard muscles. "Thanking you."

"You don't have to thank me, it's some genetic defect. I have to protect those who aren't able to protect themselves, for whatever reason. You weren't there—"

"Stop babbling, Sher. I mean for not partaking in tonight's offers."

"Huh?" The blonde's head lolled forward as Keefer's fingers worked magic on her neck.

"You didn't have sex with those girls."

Keefer's breath blew across her ear and Sheridan shivered; she hadn't even realized that the tall woman had bent down. "I told you why," she reminded her.

"Uh-huh." Keefer smirked from behind the blonde. She had a feeling that it didn't matter how they smelled or how tall they were. She had an inkling that Sheridan wasn't aware of the truth yet. A truth she was starting to comprehend herself, understanding more and more as she touched the blonde's body. *I'm totally falling for you, Sheridan.*

The blonde groaned indulgently as long fingers dug deeply into her shoulders, erasing the tension with expert ease. She felt very happy, lucky to be on the receiving end of such attentions. No one had really ever given her that much before and she almost felt guilty for accepting it so readily, but it felt good. So good, so she was surprised when her stomach suddenly felt ill like it had been doing for the last couple of days. It passed quickly and she sighed in relief.

"Am I putting you to sleep?" Keefer whispered into Sheridan's ear.

"Hell no, just the opposite." The blonde reached behind her and brushed the ticklish, long black hair off of her neck.

"Sorry, do you want me to tie it up?" Keefer pulled her hair behind her and came around to face the blonde, kneeling in front of her.

"No, I like it down." Sheridan stared deeply into the light blue eyes; it made her nervous to be allowed so much. She swallowed audibly.

"What's wrong?" Keefer let her fingers drift down the side of Sheridan's face.

"You are so beautiful," the blonde blurted, surprising herself. She was becoming nothing more than a bucket of mush lately.

Keefer blushed and her eyes darted away. She felt so much less than beautiful. Her hair was a mess, she'd just woken up, and she was sure she had sleep in her eyes. "Thank you."

"Thank you for allowing me to stare at you." *Why do I feel like this when I look at her? What's making me act like a total moron? Since when do I say things that retarded?*

Keefer gathered herself and climbed up on Sheridan's lap, laying her head in the crook of her neck. The blonde wrapped her arms around her and they both sighed in contentment. Sheridan placed a kiss on top of Keefer's head and the brunette sighed again.

I can sit like this all night long, they both thought simultaneously.

Suddenly Fifi came trotting in and sat on the floor in front of them, making a small huffing sound. When they both turned to look at her, she dropped something on the floor at Sheridan's feet.

"Is that my bra?"

"Oh, dear God..." The brunette buried her fiery face in Sheridan's neck.

"Keef?" Sheridan asked with amusement.

"I'm going to die."

"Keefer Gibson, have you been doing nasty things with my unmentionables?"

"No! God!" Keefer pulled back and looked shocked. "I did no such thing!"

"If I had your bra, it would get quite a workout."

Keefer blushed even redder, her ears the color of cherries.

Sheridan chuckled. "Looks like I have some apologizing to do. I've been blaming Pharaoh all this time."

"I only slept with it. It smelled like you." The horrified inspector still felt the need to explain.

"You know it's your fault that I'm not wearing a bra right now."

Keefer's nipples hardened as she realized her breasts were against Sheridan's. "No?"

"Uh-uh. Wanna see?" Sheridan teased, reaching down between them for the bottom of her shirt.

"Fifi's watching," Keefer sputtered.

Once Sheridan exposed her stomach, Keefer couldn't care less who was in the room watching. Her hands immediately found purchase on the hard muscles and she emitted a small groan, dropping her face back into Sheridan's neck to suck on the tasty skin.

"You have no idea how hot that makes me," the blonde whispered into dark hair.

"My hands? My mouth?"

"Your moans."

Keefer groaned again, just for Sheridan.

Chapter 22

Sheridan awoke slightly disoriented and craned her neck to look around. *Oh...Keefer's bedroom,* she remembered, dropping her head back onto the pillow heavily. *Yeah...Keefer's bedroom,* she thought this time with a broad smile, glancing at the expanse of skin to her left. She recalled how she'd gotten there as she stretched her arms over her head and resettled, draping one over the brunette's body.

They had been in the kitchen kissing and touching for a long time until Keefer had let out a yawn that threatened to swallow her head. Sheridan remembered the look of surprise on the inspector's face when she stood up and carried her into the bedroom. The construction worker was sure her face had mirrored that look when Keefer asked her to stay. Now here she was, at the crack of dawn, with hardly any sleep and she was smiling like a fool. The blonde snuggled up against Keefer's warm back and buried her nose in the messy black hair. She felt inexplicably at ease lying there with the brunette. She'd never spent the night with anyone as many times as she had with Keefer without having sex with them. Keefer seemed to be special. *Special...that's what they call Steven,* Sheridan thought with a frown. *No, she's just...different. I don't want to run away from her at all. It's almost like I never want to leave.* She furrowed her brows, deep in thought. She felt very comfortable where she was at the moment—even her arm draped perfectly around Keefer's body. *My hand isn't even numb yet. It's always numb when I hang it over Zeus,* she thought for a second before wiggling her fingers to test it. *It's like it's supposed to be there. How weird is that?*

Keefer's eyes had been open for a short time, but she was loath to move. The instant she felt Sheridan snuggle up behind her, she decided to stay exactly where she was. The blonde was breathing on her neck and it was stirring other parts of her body not usually awake at this hour. She barely contained a shiver when Sheridan breathed deeply in her hair. On the other hand, she felt so safe, so secure with the strong arm holding her around her middle. It belonged there, and she was ready to jump for joy that it was there at all. Knowing what she did of the blonde, this was probably a highly unusual situation for her, and the fact that she was awake and consciously cuddling made Keefer feel important. She tried desperately not to laugh when Sheridan suddenly wiggled her fingers, tickling the hell out of her stomach. She looked down at the hand on her belly and smiled. *I could get very used to this,* she sighed before she could catch herself.

"Hey, you up?" the blonde breathed into her warm hiding spot.

"Mmm-hmm." Keefer covered Sheridan's hand with her own, begging her not to move.

The blonde smiled at the gesture, pressing herself more securely against Keefer's back in a silent promise that she wasn't going anywhere.

Keefer suddenly sensed something she hadn't sensed before and she felt her face get hot with the realization. "You're naked?"

"Well, what do you know about that?"

Keefer's mouth watered. "When did you..."

"After you fell asleep. I hate sleeping in my underwear," Sheridan explained, suddenly aroused at Keefer's flustered state.

"I can feel...it...on my butt," the brunette whispered.

Sheridan smirked and stuck her tongue out, weaving a path through the thick dark hair until she reached skin.

A small groan escaped Keefer and she turned her head to bury her face in the pillow. "Don't you have to go to work?" she mumbled into the pillow.

"Nope. My pop owns the company. I have...privileges," Sheridan purred, using her hand to sweep the rest of the hair off of Keefer's neck.

"Oh." The inspector's answer turned into a gasp as sharp teeth nipped at the nape of her neck. She squeezed Sheridan's fingers tightly.

"Do you want me to stop?" the construction worker asked, resting her hand on Keefer's hip.

"I don't know," Keefer replied honestly.

Sheridan sat up and peered over the brunette's shoulder to see her face half buried in the pillow. She turned Keefer's face toward her. "Do you want me to stop, Keef?"

"Yes and no."

Sheridan smiled. "What's that supposed to mean?" she asked, gently rolling Keefer over until she was lying on her back.

"I want you to keep going, but I feel so grungy. I just woke up; I probably look like a horror...and my breath..."

Sheridan silenced her with a heartfelt kiss. "I think you look absolutely gorgeous like this."

Keefer didn't know what to do first—blush, hide her face in her hands, or pull the covers over her partially exposed body. The way Sheridan was looking at her spoke volumes of truth, yet Keefer didn't feel deserving. Once she looked down at their still-entwined hands, she couldn't help a smile from flittering across her lips.

Sheridan leaned completely over Keefer's body and kissed her throat. "You smell all sleepy and good."

Keefer blushed even harder. "I do?"

"Totally. I want to taste you right here." Sheridan poked a finger between Keefer's breasts and the brunette giggled nervously. "That's if you want me to."

"Right now?"

"Right now."

Green eyes darkened with hunger, causing something to awaken deep within the brunette. Her heart sped up, her palms got sweaty, and a small, pleasurable burn began between her legs. All it took was one look from Sheridan and everything changed. Keefer reached up, hooked her finger in the neck of her nightgown, and pulled it down, exposing her cleavage.

Sheridan jumped at the invitation and buried her face between the warm flesh of Keefer's breasts with a happy sound.

"Oh!" Keefer exclaimed when a hot tongue began exploring the crevice. Sheridan nodded rapidly as she licked at her skin in long, slow swipes. It took Keefer a second to realize what the blonde was so excited about. She unlaced their fingers and wound her hand loosely in sleep-ruffled blonde hair. "You really like to hear me make noise, don't you?" she asked in embarrassment.

"Uh-huh." The construction worker never stopped licking and nodded again, swinging her leg over the brunette's long body to straddle her.

Keefer wanted to moan, but didn't as the weight settled across her abdomen. It felt so good, so sexy to have the naked construction worker sitting on top of her. Her eyes traced the definition in Sheridan's arms as they held up her body; she wanted to touch the muscles and before she had time to analyze her desires, she did.

The blonde's arm twitched as long fingers softly traced her bicep, leaving a path of excitement in their wake. Sheridan stifled an amused chuckle. *Even my arm is horny for her.* Sheridan leaned all her weight on the arm Keefer was touching and moved the other one to lift the brunette's nightgown up.

Keefer took in a shaky breath; she didn't know how comfortable she'd be to be naked right then. As it was, sex first thing in the morning was a new experience.

"You all right?"

Keefer smiled and shook with a small chuckle. Sheridan looked so worried with her sexy face peering up from between Keefer's breasts in concern. She felt her heart melt a little. "A little nervous."

"Tell me what I can do, Keef. What would make you feel better?"

Keefer lifted the blanket up over Sheridan's shoulders and draped her arms around the blonde's back. She looked a little sheepish at her actions.

"Don't worry, whatever you want," Sheridan said with a reassuring smile before dropping down on both elbows to kiss her.

Keefer slowly lost all nervousness as the insistent tongue began mapping out the insides of her mouth. Sheridan's kisses were breathtaking and she dug her nails in the construction worker's back to convey that message.

"Mmm...God, yes..." the blonde mumbled in between kisses.

She liked that? Keefer dug her nails in again. Sheridan's back arched and she groaned into her mouth. *Oh, yeah...* The brunette took advantage of her new-found powers, exploring the blonde's back with her nails, digging in every so often, drawing delicious sounds from Sheridan that made her sex throb. *No wonder she likes to hear me, it's such a turn-on,* Keefer thought as she brought her hands lower and began exploring the firm muscles of the blonde's ass.

Sheridan tore her mouth away with a whimper and her head fell hard into the crook of the inspector's neck. The sound was like a shock to Keefer's core and her hips jerked in response. Sheridan gritted her teeth against the erotic sensations of those sharp nails digging into her ass; she'd never known how sensitive she was there before. It amazed her that it was Keefer who had discovered this and not one of the wild women she'd slept with. *Then again, everything this woman does to me gets me wet.* Keefer's nails delved lower and when they scraped across the backs of her upper thighs, she couldn't control herself.

Keefer let out a small "oof" as Sheridan's body fell on top of her, but she recovered quickly to savor the sensations. "Feels good?" she asked, trailing her nails back up to the small of the blonde's back.

A strangled groan preceded the reply. "Fuck yeah."

Keefer got wet. She wondered whether it was from Sheridan's exclamation or the knowledge that she had reduced her to a groaning mass of muscle. She didn't think about it long, as Sheridan gathered enough strength to prop herself up on an elbow and green eyes stared at her with undisguised hunger.

"I want you."

Keefer swallowed hard. Sheridan's eyes were making her stomach quiver; they were so expressive in their need.

"Please."

Keefer felt her sex reply before she did with a brand-new flow of arousal. "Yes."

With a triumphant growl, Sheridan slid beneath the blanket and began kissing Keefer's stomach, her hands darting up to cover the brunette's breasts, squeezing them almost roughly.

Keefer couldn't suppress the startled gasp due to all the sudden sensation. She heard Sheridan groan in response and her squeezing became harder, causing new jolts of arousal in her center. The blonde's hot tongue slithered up, climbing her ribs like a ladder. Keefer groaned with an open mouth, reaching blindly beneath the blanket to clasp Sheridan's head in her hands.

"Yes, Keef..." Sheridan's fingers began to caress and tease Keefer's hard nipples through her nightgown.

The brunette felt a new kind of excitement with the knowledge that she could bring Sheridan to this state of arousal without *really* touching her. She tightened her hold on Sheridan's hair and allowed herself to react without fear to the blonde's caresses.

Sheridan wanted to scream when Keefer's long leg wrapped itself around her body, pulling her closer. She felt like she couldn't get enough air, even though she was panting into the brunette's skin. Once their bodies made full contact, Sheridan growled with desire from the intensity of the feeling.

So did Keefer.

"God, baby..." Sheridan's head popped out from the blanket and she yanked Keefer's nightgown up over her breasts and attached her mouth to a straining nipple.

"Sher!"

"Mmm-hmm." The blonde nodded approval and sucked the nipple with abandon, her other hand locating a perfect ass cheek and squeezing it in time to her suction.

Keefer's hips rose on their own and she heard a strangled whimper from Sheridan. She lifted her head up and met burning green eyes, her need tripling as she watched the construction worker suck her breast. It was like fire was in her veins and she couldn't stop herself from burning up. Green eyes rolled shut and for a split second, Keefer wondered why— until she felt her own body pressing rhythmically into Sheridan's.

The blonde was in heaven. Keefer seemed to have lost control and she couldn't have been any more turned on; not in her wildest fantasies had she felt such a need to devour someone so thoroughly. She craved to give Keefer pleasure; she needed to hear her moan. She wormed a hand between their tightly pressed bodies and cupped Keefer's mound through her panties. *Jesus! She's soaked!*

"Ohh..." Keefer's whole body spasmed, her pelvis jerking convulsively at the touch. She had never experienced a need this great and it would have scared her if she wasn't so desperately relieved to feel rough fingers slip under her panties. "Yes," she hissed. Hearing Sheridan's answering growl, her hands left blonde hair and clenched Sheridan's back.

Keefer was so wet, Sheridan's fingers had a hard time doing anything she wanted them to do. They slipped and slid effortlessly around, never staying in one place long enough, at least as long as she wanted them to, anyway. She released the nipple and looked up into the brunette's face. "Oh, Keef..." she breathed in awe. Keefer had never looked so desirable as she did then. Her whole face was flushed and her hair was in disarray, but the expression she wore was priceless and one that the blonde would never forget. "Open your eyes," she whispered.

Blue eyes opened slowly and closed quickly when she found Sheridan staring at her.

It didn't matter, everything Sheridan needed to see was evident in the split second she was allowed. She leaned her lips down to Keefer's ear and breathed a few times to make sure she had her attention.

Keefer whimpered, pressing herself into Sheridan's hand.

"I don't know what it is about you, Keefer Gibson, that makes me so crazy." The blonde moved her fingers against the soaked flesh, causing a small groan to escape half-opened lips. "I don't even care what it is," she licked the earlobe at her lips, "but I have this need for you, a craving to make you come." She bit the earlobe and moved her fingers, making Keefer's whole body jerk. "You want that, don't you? To come for me, all over me," she whispered hotly, letting the words draw themselves out slowly in the brunette's ear.

Keefer nodded and licked her lips. Her body was on fire and she needed Sheridan to put it out. She didn't care what it took. "Yes," she replied hoarsely. When Sheridan groaned uncontrollably in her ear she begged, "Please."

"Your pussy is soaking wet. Is that for me?"

Keefer nodded and swallowed hard in embarrassment.

"I see you blushing," Sheridan breathed into the dark red ear, "but you liked it when I talked about your pussy." A hot tongue tasted Keefer's entire ear and she trembled. "You got wetter."

The brunette struggled against her embarrassment. She knew she had gotten even more turned on when Sheridan spoke like that, but she wasn't ready to admit it. Since no one had ever talked like that to her before, she'd known how much she liked it.

"Do you want me to make you come?" The blonde moved her assault to the dry lips and she sucked on one and then the other while she teased Keefer's opening with her fingers.

"Oh, please," Keefer whined desperately.

Sheridan could only take so much. In less than a heartbeat, she was kneeling under the blanket between Keefer's open legs. Not even bothering to take off her panties, she shoved them to the side and covered her dripping sex with her mouth.

"God!" Keefer blurted out in relief. "Sheridan!"

Fuck yeah! The blonde felt all the hairs on her body stand up at Keefer's shout. She had no idea what had gotten into Keefer, but she was loving every minute of it. She was pumping wetness faster than Sheridan could swallow and it drove her insane with her own need.

Keefer's stomach clenched painfully hard when the blonde's fingers entered her. She sat up and reached wildly under the covers for Sheridan, for anything she could find—she needed to feel her. Her world turned upside down when her clit was suddenly pulled into the construction worker's mouth. She groaned pathetically at the same time as she grabbed a handful of blonde hair.

Sheridan grunted in pleasurable pain as one hand became tangled in her hair and the other dug into her shoulder. Keefer kept her right where she wanted her and she would have had to be dead for anyone to try to move her. She pumped her fingers in and out a few more times before she needed to reverse her mouth and hand. She longed to feel her tongue surrounded by what her fingers were just experiencing and she didn't hesitate to switch.

Keefer's hips surged when Sheridan's tongue entered her. The sounds the blonde was emitting made her tremble. Sheridan's hums and growls made Keefer's heart burst with happiness. She was enjoying this as much as Keefer and it made the inspector crazy.

"You taste so good," Sheridan mumbled from under the blankets before plunging her tongue up and inside as far as it would go. He jaw ached from the stretching, but she couldn't get enough. Her fingers worked teasingly around Keefer's clit, not giving her what she wanted but keeping her at the edge. Keefer would only come when Sheridan wanted her to.

The inspector was sweating heavily, her breath was coming in loud gasps, and she desperately wanted to come. She closed her eyes and tried to force it, but Sheridan sensed it, withdrew her tongue and stopped moving her fingers. She was totally at her mercy.

The blonde knew it was a dangerous game she was playing—Keefer could very well retreat at any time—but she played anyway in hopes of getting what she wanted. Sheridan always got what she wanted. Keefer fell back onto the bed with a weak moan; every nerve ending was tingling with anticipation of Sheridan touching her again. When she finally did, it was electrifying. "Je...Sher...yes!"

That's it baby...talk to me...tell me... The hand clutched harder at her flesh, bruising her shoulder, her hair twisted painfully tight around Keefer's fingers. *It won't be long now.*

Keefer whimpered as Sheridan continued to tease her relentlessly. She wanted to come so bad she could scream. *Why isn't Sheridan letting me come?* She pushed the blonde's face into her sex, begging for release, but it didn't work. Instead, the construction worker switched her position again and slowly entered her with her fingers, her breath blowing dangerously hot over Keefer's pulsating clit.

Sheridan smiled in glee when Keefer once again tried to push her head down. She flicked her tongue lightly over the swollen bud, groaning in sympathy when Keefer whimpered but not giving in to her desire.

The brunette writhed and twisted, hanging at the edge of bliss. Her hair stuck to her face and her nightgown was twisted around her body, but she didn't notice. All she could focus on was that space between her legs and how desperately she needed fulfillment there. *I wanna come, dammit!* she thought in frustration before it dawned on her. "Sher, please...I wanna come!" she begged in a deep and raspy voice.

Sheridan drenched her thighs at the plea and came down on Keefer's clit like she was starving.

"Uh!" Keefer yelled unabashedly as her whole body shook with pleasure.

The blonde wrapped an arm around Keefer's hips and hung on, immersing herself in the rapture.

All the brunette could do was give up as her entire body rebelled against her. She could feel her legs wrapped tightly around the blonde's neck; she knew her fingers were bruising Sheridan, but she couldn't make them stop. Neither could she stop the series of grunts and other sounds that fell loudly from her lips. Her belly spasmed as if she were hooked up to electrodes and she could feel her sex squeezing the hell out of Sheridan's fingers. Keefer could honestly say she had never experienced anything remotely like what she was going through right then—pure and total ecstasy.

Sheridan had a small orgasm in empathy for the writhing body riding her head. She couldn't control it and she didn't even want to. Gently withdrawing her fingers, she groaned wordlessly into the inspector's center, lapping up as much of the delicious arousal as she could and, when there was no more, she licked her own fingers. She felt so completely satisfied with Keefer's response, it didn't matter to her if the brunette touched her or not. All that mattered was Keefer's pleasure and she was convinced that she was definitely feeling good.

"Sheridan...stop..."

The blonde was aware that the grip on her body had loosened, but she was so wrapped up in what she was doing, Keefer had to assist. When she felt her head being pried away from her new favorite spot, she smiled sheepishly. "Sorry," she mumbled as she slid up and out of the blanket, "I got too carried away."

Keefer could only nod as she struggled to catch her breath. The aftershocks caused her to twitch every so often, a totally new experience for her and something Sheridan seemed to be proud of. Long arms and legs lay bonelessly in every direction and blue eyes spotted the self-satisfied grin that threatened to engulf Sheridan's entire head. The brunette grinned back, partially embarrassed, but mostly because she couldn't help it.

"You okay?" Sheridan asked smugly.

"Oh yeah."

"Not going to implode or anything?" Sheridan teased.

"Gimme a minute, I just might."

Sheridan read some truth in that statement and felt the need to reassure the shy woman. She climbed all the way up and placed a devastating kiss on the flustered inspector, very pleased when the sentiments were returned. She only pulled away when her need escalated to a fevered pitch, begging for relief.

When Keefer opened her eyes after the toe-curling liplock, she was hit with a look of total hunger. Her mouth fell open at the desperation in those half-lidded green eyes.

Sheridan chose not to make her craving known. She wanted Keefer to do what ever she felt comfortable doing, but she knew if she chose not to touch her she'd have to do it herself, right then, right there.

"Sher, that was...I don't know what to say," Keefer said quietly, almost inaudibly.

"You are so hot, so delicious..." Seeing the blush rise, Sheridan cut herself off and tried to arrange Keefer's hair a little better. As she moved her body, her sex brushed against Keefer's leg and she gasped out loud with need.

Blue eyes narrowed a bit and the brunette smiled a sexy little smile. She lifted her leg up and purposely pressed it between Sheridan's legs.

"God, Keef." Sheridan's eyes closed and her head dropped forward onto Keefer's chest. She squeezed the long thigh between her legs and groaned in relief.

Keefer's eyes narrowed further at the erotic sound and intense sensations against her leg. Sheridan was very wet, and so close. She rested her hands on the blonde's hips and tugged just enough to tell the construction worker what she wanted. Sheridan arched her back and rode Keefer's leg, moaning constantly. Keefer was overwhelmed with elation, the feeling so powerful that made her moan, too.

"So close, Keefer...don't move..."

"I won't."

Within seconds, Sheridan arched into Keefer and stiffened for a few seconds. Keefer heard herself hiss in pleasure at the sight of the blonde's face before Sheridan fell back down in a fit of tremors. She threw the covers off of the blonde's body and watched all the muscles flex and move under her skin. Her eyes drank up the vision and seared it into her memory forever. "That's so beautiful," she heard herself marvel out loud.

Sheridan finally calmed down and dropped her weight heavily on top of Keefer, breathing hard and fast. She let out a piteous groan and Keefer furrowed her brows in concern. "Are you okay?" she asked, rubbing the back of the blonde's damp head.

"It never felt so good to come in my whole life."

"I know what you mean," Keefer agreed.

Sheridan slid her body over, off of Keefer's leg, but never got up. She kissed the side of her lover's breast since it was right there and sighed deeply. "Did I push you too far, baby?"

"Maybe, but it was worth it," Keefer admitted shyly.

"I needed to hear you. I'm sorry." Sheridan kissed the breast again and scooted even further to the side so she could turn her head and look up.

Keefer surprised herself by stretching her neck and suddenly kissing Sheridan. "I was embarrassed at first, but then...I couldn't help myself. You made me feel so good, I couldn't stop."

Sheridan smiled and snuggled into Keefer's body with a satisfied sigh. "It meant a lot to me. Thank you."

Keefer just nodded and softly stroked the blonde's cooling back. "Comfy?"

"I can't move. I may fall asleep if you keep doing that to my back."

"'S okay." Keefer found herself suddenly exhausted, sated and spent. "I may join you," she said, making small circles on the soft skin.

"Mmm. That feels so good, everything you do feels good," Sheridan mumbled sleepily.

Keefer digested that statement as she gazed down at the construction worker sprawled out naked on top of her. *Yeah?* She smiled, very pleased with the compliment.

"Too heavy?"

The sound of Sheridan's groggy voice warmed her heart. "Nuh-uh. Sleep," she whispered, using both hands to trace idle patterns across the expanse of skin in her reach. Keefer felt her own eyes grow heavy and she closed them, leaving the image of the relaxed blonde in her head. *Definitely falling. Hard.*

When Sheridan awoke again, she knew exactly where she was, but something was different. She was on her back and she distinctly remembered falling blissfully asleep lying on top of Keefer. *How did she get out from under me without waking me up?* Sheridan was a light sleeper and normally would have awakened the second Keefer moved. A big goofy smile spread across her face. *She wore me out.* No one had ever worn out the great Sheridan before. It pleased her, in a way, that Keefer was the one who finally had.

She could hear the shower running and for a split second thought about joining the tall woman, but thought against it just as quickly. *She'd die if I walked in there. Not yet, Sher, give her time.* The thought startled her. *Okay, so what...you're an item now? A couple? Why else would you be thinking things like that, you idiot. Admit it, no one's gotten to you like the woman in the shower has and you love every minute of it. You like her a lot, more than any other woman you've dated.* Sheridan snorted out loud. *Dated...two dates per woman, tops. That's not dating, you moron. This is dating. Hell, this is a fucking relationship.* Sheridan's eyes widened and her stomach felt fluttery. *A relationship? I'm not ready for a relationship!* She shook her head in the negative rapidly. *Am I? I can get very used to her. Fuck it, I already am.* Images of how she fell asleep came to her and she nearly purred in contentment. *A relationship?*

Opening her eyes she saw Fifi lying next to her, staring at her in such a way that she felt guilty. "What did I do?" she asked as she reached over to scratch the dog behind the ears. Fifi raised an eyebrow. "Oh, please, I'll take good care of her, I promise," she swore to the weary dog. "I'm not Danni; don't look at me like that."

Keefer stood outside the bedroom door and swallowed the lump that had formed while she eavesdropped on the construction worker. *No, you certainly aren't Danni, are you?* She thought about what Sheridan meant by her vow to take care of her. *Does that mean she feels the same way about me as I do for her?* She considered exactly what it was she felt, and the only thing she had to compare it to was something she'd only heard other people talk about, but never felt herself. To be perfectly honest, it scared her. Sheridan Landers wasn't the kind of person that she should be feeling these things about. *Is she? She's still here, isn't she? Maybe she does feel like I do. Why would she have said that to Fifi if she didn't? How do I find out? Should I ask her? Will she tell me? She's never lied to me before; she'd be totally honest with me.* A thought occurred to her. *What if she doesn't feel this way and tells me so? I don't want to hear it.* She shook it off and knocked on the door.

"Yeah?"

"Shower's free," Keefer said as she entered the room.

"Okay, thanks."

The room was awkwardly silent as the two women refused to look at each other, both struggling with their own emotions and the new feelings they had suddenly realized only moments ago.

"I'm gonna..." Keefer gestured to her robe.

Keefer watched as the construction worker moved in unusual silence. *Why is she acting that way? Did I do or say something?* "Sher? Is everything okay?"

"Yeah, it's fine. It's just that...I need to take a shower. I'll be right out," she said as she left the room, not looking at Keefer once.

The brunette sat on the edge of the bed and started to cry. *Something went wrong. She can't even look at me. She regrets what happened. I'm such a loser. Why would I think she'd want to be with me anyway?*

The blonde stood in the shower, thinking about what was going on inside of her. It was a whole new world of feelings, ones she was unfamiliar with, ones she couldn't even name. They ate at her insides like they wanted her to figure them out, yet when she tried, they went away. It puzzled her. She was normally so cool and in control, but when she had these feelings, she felt she was spinning totally out of control. It was Keefer—she made her feel like this. How could something that felt so good, be so bad? Why did the thought of kissing the brunette make her knees weak and her belly warm, and yet the thought of a relationship with her make those same knees tremble and that same belly sick? *Because I'm not ready for a relationship,* Sheridan thought while she rinsed the soap off her body. *Then why do you miss her right now? You can't answer that, can you?* her inner voice dared her. *Face it, Sher, everything's changed now. Admit it, already...you need her.*

Keefer hid her face when Sheridan walked back into the room. She didn't want to look at her and, even more, she didn't want Sheridan to know she was crying. She knew the blonde would get upset. She was saved by the phone ringing.

Sheridan sensed that something was wrong when she walked into the room, but didn't get the chance to find out what it was before the phone rang. She followed Keefer into the living room.

"Why are you calling me? Yes, I know what she did to you and from what I understand, you deserved it and more."

Sheridan frowned. *Is she crying? Is that Danni?* "No, I don't care to hear what happened, I know what happened." Keefer paused then became mad. "Don't you ever say that about her again!" Suddenly, Keefer's face got red with anger and Sheridan snatched the phone from her hands in time to hear Danni call Keefer the little slut's whore.

"Hey, dickface, this is the slut," Sheridan growled. "Did I just mistakenly hear you calling my girlfriend a whore?" She glanced at Keefer, whose mouth was agape. "Oh, I see. I thought not, because Keefer is very special to me, you see, and if I ever heard someone call my lover a name like that, I'd have to tear a hole in their side and rip out their liver. You understand that, don't you?" Sheridan braced her legs as Keefer flung herself at her. "I knew you would. Now, if you ever disturb us again, I'll have to hurt you. Yes, you, too, Danni. Have a good day." Sheridan hung up the phone and looked sideways at the woman draped all over her. "What?"

"Am I really your girlfriend? Do you mean what you said?" Keefer asked excitedly.

"Yeah, I did," Sheridan admitted with a hint of a blush.

"Thank you, Sheridan!" Keefer proceeded to kiss every inch of skin on Sheridan's face.

255

Chapter 23

The couple spent the rest of the day lounging lazily around the house, discussing anything and everything from renovations to favorite colors. Sheridan was still surprised at herself for blurting out that bit about Keefer being her girlfriend and lover, but now that she had said it, she felt a lot more relaxed while in the tall woman's company. There was less to think about and more to be happy for. Keefer was lying out on the couch with her head in Sheridan's lap, the blonde's fingers running slowly through thick black hair. She sighed deeply in contentment and it made Sheridan smile.

"What are you doing tonight? Are you going to the club?" Keefer asked with a lazy drawl.

"Probably," the construction worker replied equally languidly, enjoying the feel of the silky strands sliding through her fingers.

"You do realize that Danni will most likely be there," the brunette warned.

"Yeah, well, she better just stay clear away from me if she knows what's good for her," Sheridan said with a small growl.

Keefer reluctantly sat up to look the blonde in the eyes. "Sher, don't hit her anymore. Don't let her get to you like that." She took Sheridan's hand and squeezed it.

"If she gets in my face, she gets hit. Simple. Don't protect her."

"I'm not protecting her, I'm protecting you." Sheridan attempted to protest. "I know you can take care of yourself, that's not what I meant. I know the club means a lot to you and I want you to go there and not have to worry about confrontation. She's only going to try to rile you. She's jealous and she has every right to be."

"I think anyone who *isn't* jealous of me is a moron."

Keefer blushed. "Thank you."

"I know what you mean, Keef. I'll try to take her with a grain of salt. I just don't appreciate her talking shit about you. It pisses me off something fierce."

"I understand; it makes me mad when she says things about you, but that's what she wants. Don't give her the satisfaction, is all I'm saying," Keefer said, bringing the hand she was holding up to her lips and kissing it.

The blonde pondered that for a while and finally nodded. "Okay, I'll hang back, but if she touches me..."

"Then you can kick her ass."

Sheridan smiled and leaned in for a kiss. She was surprised when Keefer pulled her down and she wound up on top of her. She took a moment to indulge in the feeling of the sexy brunette underneath her.

"I love how you feel on top of me," Keefer whispered into Sheridan's mouth.

"I was just thinking the same thing," the blonde admitted with a nip to Keefer's bottom lip.

"Let's not start that, Sher." Keefer giggled, holding her hand over her mouth. "I'm starving."

"Me too." The blonde wiggled her eyebrows and smacked her lips.

Keefer blushed just a little. "You're always starving for that. I mean food." Blue eyes twinkled.

"Come to think of it, I could eat," Sheridan said thoughtfully.

"Want me to cook?" Keefer asked, wrapping her arms tightly around Sheridan, not even attempting to get up.

"Nope. Let's order in, I don't want to move."

Sheridan eventually made it back to her house after dinner. She took the dogs on an extended walk and promised them some special time later. They seemed to understand when she explained her reasons for being so neglectful, but she knew they'd be less than understanding should she bring Keefer into the house. She could just picture it...trying to kiss Keefer with Zeus standing on her head and Pharaoh on Keefer's. She snickered at the image. "You know, she's going to eventually come here, guys," she announced to the dogs, who paid her no mind. "You can't walk all over her like you do me," she added, knowing they weren't listening at all. "Hey, it's not like I love you any less..." She wondered what the end of that sentence would have been if she didn't end it where she did and grimaced. "Nah," she shook it off, "that's not what I was going to say."

Keefer blushed again at the memory of Sheridan standing by her door, her black bra hanging out of her pocket. "I was so busted. Thanks, Feefs." She glanced over at the dog, whose ears perked up at her name.

The tall brunette began undressing in front of her mirror and her eyes widened upon discovering the big, reddish bruise on her collarbone. "When did she...?" Pulling off all of her clothes, she revealed two more such marks and flushed with the sudden memories. "Ohh, now I remember *that* one." She smiled lazily and allowed herself to relive the memory. She blushed suddenly when she was reminded of the same marks peppering various parts of Sheridan's anatomy. "Oh, no. I did do that too, didn't I?" Keefer dressed in a long T-shirt and forwent underwear. "Yeah," she said smugly to her reflection, "I did. Let Danni read that and weep."

Sheridan knew the ribbing she was going to take from her friends if she didn't wear the turtleneck, but it was just too damned warm for it and the mock turtleneck didn't cover half of the marks anyway. Sighing, she yanked off the heavy shirt and pulled out a tank top. "Fuck it," she stated, pulling the comfortable shirt over her head. *I can take it,* she thought bravely. Giving herself the once over, the blonde grabbed her leather jacket and headed out the door.

The tall inspector snuggled down in her bed, Fifi by her feet. She stretched long and hard before getting more comfortable beneath her blanket. Once she closed her eyes, all she could think about was Sheridan. Just a few days earlier, that would have frustrated her, but now she smiled and sighed happily. *Could you believe it? She said she's my girlfriend. She called me her lover to Danni, of all people. I hope she knew what she was doing when she said that. Danni will have that news roaming through the club in no time. Poor Sheridan, her reputation will*—Keefer suddenly opened her eyes and sat up. "Uh-oh," she said, slightly panicked. "This changes everything!"

Sheridan waltzed down the stairs and into the club, just as she did every night, and wandered into the large room. She walked a few steps before she noticed most everyone staring at her in a very weird way. The blonde glanced down just to make sure her pants weren't around her ankles. She would have sworn they were. Satisfied that she was fully clothed and her nose hadn't fallen off, she moved about the sea of women like Moses parting the Red Sea. If it wasn't for the demanding thump of the bass-driven music, she would have thought she'd walked into a dream. Finding her friends at their usual space by the bar, the construction worker sidled up to them with a mock shudder. "Ooh, freaky tonight, huh?"

Marie stared at Sheridan in silence while Sharon and Dawn smirked knowingly.

Greg, on the other hand, came flying through the club with a screech and jumped in front of the now-uncomfortable blonde. "Gimme gimme!" he shouted, breathless from his flight over to the bar, and grabbed Sheridan's chin. He studied the construction worker's face a few seconds before smiling and declaring her a kept woman.

"What the fuck is wrong with everyone?" Sheridan demanded angrily. "Why is everyone acting so goddamned strange?"

Danni suddenly appeared, laughing her head off and pointing at the hostile blonde.

Angry green eyes narrowed and Sheridan made fists before she remembered her conversation with Keefer. She took a few deep breaths and turned her back on the redhead, to the astonishment of her friends.

"Whassamatta, Sheridan, Keefer tell you not to hit me anymore? I knew she would," Danni gloated.

Sheridan winced hard, wanting nothing more than to shut the redhead up via a fist to the mouth. She took a few more deep breaths and ordered a bottle of water.

"Uh, Sher? You okay?" Dawn asked in total confusion at her friend's reaction.

"Fine." The construction worker smiled unconvincingly.

"The great whore of Brooklyn...pussy whipped. Who would have thought?" Danni continued.

Sheridan turned to face the taunting woman. The look in her eyes meant certain pain, should she take one more step forward.

Danni gulped, but was confident that Sheridan wouldn't risk getting kicked out of the club again and going against Keefer's wishes at the same time. Although she wanted to scream her head off about the hickeys Sheridan was wearing so proudly, she stepped closer to the blonde, smiling brightly.

Marie put a hand on Sheridan's shoulder, just in case she was going to have to hold her back. *Jeez, Danni is so fucking stupid!*

"Wanna go outside, Sher?" Sharon asked Sheridan, pulling on her forearm. The construction worker could feel her muscles twitching under her friends' hands.

"Yeah, Sher, maybe you should go outside and cool off. You look a little hot there," Danni teased.

Sheridan broke from her friends' grasp and closed the distance between herself and the redhead. Danni panicked momentarily, but her back was against the speaker and she had nowhere to run.

Sheridan stared deadly daggers into Danni. She leaned her face in really close and snarled in her face. "Boo!" she yelled, smirking evilly when the redhead flinched.

Sharon and Dawn pulled Sheridan away and pushed her toward the stairs. "Patio, now," Dawn announced.

Danni breathed a sigh of relief. "Beats me why a woman like you would want a cold fuck like Keefer around," Danni yelled after them.

Sheridan struggled mightily on her way to the patio, her friends holding on to her for dear life.

Marie waltzed over to the laughing redhead, lifted both arms up, causing Danni to flinch again, and rested both forearms on the speaker around Danni's head. Marie was of a formidable size; she knew how to use her bulk to her advantage, especially when she leaned in as close as she did to the worried woman. "You know, Danni," she sneered angrily, "Keefer may have told Sheridan to back off, but she didn't say anything to me, so watch your fucking step, pretty girl."

Danni swallowed, focusing on the space between Marie's teeth. She had heard how it got there. Supposedly, the pizza-maker went up against an entire gang of homophobic guys and walked away with only a few teeth missing. Danni wasn't stupid and she just nodded.

"Good, 'cuz one more childish outburst like that one or one more negative word about your ex and I'll wipe the fucking floor with you."

Danni nodded again. Marie smiled sweetly and patted Danni condescendingly on the cheek before leaving to see to Sheridan.

Once on the patio, Sharon threw Sheridan in a chair and stood in front of her, blocking any attempts she might make at escape. "Chill out, now," she ordered her friend and then turned to the few people outside. "You guys get inside."

They all watched as the people obeyed out of respect for Sheridan.

The blonde breathed heavily. "I'm cool. I swear," she said in a low growl.

"Oh, that's convincing, Tiger," Dawn said as she watched the door for any signs of Danni. When it opened she tensed, but it was only Marie.

"Where were you?" Sharon asked.

"Had something to take care of." Marie winked, then squatted down in front of the construction worker.

"Please tell me she's bleeding. Please," Sheridan begged.

"Sorry, Charlie, I just warned her a little," Marie snickered. "Hey, wanna tell us what's going on? Is Danni right?"

Sheridan blew out a frustrated breath and leaned her arms on her knees. "Yeah," she said quietly.

"Start from the beginning. Are you and Keefer an item? Danni's telling everyone that you're her girlfriend," Marie said, her eyes narrowing on the big, red bruises on her friend's neck.

"I guess so. I mean...that's what I told her."

"Told who?" Sharon asked.

"Danni."

Dawn's eyebrows rose comically high. "You told *Danni* this? When?"

"Today. She called to harass Keefer and I took the phone and told her to leave my girlfriend alone. Told her I'd rip out her liver," Sheridan snickered.

Dawn, Marie and Sharon followed suit and all four of them laughed for a while, relieving the tension.

"So, uh, what gives? You guys are lovers now?" Sharon asked, not quite believing it, "or did you just say that?"

"No, I meant it when I said it. Jeez, guys, what the fuck is going on?" The blonde leaned back in the chair again and slid down, letting her head fall over the back.

"Shit, Sher, we can't tell you that," Marie replied, just as shocked as Sheridan.

"I don't know what it is about her or what she does to me. I think I knew I was in trouble the minute I saw her," Sheridan admitted while looking at the stars.

The three friends shared knowing glances.

"I'm so different with her, ya know? I say the weirdest things; I do the weirdest things...I don't know." The construction worker groaned as if she were in pain.

Marie shook her head; it bothered her to see her good friend so confused. "Hey, do you like how you feel and act when you're with her?"

Sheridan shrugged, then sat up properly in the chair, looking at all her friends and seeing nothing but sympathy. "Yeah, I guess. I mean, I never acted this way before...I never wanted to. It's new, but I guess I like it."

Dawn needed to know, it was killing her. "All those things Danni is saying about her, you know..."

"Keefer had a lot of issues, but she's not what Danni says. Danni is an uncaring shit for brains. Keefer needs some time, she needs some special attention, that's all."

Marie's eyes widened. "*You* are ready for all that?"

"I didn't think so. Hell, I convinced myself to stay the hell away from her, but I couldn't. It was crazy! All I thought about...all I wanted to do...Shit, I'm fucked, aren't I?" she whined pathetically.

Sharon looked her friend in the eyes. "Totally."

"What's that supposed to mean?" Sheridan asked hotly.

"It means, yes, you're fucked, but in a good way. Think about it, Sher, is it such a bad thing to be around Keefer, to think about her?"

"I suppose not."

"Then stop whining about it and just let it be. Be happy for a change."

Sheridan sat still and thought about what her friend just said. *I thought I was happy before Keefer. Wasn't I?* Green eyes closed and Keefer immediately popped into her head. A small smile followed the image. *No, I guess I really wasn't. Crap. Now I miss her.*

Dawn saw the range of emotions pass across her friend's face and felt bad for her. "Hey, Marie took care of Danni, let's go dance," she said with enthusiasm.

"Yeah, let's go," Sharon agreed, pulling Sheridan up out of the chair.

"Okay, but if Danni—" Sheridan's phone rang and all four women stopped in their tracks. "Hiya, baby," the blonde said with a big, bright smile on her face.

Marie mouthed one word to Dawn and Sharon—"fucked"—and they all snickered as they left their friend talking to her woman.

Sheridan turned her back to the exiting bunch and closed her eyes, picturing her girlfriend as she spoke. "What's up?"

"I couldn't sleep, I tried to, then I tried to watch television. I even turned on channel 46, but I couldn't help it, I had to call you."

Sheridan raised her eyebrows at Keefer's upset babbling. "What's wrong? Are you okay?"

"I had the strangest feelings all night. I just know Danni confronted you. I'm sorry for telling you what to do, if you want to hit her, you go right ahead..."

"Whoa, whoa, Keef, calm down. You're right; nothing gets solved when I fly off the handle. Pop's been trying to smack that sense into me for years." Sheridan snickered at her joke. When Keefer remained silent, she changed her tune. "Look, Danni gave me plenty of reasons to hit her, but I stayed cool. I have a great bunch of friends who also made sure I hung back. I'm okay."

"Are you sure? Danni can be pretty obnoxious."

"Yeah, she was, but I promise I'm okay. I think Marie scared the pants offa her, too." Sheridan smirked, imagining what her bulky friend could have done.

"Yeah? I was worried about you, Sher. I hate it that Danni plays games with you because of me...and after you told her that I was your girlfriend...I know it must have been bad. I'm sorry."

"Hey, don't apologize! I'm glad you're my girlfriend and I don't care who knows it!" the blonde said with conviction.

"I sure hope so, you said that loud enough to wake the dead."

Sheridan glanced around and found a few women scattered around the patio, looking at her with shock and disappointment. "Fuck 'em," she said, loud enough for them all to hear, "I'd be proud to walk you around this club on my arm."

"You're not going to regret being with me? Sher, your reputation—"

"My reputation can rot," Sheridan said truthfully, shocking herself.

"But you can have any woman you choose."

"That's right. And your point is..." the blonde said with a grin.

"I miss you. I wish I could hold you right now," Keefer blurted out tearfully.

"Are you crying? Why?" Sheridan asked with concern.

"Because I feel so happy; you made me feel so happy."

Sheridan felt her heart swell. No one had ever told her that without an ulterior motive in mind. Keefer meant it—she didn't want anything in return, just maybe a hug, which Sheridan wished she could deliver right that moment. "I miss you, too."

They sat in silence for a while, each happy to listen to the other breathe, both satisfied with the connection, even if it was by phone. It didn't bother Sheridan in the least that she was in her club, all by herself, on the phone with Keefer. "You watched channel 46?" she asked teasingly.

"Yes. I watched it plenty of times already," Keefer admitted.

"Oh yeah? Anything interesting?" Sheridan asked with a sexy drawl to her voice.

"Yes."

"Do tell."

"I'd rather show than tell," Keefer said seductively.

"Oh baby!" Sheridan exclaimed, suddenly horny.

"I can't believe I said that!" Keefer moaned in embarrassment.

"Me neither," Sheridan chuckled. "I liked it."

"Maybe that's why I said it. I like teasing you," the inspector said with a giggle.

"Babe, you can tease me all you want. Hey, Sharon is giving me the eye, I better get going."

"I'd like to meet your friends one day, Sher."

"You got it. Good night. And stay away from channel 46 until I get there."

"Oh, God...good night."

Sheridan chuckled and hung up her phone. "What?" she asked her friend, who was smirking at her.

"Nothing. Just liking the way it looks on you."

"The way what looks on me?"

"Love, you dope."

"Love? What would make you think...I am not...shut up, asshole."

Sharon continued to smirk.

"Come on, let's dance," Sheridan said, her mind suddenly swirling with thoughts that she needed to push away.

Keefer lay back in her bed, a big smile plastered to her face. Sheridan had made her feel so good with the things she'd said on the phone. Keefer knew what a big deal it was to have Sheridan Landers call her her girlfriend, and for her to practically yell it out in that club made her heart want to burst. At first, she was wrestling with the idea that Sheridan only said it to keep Danni away, but now after the conversation they'd just had, she knew otherwise and she felt giddy. "Feefs, this is it. I know it, I can feel it."

The dog walked around the bed, finally coming to a stop by her mommy's side. She gave the tall woman a few licks before circling and falling into a comfortable position.

Keefer petted her dog while she thought out loud. "It's like that movie that Danni made me watch, the one where the two women start out as friends but then fall in love. I think I'm falling in love with her. I don't know if that's a good thing or a bad thing. Sheridan may not want to be in love, she may not even know what it is. Heck, I didn't know what it was until I kissed her in the club that night. I didn't know it then, but now I do. It's all so perfect...the way I feel, the way I think." Keefer closed her eyes and sighed happily. "The way she makes me feel. I want to feel like this forever." She thought in silence for a while. "I don't know what I'd do if she doesn't want to be loved, 'cuz I know...I love her."

Sheridan danced her little ass off, but this time, she was dancing alone. Lost in thoughts and emotions, the blonde danced and danced, but couldn't make them go away. *Love? Shyeah, right. Imagine that,* she thought, rolling her eyes. *Me? Never.* She pounced her way around the stage, ignoring all the potential partners who threw themselves her way. *Wait! Oh, no...I called her my lover—you can't have a lover without love, can you?* Sheridan stopped dancing and sat down on the side of the stage.

Can you? She glanced around the club at some couples making goo-goo eyes at each other, totally lost in each other, oblivious to their surroundings. *Okay, Debbie and Lisa, they're in love...*Green eyes studied them and their actions carefully. They practically mirrored Keefer and her in private. Sheridan's heart picked up speed and her mouth went dry. *Okay, bad example.*

She let her eyes wander to a couple that had been together longer than the other and studied them. They smiled at each other, seemed to be more comfortable when they were touching in some way, and kissed every so often. Green eyes closed as Sheridan began to panic. *No way...love?*

Chapter 24

Keefer couldn't help it. Ever since Sheridan had told her not to watch the porno channel, she had the urge to watch it. She fought it all night and finally got to sleep, but once she'd finished breakfast and walked the dog, she couldn't think of a better way to spend her vacation than with a cup of coffee and channel 46. She wandered into the living room and turned on the television. She flipped through the channels a while, pretending that she didn't want to watch that channel, and kept passing over it on purpose. Finally, after going through every single channel there was a number of times, she turned on to 46.

"That's *not* what I was looking for." On the screen was an extreme close-up of a very sloppy blowjob. The brunette shuddered and immediately changed the channel. The images were vulgar to her and she grimaced, attempting to make them vanish from her memory. She went to the menu channel and watched that scroll by for a good amount of time before curiosity got the best of her and she went back to investigate. She wasn't disappointed—there were two women on the screen, one apparently playing butch, dressed appropriately and everything. From her experience, every porno movie had at least one lesbian scene; she chalked that up to men and their fantasy to see two women get it on.

Everything was going according to the usual script until the butch opened her jeans and produced a dildo. Keefer gasped out loud. She had been thinking about that ever since Sheridan admitted to having one. The last time she'd watched two women with a dildo, they were both pretty feminine and she hadn't known that Sheridan had one. It didn't matter that the woman wearing the dildo in the movie was brunette; all Keefer could see was Sheridan standing there, rubbing the phallus suggestively. It turned her on more than she expected and she squeezed her legs closed tightly, watching their every move with bated breath. It wasn't long before she was squirming uncomfortably, highly aroused. No matter how hard she tried to concentrate on the two women in the movie, they kept becoming Sheridan and her. Between fits of blushing, Keefer found herself watching and fantasizing, imagining she was on the receiving end of the dildo. This new fantasy surprised her; Danni didn't have one and had never even brought the subject up. Keefer never knew she'd welcome it until she began to picture Sheridan and herself in place of the actresses.

She began to think about the possibility and shook her head rapidly. "Oh no, I could never tell her about this," she said to herself. "Could I?" Keefer knew without a shadow of a doubt that Sheridan would indulge her. Happily. Especially when it came to something like this. The construction worker seemed to understand her better than Danni ever had and this gave her a newfound sense of confidence when it came to matters of sex. No matter how embarrassed she felt expressing herself in this area, she knew Sheridan would never patronize her or laugh at her.

Turning her attention back to the screen, the brunette began to wonder what it would be like, her first time. Sheridan was sure to be patient and gentle. Keefer got very nervous thinking about it and began to perspire a little. She wasn't sure she was ready for it mentally, but physically she was positive. It seemed like there was a certain level of closeness, a deeper connection achieved while making love in that manner. It intrigued her, yet scared her at the same time.

"Swallow the shit, Keef, you've been doing so well lately. Just tell her. She'll probably do a little happy dance over it." She chuckled at the image.

Sheridan made it to work early, which surprised her since she'd wiped herself out dancing the previous night. Another thing that surprised her was that she woke up before the alarm that morning, a happy smile on her face even though it was plastered to Pharaoh's butt. She pushed the dog away with a chuckle and whistled her way into the shower. She was in a good mood and didn't question its origin—she just went with it.

She took off her hard hat and sat down on a stepladder to drink her coffee. She took off the top and blew on the hot liquid. *Speaking of blowing...*Sheridan felt bad for blowing off the chick in the donut shop, but she had a girlfriend now and shouldn't be flirting with every hot woman that crossed her path. Even if she had fucked them. *No big deal. She ain't got nuthin' on Keefer anyway,* she though with a grin. It was with that thought that Bobby came stumbling up the steps.

"Hey, Patch," he said wearily, tossing his hard hat at her feet.

She looked at the yellow hat and chuckled. "Maria keeping you up all night?"

Bobby pulled up an overturned bucket and sat down next to her, opening a huge thermos of coffee. "Morning sickness will do that to ya," he said, looking for a reaction out of the corner of his eye.

"That's too bad...What?" Sheridan jumped up. "Maria's pregnant? Congratulations!" she yelled, smacking him on the shoulder, a sore and tired shoulder.

"Ow." He rubbed the spot and smiled weakly.

"Hey, isn't morning sickness supposed to be in the morning?" she asked, sipping her coffee carefully.

"That's what I thought. It sucks, Patch. By the way, I would have told you yesterday, but you were out. What's up?"

"I had things to do," she said, turning her head and refusing to make eye contact.

"Things?" he asked, wondering why she was acting that way.

"Yeah. So boy or girl?" she asked, changing the subject.

"Dunno, we want it to be a surprise."

Sheridan snickered and gave him a sideways look, then snickered again.

"What?" he asked in confusion.

"You made a baby." She laughed outright.

"And this is funny because..."

"I keep picturing you doing it." She had to put her coffee down so she wouldn't spill it as she laughed.

"That's right, yuck it up," he said, offended.

"Oh, please, I probably look just as stupid when I do it." She got up, presented him with her ass, and made humping gestures.

"Yeah, but I'd rather watch you do it than me," he snickered, earning him a smack to the back of the head.

Phil and Tony arrived together at that moment and both of them laughed.

"What, it's only ten of nine and already he's on your nerves?" Phil said, making his way over.

"Was it really bad? Can I hit him too?" Tony asked with a little too much excitement.

"Nah, I got it under control." Sheridan grinned, smacking Bobby again for good measure.

"You okay, Patch?" Phil asked seriously.

"Yeah, why?" she asked in confusion, giving herself the once-over.

"Thought you were sick or something. Your pop said he had no idea why you were out yesterday."

"I had business," she said lamely into her cup.

Tony walked over and poked a hickey. "Oh, is that what you call it now? Business?"

"Fuck off!" She jumped up out of reach.

"Hey, Tony, there's one here, too." Bobby pointed to the other side of her neck. "Come on, let's see. Any nail marks?"

"Back off," she warned, a blush creeping up her face.

"Was it good?" Phil teased. "Whoa...is that a blush?" he asked in amazement.

"Holy shit. Must have been something. Anyone we know?" Bobby teased.

Sheridan didn't know what to say. They did know Keefer. Unfortunately, her silence spoke loudly. The men glanced at each other with curious looks. Sheridan was highly interested in her coffee cup and didn't want to share details. This was very odd for the blonde, and it raised all the eyebrows in the room.

"She something special, Patch?" Phil asked, resting his hand on her shoulder.

"Sorta," she shrugged, still not looking at them.

They all had a good idea who it could be, but even if it was blatantly thrown in their faces, they still couldn't fathom Patch settling down with one woman—even if it was one hell of a good-looking brunette with legs for days.

Sheridan suddenly stood up and grabbed her hard hat. "I'm going to the john," she announced before leaving.

"It's that inspector, isn't it?" Bobby asked Phil.

"I'd bet my left nut on it," he replied.

"Damn," Bobby shook his head in disbelief. "You think this is it? You think she's in love?"

"That, I don't know. Time will tell," Tony said.

"C'mon, guys, we've all been there. She's fucking gone." Phil reminded them of their own behavior when they had fallen in love.

Bobby thought back to the few times Sheridan had acted crazy, and they all involved the tall brunette. "Poor little shit. She don't know what hit her."

"Should we talk about it? You know, give her a clue?" Tony wondered.

"Let's just see what happens. She may already have a clue."

Sheridan walked back into the room to three knowing smiles. She held up a hand to stop any conversation from starting. "Drop it, guys. I don't want to talk about it."

Sheridan was preoccupied for the rest of the day. She got her work done with a minimum of mishaps, but she still had a clumsy moment or two—especially when she started thinking. There were times when she would think about Keefer and a warm pleasant feeling would envelop her, like when you play in the snow all day and then drink hot chocolate. It was a comforting feeling and she would smile. Then there were the other times, when thinking about Keefer, she'd get the weird feeling, the one where she felt like something was about to happen and all her arm hairs stood up. That was when she was most distracted and dropped her tools or tripped over her own feet. She couldn't figure it out and it bothered her. How could the same person make her feel so drastically different things? She tried to understand it but failed, leaving her feeling confused.

Driving home, she turned up the radio loud and put her cell phone on vibrate, just in case Keefer might call. She had missed the tall woman all day and couldn't wait to see her again. She thought about calling her a bunch of times, but felt it would be better to let Keefer enjoy her days off with no interruptions. Little did she know, the inspector had picked up her phone at least a dozen times and hung it up before she dialed. Sheridan sang out loud with the radio, finally thinking of nothing else but the music.

Keefer was frustrated to tears. Typically, she'd love nothing more than a quiet day or two by herself to do nothing. However, her quiet lounging was constantly interrupted by thoughts of the construction worker. Her mind would wander at any given time, usually asking questions to which she had no answers. Occasionally, though, it would throw an image at her that made her face hot. She didn't really mind the arousing interruptions, wishing there was a way to capture those images on film so she could study them at length. Without having anything to do to occupy her mind, to keep the distractions to a minimum, she finally decided to sit back with a glass of wine and indulge her overactive imagination. She sat back on the couch with her feet up and allowed the questions and visions to overtake her mind. Usually, Keefer was a two glass maximum wine drinker; however, she managed to down half a bottle while daydreaming. Slightly tipsy and all fired up, Keefer picked up the phone.

The muscular blonde had just wrapped herself in a towel when she saw her cell phone dancing around on the dresser. "Shit, Keefer!" she yelled, cursing for forgetting to turn the ringer back on. She tripped over Zeus and stepped on Pharaoh as she ran for the phone.

"Yeah, Keef," she said, all out of breath.

"Hi," the brunette said cheerfully. "Am I bothering you?"

271

"Never, what's up?" Sheridan settled herself down on the bed to talk.

"Look, I'm probably only going to have the guts to talk about this once..."

Sheridan's heart sped up in anticipation and when Keefer paused, she got nervous. "What? Tell me," she urged, not knowing what to expect.

"Okay, well...I've been thinking about us all day. I couldn't do anything."

The blonde furrowed her brows at the way her girlfriend was talking—she just didn't seem like herself. "Are you all right?" she asked with concern.

"Oh, yeah, I think I may be drunk, but that's a good thing. Trust me," Keefer giggled slightly.

"Drunk? I can't leave you alone for a minute, can I?" Sheridan teased.

"That's just it, you didn't leave me alone for a minute all day long. Every time I blinked, I saw you, or me or both of us..." Keefer's voice trailed off.

"Yeah?" Sheridan's grin was audible. "What were we doing?" She lowered her voice to sound sexy.

"Remember that time I asked you about, you know, if you had any...toys?"

"Yeah..." Sheridan sat up straight and cocked her head in curiosity.

"That's what we were doing," the inspector blurted out bravely.

Sheridan let it sink in. Keefer must have been drunk to admit something like that and she wanted to make sure she heard it right. "You imagined us playing with toys? *Those* kinds of toys? We're not talking Barbie dolls, now, are we?"

"No, I mean yes...those kind. Before you say anything else, I'm not drunk enough to elaborate, but just enough to communicate, so use your imagination," the brunette said quickly.

The construction worker sat silently, her face a cross between shock and glee. She had many questions to ask concerning the subject, but was afraid to voice them. She also knew the more she let Keefer sit on the other end of the phone listening to her breathe, the less chance she had for discussion.

"I really hope the silence is a good thing."

"Oh, a very good thing. You told me to use my imagination," Sheridan said, trying to word her questions right. She didn't want to make Keefer shy away from this most interesting topic. "So, did Danni...?"

"No," Keefer shot out before Sheridan could finish her sentence.

The blonde thought for a moment. "Have you ever...?"

"No." Again Keefer replied quickly.

"Keef, are you sure you want me to...?"

"Positive."

"Babe, how much have you drank?" Sheridan asked worriedly. These one-word rapid-fire answers were so unlike her.

"Enough to have this conversation. I know I won't be able to talk about this again, for a while anyway, so unless you want my head to explode..."

"But how am I going to know when you want me to...?"

"Just do it. I trust you. You seem to know me better than I do."

Sheridan wondered how the hell she was going to suddenly produce a dildo when she felt as if Keefer was ready. Unless..."Hey, you wanna...?"

Keefer blew out a nervous breath. "No, if I know you're going to do it I may back out. But I want it, I really do, I'm just nervous...as usual."

Sheridan detected a note of sadness. "You know, there's nothing wrong with being nervous. I was nervous as hell the first time I made love to you."

"You made love to me, Sheridan?" Keefer asked.

The blonde had a puzzled look on her face ever since she finished her sentence. "Yeah," she said with masked uncertainty. "I did," she decided confidently and with a smile. "So, how will I know when you're ready? I mean, I'll know...I'm pretty sure I will, but how can I get to it without you knowing?"

"Sheridan...who says you have to go get it?" she said cryptically.

"But...ohh." The blonde smiled knowingly. "Ah, always be prepared, huh?"

Keefer chuckled nervously. "Yeah, something like that."

"You know, I'm glad we had this conversation. Thanks," Sheridan said with a smile.

"Don't thank me, thank channel 46 and three-quarters of a bottle of wine," Keefer snickered.

"Three-quarters? Why, Keefer, you lush!" Sheridan laughed teasingly.

"Yeah, that's me," Keefer laughed back, seemingly relieved that the conversation was over.

"You want company? I mean, what if you're too tipsy to make it into bed safely?"

"I think Ms. Landers is a little turned on by our conversation," Keefer teased playfully.

"You bet I am," Sheridan admitted easily. "So, what about that company?"

"Aren't you going out?"

"Fuck it. I can go out any time."

"That just made me feel very important. Do you know that?"

"You *are* important, and you should also know that I thought about you all day, too."

"That feels nice to hear."

"Are you sure it isn't the wine?" the blonde chuckled.

"No, it's all you. You make me feel like I've never felt before; like I can do anything."

"I know what you mean," Sheridan nodded on the phone. "Maybe you should get some sleep," she added.

"I thought I was expecting company."

"Give me half an hour, sexy."

"Sher, I'm feeling drunk now," Keefer said in a nervous whisper. "I may not wanna...I don't think I want to do anything..."

"Shh, babe, you can trust me."

Chapter 25

By the time Sheridan had showed up, Keefer was three sheets to the wind and finished with her wine. The blonde construction worker was treated to a dizzying kiss the second the door opened. She almost laughed at the way Keefer practically lifted her off of the floor. She didn't complain, though; she allowed her mouth to be totally ravished with as little resistance as possible.

Keefer had been anticipating the feel of Sheridan's lips since she hung up the phone. During the whole "toy" conversation, she kept picturing that cute little half smile she was sure her girlfriend was wearing while she spoke. Her lips were the only things she could think of during that long half-hour.

Sheridan was the first one to break the hot kiss. She remembered Keefer telling her that she was drunk and she wasn't sure that things should go any further with her in that condition. She stumbled back a few steps, shaking off the effects of such a kiss and flashed her patented grin when she saw the dreamy expression on Keefer's face. "Are you okay?" she asked, taking the larger hand in her own.

"Wonderful. Drunk, but wonderful." Keefer smiled almost demurely.

Sheridan raised an eyebrow; surely, Keefer wasn't playing shy after a greeting like that. "Let's go sit down, baby," she said as she led Keefer to the couch.

"'Kay," Keefer agreed, walking pretty steadily for someone who had declared herself drunk.

Sheridan stood there looking at her sitting girlfriend. "You sure you're drunk?" she asked, fingering the empty wine bottle.

"Shitfaced." Keefer smiled lopsidedly.

"You're pretty steady on your feet there, kiddo."

"Sheridan, would I be able to talk about what we talked about sober?" A small blush crept up on her and she tried to wipe it away with her hand.

"I suppose not. I like you drunk, you're silly."

"Horny, too."

Sheridan laughed out loud. "Now I *know* you're drunk!"

Keefer leaned toward Sheridan and buried her red face in the material of her shirt.

The construction worker cupped the back of the brunette's head and held her there. "Keef, I'm not sure we should do anything."

Keefer took a big breath and shook a little when she exhaled. "I won't regret a thing," she admitted into Sheridan's stomach.

"But you're crocked," the blonde argued, not really knowing why.

"Pretty much so, but think of the possibilities," the inspector muttered, rubbing her cheek on her girlfriend's belly. "You smell good."

Sheridan's eyes narrowed. *She knows she's drunk, she almost wants me to take advantage of that. Why?*

"Don't you want me to be less inhibited for you?" Keefer glanced up into green eyes.

Oh, fuck, I know what this is all about. Sheridan pulled out of Keefer's grasp and knelt in front of her. She looked into the bright blue eyes and spoke honestly. "Keefer, I want to be with you, not some ho at the club, or I'd be there right now. I like you just the way you are. Don't think I need some floozy to make me happy. I love how you blush; I love how shy you are. I'm willing to wait for anything...with you." *God, where did that come from?*

Keefer focused on the words and they made her want to cry. "I'm sorry. I just thought...and if I was drunk, and you could..."

"No, Keefer. Why should I take advantage of my own girlfriend? I admit I had no clue at first, but I made a commitment when I announced that little fact and I intend to stick to it. I want you to feel everything, remember everything. Don't change. Not for me, not for anyone."

"You won't regret being with a pain in the ass like me? I feel like I'm so much trouble."

"I *like* trouble," Sheridan said with a twinkle in her eyes.

"I like *you*." Keefer leaned forward and kissed her girlfriend slowly.

Sheridan sighed into the kiss. Yeah, she was horny and, yeah, she'd had every intention on throwing Keefer on the floor and getting down to business the minute she was greeted, but there was something tugging at her, telling her it wasn't right. She'd followed her gut and she was pretty glad she did. She felt tons better, even though she was still horny.

Keefer leaned back on the couch and closed her eyes. She needed to know one more thing while she was still drunk enough to ask. She glanced down at the crotch of Sheridan's sweatpants and blushed. "Did you..."

"Uh-uh. I'm not supposed to tell you, remember?"

The sexy grin on her face hit Keefer below the belt and she growled deep in her chest. Her eyebrows went up at the sound and she covered her mouth in embarrassment.

"See? I love that you get so embarrassed." The blonde stood up and took Keefer's hands, pulling her from the couch. "Let's get some sleep into you, babe. I think you need it."

Sheridan sat the tall, grinning woman on the bed and knelt down in front of her to take off her socks. Keefer had already opened her pants by the time the blonde was finished with her socks and she pulled the pants off by grabbing at the cuffs while Keefer lay down and lifted her butt off the bed to assist. Sheridan felt a pang or arousal at being in such a position, all she had to do was lean forward...*No*, she told herself, standing up and crawling onto the bed beside her girlfriend. "Sit up, babe, let me take off your shirt."

"You first," Keefer whispered seductively.

Green eyes narrowed. "Keef, I'm behaving as best as I can here." Sheridan pulled off her shirt, revealing that she was not wearing a bra.

Blue eyes widened at first and then narrowed.

"Keefer," Sheridan warned at the look on her face.

"Okay!" The tall woman held up her hands. "But I did tell you I was horny. All I thought about all day was...you know." She lifted her arms up and Sheridan peeled off her shirt.

"Where are your pj's?" the blonde asked, staring intently at the lacy bra.

"Don't want any," Keefer said, pulling the covers up over her body.

"Okay, suit yourself, but there's going to be a lot of blushing going on in here in the morning," Sheridan teased. She climbed into bed next to her drunken lover and got comfortable. "I think you should probably sleep now."

"Yeah, I'm pretty tired," Keefer yawned.

"Good night, Keef." The blonde leaned over and meant to kiss Keefer lightly, but long arms wrapped around her neck and a tongue wound up in her mouth. She shrugged and reciprocated.

Finally letting go, Keefer sighed heavily and rolled over onto her side to look at Sheridan. "Why do they call you Patch?"

"Where'd that come from?" Sheridan turned over to face Keefer.

"Just wanna know."

"You're looking at the fastest spackler in the east." Sheridan pointed to herself proudly.

Keefer smiled brightly. "Cute name," she said sleepily.

"Good night, baby."

"Good night, Patch."

Keefer's eyes popped open and she immediately searched for Sheridan, blowing out a long breath of relief when she saw her sleeping peacefully beside her. *What a dream!* she thought, wiping the sweat from her face. Her heart was beating frantically, her mouth was terribly dry, and her sex was throbbing continuously. She sat up, pulled the blanket from her overheated body, and blew on her skin. *Christ!* Her bra felt way too constricting and she opened it, running her hands over her breasts once they were freed. Her thighs flexed at the touch. *Oh, this feels good...*She glanced back at object of her dreamscape fantasy and shivered, her nipples hardening tightly beneath her hands.

Sheridan shifted suddenly and her arm fell, palm up, on Keefer's lap.

Blue eyes studied the roughened skin of the construction worker's palm and Keefer wished it were rubbing across her nipple instead of her own. She dropped her hands next to Sheridan's and smiled at the sleeping woman. *No, let her sleep; she looks so cute.* The blonde's lips were open slightly and she was breathing through her mouth.

Keefer remembered the last time she'd studied Sheridan as she slept and a small blush rose on her face along with a twinge of excitement between her legs. She looked back to the hand in her lap and had the urge to lick it. She licked her own instead and brought her wet palm up to her breast. *Mmm...so nice,* she thought as the nipple tingled under the attention. Keefer glanced back at Sheridan's lips and a pang of arousal made her whimper. *Oh please, if she woke up and saw you touching yourself she'd be thrilled.* The thought made her even hornier. She reached down into her panties and felt her wetness already seeping through them. It was too much. "Sher," she whispered. "Sheridan."

"Mmm."

Keefer tickled Sheridan's palm. "Sheridan, wake up."

"What? Whassamatter?" The blonde sat up and searched the room, her eyes falling on her topless girlfriend. She ran her hand over her face to make sure she wasn't still sleeping and her eyebrows shot up, confusion clearly evident on her face. "Was I touching you in your my sleep again?"

Keefer blushed and looked at her wet fingers, the ones she'd used to wake Sheridan.

Green eyes narrowed and Sheridan smelled her hand again. Her nostrils flared this time and she grabbed the hand Keefer was looking at, inhaling deeply. "You?" she asked in amusement.

A shy smile crept across Keefer's face and she nodded.

Sheridan was suddenly wide awake as she smelled her lover's scent, her eyes focusing on the erect nipples in front of her. Her clit tingled. "Are you still drunk?" she asked, hoping Keefer wasn't.

"Nope," Keefer whispered, slightly embarrassed for waking the construction worker.

"Horny?" the blonde asked, her tongue poking out to taste Keefer's finger.

"Mmm," the brunette hummed at the feeling, "yes."

Sheridan grinned then slipped the whole finger in her mouth, sucking on it greedily.

Keefer bit back a groan; she could feel the pulling sensations in her center. "I had this dream..."

Sheridan shifted until she was straddling her lover, sucking on two fingers now. She saw blue eyes staring at her breasts and leaned forward, placing one at Keefer's lips. When she didn't react, Sheridan took the fingers out of her mouth and rubbed them on her nipple, groaning at the contact.

Once Keefer felt the pebbled flesh under her fingers, she lost all of her embarrassment and sucked as much of Sheridan's breast into her mouth as she could, her hand reaching for the other breast.

"Shit, Keef." The blonde twitched, not expecting the hunger that Keefer displayed. "Must have been some dream," she mumbled, holding the brunette's head with one hand, covering the one on her breast with the other.

Keefer nodded and made a happy sound in her throat. She moved her tongue around the nipple as she had in her dream. The image was still so fresh in her mind, and she intended to make it a reality. However, in her dream, Sheridan was beneath her.

The blonde raised her eyebrow as Keefer leaned forward, pushing her down onto her back. *Must have been one hell of a dream.* She ran her hands from Keefer's head down to her shoulders and as far down her back as she could, loving the smooth skin with her fingers, letting Keefer know it was perfectly okay with her to be ravished.

Keefer felt the encouragement and moved her mouth from Sheridan's breast to her lips to show her gratitude. She shivered as the construction worker's hand came up and moved the hair from the back of her neck, tickling her skin. Her nipples tightened even more and she wished Sheridan would touch them.

Sheridan noticed the subtle movements against her body. She could feel Keefer's nipples drag across her own skin and she became very hungry for a taste. She broke the kiss and buried her face in the sweet-smelling neck, taking a swipe at the skin with her tongue. "Come up here," she whispered into a pink ear, tugging under the brunette's arms.

Keefer shuddered as Sheridan spoke; her voice was low and sexy, hot in her ear. She moved up a bit, not knowing exactly what Sheridan wanted until she saw the green eyes narrow as they homed in on her left nipple. She scooted up quickly, wanting very much to have that mouth on her breast.

"Mmm, yeah, that's what I want," Sheridan said before she trapped the hard bud between her lips. Keefer gasped and arched her back, sending a spark through the blonde's body, right to her sex. Sheridan glanced up and saw blue eyes watching, so she opened her mouth and let her tongue swirl around the stiff flesh, showing Keefer everything she was doing.

"Yes," Keefer breathed, watching the wet pink tongue dance around her nipple. It made her so hot she needed to feel Sheridan, and she pressed her hips down into the blonde's. Keefer suddenly stiffened, her heart beating wildly with excitement and fear.

Sheridan looked nervously into slightly panicked blue eyes and stopped what she was doing. "Keef?" she whispered against the soft flesh of her breast.

"I'm okay," Keefer whispered back, not really sure if she was, but knowing she was still as turned on as before made her confident to say that she was.

Sheridan moved her mouth to the other breast and paid the same attention to it as she had the first one, while bringing her hand down to Keefer's lower back.

The brunette let her head fall back as she concentrated on the feelings Sheridan was causing with her sucking. She paid no attention to the bulge between the blonde's legs until Sheridan pressed her body down onto it. She was scared to death but equally as aroused by it, having no idea that Sheridan had shown up "prepared" last night.

Sheridan lifted her hips slightly and kissed the breast she was loving. "Don't move too much, just get used to it being there," she whispered into Keefer's soft skin.

The taller woman nodded. She was very nervous, but she was excited, too, and knowing that Sheridan was being so patient right from the start gave her a little bit of relief. She needed to hug the blonde and show her appreciation. Pulling her breast from Sheridan's mouth, she slid down, parting her long legs on either side of the smaller ones. Her sex slid right over the hard lump between the construction worker's legs and she closed her eyes and groaned softly at the feeling. She settled on top of her lover so she could kiss her, the dildo pressing firmly into her belly.

Sheridan smiled a little shyly at Keefer when their eyes met. "Surprise." She chuckled somewhat nervously.

"Why are you scared?" Keefer asked, staring into sea green eyes.

"Because you are," the blonde answered, reaching her neck up to connect their lips.

Keefer backed up a bit. "But you must have done this a million times."

"Not with you." Sheridan tried for the kiss again and was rewarded with a smothering hug along with a hungry mouth closing over her own.

Keefer felt so good when Sheridan said things like that. She wondered if the blonde even knew that what she was saying was so important for her to hear. Keefer usually needed constant reassurance, but with Sheridan, all it seemed to take was one word or one look into her green eyes, and her confidence overtook her.

Sheridan wrapped her arms around Keefer's back, pressing their upper bodies together. She was enjoying Keefer's sudden aggressiveness and wanted to make it last as long as the tall woman was comfortable with it. She arched her shoulders off of the bed, squeezing their breasts together and groaning, telling Keefer she was enjoying this as much as she was.

Keefer had plenty of confidence when it came to making love to someone; that was something she knew she was good at. Sheridan only succeeded at raising that level higher with her sensuous sounds and constant encouragement. Keefer slipped her body lower, letting her open mouth drag over Sheridan's chin and down to her throat. She licked and sucked the slightly salty skin, causing more moans of approval from her lover.

The blonde was squirming. Keefer's body weight was pressing the dildo firmly between her legs and it was making her entirely too turned on for someone who had to be in control. She knew she needed to have a clear head when it came time for business and she was slowly losing focus the more Keefer leaned into her.

The brunette sucked greedily at Sheridan's throat, making the muscular woman grab at her hair and hold her tighter. She tried to ignore the lump pressing into her body but failed, and she found herself flexing her stomach muscles against the hardness in order to make out its shape. She was oblivious as to what this was doing to her lover until her hips started to jerk each time she flexed. Slightly distracted, she pulled back and regarded the big hickey she'd just made as she pressed herself down into Sheridan once again.

"God, Keef, you gotta stop doing that," Sheridan groaned, her hips involuntarily lifting to make firmer contact.

"Does it hurt?" Curious blue eyes locked into desperate green ones.

"Fuck no." The blonde reached down and pulled Keefer's hip slightly, telling her to move up.

The taller woman shifted until her sex was hovering over Sheridan's crotch. She allowed the blonde to push her body down until she was sitting on the dildo. The feeling was strange and very arousing. She'd never done that before and didn't know what to expect. She looked into Sheridan's eyes with as much trust as she could muster, even though she was borderline petrified, and nodded. The construction worker gyrated her hips slightly and Keefer jerked hers at the feeling. "Oh..." she whispered, watching the small smile spread across her lover's face. "Do it again," she said breathlessly, lost in her green eyes.

Sheridan's heart was pounding furiously as she watched Keefer discover the new sensations. It was a wonderful discovery for her, too. Sheridan had never taken the time or even cared about what the other woman was feeling. This was different, this was Keefer, and she was getting a pleasant rush as she watched her lover's face.

Keefer began to move, making the construction worker growl with pleasure. She didn't know what came over her; looking at Sheridan's face and seeing her obvious excitement gave her more confidence than she'd ever had before. With a sexy smile, she leaned forward and braced her hands on the bed above Sheridan's shoulders. "You feel wonderful," she whispered in the blonde's ear, making her shiver as she continued to move her lower half.

"Keef," Sheridan groaned, "you're gonna make me come."

Keefer grunted as a jolt of arousal traveled through her sex. She'd never made Danni come without using her hands or her mouth, and this excited her to the highest degree. She watched Sheridan's face intently as she pressed her sex down harder, swirling her hips.

"Oh, God," the blonde whimpered, "you *want* to make me come..." She almost chuckled at her predicament.

Keefer nodded, too excited to speak as she watched Sheridan struggle to keep control. She leaned her weight on one hand and brought the other to the blonde's breast, pinching and pulling the nipple as she danced on top of her.

"Fuck, baby..." Sheridan growled, clutching at Keefer's shoulders.

"Yes..." the brunette breathed, her panties soaking wet with arousal. She felt so good giving Sheridan the ultimate pleasure, and she could see that the blonde was hanging on the edge. She switched breasts and toyed with the other nipple roughly, watching with unbridled lust as her lover's back arched.

Sheridan groaned wordlessly as she came; her eyes closed and her hips rose off of the bed, lifting Keefer up with her. She'd never had an orgasm like that before and though it wasn't huge and overly satisfying, it was a big triumph on her lover's part. After the small spasms subsided, she opened her eyes to see Keefer's half-lidded baby blues boring into her. She looked so sexy sitting there on top of her, her breasts moving with her heavy breathing, Sheridan couldn't resist pulling her down for a much needed connection.

Keefer melted into the hungry kiss, opening her mouth wide and allowing Sheridan to devour her. Her sex was throbbing and she was covered in wetness. She'd never felt so good in her life; she actually felt a little cocky and it made her heart race.

Sheridan shifted their bodies and attempted to take off her sweatpants. Keefer raised up on her knees, never breaking their hungry liplock, and used her foot to pull down the pants. Sheridan tore her mouth away for a second. "You sure you want this?" she asked before sucking Keefer's bottom lip into her mouth.

The brunette merely groaned; she couldn't think of anything except the fire in her sex and she knew only Sheridan could put it out. She had never truly felt as if she needed to be filled inside and accepted fingers into her body as part of the whole experience, but now, with the knowledge that Sheridan was going to fill her up, she craved it badly. She knew her lover was nervous because *she* was nervous, so Keefer continued to kiss Sheridan until she was squirming. She sucked on her tongue, nibbled on her lips, and drove her insane until she was gasping for air. This calmed Keefer down as well; the act of kissing Sheridan always drove her to distraction.

Sheridan began to lift herself until she was sitting up with Keefer on her lap and the tall woman's long legs wrapped around her waist. She ran her hands along the length of Keefer's legs, making the inspector shiver and wiggle deliciously on top of her.

Keefer buried her face in Sheridan's neck and inhaled deeply the scent of her lover, calming her nervous stomach instantly. She licked the skin behind the blonde's ear as her fingers held both of her biceps tightly. She was scared, but as long as she was holding onto her lover, she felt she could do anything.

Sheridan was curious when Keefer began to lean back, pulling her on top of her long body as she lay down. Keefer was making the first move, much to Sheridan's surprise, and she couldn't have been more grateful.

The day before, she'd been certain she would know when the brunette was ready, but now she was much too nervous to know anything.

Keefer kept her face hidden in the soft sweaty skin of her lover's neck as she lay back. She wanted nothing more than to feel Sheridan inside of her, all over her at once, and she unwrapped her legs from around Sheridan and let them fall open on the bed.

Sheridan's heart palpitated at the blatant invitation and she kneeled between the open legs and fingered the elastic of Keefer's panties. "May I?" she asked with a sensuous smile.

The brunette nodded and lifted her butt off of the bed to help.

Sheridan lifted one long leg and then the other as she almost reverently peeled off the sexy garment. Green eyes drank in the most arousing sight she had seen in her life. Keefer was offering herself and it made her blood simmer. She slid her hands up the inside of the brunette's thighs, smiling at the shiver her touch caused. By the time her hands reached Keefer's sex, they were already wet. "Shit, Keefer," she breathed out in amazement. For a woman who, just a few weeks ago, had looked at her own wetness with curiosity, this was one hell of an event. It made Sheridan groan to know that she'd played a part in making her lover so hot.

Keefer watched Sheridan's face as the blonde descended between her legs. She had yet to take a good look at the dildo, but quickly forgot about the whole thing once the blonde's tongue touched her sex. Her hips jerked and she gasped loudly.

"Mmm," Sheridan hummed.

Keefer began to blush. She couldn't control her hips and Sheridan was making the most obscene noises from between her legs. She covered her face with her arms and bit her bottom lip as Sheridan's tongue worked its magic.

The blonde was in heaven. Keefer was so wet, and she made it a point to show her appreciation by slurping and sucking every drop. She didn't expect Keefer to be so embarrassed and frowned when she saw her cover her face.

Keefer peeked through her arms when Sheridan had stopped licking her. She found the blonde sitting on her heels looking right at her face.

"Don't hide, baby. You taste so good."

Keefer moved her arms away and continued to blush. She tensed up a little when Sheridan leaned forward and crawled up to face her.

"I'm only going to touch you with my fingers first, okay?"

The brunette nodded and moaned quietly as Sheridan's fingers teased her opening. Green eyes were watching her intently and, for once, she wasn't embarrassed. She stared right back and even kept her eyes open when two fingers entered her.

"God, you're so fucking wet..."

Ever the romantic, Keefer chuckled to herself, then moaned louder as Sheridan began to move her fingers. "Ohh..." She gasped when a callused finger massaged her clit. Her pelvis rocked in time to the gentle thrusts, and she reached out to hold on to her lover, grabbing both muscular shoulders tightly, wanting to feel Sheridan on top of her and inside her at the same time.

"Feels good?" Sheridan breathed out, her own level of arousal peaking by just watching the pleasure on Keefer's face.

"Yes," Keefer groaned, lifting her hips higher to get Sheridan to reach deeper inside of her. The need to be filled by her blonde lover was getting more and more persistent.

Sheridan sensed it was time and she eased her fingers out with a sexy wet noise. She positioned the tip of the dildo at Keefer's entrance and lowered her body down on top of the trembling woman. "Ready?"

"Oh yes, please," Keefer whimpered, her need skyrocketing, knowing she was about to be filled by Sheridan.

The blonde leaned her hips forward just a little, sliding just a bit of the dildo inside of her lover. Keefer tensed a bit. "Okay?"

"More."

Sheridan grinned and happily obliged, sliding in halfway, shivering when Keefer groaned languidly at the invasion. "Is it too big?"

"No," Keefer whispered throatily. "Go all the way," she begged, moving her hands from Sheridan's shoulders to her ass and pressing down. "I want to feel you."

Sheridan thrust the whole thing inside of Keefer and laid her body down on top of her, pressing them together tightly. She grunted as fingernails bit into the skin on her ass.

Keefer had never felt anything so fulfilling. This is what she was craving, and her imagination paled against the real thing. She wasn't embarrassed at all; Sheridan was staring at her and she couldn't care less. "Kiss me," she ordered the mesmerized blonde.

Their lips met softly at first, Sheridan still in gentle mode and Keefer thanking her lover for being so patient. However, once their lower bodies started moving, the kiss heated up quickly. Keefer struggled to keep herself from screaming and wound up biting Sheridan's lip instead of her own. This only managed to fuel the blonde's fire and she growled into Keefer's mouth, thrusting her tongue deep inside, wanting to mirror those actions with her hips.

Keefer thought she was going to explode with sensation. Fingers felt okay, but this was something she had never felt before. The dildo was wider and longer, and the friction was driving her to a higher state of arousal than ever. The ability to feel Sheridan on top of her while being filled her in such a way was so incredibly hot, she couldn't hold back and began letting out the sounds that were welling inside of her.

Sheridan broke the kiss to look at her lover's face. Keefer had been making little whimpering noises with every thrust and it was driving her crazy with the need to see her face in such a state. Keefer was gorgeous, and Sheridan felt the tingles of an orgasm tickling at her clit while she watched the beautiful face in ecstasy. Fingers dug deeper into her ass and she followed the lead, thrusting harder and quicker, plunging in all the way and pulling almost all the way out.

"Oh...my...god..." Keefer grunted between heavy breaths and whimpers. Sheridan was hitting spots inside her she didn't know she had. Spots that made her want to scream.

Sheridan knew Keefer was close when she wrapped a long leg around her back and her arms around her shoulders, squeezing all her limbs tightly. She buried her face in Keefer's wet neck and whispered, "Can you feel me all the way inside you?"

Keefer groaned and shivered from the hot breath. Her sex began to clench tightly around the dildo, giving her a brand new series of sensations.

"Come for me, Keefer."

The brunette whimpered and nodded rapidly, her eyes squeezing shut against the overwhelming feeling. Her hips jerked of their own will and she groaned loudly into Sheridan's hair.

The construction worker jerked too. Keefer's uncontrollable twitches pressed the harness into her clit hard; she was about to lose it before her lover and she needed this to be mutual. "Come on, Keef, come with me, baby..." She breathed out as her own orgasm started to over take her senses.

"Fuck..." Keefer shouted unexpectedly as her body tightened.

Hearing her lover shout, Sheridan pulled her head out from the sweaty crevice and watched her face as best she could as her eyes threatened to close.

The tall woman's legs pulled Sheridan impossibly deeper and her whole body shook with spasms. She groaned loudly as she trembled, holding her lover against her.

The blonde's orgasm subsided and she watched as Keefer came down from hers as well. Her black hair was stuck to her face and her mouth was open as wordless sounds escaped her. Sheridan's heart swelled at the gift

Keefer had given her. She wiped the wet hair off of her lover's face and kissed her on the lips. "You are so beautiful," she said, waiting to see those baby blues appear.

Keefer couldn't catch her breath. Her sex was twitching uncontrollably and she pulled Sheridan down on top of her, unable to look her in the eyes just yet.

"Are you all right, Keef?"

"Oh God...perfect," she groaned, letting her legs slide off of Sheridan's back and lie open on the bed. "Unbelievable."

"It was okay?" Sheridan asked nervously.

"Sheridan, I yelled," Keefer blushed, turning her head and pushing Sheridan back to look at her.

"That you did, sweetie, " the blonde chuckled, but soon stopped when she looked into those eyes.

"What?" Keefer said self-consciously.

"Nothing. You're so sexy," the blonde said with a smile. "I'm going to pull out now, okay?"

"Okay." Keefer didn't know what to expect and gasped as the lewd, wet sound echoed in the room.

"Don't you dare blush—that's the best part," Sheridan said, silencing her embarrassed lover with a kiss.

Chapter 26

The two women awoke in the same position they had fallen asleep in mere hours before. Sheridan was sprawled on top of Keefer, who was content to let her lay there as long as possible.

Keefer knew Sheridan was awake, and had been for quite a while, but the construction worker hadn't moved except for little errant shivers as the brunette traced light, circular patterns all around her muscular back with her fingernails. A smile lit the inspector's face. She was certain that her lover had never had a morning-after before and she seemed perfectly content to lie there all morning if she could. It warmed Keefer's belly to think she'd made the blonde feel that way.

Sheridan sighed in pleasure as Keefer's nails traveled to the back of her head and scratched her scalp in a very relaxing way. "I'm never going to get up if you keep doing that," she said sleepily, pressing her cheek down and rubbing it into Keefer's breast.

"It's eight o'clock already. I think you have to get moving, Sher," Keefer said reluctantly, untangling her fingers from the sleep-tousled blonde hair.

Sheridan sighed, this time in disappointment, and she lifted her upper body, resting her weight on her elbows. "Good morning," she said with a lazy smile.

Keefer smiled back. "Good morning," she replied, turning her head a little to the side.

"Let's not start that. C'mere," Sheridan ordered gently before leaning down and taking a proper good morning kiss.

"I must have sleep in my eyes and..."

"Shut up," Sheridan said with a playful grin.

Keefer narrowed her eyes in return and then laughed. "Okay, but you really have to get going," she reminded the comfortable blonde.

Sheridan tilted her head and looked down at where their bodies met, and then lifted only her eyes to meet blue ones with a sensuous smile. "Mmm, what a way to wake up, on top of the most beautiful woman I've ever seen. Naked to boot."

Keefer took a quick breath as the smaller woman began sliding down her naked body, leaving little kisses behind.

Sheridan kissed each breast softly, then each relaxed nipple, grinning at them as they began to perk up for her. She moved lower and kissed Keefer's ribs, the right side, then the left. She slid lower still and placed a sweet kiss on her lover's navel before kneeling between her legs and leaving a gentle kiss there, stopping to ruffle her nose through the soft black hairs.

Keefer was struggling not to cover her face. This was all so new to her. The way Sheridan was kissing her made her feel very special and somewhat embarrassed all at the same time. "Do you kiss all the girls good morning like that?"

"Never saw a morning with anyone else, Keef. Only you," Sheridan said with a twinkle in her eye, still crouching between her lover's legs. "I better get out of here before I really wake you up." She placed one more kiss on Keefer's center before sliding out of bed.

Keefer's eyes widened at the sight of her naked lover standing by the side of her bed, wearing a harness and a dildo. "You didn't take it off?"

"When could I? I'm going to have the worst marks from this thing now." She grimaced as she pulled the straps from her body.

"I'm sorry."

"Why? I wore it to bed in the first place, it's my own fault," the construction worker said as she examined her backside in the mirror. "Look at that," she laughed, "it looks like I'm wearing a jock strap." She showed her ass to Keefer, who giggled a little.

"Does it hurt?" the brunette asked of the red marks.

"Nah, not really, but this thing throbs a little." Sheridan pointed to the dark bruise on her throat.

Keefer blushed hotly.

"Aw, stop that, Keef. I like it, it drives me crazy when you suck on my neck." She wiggled her eyebrows and smiled.

Keefer threw a pillow at the naked blonde. "Go shower, you pig."

"Oink." Sheridan snorted her way to the bathroom, gathering her discarded clothes along the way.

Keefer stepped out of the shower with a self-satisfied grin. Sheridan was still banging around the house, which meant she didn't want to leave. The tall inspector tsked at herself as she dried between her legs. She'd expected to be sore to some extent, but she wasn't. In fact, she felt like she could have another go at it, especially after thinking about nothing else the whole time she showered.

"Keef, I gotta go." Sheridan knocked lightly at the bathroom door.

The brunette opened the door enough to stick her head out and smiled. Sheridan was holding out a cup of coffee. "For me?" Keefer asked, even as she took the cup and sipped from it.

"Open up, sexy," Sheridan said, leaning on the door, "I want a kiss to hold me over." She licked her lips and winked.

Keefer opened the door to reveal a long arm holding a short towel over her front.

Sheridan's eyes narrowed as she drank in the vision, a happy little smile gracing her lips. "Mmm, mmm, good," she hummed, running her fingers down Keefer's shower-warmed arm.

Keefer chuckled nervously and set her cup down on the vanity. She looked down at herself and winced slightly. The towel barely made it to mid-thigh, and the end she held against her breasts hardly covered them at all. She watched those green eyes drink her body in. The way Sheridan was leering at her sent a now-familiar tingle through her body, causing goose bumps to break out and her nipples begin to tighten beneath the damp towel.

"Are you cold?" Sheridan asked at the shiver that shook the tall body as she stepped closer.

"Stop," Keefer said, holding up her hand. Sheridan stopped in mid-lean, her mouth still open on its way to taste skin. Keefer stepped back and took a deep breath. "Sheridan, just the way you look at me gets me crazy."

"And this is bad, how?"

"You have to go to work."

"I can be late." The blonde shrugged and continued forward on her quest for a taste of Keefer.

The tall woman backed into the sink and held her towel tighter. She knew if she dropped it, Sheridan would pounce on her like a hungry tiger. "Didn't you get enough last night...this morning?" she asked, breathless in anticipation of Sheridan's tongue.

"Never enough."

The inspector gasped as that hot tongue and soft lips covered the top of her right breast. "Sher..." she moaned.

"Just a little taste," the blonde reasoned, switching to the top of the other breast.

291

Keefer's grip on the towel loosened without her even realizing it and Sheridan nudged it down further with her tongue.

"God...you better stop..." the brunette said shakily.

"Uh-uh." Sheridan shook her head, causing her tongue to bathe an even greater area.

Keefer let her body relax against the sink as Sheridan began to peel away the towel. She wanted to blush, but found that she enjoyed her lover's attentions more than she was embarrassed by them. She sighed in willing surrender and allowed Sheridan to pull the towel completely off, but she closed her eyes so she couldn't see the green eyes staring at her naked body.

"Fuck, you're incredible,"' Sheridan said, running her hands up and down the outsides of Keefer's thighs.

"That feels good," Keefer dared to admit.

Sheridan smiled; a surge of happiness ran through her body. Her shy lover was beginning to express her pleasure willingly and it thrilled her. She continued to run her hands up the tall woman's torso, stopping just beneath her breasts, and down, stopping just above her pubic hair. "Tell me," Sheridan whispered, standing on her toes, asking for a kiss.

Keefer met Sheridan's lips. "You make me feel good," she said before covering the blonde's lips with her own.

Sheridan groaned. Keefer's lips tasted so good; they felt so soft and sweet as they opened to accept her tongue. A small sigh of pleasure escaped the brunette as their tongues met and touched, the sound causing the construction worker's sex to twitch. She pressed her body into Keefer's bared skin and was rewarded by two long arms draping leisurely, comfortably, over her shoulders.

They kissed for long moments until Sheridan became good and aroused. She pulled away from the kiss and looked into heavy-lidded blue eyes. "Thank you for this, Keefer," she said, smiling appreciatively at her.

Keefer blushed at the compliment. She felt very good from head to toe from Sheridan's apparent gratefulness. She watched as her lover winked and smiled happily before turning and leaving the bathroom with a spring in her step. She leaned all her weight into the sink and breathed deeply, willing her heartbeat back to normal.

Sheridan stuck her head back into the bathroom to catch the dreamy, aroused expression on her lover's face. "I just needed something to tide me over for the rest of the day."

"Yeah, thanks," Keefer said sarcastically, covering her body with the towel once again.

Sheridan chuckled and really left this time.

"God...the things she does to me."

The construction worker drove like a maniac to her apartment where her babies were patiently waiting for her. *This is getting crazy! I have to invite her here soon or the kids will never forgive me*, she thought as she pulled her car in front of a fire hydrant in her haste to get upstairs.

Her key wasn't even in the door when she heard the dogs whimpering and singing with excitement at their mommy's return. She had to actually push the door open as they kept throwing themselves at the other side. "Back up, guys!" she said with a chuckle, finally opening her door.

"Hiya, kids!" she shouted with her arms open and the two dogs jumped her so hard she was on the floor in a heartbeat. "Okay.. okay..." She grabbed Zeus' snout with both hands. "Kisses," she demanded and was rewarded with many. Pharaoh was extremely excited and started gnawing on her arm, whining and growling. "Ow! Cut it out!" she yelled, shaking her arm free from the strong jaws. "You're a pit bull, for shit's sake...that hurts!" she chastised the hyper dog and pulled him under Zeus's body in order to receive her kisses. She grabbed him by both ears and kissed his wet nose and he followed her lead, bathing her whole face with his long pink tongue. "Now that's more like it!" she said as she tried to get up from the floor.

Sheridan didn't walk the dogs that day—they walked her in a very determined manner toward the park. She really didn't have time for a long run, but she felt guilty and indulged the dogs, calling the job site on her cellular to let them know she'd be late. Bobby laughed at her, saying something about not forgetting the details when she finally got there.

The blonde watched her dogs romp as she thought about why she felt weird about sharing her intimacies with the guys when it came to Keefer. When Bobby laughed, she had winced, feeling suddenly uncomfortable about him knowing why she was late. That had never bothered her before. She lived to tell of her exploits with the women; she loved watching their jealous faces in rapt attention as she gave them play-by-plays of the night before. Now, she wasn't too keen on sharing Keefer with them...with anybody, for that matter, and it made her think.

Keefer decided she intended to use her last day of vacation wisely and do nothing but relax. She took Fifi for a long walk, meandering up and down the streets of her neighborhood, and couldn't help but think about the night before. She blushed, but not as deeply and not as frequently as she used to, as she remembered what they had done. She recalled herself reacting to Sheridan with near abandon, moaning and groaning loudly, losing control of her body and wrapping her legs around the smaller woman's back. This was so unlike her, and she just wondered what Sheridan was capable of. *How far can I comfortably go with her?*

Keefer trusted the blonde construction worker more than anyone she had ever known, and she felt safe with her. She didn't have reason to feel otherwise—Sheridan had never made her feel uncomfortable, and if she did, the sexy little blonde took care of it in the blink of an eye...whether with words or with actions. Keefer always felt confident when Sheridan was around. *I miss her already*, she thought as she stepped up to her front door. *Is that normal?* she wondered, closing the door behind her and looking around her house. She felt a loss, knowing that the blonde wasn't there waiting for her, and shook her head. *You couldn't stand the thought of having Danni here all the time, why is Sheridan so different?*

Fifi climbed up on the sofa and curled up with a rawhide chew. Keefer's gaze followed the dog and she sighed, joined her on the sofa and turned on the television. That lasted until she flipped through all the channels distractedly and turned the set off. *I really do miss her already; this can't be healthy*, she thought with a small frown. She went into her bedroom and lay down on the bed, hugging the pillow Sheridan had slept on before their middle-of-the-night lovemaking. The scent of the blonde only made her crave holding her in person and Keefer closed her eyes, wishing she were there. A thought sprung to her mind unbidden and, to her great surprise, fell out of her mouth. "I love you, Sheridan Landers."

When the blonde construction worker got to the jobsite, she was met with hoots and applause. She took off her hard hat and bowed to her co-workers. Sheridan had never been late for work because of a woman—she'd never stayed anywhere but in her own bed after sex—so their little greeting made her blush a little bit, but she recovered quickly. "Eat your hearts out, guys," she said with a snicker.

"We are, we are...so tell us, was she that good?" Bobby asked, knowing full well that Sheridan wasn't going to talk about it. They all knew this was different and wanted justification for their assumptions.

"Even better," the blonde said with a wink before taking the top off of her coffee and blowing on it.

"Well...details?" Tony asked.

Sheridan squirmed uncomfortably. She wasn't sure what to say but she knew it would have nothing to do with Keefer. "Let's just say..." She pointed to the hickey on her throat.

The guys laughed as they always would, but all had knowing looks on their faces. Sheridan wasn't talking; this was exactly what they had thought.

"Why are you looking at me like that?" she asked self-consciously.

"It's written all over your face," Tony said with a sweet smile.

"What is? What the fuck are you talking about?" Sheridan said in annoyance.

"Come on, Patch, you're in love!" Phil blurted out.

Sheridan's mouth hung open and she blinked a few times. "I am not," she said indignantly.

"Please, you can lie to yourself, but you can't lie to us," Tony said as he patted her on the shoulder.

Sheridan paled slightly. *Can it be?* She put down her coffee, her stomach suddenly in knots. *Nah.* "What makes you guys the experts, anyway?" she asked with a forced chuckle.

"We've been there, *chica*, we know. There's nothing wrong with it," Bobby said reassuringly.

"Yeah, well, don't you think I'd *know* if I were in love?" Sheridan said, feeling very nervous.

They all shook their heads. "Nope." Phil spoke for all of them.

"Come on, am I really that fucking clueless?" Sheridan asked with a hint of desperation.

"Yeah." Tony nodded. "But it's not a bad thing," he added at her outraged expression.

The blonde waved her hand and snorted. "Oh, get a grip. I care a lot for this woman. She's different, that's all. I'd know if I was in love," she said with confidence she didn't feel at all.

"Okay, we'll drop the subject, but if you need to talk, we're all ears, Patch. We care about you and know what you're going through," Phil said sincerely.

"Yeah, yeah," she said. "I need to get some air."

As soon as she was out of hearing range, the muscular blonde kicked at the sand with her toe, a severe scowl on her face. *I'd know if I was in love! Who do they think they are...telling me...like they'd know...buncha losers...*She sighed heavily. *Come on, Sher, be fair. They're not losers, they're good guys, married guys...guys in love with their wives.* She blonde glanced back at the room she'd just left. *Ya think?* She wondered if, maybe, there was a chance they were right.

Keefer's mouth hung open in shock. She hadn't moved in a long time and it worried Fifi, who ran up and licked her mommy's face.

"Did you hear what I said, Feefs?" she asked the dog, who merely cocked her head. "I said I love Sheridan." The dog's tail wagged happily at the blonde's name. "If I had a tail, honey, it'd be wagging so hard, I'd take flight," Keefer laughed loudly, nervously at her own words. Blue eyes started to tear up as she laughed, and she wasn't so sure it was because she was laughing. She was confused. She shouldn't be in love with a woman with Sheridan's reputation. *Should I?* she thought as her laughter slowed down and all that was left were tears. "Why the hell am I crying?" she asked her concerned doggie, who started to whimper as she did every time Keefer cried. "I think I'm finally in love! This is a good thing, isn't it?"

Keefer got up from the bed and began to pace the length of her room, still hugging the pillow to her chest. "There's nothing to be afraid of...she's not the same Sheridan that they all talk about. She's different with me; she respects me and cares about me. I can tell; I can feel it in her touches and see it in her eyes," she said to herself. "And," she turned and faced the mirror, "she wants to show me off at the club...her club." She wiped her eyes and felt suddenly proud. "I think it's safe to assume that falling in love with Sheridan isn't as bad as it sounds," she reasoned. "Now, how does she feel about me?"

Keefer knew one thing for sure—she could not tell Sheridan that she was in love with her until the muscular blonde was ready to hear it. She was positive that her little construction worker was going to go through a few hoops before she admitted that she felt anything more than like for her. Keefer was sure that Sheridan was past the "like" stage, but the problem with a woman like Sheridan was getting her to admit it to herself.

The tall woman felt suddenly apprehensive about seeing her lover now that she knew she was in love with her. How was she going to hide that? "I don't want to scare her away! Oh no!" Keefer panicked. "She's going to see it in my eyes, she sees everything in my eyes!" She looked stricken for a moment. "Oh, but wait just a minute. I can see everything in hers, too." She smiled deviously and a chuckle escaped her lips. "She doesn't have to say anything, I'll know." Keefer suddenly felt much more at ease with her revelation. "I'll know if she feels the same, even if she doesn't."

It was coming close to lunchtime and Sheridan was getting mighty restless, so she went out to sit at her usual spot. No amount of work could take her mind off of the discussion from earlier and she wasn't hungry, either. She was going through her storage of Keefer moments, trying to find instances of herself acting like the guys had when they first met their wives-to-be. She didn't see herself acting like the goofy idiots she observed in them, but a few things did make her think. The time in the bathroom at the club when Keefer called and she'd run like her ass was on fire. The time in the car when she'd had an explosive orgasm with Keefer's name written all over it. She smiled with that memory, totally blocking out the other woman's reaction. *Then there's the first time we kissed...I swear the floor dropped out from under me.* Another smile accompanied that thought. *How she makes me feel just to be around her...so special, important, needed.*

Her smile disappeared as she tried to think of another woman making her feel the same way. There were none. *Needed. It's a nice feeling.* Sheridan felt a tickling sensation in her stomach. *She touches me and everything's okay. And making love to her...oh, yeah...there's nothing more fulfilling than giving her pleasure.* The thought felt foreign to the blonde, like someone else had said it, and she wondered about it for a long time. *I never gave a rat's ass about someone else's pleasure. One little gasp from Keefer and my chest feels like it's going to explode!* Sheridan could almost feel that exact sensation as she remembered their last time. *Those lips...so soft and perfect.* Green eyes closed with that image. *Then there's her eyes...I could get lost in them, I can see everything...she lets me see everything.* Sheridan pictured those deep blue pools of trust and her stomach flip-flopped wildly. She backed up from her own imagination. *Just what is it you see in those eyes, Sher?*

After stopping at the deli and the gourmet coffee shop, Keefer got out of a cab in front of Sheridan's construction site. She couldn't wait any longer and had to know that minute what her blonde lover was feeling. She spied the muscular woman sitting on the tailgate of a pickup truck, swinging her legs and lost in thought. Her brow was furrowed and she seemed to be troubled. Keefer approached quietly, so as not to disturb her, but walked into her line of vision so she wouldn't scare her either.

As soon as the blonde construction worker saw her, she leapt off of the truck and looked panicked. *Oh, shit! Why is she here...now?*

"Sher? Are you okay?" Keefer asked with concern at her lover's behavior. She seemed trapped.

"Yeah, yeah, I'm fine. What are you doing here?" Sheridan asked, more harshly than she intended.

"I thought I'd surprise you." The brunette held up a big paper bag. "I brought lunch."

Sheridan's trepidation from moments before suddenly disappeared once she saw Keefer look slightly hurt. "I'm sorry, Keef, I didn't mean to sound so—"

"No, that's okay. It looks like I interrupted you. It's my fault."

"Come here." The construction worker motioned with her finger, hopping back up onto the tailgate and pulling off her hard hat. *Fuck everything, I need to hold her*, she thought as she watched the long-legged inspector close the distance between them.

"I hope you're hungry," Keefer said, coming to a stop standing between Sheridan's legs.

Green eyes locked on worried blue and the blonde smiled slowly. "I wasn't before, but somehow, I suddenly have an appetite." Sheridan's smile turned into a sexy grin and her eyes fell on Keefer's lips.

Keefer noticed where Sheridan's gaze narrowed and she licked her lips impulsively, causing her lover to hum in approval. She stiffened as the blonde began to pull her hips closer. "Sher, the guys..." she protested.

"Let 'em find their own inspector," Sheridan chuckled and pulled Keefer down for a kiss.

Phil gestured wildly from the hole in the wall and Bobby and Tony ran over to see what was so important.

"Damn, would you look at Patch?" Phil whispered even though they were far away.

"Never mind her, look at whose face she's swallowing!" Tony said.

Sheridan pulled back from the kiss and held Keefer's face tenderly in her hands.

"Well, that answers our questions."

"Girlfriend's in love...big time."

The three men left Sheridan and Keefer alone and went back to work with a good feeling inside.

"Good for her," Bobby said with sincere happiness.

Keefer looked deeply into Sheridan's eyes. It seemed to her that the blonde was searching for something in hers, too, and it only made her stare deeper, unblinkingly into the sea green eyes. It was a moment Keefer would never forget—it was that exact second that she realized that Sheridan loved her. She threw herself at the blonde and Sheridan wound up on her back with Keefer on top of her in the back of the truck.

"Hey," the blonde chuckled, "what was that for?"

"Nothing, baby...nothing," Keefer gushed. She didn't have to hear it, and Sheridan could tell her when she was good and ready to, but she knew and it made her want to scream. She kissed every inch of skin on the squirming woman's face and laughed with joy as she did it.

"Wow, is this how I'm gonna get lunch from now on?" Sheridan teased, forcing them both to sit up.

Keefer locked her ankles around the construction worker's back and tried to smooth down her hat-ruffled hair. "Am I too heavy?" she asked.

"Nope," Sheridan smiled, liking this playful side of her girlfriend.

"Good." Keefer reached for the bag she had thrown in beside her lover and opened it. "Here." She pulled out a sandwich and a cup of coffee.

Phil couldn't help himself and went back to the hole in the wall in time to witness Keefer feeding Sheridan her sandwich. Hearing him laugh, the other guys came to stand beside him.

"You can never tell her we saw this," Tony said.

Phil shook his head. "I never thought I'd see the day. I kinda feel proud, don't you?"

Bobby nodded. "My wife never feeds me," he pouted.

"Smart woman," Tony joked and the three men walked back to their work stations with big smiles on their faces.

Chapter 27

Sheridan spent the rest of the workday whistling cheerfully and joking playfully with the guys. She had no idea how telling her behavior was to them and didn't even realize how drastically her mood had changed since lunchtime. All she was aware of was the way the guys kept staring at her and even though she was in a great mood, she was becoming uncomfortable from the constant scrutiny.

"Almost time to pack it in, Patch. Any plans for tonight?"

"Yeah, I'm meeting the girls at the club."

"Yeah?" Bobby asked with his eyebrows high.

"Yeah. What's your problem?" Sheridan asked defensively

"Nothing. I just thought...nothing." He took off his hard hat and walked away.

Sheridan looked at Phil and Tony, who seemed to be looking at her in a very disapproving fashion. "What? What's the fucking problem with me going out?"

"Well...after lunch and everything..." Tony began, but clammed up at Sheridan's glare.

"What about lunch?" the blonde asked with narrowed eyes.

"Well you looked pretty...involved...you know," Phil attempted to explain.

"Oh, I see. You guys saw me with Keefer, huh?" she said with a small smile, despite her annoyance.

"Keefer, yeah," Bobby nodded.

"And because I ate lunch with Keefer, I'm not supposed to go to the club with my friends?"

"Well, you know what happens when you go to the club." Phil grimaced after he spoke, knowing he'd have to further explain himself.

301

"No, why don't you tell me? And while you're all at it, maybe you can explain why you think it's a bad thing to do." Sheridan folded her arms and stood defiantly.

"You looked so, er, cozy with Keefer. We just thought maybe you guys were, ya know...a thing," Tony started.

"Yeah, and if you two are a...*thing*...then going to the club may be a bad idea," Phil finished.

"A thing," Sheridan said dryly. "Okay, so what if we do have a *thing*?"

"Come on, Patch. What if there's a hot babe at the club that wants some of what you got? Do you think you can turn it down?" Bobby asked a bit accusingly.

Sheridan thought for a while. The more she thought, the more steamed she became, totally losing their concern and reading it as being nosy. "Oh, so you think Keefer owns me or something?"

"That's not what I'm saying," Bobby defended himself.

"You think because of my *thing* with Keefer I'm not allowed to look at a hot chick?" Sheridan was on a roll now and totally off the track. "I do what I want, guys, no one tells me what to do. If I want to dance, or fuck, it doesn't matter. Keefer doesn't tell me what to do, you don't either—no one does!" she shouted before stomping out of the room.

"Fuck me." Bobby covered his face with his hands.

"Well. That went well." Tony blew out a frustrated breath.

"How can she be so fucking stupid? Now she's going to go out and deliberately prove something," Bobby said angrily.

Phil nodded and finished packing up his tools. "She's just too fucking righteous. She knows nothing about love. She's gonna fuck someone just for the sake of fucking her and suffer with Keefer because of it."

"Maybe not. Maybe she'll cool down in time, and if she doesn't, maybe she'll feel guilty and not be able to do it."

"Who are you kidding, Tony, she can do it with her eyes closed and one foot in the grave," Bobby argued.

"Yeah, but love is love. Her crotch may not know it, but her heart does. I'd hate to see her fuck it all up with that woman all because of some fear of losing control." Tony shook his head sadly.

"Let's go, guys. No sense in worrying about it when we can't do anything to stop it."

The tall inspector was having a great afternoon, all because of her impromptu lunch with Sheridan. *She seemed so relaxed and comfortable with me and even made it a point to touch me whenever she could.* Keefer smiled at the happy memory of herself sitting on the construction worker's lap, feeding her lunch. *I never wanted to do that before. I wouldn't have believed that I'd act like that in a public place if it didn't happen.*

Keefer made sure the house looked decent enough and went to the bedroom to change into something especially sexy for her lover. She was going to make dinner for them both and had every intention of having Sheridan for dessert.

Sheridan had banged around her apartment with a serious attitude ever since she'd gotten home. The dogs were getting nervous and Pharaoh started whining with uneasiness, forcing Sheridan to see how she was acting.

"Hey, buddy, come here," she signaled to the nervous animal. "That's right, Mommy's not mad at you," she said in as soothing a voice as she could muster, petting him lovingly. Once the dog was satisfied, he trotted away and lay down with a huge rawhide bone.

Sheridan was far from calm, though, and she realized she wouldn't be able to throw a temper tantrum around her traumatized dog. This made her frustrated on top of the anger she already felt. Her mind was racing with broken thoughts and not so nice sentiments for her friends at work. Not to mention she was entirely too confused about Keefer and what role the tall woman would be playing in her life.

Did I make a fucking commitment to her? No. I didn't say anything about her owning me. She's not my wife, for Christ sakes, I can go out to the club without getting shit from the guys. Keefer knows I like to go out...she doesn't have a problem with it. Instead of kicking something for emphasis, the muscular woman threw her weight into the couch and crossed her arms angrily across her chest.

What the fuck? So, if a hot chick wanted to dance with me, what's the big deal? It's not like I'm fucking her, the blonde scowled. *And if I did want to fuck her, whose business is that? It's not anybody's business except mine,* she thought defiantly.

Sheridan stomped her booted feet into the bathroom and pulled her clothes off roughly. She had been going to eat dinner, but her stomach was grinding into itself and food didn't seem like a great idea. Now all she wanted was a cool shower and to go out.

Yeah, that's right. Keefer's not my wife, she's my lover...and only 'cuz I said she was, and who ever came up with that title anyway? She's my girlfriend—not my keeper. I can do whatever and whoever I want.

She was pretty pissed off and it wasn't apparent to her that she wasn't thinking clearly at all. Sheridan had never been involved in a serious relationship and, while she knew the rules, she was in too much of a mood to realize that they applied to her as well.

Keefer let the phone ring until the voicemail picked up and then she hung up and did it again. *That's odd. Why isn't she answering her cell phone?* She had been calling Sheridan for a long time with no answer and was getting worried. *What is she doing?* The tall woman furrowed her brows in thought and her old insecurities came rushing back in a big way. *Did I do something wrong? Is she avoiding me?* Keefer's heart picked up speed as she became nervous. She replayed their time together at the job site and paled. *Oh no, the guys must have seen us and given her a hard time!* She felt tears welling up in her eyes. *She's probably angry with me for showing up there. I'm so stupid!* Keefer sat down on the floor in the living room and cried, feeling as if she'd ruined everything. She'd finally found true love and because she was being selfish, needing to see Sheridan that very minute, she had screwed it all up.

Sheridan's stomach growled as she drove toward the club. She'd never shown up so early before, and certainly not without eating. With the mood she was in, she was sure to be dancing her frustrations out and would never last the night if she didn't eat.

"Fine!" she yelled at her stomach, swerving into the Nathan's drive-through. "You're having hot dogs and loving them," she said to her empty belly, which was really counting on some home-cooked Keefer vittles.

She ate the hot dogs in the car after she parked at the club. It was strange for her to see so many available parking spaces and she was a little hesitant to enter the club if it was so empty. She turned up her radio while she waited for a few more patrons to arrive. The first song was great and she bopped along to it as she sang. Halfway through the second song, the words reminded her of Keefer and she switched the station when she started feeling the hot dogs twist around inside of her. The new station was worse, and the first words the guy sang were about Keefer, so she turned off the radio and the engine and got out, slamming the door behind her.

Keefer left a message and waited for Sheridan's call. It never came. She sat at the kitchen table and stared at the dinner she had made for the two of them. She was very upset at herself for acting like a love-struck teenager and running to the job site to see Sheridan. *I should have known better; people like Sheridan don't fall in love with people like me.* She didn't feel much like eating, but as she looked at the half-empty bottle of wine in her hand, she thought it might be a good idea to put something in her stomach besides alcohol. Pulling a plate in front of her, she began to pick the little cubes of cheese out of the salad she'd prepared. "There you go, Feefs," she said to the dog. "Wine and cheese. I'm just a regular party animal."

Fifi came over from her spot by the front door at hearing her mommy say her name. She had been waiting for Sheridan ever since Mommy had set two plates at the table.

"Here, sweetie." Keefer handed the dog a carrot, which she crunched on happily. "Your mommy's an ass," she said with a sad sigh.

Fifi sat and looked up at her mommy, her tail brushing back and forth across the floor in hopes of another bit of food. Boy, was she surprised when her mommy handed her an entire chicken cutlet.

"You lucked out tonight, girl, don't let it go to your head." Keefer popped another piece of cheese in her mouth and washed it down with a large swallow of wine. "Leave it to me. I can ruin anything, given half the chance. I should have known better."

The dog dropped the chicken on the floor and climbed up on Keefer's legs, emitting a small, curious whine.

"What? Yeah, Sheridan's not coming, I fucked it up somehow. You eat her dinner, I'll just get drunk and throw up."

Fifi whined again and climbed down—Mommy wasn't much for kisses at the moment—and took the cutlet into the living room to eat.

Sheridan felt out of place with the club being so empty, so she went to familiar territory. "Hiya, Ma."

"Hey, Sher, you're here early, huh? What gives?"

"I needed to get away."

"Trouble in paradise?" Verna teased.

"There is no paradise. Why does everyone keep thinking that?" Sheridan blurted out angrily.

"Whoa, hey, back up there, little missy. I didn't deserve that, did I?" Verna said, grabbing Sheridan's hand.

"Why does everyone think they can butt into my business?"

"'Cuz you made it that way, hon."

Sheridan looked outraged. "I did not."

"Oh, please. You and your nightly exploits and bragging...everyone knows who you fuck and for how long."

The blonde's face turned grim. "Everyone?"

"How do you think I know about you forgetting Wanda's name? Or how you marked that donut shop cashier, or..."

"I get the picture, Verna." Sheridan winced. "What do you know about me and Keefer, smart ass?"

"I know that ever since you've been with that woman, you haven't touched another. Everyone knows that. Quite frankly, if the word spreads any further, we'll lose half our customers," she chuckled.

Sheridan didn't find it funny. "You too, huh?" She glared.

"Me too, what?" The coat check lady raised an eyebrow.

"You think that Keefer has me on a leash or something?"

"Or something," Verna smirked.

"You know what?" Sheridan thought briefly about her impending tirade then shook her head. She liked Verna; she wasn't going to say something she didn't mean. "She does not, so just fuck you all."

Verna watched Sheridan disappear angrily into the club and pursed her lips. It would seem that her little Sheridan was having some big issues concerning Keefer. The blonde was confused and it was making her unjustifiably angry. The coat check woman thought she better grab Dawn and the girls before they got inside and let them in on their friend's behavior before they said the wrong thing. *Damn, and I didn't even get my sugar today,* she thought with a frown.

Keefer's pity party was well underway by the time she finished off a bottle and a half of wine, but unfortunately for her, she wasn't as drunk as she'd like to have been. She had changed into her baggy sweatpants and an oversized T-shirt and was camped out on the living room floor with a big bag of chips. The television flickered in the background, but she had long since muted the volume in order to carry on one-sided conversations with herself. Her words were slurry, but she was in control and was getting more and more frustrated by her inability to get stupid drunk. She remembered getting far more inebriated on half a bottle of wine that night with Sheridan.

"Sheridan. You just had to go and think her name, didn't you?" Keefer scolded herself, pounding her fist into her forehead. "Just you forget about her. I'm sure she's forgotten about you already." The tall woman scrunched up her face in disgust. "Probably in the middle of forgetting right this very second." Keefer's eyes narrowed and she snickered deviously as she walked on her knees toward the phone. She hit the speed dial for Sheridan's cell phone and waited until it rang four times, then hung up. "Shall we do it again, Feefs?" Keefer asked her sleeping dog and hit the redial button, the smirk still plastered to her face. "She better not have it on vibrate." As soon as she touched the phone, it rang.

Sharon was the first to arrive at the club. After Verna filled her in on Sheridan's attitude problem, the cop went outside to wait on Marie and Dawn, who eventually arrived together in Dawn's car. By the time the three women had met up and discussed tactics, it was already after midnight, which meant Sheridan had been inside for over three hours. Lord only knew what she had gotten herself into at that point. After an initial scan of the club came up with no sign of Sheridan, they decided that Sharon would check the bathrooms while Marie and Dawn scoped the corners.

Sharon was rather pleased to not find her friend's boots occupying any of the stalls in either of the bathrooms and went to share the news with the others when she quite literally tripped over Sheridan.

"Watch it, bigfoot," the blonde said, then laughed boisterously.

It was then that Marie came upon them and she stood with Sharon, taking in the scene. Sheridan was sitting on a carpeted platform with her legs stretched out in front of her. She was sitting between a girl's legs while another equally young woman straddled her lap. There were numerous empty beer bottles littering the platform as well as an ashtray full of butts. Sharon and Marie both knew that their friend only smoked that much when she drank, and that was a bad thing.

"She's toasted," Sharon said into Marie's ear.

Marie nodded. "Lemme go get Dawn. Looks like someone will be driving her home tonight."

Sharon scanned the area as all good cops do and spotted something she wished she hadn't. Danni was sitting at a small table all by herself with a bowl of pretzels from the bar, looking as if she were watching a movie, a smug smile stretched from one ear to the other. *Fuck*, Sharon thought, and made her way over to the grinning redhead.

"You see something interesting, Danni?"

"Why, yes, yes I do," she snickered. "Now get out of the way so I can see how it ends."

"Well, I'll tell you something, if Keefer finds out about this little moment of temporary insanity, I *will* haunt you."

Danni dared Sharon with her eyes.

"Don't you drive that little red car out there on the corner?" the cop smirked.

"It's too late."

"What do you mean, it's too late?" Sharon asked with a sneer.

"I already called Keefer," the redhead said with a bark of a laugh.

Sharon grabbed the woman by her shirt collar, lifted her out of her seat before thinking better of it, and threw her back down in her chair. "Fucking asshole," she muttered and slunk back into a corner.

The tall cop observed from the darkness as the girl on Sheridan's lap took the cigarette out of the blonde's mouth, took a drag off of it and then placed it back between Sheridan's lips after kissing them. The girl behind her was kneading her shoulders and back, her hands underneath the leather jacket that she always wore. Sharon knew she should stop Sheridan from doing something she'd be sure to regret, but she also knew that not only was she drunk, she was going to accuse her of interfering. Instead, the cop just stood there helplessly as the girl from behind started kissing Sheridan's neck.

"You smell so good, Sheridan," the girl said with a shiver.

"I taste even better," Sheridan replied, bending her head back to receive a kiss.

"Want another beer, Sheridan?" lap-girl asked, dangling an empty bottle between their bodies, clearly vying for attention.

"Mmm, sure, sweetie, I'll keep my lap warm for ya," the blonde drawled.

Marie and Dawn approached just as the girl from behind started to suck on their friend's neck.

"Shit," Dawn said angrily.

"No kidding. Lap-girl just went for more beer. Should I stop her at the bar?" Sharon asked her friends.

"Let me go," Marie said, narrowing her eyes at Sheridan, who was hauling the girl up onto her empty lap.

"See? I told ya, I ain't married or nuthin'," Sheridan said drunkenly, holding up her left hand for show. "It's all some sick rumor—a college prank gone wrong." She snickered at herself. The girl whispered in Sheridan's ear and the blonde shivered, then grabbed the back of the girl's head and kissed her hard.

"That's it," Dawn said loudly and walked up to Sheridan. "Hey, kissy lips, break it up."

Sheridan peeked out of one eye and waved her friend away. Dawn poked her on the shoulder repeatedly until she broke the kiss and frowned. "Uh, I'm busy, Dawn." The blonde winked dramatically, patting the girl on the ass.

"Oh, I can see that, Sheridan," Dawn smiled sweetly.

Sheridan looked puzzled for a moment then busted out laughing. "Oh, you wanna watch? Hey, no problem, buddy." She pointed to herself and grinned. "Watch the master and learn," she said cockily and resumed kissing the girl on her lap. When that kiss ended, she opened her eyes slowly and focused. "You still here? Where the hell is whassername and my beer?" She slapped the girl on the ass again and motioned for her to get up.

Sharon grimaced as Sheridan stood up and teetered slightly. "How many beers have you had, Sher?" she asked.

"Oh! Hiya, Sharon!" the blonde said loudly as she slapped the tall cop on the shoulder...hard. "How's it hangin'?" Sheridan turned to the giggling girl who seemed to be attached to her hip and attempted to whisper. "She's a cop. She has a gun."

Sharon wrapped her big hand around Sheridan's bicep and yanked her closer. "I asked you how many beers you drank."

"Ow, hey...no need to get touchy." Sheridan wiggled out of the grasp and brushed off her arm, then held up five fingers. "Two."

Giggling girl merely giggled and wrapped herself around Sheridan again. "Who are these people, Sheridan?" she whined. "Make them go away."

Sheridan smiled. "I got a better idea, why don't we go away?" She winked at the girl and they stumbled toward the bar.

"Okay, hotshot, now what?" Dawn asked.

"Nothing. We let Marie at them," Sharon snickered and pointed at the bar where Sheridan was hoisting her drunken self up onto a stool, Marie standing right at her side.

"So, who's the ho?" Marie asked.

"Excuse me?" the girl asked, planting both hands on her hips.

"Oh, Sheridan," the girl that disappeared purred, "I have your beer." She handed Sheridan the bottle and stood between her legs.

"Where the hell did you go?" the blonde asked and then drank down two long swallows of beer.

"She wouldn't let me go," the girl pouted and pointed at Marie.

"She's mine, baby, deal with it," Sheridan said to her friend, then pulled the girl tighter between her legs by wrapping them around her.

The girl that had come down to the bar with Sheridan pouted and came up behind her and whispered something in her ear. Sheridan stopped kissing the first girl and started kissing her instead.

Marie took the beer bottle out of Sheridan's hand and scowled. "So, Sheridan, how's Keefer?"

Sheridan tore her mouth away from the girl and glared at Marie. "How the fuck should I know? I'm not her keeper."

"Well, I just thought since she's your girlfriend, you'd know how she was."

The girl between Sheridan's legs crossed her arms over her chest and glared at the blonde. "You said you didn't have a girlfriend."

"Actually, I said I don't have a wife." The blonde laughed and tried to pull the girl back, but she stepped out of reach.

"That's terrible! You lied to me! You have a girlfriend and you're fucking around with not one, but two girls?"

"I'm not sleeping with ya, for Christ sakes," Sheridan chuckled. "Keefer doesn't own me."

"No, I'm sure she doesn't, but does she even know what you're doing?" The second girl came out from behind Sheridan.

"No, but she knows I like to go out..."

"You're such an ass, Sheridan!" the first girl said before stomping away.

"I can't believe you let me believe you were single," the second girl said with as much anger and she, too, fled.

Sheridan narrowed her eyes at her smiling friend. "What the hell are you trying to do?"

Marie watched as her friend swayed on her bar stool drunkenly and shook her head in disappointment. "What are *you* trying to do?"

"I'm just having a good time, is all...what does it look like?"

"It looks like you're running away from something, or some*one*."

The blonde made a face as if Marie were being ridiculous. "Me? I never run away from shit. I ain't afraid of no one," she insisted, poking herself in the chest.

"Oh, no? Where's Keefer?"

"How the hell should I know? Probably home."

Dawn came up on Sheridan's side and put a heavy hand on her shoulder. "It's a good thing she's home, Sher, 'cuz she'd be pretty pissed off if she saw you sucking face with those women."

"Why should she care? She's not my wife." Sheridan waved her hand and then became interested in it as it moved.

"You're piss-assed drunk, fucking with two girls, and your lover is at home, crying."

"She's not crying," Sheridan said confidently.

"Oh, I bet she is," Sharon said, appearing in front of the drunk blonde, holding Danni by the arm.

Sheridan's mouth went dry and she felt her heart pounding hard. "Why would she be crying?" she asked the wincing redhead.

"'Cuz I called her and told her what you were doing."

Sheridan swung an impressive right hook that would have been something if it had connected. Instead, she missed and wound up pulling herself off of the stool with the momentum and landed legs up on the floor, flat on her ass.

Danni couldn't help but laugh and Sheridan's friends had a hard time controlling themselves, too, at the sight.

"Ow," the blonde whined from the floor, getting up on all fours.

Dawn raised an eyebrow at her friend's uncharacteristic sound effect.

Sharon released Danni and let her run and hide just in case Sheridan had knocked some sense into herself.

"That sucked," the blonde said, laughing and rubbing her ass as she stood up. It would seem she had completely forgotten the conversation. "Hey, where's the chicks?" she asked, trying to push past Marie.

"You, my friend, are going home," Dawn said, pulling Sheridan by the arm.

"No, the night's just beginning! I don't wanna go home!"

"You're shitfaced, girl. You're gonna wind up doing something you'll regret," Marie said.

Sheridan looked somber for a moment. "I already did."

"So let's get you home before you really blow it."

"It's too late, guys. Keefer hates me, Danni told her I'm a slut. I'm not good enough for her. Let me go."

"Nope," Dawn said, wrapping an arm around her slurring friend. "This is when you need friends the most, buddy."

"I'm really not married to her, you know," Sheridan said seriously.

"We know that," Sharon said, "but she *is* your girlfriend and she deserves some respect. Even you know about respect, Sheridan."

The women walked outside to Dawn's car with Marie holding the drunken blonde up as she stumbled over her own feet.

"She loves me, you know. I can see it. She shouldn't love me," Sheridan said sadly, turning to face the car and resting her forehead on the window.

"Everyone deserves the chance, hon."

Sheridan shook her head rapidly. "No, not me. Not with Keefer." The blonde smiled. "Keefer. KeeferKeeferKeeferKeefer. Isn't that the coolest name?" she asked as if she'd just heard the name for the first time.

Dawn rolled her eyes. "She's gonna puke in my car."

"No, she won't," Marie said with a nervous laugh.

"Did you *see* how blue her eyes are? God, they're like, so blue...they're just...blue."

"She is so gonna puke in my car."

Sharon snickered. "I got a better idea. I'll drive her home in *her* car."

"I like that idea." Dawn smiled and turned Sheridan around. "Where's your car?"

"Huh?" The blonde closed her eyes and swayed forward.

"Great. I'll find her car, you stay here with her," Sharon said as she fished through Sheridan's pockets.

"Woo hoo! Is that your gun or are you happy to see me?"

Sharon held up the keys and shook her head, then went to look for Sheridan's car.

"Did you ever notice that when Keefer blushes one of those big blushes, she curls her toes?"

"Maybe we shouldn't talk about Keefer any more, Sher," Marie said with a knowing grin. Her friend was treading on a fine line of too much information.

"Why not? She's so perfect...everything...people should write poems about Keefer," the blonde said in all seriousness.

"Well then why don't you write one?" Dawn said, amused by the whole conversation.

"I'm such an ass!" Sheridan screamed suddenly.

"Pipe down, you idiot!" Marie said more out of fright than embarrassment.

"Keefer loves me and I'm such an asshole!"

"Good Lord, shut her up!" Dawn said looking around for spectators.

Sheridan stood in the middle of the street and yelled, "I'm the world's biggest fuckup!" She paused when she noticed the black sports car pull up. "That's my car!" Dawn slapped her hand over her mouth, so Sheridan pointed as Sharon pulled up.

"Why is she yelling? I could hear her from all the way around the corner."

"I don't fucking know!" Marie said in obvious distress.

"Just get her in the car, please," the cop rolled her eyes as the blonde fell over onto her lap, "and buckle her up."

"Are those my feet?" Sheridan asked, looking at Sharon's feet. "Boy, they're big."

"Upsy-daisy, Sher." Marie pulled her up into a sitting position.

"Whoa...head rush," Sheridan slurred.

Chapter 28

Keefer slammed down the phone and stared at it, willing it to ring, wanting Danni to call her back and tell her it was all a joke. It didn't ring. It just sat there, infuriating Keefer to the very limits of her tolerance. Her hands balled into fists and she took great heaving breaths in order to keep her hands from lashing out and hitting something. She'd never felt this angry before; no one ever had the ability to get her in this state of mind. She blamed her intolerance on the wine, right before she put a fist-sized hole in the living room plasterboard.

Moments later, as she stared at the hole in the wall, Keefer's anger bubbled over. "No!" she shouted. "I will *not* let her do this to me!" She was trembling with emotion. "Danni sounded so happy, so gleeful to hear my heart breaking," she seethed. "No way. No *fucking* way will I allow her to do this."

Keefer darted into her bedroom and threw a sweatshirt over her head, shoved her feet into her sneakers and, in a fit of rage, slammed the door behind her. At first, she didn't know where she was going, but her feet did and they were leading her to the club. She had to see for herself—she couldn't trust Danni.

"Turn off that fucking radio, will ya?" Sheridan kicked at the dashboard clumsily. "Everything is about her...they all know her...they're all in love with her."

Sharon looked sideways at her slurring friend, wondering if she was even aware of what she was saying.

"Go there," Sheridan lurched over toward Sharon and grabbed the steering wheel.

313

"What are you, fucking insane?" The cop wrestled the wheel back and punched Sheridan in the arm, a move ingrained in her from training, rendering the blonde's left arm useless.

"It's broke! I can't feel it!" Sheridan stared at her arm in horror.

"Sorry, man, I just punched you in the nerve, it's only temporary. You freaked me out," Sharon said apologetically, her heart still pounding.

"It's just hanging there..." the blonde whined pathetically. "I wanna go to Keefer."

"I'm not so sure she wants to see you right now, Sher."

"She loves me," Sheridan said with a shrug.

"Well...okay, but if she kicks your sorry ass into the street, don't say I didn't warn you."

Keefer walked past the park on the way to the club and concentrated on keeping her breathing under control. She felt miserable about going to the club, but she had to prove Danni wrong. *Please, God, be wrong,* she thought.

"Hey, Keef! Wait up!"

The tall woman stiffened and growled under her breath.

Danni jogged to catch up to the motionless woman. "I knew that was you," she said, running around to face her. "God, you look awful. I was on my way to your house to see if you were okay."

Keefer narrowed her eyes at the redhead and shouldered past her. Danni had to run to keep up with her.

"You can't ignore me."

"Apparently," Keefer muttered under her breath, counting away her anger from seeing Danni at that particular time.

"I'm the only one who understands you," Danni said with an amused lilt to her voice.

"Fuck off."

"Keefer! Wait up, will you please? Sheridan's not at the club."

Keefer stopped in her tracks.

"They took her home—she was fucking plastered!" the redhead laughed. "You should have seen her."

"Why should I believe you?" Keefer asked, turning to face Danni.

"Because I care about you. I'm looking out for you, baby. Sheridan's no good, she's nothing but a useless slut and she proved that to you tonight."

Keefer's heart started pounding in her ears and her breath came rapidly through her mouth. "Nothing's been proven. You're lying. I don't believe you."

"Oh yeah? Check her neck, the left side, I believe," Danni said with a smirk. "One of the girls was sucking on her neck like she was starving. Boy," Danni laughed in glee, "was Sheridan getting into it!"

"Stop it...now!" Keefer turned on her heel and started to walk back toward her house.

Danni followed her again. "You should have seen it, Keef. Your little slut, sucking that girl's tongue...I swore they were gonna fuck, right there on the spot."

Keefer stopped walking and breathed deeply. She closed her eyes and tried to erase the images that Danni's words had implanted in her wine-drenched mind.

"You must hate her right now. I don't blame you, sweetheart." Danni spoke close to Keefer's ear. "Let me take you home and hold you."

Keefer spun around, her infuriated, red-rimmed eyes locked on Danni's.

"I'll make it all better, I promise. You can trust me. Sheridan's nothing...she's a lowlife. I know what you need. I'll make you feel better."

Keefer's fist flew so fast that Danni didn't know what hit her. She hit the ground and no sooner than her ass touched the concrete, she was being hauled up to her feet again—with Keefer's hand wrapped tightly around her throat. Danni tried to pry the surprisingly strong fingers from her throat, but Keefer wasn't budging. Her free hand was cocked back and ready, her fingers in the shape of a claw, scaring Danni witless. Her quiet ex-girlfriend knew exactly what she was doing.

"Keef..." the redhead wheezed, watching the muscles in Keefer's cocked hand twitch with the effort to control them.

The tall woman panted with effort and loosened her grip. "I'll never need you," she spat out, her eyes wild with anger.

Danni attempted to nod, grateful that the tight grip on her windpipe had disappeared. "Thanks—"

Before she could finish her sentence, the hand Keefer had cocked back made contact with the side of her head and she hit the pavement again.

"You know something, Danni?" Keefer said loudly, adrenaline pumping through her body like wildfire. "You're right! You did make me feel good. I feel fucking fantastic!" She squatted over her stunned and bruised ex. "Now get up and let's do it again," she sneered.

"You're a fucking lunatic!" Danni yelled, pushing Keefer away from her. She was stunned when Keefer didn't even budge.

"And you're pathetic! Just for the record, Danni, this is the *only* time you made me feel fantastic."

Danni watched as Keefer stood up and strolled away. She got up on all fours and shook her cloudy head. "Who the fuck was that? And where did she learn how to do that?"

"You all right?" Sharon asked her suddenly silent friend.

Sheridan nodded and sighed.

The cop glanced over to see the saddest expression she'd ever seen on Sheridan's face. "What's wrong?"

"Keefer's going to be so mad at me," she pouted.

"At least you know that, Sher."

"I really fucked this up." Sharon smiled ruefully at her friend, whose head fell back heavily.

The Ride Of The Valkyries started playing from under the front seat.

"Your phone, Sher."

The construction worker opened her eyes and they rolled back, so she closed them again. "Fuck it," she slurred.

Sharon reached under the seat and looked at the display. "It's Keefer."

"KeeferKeeferKeeferKeefer," Sheridan murmured drunkenly and then passed out cold.

The tall woman slammed the door behind her and patted Fifi mechanically before she stripped off her sweatshirt. She couldn't believe how much she was sweating or how her heart was racing. When she still felt too hot, she took off her pants and blew down her soaked T-shirt. She had never felt like that before; she'd had adrenaline rushes, but never like that one. She flexed her hands, stretching her fingers all the way out, and winced at the feeling. "I kicked Danni's ass," she said, surprised by the revelation. "I actually laid her out." She laughed out loud, stopping abruptly when her eyes fell on the phone. "I wonder if Sheridan's all right." She picked up the phone and dialed, not surprised when no one answered. "Serves her right. I hope she gets sick all over the place," she said and then felt guilty. "Stupid idiot...how could you do that to me? To us?" she wondered out loud, her heart heavy with hurt. "I really love her. I don't want to let her go. This can't happen; I won't let her do this. I saw her eyes...she loves me, too," Keefer whined in frustration, tears coming feely once again. "Why did she run away?"

Keefer jumped as a horn blew in her driveway. "Who the hell? If that's Danni, I'll kill her this time." Keefer got herself all riled up as she went to the window and looked out. She couldn't see into the car, due to the headlights shining in her window, but she recognized it. "Sheridan? Oh god, she didn't drive here, did she?" She raised her eyebrows as she watched a woman as tall as herself slide out of the driver's side, walk around to the passenger side, open the door, and kneel down. She gasped as the woman suddenly backed out of the car with Sheridan draped over her shoulder. Keefer flung open the door in alarm and waved the woman inside.

"I believe this belongs to you," Sharon said and turned around, allowing Keefer to look at Sheridan's face.

Keefer nodded, her lips tight with disapproval at the blonde's condition. "Put her on the couch." She pointed the way.

The cop dropped Sheridan down and pulled off her boots before propping her legs up on the sofa. "I'm Sharon, pleased to meet ya."

Keefer tore her eyes away from Sheridan and saw that Sharon had offered her hand. She accepted it and was caught completely off guard when Sharon kissed her hand. Keefer blushed.

"Hey, go easy on her. I know she deserves hell, but she's really gonna feel this in the morning," the tall cop said.

"You're a good friend?' Keefer asked, staring once again at her lover.

"I like to think so, yes."

"Why did she do this?"

"She's afraid."

"What is she so afraid of?"

"You," Sharon said solemnly. "I'd better go."

"Sharon, thank you," Keefer said as she opened the front door.

"Don't thank me, just understand her," Sharon said and was gone.

Keefer watched from the window as the tall cop got into a car with two other women and surmised that they must be Dawn and Marie. After they drove away, she turned around and regarded the figure on her couch with a heavy sigh. Keefer was angry, and she had a lot of questions. She was pumped up on adrenaline and frustrated because Sheridan was out cold and couldn't hold her and tell her that everything was all right. Keefer wanted the construction worker to tell her that this whole night had been a dream; she wanted to feel her strong arms wrapped around her body, giving her that overwhelming feeling of security and contentment.

Keefer knelt down by her sleeping lover and stared at her slack face. The blonde's lips were half open, swollen and red, like she had indeed been kissing all night long. The inspector felt her heart pound hard. *The left side of her neck?* She turned Sheridan's unusually pliable body over and felt the tears well up again. *Danni wasn't lying?* She ran her finger over the big red bruise and sobbed out loud. *Why am I crying? I know who Sheridan is and what she did before she met me, so why does it hurt so much?* She stood up and turned her back on Sheridan. Just looking at her face hurt her deeply. *I romanticized, that's what happened. I was lying to myself. Sheridan isn't going to change her whole life because of me. Who do I think I am?*

The blonde groaned and kicked her feet. Keefer turned around and watched her carefully. *She stinks like a brewery, she may get sick.* Keefer sighed loudly, went to the kitchen and brought back a large pot, placing it in plain view on the coffee table. She started removing Sheridan's clothing, taking the opportunity to touch the blonde's warm skin whenever possible. It felt so good to touch her and she found she couldn't stop. Keefer touched her everywhere, feeling the smoothness of her skin, memorizing it, fearing that it was the last time she'd ever be able to feel her. Her crying blurred her vision and she stood up shakily to get a T-shirt for Sheridan to sleep in. She chuckled sadly when she realized she was clutching the blonde's bra desperately, but she didn't let it go. In fact, after she managed to get the shirt on the limp dead weight of the construction worker, she curled up on the couch behind her and brought her fist up to her face, smelling the bra and Sheridan's personal scent as she tried to relax. It wasn't long before the effects of the evening caught up with her and she fell into a deep sleep, her fist still at her nose.

Knocking...knocking...pounding...knocking...
Sheridan's head felt like it was going to explode.
Bang
Bang
*Good God...make it stop...*The blonde groaned and rolled her dry tongue around in her even dryer mouth.
Bang
"Open the fucking door...now!"
Sheridan rolled over slowly onto her back and winced painfully. Someone was banging on her door and she had no idea how she'd gotten home. *Wait a minute...where are the dogs?* A bloodshot green eye opened slightly and she furrowed her brows. *Ow.*
Bang
Bang
Where the fuck am I? The blonde began to panic, not remembering a thing from the night before. *Oh, God...I didn't...*Her eyes flew opened and it took her a moment to realize she was lying on Keefer's couch. *How the hell did I get here?*
Bang
Where is Keefer—and who the fuck is banging on the door?
Sheridan concentrated, which was hard to do with the ringing in her ears, and she heard the shower running behind the closed bathroom door. A sense of relief washed over her knowing that Keefer was there.

Bang

"Motherfucker..." she muttered as she slowly turned her body and put her feet on the floor. "When did I get undressed?" she wondered, looking down at herself as she stood up cautiously.

Bang

The blonde glared at the door as best she could under the circumstances and put her hands to her splitting head as she walked, ever so slowly, toward the infernal banging. She began to feel light-headed and sweaty. *Oh God...not a good sign...*She winced, swallowing hard.

"I know that's your car, Sheridan! Open this door, you goddamn fucking slut!"

Despite her throbbing head and dreadful nausea, the blonde construction worker's nostrils flared at the words. She flung open the door and gave the most menacing stare she could muster to the woman on the other side.

"You little fucking son of a bitch!" Danni yelled, her fist connecting with the side of Sheridan's face. The blonde fell backwards and groaned pathetically. Danni advanced on her and lifted her up by grabbing a handful of her shirt. "How many girls do you need in one fucking night, you little whore?" Sheridan saw it coming but there was nothing she could do about it, she closed her eyes and swallowed again, willing herself not to throw up on Danni and embarrass herself further.

"Danni!" Keefer screamed, just as the redhead's fist connected with Sheridan's face again.

"Oh, fuck," Sheridan whined in an unusual voice right before she lost a night's worth of beer all over Danni.

"Sher—oh my god!" Keefer grabbed the pot off of the coffee table and ran over to the door, not knowing what to do first.

"You stupid asshole!" Danni yelled, ready to attack a miserable Sheridan, who had fallen to all fours.

Keefer thrust the pot at Sheridan, who held up a hand and took a deep breath. "I think I'm okay," she rasped out.

"Who the hell do you think you are?" Keefer pushed Danni hard and the redhead fumed, pushing her back.

"You're pathetic, fucking this excuse for a human being—and after how she treats you."

"You should talk!" Keefer shouted, kneeling down next to Sheridan and picking up her head. She gasped at the way her face was bruising. "Does this make you feel good, Danni? Beating her when she's in this condition?" She stood up and came at the redhead, her fists clenching and unclenching.

319

"It's the only time she could beat me," Sheridan said in a low, pained voice as she struggled to stand up.

"You butt out!" Danni yelled angrily, pushing Sheridan back down to the ground.

Keefer raised her fist to hit her ex-lover when nightstick suddenly appeared across Danni's throat, holding her in a chokehold.

"What the hell is going on here?" Sharon asked, taking in the unusual scene.

Sheridan wanted to crawl under the furniture and refused to look up at her friend. Keefer blushed furiously. The night before she hadn't been wearing any pants when Sharon had shown up, and now she was in a towel.

"This maniac showed up at my house and beat Sheridan," Keefer explained to the cop.

"Well, it's a good thing I decided to come and check up on you then, huh, Sher?" Sharon asked, pushing Danni into her partner's hands. "Cuff her and put her in the car until I get this squared away." The cop looked at Danni and frowned. "And open the windows, will ya?"

"She fuckin' puked on me!"

"You hit her!"

"Enough, you two," Sharon said sternly. Once a protesting Danni was in the squad car, the cop squatted down and put her arm around Sheridan's shoulders. "You okay, Sher?"

"Yeah," the blonde said, looking away.

"Wanna press charges?"

"Yes," Keefer answered, "I do."

"Okay, harassment, trespassing...I'll think of a few more things."

"She pushed her," the blonde said, getting to her feet and walking slowly to the couch.

"Yeah, Danni pushed me, but she hit you. Look at you!" Keefer said angrily and hurried into the bedroom, put on her robe, and then ran into the kitchen.

"I brought you here last night, Sher; you were pretty fucked up." The cop touched her friend's face to inspect the damage.

"I kinda figured, when you said you came to check up on me. Ow! That fucking hurts."

"Here." Keefer appeared with an ice pack and handed it to Sheridan. "Are you going to press charges against her?" she asked the unusually pale and quiet blonde.

"No, but you should."

Keefer wondered why Sheridan was acting like she was and decided to talk to her about it after Sharon left.

"That's gonna be a hell of a shiner, Sher." The cop winced and scrunched up her nose.

"Did I make an ass of myself last night?" the construction worker asked quietly.

Sharon glanced nervously at Keefer, who looked away. "Yeah, you did." Sheridan looked at her in horror. "But we still love ya," the cop winked and chuckled.

Keefer looked at Sheridan through narrowed eyes, not caring to hear all the gory details, and turned to Sharon. "What do I have to do to press charges against Danni?"

"Oh, you take your time. We'll keep her comfy until you're good and ready to come down to the precinct and fill out the paperwork," the cop said with a devious grin.

"Fine by me," Keefer smiled back and walked Sharon to the door. "Hey, you really are a good friend. Maybe we can meet again under...different circumstances?" She followed the cop outside.

"I'd love to. Hey, just take care of her for now. A lot more of her is bruised right now than her face."

"I am so angry with her," Keefer started, but then shook off the thought. "Can you answer another question for me?"

"Shoot."

"Did she...um, you know...last night?"

"Last night, all she could talk about was you. No, she didn't, I don't think she could have, either. It's all about you, KeeferKeeferKeefer," the cop chuckled.

Keefer gave Sharon an odd look.

"Never mind," the cop laughed.

"Thanks."

"No problem. I know you're pissed off right now and Sheridan deserves everything you want to give to her, but go easy, she's never been in love before."

In the midst of all the emotions swirling around in Keefer's head, she felt her belly tingle from what Sharon said. *She's in love with me...*Keefer spared one last look at the sneering Danni in the back of the police car and heard her yelling something when Sharon opened her door to get in. The brunette shook her head in disgust and walked back into her house. She found Sheridan struggling to put her clothes on. "Sher, just lay down in my bed and relax," she said as she disappeared into her bedroom to get dressed.

"You have to be at work and I should get home."

321

"I called in already." Keefer reappeared dressed with her wet hair pulled back into a ponytail. "Just go to bed and give me your keys, I'll take care of your dogs."

"No, I can do it," the blonde said, bending over to put on her pants. "Oh boy..." she gasped, falling into the couch and breathing deeply.

"You're in no condition to drive." Keefer held out her hand, "Address and keys."

"You won't even look at me," Sheridan said sadly.

"I am so incredibly angry with you, but now is not the time to discuss it." She glanced at the construction worker, who looked green. *Uh-oh,* she thought just as the blonde bolted into the bathroom.

Keefer wanted to feel good that Sheridan was feeling so miserable; she wanted to go into the bathroom and taunt her, get her back for hurting her so badly, but she couldn't. The part of her that cared, felt miserable with her; she loved her too much to be vicious.

Sheridan leaned her face where no face should be and groaned pathetically. She jumped when a cold, wet rag appeared on the back of her neck and long fingers sifted through her damp hair soothingly. Keefer was kneeling behind her, and she couldn't turn and face her, no matter how much she tried. She sighed in defeat. "In my jacket pocket, left side. 6801 Nineteenth Avenue. Third floor. 3G."

"Where are the leashes?"

"On the back of the door. Take Zeus first, you can't handle both of them," the blonde bit out before she started heaving again.

Keefer rubbed Sheridan's back in circles. "You'd be surprised what I can handle."

Chapter 29

Keefer took a slow walk to Sheridan's apartment. She had been very curious to see the inside of the place for a while now. She climbed up the last flight of stairs loudly, making sure to announce her presence long before she got to the door. She was startled as the dogs started throwing themselves against the door when she put the key in the lock.

"It's not Mommy, guys. It's me. You recognize my voice, don't you?"

The dogs began whimpering and whining, one scratching at the door, and Keefer started to laugh. *Is this what she comes home to every day?* "Okay, okay, but you'll have to back up if you want me to open it!" she said, still laughing. Finally wedging herself through the door and inside the apartment, Keefer giggled and screamed as the two dogs jumped her, licking her all over her face and pulling at her clothes. The ache behind her eyes from her previous night's overindulgence took a back seat to the attention lavished upon her by the dogs. Zeus had her pinned to the back of the door, slobbering all over her neck, and Pharaoh was popping up and down like a spring, barking excitedly. It took her a long time before she was able to get the leashes on them, but no time at all to get down the three flights of stairs, as they dragged her all the way.

"God! Is this how you treat the guests?" she asked them as they ran out of the front door of the building. She allowed them to lead her, not knowing where they liked to walk, and chuckled as they headed for the park. "Oh, I see," she said. "I'll indulge you for a little while, but then I have to get home and see to your mommy."

Sheridan groaned as the shower water hit her on the head. "I am so incredibly stupid," she complained while soaping up her body. "Keefer's so mad at me that she can't even look at me, and yet she's walking my beasts so I can rest in her house."

She reached behind her and attempted to wash her lower back and winced. "Ouch! What the hell?" She twisted and turned but couldn't see what she was looking for. "I hurt my ass?" she wondered, washing said area carefully. "Gotta ask the girls," she thought out loud and prepared herself to wash her hair, which just so happened to be growing out of her throbbing head.

After her shower, she wanted to put on her own clothes, but didn't have the strength to and just put Keefer's shirt on again. She sniffed it and was disappointed to smell only fabric softener. She glanced at the bedroom, wanting so badly to take Keefer up on the offer of crawling into the big, comfortable bed and sleeping, but she didn't feel worthy of such a thing as Keefer's bed. She ended up in the den, curled up on the futon with Fifi, wondering what Keefer was doing with the dogs. She smiled, knowing the stubborn woman had walked them both at the same time and that they had probably dragged her to the park. The thought of the tall inspector cavorting with her babies gave her a good feeling in her stomach and she welcomed it after such a bad morning. She patted her empty belly and sighed. "Don't get used to the feeling. She's probably going to read you the riot act and never want to see your sorry ass again," she told herself.

After she lay around for some time, Sheridan's stomach had the audacity to growl, despite being so hung over. Fifi's ears perked up and she sniffed Sheridan's middle. "The nerve," the blonde said to her belly, knowing it would be a bad thing if she ate. She shifted on the couch and grimaced as her tailbone hit the cushion at a painful angle. "What the hell did I do?" she wondered again and got up to inspect. Standing in Keefer's bedroom, Sheridan inspected first her eye and then her jaw. "Danni sure got me good, huh, Feef?" She was sure to have a raging shiner and a bruise on her jaw. "What the hell am I going to tell the guys?" With her back to the mirror, she lifted up the shirt to find another big bruise. "Holy shit! Look at that!" she said to the dog. "How the fuck did I do that?" she asked her own reflection. She wondered what other surprises her body had in store for her and began to inspect, gasping at the huge hickey on her neck. "Oh, man," she whined. "Keefer had to see that!" She felt sick with herself and trudged sadly back into the den.

When Keefer arrived back at Sheridan's apartment, she fed the dogs their breakfast and decided to snoop around for a bit. She started in the kitchen cabinets, being that she was in there already. She was appalled at the lack of real food and the abundance of Chef Boyardee products. She grew even more disgusted when she peeked in the fridge and scrunched up her face at the frozen dinners and pizzas in the freezer. "I can't imagine how she can be in such great shape when she eats this garbage!" Thirst suddenly hit her out of nowhere and she opened the fridge again to find a large bottle of water staring back at her. She looked briefly for a glass then with a small chuckle lifted the bottle to her lips. The ice-cold water felt like heaven to her dry throat and she closed her eyes, concentrating on the cold trail that it was leaving inside her body. After drinking her fill, she stared at the bottle, a sudden thought popping into her head. *Sheridan's lips were probably on this bottle.* Keefer clicked her tongue and scolded herself, *What are you doing? Sheridan's lips have touched just about every part of your body and you're obsessing about a bottle?* She put the water away and resumed her snooping.

She found the living room small and messy, but organized. She touched the workout bench and felt a tingle in her body, knowing that Sheridan sweated and grunted while using it. She tried to lift the leg weights and struggled a bit, surprised at the little blonde's abilities. Walking around the small room, she smirked at the condition of the furniture, knowing that the dogs had a lot to do with the teeth marks in the coffee table.

Sheridan was snuggled in the den half asleep when her cell phone rang. Thinking it might be Keefer, she ran to get it. "Yeah?" she asked hurriedly.

"Honey? Where are you? Are you all right?"

"Oh, Pop, hi...Yeah, I'm fine, I guess," she said hesitantly.

"The guys said you didn't show up and you didn't call, either. I got worried, and when you didn't answer your phone..."

"Pop, I'm not home," Sheridan said to her nervous father.

"Are you sick?" he asked with concern.

"You could say that," she winced. "I drank too much last night and I'm suffering the consequences. I was pretty stupid."

"You don't get drunk, Sher, and I never knew you to be stupid. What happened?"

"Nuthin'," she shrugged. "I got drunk, got my ass kicked, and I'm paying for it now."

"Are you hurt? Who hit you?" Mr. Landers was very angry.

"Aw, Pop, calm down, I'm okay," Sheridan said with a heavy sigh.

"I should lay into you about what you did, but you sound pretty miserable already. Do you want to talk about it?"

"No, you know what they say, I made my bed..."

"Do you want me to stay home and take care of you? Why don't you come over here and spend the day. I'll make soup."

It sure sounded good to Sheridan. Having her pop pamper her and baby her all day was really tempting. "Well..." She thought about leaving, but then pictured Keefer's look of disappointment from earlier and felt a blow to her gut. Keefer was sure to be even more disappointed if Sheridan ran away from her. "No, that's all right, Pop. I'll be fine. Keefer will take care of me." *Lord knows I deserve it.*

"Keefer of the long legs?" her father teased.

"Yeah." Sheridan decided not to even try to get out of it—she didn't have the strength. "She'll make sure I'm okay." *Right before she kicks me out on my sorry, bruised ass.*

"If you insist," Mr. Landers chuckled. "You take the day off, and when you feel better, I'm going to smack you hard."

"I know. I deserve it."

"Listen, Steven is going to stay home by himself today. He's excited about it. If you feel better later, maybe you'll come by?"

"I just may. If you make that soup, you have a deal."

"You got it, sweetheart."

"Thanks. Bye, Pop."

Keefer stood outside the bedroom and hesitated, not sure if she should go in and if she could even control her impulses if she did. She peeked into the room and snorted out a laugh to find both dogs sprawled out, fat and happy, on the bed. "I bet Mommy lets you do that, too," she said to them, then approached the bed and sat down. She scratched Zeus's exposed belly and his foot moved. She laughed at that and did it again until the big dog gave her a look. "Okay, but it's funny, big guy." Keefer ran her hand over Sheridan's pillow, picturing her blonde head lying on it, her face relaxed in sleep. The tall woman sighed, not knowing if she'd ever see the construction worker sleeping again.

"Why did she do that?" she asked the dogs. "She's so...so...ooh!" Keefer couldn't find the words. "She's infuriating, is what she is." She stood up and looked around, her eyes falling on the black duffel bag by her feet. She kicked it with her toe. It was already open and she was curious. She squatted down to look inside and blushed hotly at the contents. "Well...that's an interesting color," she said of the bright purple dildo she spotted inside. She jostled the bag without touching anything and saw what looked like a blood pressure cuff with a hole in it. Her brow knitted in confusion as she tried to imagine what it was. She poked her finger inside and moved it around, wondering about its function.

She stood again and looked at the dogs guiltily. "You didn't see me snoop," she told them and left the room, returning to the living room. There were magazines on the coffee table and she went to investigate. "I wonder what she reads." The tall woman immediately thought *porno* and was surprised to find out otherwise. "*New Yorker?*" she said out loud. She nodded at the *Out* magazine and raised an eyebrow at a small catalogue. Leafing through it, she quickly turned red, realizing that it was a toy catalogue, but continued to flip through the pages in interest. She stopped dead at the picture of what she'd found in the duffel bag and giggled nervously. *Thigh harness?* She read the little blurb next to the picture and was embarrassed to be imagining Sheridan using it...with her. "Stop that, Keefer," she said with a frown. She felt sad all of a sudden and sighed heavily.

Sheridan was in the kitchen, slowly depleting Keefer's bottled water supply, when the tall woman came home. She felt her heart speed up in anticipation. She wasn't sure what she was expecting, but she was ready to take it, whatever *it* was. She saw the tall woman head right for the bedroom. "I'm in here," she called out, emerging from the kitchen.

Keefer noticed Sheridan's wet hair and slightly healthier hue. "Have you slept at all?"

"No, I couldn't," Sheridan said sadly.

Keefer looked away. "We have to talk, Sher. Are you up to it?" Keefer said, sitting down on the couch.

The blonde felt like crying when Keefer averted her eyes. "Yeah. Do you want me to come in there?" she asked from the doorway of the kitchen.

"Well, I would like to see you when I talk to you," Keefer replied.

"But you won't look at me, I just figured..."

"Do you have any idea how hard it is for me not to look at you?"

"Why won't you?" Sheridan asked, moving slowly into the living room.

"It hurts you, doesn't it." Keefer realized from the sad expression on Sheridan's face.

"Yeah, it does," the blonde admitted, sitting on the couch hesitantly.

"I don't want to hurt you, but every time I look at you, it hurts *me*."

"I'm so sorry, Keefer."

The brunette turned to face the construction worker. Sheridan was miserable and it made her sad. "Are you really?"

Sheridan raised bleary green eyes to meet blue. "Yeah." She smiled a little when Keefer held her gaze.

"I see," the tall woman sighed heavily. All this time she'd known that they had to have this talk—but still, she was at a loss for words. She stood up and walked into the kitchen to gather her thoughts, as well as something to moisten her suddenly dry mouth.

Sheridan sat patiently, albeit uncomfortably, like a child waiting to be punished. Keefer had every right to be furious with her, yet she hadn't raised her voice and it made Sheridan feel even worse. The blonde was expecting an explosion—anything other than silence—and she felt a little sick from the anticipation. When Keefer re-entered the living room, Sheridan was prepared for the worst.

"Why?" Keefer asked, fiddling with a water bottle.

"Why?" Sheridan repeated. When Keefer nodded, Sheridan met her eyes and her stomach dropped a few inches at what she saw in them. "You're disappointed in me, aren't you," she stated sadly.

"I don't know yet. I don't want to be, so answer my question. Why?"

"Why did I get drunk?"

"That's a start," Keefer said before taking a long drink of water.

"I was pissed...at the guys, for telling me not to go out." Sheridan winced, only now realizing how stupid she'd acted.

"Why did they tell you not to go out?"

"'Cuz of you." Green eyes glanced again at blue. "They saw us at lunch," Sheridan added, looking down at her feet.

"Lunch was wonderful." Keefer smiled faintly at the memory.

"It was," the construction worker agreed.

"Then why did you go out and act like an ass?" The brunette was suddenly angry again.

"I don't know," Sheridan shrugged.

Keefer lifted the blonde's chin and searched her face. "You've never lied to me before, don't start now."

Sheridan sighed and averted her eyes. "Because I'm stupid."

"Not good enough," Keefer said, fighting every instinct to touch the lips so close to her fingers.

The blonde thought a while, her urge to flee almost overwhelming, but she looked into expectant blue eyes and knew she owed Keefer at least the truth. "I went out last night and made a complete asshole of myself because I'm scared," she admitted, her heart pounding in her ears.

"What are you so scared of?" Keefer whispered, also scared to hear the answer.

"You."

Keefer's heart broke a little.

Sheridan felt panic the second Keefer's beautiful face dropped. "No, Keefer, I'm afraid of how I feel about you," she clarified, immediately relieved when Keefer's expression became pensive.

The brunette's heart picked up speed, and she took a deep breath. "Did going out, getting drunk, having women dripping all over you, getting sick and ultimately beat up make you feel better?" she asked in a slightly sarcastic tone.

I guess I deserved that. Sheridan shook her head.

Keefer wanted to give Sheridan hell. She wanted to take her by the shirt and shake her. *How could she be so stupid? I love her!* "Sheridan, remember when we were eating lunch, and I was sitting on your lap?" The blonde nodded. "Feel that right now, the way it felt to hold each other, kiss each other. Remember how I looked into your eyes?"

The blonde closed her eyes and a small smile played across her lips. "I always wanted someone to look at me like that."

"Open your eyes and look at me now. I love you." Sheridan swallowed hard and tried to look away, but Keefer held her chin tight. "Why does that frighten you?"

"I don't know!" The blonde became frustrated. *What the hell is so wrong with Keefer loving me?* She felt like crying. "Stop looking at me like that." She wrested her chin away and stood up to pace the room.

Keefer watched Sheridan become more and more nervous and she began to regret her confession of love. She stood up and blocked the blonde's path. "How do you feel about me?" she asked.

Sheridan balled her hands into fists and punched her own thighs. "How do I feel? I feel sick! I feel anxious! My eye is throbbing like hell and my head hurts so badly, I feel like my ears are going to pop off!"

"That's all well and good, and I can't say I feel bad either, but my question was, how do you feel about me? Do you love me, too?"

Sheridan had no choice but to face the tall brunette as she was cornered against the wall. Her gaze traveled all over the living room as she fidgeted.

"It's not that hard of a question."

"You have no idea."

"Oh? Try me. I know more than you think, Sheridan."

"What do you know," the blonde dared, attempting to change the subject.

"I know," Keefer took Sheridan's hands and led her to the couch, "that you feel something for me, I saw it in your eyes. I know that you got drunk last night and acted like a fool in heat because you were trying to prove something—to whom, I don't know." Keefer waited for the blonde to finish grimacing before she continued. "I also know what it was that you were trying to prove."

The smaller woman looked up through her lashes guiltily at Keefer. "I was trying to prove that I didn't need you."

"And?"

"I failed miserably." Sheridan's shoulders slumped.

Keefer smiled a little and ran her fingers down the side of the blonde's bruised face. "Not a bad lesson to learn, if you ask me. I like that you need me, 'cuz I need you, too."

Sheridan smiled back crookedly; a whole smile hurt her eye and jaw. "Ya know, it feels good inside when you say that to me."

"I'll say it forever, if you let me." Keefer couldn't resist placing a light kiss on Sheridan's lips.

The construction worker felt warm all over and was shocked to find herself blushing. "Forever, huh?" she asked nervously and Keefer nodded. "That's a long time, Keef."

"The longest. If you're not ready for it, then you have to tell me now."

Sheridan thought deeply. So many questions ran disorganized through her mind, but one thing stuck out the most: tomorrow without Keefer would be unbearable. "You really love me? Even though I'm such a shmuck?"

"Surprised the hell outta me," Keefer said seriously, "and that's going to change, Miss Landers. I want to be with you, as your lover, as your partner, and I'll take most of your shit, but if you ever pull anything as stupid as you did last night, I'll kick your ass. Now, the real question is, do you want me?"

Sheridan's eyes widened. *She needs to know right now? This very second? I haven't had time to think—Wait, stop thinking, and just do. You need her, you want her.*

Keefer was startled when Sheridan wrapped her in a bear hug and began kissing her senseless. She wasn't quite sure if it was the blonde's answer or her way of getting out of the question. She pulled away form the onslaught and caught her breath. "Well? I need to hear it, Sher."

"I want you, please deal with me...please."

Keefer pulled Sheridan back into the embrace. "I have no choice, do I?" she joked, overcome with relief.

"I promise I'll try to be a good girlfriend. I have no experience, but I'm sure you'll tell me when I fuck up, won't you? I mean, I'm not going to actually try to fuck up, but I'm sure I'll do it...often...and..."

Keefer put her hand over Sheridan's mouth. "It'll be okay. I never been in love before either, Sher. I'm scared, too. I'm going to make mistakes also and I'm hoping you won't be too hard on me." She released the blonde's mouth.

"I already forgive you for everything," Sheridan grinned.

"Hold that thought, okay?" The brunette smiled. "Now kiss me, baby."

They kissed softly at first, Keefer trying to be careful of Sheridan's bruises, but the blonde was having none of it. She wanted to pour everything she felt into her kiss. They held on to each other tightly, both afraid to let go as their mouths and tongues told each other everything they needed to know.

Sheridan suddenly pulled back and looked into Keefer's dreamy eyes and it all clicked into place. She never wanted to be without Keefer, she never wanted those baby blues to look at her with anything but adoration and pride, she never wanted to wake up alone again. "I love you," she blurted.

Keefer's mouth opened and nothing came out. She didn't think Sheridan was even aware that she loved her yet; she certainly didn't expect to hear it at that moment.

"I mean it, I love you!" Sheridan said excitedly.

"Oh God...me too, I love you, too!" Keefer finally replied, wrapping her arms tightly around her lover.

"You're choking me, Keef!" Sheridan chuckled.

Keefer let go and took inventory of Sheridan's injuries. "How do you feel?" she asked, concerned with the discoloration of her eye.

"I'm so incredibly wired! Fuck, I feel good!" the construction worker replied, getting up and doing a happy dance.

Keefer laughed, "I meant your eye, you nut job."

"Oh, that? It's okay." Sheridan shrugged.

"You look so cute in that shirt, dancing around the living room."

"I'm not wearing panties." Sheridan wiggled her eyebrows.

Keefer grinned wickedly.

The blonde became serious. "Are we okay? I mean, aren't you going to yell at me for how I acted?"

"Oh, believe me, I was going to. I was going to rip you apart, but after seeing you last night, and then this morning, I figured you pretty much suffered enough."

"I deserved it, I guess."

"No, you didn't deserve Danni—oh, my god! She's in jail!" Sheridan snickered and soon Keefer joined her. "Let her sit there," she said through her giggles.

Sheridan sat down between Keefer's open legs and leaned back on her chest. "Mmm, you feel good behind me."

331

Keefer glanced down and narrowed her eyes, then smacked Sheridan in the arm, hard.

"Hey! What the hell was that for?" the blonde twisted around to see Keefer's face.

"Don't think I missed this." Keefer poked the hickey repeatedly.

"Ow! Quit that!" The blonde swatted at her hand.

"No one, and I mean no one, is to suck on this neck." Keefer gave a final poke. "This neck and all its wonderful skin, is mine." She let loose one more smack.

Sheridan frowned and rubbed her arm. "Ooh, possessive, huh?"

Another smack and poke.

"Okay! Jeez! No one. I got it!"

"Good. You know, I don't mind one bit that you go out, dance, and hang out with the girls, but lay off the floozies. You're mine, woman."

Sheridan smiled, "Fuckin' A. Wanna prove it?"

"How would I do that?" Keefer grinned.

"Write your name all over me...with your tongue."

"Oh yeah, good idea," Keefer purred.

Chapter 30

The idea of mapping every inch of Sheridan with her tongue interested Keefer beyond words, but Sheridan had had a rough morning and the brunette was also distracted with worry for Danni. This disturbed her; after what Danni had been pulling lately, she deserved to sit and rot in jail for a long time. For some reason, however, Keefer felt a little bad about her being there...guilty for putting her there. Sheridan shifted in her position between Keefer's legs and broke her from her thoughts. "You know, as much as I'd love to lick you all over, Sher, I think you need to eat something, get some ice on that eye, and rest," Keefer said while running her fingers up and down Sheridan's muscular arm.

"That feels good," the blonde said quietly, watching the goose pimples sprout from Keefer's tickling touch. "What are you going to do? You should go to work. I'm sorry I made you stay home today."

"No problem, really. I just extended my vacation from four days to five. I originally intended on taking five anyway," Keefer said, moving her fingers up to tickle across the back of Sheridan's neck. "Maybe all the drama was for a reason. If I hadn't stayed home with you, you never would have told me you love me today."

"I guess...but I'm sure it would have came up sooner or later." Sheridan squirmed and Keefer calmed her by tickling her arms again. "Mmm. You're gonna put me to sleep."

"That's the whole point," Keefer snickered.

"You haven't answered my question. What are you going to do while I sleep?" Despite how good Keefer's fingers felt, Sheridan moved them away and twisted around to look at her lover.

"I should see about Danni," the brunette said with a remorseful smile.

Sheridan chuckled quietly. "You feel bad for her, don't you—even after she kicked my ass."

"I don't know why, but yeah." Keefer frowned.

"Hey, that's okay. That's just you. Go on and spring her from jail." The sore construction worker winced a little as she stretched her neck for a kiss.

"You don't mind? You're not upset?" Keefer asked between little pecks to the blonde's lips. She was tempted to bring her mouth lower and start that tongue-writing journey.

"Nah, to tell you the truth, I was surprised you let them take her away at all." Sheridan turned around and leaned her back against Keefer's front again, settling comfortably into Keefer's breasts.

The brunette settled her hands on Sheridan's thighs. "I was furious with her. Who did she think she was, anyway, hitting you when you were in that condition?" *Her thighs are so strong.*

"I did puke on her, though," Sheridan joked to cover her embarrassment. She felt Keefer's heart beating a bit harder against her back and grinned, covering Keefer's hands with her own.

"That you did." The brunette looked down as Sheridan's head lay heavily against her shoulder. Those beautiful green eyes were closed and the blonde's lips were partially open, giving Keefer the urge to kiss them, if she could reach. Her fingers twitched underneath the strong hands that were covering them.

Sheridan noticed the hitch in her lover's breathing and purposely licked her lips. She grinned inwardly as the beat grew stronger against her back. "What do you want, Keefer?" she asked in a low, sexy voice.

The tall woman bent her head to Sheridan's ear. "I really want to touch you...right now...like this," she whispered.

Sheridan shivered and felt her nipples harden. "I thought I was in no condition," she almost moaned as Keefer continued to breathe into her ear.

"You aren't."

"Don't tease me, Keef, I'm getting way too turned on like this." The blonde moved Keefer's hands up over her hips and stomach and rested them on her ribs, under her breasts. She dropped her hands away, leaving Keefer to roam freely.

Keefer felt Sheridan's heart beating strongly under her hands. She saw the nipples harden and poke against the fabric of the shirt and she wanted to touch them. She kissed the top of the blonde head. "Are you sure?" she asked, even as her hands slipped up to cup Sheridan's breasts.

"Oh, yeah," Sheridan breathed out as two thumbs brushed her nipples.

"Take your shirt off and come right back here," Keefer said, releasing the breasts.

Sheridan sat up and pulled off the shirt quickly, leaning back as soon as she did. "Now I'm naked and you're fully clothed," she remarked with a grin.

"Just the way I want you." Keefer grinned back, though Sheridan couldn't see her face.

"Kinky," the blonde chuckled, then gasped as Keefer went straight for her breasts again.

Keefer watched her hands as they held the two round breasts, her thumbs rubbing circles over hard nipples. Her gaze drifted down to Sheridan's comfortably bent legs, her triangle of blonde hair, and then her perfectly sculpted abs.

"Are you watching me?" the blonde asked, slightly self-consciously.

"I like looking at your body; I think it's perfect."

Sheridan felt her face get hot.

Keefer chuckled, "Sheridan Landers, don't tell me you're blushing."

"I don't believe it either." Sheridan opened her eyes and swallowed, weighing her feelings. She shivered as Keefer changed tactics and began pinching and teasing her nipples. She couldn't stop blushing and she laughed nervously.

"What is it?" Keefer asked in a whisper.

"I don't know. It just feels so...like it's the first time, and no one's ever looked at my body before."

"It is the first time, Sher...for both of us."

Sheridan hummed as one of Keefer's hands traveled down her stomach and her fingers teased her pubic hair. "I guess it is. I've never been in love before."

"Me neither." Keefer rested her chin on Sheridan's shoulder.

"It feels different...better. Very, very good."

"Good. I want to make you feel very, very good," Keefer breathed as she let her longest finger venture further downwards.

Sheridan's hips twitched as Keefer's finger brushed lightly over her clit and then retreated.

"Come on, Keef, I'm getting so wet already."

Keefer felt a sense of possession while touching Sheridan in that manner—like she was the only one allowed to do that. *I am the only one.* "Shh. Slowly, Sher, I want to watch you move for me."

"God, Keef, I feel like such an teenager!" Sheridan said in frustration.

"Me too, like I'm learning everything." Blue eyes strayed to blonde curls. "I am, you know, I never did this before. I'm thirty-five and I've never had the chance to do this," Keefer admitted, sliding both hands as far down Sheridan's legs as she could reach, watching the muscles twitch and flex under her touch. "You are so beautiful," she added, mesmerized by

335

Sheridan's body as she moved her hands back up the inside of the blonde's thighs.

"You're ...oh, God...thirty-five?" Sheridan asked between gasps of pleasure.

"Uh-huh." Keefer mapped Sheridan's entire torso with her hands, delighting in the movements of her body.

"I'm thirty-one. Never been with an older woman before." Sheridan arched her back as Keefer rubbed her palms in circles over her nipples. "Keef...please..."

"Patience," the brunette whispered breathily into Sheridan's ear. She reveled in the full-body shudder that her breath caused. "How's the old broad doing so far?" she teased.

"She's relentless." Sheridan lifted her hips up in invitation. "If she doesn't touch me, I will."

Keefer's mouth went dry. All those images from channel 46 flooded her mind, of women touching themselves and how hot it made her. Imagining Sheridan touching herself made her groan out loud. She immediately pictured Sheridan that night in bed next to her, touching herself in the dark, and her sex suddenly clenched and flooded.

"You'd like that, wouldn't you," Sheridan said, pulling on Keefer's hand and trying to bring it between her legs.

"Yeah," Keefer rasped, then swallowed to wet her dry throat.

"I will," Sheridan said.

"Don't...not now...let me." Keefer panicked, not ready to see that yet, wanting only to give Sheridan pleasure at that moment. She didn't want to lose the sense of control she was feeling. Looking down at the length of the construction worker's naked body thrilled her. Watching intently as her fingers made Sheridan dance and move, Keefer was almost giddy with the power of it all. She had never been so intrigued by a body's reaction to her touch. She couldn't have cared less what Danni looked like; she only cared enough to make her come so she'd fall asleep. At that moment, she couldn't tear her eyes away from the blonde's muscular body as it squirmed and writhed under her touch. She allowed Sheridan to hold her hand between her legs, but she didn't move her fingers. She watched through half-lidded eyes as Sheridan did the moving, bucking her hips and wiggling her ass. The surge of arousal Keefer felt was intoxicating.

"You're killing me, Keef," Sheridan panted.

Keefer slid her free hand up to the blonde's face and traced her lips with two fingers. She groaned when Sheridan's tongue came out to meet her and toyed with her fingers. With a smirk, she brought her wet fingers to a straining nipple and painted it with Sheridan's saliva, then blew over the blonde's shoulder.

A cool gust of air met Sheridan's nipple, making her twitch and moan. "Fuck, Keef..." Sheridan wondered what had come over Keefer. The brunette was normally a confident lover, but the sudden change in character excited Sheridan even more.

Keefer began moving her fingers through Sheridan's sex and hummed with approval as the construction worker writhed to meet her fingers, trying to draw them inside. "You're so wet, I didn't think you had it in you," Keefer teased.

Sheridan only nodded and bit her bottom lip. At first, she'd felt exposed while being touched that way, but now she was hotter than she could ever remember and her sex was literally aching to be touched by Keefer. No one else could ever make her feel like this, and no one else could quench her need. She was sure of that now, especially when Keefer suddenly filled her. All that blind searching with nameless women ended when Keefer ran her long fingers through her wetness. She needed Keefer to touch her—only Keefer. She groaned long and wordlessly as the knowing fingers entered her with a purpose.

"Feels good, Sher?" Keefer asked, her voice deep with arousal.

"Uh-huh." Sheridan held Keefer's arm with both hands; she didn't want her to stop. She dug her fingers into Keefer's arm and panted as she neared orgasm. Sheridan's hips moved in time with Keefer's strokes, the heel of Keefer's hand pressing against Sheridan's clit as her long fingers entered and retreated. The blonde's thighs began to tremble.

Keefer was experiencing an adrenaline rush; it felt so good to have Sheridan in this position. She had a feeling this was the first time Sheridan had let anybody have their way with her in such a manner and it felt wildly powerful. Sheridan's head moved back and forth against her breasts and Keefer spotted the ugly hickey. With a growl of possession, Keefer bent her head and sucked on Sheridan's neck, right over the bruised spot.

"Fuck!" the blonde cried through gritted teeth, her sex grabbing at Keefer's fingers, intensifying the friction.

"Yeah, Sher, come for me." Keefer sucked harder, marking the blonde with her own brand for the world to see.

Sheridan held Keefer's arm in a death grip as her body arched and stilled. Her mouth opened and a trembling moan escaped her. Her orgasm was intense and she twitched and bucked for a long time, whimpering as she did.

Keefer felt exhilarated as she watched Sheridan come in her arms. She especially loved the way her abs spasmed and had the sudden urge to lick off the sheen of sweat that appeared from them. She winced as the grip on her arm became painful, but she couldn't fault the blonde, she could only grin triumphantly as Sheridan started to finally relax her body and her grip.

Green eyes opened and Sheridan turned her face up. "God, I love you," she breathed between pants.

Keefer smiled and her heart beat furiously in her chest. "I love you, too."

Looking down at Sheridan's face as she spoke those words caused Keefer's heart to skip a beat. The blonde's face was totally devoid of any barriers, and Keefer could see the pure honesty in her eyes. Sheridan didn't speak those words spontaneously, like some people do after sex; her eyes were wider than usual and she looked slightly shocked that it was her who'd blurted those words. Keefer knew she meant them and it was everything to her. She wrapped her arms possessively around the blonde and smiled as Sheridan yawned widely. "Let's go in my room and get you tucked in."

"But you..." The blonde yawned again. "Don't you..."

"Don't worry, Sher, there will be plenty of time for that. You need to get some rest. I think it's too late for that eye, though." Keefer stood up with Sheridan, her arms still wrapped around her from behind. Once the blonde started walking, though, the tall woman had to release her or she'd be walking in a squat. Keefer indulged herself with a leer to Sheridan's naked backside when she noticed the big bruise. "What the hell happened to your butt?"

Sheridan's hands reflexively covered the spot. "I have no idea." She shrugged and continued walking into the bedroom. "You coming?"

"Sheridan! How did you get that thing? It's gotta hurt!"

"I told you, I don't know." The blonde turned in the doorway to the bedroom and met Keefer's eyes. "I don't remember," she admitted sheepishly.

Blue eyes narrowed and Keefer was angry for a moment before she realized that Sheridan probably *shouldn't* remember a bruise like that. "Well, I'm sure it's for the best. Let's go—march!" She pointed to the bed, where Fifi was already snuggled.

Sheridan was blissfully asleep minutes after her head hit the pillow, but Keefer still sat there, sifting her fingers through the soft, blonde hair. She thought over the morning's events and became upset again over Danni's actions. She felt guilty, too. Sheridan never would have gotten hurt had it not been for her. Keefer leaned over and gently kissed Sheridan's bruised face, frowning a little as the memory of Danni's blow flashed before her eyes. A smirk shaped her lips when she got to the part when Sheridan had thrown up on Danni. *Stupid thing to do, Danni.* She lightly traced the side of her lover's face with one finger and grinned at the way Sheridan's lips turned into a smile. *What is it with Danni, anyway? It's not like we had anything meaningful. Nothing at all like what I feel with Sheridan. Why is she doing this to us? She was the one who was cheating on me; she played dirty and lost.* Keefer kissed Sheridan on the forehead and wandered into the living room.

Keefer stood by the couch and contemplated the hole she had punched in the wall. She was surprised that Sheridan hadn't noticed it. *Then again, look at the shape she arrived in and all the things that had happened this morning.* She wondered if she had any spackle in the closets and her memory came up empty. *That's okay, Sheridan can fix it for me.* Keefer grimaced. *Then I'll have to tell her why it's there. I feel so stupid, losing my temper like that.* Sheridan's cell phone rang and after Keefer located it, she wondered if she should answer it. She picked up the phone and glanced at the little screen. *Pops. He may be worried about her.* She answered it nervously, "Sheridan's phone."

"Uh, hello, who's this?"

"I'm Keefer, sir, Sheridan's friend. She's sleeping at the moment."

"Poor kid. Is she all right? Is she really banged up?"

"You know what happened?" Keefer asked hesitantly.

"Yeah, she told me earlier, I was just checking up on her," Mr. Landers explained.

"Well, she's sleeping. She had a rough night, but don't worry, I'll take care of her."

"I bet you will."

The tone of his voice made Keefer believe he knew more than she thought he did.

"So, hey, whaddya say you drag her ass over to my house for dinner? Her brother's been waiting on her all morning and he'll be disappointed if she doesn't show."

Keefer became very nervous; meeting Sheridan's father was a big deal. "Uh, well...she really isn't, I mean, maybe you should ask her first?"

Mr. Landers chuckled. "No need to be nervous, honey, I like you already."

Keefer blushed. "I still think you should ask her."

"When she wakes up, tell her I called," he said.

"Will do," Keefer replied, anxious to hang up the phone.

Keefer put the phone down and stared at it, replaying the conversation. *He seemed nice—concerned about Sheridan.* She glanced toward the bedroom and sighed. *Once she hears that her brother is waiting for her, she's sure to go. Maybe I should...* Her heart beat faster. *Why am I so nervous? It's just her father; I've already met her brother.* Keefer blushed, remembering the things Steven had said about her. *Oh, it could be very interesting. He sounds nothing like Danni's father—Danni!* Keefer remembered Danni was still stewing away in jail. She checked up on Sheridan once more before writing her a note and heading out the door.

Keefer had never been to the police station and wasn't sure what to expect when she opened the door. Right in front of her was a desk with a police officer and to her left was a big counter or an enormous desk that took up the whole side of the room. There were offices and stairways and police officers milling about the rest of the room. She hadn't spotted a cell yet and wondered where Danni was being held and what it looked like.

"Can I help you, ma'am?"

Keefer looked at the officer and blushed. "Um, yes. I'm here to see..." Keefer froze, not knowing Sharon's last name. "An officer brought in a woman this morning named Danni..."

"Oh, her." The officer scrunched up his face. "You'll have to sign in here," he pointed to the book, "and I really hope you brought her some clothes."

Keefer couldn't help grimacing along with the officer. "No, I didn't. I'm actually here to press charges," she said after signing her name.

"You the one who puked on her?"

"No, that was my girlfriend, the one she assaulted."

"Oh, it's like that, huh?" the officer smirked.

Keefer narrowed her eyes. "Very much so...sir," she added with distaste.

"Go on up to the desk and tell that guy." He pointed at the proper officer.

Keefer stared at him longer than she should have and then proceeded to the desk.

It was an annoying process, lots of paperwork and no one to help her. She waited patiently for the arresting officer to show. She really wanted to talk to Sharon. She felt like everyone was staring at her and was relieved to hear the tall female cop's voice.

"Hey, Keefer, how's it hangin'?"

The brunette chuckled, "Thank God you're here. These guys are starting to make me uncomfortable."

"They're pissed 'cuz you're family." Sharon shrugged, shooting a look at the cops facing their way. "So, I just saw Danni, she heard you were here and wants to speak to you."

"I don't want to speak to her," Keefer replied quickly.

"No doubt. So, what do we have here?" Sharon indicated the report.

"So far, assault and trespassing. That's all I can come up with."

"Good enough for me. That'll give her enough shit. How's Sher doin'?"

"Okay, I guess. She's all bruised up, even on her butt."

Sharon snickered.

"You know how that happened?" Keefer asked curiously.

"Yeah, she did it at the club. She was pretty wasted and she took a swing at Danni. Flung herself off the stool and flat onto her ass." Sharon bit back a laugh.

"No kidding? Why was she going to hit—never mind, I don't want to know."

"She was protecting you," Sharon said seriously. "Keefer, I hope you weren't too hard on her; she was really confused with her feelings. She didn't do anything to intentionally hurt you."

Keefer sighed, "I really wanted to tear her head off, but after what you said last night and this morning, I thought about it more. Thank you for taking such good care of her, I bet she was a handful."

"In all honesty, she really couldn't stop talking about you. I knew before that you must have been something and now I see what she has to talk about."

The tall brunette blushed. "Thank you."

Sharon looked Keefer in the eyes. "Sheridan's been hooked on you for a while now. You really got to her. The girls and I have been worried about her, and now this..."

"I never meant for her to get hurt, I'm sick with shame over it," Keefer said, near tears.

"Hey, don't cry, I'm just looking out for Sheridan—I love the girl."

"I love her, too."

Sharon smiled, "Good to know, Keefer. Good to know. Go on, get out of here...go take care of Sheridan."

Sheridan woke up with a smile on her face. Despite the fact that her eye was throbbing, her jaw hurt, and she was face first in Fifi's belly, she felt good. Inside. *I feel good inside.* It was a foreign, yet welcome feeling. She stretched and yawned, yelling out loud at the pain from opening her mouth that wide had caused. Fifi jumped up and eyed her curiously, sniffing her face and neck. Sheridan laughed as the dog's whiskers tickled her skin. "Cut that out, you," she said, grabbing the dog by the ears and kissing her nose. "Where's Mommy?" she asked. Fifi merely kissed her back. "Your breath smells a hell of a lot better than Pharaoh's," she remarked as she dragged her sore body out of bed.

After dressing in her own clothes, Sheridan went to the bathroom and washed her face. "God, look at me!" she said in surprise. "Fucking Danni...that no-good piece of shit. What did Keefer ever see in that asshole?" She examined her face and grew more upset. "I can't believe she did this...I can't believe I let her do this," she sighed heavily. "If I hadn't been such an asshole last night, she never would have gotten away with it."

Sheridan wandered into the kitchen. Her stomach was painfully empty and she needed to eat. She spotted a bottle of water on the table along with a note. She smiled while reading Keefer's instructions to drink the water and eat a bagel from the freezer. "Mommy went to make Danni's life a little more miserable," she snickered at Fifi. "Good for her." She bent down and petted the dog. "Hey, do I look any different? You're supposed to look different when you're in love." Fifi wagged her tail and waited patiently for Sheridan to start eating. "You only love me 'cuz I feed you," she joked and got a treat for the dog. "Here, don't tell Mommy."

She made a bagel and took it into the living room to eat. She made herself comfortable on the sofa and smirked at the recent memory from that particular piece of furniture. "She sure threw me for a loop," she chuckled. "What do you do when you're in love? How does this work?" she asked the dog, who only wanted some cream cheese. Her eyes wandered around the room and fell on the hole in the wall. She stood up and inspected it, knowing there was only one way a hole like that—at that height—could appear. "Fuck," Sheridan grimaced. "I made her that mad?" The blonde felt awful; she couldn't imagine Keefer getting that angry over anything. She put down her plate and went out to her car, pulling all the materials she'd need from her trunk.

When Keefer arrived home, she found Sheridan in the driveway, putting her tools into her trunk, a scraper in her hand. "Hey, baby, what are you doing?"

The blonde's expression turned guilty. "I fixed the hole in the wall."

"Oh." Now it was Keefer's turn to look guilty. "You didn't have to."

"I wanted to, it was the least I could do after making you so mad." Sheridan took Keefer's hand and kissed the bruised knuckles. "I'm so sorry."

"We're past that, Sher."

"Thank you. I'll never make you that mad again."

"I hope not," Keefer said and then smiled. "Your dad called while you were asleep. He wants to talk to you."

"Cool, he made soup for me," Sheridan said excitedly. "Wanna go over there with me?"

"I don't know..."

"Come on." Sheridan stuck out her bottom lip and made puppy-dog eyes.

Keefer narrowed her eyes. *Damn, weakness number one.* "Come inside and we'll talk about it."

Sheridan grinned triumphantly. *I knew the lip would work.*

TJ Vertigo

Chapter 31

Sheridan finally convinced Keefer to go with her to her father's house and was forced to wait patiently as her lover changed her outfit for the third time. Sheridan chuckled at how nervous Keefer was and she actually found it cute, so when Keefer emerged from her bedroom in her next set of clothing, the construction worker found it hard not to tease.

"Well? What do you think?" Keefer asked, twirling around.

"Hmm, I dunno. Don't ya think it's a little butch?"

Keefer panicked. "Butch?" She looked down at her clothing—beige chinos and a white shirt.

"Come on, Keef, I'm just playing. You look fine. You looked fine in all the other things you had on, too. It's just my pop, calm down, will ya?"

Keefer smacked Sheridan in the shoulder. "Don't fool around, I'm too nervous."

"There's nothing to be nervous about. Honestly, my pop is cool."

"Danni's father hated me."

"Screw him. Don't worry. You'll see, everything will be okay."

"You promise?" Keefer asked worriedly.

"Yep," the blonde smiled. "Now, let's go. I need to go home and change my clothes, too."

Keefer bent down and kissed Fifi. The dog then trotted over to Sheridan, sat down and looked up expectantly at her.

"Later, Feefs." Sheridan bent down and let Fifi lick her face.

"I've never seen her attach herself to someone so fast. She usually doesn't trust people," Keefer said with a big grin.

"Well, I'm not just people," the blonde replied.

No, you're not, are you, Keefer thought as they left the house.

When Sheridan opened the door to her apartment, she was instantly jumped. The dogs were overjoyed to see her and pounced on her like she'd been gone for days. Keefer was left snickering in the hallway as the dogs threw themselves at Sheridan, slamming the door behind her in Keefer's face. The tall woman could only imagine what the dogs were doing to Sheridan as the blonde grunted and spit intermittently. Once Keefer was able to push the weight of Sheridan and the dogs along with the door, she snuck inside the apartment. The dogs began to dart back and forth between their mommy and Keefer, tripping over their own feet and each other.

Keefer laughed as Pharaoh did an imitation of a kangaroo—jumping up and trying to lick her face—and Zeus shook his tail so hard that his whole backside flew back and forth. "Hey, guys, you just saw me this morning!" Keefer giggled as she spoke.

Sheridan crawled away from the fray and lay on the floor in hysterics, watching Keefer as she tried to accommodate both dogs. "This is normal, Keef."

"Hey! Hey!" Keefer shrieked as Zeus tripped her and she fell to her knees.

A loud whistle stopped the dogs in their tracks and they both turned to look at Sheridan. "That's enough!" she said forcefully. "Now go lay down." She pointed to the living room and the panting, excited dogs slunk away.

"You didn't have to yell at them on my account," the brunette said as she got back to her feet.

"Oh, yes, I did. We'd never get out of here if I didn't."

Keefer frowned and looked toward the living room.

"God, Keef, I didn't beat them or anything," Sheridan smiled. "Fine. The treats are in the cabinet in the kitchen," she chuckled.

"I know, next to the food," Keefer said as she went right for the treats.

"Oh?" Sheridan was suddenly beside the brunette. "Do any snooping around here this morning?"

Keefer blushed and looked everywhere but at Sheridan.

"Uh-huh. Found something blush-worthy, did you?" The blonde wrapped her arms around Keefer from behind.

"Maybe," the inspector mumbled.

Sheridan kissed Keefer between the shoulders. "Found my bag o'tricks?"

Keefer turned around in Sheridan's arms with the doggie treats in her hands. She was bright red and grinning sheepishly. "I think so."

"See anything you like?" the blonde asked, wiggling her eyebrows.

"Do we have to talk about this now?" Keefer asked, trying to get out of Sheridan's grasp.

"Nope." The blonde released her lover. "I'll just have to try each thing out, one by one, and see what you like best."

"Oh God! Sheridan!" Keefer hurried out of the kitchen and into the living room.

Sheridan folded her arms over her chest and leaned against the stove. "Oh, you definitely saw something," she snickered.

Keefer handed the now-obedient dogs their treats and sat on the couch between them. "You're not going to drop it, are you?" She hid her hot face in her hands.

"Nope."

"Well, if you must know...there was one thing."

"Yeah, and..."

Keefer shook her head and sighed. "The thigh thing," she said into her hands.

"Oh yeah?" The construction worker slipped into her bedroom while Keefer hid her face and came into the living room holding said item. "This?" she asked, dangling it off her finger.

Keefer peeked from between her fingers and nodded.

"Cool. I kinda like this one myself."

"Please put it away. I can't believe we're having this conversation now. It's all I'm going to think about while I sit with your father."

"We were gonna have this conversation sooner or later. Now's as good a time as any." Sheridan chuckled at Keefer's bright red face. "Come on, Keef, you don't ever have to be embarrassed about this stuff with me, you know that." Sheridan squatted down in front of the mortified brunette.

"I know, but I can't help it. Maybe if you don't talk about it and just do it instead..."

"That seems easy enough, but I want to make sure I don't do anything you won't be comfortable with. It would really make me feel bad if I tried something and it bothered you. I'd rather know about it ahead of time."

Keefer looked into Sheridan's eyes and smiled bashfully, "You're right, we should talk about it ahead of time. I'm just such a baby when it comes to these things."

"Don't talk like that, you're *not* a baby. Keef, we both have to learn things about each other. I just don't want to play guessing games."

Keefer nodded and leaned over to kiss the blonde. "Thank you for dealing with me."

Sheridan snorted. "You? Dealing with *you*? Are you kidding? I am no walk in the park!" She pointed to her chest.

"Well, I love you anyway," Keefer grinned. "Go get dressed, and take that thing with you," she indicated the thigh harness.

Sheridan kissed her lover thoroughly before leaving the room. Keefer fell back into the couch with a dreamy sigh. "Guys, your mommy is one hell of a kisser." She scratched Zeus behind the ear and the big dog sighed. "You two must be one hell of a handful. It's a good thing you found Sheridan." Keefer was still replaying the harness conversation and was startled when the blonde began talking.

"You can turn on the TV if you want, but I shouldn't be long."

Blue eyes drank in the sight of the construction worker walking away in her underwear. Keefer nodded absently as her eyes raked over every exposed inch of her lover. *Oh, boy...that's a keeper of a vision.*

Sheridan was ready before Keefer had the chance to shake loose the sexy image, and was soon standing in front of her with a raised eyebrow. "What were you thinking about?" she asked with a knowing grin, indicating that Keefer's expression gave had already given her away.

"Oh, uh...nothing really." She stood quickly, causing the dogs to jump to attention. If Keefer thought she'd have trouble keeping her mind in the right place before, she was in even more trouble now. Sheridan looked delicious to her and her eyes kept wandering up and down the construction worker's body.

"It's just jeans, Keef," she teased.

"Easy for you to say. I think those were made for you." Keefer couldn't control herself and ran her hand across Sheridan's stomach. "And must you wear such tight shirts?"

"I love the way you look at me when I wear them."

Keefer blushed and looked away. "You're totally irresistible."

Sheridan gave her lover a sexy smile. "I think you proved that this morning."

Keefer's lips twitched with the memory. "Mmm-hmm," she grinned, her eyes narrowing as she recalled certain moments.

Sheridan swallowed hard at the look on Keefer's face. "Let's go before I tear off your clothes right this second."

The drive over was nerve wracking for Keefer, but it seemed that Sheridan didn't notice. The blonde was singing out loud with the radio, tapping her fingers on the steering wheel. Keefer found herself smiling at her lover during particularly dramatic choruses, despite her nervousness. The inspector continued to stare at Sheridan as they rode, amazed that this self-assured, cocky woman was the same one that lay submissively in her arms earlier that day and allowed her to stake claim to her body in the most intimate of ways. Keefer smiled at the trust Sheridan obviously felt for her.

"Here we are."

Keefer nearly gasped out loud. "*This* is your father's house? You grew up in *here*?"

"Huge, ain't it?" Sheridan said as she pulled up to into the driveway.

"It's gorgeous," Keefer said, taking it all in.

Sheridan beamed. "It's just one benefit of being a construction worker. I helped build that deck when I was twelve."

Keefer smiled at Sheridan's prideful expression. "You did a good job."

"Come on, Steven's probably having a cow."

Keefer had to practically crawl out of the small car and stood by the steps waiting for Sheridan, nervously shifting from foot to foot.

"I swear, Keef, no one's going to bite you." Sheridan raised her eyebrow when she realized what she'd just said and opened her mouth again.

Keefer clamped her hand over her lover's lips. "Please, don't say anything. I have enough of you on my mind already."

Before they could ring the bell, Steven flung open the door and shouted, "Sher—oh shit! What happened to your face? Damn, that—" He stopped dead once he noticed Keefer and a slow grin appeared on his face. "Cool. Keefer's here, too."

"Good observation," the blonde teased. "Move, Stevie-boy." She banged into him with her shoulder and he bolted into the house.

"Pop! Sheridan's here and she brought *Keefer*!"

Sheridan stole a glance at her lover as they walked into the house and chuckled at the redness covering her cheeks. "Ain't that something, he's got a woody for ya."

"I'm going to die," Keefer mumbled as they made their way into the living room.

"Oh, come on, you won't die." Sheridan took the brunette's hand and held it close to her chest.

"Hi honey. Ooh." Mr. Landers winced and ran his finger over his daughter's eye. "That's gotta hurt."

"Like a bitch. Pop, this is Keefer, Keefer, meet my pop, the coolest father on the planet."

"Well, will you look at you." The older man smiled warmly at Keefer then turned to Sheridan with a chuckle. "You definitely take after the old man, kiddo."

Steven suddenly appeared wearing a baseball cap and carrying a basketball. "Can we play, Sher? I wanna show Keefer my shot!"

"Not now, Steven, I'm not feeling that great."

"Well, if you didn't run around getting your ass kicked—"

"Steven, I'm sure your sister's hungry," Mr. Landers broke in.

Steven pouted.

"Maybe after I eat, okay?" Sheridan said as she stole her brother's hat and put it on her head, making Steven laugh as the hat covered her eyes and ears. "I'm starved, where's the food?" she said, rubbing her belly.

"Keefer, you wanna sit next to me? I don't spit or nothing, I swear," Steven said shyly.

Keefer looked to Sheridan, who merely shrugged. "Sure, I'd love to," she answered.

"All right!" The younger man pumped his fist in the air and took off into the dining room.

Mr. Landers chuckled. "I think your brother has a crush on your woman," he teased.

"Can you blame him? I mean, look at her!" Sheridan leered at her lover.

Keefer blushed hotly. It was very embarrassing to her that Sheridan's father knew they slept together.

Sheridan noticed Keefer's discomfort and rested her hand in the small of the tall woman's back. "I'm sorry, Keef. Pop, she's really shy."

"Well you better open up, honey, I want to know all about the woman who turned my daughter inside out."

"Um, I'm starving in here!" Steven yelled from the dining room.

"That's our cue. Go sit down and I'll get it all ready."

"Thanks, Pop, you're the greatest."

"After you, pretty lady." Mr. Landers gestured at Keefer.

"Thank you, sir," Keefer said quietly.

"Whoa! I'm no sir, call me Pop."

Keefer cleared her throat and nodded, allowing Sheridan to lead her through the house.

The second Keefer sat down, Steven began smiling. "You want a roll?" he asked her.

"No thanks," she politely declined, smiling sweetly at him.

"Okay, but if you do, if you want anything even, just ask and I'll get it for you," he said, puffing out his chest.

"Stop drooling, Stevie-boy."

"Quit it, Sheridan," he frowned. "I am not drooling. I'm just being a gentleman. Isn't that what you do when you have a gorgeous woman sitting next to you?"

Sheridan smiled. "Yeah, I guess you're right."

"Soup's on!" Mr. Landers appeared with a steaming pot and set it in the middle of the table. "I'll be right back with the ziti for those of us who didn't drink too much last night," he said, narrowing his eyes at his daughter.

"You got drunk last night, Sher? Did you throw up?"

"Yeah, I threw up."

Mr. Landers came back into the room with a pan of ziti that made Keefer's mouth water.

"Hey, enough of that talk, we're eating here." Sheridan leaned over Keefer and whispered to her brother, "Puked all over the chick that hit me."

Sheridan and Steven shared a snicker while their father looked on with distaste. "So, Keefer, what do you do?"

"I work in records, at OSHA, but I still go out on inspections." She glanced at Sheridan.

"Yeah, that's how we met," the blonde added.

"Who kicked your ass, Sher?" Steven asked around a mouthful of ziti.

Sheridan wanted to run a list of adjectives describing Danni to her brother, but she didn't want to upset Keefer. "This chick named Danni."

Steven stopped chewing and furrowed his brows in thought. "Danni—hey, isn't that the same girl from the car wash?"

"Uh, yeah. Hey, I'd like a roll, Steven," Sheridan said, quickly changing the subject.

Mr. Landers saw his daughter squirming and Keefer looking strangely at her, so he jumped in to help. "The guys were worried about you this morning, Sher. You didn't show and you didn't call. They said you all had some disagreement last night, too."

"Yeah, I was stupid. I acted like an all-around ass last night," Sheridan grimaced.

"Does Danni still think you're, um, *doing it* with her girlfriend?" Steven asked, still stuck on the subject. "Is that what she beat you up for? I didn't think she looked so tough."

"Steven, that's enough," the older man warned.

Keefer's eyebrows disappeared into her bangs as she grinned in amusement at her highly uncomfortable lover. "So, this Danni person...she's threatened you before?" she asked innocently.

"Oh yeah, she tried to act all rough, but Sheridan flexed a few times and she ran away."

"So, tell me, Steven," Keefer tried not to laugh at Sheridan's outraged expression at her brother, "what did Sheridan say about Danni's girlfriend?"

Mr. Landers watched his daughter wince and was suddenly very interested in this story.

"Well, first Sher pointed out that it was Danni's *ex-girlfriend*, and she never told Danni that she wasn't doing it, but she told me later that she couldn't *do it* with her 'cuz there's a difference between making love and doing *it*. But Danni didn't know that," Steven laughed. "She got so mad, but Sheridan scared her away."

Though Keefer tried to make sense of the story, all she heard was Sheridan *couldn't* do it. *When was this?* she wondered.

Mr. Landers put two and two together and realized that Keefer must be Danni's ex. "Okay, Steven, that's all, let's finish eating." He grinned at his daughter who seemed to have slid several inches under the table.

Keefer smiled at her lover, then at Steven. "I'll take that roll now, Steven."

"You can call me Stevie," he said with a proud grin.

Sheridan's eyes widened and then she rolled them. "Oh, brother," she mumbled.

When dinner was over, Sheridan took Keefer on a tour of the house. They started in the dining room since that's where they already were. She proudly pointed to the floor. "Pop let me and Steven help with the floor. It was the first thing we did in the house. God, Pop," Sheridan yelled into the kitchen, "what was I, six when we did the floor in here?"

"Just about. There was no way you guys were going to let me do it alone." He snickered with the memory of his daughter in a plastic tool belt and feetie pajamas.

Keefer stared at the hardwood floor and wondered what a six-year-old could have done to help. "So what did he have you do?"

"We really didn't do much else but help sand some edges..."

Steven jumped into the conversation. "Nuh-uh...we kicked the boards into place!"

"Yeah, but we really felt like we did something back then," Sheridan said with a grin.

"I'll bet," Keefer grinned back. *What a great family this sounds like.* Her gaze drifted to the wallpaper and wainscoting. "I bet you wanted to do the walls too." She nudged Sheridan with her shoulder.

"You got that right, so Pop gave us a whole other project to do to get out of his way." Sheridan led her lover into the next room, the den.

"Can I show Keefer my room?" Steven asked anxiously.

"Is it clean?" Sheridan asked, then leaned close and whispered, "You don't have underwear hanging from the chairs, do you?"

Steven bolted from the den and ran up the stairs.

Keefer took in the room and its furnishings. All of the furniture was raw wood and it looked handmade. A big rocking chair sat in front of a working brick fireplace and the mantle was gorgeous. A bamboo-type roll screen covered the large picture window and a light sisal rug covered the floor, but one wall caught her eye. From the baseboard to about four feet high were multicolored handprints, two different sizes. She couldn't help herself from smiling. "I suppose that was the project," she said, pointing to the handprints.

Sheridan chuckled, walked over to the wall and knelt down. "Yeah, it was nontoxic paints and we realized a few weeks later that they were water soluble," the blonde pointed out a smeared green handprint, "so Pop covered it over with a sealer. These hands are here forever. To paint over them, you'd have to strip off the top coat, and I don't think he has the heart to strip away the prints." Sheridan shook her head and sighed. "It's weird." She placed her hand over a much smaller handprint. "This was my hand."

"I know—it's the cutest one there." Keefer knelt down next to her lover.

Sheridan chuckled. "Come on, let's go to my room," she said with a wiggle of her eyebrow.

Keefer laughed and let Sheridan take her by the hand. After getting to the next landing, Keefer noticed that there was another flight of stairs and was curious to know where they led to. She craned her neck as she walked, trying to catch a glimpse of the next landing.

"Guest rooms and another bathroom upstairs. There's four full johns in the house, and one in the garage."

"Four bathrooms?" Keefer asked loudly in amazement.

Sheridan shrugged. "No, five—four *full* ones," she corrected. At Keefer's unblinking stare, she further explained, "Yeah, one john per bedroom, one upstairs and a half one downstairs."

"Are you serious? Wow." The brunette blinked a few times to comprehend.

"Yeah, I know, it sounds extravagant, especially for Brooklyn, but when your pop builds the house, you can have what you want." Sheridan stopped in front of a room and pushed Keefer in ahead of her.

Keefer gaped at Sheridan's bedroom. It was the size of the inspector's living room and kitchen combined, plus it had a bathroom off to the side. "Funny, I never would have thought...I mean, after seeing your apartment...just, wow." The walls were painted a very dark blue, the ceiling and molding a lighter shade of the same color. There were a few posters on the walls—most were of rock bands, and one was of a heavily muscled woman. The carpeting was gray, as were the shutters and bedding. There was a captain's bed and Keefer assumed it was king-sized, noticing that it had a row of drawers lining the base. There was a huge workout system in one corner and a television on a stand that contained shelves full of videos and video games. A chest of drawers, a nine-drawer dresser, and an enormous armoire rounded out the room. "Jesus, Sher—it's like you could fit my whole house into here!"

"My bedroom used to be on the ground floor, but we knocked down that room and added the pool. Pop made most of the renovations after Mom died. This used to be two rooms and the next floor didn't even exist. I think doing all that work kept him going...us kids, too. We helped with a lot of the work."

Keefer smiled sadly. It must have been so hard for them at that time. She wondered if Sheridan would have had the passion for building if her mom hadn't died.

"Steven's room has a kick-ass walk-in closet. My bathroom used to be a closet, one of those huge ones that you could rent out as a room, but I'd rather have the bathroom, so we built it. Steven had the option of both, so he took both. Greedy little bastard," she joked.

"I heard that!" Steven hollered. "You can bring her into my room now, no underwear!"

Keefer was so overwhelmed already that she was almost afraid to see Steven's room, but she trooped on and couldn't help but smile at his decor. It was mostly sci-fi oriented with the occasional semi-dressed female. It was painted in greens and even had a green rug. "Lemme guess, green is your favorite color," she joked.

"How cool! Sher, she guessed my favorite color!"

Sheridan threw a Star Wars figurine at him. "You're such a putz."

Keefer elbowed her lover, who scowled and rubbed the spot dramatically. Keefer rolled her eyes and turned back to Steven. "So, are you going to show me the cool closet I heard all about?"

"Yeah, look!" he said, throwing open the double doors. "You can sit down in here and think about what to wear and everything," he said, sitting down on the small bench and pretending to think.

"I see," Keefer chuckled. "I love it. Maybe I can have your sister build me one of these," she said seriously enough to get a raised eyebrow from her lover.

"Ooh, I can help! Sher, lemme help you! I can do it, I wanna help build a closet for Keefer!"

Sheridan narrowed her eyes at Keefer and glared through the lowered lids. "Maybe. We'll see."

"I think it's great idea, Sher. I bet Steven is a big help...think about it."

"You're serious? You want me to build you a closet?"

"Now that I think about it, yeah," she said with a blush, just now realizing that she'd pretty much ordered Sheridan to work.

Sheridan glanced at her doe-eyed brother, lower lip aquiver in full beg mode, then directed a withering look at Keefer. "Good thing I love you."

Steven spoke around his pout. "Is that a yes?"

Sheridan sighed and braced herself for the attack. "Yeah, it's a yes."

Both Keefer and Steven whooped and jumped on Sheridan, forcing her backwards onto the bed. The construction worker accepted the kisses from her lover and the good-natured, happy jostling from her brother, wondering what she just gotten herself into.

Chapter 32

Keefer finished her tour of the house and, after a brief bout of embarrassing "Young Sheridan" stories, Mr. Landers was bidding the couple a good night in the foyer.

"It was great meeting you, Keefer. Please don't be a stranger. If Sher gets on your nerves, you're always welcome here." He snickered as his daughter rolled her eyes. "I'm sure Steven would never object to your company."

"I'll bet," Sheridan grumbled.

Keefer grinned. "Thank you very much for dinner. I'm sure we'll be seeing each other again very soon."

"Steven! Sheridan's leaving!" the older man yelled, then turned back to Keefer. "Take care of her, will ya? Make sure she eats."

Keefer glanced at her scowling lover and smiled. "Don't you worry." She winked at Sheridan's dad, who winked back and ruffled his daughter's hair.

"Quit that." The blonde smoothed her hair and watched as her brother flew down the stairs, slid through the hallway in his socks and passed right by her.

"Bye, Keefer!" he said excitedly.

"Bye, Stevie." Keefer gave him a kiss on the cheek.

Steven blushed and broke out in a goofy smile.

"Remember, we have a date," she said in a loud whisper.

"Uh-huh, I remember." He grinned proudly.

"All I did was leave them alone for a second and they're dating behind my back," Sheridan teased good-naturedly. She really couldn't pretend to be annoyed when her brother was so excited. "So, what's this about a date?" She poked Steven in the stomach.

357

"Me and Keefer are going to watch *Star Wars* together! Why didn't you tell me she likes *Star Wars*, Sher?"

Sheridan tried not to laugh. "I forgot," she said with a snicker. They had discussed *Star Wars,* and Keefer wasn't a big fan at all.

The tall woman elbowed her lover.

Mr. Landers smirked at the two women. "You've got reading to do, Steven. Go on and get ready to take your shower."

"'Kay. Good night, Keef. Smell ya later, Sher."

"Night, Bigfoot." Sheridan snorted as her brother grinned like an idiot at her lover before running up the stairs. "We gotta go, Pop. The dogs have to go out."

"I know, hon." Mr. Landers hugged his daughter, then opened his arms for Keefer. She hesitated. "I don't bite," he smiled.

Keefer allowed herself to be hugged by a man for the first time, and it didn't feel half bad.

"Good night, you two, drive safe."

The couple drove to Sheridan's house to take the dogs out for a quick walk, with Sheridan promising them a long morning run, and then they did the same with Fifi. It wasn't very late, but they'd had a long day and just wanted to relax and unwind for the rest of the evening.

Now back in her house, Keefer sat at the kitchen table watching Sheridan prepare coffee for them. Her gaze traveled the length of the construction worker's body, slowly admiring every inch. She lingered a while at the sculpted muscles of Sheridan's shoulders and licked her lips when she stared at the arousing bulge of her biceps. She felt her breathing change as the blonde's arms flexed here and there while she reached for a spoon or stirred in sugar.

Keefer felt a thrill shiver up her spine, knowing that Sheridan was all hers—every bit of her, every hair on her body. It was a strong sense of possessiveness and the inspector liked it. *No one else will be touching Sheridan from now on, only me.* Keefer sighed contentedly as she studied the perfectly formed, round firmness of her lover's backside. Her hands twitched with the need to hold Sheridan's ass...to grab great handfuls of the solid muscle covered with baby soft skin. Her thoughts turned from admiration to want as her gaze traced the defined curve of Sheridan's thigh.

"Here ya go." The construction worker turned around with both mugs and was faced with a heavy-lidded, sultry stare from her preoccupied lover. "Hey," she said as a knowing smile slowly spread across her lips, "what ya thinking about?"

"You." Keefer accepted the coffee, never taking her eyes from Sheridan's.

Sheridan's insides melted at the low, sexy timbre of Keefer's voice. "Oh?" she asked, purposely flexing her arms as she crossed them over her chest.

Blue eyes drank in the sight hungrily. "I never felt like this about anyone...ever," Keefer said, reluctantly dragging her gaze from her lover's arms to her eyes.

"How's that?" Sheridan leaned across the table, Keefer's blue eyes burning into hers so intently that the hairs stood up on the back of her neck.

"I feel like I can't get enough of you. I'm not just talking about, you know...sex. I mean, I don't want to stop looking at *you*. If you're within my range of vision, I can't look at anything else."

Sheridan smiled as she leaned all the way across the table, closing the distance between them, and kissed her lover reassuringly. "You want to know if it's okay to feel like that." Keefer nodded. "It better be, because I feel the same way. I can't get enough of you either, Keef."

Keefer let out a relieved chuckle. "I guess we're a perfect match."

Sheridan gave her lover a series of quick kisses before answering. "Perfect." Green eyes stared into blue.

Keefer blushed and backed away slightly. "Sorry about earlier. You know, with Steven."

Sheridan chuckled and sat back in her chair. "Which time?" she asked with a smirk.

"That whole thing with Danni. It was too good to pass up." Keefer sipped her coffee; it was the perfect temperature, so she took a big swallow. "So," she looked up at Sheridan through her lashes, a playful smirk on her lips, "you *couldn't* simply sleep with me, you wanted to make love to me."

"To you, with you...I knew it then, but at the same time I didn't know it. How stupid was I? How could I not see it?" The construction worker shook her head and drank some coffee. "I loved you from the moment I saw you."

Keefer's mouth hung open as she watched Sheridan drink. She'd admitted that as nonchalantly as a weather forecast. "You did?"

"Well, yeah. I just didn't know it. I wish I did, though, it would have saved me a lot of trouble."

"Trouble?"

Sheridan thought of the women she'd used to forget about and replace Keefer. "Yeah, but I'm actually relieved to know what was wrong with me that whole time. Love? Me? Who would have imagined it?" Sheridan got up and stood between Keefer's legs. "I never would have dreamed of being in love, or being this *much* in love. I didn't understand what was going on, but now that I do..." Sheridan hesitated to find the words, "I am so lucky that it's you."

Keefer blinked back tears. "Me, too...all of it." She stared at her lover's smiling lips, tilted her head up, and closed her eyes. She anticipated the feeling of Sheridan's soft mouth covering her own so much that when their lips did touch she groaned in relief.

Sheridan knew exactly what her lover was feeling—she felt it herself. She held Keefer's face with both hands and kissed her so tenderly, she surprised herself. It was such a good feeling for her to give of herself with a simple kiss. She made a silent vow to do it again, and often.

Keefer accepted the sweet kiss and returned the sentiment, licking the outline of Sheridan's lips, softly tickling the roof of her mouth with her tongue. When Sheridan mirrored her actions, the sensations warmed Keefer's entire body, making her light-headed. She grabbed Sheridan's arms for support, as she was sure that she'd slide right off the chair and onto the floor if she didn't.

When the kiss ended, green eyes fluttered open and studied blue ones for an explanation. "That was new. Did you feel it?"

Keefer nodded, still slightly dopey from the kiss. "If that happens again, I'd better be lying down or I'll fall over."

"Yeah, wow." Sheridan slipped back into her chair, somewhat confused that a simple kiss could rock her entire world.

Keefer watched Sheridan's lips as she drank the rest of her coffee. She wanted to devour her lover whole and the feeling worried her. It was too intense. She shook it off and drained her mug. "So, when are you building me a closet?"

"As soon as you tell me to."

Keefer smiled happily. "Yesterday would be good."

Sheridan grinned back. "You do know that a herd of wild elephants wouldn't keep Steven away now."

"I want him to help. I like him a lot, Sher."

Sheridan scowled.

"Oh, please, you love him to death. You have a soft spot for your baby brother, so don't even try to hide it. It's one of the qualities I love so much about you."

"Did I tell you that I taught him how to use a table saw?"

Keefer giggled, "You don't need extra credit. I couldn't love you any more than I already do."

Sheridan's expression turned pensive. "Doesn't it scare you?"

"Yeah, a little. It's new, and that's always scary, but I trust you and I trust love. Call me romantic."

"Romantic."

Keefer threw a napkin at her grinning lover. "Wanna go snuggle in the living room for a while?"

"Thought you'd never ask." The construction worker stood up and stretched her back. "You do realize that if word got out that I snuggle, I'd have to kill you."

"I'm not afraid of you." Keefer puffed out her chest.

Green eyes narrowed at Keefer's chest. "Keep that up and there will be a lot more than snuggling on that couch."

"I'm counting on that," the inspector said with a sexy smile.

Sheridan sat on the floor and leaned back against the couch, clicking on the television as she did. Keefer stretched out her long body on the floor and lay her head on the construction worker's thigh. After a few minutes neither was paying much attention to the television. Sheridan was running her fingers through the long, silky black hair, fanning it out across her legs, wondering why it always smelled so good. Keefer had her eyes closed, savoring the feeling of her lover's hands sliding through her hair and brushing against her scalp every so often. Feeling as full and relaxed as she did, Sheridan was afraid she'd fall asleep, and watching her fingers was almost hypnotic. She focused instead on the inspector's lips as they lay slightly parted and upturned at the corners in contentment. Keefer's tongue poked out and licked her bottom lip innocently, but Sheridan found it incredibly arousing and raised an eyebrow at herself. While thinking about how she could find an innocent gesture such a turn-on, she stopped moving her hands and a blue eye popped open to investigate.

I know that look, Keefer thought. *I like that look*, she grinned inwardly. "What are you waiting for?" she asked.

"Huh?" Sheridan asked distractedly.

"I know you want to kiss me, so what are you waiting for?" Keefer said, then pursed her lips.

"Uh-uh, it's not *that* kind of kiss, missy." Sheridan slid her legs out from under Keefer and the brunette sat up, hair all askew. "Mmm, you look sexy like that."

Keefer might have blushed, had she the time, but she was being kissed thoroughly and barely had the power of thought. She wrapped her long arms around Sheridan's back and pulled her closer.

The construction worker climbed to her knees and straddled her lover's long legs, kneeling as she deepened the kiss and sucking Keefer's tongue into her mouth, knowing that it drove the brunette crazy when she did. She almost laughed at the instantaneous reaction as the tall woman pushed her down on her back and took control of the kissing, her hands traveling everywhere on the blonde's body. Now flat on her back, Sheridan relaxed and let Keefer lead. She sighed happily when the brunette began trailing kisses and licks down her neck, pushing her tongue under the neckline of her shirt and licking all her sensitive spots. She held on to Keefer's shoulders tightly as she claimed her throat, but began to push her back as she tried to lift her shirt.

Keefer lifted her head in protest and Sheridan nearly melted at the look on her face.

"Why are you stopping me?" the inspector asked, still fighting to pull off her lover's shirt.

"You had yours this morning; I want mine now," Sheridan replied with a sexy grin.

Keefer smiled a little shyly as she dropped the bottom of her lover's shirt. "Okay...but you have to take off your clothes, too," she said as she eyed the blonde's breasts.

Sheridan saw where Keefer's gaze was aimed, so she pulled off her shirt and bra at the same time. Blue eyes darted from one breast to the other and Sheridan couldn't resist the hungry stare. She leaned forward and stuck out her chest.

Keefer hesitated slightly before glancing up into green eyes. They were more than receptive, they were begging. She reached out for Sheridan's left breast as she closed her lips around the nipple. Hearing Sheridan hiss made her groan quietly and she nipped at the already hardened flesh playfully.

"Jeez, Keef," the blonde breathed, tangling her hands in Keefer's hair, pulling her closer.

Keefer switched breasts and looked up at her lover's face as she worked her tongue across the nipple. Sheridan's eyes were almost closed, her wet lips were open in pleasure, and she was watching. Keefer bit the nipple and her nostrils flared as Sheridan's lips curled into a sneer and she hissed again through her teeth. Keefer closed her eyes again as the blonde's fingers pulled her hair tighter.

"Supposed to be...mmm...my turn," Sheridan mumbled between hums of pleasure.

Keefer reluctantly let go and backed up, a devilish smile on her face. "Oops."

"I'll give you oops," Sheridan growled, pushing Keefer down onto her back and laying her body on top of her.

Keefer let out a small yelp when Sheridan grabbed the skin of her neck in her teeth and tugged at it, but Sheridan didn't stop there; she scooted down and nipped at the brunette's nipple through her shirt, making Keefer yelp again. The tall woman fought Sheridan off playfully until the blonde pinned her hands over her head. Sheridan chuckled evilly as her giggling lover struggled in her grasp.

"Ha, now I got you."

Keefer stopped wriggling and sighed heavily in surrender. "Alas, you have me fair and square. Do what you will with me," she said in an exaggeratedly breathy voice.

Sheridan let go of her lover's arms and sat up, motioning for Keefer to do the same, and pulled off the brunette's shirt slowly, then her bra, savoring each bit of skin as it was revealed.

Now topless, Keefer fought the urge to cover her breasts. It wasn't that she wanted to hide herself from Sheridan, it was just an old habit that was hard to break. She kept her hands on her thighs and felt herself turn pink under Sheridan's hot gaze. Pleased green eyes drank in her upper body with appreciation, and soon Sheridan's hands followed the same path as her eyes and began to touch her naked body. The feel of her lover's rough hands always excited her and her belly clenched visibly when Sheridan's hand traveled across it.

"Is this okay?" the blonde asked quietly, making sure Keefer was comfortable with her explorations.

The tall inspector nodded and sucked in her bottom lip. She was feeling a tiny bit exposed, but not enough to be embarrassed—not like she used to feel. This was Sheridan admiring her body, and it felt good to be looked at by her appreciative lover. True, she was topless and on display, something that a few weeks ago would have sent her screaming from the room, but this was different—it was Sheridan. Keefer took a deep breath and arched her back slightly as a callused fingertips skimmed across her right breast.

"I think you're beautiful, Keef," Sheridan said honestly.

Keefer's head cocked to the side and she met her lover's eyes. "I know. I can feel it when you look at me like this."

"Are you sure you're all right? I don't want to make you feel uncomfortable."

"I'm okay, really." Keefer's eyes wandered to Sheridan's naked torso. "Can I?"

"Any time you want to." Sheridan took both of Keefer's hands and placed them on her waist. "You never have to ask."

Keefer smiled as she looked into Sheridan's eyes—green eyes that spoke to her of nothing but honesty. Her lover was an open book and whether it was from the moment or the whole day's events, Keefer felt her eyes well up with tears.

"Hey? What happened?" Sheridan asked, deeply concerned.

"Nothing, well...something," Keefer wiped at her eyes with the back of her hands. "You really love me...just like that...you mean it."

Sheridan furrowed her brows in confusion.

Keefer smiled through her tears. "Of course, you have no idea what I'm babbling about, do you?" Sheridan chuckled slightly and shook her head. "I watch too many love stories on television, and I always cried when they finally found true love...when the heroine was swept off her feet by the handsome young man...I feel like the heroine...I mean when you look at me like you do."

The blonde smiled and sighed heavily. This was a good cry, not a bad cry, and she was infinitely relieved. Then she got nervous. "I make you feel like that? Just by looking at you?"

"You do. It's a good thing, Sher." Keefer took Sheridan's hands and put them back on her body. "Don't even worry about it."

Sheridan did worry about it, at least for a few seconds until she realized her left hand was on Keefer's breast. She looked up to see blue eyes reassuring her.

"It's your turn, remember?" Keefer squeezed Sheridan's hand, the one covering her breast, and her lips parted in a silent sigh.

"My turn," the blonde repeated with a happy grin before leaning forward and capturing her lover's lips.

The kiss was soft at first, but then Sheridan lost herself and it became a more demanding, hungry kiss. Keefer accepted the intentions and opened herself fully for Sheridan. The blonde pushed her back until she was lying on the floor again, and her rough hands mapped out every bit of exposed skin as her naturally dominant instincts took over. She wasn't being rough in her ministrations, but she was aggressive, acting on an inbred habit of taking what was hers.

Keefer enjoyed Sheridan's frantic groping. She liked it when her lover claimed her body. She never would have allowed anyone else to paw at her like Sheridan was doing, but for some reason when her lover touched her so hungrily, the adrenaline flowed through her as if she was the one in control. She arched her shoulders as two callused palms scraped her nipples and she groaned quietly when Sheridan hummed her pleasure, devouring her mouth like she was starving. The inspector wasn't lying idly by; her hands slipped under Sheridan's waistband and enveloped her backside. Her hands held the flesh she had been admiring so intently in the kitchen, squeezing the hard muscles rhythmically, pulling the construction worker's lower body tightly between her legs.

Sheridan growled as Keefer's nails dug into her skin. She'd never known herself to be so turned on by someone squeezing her ass, but then again, this was Keefer and anything Keefer did fuelled her desires. Her hands closed tighter around the tall woman's breasts and she felt her heart beat faster as the hard nipples pressed against her palms. Their frantic kissing caused Keefer's hair to become trapped between their mouths, and Sheridan pulled away from the kiss with a grunt of disapproval and worked her way down her lover's face to her neck where she began to suck.

Keefer was on fire. "Oh, Sher..." she breathed, pulling her lover's body harder into hers, wishing they were completely naked so she could feel Sheridan's powerful bare thighs within her own. The blonde slid lower, trailing her tongue down the valley between her breasts, and Keefer had no choice but to lose contact with her backside. Her hands clutched Sheridan's arms, her long fingers wrapped around taut biceps. Keefer groaned. Everything about Sheridan's body made her burn. A determined hand began opening her pants and a hungry mouth closed around her nipple. Keefer cried out in anticipation and pleasure and she did something she had never done before. She opened her eyes and watched Sheridan suck her breast.

Sheridan lifted her eyes at the sound of a gasp from her lover and it seemed all time stopped. Her pulse tripled and her sex clenched. Sheridan had read about them and heard about them, but this was the first time she'd actually seen a smoldering look, and it was all hers. Something made her stop what she was doing and she slowly crawled back up and hovered over her lover, unable to break eye contact. She was panting audibly with arousal, but didn't want to lose the moment; Keefer's eyes were boring into hers with such intensity it made her toes curl.

Keefer watched as frantic green eyes grew softer and a slow smile spread across her face. She felt something change just then and was about to speak, but Sheridan shushed her and moved to kneel between her legs. She was surprised when her lover resumed taking off her pants, slowly.

Sheridan suddenly had the urge to go slow, a reaction that took her by surprise. It wasn't usually in her nature, but she couldn't deny the urge—not after looking into her lover's eyes. She slid Keefer's pants and panties down over her hips, then stretched her legs out and lay down. She lowered her head and kissed each bared hip reverently, then slid the pants lower, kissing each thigh.

Keefer kept watching, only blinking when she had to, not wanting to miss one second of Sheridan's unwavering gaze. This was all new to the brunette, who would normally just as soon have made love quickly in the dark and not talked about it in the morning, but now...this was different. Sheridan seemed to be worshipping her body, even kissing her toes as she slid the jeans off completely. Keefer had never experienced such an intense feeling as she did with Sheridan staring into her eyes and crawling back up her body. It was unnerving, the emotion she found in those green eyes. It was scary and exciting at the same time.

Sheridan kissed her way back up Keefer's long, beautiful body and stopped once she was face to face with her. She was confused. Her body had been in overdrive moments before and now she needed to go slow, drink in every curve and dip of the brunette's body, taste every inch. It began to frighten her, this intense need, but just knowing that Keefer accepted her, trusted her, made it all better.

The inspector ran her fingers up and down her lover's arms as they supported her. Each muscle stood out in relief, sculpted and beautiful. Blue eyes traced the paths her fingers took until she felt Sheridan's nipples brush against her own. Her gaze fell to between them and her heart picked up speed as she watched Sheridan move, purposely brushing nipple against nipple. Keefer's hands followed her eyes and she reached between them to hold her lover's breasts. Seeing Sheridan watching her hands set her on fire. She opened her legs, wrapped them around the construction worker's back and lifted her hips, seeking relief. Green eyes caught blue and Keefer felt herself twitch. "Please make love to me, Sheridan."

Sheridan hesitated for a moment before standing up and taking off her pants. Keefer watched with a raised eyebrow as her lover dropped her pants in a heap and peeled off her underwear. She got a thrill from watching Sheridan undress, knowing she'd be able to feel that hard, sexy body in all its naked glory. Keefer's sex was literally throbbing, begging to be touched...and as she watched her lover drop back down between her open legs, her breath caught in anticipation.

Sheridan wanted to feel Keefer underneath her, hold her in her arms as they made love. An idea came to her mind and she lay her body on top of Keefer's. They both sighed at the contact, and Keefer's legs wrapped themselves around Sheridan quickly, squeezing her tight.

The blonde slipped her hands under Keefer's arms and held on to her shoulders. She smiled when Keefer turned her head and kissed her fingers. Sheridan had never made love to anyone that way before and she was excited that Keefer would be the first. She bent her head and sucked her lover's bottom lip into her mouth as she adjusted her body. When sex met sex, Keefer groaned and jerked her hips. Sheridan grinned around the lip she was sucking and nodded, sliding just a little bit lower. She moaned loudly at the wetness she encountered between Keefer's legs.

Keefer closed her eyes and whimpered as her lover began to press their centers together. Her hands traversed the expanse of Sheridan's back and settled on her favorite two muscles. She held the two solid globes and pressed them together harder, lifting her hips as she did. The feeling was exquisite and she groaned out loud again. She could feel Sheridan's ass flexing in her hands and when she imagined how it looked, she felt wetness pool between her legs.

Sheridan moved slowly, savoring the feeling of their bodies touching. She didn't want to go any further until she was sure that Keefer was comfortable with what she was doing. She didn't have to wait long, as strong fingers dug into her backside, pulling them together harder. Sheridan was content to just relish the feeling of their sexes touching for a while longer, but her lover had other ideas.

Keefer rubbed her center against her lover's pubic hair and gasped as her clit received the contact she craved. *This is good...too good...why didn't we do this before?* she thought, as she pulled back her hips and did it again. The feeling was just as good and she wondered why Sheridan wasn't moving. She opened her eyes and met heavy-lidded green ones staring back seductively.

"You like this?" the blonde asked, rotating her hips.

Keefer inhaled sharply at the new feeling. "Yes," she whispered, waiting for her lover to do it again.

Sheridan swiveled her hips again, but this time she slid her body up and down slightly, making the connection she wanted, groaning in relief. She watched as blue eyes fluttered closed and smiled slightly at her lover. She had a feeling this wasn't going to last long for Keefer and it was okay, as long as she got to hold her and watch her while they made love. Her eyes would be a plus, but the look on her face was just as important.

Keefer hummed as her lover began moving up and down, vaguely aware that Sheridan was watching her, but not caring—she felt too good to be embarrassed. She brought her hands up, spreading them out on her lover's back, feeling the muscles contract and relax as Sheridan moved her body. *Sensual.* That's the word she was looking for, and she never thought she'd feel anything like it. She never expected Sheridan to be a sensual lover; she was already more than satisfied with her as she was, never missing anything. *You don't miss what you don't know...God, this feels good.* She grunted as her lover picked up the speed. If she opened her eyes, she knew what she'd see and she was sure it would send her over the edge, so she squeezed her eyes tight and grasped Sheridan's shoulders.

Sheridan was lost in the feeling of Keefer's body wrapped around her, rubbing against her...their breasts mashed together. Her sex was begging her to go faster, quench the need for release, but she wanted this to last, and knew that if she gave in to her need, it would all end.

The brunette tried to pull her lover against her harder. First she used her legs and when that didn't work, she brought her hands back to Sheridan's backside and squeezed. Her lover emitted a strangled groan, but still didn't comply. Keefer's mind was full of images of what Sheridan looked like as she hovered over her, what their breasts looked like pressed against each other, what Sheridan's ass looked like as it moved so beautifully in her hands.

Sheridan had been staring at Keefer's lips; they were parted, and little sounds escaped them each time their clits touched. She knew that Keefer needed more too, and when blue eyes popped open and met hers, Sheridan was a goner.

Keefer met Sheridan's eyes, only inches away from her own, and she whimpered at the look of complete arousal she saw. The heat in her sex exploded and she felt her belly spasm with the beginnings of her orgasm. Sheridan groaned and threw her head back, arching her upper body off of Keefer's. The inspector thrust her hips up as she began to come, bringing her lover over the edge with her. She shook with the intensity and wrapped her arms tightly around Sheridan as she fell heavily on top of her.

"Keefer...shit..." the blonde groaned through clenched teeth, her lower body jerking erratically into her lover's.

Keefer clutched Sheridan to her and sought out her lips. She needed to be connected everywhere, and when their tongues met, a brand new set of clenching spasms wracked her body. She whimpered desperately into Sheridan's open mouth. The construction worker had stopped moving but was grasping her shoulders painfully hard. This was the longest orgasm Keefer had ever had and she let it flow, riding it out, milking all the pleasure she could from it—from Sheridan.

The blonde tore her mouth away from Keefer's to see the look on her face. She groaned at the expression. The look of pure pleasure was blatantly exposed and she captured Keefer's lips once again, swallowing her moans until she finally stilled.

The two lay there for a long while; Sheridan on top of Keefer, both sweaty, both panting, both extremely sated. Keefer loosened her grip on Sheridan and let her legs slide off of her back. She lay there bonelessly on the living room floor, a goofy smile on her face.

Sheridan reclaimed her arms from under her lover's body and leaned her weight on one elbow. She gently pushed the damp hair from Keefer's face and kissed her forehead, licking the salty taste off of her lips.

Blue eyes opened slowly and Keefer smiled shyly. She reached up and smoothed back blonde hair. "That was wonderful," she said dreamily.

"Sure was," Sheridan replied, bending down to kiss Keefer's lips.

Keefer grinned and blushed.

"What's that for?' Sheridan teased.

"I thought you were going to use that thigh thing."

Sheridan snickered, "I forgot it, but you do know...*you* do all the work with that thing."

Keefer's eyes widened and she ran her foot up Sheridan's bare leg. "I do?"

Sheridan narrowed her eyes playfully. "Think about it, Keef. If *I'm* wearing the thigh thing, *you're* on top."

Keefer blushed redder as she thought about that scenario. Then she playfully slapped her lover. "It doesn't have to be that way and you know it."

Sheridan laughed and slid off of Keefer, propping herself up on one arm. "No, but it would be hot."

"Stinker."

"Please think about it, Keef. I'd really like that. A lot."

Keefer smiled. "I'll think about it, but for now, we really have to get to bed. You promised the kids a long walk in the morning. Besides, I want to cuddle with you now," she added with a patented Keefer shy smile.

TJ Vertigo

Chapter 33

Sheridan slipped from sleep with the oddest feeling. Still not fully awake, she began to panic a little until she realized where she was, frowning somewhat at the unusual sensations she was experiencing. She mentally took stock of her body, starting at her feet. *Okay, definitely not Keefer, that's Fifi on my ankle. Legs are twisted up in the blanket...arms behind my head...chest exposed—Wait a minute! I'm horny as hell!* She peeked open her eyes and looked down at her very hard, very wet nipples. *Looks like someone was having her way with me.* She glanced over to her left and there was Keefer, sitting next to her shoulder, wearing her bathrobe, legs folded under her and a shy, guilty smile on her face. Sheridan raised an eyebrow and looked down at her chest, then back at Keefer.

"I opened my eyes, and there they were," Keefer explained.

Sheridan raised the other eyebrow.

"I tried to ignore them...I even left the room...but you said any time, that I don't have to ask...and you were sleeping..."

The construction worker couldn't help but chuckle at her lover's babbling. "Keef, it's all right." She smiled reassuringly.

Keefer blushed a little and tucked some hair behind her ear. "I couldn't help myself," she admitted shyly.

Sheridan sat up and flexed her legs.

Fifi sat up, too, her tail wagging as she looked at the blonde.

Sheridan narrowed her eyes. *I'm soaking wet!* "Just how long have you been at it?"

Keefer shrugged. "Well...I only touched them at first, but then I thought it was wrong, so I covered them up and went to the bathroom and when I came back, there they were again. I tried to cover them again, but you had twisted yourself up in the blanket."

"I see." Sheridan wrestled out of the blanket and crawled across the bed.

Keefer's eyes widened as her lover walked naked into the bathroom. She waited a minute to compose herself and then went to her closet to pick out the day's clothes. When Sheridan returned, she plopped herself back into bed with a strange look on her face. "What?" Keefer asked.

"I just got my jollies wiping myself."

Keefer turned pink. "I'm sorry."

"You're not going to leave me like this, are you?" Sheridan asked in a low voice.

Keefer hung the shirt she was holding on the doorknob and walked back over to the bed.

Sheridan was lying there, naked, smelling of soap and toothpaste, and she found it very sexy. "You want me to finish?"

"Either you or me—take your pick."

Keefer gulped. her choice was made instantly and she fell into Sheridan's open arms. They lay entwined for a while until Sheridan opened her arms again and brought them up over her head. "It's six o'clock, you have a half-hour, go to town."

Keefer fought the urge to blush and won. Feeling triumphant, she gathered her nerve and lay down, stretching herself out next to her lover. She reached out her hand and with one finger, circled Sheridan's left nipple, bringing her gaze back and forth from her lover's face to her finger. She watched with great interest as the flesh pebbled and grew hard. Goose bumps sprung out on Sheridan's breasts and Keefer smiled at the reaction.

Sheridan sighed in contentment and closed her eyes. She was totally comfortable with Keefer's explorations and relaxed herself, enjoying the sensations spreading through her body.

Keefer propped her head up on her hand and scooted closer to her lover's body. She could feel the heat emanating from Sheridan's skin and wished she could feel it against hers, but was a little shy about taking off her robe. She frowned. *What's wrong with you? Just take it off. This is Sheridan here.*

Sheridan opened her eyes as the hand left her body and the bed shifted. She was more than pleased to see Keefer shed her robe. She wanted to cheer for her lover, but knew she couldn't make a big deal out of it, so she closed her eyes again and groaned her approval as Keefer's soft skin met hers.

The inspector was very happy with her decision as her breasts met Sheridan's arm. Her nipples tightened on contact and she had a feeling that she would soon be asking for relief as well. Her pubic mound found her lover's hip, and she closed her eyes briefly to gather herself. *Oh yes, I'm already turned on and nothing's even happened yet.*

Sheridan forced herself not to fling herself on Keefer. It took an incredible effort to keep still when the soft hairs met her skin. She could tell by the intake of breath that Keefer was enjoying this very much. The blonde wanted to touch her lover but she was so excited that Keefer was letting go of her uncertainties and she didn't want to scare her. Sheridan jumped slightly as long black hair tickled her skin and she braced herself, knowing that the liquid heat of Keefer's mouth was soon to come. When it did, it felt like heaven.

The tall woman felt a surge of adrenaline when Sheridan shivered and groaned. She flattened her tongue and picked up where she had left off while her lover was sleeping. *It's so much better now that she's awake.* Keefer bathed the entire breast with her tongue and then zeroed in on the straining nipple. Sheridan arched her shoulders and grabbed Keefer's head, tangling strong fingers in her hair, and Keefer inhaled sharply through her nose. Becoming bolder, the brunette bit the nipple lightly, rolling it lightly between her teeth. Sheridan's fingers tightened and her thighs clenched together. Keefer knew she had done something right so she did it again, only a little harder. Her lover hissed through her teeth and brought her other hand to hold her head in place.

"Yeah, baby..." Sheridan groaned, her thighs clenching and unclenching.

Keefer hummed and released the nipple, pulling it slightly with her teeth as she did. Sheridan gasped and growled. The tall women felt very pleased with herself and began her assault on the other nipple.

Sheridan suddenly noticed her lover was pressing into her hip. She wondered if Keefer was even aware she was doing it. She decided not to bring attention to it. She bit back the urge to press back and reveled in the feelings Keefer was producing in her.

Keefer's heart beat rapidly each time Sheridan groaned, which was now almost constantly as she teased and bit her nipple. She wanted to touch Sheridan too and had been holding back due to that small part of her that was still embarrassed about making love in the morning light. *After you had your way with her on the couch yesterday morning, how can you still be afraid? Snap out of it!* She reluctantly released the nipple from her teeth—not before biting it one last time—and sat up cross-legged at Sheridan's side.

Sheridan looked over to her lover as she moved and squeezed her eyes shut when she saw how Keefer was sitting. *God! It's right there!* She made a fist in order not to reach out and touch Keefer's sex. *Let her do this*, she told herself and shuddered as a large hand appeared on her thigh.

Keefer had been watching her lover's reactions as much as she could and saw a somewhat pained expression on her face. She momentarily wondered if she was doing something wrong, but then the smell of her own arousal hit her and she blushed. She noticed Sheridan's clenched fists and rapid breathing. A ball of nervous excitement filled her belly and with a flash of courage, she took Sheridan's hand and put it between her legs.

The construction worker's eyes popped open and she looked into nervous, but aroused, blue eyes. She patted the pillow next to her head and Keefer lay down, stretching her long body out on the bed. Sheridan never took her hand away from where it was nestled firmly between Keefer's legs, the evidence of her arousal coating her fingers.

Keefer replaced her hand on Sheridan's thigh and closed her eyes. Her lover's fingers felt so good pressing into her. She wanted to move into them, but if she did, she was afraid she wouldn't be able to concentrate on Sheridan.

"Keefer..." Sheridan covered Keefer's hand with her own and moved it between her open legs.

The inspector let out a heavy breath at the heat under her fingers. It was so wet, and hot, and soft. She snapped out of her daze and tried to block out the feeling between her own legs, thoroughly wetting her fingers before moving them higher to where she knew her lover needed them.

Sheridan moaned in relief as Keefer's long fingers began to work their magic. She opened her legs wider and turned her head to look at her lover.

Keefer met Sheridan's eyes and she smiled a little cockily at the lust she found there. That is, until Sheridan began to move her hand. Blue eyes rolled back and Keefer groaned out loud. She didn't realize how stimulated she had become until Sheridan touched her, and she was hit head-on with the depth of her arousal.

Sheridan's hips began moving in time with Keefer's fingers, and she licked her dry lips and craned her neck to meet her lover's mouth. Keefer whimpered as her lips opened to accept her lover's tongue. The tall woman's legs opened wider and she thrust her tongue into Sheridan's mouth. She was very close to coming and she changed the motion of her hand to bring Sheridan to climax quickly. She didn't think she could continue if her lover kept on moving her fingers.

Sheridan thrust her hips off the bed as Keefer rubbed her clit. She knew Keefer was trying to make her come and she allowed it to happen—

it felt too good not to come. She felt it start in her toes and it exploded through her when Keefer's fingers suddenly closed around her wrist. Sheridan grunted loudly into Keefer's mouth as her body shuddered relentlessly. She came hard, her legs closing around Keefer's hand, trapping it in place to prolong the pleasure. She was aware that her fingers had stopped moving, but Keefer was still holding her there. When she was sure she had no more left in her, she opened her legs and pulled Keefer's hand out. The aftershocks still twitched through her as she began to touch her lover with a purpose. She turned over to face Keefer and the tall woman did the same, throwing her leg over Sheridan's hip, holding her forearm in a vise grip. Keefer buried her face in her lover's neck and breathed heavily as Sheridan touched her. The construction worker kissed the side of her lover's head, her mouth watering at the wetness beneath her fingers. Keefer was panting steadily in her ear, her hot breath hitting her neck like steam.

"Sher...Sher..." Keefer moaned between gasps as her inner walls began to tremble.

Sheridan's nostrils flared and she growled deep in her chest as Keefer stilled her hand and moved her body instead. The brunette's hips bucked on her fingers and the long strangled moan she breathed out covered Sheridan's whole body in goose bumps. The blonde stiffened her fingers and let Keefer ride them as she trembled and shuddered. Sheridan closed her eyes and pictured her lover's face in ecstasy.

Keefer finally came back to reality to find herself digging her nails into Sheridan's forearm. *God*, she thought, *I did that?* She released her grip and pulled her sweaty face out from its steamy crevice, slowly. She found very pleased green eyes and a sexy little smile.

"I love you," Sheridan whispered.

Anything negative Keefer was feeling was erased with those three words. Spent, she flopped over onto her back and attempted to catch her breath. She gasped as her lover removed her hand, brushing her clit as she did.

Sheridan chuckled, "Sorry."

"I bet," Keefer smiled, taking that particular hand in her own and lacing their fingers together. She lifted their hands and fought a blush at the sight of the deep nail marks in her lover's arm. "Did I hurt you?"

"Nah." Sheridan climbed up onto her knees and kissed Keefer. "Not at all. I liked it." *I loved it, you wild woman.* She knew if she said that out loud, Keefer would simply shrink up and die, but did she ever want to tell her the whole truth.

"What are you smirking about?" Keefer asked, her breathing finally under control.

"You were fantastic. It turns me on so much when you let go like that."

Keefer couldn't fight the blush, remembering her actions, but it felt good to hear Sheridan say that.

"Don't blush, baby, I mean it. God, you're hot!"

"Stop it!" the brunette protested, throwing the pillow over her face.

"I'm serious!"

The pillow groaned.

"Okay, okay, I'll drop it." Sheridan smiled at the pillow. "I'm going to take a shower."

Keefer removed the pillow once she heard the bathroom door close. "She likes me like that." She looked at her naked body, the flush just now fading. "It was kinda fun." She remembered the feeling of holding Sheridan's arm and riding it, and a tingle invaded her sex. "I *really* liked that." She got off the bed and finished picking out her clothes. *I bet I could handle that thigh thing just fine,* she smiled, a spark of excitement filling her. *Wouldn't it just blow her away if I did get on top?*

Sheridan whistled her way into work, stopping first at the donut shop, where she took a good hard look at the girl behind the counter. *Nothing. Not even a twinge.*

"Hiya, Sheridan!" the counter girl said cheerfully, then frowned. "What happened to your eye?" She reached out to touch it.

"Hi," the construction worker smiled politely. "It's nothing." She backed away from the girl's touch.

"Doing anything later?" Sara asked flirtatiously.

"As a matter of fact, I'll be with my girlfriend."

The girl giggled at first, finding it funny until she saw the blonde's face. "You really have a girlfriend?" she asked in surprise.

"Yep. Can I have a dozen mixed? I owe the guys."

"Sure," Sara said, crestfallen.

Keefer didn't get a seat on the subway that morning, but she didn't really care. She took the long ride in stride, using the trip as an opportunity to relive the last few days' events. She smiled, despite being mashed up against a man who didn't know the meaning of soap. Nothing could change her jovial mood. She thought about her life before Sheridan and sighed. Everything had changed, and she was just slightly disappointed that she'd had to hit her mid-thirties in order to start living. The disappointment faded away as she thought of her lover's honest face, looking up at her, telling her that she loved her. Her belly tingled with excitement and she smiled even wider, making those around her smile, too.

"Patch! What happened to you Friday?" Tony shouted over the din of the power tools. Sheridan looked up from the stool she had placed the donuts on and Phil shut off his saw.

"What the fuck happened to you?"

Tony whistled. "Wow-ee, Patch, who got the lucky punch?"

"It's nothing, really," she said as she adjusted her hard hat for something to do. "So, where's Bobby?"

"He's getting some nails. Are you sure you don't want to talk about it?" Phil asked.

"No," Sheridan replied quickly.

Bobby came up behind her and poked her in the neck. "Look at the size of that motherfucker!"

Phil and Tony moved to look at the huge double hickey. Sheridan fought a blush of both embarrassment and guilt, knowing why Keefer had covered the hickey with her own.

"Maybe you wanna talk about *that*," Phil said, wiggling his eyebrows.

"Maybe I don't," Sheridan said with a shrug.

Bobby looked at Phil, who looked at Tony. Patch was acting weird and from the looks of things, had a very interesting day off. They couldn't let it go.

"How's the lady friend?" Bobby asked innocently.

Sheridan narrowed her eyes in suspicion. "This is killing you, isn't it?"

"Yep," Phil replied as all three men nodded.

Sheridan sighed heavily and dropped onto a bucket. "Okay, Keefer is...she's...well...she's my girlfriend now, so no wisecracks."

Six eyebrows shot up and then three mouths grinned.

"What the hell was that all about?" Sheridan asked crankily.

"Congratulations, Patch." Bobby slapped her on the shoulder. "Keefer's one hell of a lucky woman."

"No, I'm the lucky one. She's gotta put up with me," Sheridan chuckled and stood up.

"You said a mouthful," Tony laughed.

"So you two are an item. It's about time," Bobby said, patting Sheridan on the back.

"What do you mean, *about time*?" the blonde asked, looking sideways at the guys.

"You were totally taken with that woman from the moment she walked in here. It was plain as day."

Sheridan shifted from foot to foot. The guys decided to change the subject.

"Spill it, Sher, what's with the eye?" Tony said, hands on his hips.

The blonde grimaced. "Keefer's ex popped me when I was less than ready."

"You? Not ready?"

"I was hung over. Bad."

"You did go out and get trashed then," Phil said with a frown. "We told you not to do that."

"Yeah, that's what I needed, you guys telling me not to."

"All right then, what happened?" Bobby asked in concern.

"You're not gonna have trouble with this woman's ex now, are you?" Tony worried.

"No. She's taken care of, for now. She's a little possessive—doesn't know when to let go."

"Do you love Keefer?" Phil asked.

"Yeah," the blonde mumbled

"Is she worth the ex's shit?" Tony wondered.

"Definitely."

"Okay then, you know what you're doing," Bobby said with relief. Then he smiled teasingly. "Now about that hickey..."

"Gibson!"

Keefer halted in her tracks.

"What the hell is that?" her boss pointed at her from across the hall.

Keefer looked down at herself quickly and found nothing wrong. "Sir?"

"You were smiling. Good to see, Gibson. Have a good vacation?"

"Absolutely. The best."

"Good then. It's nice to see that spring in your step."

"Thank you, sir." Keefer blushed a little as her boss winked and walked away. She entered her office and closed the door behind her, leaning against it as she looked at the mountain of paperwork that had appeared while she was gone. "Fuck."

"Not like you to curse, Keefer."

The tall woman whirled around to find Danni sitting in her chair.

"That little tough girl is wearing off on you."

"What are you doing in here?" Keefer willed her heartbeat back to normal.

"Thought I'd drop by and tell you about my stay in jail. You may be amused."

"Get out." Keefer went to the door and opened it all the way.

378

"Did you know that you're girlfriend fucked her way through just about every female officer in the precinct?"

Not Sharon, the brunette thought to herself.

"Oh, yeah, and that friend of hers, she's a real bitch. Hated that I hit her poor friend; worked me over pretty good."

Keefer couldn't help but smirk. "Danni, please leave."

"She was nice enough to give me some decent clothes to wear after your girlfriend puked on me."

Keefer closed the door. "You deserved that. You had no right coming into my house and hitting her. Hitting anybody! You're so lucky I didn't answer that door, Danni, I'd have wiped the floor with you." The inspector was angry now.

"But you didn't. Sheridan did, your little drunken whore...so cute in your T-shirt...I myself could have puked."

Keefer balled her fists and took a deep breath. "What are you really here for?"

"I just wanted to thank you for giving me the opportunity to beat up your slut. The lockup was well worth it, though I don't know that I'll get this ink off of my hands."

"I suggest you call her by her name."

"The little whore?"

Keefer had Danni by the throat before she knew what hit her. "Sheridan. Say it: Sheridan."

"I didn't think you'd do this at work. I'm impressed," Danni squeaked out.

"Sheridan." Keefer squeezed harder, cocking her other hand back in a fist.

"Okay," the redhead choked out. "Sheridan."

Keefer let go and opened the door again. This time Danni got up and left, rubbing her sore throat.

"Does the little hard hat know you're such a bruiser?"

"Fuck off, Danni."

"I wish you would have used that mouth when you were with me— I'm getting wet."

Keefer's nostrils flared.

Danni chuckled and walked away, whistling as she did.

The guys sat around the dirt yard eating their lunch, all glancing at Sheridan as she continuously fingered her cell phone.

"So, is it true what they say about lesbians?" Phil asked around a mouthful of sandwich.

Sheridan raised an eyebrow and stopped chewing. "What is it that they say, Philly?"

"You know, one date and you're moving in together?"

Tony snickered, "We'll help you pack. Hey, do the dogs like her?"

Sheridan rolled her eyes. The thought of waking up next to Keefer every morning wasn't a bad one and she fought the urge to smile like a goof. "Yeah, the dogs like her. They love her, actually. They even listen to her better than me."

"Figures," Bobby grunted.

Sheridan swung around in her seat. "Hey guys, I'm gonna need some supplies. You wanna help me get them over to Keefer's?"

"What ya building?" Tony asked, rubbing the back of his hand across his forehead. "Man, it's getting hot out today."

"A closet, a big one." Sheridan gulped from her soda bottle. "Yeah, it was already warm when I had the dogs out this morning."

"Ooh, Patch is building her girlfriend a closet. True love at its best," Bobby teased.

"Fuck off, asshole," Sheridan chuckled and kicked sand at him.

"Sure, I'd love to help. Tell me when," Phil nodded.

"This weekend, maybe; I'll let you know." Sheridan smiled, already looking forward to building a closet for Keefer that weekend. She didn't realize that she hadn't given one thought to going out.

"How romantic. Will there be mood lighting in that closet?" Tony snickered.

"You suck," Sheridan threw her empty bottle at him. "I can be romantic if I wanted to," she added defensively.

All three guys laughed.

"Well I can!" she insisted.

"What are you going to do, cook her a candlelit dinner?" Phil snorted.

"What makes you think I can't?" Sheridan countered.

The guys shut up and held back their grins.

"I thought so," the blonde said victoriously. *I can so be romantic,* she thought with a huff.

"Waiting for an important call, Patch?" Bobby asked, nodding toward her cell phone, which she was fingering again.

"What are you babbling about?"

"You've been touching that phone like it's a woman all afternoon."

Sheridan snatched her hand away from the phone. "I am not," she said, standing up and wiping the dirt from her butt.

The guys watched as she walked into the empty building.

"This is too good," Bobby laughed and the guys agreed.

Keefer scowled as she worked her way through the pile of paperwork. Her office window was wide open, but the breeze hardly cooled her off. She had stayed pissed since Danni's visit that morning. She was also angry with herself for getting jealous over something Danni said. *So what if Sheridan slept with the cops—that was before, this is now. Why should I be jealous of something that happened before we met?* She couldn't shake the feeling, and each time she thought about it, she scowled harder, hating Danni for bringing it up as much as herself for reacting to it. She flung the papers down in the finished pile and stood up, stretching her back. *Maybe I should just go eat lunch,* she thought, staring out the window. The people all scurried to and fro, and she loathed the idea of going out in the sudden heat and joining them. *Second thought, I'll order in.* Just as she touched the phone, it rang. "Keefer Gibson."

"Sheridan Landers."

Keefer smiled brightly. "Hi," she said, sitting down in her chair.

"What are you doing?"

The inspector kicked her shoes off and propped her feet up on the desk, glancing at the door to make sure it was closed. "Just thinking about lunch. You?"

"Just finished."

Keefer sensed Sheridan had something to say. "Are you okay?"

The construction worker blew out a breath. "I missed you," she said, almost in a whisper.

Keefer grinned widely. "Me too. I had a horrible morning."

"You did? What happened?"

"Danni happened."

"If she touched you, Keefer, so help me..."

"No, she didn't. It's okay. She was just being obnoxious...trying to get on my nerves."

"Keef, I'm sorry, I know none of this would have happened if I hadn't hit her in the club that day."

"This isn't your fault, Sher. I had no idea she was so unstable, honestly. I was bound to find out sooner or later. I was going to break up with her anyway. Who knows what she would have done to me, had you not been there."

"What did she say to you this morning to make you so upset?"

"Nothing, it's over," Keefer closed her eyes and shook her head.

"Keef...what did she say?" Sheridan insisted.

"Can we talk about this another time? I just want to hear your voice, I don't want to get into it."

Sheridan took a cleansing breath and blew it out. "Okay, I'm sorry, later. Now," she paused, "how are you sitting?"

"My feet are up on the desk, I took my shoes off." Keefer relaxed again and smiled.

"Those cute toes of yours are all wiggly and free?"

The inspector laughed quietly. "Yeah, except for my socks."

"You have the cutest toes," Sheridan said.

"Stop that," Keefer blushed a little.

"I love it when you blush."

Sheridan's mood lightened by the time the guys returned inside. She was doing what she did best—spackling the drywall, shaking to the beat of the radio as she worked.

Keefer once again rode the train with a big smile on her face. Sheridan's phone call had brightened her afternoon and the rest of her workday. Danni never showed up again and that, in itself, was enough of a reason to smile.

The tall woman felt a blush creep up on her, recalling where their conversation went, with Sheridan asking about her underwear. *Leave it to her to turn me on at work,* she thought with a silent laugh.

Sheridan pulled her car into a spot by her apartment and stopped to think. *Romantic. Hmph. I can be romantic. Can't I?*

Chapter 34

Keefer plopped down and put her feet up onto the futon. It had been a while since she'd spent any time in the den, and she realized that she missed it. She set her dinner on the table so she could reach the remote to turn on the television and found an interesting enough show to watch while she ate. Fifi climbed up onto Keefer's legs, giving her the most pathetic of pleading stares. The tall woman stopped the fork halfway to her mouth and rolled her eyes. "You'll survive without my dinner tonight, Feefs," she joked.

Keefer ate in silence, caught in a staredown with her dog, Fifi switched tactics when the pathetic stare didn't work and began to follow the fork from plate to mouth, ears standing alert, eyebrows raised with great interest. Keefer sighed heavily and picked some food off of her plate, offering it to the dog. "Sheridan's spoiled you already." Fifi's tail wagged and she looked toward the door, the food forgotten. *Hmm...*the tall woman wondered. Once she had the dog's attention again, she tested her theory. "Sheridan," she repeated, getting the same response from Fifi. Keefer chuckled quietly. *Looks like I'm not the only one that's fallen in love with you, Sher.*

The blonde construction worker sat patiently in front of her television, chewing slowly on her fried chicken Hungry Man dinner. Green eyes stared at the screen as Sheridan tried to absorb as much information from the Food Network as she could. There were three cooking shows on simultaneously and she was flipping back and forth between them, trying to find something that a normal person could accomplish in a normal kitchen. Most of the recipes called for spices, foods, and even machinery she had never even heard of. This particular channel had a French chef making some sort of dessert, a dubbed-over American voice giving only the barest of instructions. It was so incredibly frustrating. The blonde frowned. "Does anybody actually learn to cook from these things?" she asked her dogs.

Sheridan attempted to scrape up the remaining mashed potatoes with her fork and failed, narrowing her eyes at the little potatoes section of her TV dinner. "Fuck! I don't even know when to use a spoon, and I want to cook a romantic dinner?" she said loudly, startling Pharaoh, whose head was as close to the fried chicken as it could get without drooling on it. "Please don't make me have to ask Pop to cook for my girlfriend," she pleaded with the television.

A little while later, after Pharaoh finished licking up the mashed potatoes that the fork couldn't get to, Sheridan shut off the television, thoroughly frustrated and no more educated than before in the culinary arts. "Maybe I should just buy flowers; girls like flowers. Keefer would like them." Zeus snorted. "Okay, so I'm a chicken." Pharaoh's ears perked up at the word. "There's nothing but bones, you pig," she told the dog with a pat to his rump. The pit bull licked his lips anyway, reminding the blonde about food all over again. She glanced at the phone and wrung her hands out nervously. She picked up the receiver and dialed, taking a deep breath. "Hello, Pop?"

After washing the dinner dishes, the tall inspector settled down on the futon once again, this time taking the phone and a pillow from her bed with her. Once she was comfortable, she gave Fifi the okay to join her. Keefer sunk her head into the pillow and sighed. "It smells like your favorite person, Feefs," she said as she picked up the phone and dialed Sheridan.

"Yeah."

"Yeah, yourself," Keefer smiled.

"Oh, hi baby."

Keefer's insides warmed at the genuine happiness she heard in Sheridan's voice. "Whatchya doing?"

"Nothing. Just finished dinner. You?"

"Same. I was just thinking about you," Keefer smiled sheepishly at herself.

"I'm always thinking about you."

Keefer's smile grew. "I think Fifi's having Sheridan withdrawals."

"Is her mommy, too?"

"Maybe," Keefer said in a sexy tone of voice.

"I sure hope so, because I'll never get to sleep tonight if I don't see you."

"Aren't you sweet?" Keefer blushed. "Actually, I was thinking the same thing," Keefer admitted, sinking deeper into the pillow that smelled so good. "Is it crazy to miss you so much after only one day?"

"God, I hope not."

"So...are you going to come over here or do you want me to go there?" There was a pause and Keefer could tell that Sheridan was thinking about it for a moment, considering her options.

"It would be nice to have you here, but the kids won't give you a moment's peace and I want you all to myself."

Keefer's heart swelled. "I'll be waiting for you."

Sheridan eagerly waited for Keefer to open the door so she could look at her. It actually bothered her that she felt such a strong need to be with the tall inspector. She dismissed the niggling urge to investigate those feelings. She didn't like to be confused and was usually the first person to sort out a problem when it arose, but this was a scary feeling and Sheridan Landers was someone who didn't get scared. The door opened after an unusually long amount of time and the construction worker couldn't prevent the smile from lighting up her face.

"Hiya," Keefer said, catching and returning her lover's smile.

Fifi hopped around madly, vying for Sheridan's attention. She leapt up as high as she could in hopes of getting some recognition. Sheridan squatted down and gave the dog a hug, receiving a multitude of kisses and excited whines in return. "I missed you, too, sweetheart. You're a good baby...yes, you are...ohh, I'm getting kissies..."

Keefer watched the interaction with a grin. She had never heard Sheridan use that sweet, baby-talk voice and it almost made her chuckle.

Sheridan finally stood up and gave Keefer the once-over. "You look comfy," she said of the inspector's baggy shorts and T-shirt.

"I was hanging out in the den." The tall woman bent down and kissed the blonde, sighing happily as she did.

Sheridan returned the kiss; a small satisfied noise escaped the back of her throat as their tongues met. She was swept with a sense of relief at their connection—she was no longer anxious, but complete.

Keefer broke the kiss, but not before she tugged playfully at Sheridan's bottom lip with her teeth. "I needed that," she said dreamily.

"I didn't know how much I did either, until now," Sheridan agreed.

Feeling left out, Fifi jumped up, stood with her front paws on Sheridan's thigh, and stretched. The construction worker absently reached down to pet the dog, her attention never leaving Keefer. "Watching anything good in there?" she nodded toward the den.

"Nah, just keeping busy until you got here," Keefer said with a shy smile.

"Well, now that I'm here," Sheridan raised an eyebrow and let her gaze wander the length of Keefer's body, "what do you want to do?"

Keefer pursed her lips as if in deep thought. "Hmm...oh, I don't know," she replied, flipping her long hair over her shoulder. "Have you got any ideas?" She closed the distance between them until they were leaning on each other, face to face—or in Sheridan's case, face to breasts.

Sheridan tore her gaze away from Keefer's seductive stare and eyed the swells of flesh that were within kissing distance. "Oh, I have plenty of suggestions," she replied, her voice suddenly deeper. She ducked her head and dropped little kisses on Keefer's breasts.

The reaction was immediate. Keefer's heart beat faster and her nipples tightened. She let out a shaky breath and then kissed the top of Sheridan's head. "You make me so crazy sometimes, and you hardly touch me at all," she whispered into soft blonde hair.

Sheridan wrapped her arms around her lover and nuzzled into the inviting space between Keefer's breasts. "I've been waiting all day to do this," she said, her words muffled as she pressed her face deeper into Keefer's body.

"Let's go sit down before I fall," the tall woman suggested, her knees already weak from the gentle touches.

"Then I'd have to let go of you," Sheridan said, a little surprised at herself for saying it.

Keefer felt all fuzzy from the statement. "Yeah, but you can come right back after we sit."

Fifi followed the contented couple into the den, where all three of them settled comfortably on the futon. The couple sat side by side, bodies touching, the fingers of one hand entwined. Sheridan's head was resting on Keefer's shoulder, and the brunette's head was leaning against the wall behind her. After a few minutes of easy silence, Sheridan stood up and moved between Keefer's legs.

Keefer stared at her curiously. "What, hon?"

Sheridan grinned. *She called me* hon. "I have an urge, but I feel silly," she admitted.

"I remember the first day we made love and I said I had an urge. I do believe you said 'Go with it.'"

Sheridan smiled at the memory and crawled onto the couch, straddling Keefer's thighs, and sat tentatively on the brunette's lap. She spared an embarrassed glance at her lover before she sat her weight down and wrapped her arms around Keefer's neck.

Keefer sighed loudly, feeling incredibly special with Sheridan on her lap, their arms wrapped tightly around each other. It was deeply satisfying, filling a hole inside of her that she didn't know existed. "I like this," she breathed into the side of her lover's head.

Sheridan snuggled deeper into Keefer's neck. "I knew it would feel this good." She nodded, inhaling the distinctive scent of Keefer's skin. She had felt foolish at first, crawling onto her lover's lap like a child, but she needed the closeness and the craving was too strong to ignore.

It was late into the night when Sheridan next opened her eyes. She found herself spooned behind her lover, an arm and leg thrown protectively over the tall woman. *Now, this is more like me,* she thought with relief. She had no idea what had come over her before; she had just felt so needy all of a sudden—an overwhelming sensation that had disturbed her at the time, but faded and turned into a feeling of safety and security once she was comfortably surrounded by Keefer.

Sheridan usually felt safety in routine actions or in the club where she felt confident and wanted. There was a certain security in being wanted and sought after, and even though it was for sex—meaningless couplings with faceless strangers—the security in always having them want her was there.

With Keefer, she felt weak, something she hadn't experienced since she was a child. The blonde had made herself strong in body and mind as soon as she was old enough to understand that she could. Sometimes, all it took was a simple look from Keefer and Sheridan felt like a weak child, unable to survive until she got the hug of reassurance that she craved. It was a frightening feeling, but somehow she knew she didn't have to worry. She was sure that Keefer would always be there for her if she felt suddenly needy. Keefer wouldn't laugh or dismiss her. Keefer wasn't concerned about the blonde's reputation; she would never brush the construction worker's feelings to the side and for that, Sheridan fell in love with Keefer all over again.

Keefer woke up to the sensation of being squeezed tightly. She smiled and nestled her back securely into Sheridan's body. She felt safe with the knowledge that her lover was right there, holding her, leaning into her with her body. She knew Sheridan was loving her at the moment. She didn't need words or kisses—she felt it. She reached over and fumbled for the remote, shutting off the television and all light from the room. She placed her arms back over her lover's and squeezed, letting Sheridan know she loved her just as much.

"Shh...go back to sleep."

Sheridan's low whisper washed over Keefer and she yawned, nodding as she did. "You okay?" she asked groggily.

"Perfect," Sheridan replied, leaving a sweet kiss on Keefer's head.

Moments later, Fifi jumped on top of the couple and tried to wedge herself between them on the small futon. Finding no room, she began walking all over the two women, forcing them to get up and relocate to the bedroom.

It was hard for either one of them to get out of bed the next morning and waking up tangled together wasn't helping at all. Sheridan was the middle of a sandwich, with Fifi snuggled up against her back and Keefer against her front, practically sharing her skin. The comfortable inspector hit the snooze bar three times before rolling onto her back and untangling her limbs from her lover's. She glanced at the clock, heaved a huge sigh and ended it with an annoyed groan. "Sher, we have to get up," she grumbled, throwing an arm over her eyes.

"Unnn."

Keefer turned over to face the construction worker, who looked so comfortable that she got jealous.

Sheridan frowned and grunted when Keefer began poking her in the forehead, but didn't want to move to make her stop. "Is that very nice?" she complained without opening her eyes.

"Come on, you need to leave before me," Keefer said, moving her pokes to Sheridan's cheek.

One annoyed green eye popped open and glared at the brunette. The annoyance didn't last long when the construction worker saw the playful grin on her lover's face. "Okay, I'm up," she said as she stretched out her legs and hummed. Fifi jumped off the bed groggily and immediately curled up on the floor. "It's so nice to sleep without the boys lying all over my face. I never want to get out of this bed." Sheridan reached an arm out of the blanket and beckoned for Keefer to snuggle.

"Oh no, if I get any closer to you, I won't let you leave."

Sheridan opened both eyes and sat up. "Oh yeah?" she asked, suddenly awake.

Keefer chuckled, knowing that would rouse her lover. She leaned in and gave Sheridan a quick kiss before getting out of bed. "Shower, hon."

"You are such a tease," the blonde pouted, kicking the blankets off and standing up to stretch.

"Not really. If I hadn't hit that snooze button so many times, you would have got some this morning."

Sheridan stared at her lover's back in surprise. "Ooh, someone woke up in a mood," she teased. "What brought this on?"

"Sleeping all scrunched up against you may have had something to do with it," Keefer said, facing her closet. She was a little shocked at the things she was saying, but she couldn't hide the grin at the startled tone in Sheridan's voice. She jumped as two strong arms encircled her from behind.

"I like the way you smell in the morning," Sheridan mumbled into Keefer's back.

The tall woman leaned into the embrace. "I love the way you look in the morning, all rumpled and sexy."

Sheridan pulled away and raised an eyebrow. "What have you done with Keefer? She used to be shy."

"Oh she's still shy, trust me," the tall inspector replied, turning around to face her lover. "She just turns all sorts of crazy when she wakes up in your arms."

Sheridan beamed. "Well then, we should do that more often," she said, placing a kiss on the tall woman's chest. "If you need me, I'll be in the shower," she winked. "Naked and soapy," she added before leaving.

Keefer closed her eyes and let the image appear. "Mmm," she hummed. "One day, Sheridan. One day."

The morning and afternoon went rather quickly for both Sheridan and Keefer. There was only a bare minimum of teasing at the construction site, and Danni was nowhere to be found at the OSHA offices.

Sheridan was content to hear all about Maria's pregnancy and all the odd cravings that came with it. She actually felt relieved to not be the topic of conversation, whereas she used to make it a point in the past.

Keefer got her work done with only small bits of stress and was pretty satisfied with her productiveness. Before Sheridan, the days would drag on and on, and even then, after the longest days, she dreaded going home. She felt excited as she noted she only had one more hour left at work, knowing she would be seeing Sheridan soon. The inspector began arranging her work in neat piles for the next day when her phone rang. She answered in an unusually pleasant voice, "Keefer Gibson."

"Hiya, sexy."

A big smile spread across the brunette's face. "Look who's talking?"

"When are you leaving?" Sheridan asked in a low voice.

"In about an hour. I miss you," Keefer said with a shy smile.

"You do, huh?" Sheridan barely contained her chuckle.

Keefer narrowed her eyes at her girlfriend's teasing tone. "Yes, I do. I can't wait to get home and see you."

"Knock, knock."

Keefer furrowed her brows. "Knock, knock?" she asked in confusion.

"Yeah. Knock, knock."

Keefer raised her eyebrow. There was a knock at her office door at the exact time Sheridan said the words. "That was weird," she said to her lover.

Sheridan snorted. "Open the door, it could be important."

Keefer tucked the phone under her chin and called for whoever it was to come in. The door opened slowly and there was Sheridan.

"See? Knock, knock," the blonde said with an impish grin, closing the door behind her.

"Oh, my god!" Keefer hung up the phone and stood up, shocked that Sheridan was standing in her office.

"Do I get a kiss hello or are you just going to stand there staring at me?"

"Oh!" Keefer closed the distance between them and gave Sheridan a big kiss. "You surprised me! How did you know where my office is?"

"Well, when you first came to the site, you left your card. Philly found it today amongst the clutter and gave it to me." Sheridan walked as she talked, backing Keefer up until she was leaning against her desk.

"Sheridan..." Keefer warned her lover, reading a mischievous look in her eyes.

Sheridan flashed a sexy grin before she pulled Keefer's head down for a kiss.

The tall woman felt her toes curl from her lover's lips, but at the same time, she was very uneasy about making out in her office. She ended the kiss and leaned further back. "Anyone can walk in."

"I know, ain't it hot?" Sheridan replied with a wiggle of her eyebrow.

Keefer giggled nervously. "Sher, I mean it, my door isn't locked."

The construction worker ran to the door and locked it, returning back between Keefer's legs before the tall woman had the chance to stand up straight. "Where were we?" she whispered, moving in for another kiss.

Keefer allowed the kiss this time, feeling a bit more secure now that the door was locked, but her heart was still racing despite it. She had never even thought of making out in her office—it was scary, but the way Sheridan's mouth was moving against hers, she hardly had the time to think about it.

The blonde slid her mouth from Keefer's lips over her chin and onto her neck where she began kissing and licking. "I thought about you all day and couldn't wait until later," she said, nuzzling her face into thick, black hair.

Keefer shivered from the warm breath on her neck and ear. "I thought about you, too." She tilted her head back further.

Sheridan took advantage of the move and began nibbling at her lover's throat. "You taste so good," she groaned.

Keefer felt a zing of arousal between her legs and realized what was happening. "Sher, baby...we'd better stop."

"Why?" the blonde asked between nips and sucks.

"Oh, God..." Keefer moaned. "I can't...not here..."

Sheridan pulled away and shook her head. "You're right. I'm sorry, I don't know what came over me," she said with an embarrassed grin.

"Yeah, right." Keefer narrowed her eyes, not believing her lover for a second. "You had this planned."

"Just a little."

"How am I supposed to get any work done with you here?"

"I'll be quiet; you won't even know I'm here."

Keefer looked skeptical.

"I swear. I'll just sit here by myself," she sat in a chair, "minding my own business, thinking about how delicious you smell."

"Oh, yeah, that'll work."

Sheridan buttoned her lip, but her eyes still blazed with arousal.

Keefer didn't even attempt to go back to work. She walked over to her lover and took her by the hand. "Let's go home," she said as she led the blonde out of the office.

"Cool!" Sheridan blurted as she was led quickly down the hallway.

They retrieved Sheridan's car from the parking garage and were on their way home minutes later. Keefer was watching Sheridan smoke a cigarette with a frown, and the blonde couldn't take the looks.

"What?"

"I just never saw you smoke before," Keefer replied with a shrug.

"Well it's either smoke this cigarette or pull over right here and have my way with you."

Keefer looked around quickly at the rush hour traffic and blushed. "Smoke away," she said with a nod, opening the ashtray.

Sheridan chuckled, "I thought so."

"Do you smoke a lot?" Keefer asked.

"Not really. I smoke a ton when I drink. I mostly smoke at the club and after I eat, but I haven't really with you." She thought about that for a minute. "I suppose I get my oral fix when I'm with you," she grinned and blew a smoke ring.

Keefer watched Sheridan's lips as they wrapped around the filter and then as they blew another ring. *Should I find that so arousing?* she questioned herself. *Smoking is a terrible habit...jeez, I wish I were that cigarette.*

Sheridan put out the smoke and glanced at her distracted lover. She could tell by the expression on her face what she was thinking about and decided to make the ride through rush-hour traffic more interesting. She took a hand off the wheel and rested it on Keefer's thigh.

Keefer raised an eyebrow and looked at Sheridan's hand, then up at her face.

The blonde grinned and walked her fingers higher up Keefer's leg.

"What are you doing?" Keefer asked nervously.

"Nothing," the blonde replied innocently.

Keefer looked out the window and covered Sheridan's hand with her own. "The truck divers can see right into the car!"

"So? I'm not doing anything." Sheridan continued to stare out the windshield.

"You better not." Keefer shook her head.

Sheridan smirked and squeezed Keefer's thigh as her pinky wormed its way between the brunette's tightly closed legs.

"Sheridan," Keefer said through her teeth.

Sheridan wiggled her pinky a few times before Keefer removed her hand. "You're no fun," she pouted.

Keefer squirmed in her seat. "We're almost home," she said with relief.

"You're in a hurry to get there?' Sheridan asked with a devious grin.

Keefer gave her a narrow-eyed look.

"Oh, yeah. Me too." Sheridan nodded. "I can't wait to get you in the house and crawl on top of you." She watched Keefer gulp. "Then I'm going to kiss you until you sweat." The brunette closed her eyes. Sheridan's voice dropped an octave. "Then...I'm going to lick you from head to toe...paying special attention to each nipple...sucking them...biting them..."

"Okay! That's enough." Keefer covered her lover's mouth with her hand, having felt every word between her legs. Sheridan licked her palm and she pulled her hand away and glared.

"I'm just saying."

Keefer held up a hand. "Don't say anything more until we get inside. Then you can talk all you want."

Sheridan chuckled evilly. "I'm gonna hold you to that."

Chapter 35

The remainder of the drive went quickly, which was a relief to both women, since the air in the car was thick with sexual tension. As soon as Sheridan turned the ignition off, Keefer jumped out of the car and practically sprinted to the front door. Sheridan hastily grabbed a duffel bag from the back seat before running to catch up to the long-legged woman. She shoved her arm through the handles of the bag while she hurried, leaving both hands free to grasp Keefer's ass cheeks as the tall woman fumbled for the house keys.

"Sher...the neighbors!" Keefer gasped, failing to get the key into the lock.

Sheridan snatched the keys away and opened the door, standing aside for Keefer to enter first. Fifi greeted them with eager yelps, jumping up on the blonde and digging into her side with her paws. Sheridan patted the dog on the head as she pressed herself against her lover, attaching her mouth to the skin just below her throat. Keefer grabbed Sheridan's shoulders with both hands to steady herself as the small woman stood on her tiptoes to reach more skin, her tongue painting hot trails, leaving goose bumps in its wake.

The construction worker dropped the house keys on the floor and pulled Keefer's loose white shirt from her pants, sliding her hands under it and touching all the skin she could find. When that wasn't enough for her, Sheridan began opening Keefer's pants with one hand. The brunette nearly fell backwards from the weight of Sheridan leaning against her, so the blonde began walking, leading the inspector toward the wall, never breaking contact. They made it halfway before Fifi nearly tripped them.

"Feefs...go to bed, baby...please?" Keefer begged.

393

Sheridan left Keefer standing near the kitchen with her pants open as she went inside to retrieve a dog treat. "Here, Fifi, be a good girl and go lay down. Mommy and me have business."

To Keefer's astonishment, her dog trotted happily into the bedroom with a treat in her mouth.

Sheridan zipped back in front of her lover and slid her hands up the back of Keefer's shirt. "Where were we?"

"We're going to do this right here?" Keefer asked with a nervous chuckle, then gasped as Sheridan unhooked her bra.

"Why the hell not?" the blonde replied, opening her own pants.

Keefer got a tingly feeling watching Sheridan open her pants and she pulled the construction worker's hands away and started removing the jeans for her.

"What about you?" the blonde asked, her eyes half closed from the feel of Keefer's fingers on her skin.

Keefer let her lover's pants fall around her ankles with a small giggle. She kicked off her shoes and stuck her hips forward, inviting Sheridan to take off her pants. Sheridan wasted no time removing them; she squatted down in front of the tall woman as she slid the pants down and assisted her lover in pulling her legs out.

Keefer stood awkwardly in her underwear until Sheridan stood back up and looked at her with hunger. Her inhibitions faded into the background as she pulled the blonde against her body and bent down to connect with a kiss. They had been waiting for this moment since Keefer's office, and the anticipation showed in the frantic sparring of their tongues.

Sheridan's hands traveled as far down Keefer's bared legs as they could go, the short nails lightly scratching over the skin as she brought them back up the inside of the long legs. Keefer shuddered and sucked the blonde's tongue hungrily. Her hands slid under Sheridan's shirt and covered her breasts, squeezing and kneading them. Sheridan felt her eyes roll under her lids; she loved it when Keefer did things like that, her shyness suddenly disappearing for the moment. *Speaking of shyness...* The construction worker was reminded of the bag slung over her shoulder and she pulled away from the kiss. She looked into Keefer's slightly disappointed eyes and grinned.

Keefer found the grin to be very inviting and she let go of her lover's breasts to hold her face with both hands and began devouring her lips.

Sheridan groaned as Keefer let go of her face. One hand slid through her hair and cradled the back of her head and the other hand returned to her breast, teasing her nipple, making her squirm. The blonde was helpless. Keefer was wreaking havoc everywhere she touched. Sheridan needed to sit down, or at least lean on something. The closest thing was the kitchen counter and she began to walk backwards toward it.

Keefer giggled at herself as she tried to walk with her knees bent and not break the kiss. Keefer's hands wandered up and down Sheridan's body, and the smaller woman retaliated with much of the same; they couldn't keep their hands off of each other. Still kissing and giggling, they migrated into the kitchen until Sheridan's back was up against the counter, her pants still around her ankles. Keefer groped the construction worker's arms and shoulders, loving the way the muscles moved under the skin as Sheridan grasped and kneaded the inspector's backside.

"Mmm," Sheridan hummed, breaking away from the heated kiss.

Keefer observed the flush on her panting lover's face with great interest, her belly tingling with excitement at the knowledge that she'd caused the blonde's erratic breathing. She felt rather cocky and grinned confidently as Sheridan shrugged the bag off of her shoulder.

Green eyes twinkled with mischief as she unzipped the bag and reached inside. "I have a surprise for you," she said, trying to concentrate on what she was doing as Keefer's hands trailed up and down her torso.

"Oh, yeah?" the brunette perked up in anticipation.

Sheridan grinned slyly as she pulled out the thigh harness and held it up. "Ta da!"

Keefer stood immobile like a deer in the headlights, her heart suddenly beating a mile a minute. Amidst the momentary panic, Keefer felt a bubble of excitement rolling around inside of her. *What are you panicking for? You want this; you know you can do it.*

Sheridan felt like kicking herself as she read the expression on her lover's face. "Keef, we don't have to—"

Keefer cut her off with a finger to Sheridan's lips. "Just nervous. Ignore it, it will go away," she assured her, eyeing the harness. The dildo was already attached and just looking at it made her sex clench.

Sheridan moved Keefer's hand from her mouth. "You sure? I don't want to pressure you into anything...I could just put it away and..."

"Sher, I want it," Keefer admitted with a blush. "Trust me," she said, glancing down at her own crotch.

Sheridan followed Keefer's gaze and grinned. "Yeah? Can I see that for myself?"

Keefer's blue eyes danced back and forth between Sheridan's and the dildo. She shrugged. "Go right ahead."

Sheridan brought her free hand down to Keefer's thigh and slid it slowly up the inside of the tall woman's leg. Keefer inhaled loudly as her lover's fingers brushed across the crotch of her panties. "I'd say you want *something,*" Sheridan teased playfully, flitting her fingers lightly over the sensitive area.

Keefer nodded and brought her head down for a kiss. Her lover obliged and soon they were groaning into each other's mouths again as the kissing became frenzied and their hunger escalated. The tall woman leaned into the blonde as the fingers between her legs touched her more intently. She needed to feel Sheridan, so she slid her hands down the construction worker's back, into her underwear.

Sheridan grunted when the large hands held her ass cheeks. She didn't know whether to bring her hips forward into Keefer's body, or backwards into her hands; both would feel equally good. When she suddenly remembered that she was holding the harness, a rush of excitement zipped through her body. She wanted to use it at that very moment and see Keefer's body moving against hers. She gently pushed Keefer back and caught her breath. The heavy-lidded blue eyes staring hungrily at her made her knees tremble.

She looked at the harness and then at her lover, surprised but relieved when the tall woman merely bit her bottom lip instead of looking frightened. "You ready, baby?" she asked with a sexy smile.

Keefer struggled to get her breathing under control before she replied. "Yes, very," she admitted shyly.

With Keefer being so tall, Sheridan knew she would have to put it around her waist to do it while standing up. She handed Keefer the harness and took her by the hand, leading her into the bedroom. It didn't matter where it was strapped if they were lying down, and although she wasn't sure Keefer would go for it, she was going to attempt to have her on top. She sat at the edge of the bed and motioned for her lover to come to her.

"Where do I put it? Which one?" Keefer asked.

"Either one, anyplace," Sheridan said, her belly filling with excited tingles. Keefer knelt down between her lover's legs and paused as her eyes met the black boxer briefs. She glanced up at Sheridan's face and the construction worker grinned. "Oh, yeah, gotta take them off." She stood. "Go on."

The brunette swallowed hard and placed the harness on the bed. She hooked her fingers under the waistband and waited a moment to savor how those muscular thighs looked covered in tight black Lycra. She felt her sex swell and she shifted her weight, kneeling on the carpet as she pulled down the tight underpants. Baring the blonde patch of hair proved too much for Keefer and she leaned forward without much thought and rubbed her cheek on the soft hair.

Sheridan's eyes narrowed as she watched her lover's actions. She placed a hand lightly on the back of Keefer's head and encouraged her to do what she wanted. The brunette ruffled her nose through the light hair and inhaled deeply. Sheridan almost thrust her sex into her lover's face but reeled her urges back. Sometimes she had to remember Keefer was like an inexperienced teenager when it came to sex. Sure, she knew how to please and was even cocky enough about her abilities to do so, but she'd never taken the chance to explore, and being with Danni hadn't given her the opportunity to take her time and learn beyond the act itself.

Keefer closed her eyes and breathed in the scent of Sheridan's arousal. It was delicious and she felt her own body respond to it. She opened her eyes and focused on removing Sheridan's boxers, slowly peeling them down her legs and off of her body. Her eyes darted back to the harness and she reached for it tentatively, slightly embarrassed by the way the dildo stuck rudely out of it. She ignored the butterflies in her stomach and opened the Velcro, holding it in front of her lover's right thigh, just above the knee.

Sheridan relaxed the muscles of her leg as Keefer wrapped the harness around it. She wanted as snug a fit as possible; she didn't want to have to stop and readjust it in the middle of everything. "As tight as you can, baby," she instructed, and after the material was in place, she flexed her leg and found it perfect. "Beautiful."

Keefer felt her nervousness return as Sheridan sat on the edge of the bed. She almost changed her mind, but her curiosity and need to conquer her shyness won out. She found herself standing between her lover's legs, with green eyes studying her through their lashes. She found the look sexy and the butterflies turned into arousal.

Sheridan held Keefer's hips in her hands and pulled her closer. "You wanna do it this way, Keef? We can lay down..."

"No, I want to do it this way," the brunette said confidently as she moved to straddle Sheridan's equipped thigh.

The blonde's heart rate doubled. A gush of wetness flooded her sex as she watched Keefer slip a hand beneath her panties and uncharacteristically touch herself.

Keefer found herself to be wet enough to accept the dildo, but getting herself onto it was going to be harder than she thought. She needed a little coaxing and took a deep breath before lowering herself onto her lover's thigh.

Sheridan wasn't surprised when Keefer positioned herself away from the harness, since she still had her panties on, but she was amply startled at the amount of wetness on her leg. She'd thought her lover was too nervous to be that wet, but she was wrong. Keefer was just as excited about this as she was. She was proud of Keefer's boldness and leaned forward to express her gratitude with a kiss.

Keefer lifted up slightly and Sheridan reached between Keefer's legs to hold onto her ass, her forearm coming in contact with the heat and wetness of her center. She hummed her appreciation into the kiss.

Keefer instinctively pressed herself into the blonde's arm, groaning quietly in her throat.

Sheridan answered with a groan of her own as she pulled back from the liplock. She watched her arm as she flexed it, giving Keefer something solid to move against. The tall woman's dark green bikinis weren't particularly sexy, but they were on Keefer and that made them sexy. The warm, wet feeling of the material against her skin stoked the fires of arousal in the blonde; her own sex clenched in empathy as Keefer bore down against her muscles.

Suddenly, Keefer pulled away and Sheridan was at a loss until she saw her tall lover's face, flushed with arousal, watching her with bright blue eyes. The brunette's breasts were moving in time to her heavy breathing, and when she licked her lips, Sheridan could have sworn that she felt that tongue between her legs.

Keefer took her lover's hands and placed them at the elastic of her underwear, silently asking for Sheridan to remove them. The blonde pulled them down to mid-thigh, then helped Keefer to lift each leg and slid the wet green material off of her body completely. Keefer shifted her stance, standing with her legs far apart, straddling Sheridan's leg. She reached blindly behind her, found the dildo and wrapped her hand around it. She closed her eyes. The last sight she saw was a pair of green eyes staring raptly at her hand.

Sheridan's heart pumped loudly in her ears, she pulled off her shirt quickly and leaned back on her hands, watching as her lover moved slowly, shyly. She found the anticipation unbearable and reached to her with one hand. Confused blue eyes opened and Sheridan patted the bed between her legs, and then pulled slightly on Keefer's leg.

The tall inspector moved forward, climbing up onto the bed on her knees, her sex inches above the dildo. Sheridan held her breath as Keefer placed both hands on her shoulders. Blue eyes glanced quickly at green and Keefer found Sheridan riveted to the dildo. She lowered herself even more.

Sheridan blew out the breath she was holding as her lover's lower lips touched the toy. She looked up into nervous blue eyes and tried desperately to remain patient, but failed. "Do you need me to—" Before Sheridan could finish her sentence, Keefer slid down all the way to her thigh, engulfing the dildo completely. Both women groaned loudly.

Keefer's head fell forward, her hair covering her face like a curtain, tickling Sheridan's bare chest. The construction worker gripped her lover's hips, holding her firmly. Keefer looked up through her bangs in a silent question.

Sheridan swallowed hard before she spoke. "I'm trying to imagine how it feels to be that dick," she whispered.

Keefer's inner muscles clenched at the dildo. Her hips wanted to move; she rocked forward and shivered at the much-needed contact with her clit.

"Yeah, baby," Sheridan gasped. She wanted to talk, she needed to tell her lover how hot she looked and felt, but was hesitant. She didn't want to do anything that would make Keefer stop.

Blue eyes closed as Keefer concentrated on the feeling of being completely filled. *I told you I wanted this,* she told that shy part of herself, the one that so badly wanted to surface. Keefer was having none of that and she rocked her hips in defiance of that shyness, pushing the embarrassed part of herself firmly to the back of her pleasure-filled mind. She felt Sheridan's hands leave her hips and opened her eyes. The blonde was holding the bottom of her shirt; Keefer sat up straight and lifted her arms up, allowing the shirt and already unfastened bra to be removed from her body.

Sheridan sighed happily as two beautiful breasts were bared. She sat back and shook her head wordlessly, once again in awe of the perfection of her lover's body. "Fuck, yeah," she blurted as Keefer suddenly pushed her down on the bed. The brunette was sitting on her own legs, straddling Sheridan's thigh, her mouth half open as she breathed quickly from it, her breasts tantalizingly close to Sheridan's face. The blonde was drinking it all in with pleasure.

Keefer caught her breath and grew bold at the look of lust on her lover's face. She raised her hips up slowly, rising halfway off of the dildo, and then lowered herself again. It felt so good that she groaned, and did it again and again. She was lost in the delicious sensations, not aware of the highly erotic images she was presenting Sheridan with until she heard the blonde groan painfully and felt her strong hands clenching tightly at her hips.

Sheridan watched Keefer's breasts approach her face and then retreat. Each time they came close, she tried to catch one with her mouth.

Suddenly, Keefer arched her back, giving her access to her breasts. The brunette moaned in delight as soft wet lips engulfed her nipple and sucked. She leaned all the way forward, her elbows braced on the bed on either side of Sheridan's head, her sex filled completely. She stayed still and felt everything for long moments.

Sheridan released the nipple to speak. "Can I tell you how fucking hot this is?" she asked and then returned to the pebbled flesh for more. Keefer rocked forward again, coming up off the dildo, and back, letting out a shaky yet satisfied sigh. Her movements drove Sheridan crazy. She needed to feel the flesh against her body and she wrapped her arms around the brunette, pulling her close. "You okay?" she asked, nuzzling her nose into soft black hair.

"I really want this," Keefer replied, adjusting her neck so Sheridan had more hair to nuzzle.

The blonde wormed her hands between their bodies and palmed Keefer's breasts, rubbing them in slight circles. Her work-roughened skin caused the brunette to rasp out a groan and arch her back. With more room to maneuver, Sheridan teased the nipples with her fingers, and her breath quickened as her lover began moving her hips again, fucking her leg, making her wetness flow liberally. Touching wasn't enough and she leaned forward and captured a nipple between her lips, green eyes glancing up at blue, gauging Keefer's reaction. The tall woman's eyes rolled shut as she sucked her bottom lip into her mouth and squeezed her legs tightly around Sheridan's thigh.

Sheridan hummed happily at the sudden flow of wetness on her thigh. She released the nipple, but not before swiping at it with the tip of her tongue. She needed to watch Keefer move on top of her and leaned back on her hands again, allowing the tall woman to move freely.

Keefer knew how wet she was—she could feel it, hear it, smell it. Seeing Sheridan lick her lips and swallow, she knew she could smell it too and it made her clit twitch. She rocked forward harder, rubbing her throbbing bud against the harness each time she filled herself. She could feel the orgasm building and welcomed it, squeezing at the invasion with her inner walls.

Sheridan watched through heavy eyelids as Keefer's body rocked sensuously over hers. Her clit throbbed at the sight and she needed relief, thinking for a moment about touching herself, then realized if she moved her arm, she'd fall back on the bed from the weight of her lover, and she wanted to watch this more than anything in the world.

Keefer saw her lover wiggling her hips and read the sign loud and clear. She moved her right leg slightly until her knee made contact with Sheridan's sex. She groaned loudly; her lover was dripping wet and so hot.

"Fuck, baby!" the blonde ground out through gritted teeth.

Keefer couldn't prevent the whimper of pleasure from escaping her lips. She rocked faster, filling herself hard with each thrust. She noticed Sheridan licking her lips again and suddenly craved her mouth. She arched her back so their lips would connect, never ceasing the movements of her hips. They kissed hungrily and desperately.

Sheridan didn't care if she wound up on her back and grasped Keefer's hips tightly. The instant she moved her hands from behind her, they fell onto the bed heavily, starving mouths crashing together in a blur of teeth and tongues. The blonde grunted as the new position pressed Keefer's knee securely into her clit. She lifted her hips and shuddered at the contact, growling into Keefer's open mouth. She was surprised when Keefer growled back, the sound arousing her more than she thought possible. She moved a hand to the back of her lover's head and held her tightly, sucking her tongue into her mouth.

Keefer was going to come, she could feel it each time she filled herself and rocked forward. The dildo touched a place inside of her she wasn't aware existed and it felt like heaven. She moved quickly, losing control of the ability to kiss properly, the sweet friction inside of her and on her clit turning her senses to mush. She pulled back from her lover's face and whimpered desperately.

Sheridan knew that sound and worked her hand between their bodies, finding Keefer's clit hard and ready. She touched it purposefully, happy that Keefer was going to come, but really wishing she could see her face.

Keefer gasped and shuddered hard, the climax taking over her body. Her hips jerked wildly and her eyes squeezed shut tightly. Her sex clenched powerfully at the dildo, sending jolts of incredible sensations throughout her body. She heard herself gasp Sheridan's name as she twitched and trembled.

Sheridan's nostrils flared when Keefer breathlessly called out her name. She desperately wished she were coming with her beautiful love—just hearing and feeling Keefer explode should have sent her into ecstasy, but it didn't and her sex was on fire.

Keefer calmed down as Sheridan's strong arms held her close. She still twitched and groaned as the dildo stayed buried inside of her, her inner walls sporadically clenching it. Completely satisfied and slightly out of breath, she turned her head and kissed Sheridan's shoulder, then jerked once more. "God, Sher, take it out," she begged.

Sheridan held back the chuckle as she reached down to her leg, lifting Keefer up a little at the same time so she could pull out the dildo.

"Ohh," Keefer moaned as the toy slid out of her.

"Keef...honey...I know you're beat, but I'm dying here."

"Three minutes," Keefer mumbled into Sheridan's neck. "Can you breathe?" she asked, realizing that she was dead weight.

"I'm not complaining." Sheridan ran her hands lightly up and down Keefer's bare back.

The inspector sighed and rolled over onto her back, one of her long legs draped bonelessly over and between Sheridan's.

The construction worker turned her head and studied Keefer's profile. Her sex burned for attention and staring at her lover's satiated, flushed face made matters even worse.

Keefer felt Sheridan's hand brush against her leg and she turned her head to the side to meet the blonde's guilty grin. Keefer swallowed hard. *I've had dreams like this,* she thought excitedly.

Sheridan was slowly touching herself, in no hurry, just indulging in a little satisfaction until Keefer was ready to do it for her, but after seeing the sultry look on her lover's face, she had the urge to put on a show.

Keefer watched attentively as Sheridan brought her other hand down and held herself open. The brunette felt her own sex answer with a tingle and wished she were as bold as Sheridan. She'd have loved to touch herself too, but she couldn't, not in front of her lover—not yet, anyway. Seeing Sheridan's open sex made her mouth water and when the blonde's other hand came down to play, she heard herself groan. She wondered if Sheridan would get as turned on as she was watching her touch herself. She licked her suddenly dry lips, not realizing she was breathing through her mouth.

Sheridan stroked the length of her sex, still going slowly in fear of coming immediately. Keefer's expression of lust as she watched aroused her so much, she was afraid that she'd come the second she touched her clit. She avoided it, teasing herself as Keefer watched. She hoped Keefer would touch her too—she'd have rather come at Keefer's hand than her own, even though having Keefer watch her do it was driving her crazy.

Blue eyes fixed on Sheridan's fingers as they trailed up and down, spreading open as they neared her clit and sliding effortlessly around it. The tall woman's clit throbbed, and she wished she could touch it too, ease the ache that watching her lover caused. She groaned again quietly as she spied the amount of arousal that poured out of Sheridan. She sat all the way up and couldn't stop her hand from reaching out to it, inhaling loudly as her fingers met the wet heat at Sheridan's opening.

"Yeah, Keef, touch me," Sheridan moaned, lifting her hips up, begging for more contact.

Keefer obeyed, teasing the slick entrance with two fingers, circling it and rubbing it, but not entering it.

Sheridan groaned painfully. "You're enjoying this, aren't you."

Keefer nodded rapidly. "Immensely," she whispered, shivering at the trickle of arousal as it slid out of her center, tickling her.

Green eyes narrowed even more at the shiver. "Are you getting wet?" she asked breathlessly as Keefer's fingers continued to torture her. Keefer nodded, never taking her eyes off of her fingers. "Would you...?"

"No, I can't," Keefer whispered, glancing up at understanding green eyes.

"It's okay," Sheridan replied, her hips rising and falling rhythmically.

Blue eyes watched the construction worker's fingers as they continued to avoid contact. "Why aren't you touching it?" Keefer asked, her own fingers trailing dangerously close to Sheridan's clit.

"I'll come," the blonde panted as Keefer moved Sheridan's fingers away.

"I want you to." Keefer smiled seductively as she touched Sheridan's clit, causing the blonde's hips to jerk violently.

"God!" Sheridan let go of her sex with her other hand and reached between Keefer's legs, frustrated when Keefer backed away and shook her head. "Please," she begged, even as she knew she wouldn't last long enough to pleasure Keefer to orgasm before coming herself.

"Let me finish," Keefer breathed out, watching herself touch Sheridan's clit. The blonde opened her legs wider and whimpered. Keefer felt her own clit grow in response and she added her other hand, sliding one finger inside of her lover.

"That's it, baby," Sheridan gasped, her sex milking Keefer's long finger as her orgasm approached.

"This is so hot," Keefer whispered in fascination, not realizing she'd spoken out loud.

Sheridan clenched the blanket in her fists and stiffened momentarily before her hips rose to meet Keefer's hands. "Fuck, yeah..." she growled as she came, her stomach muscles clenching as she shook with pleasure.

Keefer didn't even know that a grin of satisfaction had formed on her lips as she worked her hands fast and hard, drawing out Sheridan's climax for her own selfish indulgences.

Sheridan pulled Keefer's hands away from her body and hugged them to her chest. "Enough, baby," she groaned, licking her lips and smiling happily.

"I didn't want to stop," Keefer said as she leaned over to kiss her satisfied lover.

"Mmm," Sheridan hummed into the kiss.

Keefer drew back and blushed slightly at her latest actions. "You do things to me, Sher."

"Oh, I'll do something to you," the blonde growled dangerously and rolled on top of her. "My turn." She grinned wickedly and wiggled her eyebrows.

Keefer giggled nervously at first, then groaned as Sheridan's hard thigh met her sex.

"Ohh, Keef, you're so wet."

Long legs wrapped around a strong back and Keefer raised her hips for more contact.

Fifi peeked her head into the room sometime later and rolled her eyes. Padding off into the den, she put her paws over her head and sighed, knowing she'd never get any sleep if they kept that up. And they kept it up all night.

Chapter 36

It was early Thursday morning, and Sheridan awoke in the same position that she had for the last few mornings. Keefer was snuggled up to the front of her and Fifi sprawled out behind her, the dog's head sharing her pillow. She sighed contentedly and kissed Keefer on the head. The brunette stirred and made a squeaky sound, and her arm came out of the blanket and reached behind her to rest on Sheridan's hip. The blonde scooted even closer to her lover, pressing their bodies together and draping her leg over Keefer's. "Morning," she whispered.

The sound of Fifi's tail thumping against the mattress made them both smile.

"Morning to you, too," Sheridan said to the dog. "Move, Feefs, I gotta get up." She nudged the dog with her elbow.

Keefer groaned in protest, pulling Sheridan's leg tighter around her.

"Baby, I gotta go. The kids," the blonde explained, not really wanting to leave the warmth of Keefer's skin.

Keefer let go of Sheridan's leg and grunted her disapproval. "Mmm...okay. I'll miss you," she grumbled.

Sheridan furrowed her brows as she climbed over Fifi, who wasn't being compliant either. The two of them, both the dog and human, made it very hard for Sheridan to leave in the morning. She stood by the door and gave a final glance to the bed. Keefer had the covers over her head and the blonde swore that Fifi raised her eyebrow at her, just to make her jealous, as she stretched and got comfortable again.

Work was nearly completed and the day had been easy for the construction worker. They were basically finished with their end of the job and all that was left was clean up in preparation for the carpenters and decorators. Usually, Sheridan was eager to leave job sites at that point, ready to take on a new project, walk into an empty shell and create. That building was different—it held memories. She'd met Keefer for the first time in that very room. A smile formed on her face as she thought of the first moment she ever laid eyes on the inspector, and she laughed quietly. *She shoulda slapped me silly with the way I behaved.*

"Hey, Patch, what are the plans for Saturday?" Phil asked, suddenly standing behind Sheridan.

The blonde popped from her daydream and turned around to face her friend. "Oh, yeah." She paused, trying to concentrate on the conversation. "You'll need to truck the plasterboard, but other than that, I got everything covered."

"You gotta give me the address," Phil said while looking around at the finished room.

"You'll meet me at Pop's house, I need to pick up some stuff and Steven first. How's about nine?"

"Cool. I'll be there."

The two of them stood in silence with Phil smiling somewhat idiotically at the blonde. Sheridan gave him a quizzical look, not really wanting to hear what he had to say, but knowing he'd say it anyway.

"So," he threw an arm around Sheridan's shoulders, "how's things in the romance department?"

The blonde winced, then gave up with a sigh. He wasn't going to let it drop and she knew it. "Can you cook, Philly?"

"Me?" He laughed loudly. "No." he shook his head rapidly.

"Fuck," Sheridan growled.

"Cooking, Patch?" Bobby asked as he entered the room.

"Yeah. I was going to cook...or something," she admitted in embarrassment.

"Ask your pop, he's a fucking great cook!"

"Oh, yeah. Right. Hey Pop, help me be romantic for my girlfriend," she said sarcastically.

"Well...I think he'd be happy to help," Bobby said.

Sheridan frowned. "Aw, shit. You're right," she admitted. She stood quietly in thought for long moments before taking a deep breath and blowing it out loudly. "Well, guys, I'm outta here." She walked over to Phil and held out her hand, "Job well done, buddy." They shook hands with big smiles on their faces.

Bobby held out his arms and Sheridan narrowed her eyes. "You just wanna cop a feel, you pig," she accused playfully.

"Damned right!"

She chuckled evilly as she leapt at him. The startled man had no choice but to support her by her ass cheeks as she wrapped herself around him.

"Cop as many as you can, you fucking perv."

Phil laughed so hard that Tony came running into the room. His eyebrows rose at the display before him as Sheridan started moaning and writhing, and he laughed himself silly.

Bobby let go of Sheridan's ass like his hands had been burned, but she clung to him like a leech. He took a few steps forward before snickering too. "Of all the dreams I've had like this, you laughing morons never once appeared."

Sheridan barked out a laugh and slid off Bobby to her feet. "Was it good for you?" She wiggled her eyebrows and wiped imaginary sweat from her forehead.

"You're such an asshole, Patch," Bobby chuckled.

The blonde grinned, then looked around again. "Really, guys, we did a great job...we should be proud. I hope I get to work with you fuckers again soon," she said, suddenly serious.

"Same here. It's not as much fun without you," Tony added.

Sheridan smiled at the compliment, then pointed at Phil. "I'll wake your ass up Saturday morning."

Phil nodded. "I'll be up, don't worry."

Sheridan took one final look around the room that held such memories, then left.

Keefer walked Fifi around the block distractedly. She was a little uptight that Sheridan hadn't called her when she got in from work; it was like some sort of ritual had been broken between them and it was disturbing to her. It wasn't that she was angry with Sheridan for not calling her; rather, she had come to expect it and when it didn't come, she'd been disappointed. She took Fifi into the house and checked the answering machine. Nothing.

The inspector sat down on the couch, releasing a heavy sigh. She wanted to call Sheridan, but she didn't want it to seem like she was checking up on her—like Danni had constantly done to her. It had driven her crazy and she didn't want to do that to Sheridan. *Then again, maybe I should. Maybe something happened...oh, my god...what if she got hurt at work?* Keefer began to panic. *No, wait, she told me there was no work left...unless...you never know what can happen at a construction site!*

Sheridan was standing side by side with her pop in front of the stove, watching carefully as he added spices to his sauce.

Steven was sitting at the kitchen table, snickering at his sister's back. "I can't believe you're wearing an apron, Sher."

"Bite me."

"Hey."

"Sorry, Pop—wait! How much of that did you throw in there?" she asked in frustration.

The older man snickered. "Honey, why don't you just take her to a romantic restaurant?"

Sheridan huffed. "I can cook," she insisted.

Mr. Landers shook his head with a knowing grin. *Stubborn as ever.* "Then why don't you cook something you already know how to do?"

"I don't think Keefer would appreciate SpaghettiOs and toast."

"Cool! I like that," Steven said from behind his sister.

"Stop hovering, your breath smells." She stuck her ass out and butted her brother in the legs.

"Does not," he said, purposely breathy.

"Quit it or you're not helping me Saturday."

Steven retreated to the chair and folded his hands.

"I thought so," Sheridan said, proud of herself.

"Stop teasing him, Sher. Why is it you two become a couple of children when you're together too long?"

Sheridan shrugged. "He's easy." She turned to meet her pop's disapproving glare, then to face her suddenly angelic brother. "You know I love you, don't ya, Stevie-boy?"

His face lit up. "But of course. You can't help it, I'm too cute," he said innocently.

Sheridan narrowed her eyes, biting back a snappy reply. Instead, she turned back around to face the stove. "You know, Pop...maybe you could cook and I'll bring it over."

The older man smiled, knowing she was going to ask sooner or later. "That's cheating, honey."

"Yeah, but—"

"Yeah, but nothing. Look, cook her something easy, like a steak. She eats meat, right? Everyone knows how to slap a steak on a grill or a broiler."

Sheridan suddenly perked up. "Yeah! You're right!" she said excitedly. "I know how to make steak, I even know how to make mashed potatoes, that's easy!"

"Throw a few ears of corn in a pot of water and you've got a meal."

"Thanks, Pop!" Sheridan couldn't get the apron off fast enough, and then she kissed her pop on the cheek. Her phone rang and she instantly realized that she had forgotten to call Keefer earlier. "Shit," she hissed to herself when she saw the incoming call was indeed Keefer. She suddenly felt awful. *She must have thought the worst after what Danni put her through—fuck, and especially after what I did at the club that night.* She grimaced as she hit the talk button. "Hi, baby," she said guiltily.

Keefer was so relieved to hear her lover's voice that she blew out a breath into the receiver.

"Ooh, is this a dirty phone call?" Sheridan joked, leaving the kitchen to find privacy.

"I was worried when you didn't call."

"I'm so sorry; I didn't think."

"No, it's okay, as long as you're all right. You are all right, aren't you?"

"Yeah, I'm fine. I just forgot. I'm really sorry, but don't ask me why I forgot...it's a secret."

"A secret, huh?" Keefer said calmly.

"Yeah," Sheridan replied with a nervous chuckle.

"I'll be patient. You know I like surprises," Keefer said, her voice dropping an octave as she added, "especially your kind of surprises."

"Oh, baby," Sheridan groaned. Keefer's voice sounded so sexy that her knees went weak.

"So, will I see you tonight?" Keefer asked hopefully.

"Certainly. The boys, and I are all fed and walked, and I can't imagine being anywhere else tonight."

"I'll be waiting for you."

Sheridan pulled into the driveway and turned off the car. Keefer's front door was open and the smiling brunette was leaning on the doorframe, Fifi waiting patiently by her feet. "Why, if it isn't my two favorite girls," the blonde said as she approached the house. Once she got to the door, she stood on her toes to reach Keefer's lips. She raised her eyebrow at the expression she spied on her lover's face before their lips met. Pulling back, she studied Keefer's face. "What are you grinning like that about?"

Keefer walked into the house and beckoned Sheridan to follow. The blonde pursed her lips. *She's hiding something,* she thought as she stood in front of her tall lover. "Why do you look like that?" she asked as all sorts of things ran across her mind.

"I have something for you," Keefer said shyly and held out her closed fist.

"Well," Sheridan indicated Keefer's fist, "it's smaller than a breadbox."

Keefer nodded and ducked her head in embarrassment.

Sheridan was intrigued. She peeled open her lover's hand and found a set of keys. Her eyebrows furrowed for a second before it dawned on her. "The keys?" she asked. "To this house?"

Keefer nodded and smiled. "You know, you leave so early in the morning and sometimes, when you go out to the club, maybe you'll want to come here afterwards..." Keefer explained, slightly flustered.

"Keef, this is so cool," Sheridan beamed, holding the keys in a tight grip. Keefer trusted her—despite her reputation, despite the way she'd acted the other night, despite Danni. Keefer trusted her.

Keefer shrugged. "The other night when you came over, I was in the den. I was so comfortable that I didn't want to move, but I had to get up to let you in. It sucked."

"Thank you," Sheridan said with a happy grin, plopping herself on the couch with her arms open wide. "Now come here and let's get a proper kiss."

Keefer giggled and straddled Sheridan's lap. She hummed when their lips met and once again when their tongues touched. When the kiss ended, she rested her head on Sheridan's shoulder and played with the hair at the back of her lover's neck. At first, she'd been hesitant to give Sheridan the keys, afraid that she would panic from the blatant symbol of the next step in their relationship. Instead, Sheridan looked genuinely excited and Keefer was thrilled with her response.

"Hey," Sheridan whispered into Keefer's hair, "I have no work tomorrow. I don't have to get up at the crack of dawn."

"Who the hell is Dawn?" Keefer joked, earning a chuckle from her lover. "No more? It's finished?" Keefer raised her head to look at Sheridan's face.

"Yep. Until the next job, but most days I'll be hanging around Pop at the office, driving him nuts."

"Do you feel sad?" the tall woman asked, tracing Sheridan's jaw line with one finger.

"A little. That building was special." Sheridan reached up and tucked some stray hairs behind Keefer's ear.

Keefer smiled and placed a loving kiss on Sheridan's lips. "I know. Every time I pass it, I'll smile."

"Me too," Sheridan agreed.

The brunette suddenly grinned. "You mean I get to cuddle with you for that extra hour in the morning?"

Sheridan grinned back. "Oh, yeah, among other things."

Keefer successfully fought a blush. "Nice," she purred. "Very nice."

Sheridan cocked her head in surprise at her lover's response. "Well, someone forgot to blush."

Keefer wiggled her eyebrows. "I think I have that under control now."

Sheridan's eyes narrowed. "We'll see about that," she dared, startling Keefer by standing up and carrying her to the bedroom.

Even though she didn't have to get up, Sheridan's eyes popped open early the next morning. Keefer's back wasn't facing her as it usually was; instead, the tall woman was sprawled out on top of her, her face buried in Sheridan's neck. The blonde closed her eyes again and draped her arm loosely across Keefer's back, concentrating on the places where her sleeping lover's naked, warm skin met her own. A smile spread across Sheridan's lips and she sighed happily, moving her fingers slightly back and forth across Keefer's back.

"Mmm. Don't stop," Keefer mumbled into Sheridan's neck.

"I like this, Keef," the construction worker said, her fingers moving across a wider expanse of skin. Lying there in the morning with Keefer on top of her was her new favorite feeling.

"Me too," the brunette said sleepily. "I'm getting goose bumps."

Sheridan lifted her head up slightly to investigate. "Yeah, I can see them." Her head fell back down and Keefer snuggled her face back into her neck.

"Why are you up?" the inspector asked with a frown, although Sheridan couldn't see it.

"I dunno," she shrugged. "Maybe I woke up so I could do this," she suggested, her fingers now running the length of Keefer's back.

"Good reason." The brunette shivered a bit when her lover's rough fingertips traveled across her ass.

"I better stop," Sheridan said, resting her hand on Keefer's butt cheek. "You have to get ready for work."

Keefer whined and turned over onto her back to stretch, then settled down with her arms folded behind her head. "What are you going to do all day?" she asked, her eyes still closed.

"First and foremost, I'm going to spoil the dogs rotten. I'm gonna take them to the park for hours and then, once they're filthy and tired, I'm gonna get 'em groomed." The blonde sat up and looked down at her lover's face. "Are you coming straight home tonight?"

Keefer's eyes opened and she gave Sheridan an odd look. "Where else would I go?"

"Just asking," Sheridan shrugged.

Keefer spied a slight bit of nervousness in her lover. "What's wrong?"

"Nothing. I just wanted to know, is all."

"Will you be here?"

"Oh, you bet," the blonde said with a smirk.

Keefer narrowed her eyes. *She's up to something,* she thought as she sat up and started to face the day.

Sheridan watched in admiration as Keefer walked out of the room naked. She chuckled cockily. Only a few days earlier, she would have taken the blanket with her. *Way to go, Sher, she's finally loosened up.*

True to her word, Sheridan took the dogs to the park. For hours she ran, chased, played, wrestled, and tugged with them, only stopping when they wanted to. She changed her mind about sending them to the groomer's. After having felt like she'd neglected them for so long, the last thing she wanted to do to her guilty conscience was to leave them at the groomer's for any length of time. Deciding to instead do it herself, Sheridan loaded the smelly, dirty, sweaty dogs into her car and took them to her pop's house to wash them in the back yard. She had no idea Steven was going to be home until she got there and the dog washing became full-out water fights between the two siblings, and the dogs had a mighty good time of it, too.

After a calming phone call to Keefer, and finally getting Steven to settle down enough to let her leave, the blonde headed back home with two sparkling-clean dogs. Once home, she paced the floors. It was still too early to begin dinner and she was full of nervous energy. "I could go shopping now," she told Zeus, who was snoring exhaustedly on the couch. "The again, what am I going to do with the food while I wait for five o'clock?" Sheridan turned on the television, but nothing interested her. She was too excited about presenting her girlfriend with her first-ever attempt at a romantic dinner. Her leg shook uncontrollably as she flipped through the channels distractedly. She glanced over to the weight bench and raised her eyebrows. "Now there's an idea."

The blonde worked out hard, efficiently burning off the excess energy and eating up the time so that she had just enough time to get into the shower and go food shopping.

Sheridan didn't go to the supermarket; instead, she went to the butcher shop for the first time. After swallowing her pride and asking for help, she was surprised to learn that a good steak was expensive, and on her way out, she glared at the cashier, warning her that they had better be good. She wandered around until she found the perfect vegetable stand and had the owner pick out the best two ears of corn. He even threw in a lesson on how to peel away the outside without leaving all the stringy things Sheridan hated. Potatoes were easy and she grabbed two of those all by herself. There was still one more stop on her agenda, and that was the bakery—not just any bakery, but Brooklyn's famous Mona Lisa Bakery. She cursed under her breath as she forgot how crowded the place usually was and reluctantly took a number and waited.

The construction worker smiled happily as she put her own key in the door to Keefer's house. Fifi was so surprised to see Sheridan entering and not her mommy that she began to carry on, barking excitedly as she hopped on her back legs for attention. "Feefs! My best girl!" the blonde yelled and the dog went crazy, emitting silly noises and dancing around her legs, her tongue licking at the air wildly, hoping to catch a bit of Sheridan somehow.

Sheridan chuckled as she shuffled toward the kitchen, arms laden with bags, afraid she'd trip over the exuberant dog. "I got something in here for you," she said in a voice she only reserved for dogs. "Yes, I do, and if Mommy says so, I'll even give you steak, too!" she said, squatting down and picking Fifi up in her arms. The dog gave Sheridan a bath, licking her face and neck excitedly. "Aw, who am I kidding, even if Mommy says no, I still have steak for you." She pursed her lips and let Fifi lick them. "I have a big, fat, juicy, new barbecue-favored rawhide bone in here, guaranteed to keep you busy for at least an hour."

Fifi didn't understand a word of what Sheridan was talking about, but as long as she used that special voice, the dog knew it was exciting and she wiggled and squirmed.

Sheridan put the dog down and went to the bathroom to wash her face. "No offense, honey, but your mother wouldn't appreciate if I let her kiss these lips after you slobbered all over them."

Fifi wasn't offended. In fact, she stood in the doorway, ears on alert, waiting for her favorite human—besides her mommy—to come back and play. Instead, Sheridan went to the phone for her afternoon Keefer fix. Once she was done, she headed back into the kitchen.

"You know, Pharaoh wasn't all too pleased to give up his bone, but once I mentioned your name, he gave in. I think he has a little crush on you."

The dog wagged her whole body as Sheridan began to empty her packages. She smelled meat, and that was terribly thrilling to her.

Sheridan started looking through the cabinets under the sink for pots and spotted a small bag of charcoal briquettes. She stopped what she was doing and looked thoughtful. "Hey, Feefs, isn't there a grill out on the porch?" She went to the door and peeked outside, spotting the grill she had been sure was there. "Bingo!" Upon closer inspection, Sheridan frowned deeply. "This hasn't been used in a hundred years. Damn, it needs a good scrubbing!"

She contemplated it for a whole second and a half before she dragged the parts inside and pulled on the yellow gloves. "Don't tell anyone you saw me wearing these, girl, it would kill my rep," she said over her shoulder, steel wool in hand.

By the time Sheridan washed the grill, seasoned the steaks, peeled and salted the ears of corn, and scrubbed the potatoes, she was exhausted. She put the steaks on the grill, partially nuked the potatoes and left them and the corn on the side of the grill before she sat down heavily on the stoop. "Damn, I'm wiped! Too much today, Feefs," she told the dog, who sat down next to her. Sheridan leaned her head on the stair post and yawned.

When Sheridan next opened her eyes, there were flames coming from the grill. "Holy shit!" she yelled, jumping up and running over to the fire. The lid was too hot to touch and she ran inside to get a towel. Opening the grill, she growled as she saw the two steaks engulfed in flames. She beat the fire down with the towel and stuck the fork in one steak, running it to the kitchen sink, then did the same with the other.

"Fucking hell!" she screamed as she walked back onto the porch. The potatoes were covered in two battalions of ants, and a fly, three bees, and a stray cat were sharing one of the ears of corn. Her beloved Fifi, her best friend, was happily gnawing on the other. She narrowed her eyes at the dog and growled angrily, "Now what do I do?" She stomped her foot in frustration, sticking her head back into the house to look at the clock. "Five forty-five?" she gasped. "Dammit! I gotta clean this shit up before Keefer gets home!" She passed by Fifi and snatched the corn from her mouth. "Gimme that, you traitor."

Chapter 37

Keefer stared out the window on the subway in thought. Sheridan had sounded so strange during their last phone call, and she didn't know what to make of it. In the past, when Danni sounded like Sheridan did, she was hiding something, and the something usually wasn't good. The brunette's stomach ached with nerves. She didn't want to think bad things, but ever since Sheridan had mentioned a secret, Keefer had been nervous. She trusted Sheridan; at least she thought she did. *Why do I feel like this if I trust her? She wouldn't hurt me...would she?* The tall woman frowned at herself. *This is ridiculous. Sheridan is allowed to have secrets. God knows she's not Danni. I really love Sheridan, with every part of me. I trust her.* Keefer stood up with an air of confidence, even though there was that tiny little bit of doubt still in her mind. She looked out of the window as the city passed by and sighed. *I love her, and I trust her,* she thought again with a determined nod of her head. The conductor bellowed over the loudspeaker that the train was going to skip some stops as it went express and the tall woman smiled. She really wanted to get home and this was a good thing.

Arriving at her house earlier than usual, Keefer stepped on the porch and looked around in confusion. "What?" she asked out loud as she spotted the cover to the barbeque on the floor, the grill missing and the charcoal burning. Her brows furrowed as she noticed the potatoes, covered with all sorts of insects eating their fill. Keefer was puzzled and put her ear to the door and heard Sheridan's muted cursing. She stepped back and thought for a second, letting her gaze wander over the cooking utensils on the side of the grill, and the strange cat eating an ear of corn. A chuckle escaped her and she had to cover her mouth so she wouldn't guffaw out loud. She tiptoed over to the window and peeked in, but was unable to get a clear view of the kitchen except for the doorway. When she saw her lover running back and forth in front of the doorway with a scowl on her face, she had to run away for fear of divulging her presence.

Keefer stifled another laugh. It was painfully apparent that Sheridan had been attempting to cook dinner and had failed miserably. The doubt that had previously tickled her senses disappeared quickly, to be replaced by a warm, loving feeling. She had the urge to run inside and hold her lover; she felt oddly protective, but she knew Sheridan's personality would not allow her to do so. A second cat came upon the first one and the first one growled. Keefer snickered. *What could have gone wrong? She must know how to use a grill!* She put her ear to the door and heard the water running and decided it was a good time to sneak in. She entered quietly, which was easy since the door was unlocked and Fifi could usually hear her keys a mile away. She snuck toward the kitchen and saw the grill in the sink, steam billowing from it as the water hit the hot metal. Sheridan was holding a humongous rawhide bone in front of Fifi.

"See this yummy, delicious, juicy bone?" The construction worker allowed Fifi to lick it and the dog's tail wagged furiously, then Sheridan took it away and held it over her head. "Well, it's going to stay up here," she put it on top of the fridge and the dog's tail fell down, "until you apologize for eating the corn." Fifi lay down and sulked.

Keefer bit her lip. Fifi would do anything for an ear of corn and Sheridan must have found that out the hard way. The blonde turned toward the sink and stabbed what appeared to once have been meat with a fork.

"Stupid steak. Shoulda took her to a restaurant," she groused as she tossed the steak in the garbage. "To think, I thought I could be *romantic*," she pouted. "I'm such a loser. The guys were right."

Keefer frowned and backed out of the house as quietly as she had entered. She sat in a chair on the porch and thought about what to do. Letting Sheridan know she was there would devastate the construction worker. Keefer pursed her lips in thought and then smiled. She stood up and shook her head. *Bless her heart, poor thing. I'll fix it.* She walked a few blocks away and stopped at a pay phone to call Sheridan. She told her lover that her train had gone out of service and that she was waiting for another one to arrive and would be about a half-hour late. *That should give her enough time.* Keefer's belly rumbled. Barbeque would have been good. She smiled. *I bet she never did that before for anyone.* The thought warmed Keefer's heart. She could hear the tremendous relief in her lover's voice when she ended the phone call and she wondered what Sheridan was going to do.

Caution: Under Construction

The tall woman settled on a bench in the park and pulled her "subway" book from her bag. *She doesn't have to try and impress me...I'll have to bring that up sometime. For now, though, I'll just wait.*

Several moments later, Keefer closed her book and smiled. She couldn't concentrate on the story—Sheridan kept popping into her head. Her blonde lover was so full of surprises, and she couldn't wait to see what was in store for her when she got home again.

Usually, if Keefer was going to be late or was stuck somewhere, Sheridan was in her car and on the way as soon as she hung up the phone. However, this time, immediately after hanging up the phone with Keefer, the blonde called the local diner and ordered two dinners as fast as possible. She did a victory dance before returning to her cleanup duties. "A half-hour, Feefs! We got time!"

She ran around like a chicken without a head. She took the trash outside to leave no evidence of her disaster and had moments to spare as she sped to the diner to pick up her order. She tipped the host rather generously for helping her out and hurried back to the house. She faltered a bit as she approached the door, suddenly worried that Keefer might have already come home. She rang the bell and Fifi started barking; she waited a little longer before putting her key in the door and letting herself in.

The tall woman was very surprised to find her house smelling the way it did when she got back. It no longer smelled like charred meat and smoke, but like food. Mouth-watering food. Her stomach let its emptiness be known the minute she closed the door behind her. Fifi was lounging on the living room floor, gnawing happily on the big bone, and Keefer smiled at Sheridan's punishment tactics. "Hey, I'm home. What smells so good?" she asked as she tossed her bag on the couch.

"Hiya, babe."

Sheridan suddenly appeared by Keefer's side and the tall inspector leaned down for a kiss. Her lover was sweaty and nervous and Keefer felt bad. She wrapped her arms around the small woman and hugged her silly, burying her face in the damp neck. "Mmm, you smell sweaty, what have you been doing?"

"You'll never know if you keep breathing on my neck."

Keefer laughed and stood back. "Why does it smell so damned good in here?" she asked as she entered the bathroom to wash her hands, Sheridan right behind her.

"I tried to make dinner."

"It smells like you've succeeded."

"Uh, not really." Sheridan looked at her feet.

417

"Come on, it can't be all that bad. What did you make?"

"A mess," Sheridan chuckled and took Keefer's hand to lead her into the kitchen. "This," she gestured to the table, "is your romantic dinner, Keef."

Keefer took in the rose and the candles, the wine and the food, and wanted to cry. She had no idea how her lover had managed to clean up the disaster that had been her kitchen, but she had, and she made it all so sweet. "Oh, Sher, it's beautiful."

"Sit, Keef, you must be starved. I know I am."

Keefer allowed Sheridan to pull out her chair and watched as the construction worker poured some wine for her.

"You don't mind if I have a beer, do you?" Sheridan asked, holding up a bottle.

"Anything you want," Keefer replied, a huge loving smile on her face. "This is so sweet, Sher. Thank you."

"Aw, don't thank me, just eat."

The tall woman inspected the plate of food. It was very apparent that Sheridan had ordered this from a restaurant, but that didn't make one bit of difference to Keefer. Sheridan was just as adorable as she'd ever seen her, smiling somewhat shyly as she studied her beer bottle. She was probably deciding whether or not to tell her that she hadn't cooked it, and Keefer found it cute. "This is so sweet. No one's ever done this for me before."

Sheridan's eyebrows went up. "No one?"

Keefer shook her head as she stuck her fork in her salad. "Nope," she smiled, "you're the first."

"Then maybe I should tell you that I didn't cook this."

"Do you really think that matters to me?" Keefer asked before filling her mouth. "Mmm, I love French dressing. You don't miss anything."

"It doesn't matter that I didn't cook it?" Sheridan asked, a little frustration in her voice.

"Why should it? It's the thought that counts. You got all my favorites here, that's all that matters. You pay attention to me—you remember the little things, like salad dressing. That means even more than if you cooked something."

Sheridan chuckled. "Keef, you have no idea what I went through today." The blonde cut into her chicken and made a kissy sound.

Keefer watched as Fifi came running to her lover and accepted the bit of food happily. "I thought you spent the day with the dogs?"

"Something like that," she snickered. "Is it good?" she asked as Keefer sampled some of the chicken.

"Fantastic. Thank you, sweetheart." Keefer winked at her satisfied lover. "To tell you the truth, if the dinner's this good, I can hardly wait for dessert."

Sheridan's eyes narrowed at the implications. "Oh, yeah."

They ate in silence, alternately smiling shyly at each other, lost in their own thoughts for quite some time before Keefer cleared her throat. "So, what did you wind up doing all day?" she asked innocently

Sheridan shrugged and swallowed a healthy gulp of beer. "Took the dogs out for a long time, then I went to Pop's to wash them. Stevie was there and we had a small water war."

"Sounds like fun. I'm jealous. I sat in my office and worked all day." Keefer stared into the flame of a candle and smiled. Even if Sheridan hadn't cooked the food, it was romantic to be sitting here in the semi-darkness, drinking wine and eating dinner. "That's all you did?"

"Well, actually..." The blonde got up from the table and went to the fridge for another beer. She opened it and drank some before replying. "I did a few other things."

Keefer scraped her chair along the floor as she pushed away from the table. She motioned for Sheridan to come over to her, and when she got close enough, Keefer wrapped her arms around her waist. "Like what?" she asked, resting her cheek on her lover's full belly.

Sheridan's head dropped forward and she rested a hand lightly on the back of Keefer's neck. It felt good to be so relaxed after such a hectic day. "I went shopping...all over Brooklyn. I tried to grill us a dinner."

Keefer smiled, turned her head, and kissed Sheridan's stomach before looking up at her with innocent eyes. "*And?*"

Green eyes turned bashful as they stared into bright blue. "I fucked it up. Bad."

Keefer lifted the bottom of Sheridan's shirt out of her pants and rested her cheek on the bare skin. It was warm and smelled sexy, and she closed her eyes in bliss. "You know, I never expected this. Just knowing that you tried to do something romantic is enough for me," Keefer said quietly from her comfortable spot. She moved her head again to kiss Sheridan's ribs, then leaned back in her chair and looked up. "Actually *doing* it was the nicest thing anyone ever did for me."

Sheridan blushed slightly and squatted down between Keefer's legs. She rested her beer bottle on her lover's thigh and seemed to be studying it as she spoke. "You wouldn't have thought so, had you come home on time."

Keefer ran her fingers through the blonde's hair, scratching her scalp lightly, in the way she knew Sheridan loved. "I doubt that you could ever disappoint me."

Sheridan looked distressed. "Don't say that, Keef. You don't know. I may disappoint you one day—even if I don't want to."

Keefer smiled reassuringly. "Shh, it's okay. I know it would never be deliberate."

Sheridan seemed to relax some and leaned her head into Keefer's fingers. "If you keep doing that, I'll fall asleep right here and we'll never get to dessert."

"That's all right. I think you need this."

Sheridan nodded and sighed happily. Keefer knew just what she needed, she always did, and it made the construction worker smile, but she was serious—she was ready to fall asleep. She suddenly stood up and held out her hand. Keefer took it and allowed Sheridan to pull her out of the chair. The blonde blew out the candles and turned Keefer around to face the doorway. "To be continued in the living room."

"I can clean up, honey."

"Nope." Sheridan shook her head, "I've really gotten quite good at cleaning today. You go change into comfy clothes. I'll be right in...to feed you dessert."

Keefer's belly tingled at that idea. She followed instructions and when she sat on the couch in her pj's, a thought occurred to her. "Hey, what about the kids?"

Sheridan walked into the living room with two plates and a box of pastries. "Stevie is going to walk them tonight. I think he's even going to sleep at my apartment. I'm all yours."

Keefer chuckled at the grin on her lover's face. "Kick off those shoes and come here." She patted the couch next to her as she peeked into the bakery box.

"I'll do one better." Sheridan grinned from ear to ear as she started to take off her clothes.

Keefer watched in appreciation as her lover stripped down to her underwear. "You're absolutely right. Much better," she said with an uncontrolled leer.

Sheridan reached over to the box and pulled out a fingerful of whipped cream. "Open up."

Sheridan awoke alone on the couch, with the blanket from the futon covering her. She stretched her arms over her head and turned over onto her side to snuggle down. Fifi must have heard the rustling of blankets, because she trotted over with the giant bone in her mouth. Sheridan grimaced as the dog dropped the rawhide on the floor and jumped up on top of her, covering her face with beef-flavored kisses.

"Pffth! Feefs!" The construction worker scrunched up her face as she fended off the attack.

Fifi finally settled down, lying half on and half off the blonde, looking back and forth between her and the bedroom.

"I don't know either, Feefs. The last thing I remember was lying on your mommy's lap...and then I woke up." Sheridan sighed and mechanically petted the dog as she tried to recall the events that led to her current position.

They'd shared dessert, from each other's fingers, lips, and tongues before Keefer pulled Sheridan's head onto her lap and began running her fingers hypnotically up and down her torso and, eventually, through her blonde hair. Sheridan remembered muttering sleepily about Keefer spoiling her and she remembered her lover's soft smile of reassurance right before she drifted off.

"I think Mommy forced me to sleep last night, Feefs. Hmm...how the hell did she know how beat I was? I know I didn't tell her. She had no idea what really happened in here before she got home." The dog cocked her head to the side and licked her lips. Sheridan began scratching Fifi behind the ears. "It's freaky, really. Sometimes she just knows exactly what I want or need. Even before I know what it is. That should scare me, huh, girl?" The blonde sat up, causing the dog to stand. "Ugh, get off my bladder," she groaned, crawling out from the blankets and making a beeline for the bathroom.

Keefer heard Sheridan talking to the dog, but couldn't make out the actual words. She had slept restlessly without Sheridan spooned up against her and had gotten up numerous times to check on her. Keefer was pleased that her lover slept through the night like a log. *Poor thing was exhausted.*

It had been hard for the inspector to get to sleep at first. With each suck of her fingers, Keefer had become more and more turned on. She had to hide her eyes at times, so her lover wouldn't read the arousal in them. She wanted Sheridan to make love to her so badly, but more than that, she wanted the construction worker to relax. She had even purposely placed Sheridan face up in her lap so the blonde wouldn't smell her. Keefer had finally slid out from under her sleeping lover and gone off to bed. At first, she had toyed with the idea of touching herself to get some relief, but then decided that the wait would make it so much sweeter.

Sheridan glanced at herself in the mirror as she brushed her teeth. Her hair was standing up all over the place and she had creases on her cheek from the couch. She snickered at herself. *No better way to wake up on Saturday morning.* The blonde spit out the toothpaste and panic overtook her. *Saturday!* She ran into the bedroom foaming at the mouth and checked the time. It was 8:15, and she blew out a relieved sigh as she walked back to the bathroom. *Gotta be at Pop's at nine—plenty of time,* she thought as she rinsed out her mouth.

Keefer laughed to herself after Sheridan left the bedroom. She'd almost lost it when her lover came bolting into the room in her underwear, hair all over the place with toothpaste all over her mouth. *She must have just realized it's Saturday. I get my new and improved closet today.* Keefer smiled to herself and turned over to get comfortable once she heard the shower running.

When Sheridan peeked into the bedroom, Keefer was sleeping, and she walked quietly to the bed and kissed her on the lips. "Babe, you have to get up. Me and the guys will be here soon."

Keefer opened her eyes and grinned. "I was just lying here waiting for you to kiss me."

"Oh?" Sheridan smirked and climbed on top of her lover. "Well, then, let me give you a proper kiss," she said before leaning down and devouring Keefer's mouth.

When the kiss finally ended, Keefer hummed dreamily, pulling Sheridan down on top of her for a hug. "You smell so clean and yummy. I don't want you to leave."

"Oh, but I have to. Steven is at my apartment. I have to go get him, shoot by Pop's and then get back over here. Hopefully Stevie walked the boys."

Keefer frowned as her lover crawled off of her and stood up. "I guess I should get up, then."

"Yeah, I don't want either of them seeing you in your nightie," Sheridan chuckled.

"What nightie?" Keefer said playfully as she rolled her naked body out from the covers and stretched long and hard.

Sheridan's jaw fell open and she stopped breathing for a second. "God, woman!" She reached out to grab for her nude lover, but Keefer backed away and walked casually to the bathroom.

"See ya soon, sweetie," Keefer teased, closing the door behind her.

"Fuck." Sheridan closed her mouth and swallowed the drool. "I just got incredibly wet," she told the dog, who had no interest in the conversation.

Sheridan pulled her car in front of a hydrant and blew the horn, hoping Steven would get the message. A few minutes later, the door to her building opened and her brother came bounding onto the street. Sheridan smiled at his enthusiasm, and at his clothes. He was wearing the exact same thing as she was—denim cut-offs, a tank top and a flannel shirt with the sleeves cut off. Work boots and sweat socks finished the ensemble, again for both siblings. She grabbed the paper bag off the floor of the car and handed it to Steven as he sat in the passenger seat.

"Morning, Sher!" he beamed and then looked in the bag "Ooh, for me? Cool!"

Sheridan chuckled as her brother bit into the powdered donut, making a mess. "Coffee's in there, too, just the way you like it."

"Nank oo," he replied around a mouthful.

Sheridan threw a napkin at him and drove off toward her pop's house. "The kids miss me?"

"Nuh-uh. I had 'em out pretty late last night. We played in the park until after dark and then they fell asleep as soon as we got home."

"You know, Pop don't like you running around the park after dark," the blonde scowled. Truth be told, she didn't like it either. Glancing at him, she rolled her eyes. *He's built like a Mack truck, and he had two big-ass dogs with him. Get over it.* "Anyway, I won't tell him, okay?"

"Cool," Steven grinned and turned on the radio. "So, who's gonna be there?"

"We're meeting Philly. He'll follow us to Keefer's and then it's just you and me, kiddo."

"Thank you for letting me help you, Sher, I'm really excited!" Steven suddenly looked scared. "Will Keefer be there the whole time?" he asked meekly.

Sheridan chuckled, "She said she's getting lost today—giving us some working space. You're not disappointed, are ya?"

"No, it's good. I don't want her to see me sweating. Or worse! What if I do something stupid and bleed in front of her? I don't want to be a retard in front of her, Sher!" His voice took on the sound of desperation.

The blonde was grateful for the red light, as it gave her a chance to pull her brother's head up from his chest. "What the fuck is that all about? I don't want you talking like that anymore. Keefer likes you just fine and if you started bleeding in front of her, she'd probably take better care of you than I ever could."

"She wouldn't laugh at me?"

"Never." Sheridan began driving again and turned onto her pop's block. "Besides, if anyone's gonna make a fool of themselves in front of Keefer, it will be me. I get so fucking stupid around her sometimes."

"I think you're in love with her."

"No shit." Not noticing Phil, Sheridan turned off the car and leaned back in her seat. "I'm definitely in love, Stevie-boy."

"Is that good or bad?"

Sheridan turned her head to glance at her brother. "Why do you ask that?"

"Cause when you said it, you looked like it hurt."

"I did?" The blonde raised both eyebrows. "Pay no attention, bud, it's a good thing."

"What's love feel like, Sher?"

"I'll tell ya later, there's Philly."

The small black sports car pulled in front of Keefer's house, allowing Philly's pickup to back into the driveway. Sheridan and Steven got out of the car, Sheridan running to open the front door, leaving Steven to assist Phil in carrying the sheetrock from the truck. "Babe? We're here! Are you decent?" Sheridan called into the house.

"As decent as I'll ever be with you around."

Sheridan blushed. Philly swallowed a chuckle at his friend's discomfort and Steven just fidgeted.

Keefer appeared in the living room and a blush overtook her features when she realized she had shouted that out loud enough for everyone to hear. "You coulda told me they were actually in here," she whispered to her lover.

Sheridan shrugged and drank in Keefer with her eyes. The tall woman was wearing short jogging shorts and a T-shirt, with cute little backless sandals. "Where are you going dressed like that?"

"There's an outdoor flea market a few blocks away, and it's already hot out." The brunette looked at her outfit self-consciously.

"Oh." Green eyes narrowed and Sheridan leaned really close to Keefer. "You look fucking edible right now."

Keefer's eyes widened and her stomach flipped. Her expression turned devious and she bent down to Sheridan's ear. "I went to bed horny last night, and I woke up even hornier this morning."

Sheridan groaned out loud.

Phil cleared his throat—the drywall was getting heavy. "Uh, any time now."

"You are a tease, Keefer," Sheridan whispered.

Keefer bent her head, glanced at Phil and Steven, who looked up at the sky, then planted a nice sensuous kiss on her frustrated lover.

"God, now I'm horny, too."

Keefer grinned playfully. "Suffer a little," she said before walking out the door with an extra sway to her hips. She glanced over her shoulder, saw Sheridan's pained expression, and felt rather cocky about it.

Changing gears quickly, she stopped by Steven and smiled brightly. "Hi, Steven! I'm so glad you're here. Now I know it will be the best closet ever. I'll be back later with lunch for you guys." She kissed him on the cheek and he blushed crimson.

"Hey, where's mine?"

"Fuck you, Philly."

"Just askin'."

Keefer chuckled as she walked away.

Chapter 38

It was apparent that Steven was terribly excited as Sheridan stepped away from the table. She stood back and folded her arms over her chest and smiled as her brother held the straightedge with a white-knuckle grip and slid the X-Acto knife perfectly along the drawn line. "Now, all you gotta do is hold the big piece and hit the smaller one—it should break evenly right along the cut."

Steven poked his tongue out of his mouth and tapped the smaller piece of plasterboard until it hung off the side of the table. A huge self-satisfied smile crossed his face and he looked to his sister for approval.

"Great. Now just slice away the paper and we're set. I'll meet ya inside," she said as she walked back into the house.

Steven puffed up with pride as he cut away the portion of plasterboard and discarded it. He hefted the larger piece up and hesitated at the door. "Hey, Sher, I'm gonna get Keefer's rug all powdery."

The blonde poked her head out of the bedroom and scowled. He was right, they were going to make tracks in and out if they didn't do something about it. "Good thinking. Tell ya what...I got some painter's plastic in my trunk. Leave that wall outside for me," Sheridan tossed him her car keys, "and you can cover a path into the bedroom."

Steven did as he was told and Sheridan took the wall into the bedroom. "I can't believe I didn't think of that," she said to herself. She heard Steven tearing tape from the other room and shook her head. "I didn't even think to tape it down, either," she laughed to herself and then stuck her head out of the room again. "What would I do without you?"

"Get Keefer's house all dirty," he answered literally.

Sheridan laughed again and returned to the task at hand. She was extending the back of the closet into an already existing walk-in closet that was accessible from the hallway. *How lucky was that?* She silently thanked the person who built the two closets back to back. All she needed was a few pieces of wall to make sections, some more closet rods and shelves. Keefer had given her full control of the project, not offering any input at all, claiming that she trusted Sheridan to do a perfect job. It had made the blonde smile at the time, but now she was nervous. Not too nervous, though. *What woman wouldn't like a closet with two different entry points?* she thought to herself. Still, she hadn't shared her idea with her lover and now she was a little anxious, especially after the damage was done and she had knocked down the back wall of the bedroom closet. She heard her brother walking along the newly laid plastic and snapped out of her thoughts.

"All done, Sher. I made a road from the door to the bedroom. OK?"

"That's great, Steven. Let's do the rest of the walls."

"All right! I can do it all by myself. You just have to draw the lines. I'm too nervous and my lines will be crooked."

"Nothing to be nervous about, buddy, it's only me, and I ain't gonna say nothing if your lines are fucked up."

"Keefer will see them."

"Nope. We're painting these babies," she said with a smile. "We need another identical wall, so just take that piece you put on the side and lay it on the new piece. Draw a line on the edge and cut it. I know you can handle that. I'll be inside. Bring it to me when you're done."

Steven beamed with excitement. "Cool shit! Will you tell Keefer I made the walls?"

"Hell yeah." Sheridan went back into the closet and started to draw lines on the walls where she was going to hang the shelves. A short time later, Steven appeared with the new wall. He was dusty and happy, and the blonde felt good at the sight of his proud smile.

"What's next, Sher?" he asked enthusiastically.

"Now I need you to help me cut the shelves. Wanna use the circular saw?"

"Fuck yeah!" he blurted in excitement.

Sheridan smacked him on the back of the neck. "Hey!"

"Why'd ya do that for? You say *fuck* all the time," he pouted.

Sheridan pursed her lips, "Yeah, I guess I do. Just don't curse in front of Pop—he'll kill me."

"Or Keefer! I wouldn't curse in front of her, I promise!"

Sheridan smiled to herself. "Oh, don't you worry about Keefer. She's heard all sorts of trash out of my mouth," the blonde snickered.

"Ooh...do you talk dirty to her?" he asked, genuinely interested.

The blonde shook her head at her brother's question. "Don't ya think that's a little personal, Stevie-boy?" She positioned the plasterboard exactly where she wanted it and stepped back to check it.

"Well, you used to tell me about the other girls," Steven argued, mimicking his sister's actions.

"Yeah, well," Sheridan frowned. "Keefer's different, is all," she replied, leaving the bedroom.

Steven followed her out and found her lifting a piece of wood from the driveway. He took it from her and took it to the table Phil had left for them. "Why is she different? Is it 'cuz you love her?"

Sheridan didn't answer right away. She took out a piece of paper with the measurements on it from her shirt pocket and unfolded it, studying it. Steven began to look at the paper, too, over her shoulder and she held it up closer to him. "Do me a favor, I'll measure the shelves and you go get the saw."

Steven quickly made the trip to Sheridan's car. "You were supposed to tell me what love is like, Sher. You said you would," he reminded his sister as she put the paper away.

"I did, didn't I," the blonde sighed heavily. "It's not so easy to explain."

"'Cuz I'm slow?" he asked seriously.

"Fuck that, it's because it's hard, that's all." Sheridan pulled the tape measure from her belt and opened it on the wood, drawing lines in the appropriate places. "Go get me another piece. I'll measure it all out and you can cut the shelves."

"Cool!"

Sheridan was content to have the conversation dropped and work in relative silence alongside her brother. The only noise was the sound of the circular saw as Steven slowly and perfectly cut the shelves. Once she was satisfied that he could do the job without supervision, she returned to the closet and started taping off the new walls. Her stomach growled and it made her look at the clock. *Man, it's almost lunchtime. Keefer should be here soon.* "Hey, Stevie! Keefer should be home any second. She said she was bringing lunch, didn't she?"

Steven was at her side with a stack of shelves in his arms. "Yeah, right after she kissed me," he blushed. "I think I love her, too," he said as he put the shelves down.

Sheridan laughed. "Do you feel all warm and tingly inside when she looks at you?"

Steven furrowed his brows. "I can't remember. I don't think so," he replied, still thinking hard.

"Do you smile just because she walked into the room?"

"No. Sometimes I get scared. Do you?" he asked wide-eyed.

The blonde nodded. "Can't help it. Love does weird things to a person."

Steven nodded as if he understood. He did, to an extent. Sheridan had been acting really goofy since she met Keefer. He saw his sister wipe her hands on her shorts and looked at his. "I have to wash up. What if I have to touch her?"

Sheridan snickered, "Maybe you are in love with Keefer, too, Stevie-boy."

"Am not. I don't get tingly."

Keefer approached the wide-open front door and sidestepped the plastic as she entered the house. She stopped in her tracks when she heard Sheridan mention her name. She stayed where she was, listening to the conversation.

Sheridan and her brother were side by side at the bathroom sink, washing their hands. Steven hip-checked his sister and she did it back. "Quit it," she complained half-heartedly.

"Where do you get the tingles?" he asked.

"Everywhere, buddy, everywhere."

"Even in your toes?"

"Especially in my toes," Sheridan teased.

"How does it feel?"

The two left the bathroom and Keefer ducked back out the front door as they sat on the plastic that was covering the living room floor.

"It's a good feeling, Stevie. Sometimes it's scary, but in a good way."

"There's no good scary."

"Oh, yes, there is."

"I don't care if it's good or not, I don't want to be scared. I'm not falling in love."

"You can't stop falling in love. Do you think I would have chosen to be in love? I mean, it scared me to death. I didn't know what was going on at all. I couldn't stop thinking about her, wanting to be with her...shit, I even smelled her in my sleep."

"She sure smells good, too. If I was ever gonna fall in love, it would be with Keefer. She's so pretty."

"She's perfect, Stevie-boy, and don't you forget it."

"Is she pretty naked?"

Keefer blushed hotly from outside the front door.

"Gorgeous, and don't you even think about her naked. Wipe it out of your head right now."

"Is sex different when you're in love?"

"Much better."

"What's the difference between fucking and making love?"

Sheridan rolled her eyes. *Where is Keefer?* "Making love is special. You only do that with someone you love."

"So you do different things when you fuck?"

"No, you pretty much do the same thing...it's just different. The tastes, the smells, the touch..."

"Do you sweat when you make love?"

Sheridan raised an eyebrow, "What the hell kind of question is that?"

"Remember when you brought that girl to Pop's for dinner and you two did it in the bathroom? You were all sweaty."

"It was a hundred degrees that day," Sheridan countered, ignoring the question.

"Does Keefer sweat? I don't think she sweats."

"She sweats, Stevie, she sweats just fine," Sheridan smiled.

"That makes you happy?"

"Oh, yeah. I like her sweat."

"'Cuz you're in love?"

"No, 'cuz I'm in love, I lick her sweat." *Oh, baby, I'd love to lick her sweat right now.*

"Ew!"

Sheridan laughed. "That my brother, is love." *I'm getting way too turned on by this conversation.* "Okay, enough about Keefer's sweat. Where is she? I'm starved."

Keefer stretched out her face to rid herself of the blush. She was sweating and was sure that this would cause a few glances between siblings. She wished there was a napkin in the many bags she was holding, but then thought even if there was, they would hear the bags rustling. She took a deep breath and made a lot of noise on the porch. "Hello?" she yelled as she walked in the house.

"Cool!" Steven jumped up to take the bags away and brought them into the kitchen.

Keefer was still flushed from eavesdropping on the conversation and Sheridan found it very arousing. "Hi, baby," she said, leaning in for a kiss.

Keefer bent her head and met her lover's lips. The kiss started out as a peck, but once the construction worker smelled her lover's perfume, she held Keefer's head in place and deepened it. The tall woman made a small noise in the back of her throat and Sheridan felt the sound between her legs. She broke the kiss and stepped back. "God, I want you so badly right now."

"If your brother wasn't in the next room, I'd let you have me."

Keefer's admission gave Sheridan an arousing tingle in her crotch. "Mmm...as soon as he leaves, baby."

"Are you guys done kissing yet? I'm hungry."

Keefer blushed slightly and Sheridan smiled. "Yeah, we're done," the blonde said with a chuckle.

Steven entered the room with a couple of sandwiches on plates and some beers. "Good, 'cuz I was afraid you'd get all tingly and want to lick her sweat or something."

Sheridan smacked him on the head and looked embarrassed.

Keefer bit her bottom lip and hid her face in her hands.

"What?" Steven asked innocently.

"Nothing, just eat," Sheridan said with exasperation.

They all sat on the floor and Steven put everything down on the plastic. Sheridan examined all three sandwiches, picked the one she liked best and grabbed a beer. "Did you get anything at the flea market?"

Keefer hid a blush and grinned shyly. "It was really crowded, I went to some stores instead."

Steven tentatively took a beer and opened it, glancing at his sister for approval.

"Go on, I won't tell Pop." The blonde looked back at her lover. "What'd you buy?"

Keefer looked at the floor.

"Sexy stuff," Steven said and punctuated it with a loud burp.

"Slob!" Sheridan yelled, backhanding him in the belly. "Where's your manners?"

"I had no idea it would make me burp like that," he said wide eyed.

Keefer smiled, "That's okay, your sister can be quite a pig at times, too."

"Sexy stuff?" Sheridan questioned.

"Oh yeah, really sexy, like the girls wear in the magazines you used to have under your bed," Steven answered.

Sheridan's eyebrows went up, as well as Keefer's.

"Oh, come on, I just read the articles," the blonde defended. Then she looked at her brother. "Why were you snooping in the bags?"

"I was looking for lunch," he said, careful not to drink his beer too fast. He still burped, but quietly. "Excuse me," he announced.

Sheridan looked at her blushing lover and grinned knowingly and excitedly. "Gonna show me what you bought later?"

Keefer nodded and bit into her sandwich so she didn't have to speak. Sheridan chuckled to herself and ate, too.

"Can I see?" Steven asked.

"No!" Sheridan blurted out. "I don't believe it, my brother has a woody for my girlfriend!"

Steven looked between his legs in horror, then relief. "I do not!" he argued. "It's the zipper!"

Keefer couldn't contain her giggles.

"Figure of speech, Stevie. If you really had a woody, I'd have to kill you."

Steven frowned and Keefer elbowed Sheridan.

"So, are you far along with the closet? Can I see it?" Keefer asked to break the tension.

"Yeah! I made the walls! I'll show you!" Steven jumped up and grabbed Keefer by the hand. She fell over backwards and gave Sheridan a hell of an eyeful. Green eyes narrowed as they focused between Keefer's legs and the blonde growled.

Keefer caught the action and looked lustily at her girlfriend as she stood up. "Later."

"Mmm," the blonde hummed.

Keefer couldn't believe the mess in her bedroom—clothes piled up on the bed, shoes scattered all over the floor, and actual rubble inside her now much larger closet. However, through it all, she saw Sheridan's planning and loved the idea.

"I cut this one, and this one!" Steven said excitedly, pointing to each wall. "And I cut all these shelves by myself," he added proudly.

"Well, I'm impressed!" Keefer said with a winning smile. "You did a fabulous job," she added, giving him a hug.

Steven pulled away from the hug in embarrassment and then smiled shyly. He looked again to the closet and nodded to himself. "Yep, it's gonna be cool."

"I have no doubt," Keefer agreed distractedly as she kicked a couple of shoes out of her way. "Where's Fifi?"

"In the den. Do you love Sheridan?"

Keefer turned to look at Steven. who looked back with genuine interest. "Yes, I do."

Steven let out a breath, "Phew. That's good, 'cuz she really loves you. She'd even lick your sweat!"

Keefer feigned surprise. "Really?"

Steven nodded rapidly, "I swear it, that's what she said. I don't think I'd ever want to do that," he said with a sour face.

"Wait until you're in love, then tell me that," Keefer said with a snicker.

"Uh, what's the holdup?" Sheridan called from the other room.

Keefer and Steven walked into the living room and Sheridan couldn't resist reaching out and stroking her lover's bare leg as she passed.

"Behave," Keefer whispered as she sat down on the plastic again.

Sheridan smirked, knowing Keefer wanted anything but for her to behave.

"This is good, Keefer, thank you," Steven said of the sandwich, then took a bite.

"You're welcome," Keefer replied and turned to Sheridan. She opened her mouth to say something when her lover gave her a devious grin and then licked her lips. Words forgotten, Keefer picked up Sheridan's beer bottle and took a healthy swallow, closing her eyes as she tilted her head back. A sudden image of her lover, naked and sweaty, flashed through her mind. Blue eyes popped open in surprise. *Where did that come from?*

Sheridan raised an eyebrow at her girlfriend's change of expression. "You all right?" she asked, taking her beer back from Keefer's hand.

"Yeah. Fine," the brunette said quietly.

Sheridan wasn't about to buy it, but she went back to finishing her sandwich anyway. While eating, she felt Keefer's eyes on her and glanced in her direction. The blonde narrowed her eyes. She knew that look—Keefer was having less than pure thoughts, and she was the object of those musings. Sheridan uncrossed her legs and bent one at the knee, leaving her crotch in full view of her fantasizing girlfriend.

Keefer's heart beat harder as her gaze traveled up the well-defined muscles of Sheridan's bare thigh and stopped between her legs. She had a perfect picture of said area in her mind...wet and open. "Oh, God," she muttered out loud without meaning to.

Sheridan grinned cockily and met her lover's eyes. "Penny for your thoughts," she teased, opening her legs wider.

Keefer swallowed hard to fight her blush and took a deep breath. "Much more than a penny," she said in a deeper voice than usual.

The construction worker's mouth watered at the tone. "Okay!" she announced, standing up suddenly. "Let's get back to work. The sooner we finish..." Sheridan gave Keefer a sexy smirk, and left the sentence unfinished.

"What?" Steven asked, standing up with his empty plate.

"Keefer and I have *business*," Sheridan replied, still staring directly into light blue eyes.

"Business?" he wondered. "You just wanna have sex, oh, make love."

Keefer's eyes widened and she made a beeline for the kitchen.

Sheridan chuckled and patted her brother on the back. "Oh, yeah, and then some," she mumbled. "Go on and start drilling holes where I marked the walls. I'll take the dishes into the kitchen."

Steven smiled confidently and practically flew into the bedroom.

Sheridan snuck up behind Keefer and wrapped her arms around her waist. "I know what you've been thinking, and I approve."

Keefer blushed slightly and turned around in Sheridan's arms. "I don't think you have any idea what I was thinking," she said, still caught off guard by her sudden visions.

"Does it have anything to do with me naked?" Sheridan asked, then leaned forward and inhaled Keefer's neck.

"Very much so," the brunette agreed, closing her eyes as her lover began licking a trail across her throat. Another vision sprung into her head—of Sheridan writhing in bliss, glistening with sweat. She pushed away from Sheridan's mouth and breathed deeply.

"Oh, baby...tell me."

"I keep seeing you, and you're—oh boy, just trying to say it and I picture it. Why is this happening?"

"Keef, at least once an hour, I see you naked," Sheridan said, backing her lover against the counter. "I hear you moaning, I smell your delicious scent." She breathed the last words into Keefer's cleavage.

The inspector shuddered as her nipples tightened from the feel of Sheridan's breath. "Please, Sher..."

Keefer's whimper caused her sex to clench and Sheridan backed away. "The very second Steven leaves, I want you," she said with a growl.

"No, I want you," Keefer half whispered.

"Hmm?" Sheridan asked, raising an eyebrow.

"I want you, I want to make love to you," Keefer said with more confidence than she felt.

Sheridan groaned. "Oh, yeah, Keef, you got me," she purred.

"Sher!"

Both flustered women looked toward the bedroom.

"You'd better go. I'm going to hide in the den—just me and my dog. I can't be around you."

Sheridan smirked. She knew exactly what Keefer was feeling. "I'll be in the other room. Working...flexing...sweating...grunting..."

Keefer closed her eyes and whimpered.

It was as if a fire had been lit under Sheridan's ass and she doubled her work efforts. Steven had no trouble keeping up, but he was curious as to the sudden rush.

"What's the hurry? We have all day."

"Never mind, Stevie-boy. Like I said, Keefer and I have business."

"Yeah, s-e-x," he muttered while avoiding his sister's paintbrush.

The blonde snickered. "Oh, yeah," she growled.

"Why don't you go do it now and I'll finish painting," he asked seriously.

"Well, Steve, this is one of those all-nighter situations."

"You can do it all night?" he asked in surprise.

"Well, girls can...most girls can, anyway," Sheridan answered with a smirk.

"Wow," he said in wonder.

Sheridan climbed over a pile of rubble and frowned. "Hey, why don't you start getting rid of the garbage; there's some trash bags on the porch. Phil is gonna drop by later to load up the shit and take it to the site dumpsters."

"Sure thing."

As soon as Steven was out of the room, Sheridan took off for the den, paintbrush in hand. She opened the door slowly and spied Fifi sleeping on the floor and Keefer relaxing on the futon, eyes closed, a shit-eating smile on her face. "Am I naked again?"

Keefer jumped. "Sheridan!" she scolded.

"Well? Am I?"

Keefer cleared her throat and blushed slightly. "Yes." She stood up and moved toward her lover.

As soon as Keefer was within range, Sheridan wrapped her free arm around the tall woman's waist and pulled her close, holding the paintbrush well out of the way. "Mm...I like the way you think," she said, nuzzling Keefer's chest.

"Sher, get back in that room and finish," Keefer said breathlessly. "The sooner you're done..."

"The sooner I'm naked," she nodded. "I hear ya." Sheridan nipped at Keefer's shoulder and ran into the bedroom.

The brunette leaned on the doorframe and sighed. "I'm like a horny teenager all of a sudden," she complained as she went to the kitchen for a drink. She leaned against the counter and drank slowly, a small grin playing at her lips as she suddenly recalled the afternoon on the couch where she'd had Sheridan at her mercy. Keefer shivered as if she could still feel the blonde's skin under her fingers. The memory of Sheridan as she lay naked, propped up against her chest, her glorious body spread out for Keefer to explore. The brunette closed her eyes as her mind began to replay the movement of her hands. She could smell the scent of the construction worker's skin as she buried her face in her neck, her hands traversing the expanse of flesh, resting in the warm, wet crevice between Sheridan's legs, the blonde's mouth opened...

"Keefer!"

Keefer jumped out of her daydream and dropped the bottle of water on the floor. "Shit!"

"Fifi's out!"

Keefer threw the dishtowel on the puddle of water and took off toward the bedroom. She bent over and grabbed Fifi, who was sporting white paint on her left side, and pulled her out of the closet.

Sheridan smirked at her lover's flushed appearance and couldn't resist fueling her fires.

Keefer gasped as Sheridan's hand slid up the back of her leg and into her shorts. Her gaze darted to Steven, who was happily cleaning up the floor, and then back to Sheridan, who was flashing a crooked grin. She removed Sheridan's hand and narrowed her eyes. "You are in big trouble later," she warned.

The blonde snickered "Hurt me, baby," then smacked her lover on the ass.

Keefer's eyes widened. "So much trouble," she added before taking her dog and leaving. "Come on, Feefs, gotta clean you up." *That should keep my mind occupied for a while,* she thought with relief.

Sheridan watched her tall girlfriend walk out of the room in a bent-over position. She had a sudden urge to run up behind her and thrust into her ass. Her groin tightened and she sighed heavily.

"Whassamatter?" Steven asked.

"Aww, nuthin'," she mumbled as she shook her head. "You wouldn't understand."

"You're probably right, but like Pop says, it don't hurt to talk about it."

"It's not a problem or nothing, it's just that I can't keep my hands off of her and I don't want her to think that's all I want her for. Can you imagine this? Me? Worried that someone thinks I only want them for sex? That's what my whole life was about...before Keefer. I don't want her to think I'm still like that. I love all of her. Of course, being as fucking hot as she is don't hurt things."

Steven looked thoughtful for long moments. He pursed his lips and made a strange sound with them while he thought. "Do you tell her that?"

"What?"

"Do you tell her that you love her for everything and not just 'cuz she's hot?"

"I think so. Maybe. I don't know." Sheridan furrowed her brow. "I should, though."

"Yeah. That way, you're sure she knows."

Sheridan smiled and patted her brother on the back. "You're all right, Stevie-boy. Thanks."

"I am? I mean, yeah." He puffed up. "You're welcome, Sher," he said proudly.

"Come on, now, we're almost done. Philly will be here soon."

"You just want to have sex."

"There's that, too," she smirked.

Chapter 39

Keefer fidgeted restlessly in the den, unable to find a comfortable position as she waited for Sheridan and her brother to finish their tasks. She alternated between staring blankly at the television and conjuring up images of her lover in various compromising positions. Most of the images were of actual instances, some of which were more recent and they gave Keefer curling feelings in her stomach. She never knew her brain could work that way; it seemed that all she had to do was look away from the TV screen and a vision of Sheridan presented itself.

At first, she was a little uncomfortable with the way she was thinking, but as time went on, she got lost in the daydreams and started to really enjoy them. She had never behaved like that before meeting her blonde lover. In fact, she started thinking that way after the day they met. That very night, after inspecting the construction site, she'd begun undressing Sheridan in her dreams.

Keefer paused from her thoughts and sighed out loud. She glanced over at Fifi, who was rubbing her newly cleaned, damp body on the side of the futon. She'd never gotten the chance to bathe the dog properly the previous night and this had been the perfect opportunity to do so. It had taken her mind off of Sheridan for the time being, but now that she was in the quiet of the den, her mind went into overdrive.

Sheridan stood back with her hands on her hips and gave the closet one last look. "I think that's all she wrote, Steven."

"I just gotta vacuum and we're done," he said, standing next to his sister and smiling proudly.

"I'll vacuum...I made most of the mess. Go pull up the plastic," Sheridan instructed and went in search of the vacuum.

Keefer heard the machine going and got a tingle of excitement, knowing the job was completed. Her mouth watered at the thought of finally having Sheridan to herself. Her eyes narrowed as another image of her girlfriend—naked, face down on the bed—assaulted her. "Oh yeah, definitely have to explore the back," she mumbled to herself.

Steven gestured from the doorway, trying to get Sheridan's attention over the noise of the vacuum.

The blonde turned off the machine and raised an eyebrow.

"Phil's here. Want me to start loading up the trash?"

"I'll help him, you finish vacuuming, okay?"

"No problem, Sher."

The blonde stomped her feet on the bedroom rug before walking into the living room. Phil was standing in the front doorway, a cup of coffee in his hands.

"I thought you could use a cup," he said, handing the coffee to Sheridan.

"Thanks! Hey, I appreciate this, I wasn't about to start getting a dumpster," she said, tearing open the little drink flap on the lid.

"Don't worry, it's nothing." Phil shrugged to make his point and hefted a trash bag into the back of his truck.

"At least let me help," Sheridan complained and grabbed for a bag.

"Fuck that, go drink your coffee. We're having a barbecue tonight; all the guys will be there, why don't you come?"

"I dunno..." Sheridan furrowed her brows and looked toward the den.

"She's invited, asshole! Invite the girls, too, it's gonna be the shit."

"Yeah? I can invite the girls, too?" Sheridan perked up. Steven appeared next to her and she offered him some coffee.

"Hey, bud, wanna come to a barbecue tonight?" Phil asked Steven.

"Are you gonna be there?" he asked his sister, after taking a drink.

"Well...I guess so," Sheridan said a little uncertainly.

"Cool! Yeah! I gotta go home and shower first. Tell Pop, will ya, Sher? Tell him you'll be there, too. You have to take me home, is that okay? You and Keefer, I mean. She's coming, too, right?"

"Yeah," the blonde said with a worried look. Steven was very excited about the barbecue; she couldn't say no now. Sheridan looked hesitantly toward the den and grimaced. *Keefer's gonna kill me,* she thought nervously. "Um, you guys finish up out here." Sheridan bit her top lip. "Give me a minute, okay?"

"No problem," Phil said with a conspiratorial wink. "Take your time."

"Yeah." *Oh boy.*

Keefer looked to the door as it opened. She was all fired up and ready for Sheridan to get within reaching distance and was surprised when her lover stood a few feet away with a very guilty look on her face. Her eyes narrowed. "What did you do?" she asked.

"Um. You see..." Sheridan got closer to her lover and kneeled between her legs. "Well, Philly's having a barbecue tonight, and I sorta said we'd go without asking you first."

Keefer blew out a breath. Her plans for the evening were shot to hell. "Really," she said, then pursed her lips in annoyance.

"I'm sorry, but once Steven heard, he was so excited and I couldn't say no." The blonde hung her head and looked ashamed.

Keefer didn't know whether to clap at her lover's performance or kiss her senseless for being such a mushball. She lifted Sheridan's head up and looked in her eyes. "I had major plans for you, Sher."

"God...I know." Sheridan groaned pitifully and closed her eyes.

Keefer shook her head. Sheridan was just as tortured as she was—no sense in punishing her for it. She leaned forward and captured the blonde's lips.

Green eyes popped open in surprise. The last thing she expected was a kiss. Feeling as if she were forgiven, she slid her arms around her lover and sighed happily into the kiss.

Mmm...coffee, Keefer thought briefly, and then groaned quietly as the strong arms surrounded her. She really had plans, and her crotch picked that moment to remind her. She thrust her tongue into Sheridan's mouth and suddenly dug her fingers into the blonde's biceps, knowing that would turn her on completely. *A little torture doesn't hurt...*

"Mmm," Sheridan moaned, climbing up to straddle Keefer's lap, never breaking the delicious kiss.

Keefer dropped her hands to her lover's ass and pulled her tightly against her, making sure Sheridan's crotch made contact with her body. The ensuing growl made her own heightened arousal worth the action.

Sheridan broke the kiss and ground herself into Keefer. "Fuck, baby, you got me all hot and bothered now."

"Too bad we have to go to that barbecue," Keefer said with mock pity.

Sheridan's eyebrows lifted in surprise. "You're doing this on purpose...you're torturing me!" she said as she feigned shock.

"You got that right. Are you all horny now?"

441

"Do you really have to ask?" the construction worker replied with another hip thrust.

"Good, now you're in the same boat as I am," Keefer said cockily. "Time for a shower; we have to go to a barbecue," she added sarcastically.

Sheridan climbed off her lover's lap. "Are you really mad at me?" she asked nervously.

Keefer shook her head and blew out a breath, "No, I'm not mad, I'm just frustrated, and annoyed. I really had plans for tonight. Okay, they weren't terribly pressing plans, they can wait, but it doesn't make it any less legitimate because my intentions were to ravish every square inch of you."

"I know, I really should have asked. Now I feel awful," Sheridan frowned.

Keefer disliked that expression on her lover's sexy face, but pressed on anyway. "Well, I know you don't want to hear me say it, but good. It's not only me who loses out," she said with a sly grin. When Sheridan groaned, Keefer felt justified. "Seriously, Sher, it's not the end of the world. I was just trying to make sure you don't do that again."

Sheridan was relieved and it showed.

"I'm really not mad," Keefer added with a wink. "In fact, I have a sudden urge for barbecue."

Sheridan smiled. "I'll go tell them we're coming. I first have to drive Steven to my house to pick up his things, feed and walk the dogs, then get him home to shower and change. I'll just shower there, too, at the same time, then shoot back here and pick you up, okay?"

"Sounds like a plan," Keefer said with a nod. "Drive carefully. I know you're in a hurry."

"Don't you worry any, I intend on being in one piece for when we get home later."

Keefer waved her hand at her lover. "Go, hurry up."

"Oh! I'm inviting the girls, too!" Sheridan remembered, and then paused in thought for a second. "Keef, this is okay with you, isn't it? I mean meeting everyone at once...I didn't overstep...I mean..."

"I'm nervous, very nervous, but I want to meet your friends. You didn't overstep, but I would appreciate it if you asked me next time. I was used to being dictated to in the past, but I kinda like having the freedom of choice you usually give me."

Sheridan quickly closed the distance between them and hugged her lover. "Fuck, Keef...I'm sorry. I pulled a Danni, didn't I?"

"Never compare yourself to her. Come on, it's no big deal. Get going so I can get into the shower," Keefer said honestly.

"You sure you're okay?" the blonde asked from Keefer's chest.

The tall woman chuckled. "I'm horny, I smell like wet dog and I'm really hungry. Other than that..."

Sheridan looked up into endless blue eyes. "I love you, Keef. You know that, don't you?"

Keefer kissed Sheridan lightly on the lips. "I know. And I love you, too. That's why I'm not mad—now go," she said with a genuine smile.

Sheridan grinned happily and backed out of the room so she wouldn't miss a second of that beautiful smile.

Keefer frowned once Sheridan left the room, and sat back down on the futon. She really was a little ticked, but Sheridan was apologetic and knew she had done the wrong thing right from the get-go. Keefer didn't want to hold a grudge, especially against her girlfriend. *My girlfriend. My sexy, muscular, hot...*

She groaned and held her head in her hands. *I can't even stay mad for a little while,* she complained to herself. Not that she wanted to stay mad at Sheridan, but she had really wanted to prove her point, which she thought she did well. Danni did such things thoughtlessly and without regard for Keefer's feelings; Sheridan only did it because she really didn't want to let her brother down. *There's a big difference there, Keef, let it go. She knew what she did was wrong.*

The tall woman stood up and began to think about the impending get-together. Nervous jitters swam around in her stomach at the thought of being surrounded by all of Sheridan's friends and acquaintances. Her lover was bound to leave her alone at some point to mingle and cut loose, and the idea terrified Keefer. She took a deep breath and pulled out the confidence she had used when she snuck into the club to spy on Sheridan. It took all she had that night, but she managed it and drew from that experience to gather the courage to face everyone. A small part of her suddenly worried that Sheridan might have bragged about their private moments and her legs felt weak, but then she waved that thought out of her mind. *No, I refuse to believe that she could have disrespected me like that.* Keefer grimaced at that sudden thought. *God, Danni really screwed me up, didn't she? Time to throw that garbage out.*

The brunette walked into the bathroom, still distracted by her train of thought, and stared at herself in the mirror. *No more Danni. Period,* she thought confidently. No sooner had she blinked a few times than Danni's laughing face taunted her mind, and she narrowed her eyes at the image. "Get out, you don't belong here anymore," she ground out insistently through gritted teeth. A little narrowing of the eyes and Danni's image blew up in a puff of smoke and Keefer smirked cockily to her reflection. "And stay out."

443

Sheridan drove Steven to her house, walked the dogs quickly, grabbed their necessary belongings and headed out to their father's house. At first, he was hesitant to allow Steven to stay out to all hours, but his son's begging and his daughter's reassurances convinced him to relent. The two siblings showered at the same time, Steven upstairs and Sheridan downstairs, having some sort of unspoken race. When Steven bolted down the stairs, still tucking his shirt into his jeans, Mr. Landers laughed out loud.

"I'm finished!" Steven yelled as he ran past the bathroom.

Sheridan opened the door and a puff of steam escaped. She stuck her head out with her toothbrush in her mouth and grinned. "Ah, but did you brush your teeth?" Steven furrowed his brows and pouted as he stomped back up the stairs. Sheridan shook her ass in triumph.

"Why do you have to do that to him, Sher?"

The blonde spit out toothpaste and rinsed her mouth out. "Aw, Pop, he knows I'm just fucking with him."

Mr. Landers watched his daughter put on her boots and pursed his lips. "He loves to be with you and all you do is tease him."

"That's so not true. He loves to be around me 'cuz I treat him like one of the guys," Sheridan replied defensively.

"Oh, Christ, he'll be drinking, smoking, and swearing by ten o'clock tonight."

Sheridan had the good sense to look guilty. "No, he won't," she replied in a childlike voice.

"I know you love him, Sher, just watch what you do around him. He worships you."

Sheridan felt awkward. "Oh please, Pop, worship?"

"Don't tell me you don't know that," the older man said seriously.

"I know he sorta looks up to me and stuff," she mumbled uncomfortably.

"Well, just be careful, and don't tease him so much."

"You know, I really only tease him when we're home. It must be the house," Sheridan joked.

"Must be, because whenever you two are together here, you both revert back to preschool behavior." He smiled and rubbed his daughter's back lovingly.

"I'll watch him. I always take good care of him." The blonde hugged him and waited for her brother. "Hey, how many teeth do you have?" she shouted.

Steven came downstairs with a bounce to his step. "I put on cologne." He stuck his tongue out. "Did you?" he teased, waving the scent from his neck at Sheridan.

"Nope," she frowned, "I didn't. You win, buddy, fair and square."
Steven did a victory dance and high-fived his father.
"Come on before you make us late," Sheridan groused playfully.

After a relaxing shower, Keefer had the opportunity to go through every item of clothing she owned, since all her things were scattered around the room. She put everything in its new and proper place in her brand-new walk-in closet and sat on her bed. Even with everything neatly organized before her, she couldn't find one single thing to wear. She wanted to make an impression on Sheridan's friends and co-workers in the worst way, but she also wanted to be comfortable. She stood up and went through every pair of pants she owned, frowning at them all. Nothing seemed appropriate. *What is Sheridan going to wear?* she wondered. *Jeans and a tank top. What else is she going to wear?*

Keefer rolled her eyes and pulled out her most comfortable jeans and a plain white T-shirt. *There. Totally barbecue-ish.* She nodded at her choice and quickly dressed before she changed her mind. *Feet...shoes...* The brunette was able to look at all her shoes at once with her new closet and after much deliberation, settled on sandals. She contemplated makeup and decided against it, choosing to wear her hair loose as well. *There, I'm totally comfortable, that's one less thing to worry about.*

Sharon had just got off duty and was picking up dinner in the supermarket when Sheridan called her. She was more than happy to chill out with some burgers and beer instead of cooking for herself and promptly told Sheridan so when she accepted the invite.

"So, where's this shindig at? Is Keefer coming?" she asked, putting her frozen dinner back in the store's freezer.

"Yeah, Keefer's coming. It's at Philly's house, you remember where that is?"

"Yeah, I remember where it is—across from the Stop and Shop. I'm glad Keefer's coming; I'd love to see her without drama. See you in about an hour." Sharon flipped her cell phone closed and left the supermarket, unaware that her entire conversation had been overheard.

When she had first seen the cop, Danni made herself scarce, wanting only to shop in peace, but then she overheard the phone call. She came out from behind the display where she had been hiding and frowned. *Keefer's going to a shindig? Willingly? A shindig is more than just a few friends. She has friends now?* The redhead's eyes narrowed. *This I have to see for myself.*

Sheridan called the rest of the girls while she drove to Keefer's and they agreed to meet her, too. She was getting very excited about hanging out with all her friends and Keefer, too. *This is gonna be so cool,* she thought. *And Steven, can't forget to keep an eye on Steven.* She turned to her brother and chuckled. "You know, Pop's worried that I'll corrupt you."

"What's that mean?" he asked with furrowed brows.

"He thinks you'll be smoking and drinking and cursing by the end of the night," she explained.

"Ew, I'll never smoke," he grimaced. "I can have a beer, right?" he asked expectantly.

"Yeah, but just one or two, and watch your mouth around Pop, okay?"

"I never curse in front of him like you do," Steven said seriously. "He'd get mad at you and then I'll feel bad."

Sheridan pursed her lips in thought. "Ya know, Stevie-boy, I'm not the best person to be setting an example, so maybe you shouldn't watch me so carefully," she said quietly.

"Huh?" Steven didn't follow.

Sheridan shifted in her seat uncomfortably. "Well, like, I curse but I tell you not to, and I drink and I tell you not to. Maybe you should hang around with people who will teach you the right stuff."

Steven understood his sister and he felt scared. "You don't want to hang around with me any more?" he asked meekly.

"No! That's not it!" she answered quickly. "It's just that I may not be the best teacher, is all."

"Are you kidding me? You teach me all the best stuff! You teach me how to use tools and cut walls and build things! You taught me how to paint the bathroom, and how to put tiles on a wall, and how to hammer and tie my shoes!" He stopped to take a breath. "You're the best teacher I have, Sher! You don't talk to me like I'm a retard, like the people in the home did, or that stupid school. I like having you teach me stuff!"

Sheridan blushed darkly. "Well...I was just sayin'..."

Steven smiled happily. "I love you, dirtbag."

"Love you, too, asshole." Sheridan put on the radio and smiled proudly, despite her embarrassed blush.

Phil waved his hand wildly when he saw Sheridan's car drive up to his house. "Come on!" he shouted over the din of the music. "Bring that sexy woman over here!"

Steven unfolded himself from the passenger side and Phil frowned.

"Hi, Phil! I'm gonna stay here while Sheridan gets Keefer," he said excitedly, his eyes darting all over the front yard.

Sheridan popped out of the car to nod in agreement. "Keep an eye on him, will ya?" When Phil nodded, she continued, "Hey, and don't say anything stupid like that when Keefer gets here. She's kinda shy and shit."

"No problem. So, you're going to get her now?"

"Yeah, they need some alone time to make kissy-face and goo-goo eyes," Steven teased.

"Ooh." Phil and Tony whistled and hooted.

"Bite me," Sheridan snickered in embarrassment before she got back in her car and drove off.

Keefer was still nervous and almost ready to face the evening. When Sheridan pulled into the driveway, her heart started beating furiously. She took a deep breath and closed the door behind her, hoping the smile she was wearing would convince her lover that she was happy, and not terrified.

Sheridan turned off the car and met her halfway, stopping Keefer in her tracks and stretching for a kiss. They kissed briefly until Keefer pulled away.

"Steven's already there; I thought you and I could be alone for a few. Are you okay?"

Keefer sighed nervously. "Sher, I'm really not comfortable with public displays and I know how you get, especially if you drink...and..."

"Babe, don't worry...I know," the blonde reassured her. "I'll be on my best behavior, I promise. I already fucked up once today." She smiled and blinked rapidly, once again asking forgiveness.

Keefer grinned. "I told you, I'm not mad. Thank you for understanding me."

"Hell, Keef, I don't ever want to do anything to upset you, at least not twice in one day."

Keefer's grin turned into a smile. "I know. Come on, before I chicken out completely."

Sheridan grabbed her girlfriend's arm as she started to walk. "If you don't want to go, we don't have to, Keefer. Don't do something that makes you uncomfortable for my sake. That would really suck."

"No, it's not like that. If I really didn't want to go, I wouldn't. I'm nervous about it, but kind of excited to meet everyone at the same time. I want to know your friends; they make you happy."

"You make me the happiest."

Keefer grinned shyly. "That's the second time you said something mushy to me today. What's gotten into you?"

Sheridan shrugged, hearing Steven's words of wisdom far off in her head. "I just want to make sure you know it. You don't mind, do you?"

The tall woman bent down and kissed Sheridan lovingly. "Not at all. Thank you. Even though I know it, sometimes it's good to hear it."

There were no parking spots left when the couple arrived at Phil's house, making Keefer even more nervous. "There must be a lot of people there," she worried out loud.

"Yeah, you'd think, but it's just that they all have big cars. Dykes love trucks as much as those guys do." Sheridan gestured to Tony and Bobby who were walking over to greet them. "Must be penis-oriented."

Keefer giggled at her girlfriend's statement, then became startled as her door opened suddenly. A large hand, followed by Bobby's face, filled her view and she turned to Sheridan in question.

"'S okay, Keef, Mr. Chivalry over there is Bobby."

The brunette hesitantly accepted the hand and squeaked when Bobby literally pulled her from the car. She blushed as he took a long look at her, up and down, side to side.

"Whoo-ee," he commented with a big grin. "Pleased to meet you, Inspector."

"Keefer, please," she responded, still blushing at his appraisal.

"Bobby, knock it off, you're embarrassing the woman," Tony yelled from the other side of the car, even though he couldn't take his eyes off of her either.

Keefer looked over the car to her lover, who was grinning from ear to ear. *What the heck is that all about?* she wondered of her girlfriend's cocky expression.

Sheridan came around to Keefer and took her hand, leading her away from the guys. "They can't help it, you're too hot to ignore."

Uh-huh. Now I see. "And this makes you feel good, huh."

"Very. Let's go, I want you to meet everyone. You ready?"

"As I'll ever be." Keefer nodded and swallowed.

"Wanna hang back for a while and I'll show you who everyone is before you meet them?" Sheridan asked, halting their movement.

Keefer thought about it. "Yeah, maybe that would be easier, but no, let's just get it over with." She squeezed Sheridan's hand tightly. "Thank you for that, though. You're sweeter than you know."

"Aw, quit it."

Marie and Dawn noticed Keefer immediately and motioned to Sharon. The tall cop walked over to meet the couple and handed Sheridan a beer. "Hi, guys. Glad you came, Keefer, I finally get to meet you under good circumstances." Sharon smiled brightly, making Keefer feel at ease.

"Good to see you again, too," she smiled back, already relieved a little. *If they're all this nice, I can deal with it.*

"Hey, Sher! Over here!" Steven called out from the grill.

Keefer and Sheridan smiled at each other. Steven was wearing a big chef's hat and was manning the grill. They made their way over and Sheridan couldn't resist teasing him. "Hey we've got Emeril on the job tonight!" She snuck up behind him and yelled, "Bam!"

Steven jumped but didn't drop anything. "You suck!" he yelled.

Sheridan narrowed her eyes and looked at Keefer, then thought better of the comment she had. "Yeah, well, made ya jump."

"Phil is letting me cook hot dogs and hamburgers! This is so cool! You want one Sher? Keefer, I made a special hamburger just for you, you want it now?"

"You made me a special hamburger?" she asked in puzzlement.

"Yeah, it's a perfect circle, it looks just like a hamburger is supposed to. The others just look like blobs. When I saw this one, I thought you have to have the perfect one." He pointed at it with the spatula.

Keefer blushed and Sheridan snickered.

"So, you want it?"

"In a minute." Keefer leaned in close to him. "can you keep it safe for me?" she whispered.

Steven nodded solemnly. "Totally."

"We'll be back, Stevie-boy, we're gonna make the rounds," Sheridan said, dragging Keefer off to the rest of the people. "Yo, Marie!"

Keefer braced herself for the girls. They were Sheridan's closest confidantes. They knew everything about the blonde that she didn't know, and then some. She looked at Marie and liked the smile on her face. It wasn't phony or contrived. She was genuinely pleased to see her and it made her smile shyly back.

"Well, hello, Keefer," Marie said sweetly, extending her hand. "Finally, I get to meet the woman who can put Sheridan in her place."

Keefer accepted Marie's hand and shook it briefly. She noted the other woman approaching, also smiling brightly. "So, I put her in her place?"

"Oh, yeah. Taught girlfriend here a few lessons."

"Cut it out," Sheridan scoffed.

Keefer looked to her fidgeting lover and pondered that while the next woman introduced herself.

"Hey, Keefer, I'm Dawn, very pleased to meet you."

"Same here. Sheridan talks so much about you, I feel as if I know you already," Keefer said to the both of them.

"Don't we know it. You fried our girl's brain."

Keefer looked confused.

"That's a good thing, baby," Sheridan said, wrapping her arm around Keefer's waist.

Baby? Oh Lord, both Dawn and Marie thought simultaneously.

"Hey, there's Philly, lemme go say hello. You wanna stay here or come with me?" Sheridan asked Keefer.

"I'll come with you," the tall woman replied, liking the feel of Sheridan's arm wrapped securely around her.

Dawn, Sharon and Marie migrated to a corner and watched their friend and her lover.

"Keefer, in the flesh. Damn, but she really is gorgeous," Dawn said.

"Without makeup, in jeans and a T-shirt. Oh yeah, I can see what got Sher," Marie agreed.

"Yep. She really loves Sheridan, too. I think it's really sweet," Sharon added.

"Do you see how she is with Steven? He practically shines around her," Dawn said with a smile, watching as Steven prepared Keefer a hamburger.

"Like brother, like sister. Sheridan's so fucking gone," Sharon laughed. "Look at her!"

They watched as Sheridan leaned against a tree and watched her lover with a big stupid smile on her face. The blonde never took her eyes off of Keefer, even as she spoke to Phil and drank her beer.

"If it can happen to her, it can happen to all of us," Sharon noted.

"Amen, sister friend," Dawn agreed.

"She's a real looker, Patch."

"Oh yeah," Sheridan agreed dreamily, then suddenly smacked him in the belly "Hey, don't stare at her like that, you pig."

"I'm not! I'm just looking." He snickered at his friend's protectiveness. "Can't help it, anyway. You have one hell of a girlfriend, hon."

"Don't I know it." Sheridan puffed out proudly. "I'll be back," she said and walked off toward Keefer.

Keefer looked up to see her lover approach. "I made you a plate, I know you're hungry." She handed Sheridan a plate of food.

The blonde smiled and walked them over to the table. "Are you having fun?"

"Yeah, I am. I'm glad I came. It's not so bad, everyone is so nice to me." Keefer held up her perfect hamburger and waved it at Steven before taking a bite. She made happy faces as she chewed, causing Steven to beam.

"He thinks you're a goddess, you know," Sheridan said off-handedly.

"He does not. He just has a crush," Keefer said, blushing.

"Oh no, he lurves you."

"Stop that," Keefer scolded, smacking her lover's hand.

Sheridan pouted and Keefer kissed her finger, looked around, and then touched Sheridan's lip.

"Oh man, did you see that?" Sharon said, her eyes wide in disbelief.

"She fucking pouted!" Marie said in amazement.

"Check out Patch." Bobby elbowed Phil.

"She's actually making goo-goo eyes. Damned if Steven wasn't right!"

Fucking gross, Danni groused from in her car. *What the fuck does Sheridan have that I don't have? Look at her! She's holding hands...above the table...people are watching!* Danni slunk down in her seat and frowned. "Fucking slut stole my girlfriend."

Marie happened to glance beyond the hedges and noticed a car double-parked by the driveway. "Hey, someone's gonna get a ticket," she worried.

Sharon looked up and cursed, "Fuck. It's Danni."

"Danni? What the hell is she doing here? How did she now about this?" Marie wondered.

"Holy shit! Do you think she's stalking Keefer?" Dawn asked nervously.

"I hope to God she is. That's jail time, ladies," Sharon said with an evil grin.

Marie looked to Sheridan and Keefer, who were now sitting on the same side of the table, and then back to Danni. "Do you think we should tell her?"

"Who do we tell? Keefer or Sheridan?"

"Fuck, I don't know." Dawn blew out a frustrated breath.

"Maybe I should just handle it," Sharon said.

"Uh-oh, they're coming over," Dawn said behind her beer can.

"Hey, why the serious faces?" Sheridan asked curiously.

"Uh, nothing. What are you guys doing after? Wanna go to the club?" Marie asked nervously.

Sheridan cocked her head and raised an eyebrow at her friend's behavior, then looked at Keefer with a devastating grin. "Nope. We have *business.*"

Keefer backhanded Sheridan in the side. "Sher!" she blushed.

"What?" the blonde asked innocently.

Sharon smiled knowingly, "That's cool. I wish I had business."

"I'd settle for a silent partner," Dawn joked.

Danni fumed. Keefer was blushing, laughing and having a great time. *She's not supposed to be laughing with her.*

Chapter 40

Danni watched from her car as Keefer laughed and enjoyed herself with her new friends at the barbeque. She grew more hostile by the minute and the angrier she got, the more unreasonable she became.

Sheridan, Keefer, Dawn, and Marie sat in a circle and chatted casually, while Sharon stood off to the side, talking with Steven. She wanted to keep an eye on Danni and didn't want to look conspicuous, so she distanced herself from the group, and at the same time gave herself a clear view of the redhead.

Keefer jumped slightly when Sheridan's hand was suddenly on her thigh. The blonde was engrossed in telling a tale to her friends and it seemed as if she had no idea that she'd even placed it there. Keefer looked down when the hand didn't leave and blushed as her lover's fingers began caressing her thigh. Blue eyes quickly scanned the group, and Keefer swallowed nervously when she saw the girls trying hard not to focus on Sheridan's actions. Their eyes darted between the construction worker's hand and her face as she spoke.

The brunette's heart picked up speed and her libido resurfaced quickly as the blonde's fingers stroked the inside of her thigh, her pinky and ring finger venturing dangerously close to Keefer's crotch. Keefer rested her hand on top of Sheridan's and halted its movements, causing Sheridan to stop talking and look at their hands. It was apparent from the expression on her face that Sheridan had no idea what her hand had been doing and she was slightly embarrassed. She flashed an apologetic grin at her lover, which Keefer accepted, and laced their fingers together, holding their hands on her leg.

Sharon's hackles went up as she saw Danni's fists beat against the steering wheel in frustration. She looked toward her friends and saw the reason for Danni's dismay. Keefer was staring lovingly at Sheridan's face as the blonde laughed and talked with Dawn and Marie. She couldn't help the goofy grin from forming on her lips as she watched her new friend. Keefer was obviously very smitten with Sheridan, and the cop couldn't be happier for Sheridan. She deserved this, and it was about time. Her grin faded as she thought about the potential threat Danni was posing to her friends' happiness.

Sheridan got up to get Keefer a drink; she'd had two beers and wasn't drinking any more, since she was driving. Keefer had already scolded her for having the second beer and she didn't want Keefer to ever be disappointed in her, so she'd switched to soda. However, the brunette was not going to be driving and seemed to be enjoying herself, so Sheridan had no qualms about letting her have another drink. She snuck up behind Bobby and grabbed his ass with both hands. "Ooh, baby!" she purred loud enough for the others around to hear.

"Oh please, Patch." Bobby rolled his eyes as the guys laughed. "What the hell do you want with my ass when you got that one over there?" He pointed his thumb over his shoulder at Keefer.

Sheridan grinned proudly. "Too true," she agreed as she reached into the pail of beers and pulled out a cold one.

"You two are perfect for each other," Phil said.

"I like to think so." Sheridan nodded as she wiped the bottle of beer dry with a napkin and opened it.

Tony grinned at the action. "Ya know, my wife just throws the wet bottle at me from the kitchen."

"Yeah, well..." the blonde mumbled in embarrassment.

"I envy you, Patch," Phil said seriously. "It's been a long time since my wife looked at me the way she looks at you."

"Aw, cut it out."

"No, he's right. She stares at you like you're a god," Bobby agreed.

Sheridan couldn't prevent her cocky grin. "Oh yeah, boys, I *am* a god," she said with an evil little chuckle and a rude, humping gesture.

"I wouldn't be surprised if you know how to work one of those things better than we do," Phil laughed.

"Wouldn't you like to know," Sheridan replied, puffing out her chest.

"We could always ask her," Tony teased.

Sheridan paled. "Don't you dare! Please, don't even joke like that!" She panicked. *Keefer would shrivel up and die on the spot!*

The guys raised their eyebrows collectively.

"Hey, I'm only kidding, chill out," Tony said.

"Well, don't. Not about sex. Please." Sheridan relaxed a bit and smiled weakly.

Oh, yeah! Phil thought. *This is the woman with the issues.*

"I better get back over there before she misses me."

They watched Sheridan walk off and shared curious looks.

"Would you ever imagine that?" Bobby asked.

"No way, never. She's being considerate, compassionate and damn...she's really in fucking love with Keefer!" Tony said, watching as Sheridan gave Keefer the beer and sat cross-legged on the ground between her legs.

"Hey, know why she panicked?" Phil asked. The guys looked at him expectantly. "Remember she said Keefer had issues? I think it has something to do with sex. She never would have reacted like that otherwise."

"Wow. I wonder what, though," Tony said curiously.

"Beats me, but it's astounding that she even thought to hook up with someone with *those* kind of issues," Bobby said.

Sharon's eyes narrowed as Danni suddenly sat up straight, her mouth working angrily. The cop couldn't make out what the redhead was saying, but the venom was clearly apparent. She glanced at her friends and cursed under her breath. The tall woman was sitting in a chair and Sheridan was sitting between her legs. Keefer was running her fingers through Sheridan's hair and seemed to be totally engrossed in her hand as she stared at it half-lidded while it slid through the blonde hair. She was certain that Sheridan was purring, from the expression of pure bliss on her face. The blonde moved her head and gazed up at Keefer with a look of pure love. Sharon didn't even bother to look at Danni as she read the impending kiss loud and clear. She put down her beer and excused herself from Steven.

Danni's mouth dropped open and she watched in horror as Keefer lowered her face to Sheridan's. She squeezed her eyes closed as their lips met but couldn't keep them closed long enough to miss the entire thing. "Motherfucker! She kissed the goddamned whore right there in front of God and everybody! Son of a bitch!"

Keefer yelped out in surprise as she was suddenly pulled from her chair and held forcibly behind Sharon.

"What the fuck are you doing?" Sheridan jumped up and shouted at Sharon.

Marie and Dawn were a little too drunk and it took them a second to process what was going on. Sheridan's shout brought the guys over to the group and they watched, curious and on alert.

"Trust me on this one. Keefer, maybe you should go inside."

Dawn snapped out of her haze first and remembered Danni. She spun around quickly and saw the redhead approaching them at a fast pace. "Fuck! Sher, look."

Sheridan tore her eyes away from Sharon and Keefer to see Danni heading right for Keefer. She dropped her soda on the ground and stepped into Danni's path. She could see from where she was that the redhead was beyond reason and probably would have to be either knocked unconscious or physically restrained from getting whatever it is she wanted. She saw the fist long before Danni could connect and caught it with her left hand.

"Let go, you fucking slut!"

Marie grabbed the redhead from behind and held her tightly. "You weren't invited, Danni. I think you'd better go."

"I'm not going anywhere without Keefer!"

"Like hell you're not," Sheridan snarled. "Unless you want me to beat the living shit out of you right here in front of everyone, you better go on your own."

"Fuck you." Danni spat at Sheridan, and the blonde jumped away just in time.

"No! I said no more!" Keefer yelled cryptically. Sharon struggled to hold her in place.

"Keefer, I think you should get lost, really," Sharon said over her shoulder.

"This is crazy!" Keefer said, the frustration clear in her tone.

Steven stepped out of the house to see the scene unfolding. He recognized the redhead and also remembered that she had beat up his sister. His eyes narrowed and he got angry, but then he remembered that Sheridan had puked on her and he grinned.

"Steven, maybe you oughtta bring Keefer inside and sit with her," Sharon said in desperation. There was a scene unfolding that by all rights she should stop immediately, but if she let go of Keefer, the tall woman was going to run the wrong way.

"Hell no! I wanna see Sheridan kick her ass!"

"Steven, please!"

Steven folded his arms over his chest and shook his head in defiance like a petulant child.

Sharon rolled her eyes and attempted to push the stronger than she thought brunette further away.

Danni struggled mightily as Sheridan held her arms and Marie held her body. Sheridan could feel the redhead trembling in fury and was a little worried about what might happen.

"Hey, want me to call the cops?" Phil asked

"Yeah, please," Sharon yelled with a nod.

"Keefer! Get the fuck over here. Tell them that you're my girlfriend. You love me! You told me!"

"Fuck off, she loves me, asshole," Sheridan taunted.

Danni wrestled her fist out of the blonde's grasp and swung blindly, just missing Sheridan.

"You're going to jail, now, Danni, hope you enjoy it. No one's gonna bail your sorry ass out this time," Sheridan sneered.

"Fuck, Sher, quit it, she's strong!" Marie struggled as Danni went crazy in her arms.

"Keef! Just tell them! Come on, come home with me, where you belong. I love you, I'm the only one who understands you. I can make you happy. You know I can. Baby...please...you can't possibly love this loser whore, she's nothing but bad news, honey!" Danni begged desperately. "She's gonna hurt you, I promise! She's gonna use you and hurt you. She'll make you cry, she's worthless—" Danni stopped speaking as Sheridan's fist connected with her mouth.

Marie winced as the blood splattered from Danni's mouth. "God, Sher, *I* fucking felt that!"

Sheridan screamed in Danni's face. "Shut the fuck up! You're useless, you fucking mental case, leave her alone!"

"Sheridan! Stop it!" Keefer cried. She couldn't believe what was happening. One second she'd been as content as she could ever be, and the next second all hell broke loose. Tears of frustration fell down her cheeks and she watched her lover hit her ex-girlfriend again, this time in the stomach.

Steven panicked when Keefer cried and yelled. Didn't she understand that the woman had beat Sheridan when she was hung over and defenseless? He ran over to Keefer and Sharon in confusion.

Sheridan saw red; she'd held herself in check for as long as humanly possible, but once she lost it and felt the satisfying connection with Danni's face, she was helpless to stop herself from hitting her again. All the anger and embarrassment the other woman had caused her came rushing back, throwing her into a blind rage. She could hear Keefer screaming at her to stop, but was powerless to do so. She cursed, growled, and lashed out, throwing punch after punch until she was suddenly restrained.

Danni pitched forward as she gasped for breath through what Dawn was sure were broken ribs. Initially, Dawn was stunned motionless, as was everyone else, while Sheridan displayed her rage. The alcohol they'd consumed made them a little disconnected and it took longer than it normally would for someone to stop Sheridan's tirade.

Eventually, Phil and Tony ran and grabbed their out-of-control friend before she killed the redhead. Marie loosened her grip on Danni in an act of mercy, allowing her the freedom to fight back if she wanted. Unfortunately, the way Sheridan was beating into her with such force, the redhead couldn't even protect herself, much less have the opportunity to fight back.

Sheridan's chest heaved as she fought to breathe; she was completely restrained and freaking out. The adrenaline was rushing through her bloodstream at a furious pace and she could hardly see straight. Keefer was yelling at her. She knew she should turn her head and look at her lover, but the sound of Keefer crying was enough to break her heart and she was sure the tall woman wouldn't ever forgive her for what she'd just done. She hung her head and panted heavily, feeling like the world's biggest asshole. She began crying without even knowing why.

Steven got frightened when Sheridan started to cry. He was very confused with the whole episode. He looked back and forth between everybody there and was at a loss as to why they all looked so upset. In his mind, Danni deserved the beating.

Phil heard his friend muttering apologies under her breath and looked at Keefer, who broke away from Sharon and ran toward them. He let go of Sheridan and she fell to her knees, crying in shame and frustration. Keefer knelt down and immediately wrapped her arms around her sobbing girlfriend and held her.

"I'm so sorry, Keef...I couldn't stop...she said I'd hurt you...she was right, I made you cry..."

Keefer bit her top lip in an effort to stop the tears. "It's all right, baby." Her crying was destroying the blonde, and she had to make it stop. "I'm okay, I was just scared." Sheridan looked up to see the truth in Keefer's eyes, and her pitiful tear-streaked face made Keefer feel horrible. She wiped away Sheridan's tears and kissed her tenderly, smiling slightly at the salty taste on her lips. "I swear, I'm okay. You didn't make me cry, honest."

A symphony of sirens could be heard in the background and Keefer took a second to thank God that someone had thought to call an ambulance as well as the police. Sheridan had really hurt Danni and at one point, the brunette had been afraid she was going to kill her. She shuddered at the thought and held her girlfriend tighter.

Danni had fallen to all fours, her breathing labored, blood dripping down her chin from her nose and mouth. She coughed loudly and gagged on the blood as she spit it out. She lifted her head with effort and stared evilly at Sheridan and Keefer, who were entwined in each other's arms. She made a sour face and used a mocking voice to taunt them. Blood sprayed from her mouth as she spoke. "I love you, sweet pea...you're my angel pie, honey bun. So fucking sweet, I could puke."

Sheridan suddenly exploded up from Keefer's embrace and was on Danni in a heartbeat, pulling her upright by a handful of hair. "Let me fucking help you, you son of a bitch!" She kneed the redhead in the stomach and threw her on the ground.

Keefer and Phil ran to get Sheridan away. The cops had just pulled up and were approaching the scene, and the last thing they wanted was for Sheridan to wind up in jail, too. They dragged her away from the bleeding, beaten woman and held her.

Keefer was alarmed at the fury coursing through her lover's body. Sheridan was shaking on the inside; her fists clenched so hard that her knuckles were white, her jaw muscles were working a mile a minute, and she was breathing very heavily. The tall woman held tightly to Sheridan's biceps while they watched in disgust as Danni retched pathetically.

"You fucking loser asshole. You leave my woman alone or I swear I'll kill you next time," Sheridan growled, her voice low and her anger barely controlled.

"You hear that, Officer?" Danni choked out between gasps.

"I heard nothing. What's the problem here?"

A myriad of responses burst forth.

Keefer tried to soothe her lover by stroking her back; she could feel the muscles coiled tight under her hand. Her belly clenched, and she blushed at her body's uncontrolled reaction to Sheridan's. She moved her hand to the blonde's arm and caressed it lovingly. "Maybe you should talk to the police, Sher."

Sheridan closed her eyes and tried desperately to concentrate on her lover's soothing touch. She nodded and took several deep breaths before opening her eyes and finding a sea of understanding in Keefer's gentle blue eyes. "You're not mad at me?" she whispered, not believing her girlfriend could be so wonderful.

"No," Keefer offered a watery smile, "I understand what just happened. In fact, I feel guilty."

"I lose my mind and *you* feel guilty? Why?"

"Danni's my garbage—"

"Hold it right there, Keef. Danni is a mental case; she's not your responsibility. She's a fucking fruit loop who doesn't get the concept of the word *no*. Why the hell would you blame yourself for that?" The blonde leaned into Keefer's touch, little shivers traveling up her spine from the feel of the long fingers stroking her bare skin.

"If I never knew her, this wouldn't have happened."

"Keefer, if you never knew her, we would have never had a chance."

The tall inspector furrowed her brows for a while, then a grin slowly appeared on her face. "There is that," she agreed with a chuckle.

The both watched with different degrees of satisfaction as Danni was strapped to a gurney and wheeled into an ambulance.

"I better go talk to the cops," Sheridan said with a sigh.

Keefer reluctantly released her hold on her lover and watched as she trod sadly toward the fray. She could see that the blonde was blaming herself for what had happened and felt miserable. Keefer shook her head and thought, *What can I do? How do I fix this and make her feel better?*

"Some party, huh?" Phil said with a wry chuckle.

Keefer jerked at the voice and offered a half smile to the speaker. "Yeah," she chuckled back, then gave Phil a determined look. "She feels horrible. You know her, what should I do?"

Phil blew out a breath through pursed lips. "I honestly don't know. Maybe you should ask the girls. I'm sorry."

"'S okay. I just feel sort of helpless right now. This is all new to me," Keefer admitted.

"Hey," Phil put his hand on Keefer's shoulder, "it's new to all of us. Don't beat yourself up over it. It's not your fault."

Keefer grinned sadly. "That's going to take a while."

"Well, Inspector," he rubbed her shoulder reassuringly, "you're not alone."

"Thank you," she said, giving Phil a genuine smile. "Good to know." She excused herself and made her way over to Sharon, who surprised her by pulling her into a heartfelt hug. It felt good and she relaxed into it.

"Thank you, Keefer."

The brunette pulled away with a puzzled look. "What for? I ruined the party!"

"Thank you for loving Sheridan. If you weren't there for her, fuck only knows what would have happened to her tonight. I've never seen her like that before; it was frightening. And how did you ruin anything? What the hell did you do?"

"Danni is my ex. I feel responsible."

"Fuck that! Look at Sheridan! She feels responsible for the world right now. Never mind Danni, what are we going to do about that?" She pointed at Sheridan, who was sitting with her head in her hands.

"I better go over there," Keefer said nervously. "How do I fix this?"

460

"You love her, I trust that you'll do the right thing."

Keefer nodded disbelievingly but went on anyway. She stopped a few feet away from her lover as Steven trotted to Sheridan's side. Keefer didn't want to overhear the conversation, but she didn't want to be far away from her distraught girlfriend. She was suddenly flanked by Dawn and Phil, who both put comforting hands on her shoulders, and she closed her eyes for a second to memorize what it felt like to have this much support.

"Sher, please don't cry," Steven said with a crack to his voice. He knelt down next to his sister and tried to look at her face. "It hurts my stomach, please stop."

"I'm okay, Stevie-boy," she answered unconvincingly.

"You're still crying...why? Tell me!" he almost demanded.

Sheridan wiped her face hastily with her hands, then turned to look into his panicked face. "Well, it's like this..." she started, then grimaced, not knowing how to explain.

"Tell me, my stomach really hurts and my heart is beating so fast, I'm scared!"

"It hurts me inside." She pounded on her chest. "It hurt so bad that it made me cry."

"Why, though? She didn't hit you, I saw everything!"

"No, no...it wasn't physical, well, it is a physical pain..." She blew out a frustrated breath. "Steven, have you ever felt like you may have disappointed me, you know, thought that I hated you?"

He nodded, wide eyed. "Oh yeah, plenty."

"How did you feel inside when you thought you had let me down?"

"Really sick. I felt so sad and so..." The light bulb was practically visible. He nodded again, this time in sympathy.

"I thought that I disappointed Keefer. I thought that she hated me for what I did and how I acted and it hurt so bad inside that I..." Tears welled up in Sheridan's eyes from the mere thought. "I couldn't do anything but cry."

Steven looked at Keefer, then back to his sister. "But she doesn't hate you, she loves you." He became suddenly alarmed. Why wasn't Keefer hugging Sheridan? Didn't she know it was the only thing to make her feel better? "She does love you...doesn't she?" he asked nervously.

Sheridan chuckled mirthlessly, "Yeah. Go figure."

Keefer began to cry again at her lover's outright fear of hurting her.

Feeling relieved, Steven stood up in front of Keefer and studied his sister's face and how she was hugging her stomach. "Hey, Keefer? Know what always makes me feel better when I have to hold my stomach like that? A hug. Pop always hugs me when I cry."

Keefer smiled through her tears. "I'll go do that, Steven," she replied and knelt down next to her lover.

Sheridan jumped a little when Keefer touched her shoulder. She felt awful...weak and stupid. She didn't want Keefer to see her like that and shied away from the tall woman's touch.

Keefer raised her eyebrows when her lover slid further away, but persisted and followed her. She changed her gentle touch to a firmer more convincing grip and pulled the blonde closer.

"I'm fine, Keef, why don't you go and hang out with the girls or something."

The brunette felt as if she'd just been slapped and she fought the urge to run away like she'd been told. *No, she needs me now.* "That's okay, I'd rather sit here with you," she said in a lighter tone than she felt like using.

Sheridan sniffed and then sighed heavily. "I'm really sorry I ruined the night. I don't know what happened—I couldn't help myself," she admitted quietly, her head still hanging low.

Keefer set her jaw, and with her hand turned Sheridan's face toward her own. Her expression softened when she saw just how upset her lover really was. "It's all right. I'm not angry with you—I was scared. It all happened so fast and I was confused."

"You swear?" Sheridan asked, narrowing her eyes.

Keefer rearranged Sheridan's sweaty hair and smiled. "I swear. Actually, I still feel like it was my fault. If she hadn't come looking for me, none of this would have happened."

"I told you, she's a nut case. It's not your fault. If I didn't lose control like some maniac..." The blonde made a fist and wanted to punch herself in the head for being such a loser.

Keefer sighed. It was going to be a long conversation and her ankles hurt from crouching. She took her lover's balled-up hand and pulled her to her feet. "Come on. We're going home, we need to talk."

"Wait, we can't go home now...what about Steven?" the construction worker asked in concern.

"Wait right here, don't move a muscle," Keefer instructed and went off toward the others, who were trying hard to look busy with other things.

Sharon met Keefer halfway with a look of expectation on her face. "How is she?"

"Rotten. She thinks everything is her fault, she thinks I'm mad at her, too," Keefer blurted out.

Sharon gave Keefer the once-over. "What about you? How are you taking all of this?"

"Danni is my ex; I feel responsible, in a way. She came here looking for me and that's how this all started. Sheridan says if it weren't for Danni, we would have never had a chance, and she's right, but what do I have to do to get rid of her? If she continues to do things like this, I'm afraid Sheridan will be the one in jail."

"I don't know what to tell ya, Keefer. It's not your fault, but you won't believe it from me. You need to convince your own self of that." The tall cop glanced over at Sheridan. "She scared me, too. I never saw her like that before."

"We need to go home and talk, do you think someone can get Steven home in one piece?"

"I'll do it. No problem," Sharon smiled. "Thank you. I owe you one."

"Shyeah, right, you don't owe me nothing." Keefer smiled genuinely as she headed back to her lover.

Sheridan allowed Keefer to pull her to the car. She didn't want to talk, she wanted to go somewhere and beat herself up over her actions. She was convinced that Keefer was either afraid of her now or angry over the extent of Danni's beating. Sheridan didn't even know why she'd gone berserk. *How am I going to explain that to Keefer? She's probably going to be careful not to make me mad now. Fuck. Why couldn't I just walk away like she told me to?*

"Come on, Sher, let's go home."

The blonde plunked herself into the car reluctantly and paused when she put the key in the ignition. *Home? She didn't say my house, she said home.* She thought for a minute and then turned the key, a frustrated noise escaping her throat. *She still loves me? Why?*

After driving in strained silence for a while, Keefer sighed heavily and turned to face her lover. She felt the need to mother Sheridan for some reason, an urge that she had never felt before with a human being. She'd had the need with Fifi when she first saw her and, while it was a similar feeling, it was ten times more overwhelming as she looked at her distraught lover. However, she knew the feeling was not mutual and that Sheridan would probably shy away from her. That would hurt Keefer, even though she knew her lover wouldn't do it on purpose. "Sher, I understand if you want to be alone. I can feel it, and I don't want to force you into anything."

The blonde made a sour face and shrugged.

"I'm serious. I want to sit and hold you and make you feel better, but I'm sensing that you don't want that. Am I right?"

"I guess so. I don't know. I don't want you to go away right now, but I don't know if I can feel better, either," Sheridan explained.

"Okay. So, what do you want to do?" Keefer asked, hiding her frustration.

The blonde parked the car in front of Keefer's house and sighed. She stared at her hands as they continued to grip the steering wheel.

"Sher! Your hand is bleeding!"

Sheridan shrugged in indifference and stretched out said hand to inspect. "Danni's teeth," she mumbled.

"At least come inside and let me fix that. You can go home if you want afterwards, or you can sleep in the den if you want. The choice is yours, but just know that I really want to hold you right now. I feel like I need to." Keefer fought back tears; the urge was so strong to pull Sheridan to her and hug her senseless. She felt like something big had worked its way between them, even though she knew that this was just an aspect of her lover's personality that she had to endure. She needed the physical connection to know everything was going to be all right.

Sheridan opened her door and got out of the car. Keefer composed herself and followed. They both entered the house in silence and greeted Fifi with more enthusiasm then they felt.

"Go wash your hands in the bathroom, I'll be right there," Keefer instructed.

"'Kay," Sheridan said sadly.

"Feefs, what am I going to do?" Keefer asked the dog, who was beginning to sense a problem. She put her tail down slowly and trotted carefully to the bathroom.

Sheridan winced as the soap burned the wound on her hand. She looked in the mirror and hated her miserable appearance. Just an hour ago, she'd felt the most wonderful sense of peace while Keefer stroked her head. Now she felt like shit. A panicked feeling overtook her. *I fucked it all up!* She ran her wet hands over her face and through her hair.

Keefer approached the bathroom to see her lover with her hands on the back of her head and her face showing her fear. She stood in the same spot for a while as the blonde turned off the water and sat heavily on the side of the tub. Sheridan was in turmoil; apparently, she was making a mountain out of a molehill, causing herself more grief than was necessary. Keefer didn't understand this behavior. *I told her it was okay. Why doesn't she believe me? Okay, yeah, I was crying, but I was scared...for both of them. Maybe that's why she's upset? Does she think I still care for Danni? That's ridiculous. She wouldn't think that, would she? Why else is she so sad?*

"Keef? Are you coming?"

Keefer straightened herself up and walked into the bathroom. Sheridan was petting Fifi, who was staring expectantly at her. The dog knew her favorite friend was not right and she wagged her tail in hopes of making her talk in that special voice to her. "Feefs, you're going to have to move for a minute," Keefer said sweetly as she crouched down in front of her lover. The dog sat right where she was, staring at Sheridan with her head cocked.

"Hey, sweetie," Sheridan started, "go inside for a second and when mommy's done with me, I'll give you a cookie." The blonde leaned over and kissed Fifi on the snout.

Keefer watched in amusement as the dog obeyed. "I think you're her favorite," she said lightly.

Sheridan forced a grin.

"Okay, let me clean this properly. It's gonna burn, so get ready," the brunette warned as she soaked a cotton ball with peroxide. "You know, there are so many germs in the mouth," she said as she dabbed the cuts. Sheridan flinched a bit but didn't make a sound. "It hurts?"

"Burns a little."

Keefer blew gently on her lover's hand and smiled when Sheridan sighed. *She's in there, just gonna take a bit of work. She's letting me do this, so it can't be all that bad.* "Okay, you want a bunch of Band-aids or one big, sexy gauze pad?"

"Don't matter."

Keefer frowned at Sheridan's toneless responses. "Okay then, a macho-looking bandage coming up."

"It's not an award, Keef. I did something stupid and I wish I hadn't."

Keefer furrowed her brows. "I don't know what you mean."

"I'm going to see the bandage and remember why it's there."

"Well, I have to cover them—they're still bleeding, Sher. What do you want me to use?"

"Never mind."

Keefer got a little angry. "Honey, I know you feel terrible over what happened tonight, but you can't make it go away. It happened and it's over. Let's move on."

"Says she who believes it was all her fault."

Keefer narrowed her eyes. *Damn. Practice what you preach, Keefer.* She finished with the bandage and Sheridan flexed her hand and stood up. "Are you going home now?"

"I dunno."

"I don't want you to. I want you to stay here. I don't want you going away now, in this mood." *You might not come back.*

"I'll be in the den. Good night, Keef."

Keefer swallowed heavily. This was hurting her more than anything. "Good night, Sher."

Sheridan closed the door behind her and sat on the futon. "She acts like nothing's wrong! I beat up Danni and she never even tried to hit me back. Only assholes do shit like that." She lay down and sighed. "She still loves me, though," she said as she looked at her bandage, "that's for sure." There was scratching at the door and she looked at it for a moment before deciding to let the dog in.

Keefer watched as Sheridan opened the door long enough for Fifi to enter and then closed it again. *I don't know what to do or say. This is so confusing. Maybe I should call someone? Maybe Sharon? Maybe her father? No, that would look like I don't know what I'm doing...but I don't.* Keefer went into her bedroom and changed into her pajamas. *She's right in the other room and I feel so alone.*

Sheridan sat on the floor with the dog and thought out loud. "Mommy still loves me. Why am I acting like this? I didn't really blow it, did I?" She scratched Fifi behind the ear and the dog closed her eyes. "You like that, don't you? It feels good to be loved, huh." Sheridan thought about what she'd just said. "Mommy does this so good...she can make everything go away." The blonde bit her bottom lip. "She said she wants to hold me. I didn't want it before, but it would sure feel good now."

Fifi rolled over onto her back, displaying her belly. Sheridan moved her scratches to the dog's chest. "I'm being stupid. I obviously want to be with her or I would have gone home. I didn't want to go home, I wanted to be with her and now I locked myself in this room." Sheridan pursed her lips and furrowed her brows. "Do ya think Mommy would think I'm crazy if I went inside now? After the way I acted?" Fifi snorted. "Well, okay then."

Keefer was lying in the dark, wondering what to do when she heard the den door open. *Okay, Keef, you know what to say...*

"Baby?" Sheridan's sheepish voice made the brunette smile, despite the situation.

"Yes?"

"Can I come in?"

Keefer sat up. "Of course. You don't have to ask."

Sheridan slowly made her way to the bed and sat on the side next to Keefer. "Um...you still love me, right?"

Is that what this is about? "Are you crazy?"

"Depends who you ask," Sheridan joked weakly.

"Get over here," Keefer said strongly. When Sheridan slid under the covers next to her, she wrapped her arms around the blonde like she'd been waiting to do all night. "Just because you make a mistake doesn't mean I don't love you! How could you think that?"

"You were so upset, you were screaming at me and I didn't listen. I just kept doing what was making you upset."

"Sher, we all freak out. I punched a hole in my living room wall, for Christ sakes. It's okay, I still love you." Long fingers drifted up to the back of the construction worker's neck.

Sheridan sighed and slid down into Keefer's arms. "I really couldn't stop. I think it was 'cuz of all the shit she put you through, and how she hit me when I was hung over and—"

"You don't have to explain. In a way—a small way—don't get all cocky, now," Keefer teased. "In a small way, I felt good. You were protecting me."

"If she so much as breathed on you, Keef, I swear I would have killed her."

"I know that, and it makes me proud, but it doesn't mean you can go around beating people up."

"I'm sorry. I disappointed you."

"Oh no, you don't." Keefer turned her lover around to face her. "Don't go assuming anything. You didn't disappoint me. You scared me. Completely different things." *This disappointment thing is a big deal!*

Sheridan squirmed a bit before Keefer began stroking her back and she settled down. "Can I apologize for scaring you?"

"Yes."

"I'm sorry for scaring you."

"You're forgiven."

"Wow. You're easy."

"Don't let it get around," Keefer snickered. She let her fingers drift under Sheridan's shirt and lightly scratched her back.

"Keef?"

"Hmm?"

"Can you just do that until I fall asleep?"

"My pleasure." Keefer smiled, almost giddy that things were okay again. "I love you, Sheridan."

"I love you, too, baby."

Chapter 41

Sleep came easily for the two lovers. It was had been a harrowing night for them, and once the fear and confusion subsided, exhaustion set in. Sheridan lay in Keefer's arms, snoring and contented. Keefer slept peacefully, too. She had attempted to stay awake and try to figure out how to approach this new facet of Sheridan's personality. The construction worker had been virtually devastated, assuming she had disappointed the brunette. Keefer pondered the situation briefly, but the feel of Sheridan in her arms and the blonde's even, deep breathing lulled her to sleep peacefully.

Somewhere in the middle of the night, Fifi circled the bed a few times, looking for a good spot to jump up on without disturbing her mommy and her best friend. There wasn't really room for her to do so; the two women were sprawled out all over the big bed, leaving very little space for the dog to cuddle. Fifi pouted as best she could. Sheridan was up on that bed and she needed to be there, too. Raising her fluffy and uneven eyebrows, the mutt hopped up on her hind legs and rested her front paws on the mattress, surveying the situation. Finally seeing an opening, she leapt up as smoothly as she could and slowly wormed her way into the spot. Sighing heavily in contentment, Fifi closed her eyes and fell asleep.

A bird chirped outside the window, causing Keefer to stir. The first thing she became aware of was her lover's firm grasp on her breast. *Oh, yeah, this is how I want to wake up!* Squinting open an excited blue eye, Keefer was surprised to see Sheridan was still sleeping. *Rats.* Her pout soon turned to amusement as she noticed Fifi. Keefer stifled a laugh and bit her bottom lip. Sheridan was bound to have a stiff neck when she woke up—Fifi was draped across the pillow, her body molded perfectly around Sheridan's head. The tall woman couldn't prevent the silent chuckles from consuming her and when they did, her eyes widened as Sheridan's fingers tightened their hold on her breast. *Baby, you have no idea what you're doing to me,* she thought with a quiet groan. Her nipple hardened considerably under her lover's touch, and even though Sheridan was sleeping, Keefer's body couldn't have cared less. Blue eyes stared at the hand, willing it to move, just a little, and feed her need. It didn't. Keefer inhaled deeply, and Sheridan's palm pressing into her nipple was too much to take. She removed the hand from her body and sat up. *I'm horny all over again. Why do you do this to me?* She looked at her sleeping lover with an accusing glare. *Yeah, you. Why do you turn me on in your sleep?*

Keefer sighed out loud, alerting Fifi to an awake human. The dog's tail began wagging, smacking Sheridan in the face repeatedly. Keefer watched with a smile as Sheridan woke up. The blonde grimaced and tried to wipe the offending annoyance from her face but it didn't work, it kept hitting her. Her eyes opened quickly to find the source, and the look of confusion on her face made Keefer laugh. Green eyes widened and Sheridan grabbed Fifi's tail, stilling it. She followed the tail with her eyes and laughed. "Okay, your pillow is awake now, Feefs. Time to get up," she said in a sleep-roughened voice.

Keefer narrowed her eyes. Even Sheridan's morning voice turned her on. *Hell, anything she does right now will turn me on.* "Morning," she said with a sexy grin.

Noticing the look on her lover's face, Sheridan wiggled her eyebrows. "Morning, sexy. Care to get your dog off my head?"

"Come on, Feefs, let's go," Keefer said sternly.

The dog obeyed and made sure to step all over both women as she made her way from the bed.

"Thanks. Did ya sleep good? I feel like I fell into a coma."

"I slept well. Had a few dreams..." the brunette said with a shy smile.

"Oh? What kind of dreams?" Sheridan stretched and groaned. "Ow."

In a way, Keefer wanted to confess her lusty dreams and make them reality that very second, but she was hesitant due to the events of the previous night. She wasn't sure about her lover's emotional state and didn't know if she'd want to make love. She avoided the question altogether. "I knew she'd do that to you. Come here, let me rub your neck."

Sheridan was more than happy to comply and scooted over between Keefer's legs. "Oh, yeah, baby." she moaned as the long fingers dug into her stiff muscles.

Keefer fought a shiver. *God, she's so hot when she wakes up.* She tried to discreetly smell the back of her lover's neck but Sheridan sensed it and turned around.

"What are you doing?" she asked playfully.

"Smelling you," Keefer replied with a small blush.

"Oh, well then, carry on," the blonde said with a chuckle and turned back around.

"I'd better not." Keefer resumed her massage and contained her strong urges.

Sheridan had a feeling she knew what was going on with her lover. "Keef?"

"Yeah?"

"What kind of dreams did you have?"

Keefer blushed. "Oh, you know."

Sheridan grinned knowingly. "Nope. Tell me."

"Um, well..." Keefer sighed. "Sex dreams," she said quietly.

"Were you...on top?"

"Yeah," the brunette admitted sheepishly.

"Mmm...wanna show me what you dreamed?" the blonde asked in a sultry tone.

Thank God! "If you're in the mood."

Sheridan turned around and faced Keefer, her eyebrow raised high. "Silly thing to say. I always want you." She let her eyes close halfway and licked her lips.

Keefer's nostrils flared before she lunged forward and captured Sheridan's lips. She leaned heavily against the smaller woman until she was on her back. The blonde allowed her suddenly aggressive lover to push her down onto the bed, though if she had to admit it, the display of control turned her on even more. Keefer's hands were everywhere at once and Sheridan groaned her approval.

The tall inspector felt a surge of need, an overwhelming urge to devour Sheridan and, seeing as her lover was being so compliant, she acted on it. All traces of her own arousal faded into the background as she sucked the blonde's tongue.

Sheridan broke the steamy kiss long enough to stretch her legs out underneath them and then pulled Keefer back down to her by her shoulders, giving her every signal for her to continue. The brunette didn't hesitate to resume sucking the blonde's lips into her hot mouth.

Keefer arched up off of Sheridan, and her large, insistent hands pulled the construction worker's shirt up over her breasts in order to touch them without interference. The muscular woman beneath squirmed under the onslaught of lips and hands. "Mmm!" she mumbled, tearing her mouth away. "I want to touch you, too," she panted.

"No. All for you, okay?" Keefer replied breathlessly.

Sheridan's breath caught. Her lover's eyes blazed with hunger and it made her clit twitch in anticipation. She nodded and lifted her hands over her head. "I'm all yours, baby."

Blue eyes narrowed and a shy grin spread across Keefer's lips. "Thank you."

Sheridan closed her eyes and licked her lips, inviting Keefer to capture them again. Her kisses were so delicious, and she waited with excited anticipation. Instead, she felt her shirt being lifted and removed, then her shorts. She lay there, naked, with her eyes closed, knowing Keefer was staring at her. It made her hot and she squirmed. "Please, Keef."

"I don't know where to start."

Sheridan arched her back, presenting her breasts.

Keefer licked her lips and moved to straddle her naked lover. She felt a little dirty, ogling Sheridan's naked body when she herself was fully dressed, but it turned her on at the same time that it made her feel like a letch. It was exciting to have all that muscle and flesh at her disposal.

Warm hands cupped both breasts and Sheridan was surprised when she felt Keefer's tongue swipe at her bottom lip; she was sure her tits were the next item on the menu. She parted her lips and accepted Keefer's tongue, sliding her own against the soft, wet muscle invading her mouth. Keefer's thumbs began to brush back and forth across her nipples and Sheridan moaned into her mouth. This little control thing was getting her so wet.

The tall woman stretched herself out on top of her lover, sliding a long leg between two muscular ones. She made a satisfied little groan in the back of her throat as those two legs trapped her own and squeezed. She reveled in the feel of Sheridan's pubic hair against her skin and the heat emanating from her center. She pressed into the damp flesh and was rewarded with a deep moan.

The blonde turned her head away from the kiss and took a deep breath. "Oh, yeah, Keef," she whimpered as her lover's fingers began teasing her nipples more insistently. Each time Keefer pulled and pinched at her nipples, she felt an answering pull in her sex. Her hips began moving, her body begging for more.

"No, Sher, not yet," Keefer whispered against her lover's lips, removing her leg from between Sheridan's. The blonde whimpered and her hands grabbed at Keefer's leg. "All mine, remember?"

Sheridan grimaced. She was happy that the tall woman was displaying some control over her, but she had no idea Keefer would be able to tease her so thoroughly. She had a feeling she was in for more than she could handle. "But I've been horny for days," she pleaded.

"Me too," Keefer agreed. "But I want you so much right now," she admitted, lowering her lips to Sheridan's throat.

"Oh, God," the blonde groaned as teeth and lips explored her skin, working their way down to her chest, her lover's tongue hot against her flesh. She opened her legs as wide as she could, but Keefer's knees prevented her from really spreading them. "Come on, touch me, Keef," she whined.

"I will," the taller woman breathed into damp cleavage.

Keefer's tongue met her fingers on Sheridan's breast and she bathed the nipple lovingly, sliding her hand lower, resting it on top of blonde curls, while she sucked at the pebbled flesh in her mouth. Sheridan's hips rose high off the bed, begging Keefer to touch her, but the brunette refused her silent plea. She switched breasts and sucked the other nipple hungrily, forcing a strangled whimper form her frustrated lover. The sound sent a shock wave between her own legs and Keefer suddenly became aware of how incredibly wet she had become. She spread her knees wider and felt her lower lips open, the wetness soaking her panties.

Sheridan took advantage of the situation and spread her legs wider as well, again meeting the resistance of Keefer's knees. "Baby...I'm so wet..."

The inspector nodded in agreement, taken completely off guard at how incredibly turned on she had become. Her ass swayed as she began licking and kissing her way down Sheridan's body. The blonde groaned miserably at the sight, and her hands moved to clutch at Keefer's shoulders, pushing her down.

"Patience," Keefer breathed into her lover's navel. *God, I can smell myself!*

"Fuck, Keef! You're going to touch it once and I'm gonna come," Sheridan warned.

Keefer grinned into Sheridan's belly. "Then I'll just have to do it again."

Sheridan closed her eyes and whimpered. Keefer was driving her insane and she could swear she smelled her. "You're wet, baby, I can smell it. Let me touch you," she purred.

Keefer stopped moving for a second. She was so wet, and so hot, and she wanted to feel Sheridan's touch so badly, but then she'd never get to finish what she was doing. She stretched her body out on the bed between Sheridan's legs and gasped as her sex met the blanket. She clenched inside and felt a new flow of wetness as she inhaled her lover's scent. Her hips jerked and she groaned quietly as her clit received its desired contact.

*There's always that...*she thought as she pressed herself into the blanket again.

"Please...let me touch you..."

Keefer didn't answer; instead, she licked the length of Sheridan's sex, slowly.

"Shit!"

The brunette closed her eyes and clenched her thighs again. A jolt of heat spread through her core and she grunted from the intensity. Tasting Sheridan drove her crazy and she was on the verge of coming just from doing so.

Sheridan grabbed Keefer's head and held tightly. She hadn't been kidding, she was almost there. "Don't touch it yet, baby."

Keefer groaned and speared her tongue deep inside of her lover, holding her hips down as they surged. She let her tongue stay there, marveling at the way Sheridan's muscles pulled at it and clenched around it. Her own clit throbbed painfully and she took care of the building pressure with another clench. She'd never come from making love to another before, and she was excited about the prospect. She knew that she'd never be able to touch herself in someone else's presence, no matter how horny she'd become. With Sheridan, however, it was becoming a daily urge and she was thrilled that she could get away with humping the blanket, because she was so horny and wet that she was sure she'd explode if she didn't get some relief. She plunged her tongue faster in and out of her lover, and as she did, she could feel herself throb with every thrust. A loud groan escaped her as she pressed her clit into the bed.

Sheridan lifted her head at the sound, curious to know what had caused it. She saw Keefer's ass flex as she ground herself into the bed. "Oh, yeah, baby," she whimpered. The sight of Keefer getting herself off made her twitch uncontrollably.

Sheridan's grip tightened in her hair and Keefer knew what she needed. She withdrew her tongue from its nest and flattened it over her lover's hard clit. Sheridan arched and Keefer grinned with an open mouth. She briefly wondered why Sheridan was propped up on her elbows, but that thought fled as a new flood of wetness poured out of the blonde's opening. Keefer shook her whole head back and forth as she worked her tongue over Sheridan's clit.

Sheridan groaned loudly as Keefer's ass flexed more rapidly. She could feel her lover's breath coming in spurts against her sex, and it made her whole body throb to know Keefer was going to come. The brunette suddenly wrapped her lips around her clit and Sheridan was a goner. "Oh, God!"

Keefer's hips jerked erratically into the bed as her lover cried out. She felt her own orgasm bubbling up quickly as it spread through her lower belly. She didn't even need to move, Sheridan's climax had brought on her own and she whimpered around the blonde's clit, sucking it hard.

"Keef, god, yes..."

The brunette's orgasm wasn't all encompassing, but it was satisfying and the short length of it allowed her to concentrate more fully on Sheridan. She batted her tongue quickly across the tip of her clit as her lips pulled at the hard, twitching flesh. Sheridan was groaning and shuddering and Keefer was exploding with joy that she had made her feel so good.

"Fuck...stop...Keef!" Sheridan fought to pull her lover from between her legs.

Keefer gave one final suck and then rested her head on Sheridan's thigh. The blonde grabbed at her shoulders and tried to pull her up. Keefer complied and climbed up the blonde and settled with her head on her shoulder.

"Wow," Sheridan sighed, wrapping her arms around her sweaty lover.

"Oh, yeah. Wow," Keefer agreed, smiling at what she thought was her secret.

Once Sheridan caught her breath, her hands began wandering down Keefer's back, she smiled slyly at the shiver it caused, and then she scratched her short nails slowly across Keefer's ass cheeks.

"Mmm, good," Keefer sighed, lifting her head to look meet green eyes.

Sheridan strained her neck to reach for a kiss and Keefer adjusted herself to help. The taller woman was now straddling Sheridan; the wet crotch of her panties on her lover's skin bore the evidence of her orgasm. The blonde smiled into the kiss, flexing her stomach muscles against Keefer's sex. The tall inspector inhaled sharply through her nose and Sheridan almost chuckled. She lightened the kiss and ended it with a series of smaller, gentler ones.

Satisfied and happy, Keefer climbed off of the construction worker and lay next to her on the bed, a cute grin on her slightly swollen lips.

Sheridan sat up and studied her lover. Her rumpled clothes, sexy smile, sparkling blue eyes, and full wet lips made her tingle all over again. "Hey," she whispered, dragging her fingertips down Keefer's torso. "Can I touch you now?" she asked, even though her hand kept traveling lower.

Keefer blushed slightly as her lover's fingers touched her wet panties.

"Well," Sheridan raised her eyebrow, "what do we have here?"

Keefer chuckled nervously and covered her face with her hands.

Sheridan made a show of leaning down and smelling Keefer. "Mmm. You know honey, if I didn't know better..." the blonde climbed up and nibbled on Keefer's neck, just below her ear, "I'd think you already came," she whispered breathily.

Keefer shuddered as Sheridan's words blew across her ear. "Maybe," she mumbled in embarrassment.

Sheridan smiled knowingly and brought her lips to meet Keefer's. "Maybe?" she asked in a purr, and kissed her hiding lover reassuringly. "Do you know how much it would turn me on to know you came from making love to me?" she asked, gently prying Keefer's hands from her face.

The red-faced inspector bit her top lip and fought to look at Sheridan.

"God, that's so hot," the blonde said with a groan, imagining Keefer's ass clenching and flexing as she humped the blanket.

"That never happened before," Keefer admitted in a shy whisper.

"Oh, baby!" Sheridan growled before she wrapped her arms around her lover and kissed her thoroughly.

Keefer relaxed into the attention and sighed deeply in relief.

Sheridan moved her kiss to Keefer's ear. "You have nothing to be ashamed of. In fact," she stopped to tongue the ear at her lips, "you got me turned on all over again."

"Yeah?" Keefer breathed out distractedly. Sheridan was doing wonderful things to her ear.

"Oh yeah," the blonde growled.

Keefer groaned, her sex growing wetter as her lover licked her neck. "Can I do anything about it?"

"You most certainly can," Sheridan said as she licked a trail across the brunette's throat. "Want me to tell you?"

Keefer's entire lower body clenched as she imagined Sheridan telling her what to do. She nodded, digging her nails into muscular shoulders. Sheridan moved so she was kneeling, hovering over her lover's body, her hands holding her weight on either side of Keefer's head.

Blue eyes roamed the scene before her and Keefer's heart beat rapidly. She was getting so turned on, all over again.

"I know it gets you hot when I talk to you, baby." Sheridan wanted Keefer to touch herself so badly that she was willing to go for broke to make it happen.

Keefer closed her eyes. It was true—she couldn't hide from it. She took a deep, ragged breath in anticipation of her lover's sultry voice telling her where and how to touch.

"Keef?" When blue eyes opened slowly, Sheridan continued. "Are you okay with this?" she asked sincerely.

Keefer smiled shyly. "I'm very okay," she admitted.

A sexy grin spread across Sheridan's lips and she bent down, brought their lips together ,and spoke against them, "I want you to touch me so badly. I want to feel your long sexy fingers...mmm..." She was stopped by Keefer's tongue as it speared through her lips.

Sheridan's heart pounded as a result of Keefer's attack. The tall woman had wrapped her arms around the blonde's neck, making sure she knew this was not a quick peck. Keefer's tongue hungrily probed the recesses of Sheridan's mouth and the construction worker groaned loudly in response. Her arms shook from the effort it took to hold her up. She wanted to fall down on top of Keefer and meld their skin together, but Keefer was still dressed. Sheridan shifted her weight to one arm and began to lift the inspector's shirt.

The brunette arched her back off of the bed, allowing her shirt to be lifted as far as possible without breaking their hungry kiss. She groaned as a strong hand covered her breast, squeezing it hard, conveying Sheridan's hunger. She broke the kiss, panting with arousal, and reached down to grasp Sheridan's hips.

The blonde held her ground as Keefer tried to pull her down. Her mouth was open and she breathed heavily, loudly, caught in a staring match with her determined lover. She was denying Keefer contact, desperately wanting the tall woman to touch herself. It was a quest. She tore her gaze from the electric blue eyes below her and watched her fingers as they teased Keefer's hard nipples, reveling in the erratic rise and fall of her lover's chest. "Take off your panties, baby," she instructed in a raspy voice.

Keefer released Sheridan's hips and pulled her underwear down as far as her arms would take them, and then used her feet to take them off completely. Blue eyes met heavy-lidded green and Keefer swallowed hard, her lover's sultry look making her mouth dry.

"How wet are you, Keef?"

Keefer closed her eyes briefly at the deep sexy timbre of Sheridan's purr. "Very."

Sheridan groaned and took hold of a large hand, bringing it between Keefer's legs. "Show me how wet you are...do it for me, baby," she urged, removing her hand from Keefer's.

The inspector blushed as she quickly reached lower to touch her wetness then, with a shaky breath, showed Sheridan her glistening fingers.

The construction worker's sex throbbed hard at the sight. She sat back on Keefer's belly and took the wet hand to her lips, sucking on the fingers with a hungry groan.

Keefer's hips rocked uncontrollably; it was as if she could feel her lover's lips and tongue between her legs.

477

"You taste so good," the blonde purred as she brought Keefer's hand between her legs and lifted up onto her knees. "Touch me," she whispered.

Keefer gasped at the heat against her fingers and the delicious sound Sheridan made when she moved them. She watched her lover's face intently, excitedly as she pleasured her. Her own sex begged for attention and she squirmed when Sheridan grabbed her arm with both hands.

"Feels so good, Keef." Sheridan exhaled loudly and began to move against Keefer's hand. The brunette crossed her thighs and shuddered. Sheridan looked so sexy—her sweaty, naked body riding her hand. Sheridan suddenly fell forward and leaned on her hands. "Rub my clit, but don't make me come."

Keefer licked her lips and did as she was told. Her lover's sexy, aroused voice sent shocks to her clit and she squeezed her thighs together tighter, trying to stop the throbbing.

"Oh yeah...baby...that's it..."

Keefer's heart beat so hard that she could see her chest moving. She was so turned on by Sheridan's raspy breathing and her barely spoken praise. The blonde rocked forward and back, her breasts coming so close to Keefer's face that she craned her neck and tried to catch one in her mouth.

"Baby, I want to feel your tongue...slide down."

Keefer's mouth and sex flooded simultaneously at the thought of Sheridan sitting on her face. She kept her hand in its wet haven and scooted down the bed until she was looking up into Sheridan's center. She watched her fingers moving there and groaned.

"Looks so hot, don't it?"

"Oh yeah, so much so..." Keefer replied before she could stop herself.

"Taste it." Sheridan swayed over Keefer's face, watching blue eyes almost roll in pleasure.

Keefer held Sheridan's hips with both hands and pulled her down, her outstretched tongue slipping effortlessly inside her wet lover. The feeling of Sheridan in this new position was nearly overwhelming and she groaned deeply.

"Oh, fuck, yeah," the blonde grunted, holding Keefer's head in place.

The brunette's sex gushed, and she felt the slick trail slide down between her ass cheeks as she tasted and listened to Sheridan. She opened her eyes and looked up the length of her lover's body, groaning at the vision. Sheridan's strong thighs surrounded her head, her hands clutched at her hair and stomach muscles rippled. Keefer thrust her tongue hard and fast, driven by the writhing blonde on top of her. Her sex ached for attention and she wished Sheridan would touch her. Her legs uncrossed and splayed open in an unconscious invitation. Her hands roamed up

Sheridan's body, feeling as much of her as they could, and she dragged her nails down every inch of sweat-dampened skin she touched. Keefer thrust her tongue deeply, taking breaths sporadically as Sheridan leaned heavily into her nose.

"Oh, Keef, baby...I bet you're so hot right now...watching me...tasting me..."

Keefer groaned pathetically, bending her knees and closing her thighs. She was damned horny and so very wet; she began to entertain the thought of touching herself.

Sheridan looked down at her lover's face and her sex clenched painfully at the blue eyes looking back at her. She could feel Keefer's legs opening and closing behind her; she could see the desperation in those eyes. Her mouth watered as she thought of how the brunette might taste right that moment. Her nipples hardened and she twitched on Keefer's face, flooding her mouth with wetness. Her lover whimpered as she greedily lapped up the offering, and Sheridan bit her bottom lip hard. *I will not flip around and lick her. I want her to touch herself. There is no way I will...* "Fuck, Keef!"

The brunette grunted as she took Sheridan's clit into her mouth. The blonde was trembling, her abs jumping and her legs closing around her head. Keefer couldn't stop her own body from moving in time with her mouth, and her hips wiggled and pumped.

Sheridan glanced over her shoulder at Keefer's writhing body and growled. She lifted herself off of Keefer and twisted around until she was facing her lover's soaking wet sex. *Fuck it, she'll touch herself another time, I need to taste her now!*

Keefer's lower body came high off the bed and she nearly bit her lover. "Oh, Sher, yes!" she grunted into the blonde's sex before devouring it with renewed vigor. This felt incredible, and she wasn't sure she was going to be able to keep up with her lover while she reciprocated the pleasure. *Her clit, Keef, go back to her clit,* she told herself, falling quickly into pre-orgasmic bliss.

Sheridan groaned happily. Keefer was going to come already and she couldn't wait to join her. She slid two fingers inside her receptive lover and worked them in and out quickly as she neared her own peak.

Keefer's hips jerked erratically and she whimpered around the flesh between her lips. She wrapped both arms around Sheridan's hips as they began to dance wildly, her own body following suit, and they both moaned and groaned as they came together.

Keefer thrust down on Sheridan's fingers and stayed that way as her insides trembled and spasmed around them. Her clit felt like it was on fire as her lover sucked it expertly, drawing out every last ounce of pleasure.

Sheridan gasped and stilled as Keefer brought her to the ultimate pleasure.

When they both returned back to reality, Sheridan turned herself around after one last kiss to Keefer's sex. She settled on top of her lover and sighed a loud, satisfied sigh. "Oh, baby...I can't move."

Keefer slapped the blonde's shoulder playfully.

"What was that for?" Sheridan asked, feigning hurt.

"You drove me crazy!"

Sheridan chuckled and lifted herself onto her elbows to look at Keefer. "Yeah, I did. I wanted you to touch yourself."

Keefer giggled shyly and blushed. "I almost did, but you turned over and beat me to it," she admitted.

"Son of a bitch! So close!" Sheridan dropped back down on top of her lover with a thud.

Keefer giggled again. "Oh well," she shrugged.

"I was this close!" Sheridan whined. "I'll never get you there again."

"You never know," Keefer said shyly. "It was almost painful for a while there."

Sheridan pumped her fist in the air. "There's still hope," she grinned.

"Shut up and kiss me."

Sheridan tipped her head and obeyed, kissing her sensuously, humming her pleasure as she did. She hadn't known that kissing could be so wonderful until her lips touched Keefer's for the first time. Long arms tightened around her back and she sighed in contentment, drinking up the feeling of being held securely in her lover's grasp.

Keefer eventually broke the kiss and her eyes opened slowly. She giggled as Sheridan's goofy smile came into focus. "You're adorable," she said as she rubbed her nose against her lover's.

"You're not so bad yourself," Sheridan replied before burying her face in Keefer's neck and inhaling the warmth. "I love the way it feels to be on top of you like this."

Keefer squeezed Sheridan tighter as her belly filled with warm tingles. "It feels good," she agreed, "but you know what feels better?"

Sheridan lifted her head and gave Keefer a questioning look. She grunted as Keefer rolled them over until she was on top, with strong arms encircling her protectively.

"This," the brunette sighed. "This feels better."

Sheridan couldn't disagree; she nodded as she reached up to smooth Keefer's unruly black hair.

Fifi peeked her head into the room and her tail wagged fast when she saw they had finally settled sown. She jogged in quickly and jumped on the bed.

Keefer protested as her dog walked across her bare butt, then laughed when Fifi went directly to Sheridan and licked her face enthusiastically.

"Morning, honey!" the blonde greeted the dog happily. "Does someone want to go out?"

Keefer groaned. "Oh, Feef, can't you use the toilet?"

"It's okay, Keef, I'll take her. I have to get up, anyway. The boys are waiting for me at home."

"Oh, all right." the inspector rolled off of Sheridan reluctantly and pouted.

The blonde kissed her lover's protruding bottom lip. "I'll be back, baby," she said with a wink. "Go play in your new closet."

Keefer threw a pillow at her lover. "You may be sorry if I do," she warned playfully.

Sheridan looked at Keefer curiously. "I'll be sorry?"

"Yes. Now that I have such a big closet, I might have the need to fill it up."

Sheridan's eyebrows lifted. "Shopping?"

Keefer smiled deviously. "Shopping," she confirmed.

The construction worker groaned and dragged her feet all the way into the bathroom.

Chapter 42

It was a lazy Sunday for Keefer, who didn't even get out of bed until her lover had left. She took a long, hot shower and then straightened up the house before taking Sheridan's advice. Standing in the closet, she began pulling out various clothes and throwing them on the bed. The first things in her Goodwill pile were things that Danni had bought for her; she couldn't even stomach looking at them. The next items she pulled out were the ones that were old or dated, and then she tackled her shoes. By the time she was done, she had two trash bags full of clothes and her closet was looking pretty bare. Keefer was on a roll. The next thing on her agenda was her dresser drawers, she knew there were *Danni things* in there.

Sheridan was sweaty and out of breath by the time her dogs decided it was time to go home. She peeled off her shirt and pulled her bra out of her pants pocket, tossing it onto her bed. "Jeez, guys, you wore me out!"

This is no good, she thought. *I can't keep running back and forth like this all the time. I'm neglecting my kids.* A sour look crossed her face. *What am I supposed to do about it?* She didn't have much time to think about it as Pharaoh stealthily slipped in and stole her bra. "Hey! That's my last white one, you thief!"

Keefer hauled the bags of clothing onto the porch and sat down on one of the plastic chairs. She let her eyes wander over the wooden boards of the floor and pursed her lips in thought. *Pretty ugly, isn't it?* she sighed. It had been so long since she'd actually cleaned house, and now that she did, there was something new she wanted to change each time she looked.

I should get motivated and start fixing things. She glanced toward the front door and shook her head. *There's so much to do, though.* Her eyes lit up suddenly. *Ah, but I have my own personal construction worker, don't I?*

Sheridan had been lying on her couch for some time after unsuccessfully chasing her dog. She'd let Pharaoh have the bra, feeling that he had every right to tear it up; she had been spending so little time with her dogs, he deserved it. Zeus walked up to the couch and laid his big head in her lap, huffing and grunting for some attention. "I'm sorry, sweetie," she said apologetically as she scratched his head. "I love you, really."

After a few minutes, Pharaoh abandoned the now-shredded bra and joined his brother, both dogs competing for their scratches. "Maybe I should stay home with you guys today," she said guiltily.

The tall inspector began making a list of things that needed repair or replacing. She started on the porch and moved through the house slowly. She paused as she stood outside the bathroom, a pleasant smile on her face. *This room needs nothing,* she thought with a chuckle. She closed her eyes as she remembered Sheridan and herself crammed together in the bathtub, smashed against each other by the sink, and again by the wall. She could feel that heated kiss, laden with frustration and want. She laughed out loud at how desperate Sheridan had been that day, and how she'd held herself in check. *Poor thing, I practically tortured her with kisses and yet she behaved.*

Keefer walked away from the bathroom with a big grin on her face as she recalled the day after the big bathroom remodeling vividly. *The first time we made love.* She stopped walking and groaned as her nipples hardened, then looked down at them and shivered. *Sheridan literally worshipped them that day.* She reached up and pressed her palms into her breasts, attempting to push her nipples back in. *She hasn't done that since...I liked it so much.* The brunette rubbed her hands over her breasts a few times, her list of repairs forgotten. *Gotta get her to do that again. Where is she, anyway?*

Sheridan stretched and wrinkled her nose, "Shit, I stink." She climbed out from under her dogs and turned on the shower, taking off her remaining clothes. She was about to get into the tub when the phone rang.

"Hiya, sweetie," she said happily into the phone.

"I miss you," Keefer replied.

Sheridan sighed. "I miss you too, baby, but I'm having a problem with my dogs."

"Problem? Is everything okay? Are they okay?"

The blonde chuckled. "Calm down, honey, they're okay, they just miss me. I've been neglecting them badly."

Keefer paused. "So...what are you going to do?"

"I don't know. I want to be with you in the worst way, but I feel guilty about the boys. I've never left them alone so much in their lives."

"Bring them here," Keefer said seriously.

"There? To your house?" Sheridan's eyebrows rose in question.

"Yes, why not? They get along with Fifi, and they like me..."

The blonde lit up excitedly. "Shit! Why didn't I think of that? I was sitting here all torn up about separating my time between you both. Cool, Keef!"

Keefer laughed, then turned serious. "You were torn up?"

"Hell, yeah. I want to be with you, and the boys need me, too. I was afraid I'd have to cut my Keefer time down."

"I love you, baby," Keefer said.

"I love you, too. Hey, I got the water running, I'm about to go in the shower."

"You're naked?" Keefer asked.

"Totally," Sheridan purred.

"Mmm. Go take your shower," the brunette urged.

"I will, baby, and I'll think about what you did to me this morning while I wash my parts."

Keefer groaned. "We can't spend every waking minute in bed, Sher."

"I know, baby, but you make me so hot...all the time."

"Don't I know the feeling. Go, take your shower."

"I'll be over afterwards."

"Can't wait to smell you."

Sheridan showered and indeed *did* think about Keefer as she washed herself. However, she thought about her the *whole* time, not just as she washed her *parts*. She thought about Keefer's naked ass, gyrating and flexing as the brunette made love to her, and about Keefer's admission that she'd almost touched herself. By the time Sheridan was done with her shower, she was ready for another. "Stop it. Keefer is right; we can't just live on sex. Enough," she told her crotch as she patted it dry—extremely carefully. "We're going shopping. Can't be any harm in shopping," she said as she put on her deodorant. "In fact, I'm just gonna give her a little kiss when I walk in the door. Nothing fancy, just a peck." She looked at herself in the mirror and set her jaw firmly. "A day at the mall, that's it."

Keefer hung up the phone and groaned. "Okay, stop this!" she scolded herself. "We can have a day without sex." She nodded, trying to convince her body of her statement. "She'll come over with the boys, we'll kiss hello...gently...and then after the dogs are all settled in, we'll go shopping. That's that," she said firmly. "Oh, all right, we'll make out, *then* we'll go shopping." Keefer frowned, then put her foot down. "No. A little kiss, and maybe a hug. That's what we'll do."

She stood in her bra and panties, studying her clothes. She wanted something that would be easy to take on and off in the fitting rooms, but didn't want to look frumpy. She held up a pair of nylon shorts, holding them against her. "This is okay, no buttons or zippers." She also went for a tank top, figuring she could just put shirts on over it instead of taking it off. Dressed and ready, she stood in front of the mirror and stared at herself. She looked plain, and she frowned. A devious smile suddenly lit up her face and she chuckled out loud. "Oh yeah, I know just the thing," she said as she fished through her drawer. "No one will even know."

Sheridan had no trouble loading the dogs into the car. The trouble was in getting their dog bowls and food in with them and making sure the animals didn't tear into the bag of food while she was driving. She drove slowly as the two dogs bounced excitedly around in the car. She had made the mistake of telling them they were going to see Keefer and now they were hyper about the trip, tangling their leashes into one big knot.

Keefer watched in amusement as her lover tried to corral the dogs and their belongings in her little car. She laughed when Sheridan's seat suddenly fell backwards and Zeus was sitting on top of her, his head hanging out of the driver's window. She didn't dare call the dog, knowing that he was likely to jump out the window and strangle his mommy. Instead, she sat down on a chair with a hand covering her mouth and watched the scene unfold.

Sheridan managed to get the seat back into an upright position and held the tangled leashes in one hand, the fingers of her other gripping Pharaoh's collar tightly. "Keef? You wanna give me a hand?"

Keefer began clapping from her chair.

"Oh, you're a riot," Sheridan shouted as her door opened.

Fifi heard Sheridan and came running from the bedroom to greet her. She stopped short at the door and cocked her head to the side.

Keefer snickered and stood up. "Let Zeus go, I'm right here."

"I can't, their leashes are all tangled up!" Sheridan yelled as both dogs tried to get out of her door at the same time, stepping all over her.

The frustration was evident in her lover's voice, but Keefer couldn't contain her laughter. "Unhook them then, they'll come to me either way."

Sheridan blushed at her stupidity and unhooked the leashes. The dogs bolted from the car and ran fast and furious at Keefer. Now it was

Sheridan's turn to laugh as Keefer was on her back in a heartbeat with two massive dogs on top of her.

Fifi, in a fit of jealousy, ran out the door, jumped into the pile and started to bark at her mommy.

Sheridan crawled out of the car and sat on the driveway, holding her stomach from laughing so hard. Just to be a wise ass, she started applauding.

"Sheridan! Help!"

Keefer's loud giggling gave Sheridan a happy feeling that warmed her heart. She waited a little longer before untangling the leashes and hooking them back on the proper dogs.

Once the big boys were pulled off, Fifi stopped barking and also climbed off of Keefer.

"Good Lord!" Keefer gasped through her laughter. "They licked me to death!"

"They have good taste," Sheridan commented, giving Keefer a helping hand.

The tall woman picked up her jealous dog and kissed her nose. "Feef, now you be good, and share with the boys." Keefer put Fifi down on the floor and nodded to her lover.

Fifi looked at her mother in horror as Sheridan led the dogs into the house.

"Okay guys, this is Fifi's house, you'd better behave," Sheridan warned, pointing a stern finger at them. She unleashed Zeus, who went right into the kitchen, then Pharaoh, who immediately jumped on Keefer again. Sheridan knelt down and grabbed Fifi, picked her up and hugged her. "Who's a good girl? You're a good girl!" she said in her most affectionate baby voice.

Fifi felt somewhat better that Sheridan ignored the other dogs and held her. She wagged her tail happily and licked the blonde's face. Soon the two big dogs finished their inspection of the house and came back to the two women. Sheridan put Fifi down and got her a treat, petting her as she ate it, while Keefer did the same for the boys.

The tall woman watched the muscles in Sheridan's arm move as she petted Fifi. Her mouth watered with visions of those same muscles engaged in entirely different acts. Her gaze shifted to her lover's lips as she cooed at the dog and she had a strong urge to kiss them, and not the little peck she had been planning. Blue eyes closed as Keefer shook the image out of her head.

Sheridan stood up straight and raised an eyebrow at her lover. The tall woman's eyes were closed and she was biting her top lip. *God, I want to suck her face off.*

487

Keefer opened her eyes and found green eyes staring at her intently. She took a deep breath and clenched her fists so she wouldn't grab and maul her lover.

Sheridan took a step forward and tilted her head up, asking for a kiss.

They came together hard, their momentum propelling Keefer's back against the wall. Tongues plunged and retreated, lips moved hungrily and hands tried to touch everything at once. Sheridan emitted a guttural groan, causing Pharaoh to jump up on them and investigate. Fifi wasn't happy with the big dog climbing up *her* Sheridan, and she jumped up the blonde's other leg.

Keefer tore her mouth away and panted heavily, her eyes half closed and fixated on her lover's lips. "Someone's jealous," she breathed out.

"They'll have to learn to share. You're mine," Sheridan replied, dropping her forehead onto Keefer's shoulder.

Keefer reached up and held the back of Sheridan's head, keeping her close. "Sher, we should stop."

"Why?" the blonde mumbled, rubbing her cheek on Keefer's breast.

"We agreed to go shopping today. Besides, I know we can have *one* productive day without sex."

Sheridan nodded. She was suddenly determined to have a normal day out with her lover, even if it meant shopping at the mall, something she really hated. It seemed important enough to Keefer. She peeled herself off of her lover and thrust her hands in her jeans pockets. "Yeah, we can have fun doing something other than sex," she agreed, still staring hungrily at her lover.

Keefer shivered and then broke the heavy stare. "Give me those bowls," she said, grabbing them and the bag of food from where they lay on the floor.

Sheridan watched her lover as she walked into the kitchen, all the dogs trailing after her. "Just set down some water, we'll feed them later."

Keefer returned shortly, giving her girlfriend the once-over. Suddenly her eyes widened. "You're wearing a white T-shirt without a bra?" she asked loudly in disbelief.

Sheridan shrugged. "Yeah, what's the problem?"

"Are you trying to drive me crazy?" Keefer asked in distress.

"The boys ate my last white bra," she offered as an explanation.

"Well then, that's the first thing on the agenda at the mall...buying you a bra."

"Come on, Keef," Sheridan whined.

"No arguments. I will not have you walking around with these," she poked Sheridan in the breasts, "winking and smiling at everyone we see."

Sheridan grinned in amusement. "I like it when you get all butch," she teased.

Keefer narrowed her eyes playfully. "Come on, Nipples, let's go get you covered up." She opened the door and held it for her lover.

The dogs heard the door open and came to investigate. Sheridan knelt down next to Zeus. "You guys be good, and play nice with Fifi. We'll be back with new bones for all of you."

The construction worker stood forlornly by the garbage pails, surrounded by bag-laden husbands and boyfriends as Keefer shopped. Green eyes stayed riveted to the tall brunette as she meandered through the shop, picking things up occasionally and studying others. Sheridan looked around at her peers, all confined to the benches as she was. Everyone had the same blank stare, and the same expectant expression popped up each time a woman exited a nearby store. She wondered if they were in the same boat as she was, admonished to the bench by their wives and girlfriends. Exiled for a momentary lack of control.

Sheridan grimaced with guilt as she recalled the look on her lover's face before she pointed wordlessly to the garbage pail. The blonde had tried to apologize but Keefer insisted that she stand where she was pointing and not move. *Okay, so maybe I shouldn't have blurted out how fuckable she'd be in that skirt,* Sheridan thought ruefully. *How did I know there were all those people behind me?*

Keefer suddenly appeared by her side and Sheridan smiled apologetically, hoping this time it would work. "I'm sorry, honey. I'll behave," she promised. "Don't leave me here again."

Keefer looked skeptical. "Do you think you can control yourself?"

"I will. I promise."

Keefer chuckled. "Okay," she said disbelievingly.

Sheridan followed Keefer happily through the mall. She was just so glad to be away from that horrible bench that she didn't even notice where they were heading. When they stopped outside of the lingerie store, Sheridan swallowed hard and her eyes went wide.

"You promised to behave," Keefer reminded her with a playful twinkle in her eye. Sheridan pursed her lips and nodded, dragging her feet reluctantly after her girlfriend. Keefer smiled and bit back a laugh. It was going to be torture for Sheridan to behave herself in that store, and Keefer wanted to see how long it would take before she lost it. "Come on, we need to get you a bra, and I need some pj's."

"I don't wear these bras, Keef!" Sheridan said in a panic, eyeing all the frilly, lacy garments.

"They have sports bras, too, Sher," she said, pointing to a section in the back of the store.

Sheridan's eyes followed her lover's finger and they narrowed. "I don't see any sports bras."

Keefer chuckled. "They're there, trust me." Sheridan gave her a disbelieving glare. "Why don't you wander around, *behaving* yourself, and find me some cute pajamas?"

"You trust me to pick out your pj's?" Sheridan asked, wide-eyed.

"I do." *I trust you more by yourself than with me in this store,* Keefer thought.

The blonde lit up excitedly. "Cool, babe! I'll go find you something!" she said before she took off.

"God help me."

Sheridan was like a kid in a candy store for the most part, fingering and touching things, to the saleswoman's dismay.

"May I help you?"

Sheridan shifted the bags she was holding and flashed a charming smile at the woman. "Nope. I got it covered."

"Are you sure? Because *that*," she indicated the negligee Sheridan was rubbing on her face, "isn't your size," she huffed.

"Yes, I'm sure," the blonde replied distractedly as she spied some camisoles. She released the silky garment she had been molesting and wandered away. She stood in front of the mannequin that had caught her eye, picturing Keefer in the black and red outfit without a care in the world.

"Is there something in particular that you're looking for?"

Sheridan frowned, having been rudely snapped out of her daydream by the annoying woman. "Look, lady, I don't need any help," she bit out.

"Perhaps if you tell me—"

"Perhaps if you take a walk..."

The woman stepped away a few feet, but still kept her eye on the blonde.

"What? Because I don't look like I wear this stuff, you're gonna harass me the whole time?"

The lady backed away further.

"Stupid, ignorant people...oughtta get a life," Sheridan mumbled. "Ooh!" Her mood changed dramatically as she found herself in front of yet another daydream-worthy display.

Keefer signaled to her lover that she was heading to the try-on rooms and Sheridan nodded, confident that she'd picked out something perfect for Keefer.

"Open up, Keef," Sheridan said as she knocked on the door, "it's me." The lock opened and the blonde continued into the dressing room. "I have something that I—" Sheridan stopped talking and her mouth hung open. Keefer was standing there in a tiny little camisole and lace panties. "Fuck, yeah! That's what I call underwear!" she said with a lascivious leer. "Buy it," she urged.

Keefer blushed hotly. "I wore it here."

"You wore it...oh, baby!" Sheridan grinned evilly, her gaze traveling the length of Keefer's body repeatedly. "I don't know why, but damn..."

"I wanted to feel sexy," Keefer said shyly.

Sheridan dropped the bags, opened her arms, and licked her lips. "Come over here and I'll tell you how you feel."

"Sheridan," Keefer warned, "these mirrors are usually two way."

The blonde stared at the mirror, then lifted her shirt and flashed it. "There, that oughtta keep 'em happy. Buncha pervs, watching my woman take her clothes off!"

Keefer blushed harder. "Sheridan!" she whisper-shouted. "Here," she thrust a hanger at her lover, "try this on if you're going to be taking off your shirt."

Sheridan eyed the bra suspiciously. "That don't look like a sports bra."

"It's called a bralette."

The blonde narrowed here eyes. "Bralette? How...cute."

"Just try it on. I'm sure you'll like it."

"Okay, but only if you try this on," she handed Keefer one of the hangers she'd been holding.

"Sheridan, these aren't pajamas. It's a G-string."

"I know. No one says you can't wear it to sleep, though," Sheridan replied, once again leering at her lover.

Keefer blushed. "Okay, no way. You have to get out of here."

"Please let me stay! I'll try on the chiclet!"

"Bralette."

"Whatever. Please?" Sheridan tried to look innocent but failed. "I'll be good," she fairly purred, once again staring at her lover's outfit.

Keefer felt a jolt of excitement in her loins and she gulped. Suddenly, the idea of being in that dressing room with Sheridan was a huge turn-on. "Um, all right...but hands to yourself."

Sheridan smiled so wide it looked painful and sat down with her hands folded in her lap.

"You're not going to just sit there stock-still and stare at me like that, are you?" Keefer wondered.

"Probably not. I have a feeling I'll be squirming a bit," Sheridan said with a sly smile.

Keefer's ears turned pink, even though her heart sped up in anticipation of doing a little sexy fashion show for her lover.

"Keef, it's just us," Sheridan said reassuringly. She spread herself out in front of the mirror and winked. "And the guy behind the mirror."

Keefer snickered and relaxed. She held up a pair of satiny blue lounge pants and Sheridan nodded in approval. Keefer bent over to put her foot in the pants leg and her nipples strained against the smooth fabric of her camisole, causing them to pucker instantly. She ignored the pleasurably tingling sensations and continued to put on the pants. However, when she stood up again and looked over at her lover, the tingling turned into throbbing. Sheridan's eyes were riveted to her left nipple and, if possible, it hardened even more under her stare.

"Oh yeah, you should wear these things more often, baby," Sheridan said in a deep, sexy voice.

A myriad of emotions flew through Keefer and she tried hard to not let any of them show. She was embarrassed, horny, brave, and self-conscious, all at the same time. She plastered a confident look on her face and even pushed out her chest a little.

"Mmm, pretty cocky about those tits, are you?"

Keefer looked down at them, then at Sheridan's lusty expression, and smiled. "You like them, don't you."

"Fuck, yeah, baby. There's no bra under there, just a thin layer of sexy material between your beautiful tits and my eyes," Sheridan purred.

Keefer felt pretty good about her body at that moment. The way Sheridan was drinking her in—not only her breasts, but from head to toe—made her feel really desirable. She gestured to the pants. "What do you think?"

"Hot, definitely hot. I can't wait to feel you lying next to me in them."

Keefer turned around, giving Sheridan a nice view of her ass as she bent down and pulled them off. Hearing her lover's loud intake of breath gave her even more confidence, not to mention how hot it made her feel. She stood upright and tossed the pants to Sheridan. "Hold those," she said and bent over at the waist to pick up another piece of clothing.

Sheridan raised an eyebrow at her lover's display of obvious sexuality. It was turning her on immensely and she wished that they were anywhere but in that dressing room where she'd promised to behave.

Keefer shimmied into a pair of soft pink boxers and a little matching shirt. She tried to look at herself in the mirror, but Sheridan was in the way.

Caution: Under Construction

"Don't be showing the pervert in the mirror anything. I'll tell you what I think."

Judging from her lover's grin, Keefer figured this set was a keeper, too. She had an inkling that anything she tried on that was made of something small and shiny would be just fine with Sheridan. She struck a dramatic pose and the blonde applauded.

"Oh yeah, baby, you work it." Sheridan nodded enthusiastically.

Keefer pursed her lips and tossed her hair back, biting back a chuckle. "How's this?"

"Beautiful, baby, now try on the nightie." Sheridan wiggled her eyebrows and held up said item.

"Okay, but you have to try on the bra first."

"You got it." Sheridan peeled her shirt off in one motion and held up the bra to inspect. "Not bad. Feels flimsy, though."

"It'll work, trust me," Keefer assured, blue eyes narrowing on Sheridan's breasts.

Sheridan smirked at her lover's stare and jutted her chest out. "Wanna help?"

Keefer coughed a little and stepped back. "Oh, no, no you don't," she warned. "You know, if I get that close...anyway, we made a deal."

"Aw, baby. That was before."

"No, we made a deal. No sex today." As she said it, Keefer's sex twitched.

Sheridan got into the bra and adjusted the straps. "Hey, looks good. Feels great!"

"I told you. We'll get you some other colors when we leave," Keefer said proudly. She was glad she could pick something out that Sheridan would like.

"Your turn now," Sheridan said, hands on hips. "Nightie, please."

"How come I get the feeling that you'll be happy with whatever I try on?" Keefer asked with a grin.

"Keef, if it's on your body, how can it possibly look bad?"

The brunette blinked in shock a few times before gathering herself. Sheridan just said things like that out of the blue. Just when she thought she was going to continue to be her piggy self, Sheridan came out with a sweet thing like that and threw her for a loop.

"What? No more?" the blonde pouted.

Keefer squatted down and initiated a long sensual kiss, the aftereffects of which sent Sheridan crashing into the mirror and falling on her ass. Once she was upright again, she put her finger to her lips. "Shh, Keef! You don't want Cruella finding us in here."

"Is everything all right in there?"

493

"See? It's her! Answer her, tell her you tripped on the chiclet or something."

Keefer tried to hold it in, but busted out laughing anyway. Sheridan stared wide-eyed at her lover.

"Bralette," Keefer squeaked out as she laughed. "I tripped on a bralette!"

Sheridan snorted loudly before she fell into a fit of hysterics, too.

"Excuse me, but is there more than one person in the fitting room?"

The horror in the disembodied voice only made them laugh harder.

"I'm getting the manager!"

They heard the woman walk away in a huff and laughed even louder.

"You should see her, Keef, she looks like she sucked on a pickle." Sheridan imitated the saleswoman's pinched face of disapproval. "She's so stuck up and anal, her legs are probably sewed shut at the knee."

"Probably runs naked through the store with a thong tied around her head after hours," Keefer added through fits of laughter.

By the time the woman came back and opened the locked door with a key, Sheridan was laying on her back, wearing the bralette, her legs in the air, holding her sides from the laughter. Keefer was on her knees, the G-string on her head and her hands between her legs holding herself. "Stop! I'm gonna pee!" she declared through hysterics.

Sheridan sat on the bench, surrounded by husbands and boyfriends, clutching the bags and staring at her feet. A red-faced Keefer approached rapidly, her long legs eating up ground in an attempt to get as far away from the store as fast as she could without running. Sheridan winced when she saw her lover's shoes standing in front of her. "You can't blame that all on me, you know," she said with a pout.

"I've never been so embarrassed in my life!" Keefer said, thrusting a bag at her lover.

Sheridan looked into the bag. She felt guilty when she saw her bra in three different colors. *Even after being totally mortified, she still got me my bras.* "Heh, I see you bought the pink outfit."

"They *made* me buy the pink outfit," Keefer growled, walking quickly toward the exit. Sheridan practically ran in order to keep up.

"Made you?"

"Yes. Even after I convinced them I didn't *actually* pee in it," she replied, tight-lipped.

Sheridan groaned. She knew that this was one of those situations where she was going to have to take full responsibility, even if she wasn't the only one to blame. People like Keefer didn't get kicked out of classy lingerie stores. *Crap.* "I'm sorry."

"Sheridan, that was my favorite underwear store! I'll never be able to show my face in there again. Do you know how awful it was to be escorted to the desk by a security guard?" she asked, opening the door to the parking garage.

Sheridan smiled guiltily. She knew she should not tell Keefer she knew what it felt like, so she simply smiled and looked penitent. "I love you, Keef."

Blue eyes narrowed and glared.

Okay, not a good time to pull out that one. Green eyes scanned the area for an errant flower salesman. "Hey, let's go to that really cool Italian seafood restaurant that you like so much. I'll buy you dinner and you can have wine."

Keefer's glare softened. "Can I get lobster?"

"Absolutely." The blonde nodded rapidly, throwing the bags in the trunk of her car.

Keefer smiled. "Okay."

Sheridan sighed mightily. *Phew! Pulled that out of the fire.*

Keefer slid into the passenger side and put on her seat belt. "You know, she really did look like she sucked on a pickle."

Chapter 43

The couple shared snickers over dinner as they relived the events in the mall. Keefer had finally settled down and found the humor in the situation, although it was still all Sheridan's fault. If the construction worker hadn't come into the changing room in the first place, none of it would have happened.

Sheridan took the blame, chalking it up to just one of the many times she would be wrong. She didn't mind, though. If Keefer was going to let her off the hook this easily in the future, her life was going to be a piece of cake. Besides, she'd had a lot of fun getting into trouble.

When the two women finally arrived home, Sheridan mentioned that it might be a good idea if she opened the door and took the brunt of the boys' enthusiasm. Keefer agreed and stood back on the porch with the shopping bags, already grinning in anticipation of her lover being jumped.

Sheridan shushed Keefer and put her ear to the door, listening intently. "I don't hear anything," she whispered. "That can be a bad thing."

"What do you mean, *bad thing*?" Keefer asked, putting her ear to the door, as well.

"Trust me. Those two are never quiet. Something's up," Sheridan whispered nervously. She put the key in the door and waited. Nothing happened. She opened the door slowly—still, nothing happened. She stuck her head in the door, gasped, closed the door quickly and gave Keefer a panicked look.

"What?" Keefer asked nervously.

"Keef...we don't know for sure it was the boys' fault...I mean, you could have been robbed or something."

Keefer's eyes widened in horror, then narrowed and she tried to push open the door.

"Now, now...Keef...don't get upset..."

The tall woman growled and shoved open the door. "Holy shit!" she gasped, dropping the shopping bags on the floor. "Holy goddamned shit!"

Sheridan ran inside ahead of her and blocked her path. "I'm sure Fifi had something to do with this."

"Fifi! Get in here!" Keefer ground out, her arms folded over her chest, foot tapping angrily.

Sheridan winced. "You guys better get in here, *now!*"

Toenails were heard in the kitchen, a snort was heard from the bathroom, and Fifi came running obediently from the bedroom to sit down in front of her mommy.

Keefer pointed to the utter destruction that was once her couch. "What did you do?" she asked the dog sternly.

Fifi cocked her head to the side and raised and dropped each eyebrow independently of the other, all the while looking very innocent.

Sheridan suddenly felt bad for the dog and reached down to discreetly remove a piece of fluff from Fifi's fur.

"Don't protect her, Sher, she's guilty, too."

Zeus, remembering Mommy's promise of a treat, loped slowly into the room and went directly to the shopping bags, sticking his fat head inside of one.

Sheridan snatched the bag away and held it up in the air. "Oh, no. No, no, no. Are you nuts?"

Pharaoh came in slowly, too, and sat on Sheridan's feet, looking up guiltily, asking for forgiveness.

"What am I going to do with you now?" Sheridan asked in frustration, pointing to the mess. "Keefer let you stay here so I didn't have to run back and forth like a maniac every morning and night and you destroy her living room!"

Keefer pursed her lips in thought. Sheridan had a point, But still...

"Bad! Both of you!" Sheridan stomped her foot and Pharaoh winced. "Oh no, don't play that game with me, you tore apart that couch." She pointed again to the couch and Zeus put his head down. "Now you can't come here anymore, and that makes it much harder on me."

And me! Keefer frowned.

Sheridan took a deep breath and glared at her dogs. "Thanks a lot, kids."

"I can get a new couch, Sher."

"Keef, you can't just let them get away with—"

"No, it's okay. Seriously. I've been thinking about the house lately and I really want a new couch."

Sheridan stared blankly at her calm lover as she stood there, completely surrounded by couch innards. "But still, I feel awful. They don't do this in my house!"

Keefer kicked a pile of stuffing and watched as it floated back down. She picked up a mangled cushion, showing it to Zeus, who turned his head away in an attempt to ignore it. "Zeus, I'm not happy. That goes for you, too, Pharaoh." The large pit bull came over to Keefer and leaned into her legs. "You are both bad boys and I'm mad at you," she said with disappointment in her voice.

Sheridan watched in awe as her hyperactive pit bull climbed delicately up Keefer's legs and whined.

"Is that all you've got?" Keefer asked the dog. Pharaoh rested his head on Keefer's hip and whimpered. "Okay, well...give me a kiss and I'll think about it," Keefer said, bending down to receive the sloppy kiss.

Sheridan's jaw fell further as Zeus inched his way toward Keefer, head down, and flopped over on his back in a display of submission.

"Why do I have a feeling that you may have instigated this whole thing?" Keefer asked the Rottweiler. He licked his lips and arched his back. "Okay, how about I let you both off the hook," Keefer said, reaching over to scratch the dog's exposed belly.

"You guys are such traitors!" Sheridan pouted.

Keefer flashed a sweet smile. "When you got it, you got it."

The blonde rolled her eyes.

Fifi looked incredulously at the scene, then walked over and blinked demurely at Sheridan.

"You're not so innocent yourself, young lady, so don't you play coy with me."

The dog slinked over to her mommy and eyed Sheridan. When Keefer petted her head, the blonde could have sworn she saw Fifi stick out her tongue at her.

Sparing one last look to the destruction, Sheridan sighed heavily. "Okay, the love fest is over. Who wants dinner?" she asked.

All three dogs ran to follow Sheridan into the kitchen. Keefer brought the bags into the bedroom and began to unpack them. She heard her lover yell and was startled by a loud crash and scattering sound. "Sher?" she asked, making her way toward the kitchen.

"It's all your fault," the blonde yelled back.

Keefer tried really hard not to laugh as she watched her lover crawling around on the floor, picking up pellets of dog food one at a time, while trying to keep the boys from eating it all. She quietly went and retrieved the broom, smacking Sheridan on the butt with it.

The blonde glared up at her lover, but once she saw the mirth clearly evident on Keefer's face, she chuckled. "Yeah, a broom would help," she said with a shake of her head.

Sheridan flopped down on her belly and buried her face in the pillows. She lay bonelessly exhausted, silently mumbling obscenities regarding the dogs.

By the time Keefer entered the bedroom, freshly showered and wearing her new pink outfit, the construction worker was snoring loudly. Keefer sighed. "Well, I suppose we *did* have an agreement." She crawled into bed and stared at her sleeping lover. "If you hadn't felt so guilty and insisted that you clean up everything by yourself..." Keefer leaned over, placed a gentle kiss on Sheridan's shoulder and then pulled the covers up over it. Blue eyes traced the outline of Sheridan's body under the covers and closed as Keefer groaned. *Why does she have to be so hot?*

The brunette sighed again and watched her lover's back rise and fall evenly as she slept. She raised an eyebrow and bit her bottom lip as she reached out and, with one finger, moved the blanket down a little bit. She drank in the smooth skin with her eyes, her mouth watering at the sight. She held her breath as she pulled the covers away further, slowly, until the construction worker was bared all the way to the backs of her thighs.

Keefer sat back against the headboard and studied the soft skin. Every curve was traced with her heavy blue gaze. She did her job well as every inch of flesh was investigated, hungrily. Her belly tightened and she crossed her thighs, squeezing away the ache that had been there all day. Groaning, she traced the curve of Sheridan's ass cheek with her fingertip, dragging it lightly up the construction worker's muscled back until she reached her shoulder. Goose bumps broke out across Sheridan's body and Keefer shivered in sympathy. *Oh, God...this is torture!* She quickly covered her lover and threw herself into her pillows. *Great, now you're seriously horny again. Good going, Keef.*

She sighed and poked Sheridan in the side, but the blonde slept on. "Fine," Keefer pouted and turned over to go to sleep.

Sheridan woke suddenly in the middle of the night. She tried to sit up but couldn't, due to the big pit bull sprawled across her belly. "Pharaoh, get up!" she whispered, wiggling her hips. The dog didn't budge. Neither did the one smushed up into her neck, breathing on her face. "Feeeeefs..." she groaned, "You're gonna give me a stiff neck again." The dog merely tasted something in her sleep and sighed. The blonde craned her neck to hunt for Zeus and snickered when she spotted him. He was spooning with her lover, his big fat head sharing the pillow, Keefer's long arm draped over his body. *We need a bigger bed,* she laughed to herself.

Looking at her lover, all curled around her dog, Sheridan smiled happily. *It takes a special kinda woman to love these guys, especially after last night.* Sheridan briefly thought about the couch and winced. I lucked out big time, she thought with a contented sigh. She dislodged her arm from under Pharaoh and reached over, fishing around under the blanket until she found Keefer. She stroked her lover's back a while, enjoying the feel of the soft material as it moved under her hand. When that wasn't enough, she slipped her hand under the silk boxers and held Keefer's butt cheek. Before she knew it, she was again sound asleep.

Keefer awoke to find that the warm body she had been snuggling was not the same body she had been dreaming about. She sat up and looked over at her lover, buried under dog, and snickered. She patted the Rottweiler on the rump and pushed him toward the edge of the bed. Zeus rolled over and crawled out of the covers, stretching and yawning as soon as his feet hit the floor. He looked around to gather his bearings and started to walk over to Sheridan's side of the bed when Keefer stopped him.

"Let your mommy sleep, big guy. Come with me and I'll feed you breakfast," Keefer said around a yawn.

Hearing the "b" word, Pharaoh's good ear perked up and he stood also, stretching on top of the bed and gingerly jumping over Sheridan to follow Keefer. Fifi strolled along casually, bringing up the rear. Keefer laughed silently and shook her head again, knowing her mornings would never be the same.

The brunette couldn't believe how fast the big dogs devoured their breakfast. They inhaled it immediately as Fifi and Keefer looked on in amazement. The smallest dog ran to her dish and stood guard. The boys also sloppily slurped up what seemed to be a gallon of water, then shook themselves dry, spraying both the disgusted-looking Fifi and the stunned Keefer with the wet debris. The tall woman wiped herself off and made a sour face. Not only just her mornings, but her kitchen would never be the same, either. "I suppose you want to go for a walk now?"

Five ears stood at attention and Keefer giggled. "This is going to be fun," she mused. "Okay, I'm going to get dressed. Fifi, keep the boys in line, will you?" The small dog wagged her tail and sat on top of her food bowl.

Keefer stood by the side of the bed and watched her lover sleep. She had the urge to climb on top of Sheridan and just revel in the feel of the construction worker beneath her. She fought the need, though, giving Sheridan her peace to sleep in and enjoy her newly acquired days off. The blonde made a tiny noise as she rolled over onto her side, the blanket exposing her shoulders. Keefer stared at the relaxed muscles under the smooth skin and groaned. "We don't have any deals for today, Ms. Landers. You better be prepared for me when I get home," she warned the sleeping blonde.

Sheridan stretched loudly and made spitting sounds as the fur stuck to her lips. She didn't have to open her eyes to know the culprit, but did anyway. "Feef, why must you always be on my head?" She asked, pushing the small dog away. Scanning the bed, she found Zeus on his back at the foot and Pharaoh draped over Keefer's side. "Keef?" the blonde called out before another long stretch overtook her. "Keef?" she asked again and then looked at the clock. "Wow, ten-thirty! I slept until ten-thirty?" She got out of bed and did her morning necessities before coming back in with Keefer's pajama bottoms in one hand, a note in the other. "So, Keefer fed, watered and walked you guys, huh?" The blonde laughed to herself, imagining Keefer and the beasts, plus one. "The neighbors must be dying to know what that was all about," she snickered.

The construction worker sat down on the bed and held Keefer's silk boxers to her cheek, rubbing them a few times and purring. "Mmm. I can't believe I fell asleep." she mumbled, burying her face in the sexy material. "Oh?" she asked as she inhaled again. "Keefer," she groaned, smelling the remnants of her lover's arousal, "why didn't you wake me up?"

Sheridan pouted a while before a thought popped into her head. "Ooh, did you touch yourself last night while I slept, Keefer?" Just the idea made Sheridan's nipples hard. "Oh, baby!" The blonde fell backwards onto the bed with the shorts on her face and began to daydream.

Keefer left the ladies room with a tight-lipped expression that barely hid her amusement. That was her second trip to the bathroom to "freshen up" since she'd arrived at work. She couldn't stop daydreaming about Sheridan's naked back and in turn, had to go and wipe up the effect that her imagination was having on her body. Shaking her head and squaring her shoulders, she closed her office door behind her, determined to do work. "You're a professional. Stop acting like a horny teenager and get to work."

This determination worked for about an hour and Keefer actually managed to get lost in her work until her phone rang and her lover's voice broke her concentration.

"Hi, baby," Sheridan breathed sexily into the phone.

Keefer closed her eyes and pictured Sheridan's thighs. "Hello. Are you enjoying your day off so far?"

"Oh, yeah," the blonde purred.

Keefer's eyebrow went up. "What are you doing?"

"Lying on the bed, smelling your boxers."

Keefer blushed. "Sher, you are not!"

"Mmm...yes, I am."

"Oh, God." Keefer hid her face in her hand.

"Did you have a nasty dream last night? 'Cuz it smells so good."

"Sher!" Keefer whispered in embarrassment, her eyes popping open to look around the office as if someone could hear what her lover was saying.

"Well?" Sheridan asked.

"No, I went to sleep...like *that*."

"Mmm," Sheridan moaned. "Did you touch yourself?"

"No." Keefer squirmed in her chair.

"What were you thinking about? What made you so horny?"

"You, what else?"

"What was I doing?" Sheridan asked in a deep breathy tone.

Keefer closed her eyes again as her lover's voice shot a spark between her legs. "Believe it or not, you were sleeping."

"I was sleeping and you got so wet? Imagine if I was touching you then," Sheridan groaned.

Keefer groaned right back at the thought. She had wanted Sheridan to touch her for a day and half now.

"Oh, yeah, you'd like that, wouldn't you...if I touched you."

"Sher—stop that," Keefer said quietly in a slightly shaky voice.

"Are you getting wet again?"

"Yes, and it's not nice what you're doing," the tall woman said with frustration.

"What's wrong, baby?"

"You know very well what's wrong, Sheridan."

"You're getting all hot and wet and I'm not there to touch you...lick it up?"

Keefer's legs opened and closed all by themselves and she stood up to make them stop. "Sheridan! Did you call just to make me crazy?"

"No, I want you to touch yourself."

"I can't do that!" Keefer looked around her office nervously. "Not here. Not now."

Sheridan groaned loudly. "Oh yeah, you just thought about it, though. Are you that horny?"

Keefer closed her blinds and sat back down in the chair. "Baby...don't do this to me," she pleaded.

"Come on...please?" Sheridan begged in a breathy, seductive voice.

Keefer's belly clenched. "Don't use that voice, Sher."

The blonde purposely lowered her tone. "Mmm...I wish I were there now. I'd crawl under your desk and just breathe between your legs."

"Sher..." Keefer groaned, closing her legs.

"Go on, Keef...lock your door...come on, baby..."

Keefer surprised herself by following Sheridan's orders, then leaned her back against the locked door. "No, Sheridan...I can't."

"I bet I can coax you. You haven't hung up the phone yet, so I know you want to."

Keefer blushed and scanned the room again.

"I bet I can make you so wet you can't help but touch yourself...pretending it's me...and my fingers, my mouth, my tongue." Sheridan groaned loudly.

Keefer's heart beat quicker at the words, and harder at the groan. "Are you touching yourself?" she asked, really hoping her lover would answer in the negative. She didn't need that image if she was going to be able to control herself.

"Oh yeah, just lying naked on the bed...legs spread wide...wishing you were here."

Keefer actually felt the wetness seep out of her. "God, baby...you are?" she asked in a tortured whisper, flopping back down in the chair.

"Mmm-hmm."

Keefer couldn't stop the image from forming and her hand fell into her lap, her heart pounding in her chest. "I can't."

"Does that mean you almost did?"

"Maybe."

"Oh, yes you can...just touch it...outside your pants."

Keefer swallowed hard and opened her legs a little more to allow her hand more room, but she didn't move it any further. She listened to Sheridan breathe into the phone and was convinced her lover was indeed touching herself. Keefer's sex clenched under her hand and she moaned pathetically, "You can't just call and do this to me..."

"You can hang up any time, baby," the blonde said in a deep, sexy purr. "Oh, Keef, you'd love how wet I am."

Keefer groaned and closed her thighs around her hand, the pressure easing some of the ache. "Sher," she tried to warn her lover, not sure if she wanted Sheridan to stop or not.

"Can you feel my mouth on your belly, my open lips dragging slowly against your skin as I slide lower?"

Keefer's fingers added pressure between her legs and she inhaled loudly at the exquisite relief. Her eyes flew open and she looked around nervously.

"You just touched yourself, didn't you...mmm...you can feel it then..."

The inspector closed her eyes again and nodded, then realized she had to speak. She licked her lips and replied quietly, "Yes."

"I bet if I were really on my knees under your desk, I'd smell you. God, you smell so good. I can't wait to taste you. You want me to taste you, don't you?"

"Uh-huh." Keefer shifted in her chair and started to move her fingers up and down the seam of her chinos. She blushed as she did, not really believing she was doing this at work.

"Oh, Keef," Sheridan groaned, "I want to slide my tongue from the bottom to the top...I want to wrap my lips around your clit. Is that what you want?"

Keefer swallowed hard again and licked her dry lips nervously. "Yeah."

"Open your pants. Touch it, Keef, pretend it's my mouth," Sheridan coaxed.

Keefer pulled open the button on her pants and lowered the zipper. It sounded hideously loud to her. Her heart pounded quickly and her breath came in rapid spurts as she did. She slid her fingers inside her underwear and stopped before she touched anything vital. "I can't, Sher," she breathed, even though she could feel herself throbbing for release.

"I'm doing it, Keef. I'm pretending that it's your fingers...your long...sexy...fingers...stroking me." Sheridan faded off at the end of the sentence, clearly involved in her ministrations.

Keefer's clit twitched at the picture drawn in her head. She slid her hand lower and gasped as she reached her goal.

"No one can see you, baby...oh yeah...you feel so good. Go on, Keef, let me taste you..."

The tall woman groaned and imagined Sheridan's lips where her fingers were. The sound of her blonde lover's aroused voice was as much of a turn-on as if she were there touching her. She wanted Sheridan to keep talking, even though her labored breathing was doing a very good job by itself.

"Are you touching yourself, honey?"

"Yeah," Keefer admitted breathlessly. "Are you?"

"Oh, yeah," Sheridan purred. "Mmm. Can you feel me? Can you feel how wet I am...how badly I want you?"

Keefer's sex clenched painfully. "Oh, God..." she moaned, her fingers slipping lower effortlessly through the wetness. She couldn't believe what she was doing, but at the same time, the whole idea of it being dangerous made it so much better. Listening to Sheridan's breathy moans, she opened her legs wider and touched more purposefully.

"Oh, Keef...you feel so good...what am I doing to you, baby? Tell me."

Keefer blushed and wet her dry mouth with her tongue. "Your mouth," she said, dipping her fingers down again to tease, just the way Sheridan would with her tongue. Groaning, she slid lower in the chair.

"My mouth...am I licking you or sucking you, Keef?" Sheridan asked between breaths.

The brunette bit her bottom lip, unable to reply due to Sheridan's imaginary mouth. Instead, she breathed out a whimper.

"Oh yeah, baby...it feels so good, doesn't it? You're gonna make me come soon."

"Yeah," Keefer agreed breathlessly, her fingers, her lover's tongue, bringing her extremely close.

"Touch me, Keef, make me come."

Blue eyes opened, unfocused. The images in her head had been so vivid that she had to verify that she was still in her office. Her eyes closed quickly, though, as she imagined her lover's face at that moment, her erratic breathing indicating that she was about to come. That knowledge and the picture her mind drew of Sheridan's face brought her to the brink; all she needed was a final push.

Sheridan groaned deeply as she started to climax. "Keef...yes," she hissed into the phone.

Keefer's hips jerked from the sounds and the images. Her thighs closed on her hand and she whined quietly into the receiver as Sheridan's lips drew out her orgasm.

Heavy breathing accompanied by a few satisfied sighs filled the phone connection as the two women relaxed.

"Keef, you okay?"

"Perfect," she murmured, her face red as she became more and more aware of what she'd just done and where. "I can't believe I did that," she whispered in embarrassment, closing her pants quickly.

"I'm so glad you did. Oh, baby, you are so hot," the construction worker purred.

"Sheridan Landers...don't you purr at me!" Keefer said, a hint of teasing in her voice. "That's how this all started."

Sheridan chuckled and blew a loud kiss into the phone. "It was fun, but I missed you."

"That was sweet, Sher," Keefer said with a warm smile.

"It's true. I want to feel you and see you. Fantasy is fun, but the real thing is so much better."

"Amen," Keefer agreed. A knock on the door startled her and she sat straight up in her chair. "I gotta go, love you," she whispered and hung up before Sheridan had a chance to say anything.

The tall, distracted inspector checked the clock again, disappointed to see that only ten minutes had passed since the last time she'd looked. She had been thinking of the phone call all day long, her mind occasionally able to concentrate on work. When her boss came in earlier, Keefer blushed hotly, physically hiding her hand as if by looking at it, he could know what she had just done with it. She couldn't wait to run to the bathroom and wash up; the smell of herself on her fingers was killing her. It only reminded her of the phone call, Sheridan's breathy voice, and the delicious sensations she'd experienced.

Her boss kept her from getting to the ladies room, burying her in his office under piles of files that she wanted nothing to do with and could care even less about. Finally left alone, Keefer escaped to the bathroom, thoughts of Sheridan's lips overpowering just about every thing else. *I am going to kill her for this,* she thought.

By dinnertime, Sheridan had cleaned the house, done the laundry, and taken all the dogs to the park and now sat on the couch watching TV. Keefer had left a message on the machine that she was going to be swamped with work for the rest of the day, but would still be home by her regular time. Without the opportunity to speak to her lover, Sheridan was left to daydream all day about their earlier phone call. Each time she did, she smiled more triumphantly. "My baby's not so shy anymore," she announced proudly.

The blonde heard the keys jingling outside the front door and strolled over with a cocky expression to greet her tall lover. The door opened and Keefer stepped inside, kicking her shoes off and opening her pants. She had a look in her eye that caused Sheridan's stomach to clench. Blue eyes narrowed and zeroed in on the blonde's lips. "Keef?" she asked and licked her scrutinized lips.

Keefer pushed her lover against the wall, squatting down and wrapping her arms under Sheridan's legs. When she stood back up, the blonde's legs had no choice but to encircle her waist as their lips met hungrily.

Sheridan pulled away from the assault long enough to groan her delight. "Oh, baby! What's this for?"

"Today, when you called me." Keefer captured Sheridan's lips with hers and sucked them. "I had already been thinking about you..." she pressed her belly into Sheridan's crotch and the blonde groaned.

"Yeah?" Sheridan asked, pressing back into Keefer.

"Uh-huh. And that phone call..." Keefer ran her tongue over her lover's lips.

"Yeah?" was the only thing Sheridan could seem to say.

"That phone call wasn't *nearly* enough." The taller woman bit the sensitive spot under Sheridan's chin and they both slid to the floor, Keefer on her knees, Sheridan still wrapped around her.

Upon hearing her mommy's keys in the door, Fifi had run into the living room. Once she saw the two women wrapped around each other, she came to a skidding halt right outside the foyer. With a heavy sigh, she turned to the boys, who were right behind her. "Don't bother," she told them. "When they do this, you are the last thing on their minds."

Pharaoh lay down on his belly and rested his head on his paws. "What do you mean? When are we gonna eat?"

Fifi smiled. "When all the yelling is over and Mommy starts breathing again."

Zeus harumphed, never having seen his mommy in this position. "But I'm hungry," he whined.

"Get over it, big head."

Chapter 44

Sheridan woke late the next morning, feeling like she had never gone to sleep at all, but she didn't mind one bit. She patted Fifi on the back and rearranged her so that she wasn't hogging the whole pillow. Taking a deep, satisfied breath, the construction worker smiled somewhat sleepily as she recalled the previous evening's activities.

Keefer had been in rare form when she came home from work. Sheridan was pleasantly surprised by her lover's behavior, with Keefer catching her completely off guard. The blonde grinned and chuckled as she remembered the way Keefer had overpowered her in the foyer.

Keefer was on her knees, sitting on her heels, with Sheridan's legs wrapped around her middle. The tall woman was devouring her lover's mouth, hungrily and lustfully, while pressing her abdomen into Sheridan's sex, driving her crazy. Long arms slid around the construction worker's back as she was lowered to the floor. Keefer stretched out her long legs and Sheridan's unfastened from around her back. A pause in the oral assault allowed Sheridan to read the hunger in her lover's half-lidded baby blues. Her heart pounded and her sex throbbed. She'd never seen that look on Keefer's face and it turned her on tremendously. Further study of her panting lover's gorgeous eyes allowed the blonde to catch a glimpse of a question hidden under all the need. A slow smile formed on Sheridan's lips. "Do it, Keef," she breathed excitedly. Keefer was going to take her in a way she had never thought her lover was capable of. Her stomach clenched and her sex twitched in anticipation.

The tall woman didn't know what had come over her; this desire, this all-consuming need to have her lover was so strong it actually scared her at first. She had thought about nothing else on the subway ride home. She didn't know how it happened, but she felt as if a thousand pounds were lifted off of her shoulders. Something had occurred...gotten through to another part of her soul, and it felt like the walls had come tumbling down. Keefer had never felt more free or light as she had while sitting in that subway car.

Her mind wandered, as it had been all day, to the phone call and the moment she'd lost all her insecure inhibitions and touched herself. For her lover. Keefer's nostrils flared when she thought about it. First in arousal, as she remembered her lover's heavy breathing, then in anger when she thought about how much pleasure she had missed out on in her life. Not that sex was the most important thing, but she felt like a whole new world had opened up for her. Her heart swelled for Sheridan, she loved her even more than ever. Her sex swelled too...she had a lot of catching up to do.

Sheridan was oblivious as to what caused the change in her lover, but she was certainly pleased. While Keefer was a very good lover, she had never been so aggressive or determined to have her way. Sheridan felt a twinge of nervousness when Keefer slid down and yanked the jeans and underwear off of her legs with one pull, but that faded away as the tall woman tugged off her own shirt and bra. The blonde swallowed hard as her lover purposely teased her with her breasts, bringing them close enough to lick, but backing away just before she could have a taste.

Keefer lifted Sheridan's shirt up over her breasts and palmed them both, breathing hard though wet lips. Her gaze focused on darkened green eyes. "I want..." she started, unable to finish.

"What, Keef? Tell me, baby," Sheridan gasped as her lover kneaded her breasts.

Keefer bent over her lover, her nipples hardening as they brushed against the backs of her own hands. Her hair fell around Sheridan's face and she breathed hotly into the blonde's ear.

Sheridan groaned and arched her back. "What, baby..."

Keefer licked her lips and brought them in contact with Sheridan's ear. "I want to fuck you, Sheridan. Will you let me?"

Sheridan growled and again wrapped her legs around Keefer's back. The soft cotton of the inspector's chinos pressed tantalizingly into her naked, moist sex, making her groan. Keefer's bluntness excited her to new heights; even hearing her lover say the word fuck *made her wet. "How bad do you want to fuck me?" the blonde growled as her lover kept an insistent pressure between her legs.*

Keefer blushed momentarily after actually speaking her desires so blatantly, but composed herself quickly. Sheridan's skin felt so hot beneath her, and she was so turned on that her heart raced. She pulled her face out of Sheridan's neck and touched their lips together. "Really bad," she replied, her voice unusually raspy, flooded with arousal.

Sheridan covered one of Keefer's hands with her own and dragged it off of her breast, downward. When their hands reached her wet center, the construction worker unwrapped her legs from Keefer's back and let them fall open on the floor, knees up in a lewd invitation. "Then do it," she said, pressing Keefer's hand into her sex.

"Baby?"

Sheridan was brought back to the present by Keefer's sleep-roughened voice. "Hmm?"

"Your eyes were open, but I could have sworn you were dreaming," she joked about the look on her lover's face. "What were you thinking about?"

"Last night," Sheridan replied with a sly grin.

"Last night, huh?" Keefer repeated with a small blush. "Which part?" she asked coyly.

Sheridan sat up and stared at her lover in amusement. "Now I know where Fifi gets it from," she commented. "Don't you even think you can get away with that shy thing after you had your nose up my ass."

Keefer turned so red she looked like an apple. Her eyes widened and her mouth hung open.

"That's right, missy. You had me every which way but loose! I had my first tongue bath, which, by the way, was too fucking good, and you have the nerve to blush," Sheridan teased, watching the steam rise off of her mortified lover.

"Sheridan!" Keefer protested.

The blonde jumped over Zeus and tackled Keefer, pinning her arms over her head. "I should take advantage of this situation." She bent down and kissed Keefer, much to Zeus's dismay as the big dog tried to squeeze back between the two women.

"You'd take advantage of lil ol' me?" Keefer asked in mock fear.

Sheridan pretended to think about it as she hip-checked the big Rotty. "Nope, I'm too busy trying to figure out how to get you to jump me again like you did last night." The blonde buried her face in Keefer's neck and purred, "Mmm...you were in such a mood last night...my little wild woman." Sheridan licked her lips and grinned wildly. "I loved it!"

Keefer felt pretty sure of herself after that remark. "You certainly weren't complaining."

"Complain?" Sheridan laughed. "How could I complain? I could hardly breathe half the time."

Fifi walked over, sat on Keefer's legs behind Sheridan, and leaned into the blonde's back. "I think someone's jealous again," Sheridan whispered in Keefer's ear.

Keefer eyed the big pathetic face to her left and the obvious pout to her right. "I think all the someone's are jealous."

"I'll take care of them today—you go shower in peace," Sheridan said as she climbed off her lover.

The day slipped by effortlessly as the two lovers fell into a comfortable routine. While Keefer was at work, Sheridan stopped at home to pick up some clothes and necessities and then stopped by her pop's office to see if he needed her anywhere. She was growing antsy. The construction worker liked to work; she enjoyed the healthy sweat that a day of hard, productive labor caused. Working out was keeping her occupied, but it wasn't enough. Finding nothing to do work-wise, the blonde went back to Keefer's house to lounge around.

Eventually, after the television bored her to death, she started to walk around the old house with a work-oriented mindset.

Keefer came home to a very enthusiastic greeting from all three dogs, causing her to wonder where her lover was. Sheridan usually held back at least one of the boys so Keefer could walk into the house without too much excitement. The radio was playing loudly and the tall woman sought out her lover instead of yelling for her. When she entered the kitchen, she was greeted with the sight of Sheridan's butt sticking out from under the sink. She watched it for a while with a dopey smile on her face as her lover apparently worked on something or other. "Now that's a hello!" she finally said.

Sheridan backed out of the cabinet with a semi-guilty expression. "There was a leak," she explained, holding up the wrench for emphasis.

Keefer grinned knowingly. She'd known for a fact that Sheridan would go stir-crazy sooner or later; she just didn't expect it to be sooner. "Uh-huh, and what else did you find that needed fixing?" she asked with an amused smile.

"Only a few things, really. Some loose doorknobs, the float in the toilet tank needed adjusting, I painted over the spackle in the living room..."

"There's no work for you yet, huh?" Keefer asked sympathetically as she crouched down in front of her lover for a kiss.

Sheridan sighed after the kiss. "Nope. Only one in the Bronx, and I don't want it."

Keefer stood up and watched Sheridan replace all the things she had taken out of the cabinet. She looked so sad and it made Keefer frown. "You know, if you want, and there's nothing else to do..."

Sheridan raised her eyebrow in question.

"The porch could use some work," Keefer said, nodding her head in the direction of the front door.

Sheridan lit up like a Christmas tree. "Yeah! I was looking at it today. We could extend it into a deck...maybe another set of steps by the driveway. I saw some really cool latticework for the railing—" she went on excitedly before realizing Keefer was smiling at her. "Well, that's if you want," she added shyly.

"You're so adorable when you're excited."

It was early Thursday morning and Sheridan was sitting up in bed, staring at her lover. Keefer was lying on her back, one arm extended over her head and the other draped over her abdomen. She had kicked off the sheet that had covered her and was lying there in panties and a tank top, her breasts barely covered by the material. Sheridan stared with undisguised lust at her half-naked lover. The sun was barely up, but the blonde had been awake for some time, entertaining thoughts of pouncing on Keefer and devouring her. Sheridan's mouth watered as her gaze followed the curve of Keefer's left breast, the baby-soft skin of which peeked out at her, tantalizing her. Blinking rapidly and swallowing hard, the blonde allowed her gaze to travel down over a flat abdomen to linger on the cutest bellybutton she'd ever seen, then further down to the apex of her lover's long legs. Bikini panties covered no more than Keefer's pubic hair, the strings on the side of the panties framing her sexy hips.

Sheridan breathed deeply, wanting so badly to reach over and touch her sleeping lover, but Keefer looked so peaceful with her lips barely open and her facial muscles relaxed. The blonde climbed to her knees and carefully leaned as close as she could and placed a tiny kiss on Keefer's belly. The brunette didn't even flinch, and Sheridan raised an eyebrow in thought. She leaned over further and placed a light kiss on Keefer's thigh. Again, no movement. Sheridan smiled deviously and kissed her lover's center. Keefer moved a little but stayed asleep.

Sheridan assessed the situation, crawled carefully off of the bed, and stood at the foot, between Keefer's feet. She slowly laid her hands gently on her lover's ankles and inched apart her legs. She climbed ever so carefully onto the bed and settled on her knees and elbows between Keefer's open legs, her face inches away from her lover's sex. She stared at the material that covered her goal and pursed her lips in thought. She knew once she touched Keefer there, Keefer would wake right up.

Making her decision, Sheridan lowered her head and just breathed on Keefer's center, long hot breaths, evenly spaced. Patiently, she sat there until she could smell her lover's warm scent. Her eyes closed as she anticipated the taste, then she barely touched her tongue to the material of Keefer's panties and tickled it lightly up the length of her sex. The brunette inhaled hard and exhaled a little moan, opening her legs wider in her sleep. Sheridan grinned cockily and repeated the motion several times, all the while watching Keefer's nipples harden under the thin cotton tank top. Her own sex clenched as she continued to lick her lover, slowly and gently. Keefer squirmed a bit, raising her hips, flexing her legs and arching her back, but all subtly. She was still asleep.

Sheridan was becoming progressively wetter as she teased her sleeping lover. She sat up on her knees and studied Keefer's face. The tall woman's brows were a bit furrowed, like she was concentrating on something, and her mouth was open much more than a moment ago. She looked delicious and so very inviting. Sheridan dropped back down and traced the edge of Keefer's panties with one finger, stopping when she got to the wet spot between her legs. Slowly hooking the finger under the fabric, she pulled the panties to the side, exposing the object of her adoration. Green eyes narrowed at the glistening wetness her tongue had caused. She glanced up at Keefer's face and grinned when she noticed her expression hadn't changed.

Sheridan lowered her mouth to Keefer's fragrant center and poked out her tongue, barely touching the hair guarding her opening. Her mouth watered instantly and she had to swallow before she tasted her lover again. The ache deepened between her own legs as she dragged her tongue deeper into the furrow of Keefer's nether lips. A gloating self-satisfied expression formed on her face as she inhaled the aroma, and buried her tongue deeper.

"Mmph!"

The cocky expression was replaced by wide-eyed surprise as a long leg wrapped around her neck and a strong hand clutched the back of her head. Green eyes looked up into highly aroused blue. Sheridan hummed as she closed her eyes and continued to make love to Keefer.

"Sher," Keefer gasped, surprised at how far Sheridan had gotten and how aroused she was.

"Mmm," the blonde replied, doubling her efforts and slipping two fingers inside her lover.

"Oh, yeah," Keefer whispered breathily, propping herself on her elbows. She was still a bit disoriented but well aware of how wet she was.

Sheridan worked her fingers in and out and rested her chin on Keefer's pubis. "What took you so long?" she drawled in a sensual voice.

"Oh, God...how long...have you been at this?" Keefer asked between gasps of pleasure.

Sheridan flashed a lopsided grin as a reply.

Keefer's head hit the pillow heavily as she fell back onto the bed.

"I love you, Keefer," Sheridan whispered before wrapping her lips around Keefer's clit.

Keefer groaned loudly, unable to return the sentiment. She held the blonde's head tightly in her clenching fingers, keeping her in place. Her leg tightened around Sheridan's neck and her whole body shook as her lover brought her over the edge.

Sheridan groaned back as Keefer's body trembled, the orgasm feeding her own need. She whimpered in sympathy as the long fingers spasmed and dug into her scalp.

When Keefer relaxed, she released Sheridan's head and neck and breathed heavily. Her eyes met twinkling green and she chuckled. "That's a first," she breathed.

Sheridan climbed up on top of her lover and kissed her wetly, hotly, running her hands up and down Keefer's body. She broke the kiss only to allow the brunette time to catch her breath and watched her lover's satisfied face as she did. "You're so beautiful."

Keefer didn't think about her hair, or the sleep in her eyes, or her morning breath. She simply smiled and pulled Sheridan down for another kiss.

Keefer floated through much of the morning at work. Her secretive grin at having been woken up in such a pleasant way had everyone guessing as to the usually emotionless woman's thoughts.

The rumor mill was in full swing by noon, generating many speculations as to why Danni had returned to work all bruised and broken. When asked, the redhead muttered something about being in an accident, but refused to elaborate. Keefer feigned pity whenever it was brought up in her presence, but silently chuckled as she watched her ex hobble past her office door. The clincher, the thing that gave Keefer the ultimate high, was when she was standing in the elevator on her way to the files room and Danni walked in, then ran back out and let Keefer have the elevator to herself.

The tall woman was unable to hold her tongue.

"There's plenty of room," she said with an innocent expression. "I don't bite," she added with a devious grin.

"No, but your attack dog does," Danni replied with barely hidden fear.

Keefer laughed loud enough for Danni to hear her as the elevator door closed. She was surprised that she didn't even feel the slightest twinge of guilt. All she had to do was recall the crazy look in Danni's eyes that night at the barbecue and she knew Danni had deserved all that she got.

The tall inspector sat behind her desk and smiled, thoughts and visions of her muscular blonde lover invading her idle moments. She was much better that day, more able to concentrate on work, but she still indulged in the errant daydream when she had a moment.

"Gibson?"

Keefer looked up slowly at her colleague. "Yes?" she asked, knowing that her daydreams were over for the time being.

Sheridan decided to spend the afternoon with Steven at her pop's office and was soon embroiled in a serious flickball match with her brother. She held up her hands, thumbs touching as a goalpost, while Steven lined up the small wad of paper. It was a 15-point game and he had 14. Sheridan made a hideous face as her brother prepared his shot. Ignoring her, he flicked the paper ball confidently and watched proudly as it sailed between Sheridan's thumbs. Sheridan ducked her head down and caught the wad of paper in her mouth.

"Hey! Why'd you eat it?"

"No shot. Goalie interference," Sheridan said, spitting out the paper.

"Big fat cheater! I won!" Steven said, sticking out his tongue and doing a victory dance.

"You dance like a chicken."

"You dance like a monkey," he countered, imitating a monkey dancing.

"I do not. Chicken dancer," Sheridan argued, dancing like a chicken.

The two siblings danced around the workshop clucking and making monkey noises when a bright flash suddenly froze them in place. Both turned around, stunned, to find the elder Landers waving a camera around in the air.

"Just thought this should go up on the brag wall," he said with a smug smile.

Sheridan put her hands on her hips. "You wouldn't."

"Oh yes, I will," Mr. Landers laughed, leaving the room.

Steven turned to Sheridan with a look of horror. "Look what you did!" he said pointing to the empty doorway.

"Me?" Sheridan poked herself in the chest.

"Yeah, you...monkey," he said, while trying to keep a straight face.

"Chicken," Sheridan said with a snort of laughter.

By the time they stopped laughing, tears were rolling down their faces.

"Now everyone is going to see how stupid you look when you dance," Steven said, wiping his eyes on the backs of his hands.

"Hey, I wasn't the only one in that picture."

"Yeah, but I'll cut it in half and hang your half on the wall," he said, then laughed. "Even better, I'll show your half to Keefer."

Sheridan chuckled, "I'll show *your* half to Keefer."

Steven panicked. "Pop!" he yelled, running from the room.

Keefer braced herself at the front door. She had stopped on the way home and picked up Chinese for dinner and knew she'd never make it past the dogs if she didn't plan a strategy. She put the key in the door and opened it a crack. The dogs came barreling to the door and slammed it shut in her face. Keefer pursed her lips and furrowed her brows, fidgeting on the porch. She forced open the door once more and yelled inside. "Sher? Some help here." The dogs went crazy at her voice and started jumping up and throwing themselves at the door, barking and whining.

Keefer sighed heavily and glanced around, just then noticing that her lover's car wasn't in the driveway. "Damn!" she blurted out and juggled her bags to read her watch. It wasn't early, if anything she was a bit late. Frowning, she threw herself in a lounge chair and waited.

Sheridan pulled up to the house to find Keefer in the midst of a serious pout. She climbed out of her car and chuckled at the look on her lover's face. "Kinda feels like the bench at the mall, I bet."

"Shut up."

Sheridan raised an eyebrow. "Ooh, what's wrong?" she asked, bending down for a kiss.

Keefer pursed her lips, but that was all she did.

"What did I do?" the blonde asked nervously.

"Your dogs wouldn't let me in the house!" Keefer said, clearly blaming Sheridan.

"And this is my fault...how?"

"They're your horses." The inspector resorted to pouting. "I'm hungry, I'm PMS-ing, and the food is getting cold," she whined.

Sheridan raised both eyebrows in fright and took a step back. *Oh, fuck me...*"Baby, you just sit there and I'll get us inside," she said sweetly.

Keefer leveled a glare at Sheridan.

"Now what?" the blonde construction worker asked in frustration.

Keefer frowned. "Nothing." Sheridan made sure her back was turned before she rolled her eyes. *PMS...just what I need. Why didn't she have PMS last month?* she wondered.

The dogs came flying at her the minute she forced open the door, and the blonde grimaced. "Back up, will ya!" she yelled. The dogs didn't listen and she allowed them a moment to adore her before she grabbed them by their collars and dragged them inside. "Okay, Keef, it's safe."

Keefer went straight for the kitchen, Fifi hot on her heels. The tall woman shook her head at the way Sheridan was holding back the big boys. She petted Fifi attentively and started to feel slightly guilty and more forgiving of the large male dogs. Going into the living room, she watched her lover struggle before making up her mind. "Let them go, Sher."

The blonde looked skeptical. "Are you sure?"

"Yes, let 'em go." Keefer squatted down and prepared for the onslaught.

Sheridan released their collars with a puzzled look on her face. She didn't understand women or PMS at all.

Keefer allowed the boys to lick and paw her senseless while she showered them with love and hugs.

Sheridan picked up Fifi, who had run to her for protection once the boys came barreling at her mommy. The blonde held the small dog and watched the love fest. Once the carrying on calmed down, she stared at her lover intently. "Are you okay?"

"Yeah," Keefer sighed. "Just had a little tantrum, that's all," she said as she sat heavily on the couch.

Sheridan watched as Keefer took off her shoes and picked her feet up onto the couch. *Maybe I should be doing something—Oh! Dinner!* "Do you want me to set the table, or would you rather I bring a few forks in here?"

"We can eat in here," Keefer replied with little emotion.

"Can I ask you a question?" Sheridan asked hesitantly.

"Yes."

"How come you didn't have PMS last month? I know I would have noticed it."

Keefer chuckled wryly. *Poor Sheridan hasn't been in a relationship. She never stayed with one person long enough to experience hormone hell.* "I worked around it, hon," Keefer said with a small smile.

"Well, don't pretend things are good when they're not on my account. I love all of you, Keef."

Keefer looked like she might cry. "That was so sweet," she said tearfully.

Sheridan's eyes widened. *What the hell?* She went straight to the couch and stood between Keefer's legs. She thought really hard, back to conversations she had purposely tried to ignore—discussions between the girls about PMS and the like. Suddenly a light bulb went off over her head.

Keefer watched with great interest as her lover sat on the couch and pulled her long legs across her lap. She couldn't resist the groan when Sheridan began to rub her foot. "Oh, Sher...that feels so good."

Outwardly, the blonde smiled and inwardly, she chastised herself for reacting to the languid moan. "Tell me if I hurt you, okay?"

"Oh God, no...that's perfect," the tall woman purred.

Again, the blonde's belly tingled and tightened and she narrowed her eyes in a silent gesture of defiance. *Stop it!* she warned her libido.

Keefer was in heaven and even though her stomach was growling, she was loath to give up the foot massage.

Hearing her lover's belly gurgle, Sheridan stood up. "Oh! Keef! The food! I'm sorry, baby, I'll go get it. You can eat while I rub your feet."

Keefer's mouth hung open in surprise. "Baby, you should eat, too, there's plenty of time for that."

"No," Sheridan insisted from the kitchen, the dogs surrounding her. "I think you need some TLC."

Feeling bad for Sheridan, Keefer offered a deal she was sure the construction worker would agree to—one she was going to benefit greatly from. "How about we eat, then afterwards, I take a long hot bath and you rub my whole body."

Sheridan returned from the kitchen with a sexy lopsided smile on her face. "Oh yeah, you have a plan."

Keefer lay on her belly, naked and relaxed while her lover sat on the backs of her thighs, working her strong hands into the tight muscles. The blonde's hair was still wet and she was wearing only her boxer briefs when she reappeared in the bedroom, giving Keefer a very enticing image to think of when she closed her eyes. She lay there and groaned as her lover's fingers dug deliciously into her back.

Sheridan, although concentrating on her task, was growing increasingly warm as she navigated the expanse of smooth skin laid out before her. Her eyes kept wandering to Keefer's perfectly shaped buttocks, and each time they did, the blonde bit her lips to control herself.

"Mmm...Sher...so nice," Keefer murmured into her folded arms.

Sheridan moved lower and smiled happily. She was making Keefer feel good and that made her feel good, too. Everywhere. She kneaded and rubbed the tight muscles, reveling in the feel of Keefer beneath her and between her legs.

"PMS isn't going to be such a bad thing if you treat me like this every month," Keefer groaned.

Sheridan had to find her tongue before speaking; her brain had it everywhere else but inside her mouth. "You deserve to be pampered."

"You *fed* me, Sheridan," Keefer chuckled. "You'll spoil me."

Sheridan puffed up. "Good."

Keefer stretched long and hard, then sighed, placing a kiss on Sheridan's shoulder, which was right at her lips. The blonde construction worker had collapsed on top of her and was in the midst of catching her breath. Keefer laughed at the situation. One second she was one breath away from sleep, the next second—and she don't know how it happened—she was face up under her very amorous lover. Now, said lover was kissing her neck in the most gentle of fashions, and she purred.

"Sorry, Keef, I don't know what happened," Sheridan said sheepishly.

"Oh yeah, it was so horrible for me to endure."

Sheridan grinned and lifted herself up on her elbows. "I bet," she said, adding a kiss to her lover's nose.

Keefer sighed in contentment and pulled Sheridan back down on top of her. She loved the feel of their warm bodies meeting, and she moaned quietly. She felt protected, comforted, and very loved. She was positive that she was the luckiest woman on the face of the earth to have a lover like Sheridan. She ran her nails gently up and down the blonde's back as she smiled, burying her nose in Sheridan's neck. The construction worker was so surprisingly sweet and attentive, and Keefer loved her so very much at that moment. She thought back to their first meeting, in the empty building—and how sexy Sheridan looked in her tool belt and work boots. Keefer's belly tingled as she recalled how that moment had changed her life. Her mind wandered to the first time she'd seen Sheridan in the club, in her tight jeans and T-shirt, defending her honor. Her heart swelled. She smiled from ear to ear when she thought of their first kiss. Sheridan had smelled so good that night. She loved the way her lover looked and smelled when she was going out to the club.

Hmm, she hasn't been to the club in a while now. Keefer frowned. *I wonder if I'm stopping her from going out. Not that I really want her to go, I want her to stay right here with me...on top of me...breathing on my neck...all night long.* Keefer bit her bottom lip guiltily. *You selfish woman, Keef.* A pensive expression crossed her features. *That's not fair.* She slid her hand into Sheridan's hair and scratched her scalp. "Sher?"

"Mmm?"

"You know, it's Thursday night, ladies' night at the club, if I'm not mistaken."

"Yeah, so?"

"Don't you want to go out with the girls?"

Sheridan raised an eyebrow and lifted her head to study her lover. *This could be a PMS test.* "I suppose. Are you trying to get rid of me?" she joked.

"No, it's just that you haven't been out in so long, and I know you must want to be with your friends."

Okay, no hint of turmoil...maybe she really does mean it? "Are you *sure* you want me to go out?"

"Positive," Keefer said with a nod of her head.

"Well, I do feel like dancing." She watched Keefer carefully. "Are you sure you won't mind?"

Keefer patted Sheridan on the butt. "Not at all," she replied with a smile.

Sheridan sat up on her knees. "Cool! I'll go call the girls," she said and kissed Keefer excitedly.

Keefer watched her lover's naked behind as it disappeared out of the room. *I mean, she hasn't gone out in a long time. I know she needs it every so often. I have her every other night, anyway. I really shouldn't be so selfish. Should I? No. She deserves to go out with her friends. I can survive a night without her; I have the boys to keep me occupied.*

"Keef?" Sheridan called from the living room.

Keefer slid slowly out of bed and wrapped the sheet around her as she padded to the living room. "Yeah?"

"I've been thinking. It really won't be any fun without you."

"What?" Keefer asked, just to make sure she'd heard right.

"I want you to come with me. I know you hate loud music and your hair smells when you leave, but if I go without you, I'll only be thinking about you the whole time. If you don't want to go, I don't either. I'd rather stay home with you."

Keefer whooped as she jumped on top of her startled lover, knocking her to the couch. "Of course I want to come with you!" she said excitedly. "Thank you, baby!" Keefer kissed Sheridan so hard, the blonde's lips hurt.

What just happened? The blonde pushed Keefer upright and sat on her lap. "You're adorable, baby." Sheridan chuckled at her lover's exuberance. "We better get in the shower if we ever plan on getting out of here tonight."

"Aren't you going to call the girls?" Keefer asked in puzzlement as Sheridan climbed off of her lap.

"No, let's surprise them." *I want to avoid the teasing for as long as I can.*

Chapter 45

Butterflies fluttered around violently in Sheridan's stomach as they approached the club. She'd never, in all her years, walked into the club with a woman already on her arm. She was sure everyone knew about Keefer—the rumors must have been fast and furious when she hadn't shown up in such a long time. She almost felt nauseous with nerves. Glancing over at her lover, seeing the excited expression on her face, made her think. *Look at how happy this is making her...and to think I almost went without her. I can't even imagine having a good time at the club alone anymore. I'd be thinking about her all night long...missing her.*

The blonde sighed and Keefer turned around to see why. "What's wrong?" she asked, reaching over and covering Sheridan's hand with her own.

"Nothing, baby. Everything's all right now," she assured her.

"I'm a little nervous," Keefer admitted. "This is going to be hard on you, isn't it?"

"Yeah, but I can take it," Sheridan said, puffing out her chest.

"My big, tough girl," Keefer teased, knowing Sheridan was in for a lot of squirming.

Sheridan chuckled as she pulled into a parking spot. "You know, there's going to be a lot of evil stares directed at you, Keef. Lotta broken hearts."

"You cocky little thing, you!" Keefer said with both eyebrows raised.

"Well, I'm just warning you."

"I happen to think you're worth those glares, Sher."

Sheridan smiled and leaned over for a short kiss. "You, too. Now git, woman."

"Ooh, I love it when you're forceful," Keefer purred.

"Don't start that, Keef; we'll never leave the car."

The couple walked toward the club, hand in hand. Sheridan braced herself as they opened the door. The doorman smiled knowingly, letting them both in for free. Sheridan went straight to Verna, who would never let her live it down if she walked by without stopping.

"Hi, Sheridan. Hi, Keefer, pleased to meet you!" the coat check woman said sincerely. "May I get my sugar, Keefer?"

The tall woman looked at Sheridan in confusion.

"She wants a kiss hello. She calls it *sugar*," the blonde explained, blushing slightly.

"By all means." Keefer waved her hand and giggled at her lover's embarrassment.

After kissing Verna on the cheek, Sheridan was quick to grab Keefer's hand again. "Well, time to face the music, Ma."

"Oh, screw 'em! This woman is good for you, honey. I've never seen you look so good!" Verna leaned over and whispered, "You better treat her right, Sheridan."

Keefer blushed.

"I have every intention of spoiling her rotten," Sheridan said confidently, squeezing Keefer's hand for emphasis. "Are you ready?" she asked her.

Keefer nodded and took a deep breath as they headed for the large main room of the club.

The first person to see them was Greg. He screamed and jumped off of the stage, running right for them. Keefer looked horrified as he ran through the club shrieking with his hands waving in the air, sure that every pair of eyes would now be trained on them.

"Oh my god! Is that really Sheridan?"

"Fuck off, Greg," the blonde said, rolling her eyes.

"No, really! And who is this divine work of art?"

Keefer blushed as Greg took her hand and kissed it. She smiled shyly and introduced herself. "I'm Keefer," she shouted over the din.

"She smells delicious, Sheridan," he commented. "I'm Greg. It's my ultimate pleasure to meet you."

"Oh, knock it off, Gregory. Where're the girls?"

"They're over by the bar. Did they know you were coming?"

"Nope," Sheridan shook her head, "it's a surprise."

Greg clapped his hands excitedly. "Coolness!"

Sheridan chuckled at his enthusiasm. "Go work off some of that energy, bro," she said as she smacked him on the ass. "I got a woman to show off."

Keefer smiled at Sheridan and squeezed her hand.

"Come on babe, let's go," the blonde said to her lover, pulling her slightly toward the bar.

Marie noticed the couple and elbowed Dawn, who nudged Sharon. All three women stood up a little straighter as Sheridan and Keefer worked their way through the crowd at the bar.

"Hey ladies, what's up?" Sheridan asked, pushing her way to the front of the crowd.

"Hi, Sher. Hey Keefer!" Sharon approached Keefer with open arms.

Keefer accepted the hug and kiss on the cheek with a shy smile. "Hi, Sharon. Sure is crowded tonight," she said while looking around.

The tall cop noticed the death grip Keefer had on Sheridan's hand and smiled. "Yeah, but I like it like that." She waggled her eyebrows and chuckled.

Keefer laughed and shook her head. "I suppose you would." She looked over at her lover, who was having a one-handed, animated conversation with Dawn and Marie, so she let go of Sheridan's other hand to allow her to use it.

The blonde's head turned immediately at the loss and she questioned Keefer with a raised eyebrow. "You okay?" she mouthed.

Keefer nodded and smiled, feeling safe with Sharon by her side. As they chatted, Keefer took the time to look around. Many eyes were on her, and a few people were even pointing and talking to each other. The tall woman, feeling very uncomfortable, inched her way forward until her body was pressed up against Sheridan's back. As the construction worker leaned into her she felt a hundred times better.

"It's weird, huh?"

Keefer looked over at Sharon in confusion. "What's weird?"

"Being the center of attention. Sheridan is so used to being watched, she doesn't even realize it's happening," Sharon clarified.

"Yeah, it's very unsettling," Keefer replied, reaching for Sheridan's hand.

"Don't sweat it. They're all jealous of you; you should feel proud to have what they all want."

"I should, but I don't. I feel uncomfortable, but happy that she wanted to bring me here tonight."

"That's a huge deal, Keefer," Sharon said seriously. "Hey, maybe you want a drink?"

"Excuse me, but are you trying to get my woman drunk?" Sheridan interjected, turning around to face Keefer.

Sharon chuckled and shook her head. "Wouldn't dream of it."

Sheridan studied her lover's eyes. "Do you want to go out onto the patio? There's less people out there."

"No, I'm okay, but I think I would like that drink," Keefer said with a small hint of a smile.

"You're uncomfortable. I can tell. Baby, we can go if you want," Sheridan said with a frown.

Keefer reached up and smoothed Sheridan's brow. "Sher, I'm okay, really," she reassured her.

The blonde looked skeptically at her lover, but didn't want to draw it out any further. PMS was iffy and she didn't want the tides to change any time soon. "Okay. White wine or beer?"

"I'll be daring and have beer," Keefer replied, wanting so badly to kiss her lover to reassure her, but unsure if she should.

Sheridan ordered two beers and turned to look at Keefer. The urge to kiss the tall woman was strong, but she wasn't sure how Keefer would react under all the scrutiny. Suddenly, a song came on that caused Sheridan to begin dancing in place.

Keefer's heart beat rapidly as she watched her lover's body move to the beat. She narrowed her gaze to Sheridan's backside as it moved, not noticing as half the club did the same thing. The blonde spun around and handed Keefer a beer, and the tall woman drank down a healthy swallow.

"This is a great song," Sheridan said, leaning heavily into her lover.

Keefer's breathing changed as she felt Sheridan's body move against her own. She stared at her lover's full lips and was about to bend down and kiss her when she was rudely interrupted.

"Hey, wanna dance, Sher?"

Keefer glared at the stranger, assessing her. Short, hippy, and young. She folded her arms over her chest and glared.

"Uh, no," Sheridan replied, turning back around to face Keefer.

The girls watched in amusement as Keefer's stance became possessive.

"But you always dance with me to this song!" the girl whined.

"Hey, sorry, but I'm here with my woman. You'll have to find another dance partner," Sheridan said, wrapping her arm around Keefer's waist.

The girl's eyes widened. "Your *woman*?" she asked in disbelief.

Marie stepped forward. "Yeah, her woman, now shoo."

The girl wandered off in astonishment.

Keefer was surprised at the strong feeling of jealousy that had bubbled up inside of her. "I'm sorry, Sher. If you wanted to dance..."

"Are you fucking nuts?" Sheridan asked.

Keefer stepped back at the question.

"I'd much rather stand here all night with you than dance with any of these hos."

Keefer chuckled. "Thank you."

"So, Keefer, what's been happening?" Marie asked, trying to make the tall woman more comfortable.

"Nothing really," Keefer answered with a shrug.

Marie looked around at the many eyes glued to the tall beautiful woman and couldn't help but wonder if they weren't all envious of Sheridan and not the other way around. "You look great, hon. Glad you made it out."

Keefer smiled shyly. "Thank you." She looked down at her clothing and found nothing extraordinary about it.

"Then again, you could make a paper sack look good," Marie added.

Keefer blushed. "Oh, stop that," she said in embarrassment, clinging tighter to Sheridan.

"Sheridan looks good, too. You make her look good."

"She always looks good," Keefer said, looking her lover up and down. "I have nothing to do with it."

"Oh, yes you do. Love does wonders for a person," Marie smiled.

Then I must look fabulous, Keefer mused, her heart flooding with love while she watched the construction worker sway to the beat as she talked to Dawn and Sharon.

"Hey, guys." Sheridan turned to Keefer and Marie. "We're going out on the patio. Come on."

"But you won't hear the music out there," Keefer argued, wanting to watch her lover dance all night long.

Sheridan grinned and leaned into Keefer seductively. "I'll dance just for you...later," she said with a wink.

Keefer's heart pounded and she swallowed. Her eyes followed Sheridan's butt as she began to walk away. To Keefer's dismay, Sheridan was stopped repeatedly as they made their way to the patio. Women draped themselves all over her, asking her to dance, wanting a kiss hello, asking her who Keefer was. The tall woman was barely tolerant of all the touching and she began to feel very uncomfortable again. She felt like she didn't belong in Sheridan's club, like she was making trouble for her lover in the only place she could go to escape. The tall woman backed up a few paces and disassociated herself from the smaller blonde.

Marie and Sharon were in the front of the pack; Dawn was behind Keefer and noticed her discomfort. "Keefer, don't be upset. They don't know, or they don't want to know, that she's with you."

"She's going to resent bringing me here. I just know it."

Dawn stepped in front of the distraught inspector. "No, she won't. Word will get around that you are her lover and it will stop, save for a few assholes. Just give it time, don't feel that way."

"Keef?" Sheridan hollered, fending off yet another admirer.

The tall woman reluctantly made her way to the blonde's side. "I'm ruining your night, Sheridan, I should have stayed home."

Sheridan looked angry and frustrated. It wasn't Keefer's fault that the women were acting like that. It was hers, for being having been such a slut in the first place. Not knowing what to do, and not wanting to admit her own guilt at the behavior of the women, Sheridan blew out a loud breath. "Keefer, I won't have you feeling like that," she said, grabbing her hand. "I love you, and if I have to announce it over the microphone I will."

"But I'm causing so much trouble."

"You're doing no such thing." Sheridan shot a glare at the approaching woman but continued to talk to Keefer. "It's my fault, not yours. Back off!" Sheridan yelled at the woman who wedged herself between Keefer and her.

"I just wanted my kiss hello," the woman pouted.

Sheridan threw her hands up in the air in frustration. Dawn and Marie pushed her toward the patio. Sharon took Keefer's hand and led her outside, too.

"Sheridan, this is turning out very badly. Keefer's feeling awful," Dawn said close to the blonde's ear.

"I know!" Sheridan agreed loudly. "But what can I do?"

Sharon took the beers away from the couple's hands and placed Keefer directly in front of Sheridan. "I think you two need to hug before you both lose it."

Sheridan threw herself into Keefer's body and the tall woman caught her, wrapping her arms tightly around her.

The girls watched in happiness as the two women seemed to physically droop in the embrace.

"I'm sorry, Keef, but I don't know what to do to make them stop. This was a bad idea."

"No, it wasn't," Marie offered. "It'll be all right. Soon the news is gonna spread and they'll all back off."

"I don't know about that. It seems they all want to test Sheridan," Keefer said, rubbing her hands up and down her lover's tense, muscular back.

The blonde lifted her head from Keefer's chest. "I have an idea, baby," she said with a cockeyed smile.

Keefer warmed all over at the smile. "What?"

"Dance with me?"

"Here? Now?" Keefer asked, blushing at the thought.

"No, inside, on the stage. Dance with me so everyone can see that I'm with you."

"Sher, I don't know," Keefer said nervously.

"Yeah! That's perfect!" Sharon agreed.

"All they'll have to see is the way you two look at each other and they'll know!" Dawn piped in.

"I don't think I can do that, in front of all these people. I don't even know how to dance, " Keefer stammered.

"Okay, okay...we don't have to dance, baby," Sheridan soothed her, once again placing her head on Keefer's chest, listening to her frantic heartbeat. "We can stay like this all night if you want."

"I'd want nothing more, but this is your place and I want you to have a good time. I shouldn't take away from that."

Sheridan lifted her head again and looked into Keefer's eyes. "Don't be upset. I'm perfectly content to sit on that chair over there and hold your hand all night long." Green eyes focused on Keefer's lips as the tall woman licked them distractedly. She fought the urge to kiss them, knowing her lover was tense and probably not receptive to it.

Keefer watched Sheridan stare at her lips and she relaxed. If anything, it made her realize that Sheridan wanted her. Even amidst the sea of women throwing themselves at her, the construction worker still wanted her. She smiled and sighed, "Honey, if you want to dance, don't let me stop you."

"Keef, I could never—" Sheridan stopped when her lover's hand covered her mouth.

"You didn't let me finish. You can dance, but only with Marie, Dawn, Greg, or Sharon."

Sheridan chuckled and kissed Keefer's palm. "Gotcha. There are rules," she smiled.

"Oh, yeah. You're *mine*," Keefer replied confidently.

Sheridan winked at Keefer and rubbed her body against hers. "You sure you don't want to dance with me?"

Keefer groaned and closed her eyes. "I can't. As much as I want to..."

Sheridan smiled cockily. She loved to turn Keefer on in public and get her all shy. She still liked that bashful part of her lover and hoped it would always be there. "So I can go dance with the girls?"

Blue eyes opened slowly. "Yeah," she said quietly, watching Sheridan's lips shine after she'd licked them.

"Thank you, baby. You're the best." Sheridan turned to look at the girls, who were all feigning innocence as they eavesdropped on the conversation. "Hey, who wants to dance?"

Everyone feigned boredom and shrugged indifference.

"Please...I know you were all listening, so don't play that shit," Sheridan laughed. "All right, I'd rather you all stay with Keefer, anyway. I'll go dance with Greg."

Keefer sighed in relief. She'd much rather have all the girls with her. She released her grasp on Sheridan and they followed the blonde back into the club.

Four sets of eyes watched as Sheridan worked her way through the sea of women on her way to the stage. One set of eyes—blue ones, in fact—watched with excited anticipation. Keefer couldn't wait to see her lover lose herself in the music. She licked her lips as Sheridan climbed up onto the stage and stood in front of Greg, her back facing him. Soon the duo began moving as one, shaking, swaying, thrusting, and gyrating, perfectly in synch.

As usual, when Sheridan and Greg got to dancing together, a small crowd formed at the base of the stage. They, too, swayed to the beat, but no one outshone the couple on the stage.

Keefer was riveted. Sheridan looked so happy and carefree. When her face wasn't reflecting her concentration, it was lit up with a genuinely bright smile. Keefer smiled too, caught up in her lover's joy. She lowered her gaze from Sheridan's radiant smile and let it creep slowly down the blonde's body.

The construction worker's hands were on her hips as she moved that particular body part with abandon, causing Keefer to swallow hard. Blue eyes narrowed as they watched the muscles in Sheridan's thighs flex and dance along with the rest of her body. The tall inspector felt a tingle of arousal as she observed her lover. Suddenly remembering where she was, Keefer looked around at the crowd of women ogling Sheridan, watching her in rapt attention. Some trying to catch the dancing woman's eye, others vying for a spot in front of the stage for a better view. Keefer felt her ears get red and she forced herself to calm down. Her lover had a reputation in this club, and Keefer couldn't wipe that slate clean just by showing up one Thursday night. She'd have to learn to deal with it. These women will always look at her lover like that; there would always be tests.

I trust her, I really do. It's these sluts that I don't trust, she thought sourly. She walked away from Marie, Dawn, and Sharon to lean on the railing of the top level. She rested her elbows on the rail and leaned forward, unaware that she, too, had gathered an audience of whispering women.

The three friends joined Keefer at the railing, lining up on her right side, with Sharon next to Keefer. They figured it was safer if she wasn't left alone for some jealous woman to harass. They observed her reaction to seeing Sheridan doing what she did best, and all three shared a knowing smile. Keefer was just as rapt as the rest of the audience. However, blue eyes darted into the crowd every so often, silently staring holes into the backs of some overenthusiastic heads.

Keefer wasn't close enough to Sheridan for her liking, so she scouted out a spot on the lower level. "I think I want to go down there," she said to Sharon.

The tall cop looked to where Keefer indicated and found there wasn't enough room on the lower railing for all four of them, but agreed anyway. They made their way down with a small amount of effort. It was very crowded in the club that night, and she wondered how long it would be before Keefer finally had enough of the pushing, staring, and whispering.

Keefer settled herself in the same position against the lower railing and watched her lover intently, trying to block out the swarm of women doing the same. It was hard, since the crowd had gotten bigger. Sheridan wasn't helping matters much, as her dancing became more sexual. Keefer could feel the effect of her lover's thrusting hips from where she stood and couldn't help but wonder what the women in front of Sheridan were feeling. Her heart pounded loudly in her ringing ears as two women came out of nowhere and flanked Sheridan, rubbing their bodies on the blonde's, touching her freely.

Sheridan was startled by the women and tried to politely move away from them, but they were persistent. A surge of guilt washed over her and she began to feel closed in by the women. She stepped away, shrugging them off of her body and glared at them, her eyes darting to find Keefer as soon as she freed herself.

Keefer noticed the way her lover was behaving and she began to get angry with the two women who wouldn't take the hint. Sure, Sheridan had welcomed this kind of behavior just a few weeks ago, but it was apparent she didn't welcome it now. Keefer's sucked her bottom lip into her mouth and turned around to face the girls. Marie wrapped her arm around Keefer and squeezed. "It's gonna take a while, Keefer, just wait it out."

"It's pissing me off," the tall woman admitted.

"It should!" Dawn agreed. "That's *your* woman they're pawing at!"

Keefer narrowed her eyes. "Wait it out, huh?" she said mostly to herself. She turned back around and watched as her lover was now fending off a whole bunch of women. She sneered at them and stared at Sheridan. *Why is she still dancing? She should just come back here if that's what is going to happen,* she thought angrily. Suddenly, green eyes met blue and Keefer's anger faded. Sheridan's eyes told a story with just one look and Keefer felt guilty for wanting her lover to stop doing what she enjoyed just because she was jealous. There was nothing to be jealous of—those women meant nothing to her lover—and with the one look Sheridan gave her, she knew that she was all that mattered.

Without telling the girls, Keefer left her spot on the railing and boldly went down toward the dance floor. She didn't get close to the crowd, but she was close enough to see the shine of the lights as they bounced off of Sheridan's lips. They looked so inviting, half open and wet. The music began to fade away and the crowd became silent as Keefer stared at her lover. In her eyes, Sheridan was a work of art, and she had to catch her breath when she thought of how much the construction worker had given up to be with her. *She loves me, only me.* A big happy smile spread across Keefer's lips as she remembered looking into Sheridan's eyes and hearing her say "I love you."

She edged closer to the stage, never taking her eyes off of her lover. She leaned her shoulder against a giant speaker cabinet and folded her arms over her chest. The crowd of women became nothing more than a blur as she watched Sheridan dance with Greg. The blonde construction worker shimmied and danced, each movement filling Keefer with pride and lust. *She's mine*, she thought possessively.

"She's something, ain't she."

Keefer blinked a few times before she realized she was being spoken to. She looked down at the short woman standing next to her and nodded.

"Oh, yeah, very easy on the eyes," the woman again commented, adding a leer.

Keefer stood up a little straighter and cocked her head to the side.

"I hear she has a girlfriend now."

The tone of the woman's voice was that of disgust and it raised Keefer's hackles. "So I hear."

"I tell you, whoever it is, is one hell of a lucky shit. That woman up there," she pointed at Sheridan, "is one freaking catch," she said sadly.

"I'd like to think so," Keefer said confidently.

The small woman looked up at Keefer with astonishment. *"You're* her lover?"

Keefer blushed. "Yes."

"Well, hell...look at you!"

Keefer blushed harder.

"Why the hell ain't you up on that stage staking your claim? That's *Sheridan*, for chrissakes!"

Keefer shrugged, not wanting to admit her fear to a stranger.

"There isn't a woman in this club who doesn't want to be in your shoes, and you just let her dance up there all by herself?" she asked, both hands gesturing wildly.

Keefer thought about it as she watched her lover dance. *She's right. I could go...oh, God, no. If she moved like that against me, I'd die!*

"I mean...*look* at her!"

Keefer watched as the women flung her hands in the air in frustration and stomped away. *Maybe I should show everyone that she's with me. Oh, please...how are they going to know that I'm not just another hanger-on?* she thought with a frown. Sharon and Dawn suddenly appeared and Keefer smiled lamely at them.

"You okay?" Dawn asked.

"Yeah. She was a little nutty, but okay."

"What'd she say? You look upset," Sharon asked.

"She just voiced the opinions of women in general," Keefer said with a chuckle. "She wanted to know why Sheridan's up there and I'm down here."

"Well?" Dawn asked.

"I'm too embarrassed...I couldn't..."

"Yeah well, *she* can," Sharon said of the woman who was attempting to wrap herself around the construction worker.

Keefer's nostrils flared.

Sheridan effectively lost the woman and sought out Keefer's eyes. She offered a lopsided grin and Keefer felt immediately at ease.

The music changed; the beat was slow and seductive and couples began filling the dance floor and the stage. Greg and Sheridan stood there, arms folded over their chests, staring at Keefer. Greg had his eyebrows raised and Sheridan smiled sexily at her. Keefer's belly flipped. They were waiting for her, and she could never get up there and dance. Sheridan moved to the very edge of the stage and began tapping her foot. It seemed like everyone in the club was staring at her, and Keefer's knees began to shake.

"Someone's waiting for you, Keefer," Marie said with a grin.

"Go get her, babe," Dawn urged, with a small shove.

"Show 'em who's boss, Keefer!" Sharon said, pushing Keefer forward.

The tall woman swallowed back her fear and started walking toward the stage. She excused herself as she squeezed through the crowd, and forced herself to go forward. Sheridan had her hand out, waiting for her to reach the stage, and Keefer focused on that hand, trying to block out the throngs of women staring at her with various expressions. Once she made it to the stage, it was still a huge effort to take Sheridan's hand. She knew that when she did, there was no turning back. She was going to be on the stage, on display, in front of the entire club.

Sheridan's heart pounded hard in her chest. Keefer was coming to her; she was going to know what it felt like to hold her in her arms and dance with her. She couldn't wait to wrap her arms around the tall woman and she had to stop herself from jumping up and down on the stage in excitement. Once Keefer's hand touched hers, she couldn't hold back and she smiled like a fool.

Keefer felt herself being yanked up on stage and she allowed herself to be pulled. She climbed on the stage with shaky legs and stood with her back to the others. Looking into Sheridan's eyes overwhelmed her and she had to close hers. Strong arms wound their way around her body and she relaxed into them, pretending it was only the two of them, in her living room. Sheridan pressed her cheek into her chest and Keefer's hand automatically claimed the back of the blonde's head.

The couple swayed slowly to the music, arms wrapped around each other, lost in the feeling. They both had been hesitant to get close to each other, not knowing if the other would be comfortable with the closeness. Now, as they melted into each other, they both wondered what they'd been waiting for.

Keefer rested her cheek on top of Sheridan's head, oblivious to the slack-jawed looks they were receiving. Anyone who looked at the couple could see plainly that Keefer was not just one of Sheridan's toys. This was real, and it forced some onlookers to smile, despite their disappointment at seeing Sheridan off the market. The two women looked perfect; they fit together in a way that the others only wished they could fit with someone.

Keefer inhaled the scent of Sheridan's hair and smiled contentedly. Nothing mattered except Sheridan as she allowed herself to be led to the music. She relished the feeling of her lover's body pressed against hers, swaying to the slow, erotic beat. The tingle of arousal she had felt before came back stronger and she chuckled to herself at the circumstances. Here, on the stage, in front of hundreds of jealous women, Sheridan could make her horny without even trying.

The blonde felt her lover laugh and pulled her head back to see what was so funny. Once their eyes met, Sheridan forgot everything except how wonderful it felt to be captured in Keefer's gaze. Drawn together by some unseen force, the two women's lips met in a kiss that affirmed their love, connecting them in a way that only a kiss could. Somewhere in the backs of their minds, they could hear cheers and hoots, along with applause and whistles, but the couple didn't care. They wrapped their arms tighter around each other and the kiss became passionate. Tongues met and caressed, arms closed tightly—their union complete.

Epilogue

Keefer lounged in the recliner on her new porch and extended deck. She raised the glass of iced tea to her lips as she watched the goings-on around her.

Steven and Sheridan were busy showing off their handiwork to their father, who beamed with pride, intermittently reaching out and touching a piece of wood fondly. Phil was busy flipping burgers on the outrageously expensive grill that Sheridan just had to have as Sharon and Dawn were play fighting with him to get a hold of the spatula. Bobby, Marie, and Tony were having the time of their lives with the hose and the dogs—the four-legged "humans" occasionally getting the better of the two-legged sort. The guy's wives were all huddled together, fussing over potato salad.

Keefer sighed happily and stretched in contentment. In a million years, she never would have thought she'd be where she was now. Her life had never seemed worth getting up in the morning for and now she looked forward to each day with more joy than she thought possible. She was confident, secure with herself, and so helplessly in love.

Sheridan had changed everything, made her feel alive. Keefer wanted to smell the flowers and touch the sky. No longer simply existing, but living. Waking up every morning next to her lover was a gift, one she wanted to cherish forever. Blue eyes sought out Sheridan and Keefer smiled proudly when the construction worker winked. It never failed, all Sheridan had to do was look at her and she felt warm inside.

Keefer glanced at the front door of their house and grinned. It had taken a few months, but Sheridan had transformed the house into their home. With the help of her brother and, on occasion, the guys, the small blonde had created the perfect nest, a place Keefer wanted to come home to, kick her feet up and sigh. Everywhere she looked inside were little bits of Sheridan, and that made her more content, more excited about coming home than ever before. It wasn't her grandmother's house anymore—it was *theirs.*

"What ya thinking?"

Keefer looked into Sheridan's twinkling eyes and pursed her lips. "You. I love you."

Sheridan beamed. "Right back at ya," she said, reaching for Keefer's iced tea.

"Hey, you go get your own," Keefer mock-pouted.

"I want this one; it tastes better."

The tall brunette chuckled. She knew what Sheridan meant. Everything her lover's lips touched tasted far better than if they hadn't. "Well, just leave me a sip, or you'll have to get me another one."

Sheridan left a drop in the glass, plopped it down next to Keefer's lounge chair and, with a charming grin, was gone.

Keefer sighed and shook her head. She should have known better. With a smile, she looked around at the people gathered and leaned back in her lounge. *The iced tea can wait.*

Sheridan ambled over to a tree and leaned against it, taking in everything around her—her family, her friends and, most importantly, her Keefer. A smile formed on her lips as she looked at her relaxed lover. Keefer looked so serene, genuinely happy, and at seeing the woman who held her heart so content, Sheridan felt content.

The blonde construction worker's life had changed, forever. She'd finally found what she was looking for, what she'd been lacking all those years. Keefer. The tall, beautiful inspector who had happened upon her job site one day. Nothing would ever be the same, and she didn't want it to be. Sheridan Landers had everything she ever wanted.

THE END

Caution: Under Construction
By Vertigo
Limitless Dare2Dream Publishing
100 Pin Oak Court, Lexington, South Carolina, 29073
http://www.limitlessd2d.net
ISBN: 0974412198 $18.00

In Caution: Under Construction, author Vertigo provides readers with a series of love stories that touch the heart and tickle the funny bone. The main story is about a new love between two women, Sheridan Landers and Keefer Gibson. But in getting to know these women, readers also are treated to lessons about family love, love between friends and the love of self that allows us the confidence to open up and be vulnerable with others.

Vertigo's novel stands out from dozens of other lesbian romance titles because her words allow readers to feel the passion her characters experience. Reading the story, one stops thinking about Sheridan and Keefer as fictional characters and starts seeing them as friends, real people we wish we encountered in our own lives.

Sheridan Landers is an attractive, muscular, blonde construction worker whose success with women is the envy of her male coworkers, to whom she brags regularly. She rules the club scene at night, dancing to expel energy and torture women until she chooses one to be her object for a night. Her sexual encounters are fast and anonymous as she allows her libido to lead her life.

But Sheridan also has a loving, caring side that few see. Readers experience it in the way she interacts with her developmentally disabled brother Steven. He worships the ground she walks on and Sheridan in return is equally devoted to her sibling. Among the other important men in Sheridan's life are her two dogs, who she treats as spoiled children, allowing them to squish her at night sleeping on her bed and talking baby talk to them when no one is around.

Sheridan's sexual persona crashes with her softer side when she meets Keefer Gibson, a gorgeous OSHA inspector who unintentionally captures the attention of men and women wherever she goes. Keefer doesn't realize

A

the extent of her attractiveness and is instead sexually repressed. Trapped in a loveless, abusive relationship she has no confidence in her ability to love or be loved. Naturally when Sheridan makes her move on Keefer she is rejected. And even though both feel an immediate pull to the other, they are thrown into conflict as they experience new feelings.

As Sheridan learns more about Keefer, she experiences feelings of concern that are foreign to her. Feeling love is so out of character for Sheridan, her co-workers debate whether they should explain to their friend what her new emotions mean.

When Keefer and Sheridan discover Keefer's girlfriend Dani cheating, sparks and fists fly and a chain of events begins that will lead the ladies to learn the meaning of love. While fighting off Dani, who becomes a stalking maniac, Sheridan becomes patient with her new lover and starts to consider someone's needs other than her own. Keefer starts to trust again and believe that she is not only worthy of love, but also capable of satisfying Sheridan's desires.

Caution: Under Construction is sensual, romantic story that deserves a place on every lesbian bookshelf.

Press Release

New author finds love is always under construction

TJ Vertigo, known by hundreds as a writer of online fan fiction, has expanded from the computer world to the printed page and released her first published novel with Limitless Dare2Dream Publishing.

The New York resident wrote *Caution: Under Construction* based, in part, on her life in her early 20s.

"It is a story about learning, growth and happiness, and the pains it can take to achieve it. Mostly, it is about love, in all its aspects, from blinding passion for another, to love of family, and children of the four-legged variety."

The message of the novel, Vertigo said, is that "there's always work to do. Nothing is ever perfect when it comes to love. It's always under construction."

The book focuses on Sheridan Landers and Keefer Gibson.

Sheridan is an attractive muscular little blonde, flirtatious and somewhat cocky construction worker who "thinks" she has the world by the balls. By day, she works for her father's construction company and gives as good as she gets, just like one of the guys. At night however, she becomes the ultimate object of desire for every woman in the club as she dances for her pleasure and theirs. Never at a loss for companionship, Sheridan's ego, among other things, is constantly stroked.

But, she has another side that most never see, a solid family that includes her beloved developmentally disabled brother, Steven. A quixotic young man, he has clear bouts of genius at unexpected times, not to mention no edit mode verbally. Together they form a marvelous pair and keep us in stitches. Their love for each other is palpable and it is clear, he adores the ground she walks on, and she him. Last but definitely not least…Sheridan's two "boys" (dogs) Zeus and Pharaoh…not exactly the best mannered four-legged gentlemen, but they give her joy and show us her softer side and something more.

C

Enter Keefer Gibson, a leggy, graceful, somewhat self-effacing beauty of thirty-something with cerulean eyes. She is an inspector for OSHA. The woman is somewhat sexually repressed and trapped in a loveless, abusive relationship with a domineering, moderately unhinged woman by the name of Dani. Keefer's greatest love and solace is her loving disfigured dog Fifi, a real little trooper and like her mom a consummate lady. The inspector's days go on and on and she accepts what life has given her, little does she know what is to come.

The inspector and construction worker meet on a job and are instantly attracted to one another. Sheridan decides she "will" have this one. Keefer feels something too, but frightened, she runs as fast as she can away from Sheridan. The story lets readers watch as these two women grow into love cautiously and passionately, forever under the stalking gaze of the maniacal and somewhat dangerously jealous eyes of Dani, Keefer's ex, who will stop at nothing to put a spanner in the works. Will she succeed? Well, read the story. Time will tell, because here you have love under construction.

Vertigo started writing fiction as a hobby about three years ago when she became involved in the world of Xena fan fiction.

Caution: Under Construction was written largely because of fan demand.

"My fans talked me into it. Not a day went by when I didn't receive a note asking me when I was going to publish. I was afraid of the whole process; especially the editing, and outright refused. Eventually, the pushing became shoving and while this was going on, the idea of having an actual book with my name on it didn't sound so bad," she said.

Fans influenced Vertigo more than just by asking for her book. When she posted her previous work online, she allowed readers to comment on the stories as they developed, and sometimes, she let them have too much control.

"*Caution: Under Construction* comes on the heels of another story I wrote that I was unhappy with. There came a point in the previous story where I stopped writing for me, and only wrote to please everyone else. I felt like I had cheated and wanted to prove that I actually could write a good story, with complex characters, and a real plot," Vertigo said.

D

Vertigo said the most rewarding part of the novel was proving she could do it and receiving such tremendous praise for it.

"People wrote me telling me my story helped them deal with their own problems. People told me that I made them laugh and they loved it. I had over 300 people join my mailing list as I was writing this story. It was a story I began writing to show everyone I had more to offer than my last story and it worked," Vertigo said.

Caution: Under Construction can be ordered at
http://www.limitlessd2d.net/catalogue/caution.html

For more information or to schedule an interview or appearance, please contact:
Samantha E. Ruskin or Anne M. Clarkson
Limitless D2D Promotions
803-356-8231
limitlessd2d@aol.com

F

Q& A with Vertigo

Question: How long have you been writing fiction? How did you get started?
Answer: I have been writing fiction for three years. I got started with fan fiction and it just took off from there.

Question: Who or what inspires you to write?
Answer: The characters speak to me and want to be heard so I write their stories down.

Question: Do you write full time or do you have another 'day job?"
Answer: I work in an animal hospital and it affects my writing tremendously. In my new story, I put some of my real clients in as characters and they are a big hit with the readers.

Question: Do you consider your writing to be "lesbian fiction?"
Answer: I think it's very safe to say my writing is strictly lesbian fiction. I am out, have been for years.

Question: Why do you write?
Answer: I enjoy sharing the voices in my head with everyone else.

Question: Is there a central or common theme you see in your books and writing?
Answer: There's always love. Other than that, my characters and storylines are all different.

Question: When you write, how much of the story is based on your actual experiences?
Answer: Quite a bit! Almost every character is based on a real person that I know.

Question: What's the most difficult part of writing in general?
Answer: Sitting down and typing it. I have a terrible time of it. I have no trouble putting it down on paper, or conjuring it up in my head.

Question: What is the most rewarding part of writing in general?
Answer: The positive feedback. I thrive off of it.

Question: Which writers have influenced your work? Who do you read?

G

Answer: I can't say any writers influenced my work, I write from my own head and experiences. Oddly enough, I don't read books. I only started reading and writing myself a few years ago, and that was solely inspired by fan fiction. I have favorite writers, but if I start to name them I'm afraid I'll leave someone out.

Question: What were your thoughts behind Caution: Under Construction? How did you come up with this story?
Answer: Ah, well, CUC comes on the heels of another story I wrote that I was unhappy with. There came a point in the previous story where I stopped writing for me, and only wrote to please everyone else. I felt like I had cheated and wanted to prove to myself and the world that I actually could write a good story, with complex characters and a real plot. I tend to write what I know, so I based one of the main characters in CUC on myself at 20 years old. I usually have the whole story played out in my head by the time I start writing. The characters start to write themselves once I become familiar with them.

Question: What's your favorite thing about this book?
Answer: The fact that everyone loved it and I DID prove that I could do it.

Question: Which of your characters do you most identify with? Why?
Answer: Sheridan. I wrote her totally based on myself as a 20 year old. Of course it's not perfectly based on my life, but it's very close.

Question: What was the most difficult part of writing Under Construction?
Answer: A lot of time, I have a passage in my head, a clear idea of what I am aiming for, and then I have a hard time getting to that point because I am so eager to get there. It happened a lot with CUC.

Question: What was the most rewarding aspect of writing Under Construction?
Answer: People writing me and telling me my story helped them deal with their own problems. People telling me that I made them laugh, and the fact that everyone loved it. I had over 300 people join my mailing list as I was writing this story. It was a story I began writing to show everyone I had more to offer than my last story and it worked.

Question: What does the title mean to you?
Answer: It means that there's always work to do. Nothing is ever perfect when it comes to love. It's always under construction.

Vertigo, aka, "TJ", was born and raised in Brooklyn, NY, and currently resides there with a lovely little gentleman of the canine variety named Sake.

/|\^..^/|\
Step into Vertigo's World--------->
www.angelfire.com/tv/Vertigo/index.html

I

Order These Great Books Directly From Limitless, Dare 2 Dream Publishing

Title	Price	Note
The Amazon Queen by L M Townsend	20.00	
Define Destiny by J M Dragon	20.00	The one that started it all…
Desert Hawk,revised by Katherine E. StandelI	18.00	Many new scenes
Golden Gate by Erin Jennifer Mar	18.00	
The Brass Ring By Mavis Applewater	18.00	HOT
Haunting Shadows by J M Dragon	18.00	
Spirit Harvest by Trish Shields	15.00	
PWP: Plot? What Plot? by Mavis Applewater	18.00	HOT
Journeys By Anne Azel	18.00	NEW
Memories Kill By S. B. Zarben	20.00	
Up The River, revised By Sam Ruskin	18.00	Many new scenes
	Total	

South Carolina residents add 5% sales tax.
Domestic shipping is $3.50 per book

Visit our website at: http://limitlessd2d.net

Please mail your orders with credit card info, check or money order to:

Limitless, Dare 2 Dream Publishing
100 Pin Oak Ct.
Lexington, SC 29073-7911

Please make checks or money orders payable to: Limitless.

I

Order More Great Books Directly From Limitless, Dare 2 Dream Publishing

Daughters of Artemis by L M Townsend	18.00	
Connecting Hearts By Val Brown and MJ Walker	18.00	
Mysti: Mistress of Dreams By Sam Ruskin	18.00	HOT
Family Connections By Val Brown & MJ Walker	18.00	Sequel to Connecting Hearts
A Thousand Shades of Feeling by Carolyn McBride	18.00	
The Amazon Nation By Carla Osborne	18.00	Great for research
Poetry from the Featherbed By pinfeather	18.00	If you think you hate poetry you haven't read this
None So Blind, 3rd Edition By LJ Maas	16.00	NEW
A Saving Solace By DS Bauden	18.00	NEW
Return of the Warrior By Katherine E. Standell	20.00	Sequel to Desert Hawk
Journey's End By LJ Maas	18.00	NEW
	Total	

South Carolina residents add 5% sales tax.
Domestic shipping is $3.50 per book
Please mail your orders with credit card info, check or money order to:
Limitless, Dare 2 Dream Publishing
100 Pin Oak Ct.
Lexington, SC 29073-7911
Please make checks or money orders payable to: Limitless.

II

Name:
Address:
Address:
City/State/Zip:
Country:
Phone:
Credit Card Type:
CC Number:
EXP Date:
List Items Ordered and Retail Prices:

List Items Ordered and Retail Prices:	

You may also send a money order or check. Please make payments out to: Limitless Corporation.
You may Fax this form to us at: 803-359-2881 or mail it to:
Limitless Corporation
100 Pin Oak Court
Lexington, SC 29073-7911

South Carolina residents add 5% sales tax.
Domestic shipping is $3.50 per book

Visit our website at: http://limitlessd2d.net

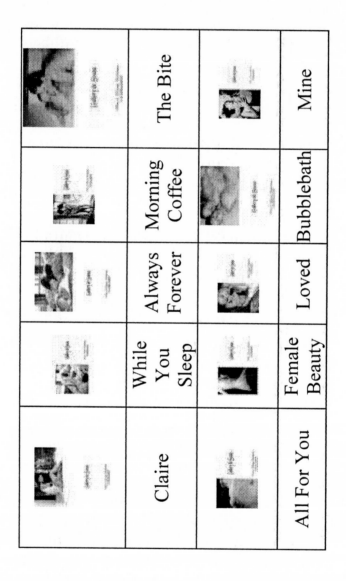

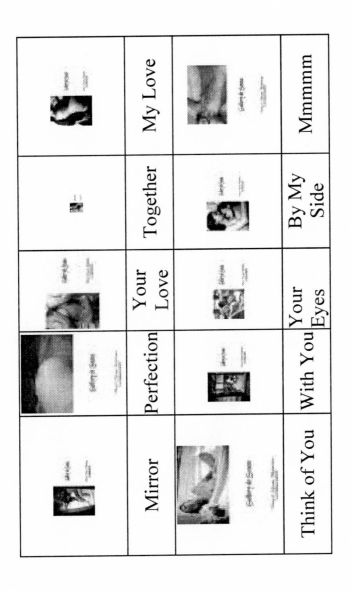

Think of You	Mirror	Perfection	With You	Your Love
Your Eyes	Together	By My Side	My Love	Mmmmm

Unless otherwise specified the cards will come blank, with no printing inside. You may, however, request something be printed inside at no extra cost.

Personalizing the cards will be done upon request or you may choose to have a pre-determined text printed.

- Photo Cards are $5.00 each US funds or $4.00 each when purchased in lots of 10 or more. Shipping is $.75 per card within the continental US Shipping outside the United States will be determined on an individual basis so that we may charge you only the actual shipping cost. At Dare 2 Dream you will never be charged a handling fee.

- Post Cards are $3.50 each US funds or $3.00 each when purchased in lots of 10 or more. Shipping is $.50 per card within the continental US For shipping outside the United States, see photo cards.

- 8 X 10 Photos of the images are available in glossy or matte finish for $8.00 each US funds Shipping is $1.50 per print within the continental United States For shipping outside the United States, see photo cards.

South Carolina residents add 5% sales tax.

Learn more about the photographer and the Gallery de Souza

Introducing...
Art By Joy

By JoyArgento

Hi, allow me to introduce myself. My name is Joy Argento and I am the artist on all of these pieces. I have been doing artwork since I was a small child. That gives me about 35 years of experience. I majored in art in high school and took a few college art courses. Most of my work is done in either pencil or airbrush mixed with color pencils. I have recently added designing and creating artwork on the computer. Some of the work featured on these pages were created and "painted" on the computer. I am self taught in this as well as in the use of the airbrush.

I have been selling my art for the last 15 years and have had my work featured on trading cards, prints and in magazines. I have sold in galleries and to private collectors from all around the world.

I live in Western New York with my three kids, four cats, one dog and the love of my life. It is definitely a full house. I appreciate you taking the time to check out my artwork. Please feel free to email me with your thoughts or questions. Custom orders are always welcomed too.

Contact me at ArtByJoy@aol.com . I look forward to hearing from you.

Making Love

Towel Cuddling

Motorcycle Women

Joy Argento

Check out her work at
LimitlessD2D or at her website.
Remember: ArtByJoy@aol.com !

Printed in the United States
25100LVS00002B/86